RAVES FOR JOSEPH WAMBAUGH AND . . .

## THE BLUE KNIGHT

"MARVELOUS . . . REALISTIC, FRIGHTENING, TOUCHING IN ITS HUMANITY."
—*Detroit Free Press*

"AN EXTRAORDINARY PIECE OF CRAFTS-MANSHIP."
—*Los Angeles Times*

"ENTERTAINING, EXCITING, BELIEVABLE."
—*Chicago Sun-Times*

"HARD-HITTING, TOUGH-TALKING, UTTERLY REALISTIC."
—*Publishers Weekly*

"BEYOND THE ADVENTURE, BEYOND THE REVELATION OF DAILY LIFE, THERE IS AN-OTHER KIND OF SUSPENSE . . . the gradual and surprising tale of a human being emerging from a stereotype."
—*Los Angeles Times Calendar*

*Books by Joseph Wambaugh*

THE NEW CENTURIONS
THE BLUE KNIGHT
THE ONION FIELD
THE CHOIRBOYS
THE BLACK MARBLE
THE GLITTER DOME
THE DELTA STAR
LINES AND SHADOWS
ECHOES IN THE DARKNESS
THE SECRETS OF HARRY BRIGHT
THE BLOODING
THE GOLDEN ORANGE
FUGITIVE NIGHTS

# THE BLUE KNIGHT

Joseph Wambaugh

A DELL BOOK

Published by
Dell Publishing
a division of
Bantam Doubleday Dell Publishing Group, Inc.
1540 Broadway
New York, New York 10036

ISBN: 0-440-10607-9

Reprinted by arrangement with Little, Brown and Company in association with The Atlantic Monthly Press

Printed in the United States of America

One Previous Dell Edition

April 1987

20   19   18   17

RAD

TO MY PARENTS
AND TO
UPTON BIRNIE BRADY

I often remember the rookie days and those who had
discovered the allure of the beat. Then I thought
them just peculiar old men. Now I wish they were all
still here and that they might approve of this book.

# Wednesday,
# the First Day

# 1

THE WHEEL HUMMED and Rollo mumbled Yiddish curses as he put rouge on the glistening bronze surface.

"There ain't a single blemish on this badge," he said.

"Sure there is, Rollo," I said. "Look closer. Between the *s* in *Los* and the big *A* in *Angeles*. I scratched it on the door of my locker."

"There ain't a single blemish on this badge," said Rollo, but he buffed, and in spite of his bitching I watched bronze change to gold, and chrome become silver. The blue enameled letters which said "Policeman," and "4207," jumped out at me.

"Okay, so now are you happy?" he sighed, leaning across the display case, handing me the badge.

"It's not too bad," I said, enjoying the heft of the heavy oval shield, polished to a luster that would reflect sunlight like a mirror.

"Business ain't bad enough, I got to humor a crazy old cop like you." Rollo scratched his scalp, and the hair, white and stiff, stood like ruffled chicken feathers.

"What's the matter, you old gonif, afraid some of your burglar friends will see a bluesuit in here and take their hot jewelry to some other crook?"

"Ho, ho! Bob Hope should watch out. When you get through sponging off the taxpayers you'll go after his job."

"Well, I've gotta go crush some crime. What do I owe you for the lousy badge polishing?"

"Don't make me laugh, I got a kidney infection. You been freeloading for twenty years, now all of a sudden you want to pay?"

"See you later, Rollo. I'm going over to Seymour's for breakfast. He appreciates me."

"Seymour too? I know Jews got to suffer in this world, but not all of us in one day."

"Good-bye, old shoe."

"Be careful, Bumper."

I strolled outside into the burning smog that hung over Main Street. I started to sweat as I stopped to admire Rollo's work. Most of the ridges had been rounded off long ago, and twenty years of rubbing gave it unbelievable brilliance. Turning the face of the shield to the white sun, I watched the gold and silver take the light. I pinned the badge to my shirt and looked at my reflection in the blue plastic that Rollo has over his front windows. The plastic was rippled and bubbled and my distorted reflection made me a freak. I looked at myself straight on, but still my stomach hung low and made me look like a blue kangaroo, and my ass was two nightsticks wide. My jowls hung to my chest in that awful reflection and my big rosy face and pink nose were a deep veiny blue like the color of my uniform which somehow didn't change colors in the reflection. It was ugly, but what made me keep looking was the shield. The four-inch oval on my chest glittered and twinkled so that after a second or two I couldn't even see the blue man behind it. I just stood there staring at that shield for maybe a full minute.

Seymour's delicatessen is only a half block from Rollo's jewelry store, but I decided to drive. My black-and-white was parked out front in Rollo's no parking zone because this downtown traffic is so miserable. If

it weren't for those red curbs there'd be no place to
park even a police car. I opened the white door and
sat down carefully, the sunlight blasting through the
windshield making the seat cushion hurt. I'd been
driving the same black-and-white for six months and
had worked a nice comfortable dip in the seat, so I
rode cozy, like in a worn friendly saddle. It's really not
too hard to loosen up seat springs with two hundred
and seventy-five pounds.

I drove to Seymour's and when I pulled up in front I
saw two guys across Fourth Street in the parking lot at
the rear of the Pink Dragon. I watched for thirty seconds or so and it looked like they were setting something up, probably a narcotics buy. Even after twenty
years I still get that thrill a cop gets at seeing things
that are invisible to the square citizen. But what was
the use? I could drive down Main Street anytime and
see hugger-muggers, paddy hustlers, till-tappers, junk-
ies, and then waste six or eight man-hours staking out
on these small-timers and maybe end up with nothing.
You only had time to grab the sure ones and just make
mental notes of the rest.

The two in the parking lot interested me so I decided to watch them for a minute. They were dumb
strung-out hypes. They should've made me by now.
When I was younger I used to play the truth game. I
hardly ever played it anymore. The object of the game
is simple: I have to explain to an imaginary black-robed
square (His Honor) how Officer William A. Morgan
*knows* that those men are committing a criminal act. If
the judge finds that I didn't have sufficient probable
cause to stop, detain, and search my man, then I lose
the game. Illegal search and seizure—case dismissed.

I usually beat the game whether it's imaginary or
for real. My courtroom demeanor is very good, pretty
articulate for an old-time copper, they say. And such a
simple honest kisser. Big innocent blue eyes. Juries
loved me. It's very hard to explain the "know." Some
guys never master it. Let's see, I begin, I *know* they

are setting up a buy because of . . . the clothing. That's a good start, the clothing. It's a suffocating day, Your Honor, and the tall one is wearing a long-sleeved shirt buttoned at the cuff. To hide his hype marks, of course. One of them is still wearing his "county shoes." That tells me he just got out of county jail, and the other one, yes, the other one—you only acquire that frantic pasty look in the joint: San Quentin, Folsom, maybe. He's been away a long time. And I would find out they'd just been in the Pink Dragon and no one but a whore, hype, pill-head, or other hustler would hang out in that dive. And I'd explain all this to my judge too, but I'd be a little more subtle, and then I'd be stopped. I could explain to my imaginary jurist but never to a real one about the instinct—the stage in this business when, like an animal, you can *feel* you've got one, and it can't be explained. You *feel* the truth, and you know. Try telling *that* to the judge, I thought. Try explaining *that*, sometime.

Just then a wino lurched across Main Street against the red light and a Lincoln jammed on the binders almost creaming him.

"Goddamnit, come over here," I yelled when he reached the sidewalk.

"Hi, Bumper," he croaked, holding the five-sizes-too-big pants around his bony hips, trying his best to look sober as he staggered sideways.

"You almost got killed, Noodles," I said.

"What's the difference?" he said, wiping the saliva from his chin with the grimy free hand. The other one gripped the pants so hard the big knuckles showed white through the dirt.

"I don't care about you but I don't want any wrecked Lincolns on my beat."

"Okay, Bumper."

"I'm gonna have to book you."

"I'm not that drunk, am I?"

"No, but you're dying."

"No crime in that." He coughed then and the spit

that dribbled out the corner of his mouth was red and foamy.

"I'm booking you, Noodles," I said, mechanically filling in the boxes on the pad of drunk arrest reports that I carried in my hip pocket like I was still walking my beat instead of driving a black-and-white.

"Let's see, your real name is Ralph M. Milton, right?"

"Millard."

"Millard," I muttered, filling in the name. I must've busted Noodles a dozen times. I never used to forget names or faces.

"Let's see, eyes bloodshot, gait staggering, attitude stuporous, address transient. . . ."

"Got a cigarette?"

"I don't use them, Noodles," I said, tearing out the copies of the arrest report. "Wait a minute, the night-watch left a half pack in the glove compartment. Go get them while I'm calling the wagon."

The wino shuffled to the radio car while I walked fifty feet down the street to a call box, unlocked it with my big brass key, and asked for the B-wagon to come to Fourth and Main. It would've been easier to use my car radio to call the wagon, but I walked a beat too many years to learn new habits.

That was something my body did to me, made me lose my foot beat and put me in a black-and-white. An ankle I broke years ago when I was a slick-sleeved rookie chasing a purse snatcher, finally decided it can't carry my big ass around anymore and swells up every time I'm on my feet a couple of hours. So I lost my foot beat and got a radio car. A one-man foot beat's the best job in this or any police department. It always amuses policemen to see the movies where the big hood or crooked politician yells, "I'll have you walking a beat, you dumb flatfoot," when really it's a sought-after job. You got to have whiskers to get a foot beat, and you have to be big and good. If only my legs would've held out. But even though I couldn't travel it too much on foot, it was still *my* beat, all of it. Everyone knew it all belonged to me more than anyone.

"Okay, Noodles, give this arrest report to the cops in the wagon and don't lose the copies."

"You're not coming with me?" He couldn't shake a cigarette from the pack with one trembling hand.

"No, you just lope on over to the corner and flag 'em down when they drive by. Tell 'em you want to climb aboard."

"First time I ever arrested myself," he coughed, as I lit a cigarette for him, and put the rest of the pack and the arrest report in his shirt pocket.

"See you later."

"I'll get six months. The judge warned me last time."

"I hope so, Noodles."

"I'll just start boozing again when they let me out. I'll just get scared and start again. You don't know what it's like to be scared at night when you're alone."

"How do you know, Noodles?"

"I'll just come back here and die in an alley. The cats and rats will eat me anyway, Bumper."

"Get your ass moving or you'll miss the wagon." I watched him stagger down Main for a minute and I yelled, "Don't you believe in miracles?"

He shook his head and I turned back to the guys in the parking lot again just as they disappeared inside the Pink Dragon. Someday, I thought, I'll kill that dragon and drink its blood.

I was too hungry to do police work, so I went into Seymour's. I usually like to eat breakfast right after rollcall and here it was ten o'clock and I was still screwing around.

Ruthie was bent over one of the tables scooping up a tip. She was very attractive from the rear and she must've caught me admiring her out of the corner of her eye. I suppose a blue man, dark blue in black leather, sets off signals in some people.

"Bumper," she said, wheeling around. "Where you been all week?"

"Hi, Ruthie," I said, always embarrassed by how glad she was to see me.

Seymour, a freckled redhead about my age, was putting together a pastrami sandwich behind the meat case. He heard Ruthie call my name and grinned.

"Well, look who's here. The finest cop money can buy."

"Just bring me a cold drink, you old shlimazel."

"Sure, champ." Seymour gave the pastrami to a take-out customer, made change, and put a cold beer and a frosted glass in front of me. He winked at the well-dressed man who sat at the counter to my left. The beer wasn't opened.

"Whadda you want me to do, bite the cap off?" I said, going along with his joke. No one on my beat had ever seen me drink on duty.

Seymour bent over, chuckling. He took the beer away and filled my glass with buttermilk.

"Where you been all week, Bumper?"

"Out there. Making the street safe for women and babies."

"Bumper's here!" he shouted to Henry in the back. That meant five scrambled eggs and twice the lox the paying customers get with an order. It also meant three onion bagels, toasted and oozing with butter and heaped with cream cheese. I don't eat breakfast at Seymour's more than once or twice a week, although I knew he'd feed me three free meals every day.

"Young Slagel told me he saw you directing traffic on Hill Street the other day," said Seymour.

"Yeah, the regular guy got stomach cramps just as I was driving by. I took over for him until his sergeant got somebody else."

"Directing traffic down there is a job for the young bucks," said Seymour, winking again at the business-man who was smiling at me and biting off large hunks of a Seymour's Special Corned Beef on Pumpernickel Sandwich.

"Meet any nice stuff down there, Bumper? An airline hostess, maybe? Or some of those office cuties?"

"I'm too old to interest them, Seymour. But let me tell you, watching all that young poon, I had to direct traffic like this." With that I stood up and did an imitation of waving at cars, bent forward with my legs and feet crossed.

Seymour fell backward and out came his high-pitched hoot of a laugh. This brought Ruthie over to see what happened.

"Show her, Bumper, please," Seymour gasped, wiping the tears away.

Ruthie waited with that promising smile of hers. She's every bit of forty-five, but firm, and golden blond, and very fair—as sexy a wench as I've ever seen. And the way she acted always made me know it was there for me, but I'd never taken it. She's one of the regular people on my beat and it's because of the way *they* feel about me, all of them, the people on my beat. Some of the smartest bluecoats I know have lots of broads but won't even cop a feel on their beats. Long ago I decided to admire her big buns from afar.

"I'm waiting, Bumper," she said, hands on those curvy hips.

"Another funny thing happened while I was directing traffic," I said, to change the subject. "There I was, blowing my whistle and waving at cars with one hand, and I had my other hand out palm up, and some little eighty-year-old lady comes up and drops a big fat letter on my palm. 'Could you please tell me the postage for this, Officer?' she says. Here I am with traffic backed up clear to Olive, both arms out and this letter on my palm. So, what the hell, I just put my feet together, arms out, and rock back and forth like a scale balancing, and say, 'That'll be twenty-one cents, ma'am, if you want it to go airmail.' 'Oh *thank* you, Officer,' she says."

Seymour hooted again and Ruthie laughed, but things quieted down when my food came, and I loosened my Sam Browne for the joy of eating. It annoyed me though when my belly pressed against the edge of the yellow Formica counter.

Seymour had a flurry of orders to go which he took care of and nobody bothered me for ten minutes or so except for Ruthie who wanted to make sure I had enough to eat, and that my eggs were fluffy enough, and also to rub a hip or something up against me so that I had trouble thinking about the third bagel.

The other counter customer finished his second cup of coffee and Seymour shuffled over.

"More coffee, Mister Parker?"

"No, I've had plenty."

I'd never seen this man before but I admired his clothes. He was stouter than me, soft fat, but his suit, not bought off the rack, hid most of it.

"You ever met Officer Bumper Morgan, Mister Parker?" asked Seymour.

We smiled, both too bloated and lazy to stand up and shake hands across two stools.

"I've heard of you, Officer," said Parker. "I recently opened a suite in the Roxman Building. Fine watches. Stop around anytime for a special discount." He put his card on the counter and pushed it halfway toward me. Seymour shoved it the rest of the way.

"Everyone around here's heard of Bumper," Seymour said proudly.

"I thought you'd be a bigger man, Officer," said Parker. "About six foot seven and three hundred pounds, from some of the stories I've heard."

"You just about got the weight right," said Seymour.

I was used to people saying I'm not as tall as they expected, or as I first appeared to be. A beat cop has to be big or he'll be fighting all the time. Sometimes a tough, feisty little cop resents it because he can't walk a foot beat, but the fact is that most people don't fear a little guy and a little guy'd just have to prove himself all the time, and sooner or later somebody'd take that nightstick off him and shove it up his ass. Of course I was in a radio car now, but as I said before, I was still a beat cop, more or less.

The problem with my size was that my frame was made for a guy six feet five or six instead of a guy barely six feet. My bones are big and heavy, especially my hands and feet. If I'd just have grown as tall as I was meant to, I wouldn't have the goddamn weight problem. My appetite was meant for a giant, and I finally convinced those police doctors who used to send "fat man letters" to my captain ordering me to cut down to two hundred and twenty pounds.

"Bumper's a one-man gang," said Seymour. "I tell you he's fought wars out there." Seymour waved at the street to indicate the "out there."

"Come on, Seymour," I said, but it was no use. This kind of talk shriveled my balls, but it did please me that a newcomer like Parker had heard of me. I wondered how special the "special discount" would be. My old watch was about finished.

"How long ago did you get this beat, Bumper?" asked Seymour, but didn't allow me to answer. "Well, it was almost twenty years. I know that, because when Bumper was a rookie, I was a young fella myself, working for my father right here. It was real bad then. We had B-girls and zoot-suiters and lots of crooks. In those days there was plenty of guys that would try the cop on the beat."

I looked over at Ruthie, who was smiling.

"Years ago, when Ruthie worked here the first time, Bumper saved her life when some guy jumped her at the bus stop on Second Street. He saved you, didn't he, Ruthie?"

"He sure did. He's my hero," she said, pouring me a cup of coffee.

"Bumper's always worked right here," Seymour continued. "On foot beats and now in a patrol car since he can't walk too good no more. His twenty-year anniversary is coming up, but we won't let him retire. What would it be like around here without the champ?"

Ruthie actually looked scared for a minute when Seymour said it, and this shook me.

"When is your twentieth year up, Bumper?" she asked.

"End of this month."

"You're not even considering pulling the pin, are you Bumper?" asked Seymour, who knew all the police lingo from feeding the beat cops for years.

"What do *you* think?" I asked, and Seymour seemed satisfied and started telling Parker a few more incidents from the Bumper Morgan legend. Ruthie kept watching me. Women are like cops, they sense things. When Seymour finally ran down, I promised to come back Friday for the Deluxe Businessman's Plate, said my good-byes, and left six bits for Ruthie which she didn't put in her tip dish under the counter. She looked me in the eye and dropped it right down her bra.

I'd forgotten about the heat and when it hit me I decided to drive straight for Elysian Park, sit on the grass, and smoke a cigar with my radio turned up loud enough so I wouldn't miss a call. I wanted to read about last night's Dodger game, so before getting in the car I walked down to the smoke shop. I picked up half a dozen fifty-cent cigars, and since the store recently changed hands and I didn't know the owner too well, I took a five out of my pocket.

"From you? Don't be silly, Officer Morgan," said the pencil-necked old man, and refused the money. I made a little small talk in way of payment, listened to a gripe or two about business, and left, forgetting to pick up a paper. I almost went back in, but I never make anyone bounce for two things in one day. I decided to get a late paper across the street from Frankie the dwarf. He had his Dodger's baseball cap tilted forward and pretended not to see me until I was almost behind him, then he turned fast and punched me in the thigh with a deformed little fist.

"Take that, you big slob. You might scare everybody else on the street, but I'll get a fat lock on you and break your kneecap."

"What's happening, Frankie?" I said, while he slipped a folded paper under my arm without me asking.

"No happenings, Killer. How you standing up under this heat?"

"Okay, I guess." I turned to the sports page while Frankie smoked a king-sized cigarette in a fancy silver holder half as long as his arm. His tiny face was pinched and ancient but he was only thirty years old.

A woman and a little boy about four years old were standing next to me, waiting for the red light to change.

"See that man," she said. "That's a policeman. He'll come and get you and put you in jail if you're bad." She gave me a sweet smile, very smug because she thought I was impressed with her good citizenship.

Frankie, who was only a half head taller than the kid, took a step toward them and said, "That's real clever, lady. Make him scared of the law. Then he'll grow up hating cops because *you* scared him to death."

"Easy, Frankie," I said, a little surprised.

The woman lifted the child and the second the light changed she ran from the angry dwarf.

"Sorry, Bumper," Frankie smiled. "Lord knows I'm not a cop lover."

"Thanks for the paper, old shoe," I said, keeping in the shade, nodding to several of the local characters and creeps who gave me a "Hi, Bumper."

I sauntered along toward Broadway to see what the crowds looked like today and to scare off any pickpockets that might be working the shoppers. I fired up one of those fifty-centers which are okay when I'm out of good hand-rolled custom-mades. As I rounded the corner on Broadway I saw six of the Krishna cult performing in their favorite place on the west sidewalk.

They were all kids, the oldest being maybe twenty-five, boys and girls, shaved heads, a single long pigtail, bare feet with little bells on their ankles, pale orange saris, tambourines, flutes and guitars. They chanted and danced and put on a hell of a show there almost every day, and there was no way old Herman the Devil-drummer could compete with them. You could see his jaw flopping and knew he was screaming but you couldn't hear a word he said after they started *their* act.

Up until recently, this had been Herman's corner, and even before I came on the job Herman put in a ten-hour day right here passing out tracts and yelling about demons and damnation, collecting maybe twelve bucks a day from people who felt sorry for him. He used to be a lively guy, but now he looked old, bloodless, and dusty. His shiny black suit was threadbare and his frayed white collar was gray and dirty and he didn't seem to care anymore. I thought about trying to persuade him one more time to move down Broadway a few blocks where he wouldn't have to compete with these kids and all their color and music. But I knew it wouldn't do any good. Herman had been on his beat too long. I walked to my car thinking about him, poor old Devil-drummer.

As I was getting back in my saddle seat I got a burning pain in the gut and had to drop a couple acid eaters. I carried pockets full of white tablets. Acid eaters in the right pocket and bubble breakers in the left pocket. The acid eaters are just antacid pills and the bubble breakers are for gas and I'm cursed with both problems, more or less all the time. I sucked an acid eater and the fire died. Then I thought about Cassie because that sometimes settled my stomach. The decision to retire at twenty years had been made several weeks ago, and Cassie had lots of plans, but what she *didn't* know was that I'd decided last night to make Friday my last day on duty. Today, tomorrow, and Friday would be it. I could string my vacation days together and run them until the end of the month when my time was officially up.

Friday was also to be her last day at L.A. City College. She'd already prepared her final exams and had permission to leave school now, while a substitute instructor took over her classes. She had a good offer, a "wonderful opportunity" she called it, to join the faculty of an expensive girls' school in northern California, near San Francisco. They wanted her up there now, before they closed for the summer, so she could get an idea how things were done. She planned on leaving Monday, and at the end of the month when I retired, coming back to Los Angeles where we'd get married, then we'd go back to the apartment she'd have all fixed up and ready. But I'd decided to leave Friday and go with her. No sense fooling around any longer, I thought. It would be better to get it over with and I knew Cruz would be happy about it.

Cruz Segovia was my sergeant, and for twenty years he'd been the person closest to me. He was always afraid something would happen and he made me promise him I wouldn't blow this, the best deal of my life. And Cassie *was* the best deal, no doubt about it. A teacher, a divorced woman with no kids, a woman with real education, not just a couple college degrees. She was young-looking, forty-four years old, and had it all.

So I started making inquiries about what there was for a retired cop around the Bay area and damned if I didn't luck out and get steered into a good job with a large industrial security outfit that was owned by an ex-L.A.P.D. inspector I knew from the old days. I got the job of security chief at an electronics firm that has a solid government contract, and I'd have my own office and car, a secretary, *and* be making a hundred more a month than I was as a cop. The reason he picked me instead of one of the other applicants who were retired captains and inspectors is that he said he had enough administrators working for him and he

wanted one real iron-nutted street cop. So this was
maybe the first time I ever got rewarded for doing police work and I was pretty excited about starting
something new and seeing if real police techniques
and ideas couldn't do something for industrial security
which was usually pretty pitiful at best.

The thirtieth of May, the day I'd officially retire,
was also my fiftieth birthday. It was hard to believe
I'd been around half a century, but it was harder to
believe I'd lived in this world thirty years before I got
my beat. I was sworn in as a cop on my thirtieth birthday, the second oldest guy in my academy class, the
oldest being Cruz Segovia, who had tried three times
to join the Department but couldn't pass the oral
exam. It was probably because he was so shy and had
such a heavy Spanish accent, being an El Paso Mexican. But his grammar was beautiful if you just bothered to listen past the accent, and finally he got an oral
board that was smart enough to bother.

I was driving through Elysian Park as I was thinking these things and I spotted two motor cops in front
of me, heading toward the police academy. The motor
cop in front was a kid named Lefler, one of the
hundred or so I've broken in. He'd recently transferred
to Motors from Central and was riding tall in his new
shiny boots, white helmet, and striped riding britches.
His partner breaking him in on the motor beat was a
leather-faced old fart named Crandall. He's the type
that'll get hot at a traffic violator and screw up your
public relations program by pulling up beside him and
yelling, "Grab a piece of the curb, asshole."

Lefler's helmet was dazzling white and tilted forward, the short bill pulled down to his nose. I drove
up beside him and yelled, "That's a gorgeous skid lid
you got there, boy, but pull it up a little and lemme
see those baby blues."

Lefler smiled and goosed his bike a little. He was
even wearing expensive black leather gloves in this
heat.

"Hi, Bumper," said Crandall, taking his hand from the bar for a minute. We rode slow side by side and I grinned at Lefler, who looked self-conscious.

"How's he doing, Crandall?" I asked. "I broke him in on the job. He's Bumper-ized."

"Not bad for a baby," Crandall shrugged.

"I see you took his training wheels off," I said, and Lefler giggled and goosed the Harley again.

I could see the edge of the horseshoe cleats on his heels and I knew his soles were probably studded with iron.

"Don't go walking around my beat with those boots on, kid," I yelled. "You'll be kicking up sparks and starting fires." I chuckled then as I remembered seeing a motor cop with two cups of coffee in his gloved hands go right on his ass one time because of those cleats.

I waved at Lefler and pulled away. Young hotdogs, I thought. I was glad I was older when I came on the job. But then, I knew I would never have been a motor officer. Writing traffic tickets was the one part of police work I didn't like. The only good thing about it was it gave you an excuse to stop some suspicious cars on the pretext of writing a ticket. More good arrests came from phony traffic stops than anything else. More policemen got blown up that way, too.

I decided, what the hell, I was too jumpy to lay around the park reading the paper. I'd been like a cat ever since I'd decided about Friday. I hardly slept last night. I headed back toward the beat.

I should be patrolling for the burglar, I thought. I really wanted him now that I only had a couple days left. He was a daytime hotel creeper and hitting maybe four to six hotel rooms in the best downtown hotels every time he went to work. The dicks talked to us at rollcall and said the M.O. run showed he preferred weekdays, especially Thursday and Friday, but a lot of jobs were showing up on Wednesdays. This guy would shim doors which isn't too hard to do in any hotel since they usually have the world's worst security, and he'd burgle the place whether the occupants were in or not. Of course he waited until they were in the shower or napping. I loved catching burglars. Most policemen call it fighting ghosts and give up trying to catch them, but I'd rather catch a hot prowl guy than a stickup man any day. And any burglar with balls enough to take a pad when the people are home is every bit as dangerous as a stickup man.

I decided I'd patrol the hotels by the Harbor Freeway. I had a theory this guy was using some sort of repairman disguise since he'd eluded all stakeouts so far, and I figured him for a repair or delivery truck. I envisioned him as an out-of-towner who used the convenient Harbor Freeway to come to his job. This burglar was doing ding-a-ling stuff on some of the jobs, cutting up clothing, usually women's or kids', tearing the crotch out of underwear, and on a recent job he stabbed the hell out of a big teddy bear that a little girl left on the bed covered up with a blanket. I was glad the people weren't in when he hit *that* time. He was kinky, but a clever burglar, a lucky burglar. I thought about patrolling around the hotels, but first I'd go see Glenda. She'd be rehearsing now, and I might never see her again. She was one of the people I owed a good-bye to.

I entered the side door of the run-down little theater. They mostly showed skin flicks now. They used to have a halfway decent burlesque house here, with some fair comics and good-looking girls. Glenda was something in those days. The "Gilded Girl" they called her. She'd come out in a gold sheath and peel to a golden G-string and gold pasties. She was tall and graceful, and a better-than-average dancer. She played some big-time clubs off and on, but she was thirty-eight years old now and after two or three husbands she was back down on Main Street competing with beaver movies between reels, and taxi dancing part-time down the street at the ballroom. She was maybe twenty pounds heavier, but she still looked good to me because I saw her like she used to be.

I stood there in the shadows backstage and got accustomed to the dark and the quiet. They didn't even have anyone on the door anymore. I guess even the weinie waggers and bustle rubbers gave up sneaking in the side door of this hole. The wallpaper was wet and rusty and curling off the walls like old scrolls. There were dirty costumes laying around on chairs. The popcorn machine, which they activated on weekend nights, was leaning against the wall, one leg broken.

"The cockroaches serve the popcorn in this joint. You don't want any, Bumper," said Glenda, who had stepped out of her dressing room and was watching me from the darkness.

"Hi, kid." I smiled and followed her voice through the dark to the dimly lit little dressing room.

She kissed me on the cheek like she always did, and I took off my hat and flopped down on the ragged overstuffed chair behind her makeup table.

"Hey, Saint Francis, where've all the birdies gone?" she said, tickling the bald spot on my crown. She always laid about a hundred old jokes on me every time we met.

Glenda was wearing net stockings with a hole in one leg and a sequined G-string. She was nude on top and didn't bother putting on a robe. I didn't blame her, it was so damn hot today, but she didn't usually go around like this in front of me and it made me a little nervous.

"Hot weather's here, baby," she said, sitting down and fixing her makeup. "When you going back on nights?"

Glenda knew my M.O. I work days in the winter, nightwatch in the summer when the Los Angeles sun starts turning the heavy bluesuit into sackcloth.

"I'll never go back on nights, Glenda," I said casually. "I'm retiring."

She turned around in her chair and those heavy white melons bounced once or twice. Her hair was long and blond. She always claimed she was a real blonde but I'd never know.

"You won't quit," she said. "You'll be here till they kick you out. Or till you die. Like me."

"We'll both leave here," I said, smiling because she was starting to look upset. "Some nice guy'll come along and . . ."

"Some nice guy took me out of here three times, Bumper. Trouble is I'm just not a nice girl. Too fucked up for any man. You're just kidding about retiring, aren't you?"

"How's Sissy?" I said, to change the subject.

Glenda answered by taking a package of snapshots out of her purse and handing them to me. I'm farsighted now and in the dimness I couldn't really see anything but the outline of a little girl holding a dog. I couldn't even say if the dog was real or stuffed.

"She's beautiful," I said, knowing she was. I'd last seen her several months ago when I drove Glenda home from work one night.

"Every dollar you ever gave me went into a bank account for her just like we agreed at first," said Glenda.

"I know that."

"I added to it on my own too."

"She'll have something someday."

"Bet your ass she will," said Glenda, lighting a cigarette.

I wondered how much I'd given Glenda over the past ten years. And I wondered how many really good arrests I'd made on information she gave me. She was one of my big secrets. The detectives had informants who they paid but the bluesuits weren't supposed to be involved in that kind of police work. Well, I had paid my informants too. But I didn't pay them from any Department money. I paid them from my pocket, and when I made the bust on the scam they gave me, I made it look like I lucked onto the arrest. Or I made up some other fanciful story for the arrest report. That way Glenda was protected and nobody could say Bumper Morgan was completely nuts for paying informants out of his own pocket. The first time, Glenda turned me a federal fugitive who was dating her and who carried a gun and pulled stickups. I tried to give her twenty bucks and she refused it, saying he was a no-good asshole and belonged in the joint and she was no snitch. I made her take it for Sissy who was a baby then, and who had no dad. Since then over the years I've probably laid a thousand on Glenda for Sissy. And I've probably made the best pinches of any cop in Central Division.

"She gonna be a blondie like momma?" I asked.

"Yeah," she smiled. "More blond than me though. And about ten times as smart. I think she's smarter already. I'm reading books like mad to keep up with her."

"Those private schools are tough," I nodded. "They teach them something."

"You notice this one, Bumper?" she smiled, coming over to me and sitting on the arm of the chair. She was smiling big and thinking about Sissy now. "The dog's pulling her hair. Look at the expression."

"Oh yeah," I said, seeing only a blur and feeling one of those heavy chi-chis resting on my shoulder. Hers were big and natural, not pumped full of plastic like so many these days.

"She's peeved in this one," said Glenda, leaning closer, and it was pressed against my cheek, and finally one tender doorbell went right in my ear.

"Damn it, Glenda!" I said, looking up.

"What?" she answered moving back. She got it, and laughed her hard hoarse laugh. Then her laugh softened and she smiled and her big eyes went soft and I noticed the lashes were dark beneath the eyes and not from mascara. I thought Glenda was more attractive now than she ever was.

"I have a big feeling for you, Bumper," she said, and kissed me right on the mouth. "You and Sissy are the only ones. You're what's happening, baby."

Glenda was like Ruthie. She was one of the people who belonged to the beat. There were laws that I made for myself, but she was almost naked and to me she was still so beautiful.

"Now," she said, knowing I was about to explode. "Why not? You never have and I always wanted you to."

"Gotta get back to my car," I said, jumping up and crossing the room in three big steps. Then I mumbled something else about missing my radio calls, and Glenda told me to wait.

"You forgot your hat," she said, handing it to me.

"Thanks," I said, putting the lid on with one shaky hand. She held the other one and kissed my palm with a warm wet mouth.

"Don't think of leaving us, Bumper," she said and stared me in the eye.

"Here's a few bucks for Sissy," I said, fumbling in my pocket for a ten.

"I don't have any information this time," she said, shaking her head, but I tucked it inside her G-string and she grinned.

"It's for the kid."

There were some things I'd intended asking her about some gunsel I'd heard was hanging out in the skin houses and taxi-dance joints, but I couldn't trust myself alone with her for another minute. "See you later, kid," I said weakly.

"Bye, Bumper," she said as I picked my way through the darkness to the stage door. Aside from the fact that Cassie gave me all I could handle, there was another reason I tore myself away from her like that. Any cop knows you can't afford to get too tight with your informant. You try screwing a snitch and you'll be the one that ends up getting screwed.

**2**

AFTER LEAVING GLENDA it
actually seemed cool on the street. Glenda never did
anything like that before. Everyone was acting a little
ding-a-ling when I mentioned my retirement. I didn't
feel like climbing back inside that machine and listening to the noisy chatter on the radio.

It was still morning now and I was pretty happy,
twirling my stick as I strolled along. I guess I *swaggered* along. Most beat officers swagger. People expect
you to. It shows the hangtoughs you're not afraid, and
people expect it. Also they expect an older cop to cock
his hat a little so I always do that too.

I still wore the traditional eight-pointed hat and
used a leather thong on my stick. The Department
went to more modern round hats, like Air Force hats,
and we all have to change over. I'd wear the eight-
pointed police hat to the end, I thought. Then I
thought about Friday as being the end and I started a
fancy stick spin to keep my mind off it. I let the baton
go bouncing off the sidewalk back up into my hand.
Three shoe shine kids were watching me, two Mexican, one Negro. The baton trick impressed the hell out
of them. I strung it out like a Yo-Yo, did some back
twirls and dropped it back in the ring in one smooth
motion.

"Want a choo chine, Bumper?" said one of the Mexican kids.

"Thanks pal, but I don't need one."

"It's free to you," he said, tagging along beside me for a minute.

"I'm buying juice today, pal," I said, flipping two quarters up in the air which one of them jumped up and caught. He ran to the orange juice parlor three doors away with the other two chasing him. The shoe shine boxes hung around their necks with ropes and thudded against their legs as they ran.

These little kids probably never saw a beat officer twirl a stick before. The Department ordered us to remove the leather thongs a couple years ago, but I never did and all the sergeants pretend not to notice as long as I borrow a regulation baton for inspections.

The stick is held in the ring now by a big rubber washer like the one that goes over the pipe in the back of your toilet. We've learned new ways to use the stick from some young Japanese cops who are karate and aikido experts. We use the blunt end of the stick more and I have to admit it beats hell out of the old caveman swing. I must've shattered six sticks over guys' heads, arms and legs in my time. Now I've learned from these Nisei kids how to swing that baton in a big arc and put my whole ass behind it. I could damn near drive it through a guy if I wanted to, and never hurt the stick. It's very graceful stuff too. I feel I can do twice as well in a brawl now. The only bad thing is, they convinced the Department brass that the leather thong was worthless. You see, these kids were never real beat men. Neither were the brass. They don't understand what the cop twirling his stick really means to people who see him stroll down a quiet street throwing that big shadow in an eight-pointed hat. Anyway, I'd never take off the leather thong. It made me sick to think of a toilet washer on a police weapon.

I stopped by the arcade and saw a big muscle-bound fruit hustler standing there. I just looked hard

at him for a second, and he fell apart and slithered
away. Then I saw two con guys leaning up against a
wall flipping a quarter, hoping to get a square in a
coin smack. I stared at them and they got nervous and
skulked around to the parking lot and disappeared.

The arcade was almost deserted. I remember when
the slime-balls used to be packed in there solid, asshole to belly button, waiting to look at the skin show
in the viewer. That was a big thing then. The most
daring thing around. The vice squad used to bust guys
all the time for masturbating. There were pecker
prints all over the walls in front of the viewer. Now
you can walk in any bar or movie house down here
and see live skin shows, or animal flicks, and I don't
mean Walt Disney stuff. It's women and dogs, dykes
and donkeys, dildos and whips, fags, chickens, and
ducks. Sometimes it's hard to tell who or what is doing
what to who or what.

Then I started thinking about the camera club that
used to be next door to the arcade when nudity was
still a big thing. It cost fifteen bucks to join and five
bucks for every camera session. You got to take all the
pictures of a naked girl you wanted, as long as you
didn't get closer than two feet and as long as you
didn't touch. Of course, most of the "photographers"
didn't even have film in their cameras, but the management knew it and never bothered putting in real
camera lights and nobody complained. It was really so
innocent.

I was about to head back to my car when I noticed
another junkie watching me. He was trying to decide
whether to rabbit or freeze. He froze finally, his eyes
roaming around too casually, hitting on everything but
me, hoping he could melt into the jungle. I hardly ever
bust hypes for marks anymore, and he looked too sick
to be holding, but I thought I recognized him.

"Come here, man," I called and he came slinking my
way like it was all over.

"Hello, Bumper."

"Well, hello, Wimpy," I said to the chalk-faced hype. "It took me a minute to recognize you. You're older."

"Went away for three years last time."

"How come so long?"

"Armed robbery. Went to Q behind armed robbery. Violence don't suit me. I shoulda stuck to boosting. San Quentin made me old, Bumper."

"Too bad, Wimpy. Yeah, now I remember. You did a few gas stations, right?"

He *was* old. His sandy hair was streaked with gray and it was patchy. And his teeth were rotting and loose in his mouth. It was starting to come back to me like it always does: Herman (Wimpy) Brown, a life-long hype and a pretty good snitch when he wanted to be. Couldn't be more than forty but he looked a lot older than me.

"I wish I hadn't never met that hangtough, Barty Mendez. Remember him, Bumper? A dope fiend shouldn't never do violent crime. You just ain't cut out for it. I coulda kept boosting cigarettes out of markets and made me a fair living for quite a while."

"How much you boosting now, Wimpy?" I said, giving him a light. He was clammy and covered with gooseflesh. If he knew anything he'd tell me. He wanted a taste so bad right now, he'd snitch on his mother.

"I don't boost anywhere near your beat, Bumper. I go out to the west side and lift maybe a couple dozen cartons of smokes a day outta those big markets. I don't do nothing down here except look for guys holding."

"You hang up your parole yet?"

"No, I ain't running from my parole officer. You can call in and check." He dragged hard on the cigarette but it wasn't doing much good.

"Let's see your arms, Wimpy," I said, taking one bony arm and pushing up the sleeve.

"You ain't gonna bust me on a chickenshit marks case, are you, Bumper?"

"I'm just curious," I said, noticing the inner elbows were fairly clean. I'd have to put on my glasses to see the marks and I never took my glasses to work. They stayed in my apartment.

"Few marks, Bumper, not too bad," he said, trying a black-toothed smile. "I shrink them with hemorrhoid ointment."

I bent the elbow and looked at the back of the forearm. "Damn, the whole Union Pacific could run on those tracks!" I didn't need glasses to see those swollen abscessed wounds.

"Don't bust me, Bumper," he whined. "I can work for you like I used to. I gave you some good things, remember? I turned the guy that juked that taxi dancer in the alley. The one that almost cut her tit off, remember?"

"Yeah, that's right," I said, as it came back to me. Wimpy *did* turn that one for me.

"Don't these P.O.'s ever look at your arms?" I asked, sliding the sleeves back down.

"Some're like cops, others're social workers. I always been lucky about drawing a square P.O. or one who really digs numbers, like how many guys he's rehabilitating. They don't want to *fail* you, you know? Nowadays they give you dope and call it something else and say you're cured. They show you statistics, but I think the ones they figure are clean are just dead, probably from an overdose."

"Make sure *you* don't O.D., Wimpy," I said, leading him away from the arcade so we could talk in private while I was walking him to the corner call box to run a make.

"I liked it inside when I was on the program, Bumper. Honest to God. C.R.C. is a good place. I knew guys with no priors who shot phony needle holes in their arms so they could go there instead of to Q. And I heard Tehachapi is even better. Good food, and you don't hardly work at all, and group therapy where you can shuck, and there's these trade schools there where you can jive around. I could do a nickel in those places and I wouldn't mind. In fact, last time I was sorta sorry they kicked me out after thirteen months. But three years in Q broke me, Bumper. You know you're really in the joint when you're in that place."

"Still think about geezing when you're inside?"

"Always think about that," he said, trying to smile again as we stopped next to the call box. There were people walking by but nobody close. "I need to geez bad now, Bumper. Real bad." He looked like he was going to cry.

"Well, don't flip. I might not bust you if you can do me some good. Start thinking real hard, while I run a make to see if you hung it up."

"My parole's good as gold," he said, already perking up now that he figured I wasn't going to book him for marks. "You and me could work good, Bumper. I always trusted you. You got a rep for protecting your informants. Nobody never got a rat jacket behind your busts. I know you got an army of snitches, but nobody never got a snitch jacket. You take care of your people."

"You won't get a jacket either, Wimpy. Work with me and nobody knows. Nobody."

Wimpy was sniffling and cotton-mouthed so I unlocked the call box and hurried up with the wants check. I gave the girl his name and birthdate, and lit his cigarette while we waited. He started looking around. He wasn't afraid to be caught informing, he was just looking for a connection: a peddler, a junkie, anybody that might be holding a cap. I'd blow my brains out first, I thought.

"You living at a halfway house?" I asked.

"Not now," he said. "You know, after being clean for three years I thought I could do it this time. Then I went and fixed the second day out, and I was feeling so bad about it I went to a kick pad over on the east side and asked them to sign me in. They did and I was clean three more days, left the kick pad, scored some junk, and had a spike in my arm ever since."

"Ever fire when you were in the joint?" I asked, try-ing to keep the conversation going until the informa-tion came back.

"I never did. Never had the chance. I heard of a few guys. I once saw two guys make an outfit. They were expecting half a piece from somewheres. I don't know what they had planned, but they sure was making a fit."

"How?"

"They bust open this light bulb and one of them held the filament with a piece of cardboard and a rag and the other just kept heating it up with matches, and those suckers stretched that thing out until it was a pretty good eyedropper. They stuck a hole in it with a pin and attached a plastic spray bottle to it and it wasn't a bad fit. I'd a took a chance and stuck it in my arm if there was some dope in it."

"Probably break off in your vein."

"Worth the chance. I seen guys without a spike so strung out and hurting they cut their arm open with a razor and blow a mouthful of dope right in there."

He was puffing big on the smoke. His hands and arms were covered with the jailhouse tattoos made from pencil lead shavings which they mix with spit and jab into their arms with a million pinpricks. He probably did it when he was a youngster just coming up. Now he was an old head and had professional tat-toos all over the places where he shoots junk, but nothing could hide those tracks.

"I used to be a boss booster at one time, Bumper. Not just a cigarette thief. I did department stores for good clothes and expensive perfume, even jewelry counters which are pretty tough to do. I wore two-hundred-dollar suits in the days when only rich guys wore suits that good."

"Work alone?"

"All alone, I swear. I didn't need nobody. I looked different then. I was good looking, honest I was. I even talked better. I used to read a lot of magazines and books. I could walk through these department stores and spot these young kids and temporary sales help and have them give me their money. *Give* me their money, I tell you."

"How'd you work that scam?"

"I'd tell them Mister Freeman, the retail manager, sent me to pick up their receipts. He didn't want too much in the registers, I'd say, and I'd stick out my money bag and they'd fill it up for Mister Freeman." Wimpy started to laugh and ended up wheezing and choking. He settled down after a minute.

"I sure owe plenty to Mister Freeman. I gotta repay that sucker if I ever meet him. I used that name in maybe fifty department stores. That was my real father's name. That's really *my* real name, but when I was a kid I took the name of this bastard my old lady married. I always played like my real old man would've did something for us if he'd been around, so this way he did. Old Mister Freeman must've gave me ten grand. Tax free. More than most old men ever give their kids, hey, Bumper?"

"More than mine, Wimpy," I smiled.

"I did real good on that till-tap. I looked so nice, carnation and all. I had another scam where I'd boost good stuff, expensive baby clothes, luggage, anything. Then I'd bring it back to the salesman in the store bag and tell him I didn't have my receipt but would they please give me back my money on account of little Bobby wouldn't be needing these things because he smothered in his crib last Tuesday. Or old Uncle Pete passed on just before he went on his last trip that he saved and dreamed about for forty-eight years and I couldn't bear to look at this luggage anymore. Honest, Bumper, they couldn't give me the bread fast enough. I even made *men* cry. I had one woman beg me to take ten bucks from her own purse to help with the baby's funeral. I took that ten bucks and bought a little ten-dollar bag of junk and all the time I was cutting open that balloon and cooking that stuff I thought, 'Oh you baby. You really are my baby.' I took that spike and dug a little grave in my flesh and when I shoved that thing in my arm and felt it going in, I said, 'Thank you, lady, thank you, thank you, this is the best funeral my baby could have.'" Wimpy closed his eyes and lifted his face, smiling a little as he thought of his baby.

"Doesn't your P.O. ever give you a urinalysis or anything?" I still couldn't get over an old head like him not having his arms or urine checked when he was on parole, even if he *was* paroled on a non-narcotics beef.

"Hasn't yet, Bumper. I ain't worried if he does. I always been lucky with P.O.'s. When they put me on the urine program I came up with the squeeze-bottle trick. I just got this square friend of mine, old Homer Allen, to keep me supplied with a fresh bottle of piss, and I kept that little plastic squeeze bottle full and hanging from a string inside my belt. My dumb little P.O. used to think he was sneaky and he'd catch me at my job or at home at night sometimes and ask for a urine sample and I'd just go to the john with him right behind me watching, and I'd reach in my fly and fill his little glass bottle full of Homer's piss. He thought he was real slick, but he never could catch me. He was such a square. I really liked him. I felt like a father to that kid."

The girl came to the phone and read me Wimpy's record, telling me there were no wants.

"Well, you're not running," I said hanging up the phone, closing the metal call box door, and hanging the brass key back on my belt.

"Told you, Bumper. I just saw my P.O. last week. I been reporting regular."

"Okay, Wimpy, let's talk business," I said.

"I been thinking, Bumper, there's this dog motherfucker that did me bad one time. I wouldn't mind you popping him."

"Okay," I said, giving him a chance to rationalize his

snitching, which all informants have to do when they start out, or like Wimpy, when they haven't snitched for a long time.

"He deserves to march," said Wimpy. "Everybody knows he's no good. He burned me on a buy one time. I bring him a guy to score some pot. It's not on consignment or nothing, and he sells the guy catnip and I told him I knew the guy good. The guy kicked my ass when he found out it was catnip."

"Okay, let's do him," I said. "But I ain't interested in some two- or three-lid punk."

"I know, Bumper. He's a pretty big dealer. We'll set him up good. I'll tell him I got a guy with real bread and he should bring three kilos and meet me in a certain place and then maybe you just happen by or something when we're getting it out of the car and we both start to run but you go after him, naturally, and you get a three-key bust."

"No good. I can't run anymore. We'll work out something else."

"Any way you want, Bumper. I'll turn anybody for you. I'll roll over on anybody if you give me a break."

"Except your best connection."

"That's God you're talking about. But I think right this minute I'd even turn my connection for a fix."

"Where's this pot dealer live? Near my beat?"

"Yeah, not far. East Sixth. We can take him at his hotel. That might be the best way. You can kick down the pad and let me get out the window. At heart he's just a punk. They call him Little Rudy. He makes roach holders out of chicken bones and folded-up matchbooks and all that punk-ass bullshit. Only thing is, don't let me get a jacket. See, he knows this boss dyke, a real mean bull dagger. Her pad's a shooting gallery for some of us. If she knows you finked, she'll sneak battery acid in your spoon and laugh while you mainline it home. She's a *dog* motherfucker."

"Okay, Wimpy, when can you set it up?"

"Saturday, Bumper, we can do it Saturday."

"No good," I said quickly, a gas pain slicing across my stomach. "Friday's the latest for anything."

"Christ, Bumper. He's out of town. I know for sure. I think he's gone to the border to score."

"I can't wait past Friday. Think of somebody else then."

"Shit, lemme think," he said, rapping his skinny fingers against his temple. "Oh yeah, I got something. A guy in the Rainbow Hotel. A tall dude, maybe forty, forty-five, blondish hair. He's in the first apartment to the left on the second floor. I just heard last night he's a half-ass fence. Buys most anything you steal. Cheap, I hear. Pays less than a dime on the dollar. A righteous dog. He deserves to fall. I hear these dope fiends bring radios and stuff like that, usually in the early morning."

"Okay, maybe I'll try him tomorrow," I said, not really very interested.

"Sure, he might have lots of loot in the pad. You could clear up all kinds of burglaries."

"Okay, Wimpy, you can make it now. But I want to see you regular. At least three times a week."

"Bumper, could you please loan me a little in advance?"

"You gotta be kidding, Wimpy! Pay a junkie in advance?"

"I'm in awful bad shape today, Bumper," he said with a cracked whispery voice, like a prayer. He looked as bad as any I'd ever seen. Then I remembered I'd never see him again. After Friday I'd never see any of them again. He couldn't do me any good and it was unbelievably stupid, but I gave him a ten, which was just like folding up a sawbuck and sticking it in his arm. He'd be in the same shape twelve hours from now. He stared at the bill like he didn't believe it at first. I left him there and walked back to the car.

"We'll get that pothead for you," he said. "He's sloppy. You'll find seeds between the carpet and the molding outside the door in the hall. I'll get you lots of probable cause to kick over the pad."

"I know how to take down a dope pad, Wimpy," I said over my shoulder.

"Later, Bumper, see you later," he yelled, breaking into a coughing spasm.

# 3

I ALWAYS TRY to learn something from the people on my beat, and as I drove away I tried to think if I learned anything from all Wimpy's chatter. I'd heard this kind of bullshit from a thousand hypes. Then I thought of the hemorrhoid ointment for shrinking hype marks. That was something new. I'd never heard that one before. I always try to teach the rookies to keep their mouths shut and learn to listen. They usually give more information than they get when they're interrogating somebody. Even a guy like Wimpy could teach you something if you just give him a chance.

I got back in my car and looked at my watch because I was starting to get hungry. Of course I'm always hungry, or rather, I always want to eat. But I don't eat between meals and I eat my meals at regular times unless the job prevents it. I believe in routine. If you have rules for little things, rules you make up yourself, and if you obey these rules, your life will be in order. I only alter routines when I have to.

One of the cats on the daywatch, a youngster named Wilson, drove by in his black-and-white but didn't notice me because he was eyeballing some hype that was hotfooting it across Broadway to reach the crowded Grand Central Market, probably to score. The doper was moving fast like a hype with some gold in his jeans. Wilson was a good young copper, but sometimes when I looked at him like this, in profile when he was looking somewhere else, that cowlick of his and that kid nose, and something else I couldn't put my finger on, made me think of someone. For a while it bothered me and then one night last week when I was thinking so hard about getting married, and about Cassie, it came to me—he reminded me of Billy a little bit, but I pushed it out of my mind because I don't think of dead children or any dead people, that's another rule of mine. But I *did* start thinking of Billy's mother and how bad my first marriage had been and whether it could have been good if Billy had lived, and I had to admit that it *could* have been good, and it would have lasted if Billy had lived.

Then I wondered how many bad marriages that started during the war years had turned out all right. But it wasn't just that, there was the other thing, the dying. I almost told Cruz Segovia about it one time when we used to be partners and we were working a lonely morning watch at three a.m., about how my parents died, and how my brother raised me and how he died, and how my son died, and how I admired Cruz because he had his wife and all those kids and gave himself away to them fearlessly. But I never told him, and when Esteban, his oldest son, died in Vietnam, I watched Cruz with the others, and after the crushing grief he still gave himself away to them, completely. But I couldn't admire him for it anymore. I could marvel at it, but I couldn't admire it. I don't know what I felt about it after that.

Thinking all these foolish things made a gas bubble start, and I could imagine the bubble getting bigger and bigger. Then I took a bubble buster, chewed it up and swallowed it, made up my mind to start thinking about women or food or something good, raised up, farted, said "Good morning, Your Honor," and felt a whole lot better.

**4**

IT ALWAYS MADE ME feel
good just to drive around *without* thinking, so I turned
off my radio and did just that. Pretty soon, without
looking at my watch, I knew it was time to eat. I
couldn't decide whether to hit Chinatown or Little
Tokyo today. I didn't want Mexican food, because I
promised Cruz Segovia I'd come to his pad for dinner
tonight and I'd get enough Mexican food to last me a
week. His wife Socorro knew how I loved *chile relleno*
and she'd fix a dozen just for me.

A few burgers sounded good and there's a place in
Hollywood that has the greatest burgers in town.
Every time I go to Hollywood I think about Myrna, a
broad I used to fool around with a couple years ago.
She was an unreal Hollywood type, but she had a
good executive job in a network television studio and
whenever we went anywhere she'd end up spending
more bread than I would. She loved to waste money,
but the thing she really had going as far as I was concerned is that she looked just like Madeleine Carroll
whose pictures we had all over our barracks during
the war. It wasn't just that Myrna had style and elegant, springy tits, it's that she really looked like a
woman and acted like one, except that she was a stone
pothead and liked to improvise *too* much sexually. I'm

game for anything reasonable, but sometimes Myrna
was a little too freaky about things, and she also insisted on turning me on, and finally I tried smoking pot
one time with her, but I didn't feel good high like on
fine scotch. On her coffee table she had at least half a
key and that's a pound of pot and that's trouble. I
could just picture me and her getting hauled off to jail
in a nark ark. So it was a bummer, and I don't know if
it's the overall depressant effect of pot or what, but I
crashed afterwards, down, down, down, until I felt
mean enough to kick the hell out of her. But then,
come to think of it, I guess Myrna liked that best of all
anyway. So, Madeleine Carroll or not, I finally shined
her on and she gave up calling me after a couple
weeks, probably having found herself a trained gorilla
or something.

There was one thing about Myrna that I'd never
forget—she was a great dancer, not a good dancer, a
*great* dancer, because Myrna could completely stop
thinking when she danced. I think that's the secret.
She could dig hard rock and she was a real snake.
When she moved on a dance floor, often as not, everyone would stop and watch. Of course they laughed at
me—at first. Then they'd see there were *two* dancers
out there. It's funny about dancing, it's like food or
sex, it's something you do and you can just forget you
*have* a brain. It's all body and deep in your guts, especially the hard rock. And hard rock's the best thing to
happen to music. When Myrna and me were really
moving, maybe at some kid place on the Sunset Strip,
our bodies joined. It wasn't just a sex thing, but there
*was* that too, it was like our bodies really made it together and you didn't even have to *think* anymore.

I used to always experiment by doing the funky
chicken when we first started out. I know it's getting
old now, but I'd do it and they'd all laugh, because of
the way my belly jumped and swayed around. Then
I'd always do it again right near the end of the song,
and nobody laughed. They smiled, but nobody

laughed, because they could see by then how graceful
I really am, despite the way I'm built. Nobody's chick-
en was as funky as mine, so I always stood there flapping my elbows and bowing my knees just to test
them. And despite the raw animal moves of Myrna,
people also looked at *me*. They watched both of us
dance. That's one thing I miss about Myrna.

I didn't feel like roaming so far from my beat today
so I decided on beef teriyaki and headed for J-town.
The Japanese have the commercial area around First
and Second Streets between Los Angeles Street and
Central Avenue. There are lots of colorful shops and
restaurants and professional buildings. They also have
their share of banks and lots of money to go in them.
When I walked in the Geisha Doll on First Street, the
lunch hour rush was just about over and the mama-san
shuffled over with her little graceful steps like she was
still twenty instead of sixty-five. She always wore a silk
slit-skirted dress and she really didn't look too bad for
an old girl. I always kidded her about a Japanese
wearing a Chinese dress and she would laugh and say,
"Make moah China ting in Tokyo than all China. And
bettah, goddamn betcha." The place was plush and
dark, lots of bamboo, beaded curtains, hanging lan-
terns.

"Boom-pah san, wheah you been hide?" she said as I
stepped through the beads.

"Hello, Mother," I said, lifting her straight up under
the arms and kissing her on the cheek. She only
weighed about ninety pounds and seemed almost brittle, but once I didn't do this little trick and she got
mad. She expected it and all the customers got a kick
out of watching me perform. The cooks and all the
pretty waitresses and Sumi, the hostess, dressed in a
flaming orange kimono, expected it too. I saw Sumi
tap a Japanese customer on the shoulder when I
walked in.

I usually held the mama-san up like this for a good
minute or so and snuggled her a little bit and joked

around until everyone in the place was giggling, especially the mama-san, and then I put her down and let her tell anyone in shouting distance how "stlong is owah Boom-pah." My arms are good even though my legs are gone, but she was like a paper doll, no weight at all. She always said "*owah* Boom-pah," and I always took it to mean I belonged to J-town too and I liked the idea. Los Angeles policemen are very partial to Buddha heads because sometimes they seem like the only ones left in the world who really appreciate discipline, cleanliness, and hard work. I've even seen motor cops who'd hang a ticket on a one-legged leper, let a Nip go on a good traffic violation because they contribute practically nothing to the crime rate even though they're notoriously bad drivers. I've been noticing in recent years though that Orientals have been showing up as suspects on crime reports. If they degenerate like everyone else there'll be no *group* to look up to, just individuals.

"We have a nice table for you, Bumper," said Sumi with a smile that could almost make you forget food—almost. I started smelling things: tempura, rice wine, teriyaki steak. I have a sensitive nose and can pick out individual smells. It's really only *individual* things that count in this world. When you lump everything together you get goulash or chop suey or a greasy stew pot. I hated food like that.

"I think I'll sit at the *sushi* bar," I said to Sumi, who once confessed to me her real name was Gloria. People expected a geisha doll to have a Japanese name, so Gloria, a third generation American, obliged them. I agreed with her logic. There's no sense disappointing people.

There were two other men at the *sushi* bar, both Japanese, and Mako who worked the *sushi* bar smiled at me but looked a little grim at the challenge. He once told Mama that serving Boom-pah alone was like serving a *sushi* bar full of *sumos*. I couldn't help it, I loved those delicate little rice balls, molded by hand

and wrapped in strips of pink salmon and octopus, abalone, tuna and shrimp. I loved the little hidden pockets of horseradish that surprised you and made your eyes water. And I loved a bowl of soup, especially soybean and seaweed, and to drink it from the bowl Japanese style. I put it away faster than Mako could lay it out and I guess I looked like a buffalo at the *sushi* bar. Much as I tried to control myself and use a little Japanese self-discipline, I kept throwing the chow down and emptying the little dishes while Mako grinned and sweated and put them up. I knew it was no way to behave at the *sushi* bar in a nice restaurant, this was for gourmets, the refined eaters of Japanese cuisine, and I attacked like a blue locust, but God, eating *sushi* is being in heaven. In fact, I'd settle for that, and become a Buddhist if heaven was a *sushi* bar.

There was only one thing that saved me from looking too bad to a Japanese—I could handle chopsticks like one of them. I first learned in Japan right after the war, and I've been coming to the Geisha Doll and every other restaurant here in J-town for twenty years so it was no wonder. Even without the bluesuit, they could look at me click those sticks and know I was no tourist passing through. Sometimes though, when I didn't think about it, I ate with both hands. I just couldn't devour it fast enough.

In cooler weather I always drank rice wine or hot sake with my meal, today, ice water. After I'd finished what two or three good-sized Japanese would consume, I quit and started drinking tea while Mama and Sumi made several trips over to make sure I had enough and to see that my tea was hot enough and to try to feed me some tempura, and the tender fried shrimp looked so good I ate a half dozen. If Sumi wasn't twenty years too young I'd have been awful tempted to try her too. But she was so delicate and beautiful and so *young*, I lost confidence even thinking about it. And then too, she was one of the people on my beat, and there's that thing, the way they think about me. Still, it always helped my appetite to eat in a place where there were pretty women. But until I was at least half full, I have to say I didn't notice women or anything else. The world disappears for me when I'm eating something I love.

The thing that always got to me about Mama was how much she thanked me for eating up half her kitchen. Naturally she would never let me pay for my food, but she always thanked me about ten times before I got out the door. Even for an Oriental she really overdid it. It made me feel guilty, and when I came here I sometimes wished I could violate the custom and pay her. But she'd fed cops before I came along and she'd feed them after, and that was the way things were. I didn't tell Mama that Friday was going to be my last day, and I didn't start thinking about it because with a barrel of *sushi* in my stomach I couldn't afford indigestion.

Sumi came over to me before I left and held the little teacup to my lips while I sipped it and she said, "Okay, Bumper, tell me an exciting cops-and-robbers story." She did this often, and I'm sure she was aware how she affected me up close there feeling her sweet breath, looking at those chocolate-brown eyes and soft skin.

"All right, my little lotus blossom," I said, like W. C. Fields, and she giggled. "One spine tingler, coming up."

Then I reverted to my normal voice and told her about the guy I stopped for blowing a red light at Second and San Pedro one day and how he'd been here a year from Japan and had a California license and all, but didn't speak English, or pretended not to so he could try to get out of the ticket. I decided to go ahead and hang one on him because he almost wiped out a guy in the crosswalk, and when I got it written he refused to sign it, telling me in pidgin, "Not gear-tee, not gear-tee," and I tried for five minutes to explain that the signature was just a promise to appear and he

could have a jury trial if he wanted one and if he
didn't sign I'd have to book him. He just kept shaking
his head like he didn't savvy and finally I turned that
ticket book over and drew a picture on the back. Then
I drew the same picture for Sumi. It was a little jail
window with a stick figure hanging on the bars. He
had a sad turned-down mouth and slant eyes. I'd
showed him the picture and said, "You sign now,
maybe?" and he wrote his name so fast and hard he
broke my pencil lead.

Sumi laughed and repeated it in Japanese for
Mama. When I left after tipping Mako they all
thanked me again until I really *did* feel guilty. That
was the only thing I didn't like about J-town. I wished
to hell I could pay for my meal here, though I confess
I never had that wish anywhere else.

Frankly, there was practically nothing to spend my
money on. I ate three meals on my beat. I could buy
booze, clothes, jewelry, and everything else you could
think of at wholesale or less. In fact, somebody was always giving me something like that as a gift. I had my
bread stop and a dairy that supplied me with gallons
of free ice cream, milk, cottage cheese, all I wanted.
My apartment was very nice and rent-free, even including utilities, because I helped the manager run the
thirty-two units. At least he thought I helped him.
He'd call me when he had a loud party or something,
and I'd go up, join the party, and persuade them to
quiet down a little, while I drank their booze and ate
their canapés. Once in awhile I'd catch a peeping tom
or something, and since the manager was such a
mouse, he thought I was indispensable. Except for
girlfriends and my informants it was always hard to
find anything to spend my money on. Sometimes I actually went a week hardly spending a dime except for
tips. I'm a big tipper, not like most policemen.

When it came to accepting things from people on
my beat I did have one rule—no money. I felt that if I
took money, which a lot of people tried to give me at

Christmas time, I'd be getting bought. I never felt bought though if a guy gave me free meals or a case of booze, or a discounted sport coat, or if a dentist fixed my teeth at a special rate, or an optometrist bounced for a pair of sunglasses half price. These things weren't money, and I wasn't a hog about it. I never took more than I could personally use, or which I could give to people like Cruz Segovia or Cassie, who recently complained that her apartment was beginning to look like a distillery. Also I never took anything from someone I might end up having to arrest. For instance, before we started really hating each other, Marvin Heywood, the owner of the Pink Dragon, tried to lay a couple cases of scotch on me, and I mean the best, but I turned him down. I'd known from the first day he opened that place it would be a hangout for slimeballs. Every day was like a San Quentin convention in that cesspool. And the more I thought of it, the more I got burned up thinking that after I retired nobody would roust the Dragon as hard as I always did. I caused Marvin a sixty-day liquor license suspension twice, and I probably cost him two thousand a month in lost business since some of the hoods were afraid to come there because of me.

I jumped in my car and decided to cruise by the Dragon for one last shot at it. When I parked out back, a hype in the doorway saw me and ran down the steps to tell everybody inside the heat was coming. I took my baton, wrapped the thong around my hand which they teach you not to do now, but which I've been doing for twenty years, and I walked down the concrete stairway to this cellar bar, and through the draped doorway. The front is framed by a pink dragon head. The front doorway is the mouth of the beast, the back door is under the tail. It always made me mad just to see the big dumb-looking dragon-mouth door. I went in the back door, up the dragon's ass, tapping my stick on the empty chairs and keeping my head on a swivel as I let my eyes get accustomed to the gloom.

The pukepots were all sitting near the back. There were only about ten customers now in the early afternoon, and Marvin, all six feet six inches of him, was at the end of the bar grinning at a bad-looking bull dyke who was putting down a pretty well-built black stud in an arm wrestle.

Marvin was grinning, but he didn't mean it, he knew I was there. It curdled his blood to see me tapping on the furniture with my stick. That's why I did it. I always was as badge heavy and obnoxious as I could be when I was in there. I'd been in two brawls here and both times I knew Marvin was just wetting his shorts wishing he had the guts to jump in on me, but he thought better of it.

He weighed at least three hundred pounds and was damned tough. You had to be to own this joint, which catered to bookmakers, huggermugger whores, paddy hustlers, speed freaks, fruits and fruit hustlers, and ex-cons of both sexes and all ages. I'd never quite succeeded in provoking Marvin into attacking me, although it was common knowledge on the street that a shot fired at me one night from a passing car was some punk hired by Marvin. It was after that, even though nothing was ever proved, that I really began standing on the Dragon's tail. For a couple of months his business dropped to nothing with me living on his doorstep, and he sent two lawyers to my captain and the police commission to get me off his back. I relented as much as I had to, but I still gave him fits.

If I wasn't retiring there'd be hell to pay around here because once you get that twenty years' service in, you don't have to pussyfoot around so much. I mean no matter what kind of trouble you get into, nobody can ever take your pension away for any reason, even if they fire you. So if I were staying, I'd go right on. Screw the lawyers, screw the police commission. I'd land on that Dragon with both boondockers. And as I thought that, I looked down at my size thirteen triple E's. They were beat officer shoes, high top,

laces with eyelets, ankle supporting, clumsy, round
toes, beat officer shoes. A few years ago they were actually popular with young black guys, and almost
came into style again. They called them "old man
comforts" and they were soft and comfortable, but
ugly as hell, I guess, to most people. I'd probably always wear them. I'd sunk my old man comforts in too
many deserving asses to part with them now.

Finally Marvin got tired watching the arm wrestlers
and pretending he didn't see me.

"Whadda you want, Morgan," he said. Even in the
darkness I could see him getting red in the face, his
big chin jutting.

"Just wondering how many scumbags were here
today, Marvin," I said in a loud voice which caused
four or five of them to look up. These days we're apt to
get disciplinary action for making brutal remarks like
that, even though these assholes would bust their guts
laughing if I was courteous or even civil.

The bull dyke was the only righteous female in the
place. In this dive you almost have to check everybody's plumbing to know whether it's interior or exte-
rior. The two in dresses were drags, the others were
fruit hustlers and flimflam guys. I recognized a sleazy
bookmaker named Harold Wagner. One of the fruit
hustlers was a youngster, maybe twenty-two or so. He
was still young enough to be offended by my remark,
especially since it was in front of the queen in the red
mini who probably belonged to him. He mumbled
something under his breath and Marvin told him to
cool it since he didn't want to give me an excuse to
make another bust in the place. The guy looked high
on pot like most everyone these days.

"He your new playmate, Roxie?" I said to the red
dress queen, whose real name I knew was John Jeffrey
Alton.

"Yes," said the queen in a falsetto voice, and motioned to the kid to shut his mouth. He was a couple
inches taller than me and big chested, probably shack-

ing with Roxie now and they split what they get hustling. Roxie hustles the guys who want a queen, and the kid goes after the ones who want a jocker. This jocker would probably become a queen himself. I always felt sorry for queens because they're so frantic, searching, looking. Sometimes I twist them for information, but otherwise I leave them alone.

I was in a rotten mood thinking nobody would roust the Dragon after I was gone. They were all glaring at me now, especially Marvin with his mean gray eyes and knife mouth.

One young guy, too young to know better, leaned back in his chair and made a couple of oinks and said, "I smell pig."

I'd never seen him before. He looked like a college boy slumming. Maybe in some rah-rah campus crowd beer joint I'd just hee-haw and let him slide, but here in the Pink Dragon the beat cops rule by force and fear. If they stopped being afraid of me I was through, and the street would be a jungle which it is anyway, but at least now you can walk through it watching for occasional cobras and rabid dogs. I figured if it weren't for guys like me, there'd be no trails through the frigging forest.

"Oink, oink," he said again, with more confidence this time, since I hadn't responded. "I sure do smell pig."

"And what do pigs like best?" I smiled, slipping the stick back in my baton ring. "Pigs like to clean up garbage, and I see a pile." Still smiling I kicked the chair legs and he went down hard throwing a glass of beer on Roxie who forgot the falsetto and yelled, "Shithouse mouse!" in a pretty good baritone when the beer slid down his bra.

I had the guy in a wristlock before he knew what fell on him, and was on my way out the door, with him walking backwards, but not too fast in case someone else was ready.

"You bastard!" Marvin sputtered. "You assaulted my

customer. You bastard! I'm calling my lawyer."

"Go right on, Marvin," I said, while the tall kid screamed and tippy-toed to the door because the upward thrust of the wristlock was making him go as high as he could. The smell of pot was hanging on his clothes but the euphoria wasn't dulling the pain of the wristlock. When you've got one that's really loaded you can't crank it on too hard because they don't react to pain, and you might break a wrist trying to make them flinch. This guy felt it though, and he was docile, ow, ow, owing all the way out. Marvin came around the bar and followed us to the door.

"There's witnesses!" he boomed. "This time there's witnesses to your dirty, filthy false arrest of my customer! What's the charge? What're you going to charge him with?"

"He's drunk, Marvin," I smiled, holding the wristlock with one hand, just in case Marvin was mad enough. I was up, high up, all alive, ready to fly.

"It's a lie. He's sober. He's sober as you."

"Why, Marvin," I said, "he's drunk in public view and unable to care for himself. I'm obliged to arrest him for his own protection. He *has* to be drunk to say what he did to me, don't you agree? And if you're not careful I might think you're trying to interfere with my arrest. You wouldn't like to try interfering with my arrest would you, Marvin?"

"We'll get you, Morgan," Marvin whispered helplessly. "We'll get your job one of these days."

"If you slimeballs could have my job I wouldn't want it," I said, let down because it was over.

The kid wasn't as loaded as I thought when I got him out of there into the sunshine and more or less fresh Los Angeles air.

"I'm not drunk," he repeated all the way to the Glass House, shaking his mop of blond hair out of his face since I had his hands cuffed behind his back. The Glass House is what the street people call our main police building because of all the windows.

"You *talked* your way into jail, boy," I said, lighting a cigar.

"You can't just put a sober man in jail for drunk because he calls you a pig," said the kid, and by the way he talked and looked, I figured him for an upper-middle-class student hanging out downtown with the scumbags for a perverse kick, and also because he was at heart a scumbag himself.

"More guys talk themselves into jail than get there any other way," I said.

"I demand an attorney," he said.

"Call one soon as you're booked."

"I'll bring those people to court. They'll testify I was sober. I'll sue you for false arrest."

"You wouldn't be getting a cherry, kid. Guys tried to sue me a dozen times. And you wouldn't get those assholes in the Dragon to give you the time of day if they had a crate full of alarm clocks."

"How can you book me for *drunk?* Are you prepared to swear before God that I was drunk?"

"There's no God down here on the beat, and anyway He'd never show His face in the Pink Dragon. The United States Supreme Court decisions don't work too well down here either. So you see, kid, I been forced to write my own laws, and you violated one in there. I just have to find you guilty of contempt of cop."

## 5

AFTER I GOT the guy booked
I didn't know what the hell to do. I had this empty
feeling now that was making me depressed. I thought
about the hotel burglar again, but I felt lazy. It was
this empty feeling. I was in a black mood as I swung
over toward Figueroa. I saw a mailbox handbook
named Zoot Lafferty standing there near a public
phone. He used to hang around Main and then Broadway and now Figueroa. If we could ever get him another block closer to the Harbor Freeway maybe we
could push the bastard off the overpass sometime, I
thought, in the mood for murder.

Lafferty always worked the businessmen in the area,
taking the action and recording the bets inside a self-
addressed stamped envelope. And he always hung
around a mailbox and a public phone booth. If he saw
someone that he figured was a vice cop, he'd run to
the mailbox and deposit the letter. That way there'd
be no evidence like betting markers or owe sheets the
police could recover. He'd have the customers' bets
the next day when the mail came, and in time for col-
lection and payment. Like all handbooks though, he
was scared of plainclothes vice cops but completely ignored uniformed policemen.

So one day when I was riding by, I slammed on the

binders, jumped out of the black-and-white, and fell on Zoot's skinny ass before he could get to the mailbox. I caught him with the markers and they filed a felony bookmaking charge. I convicted him in Superior Court after I convinced the judge that I had a confidential reliable informant tell me all about Zoot's operation, which was true, and that I hid behind a bush just behind the phone booth and overheard the bets being taken over the phone, which was a lie. But I convinced the judge and that's all that matters. He had to pay a two-hundred-and-fifty-dollar fine and was given a year's probation, and that same day, he moved over here to Figueroa away from my beat where there are no bushes anywhere near his phone booth.

As I drove by Zoot, he waved at me and grinned and stood by the mailbox. I wondered if we could've got some help with the Post Office special agents to stop this flimflam, but it would've been awful hard and not worth the effort. You can't tamper with someone's mail very easy. Now, as I looked at his miserable face for the last time, my black mood got blacker and I thought, I'll bet no other uniformed cop ever takes the trouble to shag him after I'm gone.

Then I started thinking about bookmaking in general, and got even madder, because it was the kind of crime I couldn't do anything about. I saw the profits reaped from it all around me, and I saw the people involved in it, and knew some of them, and yet I couldn't do anything because they were so well organized and their weapons were so good and mine were so flimsy. The money was so unbelievably good that they could expand into semilegitimate businesses and drive out competition because they had the racket money to fall back on, and the legitimate businesses couldn't compete. And also they were tougher and ruthless and knew other ways to discourage competition. I always wanted to get one of them good, someone like Red Scalotta, a big book, whose fortune they say can't be guessed at. I thought all these things and how mad I get everytime I see a goddamn lovable Damon-Runyon-type bookmaker in a movie. I started thinking then about Angie Caputo, and got a dark kind of pleasure just picturing him and remembering how another old beat man, Sam Giraldi, had humbled him. Angie had never realized his potential as a hood after what Sam did to him.

Sam Giraldi is dead now. He died last year just fourteen months after he retired at twenty years' service. He was only forty-four when he had a fatal heart attack, which is particularly a policeman's disease. In a job like this, sitting on your ass for long periods of time and then moving in bursts of heart-cracking action, you can expect heart attacks. Especially since lots of us get so damned fat when we get older.

When he ruined Angie Caputo, Sam was thirty-seven years old but looked forty-seven in the face. He wasn't very tall, but had tremendous shoulders, a meaty face, and hands bigger than mine, all covered with heavy veins. He was a good handball player and his body was hard as a spring-loaded sap. He'd been a vice officer for years and then went back to uniform. Sam walked Alvarado when I walked downtown, and sometimes he'd drive over to my beat or I'd come over to his. We'd eat dinner together and talk shop or talk about baseball, which I like and which he was fanatic about. Sometimes, if we ate at his favorite delicatessen on Alvarado, I'd walk with him for a while and once or twice we made a pretty good pinch together like that. It was on a wonderful summer night when a breeze was blowing off the water in MacArthur Park that I met Angie Caputo.

It seemed to be a sudden thing with Sam. It struck like a bullet, the look on his face, and he said, "See that guy? That's Angie Caputo, the pimp and bookmaker's agent." And I said, "So what?" wondering what the hell was going on, because Sam looked like he was about to shoot the guy who was just coming out of a bar and getting ready to climb aboard a lavender Lincoln he had parked on Sixth Street. We got in Sam's car, getting ready to drive over to catch the eight o'clock show at the burlesque house out there on his beat.

"He hangs out further west, near Eighth Street," said Sam. "That's where he lives too. Not far from my pad, in fact. I been looking to see him for a few days now. I got it straight that he's the one that busted the jaw of Mister Rovitch that owns the cleaners where I get my uniforms done." Sam was talking in an unnaturally soft voice. He was a gentle guy and always talked low and quiet, but this was different.

"What'd he do that for?"

"Old guy was behind on interest payments to Harry Stapleton the loan shark. He had Angie do the job for him. Angie's a big man now. He don't have to do that kind of work no more, but he loves to do it sometimes. I hear he likes to use a pair of leather gloves with wrist pins in the palms."

"He get booked for it?"

Sam shook his head. "The old man swears three niggers mugged him."

"You sure it was Caputo?"

"I got a good snitch, Bumper."

And then Sam confessed to me that Caputo was from the same dirty town in Pennsylvania that he was from, and their families knew each other when they were kids, and they were even distant relatives. Then Sam turned the car around and drove back on Sixth Street and stopped at the corner.

"Get in, Angie," said Sam, as Caputo walked toward the car with a friendly smile.

"You busting me, Sam?" said Caputo, the smile widening, and I could hardly believe he was as old as Sam. His wavy hair was blue-black without a trace of gray, and his handsome profile was smooth, and his gray suit was beautiful. I turned around when Caputo held out a hand and smiled at me.

"Angie's my name," he said as we shook hands. "Where we going?"

"I understand you're the one that worked over the old man," said Sam in a much softer voice than before.

"You gotta be kidding, Sam. I got other things going. Your finks got the wrong boy for this one."

"I been looking for you."

"What for, Sam, you gonna bust me?"

"I can't bust you. I ain't been able to bust you since I knew you, even though I'd give my soul to do it."

"This guy's a comic," said Caputo, laughing as he lit a cigarette. "I can depend on old Sam to talk to me at least once a month about how he'd like to send me to the joint. He's a comic. Whadda you hear from the folks back in Aliquippa, Sam? How's Liz and Dolly? How's Dolly's kids?"

"Before this, you never really hurt nobody I knew personally," said Sam, still in the strange soft voice. "I knew the old man real good, you know."

"He one of your informers, Sam?" asked Caputo. "Too bad. Finks're hard to come by these days."

"Old guy like that. Bones might never heal."

"Okay, that's a shame. Now tell me where we're going. Is this some kind of roust? I wanna know."

"Here's where we're going. We're here," said Sam, driving the car under the ramp onto the lonely, dark, dirt road by the new freeway construction.

"What the fuck's going on?" asked Caputo, for the first time not smiling.

"Stay in the car, Bumper," said Sam. "I wanna talk with Angie alone."

"Be careful, *fratello*," said Caputo. "I ain't a punk you can scare. Be careful."

"Don't say *fratello* to me," Sam whispered. "You're a *dog's* brother. You beat old men. You beat women and live off them. You live off weak people's blood."

"I'll have your job, you dumb dago," said Caputo, and I jumped out of the car when I heard the slapping thud of Sam's big fist and Caputo's cry of surprise.

Sam was holding Caputo around the head and already I could see the blood as Sam hammered at his face. Then Caputo was on his back and he tried to hold off the blows of the big fist which drew back slowly and drove forward with speed and force. Caputo was hardly resisting now and didn't yell when Sam pulled out the heavy six-inch Smith and Wesson. Sam knelt on the arms of Caputo and cracked the gun muzzle through his teeth and into his mouth. Caputo's head kept jerking off the ground as he gagged on the gun muzzle twisting and digging in his throat but Sam pinned him there on the end of the barrel, whispering to him in Italian. Then Sam was on his feet and Caputo flopped on his stomach heaving bloody, pulpy tissue.

Sam and me drove back alone without talking. Sam was breathing hard and occasionally opened a window to spit a wad of phlegm. When Sam finally decided to talk he said, "You don't have to worry, Bumper, Angie'll keep his mouth shut. He didn't even open it when I beat him, did he?"

"I'm not worried."

"He won't say nothing," said Sam. "And things'll be better on the street. They won't laugh at us and they won't be so bold. They'll be scared. And Angie'll never really be respected again. It'll be better out here on the street."

"I'm just afraid he'll kill you, Sam."

"He won't. He'll fear me. He'll be afraid that *I'll* kill *him*. And I will if he tries anything."

"Christ, Sam, it's not worth getting so personally tied up to these assholes like this."

"Look, Bumper, I worked bookmaking in Ad Vice and here in Central. I busted bookmakers and organized hoodlums for over eight years. I worked as much as six months on *one* bookmaker. Six months! I put together an investigation and gathered evidence that no gang lawyer could beat and I took back offices where I seized records that could prove, *prove* the guy was a millionaire book. And I convicted them and saw them get pitiful fines time after time and I *never* saw a bookmaker go to state prison even though it's a felony. Let somebody else work bookmaking I finally decided, and I came back to uniform. But Angie's different. I know him. All my life I knew him, and I live right up Serrano there, in the apartments. That's *my* neighborhood. I use that cleaners where the old man works. Sure he was my snitch but I liked him. I never paid him. He just told me things. He got a kid's a schoolteacher, the old man does. The books'll be scared now for a little while after what I done. They'll respect us for a little while."

I had to agree with everything Sam said, but I'd never seen a guy worked over that bad before, not by a cop anyway. It bothered me. I worried about us, Sam and me, about what would happen if Caputo complained to the Department, but Sam was right. Caputo kept his mouth shut and I admit I was never sorry for what Sam did. When it was over I felt something and couldn't put my finger on it at first, and then one night laying in bed I figured it out. It was a feeling of something being *right*. For one of the few times on this job I saw an untouchable touched. I felt my thirst being slaked a little bit, and I was never sorry for what Sam did.

But Sam was dead now and I was retiring, and I was sure there weren't many other bluesuits in the division who could nail a bookmaker. I turned my car around and headed back toward Zoot Lafferty, still standing there in his pea green slack suit. I parked the black-and-white at the curb, got out, and very slow, with my sweaty uniform shirt sticking to my back, I walked over to Zoot who opened the package door on the red and blue mail box and stuck his arm inside. I stopped fifteen feet away and stared at him.

"Hello, Morgan," he said, with a crooked phony

grin that told me he wished he'd have slunk off long before now. He was a pale, nervous guy, about forty-five years old, with a bald freckled skull.

"Hello, Zoot," I said, putting my baton back inside the ring, and measuring the distance between us.

"You got your rocks off once by busting me, Morgan. Why don't you go back over to your beat, and get outta my face? I moved clear over here to Figueroa to get away from you and your fucking beat, what more do you want?"

"How much action you got written down, Zoot?" I said, walking closer. "It'll inconvenience the shit out of you to let it go in the box, won't it?"

"Goddamnit, Morgan," said Zoot, blinking his eyes nervously, and scratching his scalp which looked loose and rubbery. "Why don't you quit rousting people. You're an old man, you know that? Why don't you just fuck off outta here and start acting like one."

When the slimeball said that, the blackness I felt turned blood red, and I sprinted those ten feet as he let the letter slide down inside the box. But he didn't get his hand out. I slammed the door hard and put my weight against it and the metal door bit into his wrist and he screamed.

"Zoot, it's time for you and me to have a talk." I had my hand on the mailbox package door, all my weight leaning hard, as he jerked for a second and then froze in pain, bug-eyed.

"Please, Morgan," he whispered, and I looked around, seeing there was a lot of car traffic but not many pedestrians.

"Zoot, before I retire I'd like to take a real good book, just one time. Not a sleazy little handbook like you but a real bookmaker, how about helping me?"

Tears began running down Zoot's cheeks and he showed his little yellow teeth and turned his face to the sun as he pulled another time on the arm. I pushed harder and he yelped loud, but there were noisy cars driving by.

"For God's sake, Morgan," he begged. "I don't know anything. Please let my arm out."

"I'll tell you what, Zoot. I'll settle for your phone spot. Who do you phone your action in to?"

"They phone *me*," he gasped, as I took a little weight off the door.

"You're a liar," I said, leaning again.

"Okay, okay, I'll give you the number," he said, and now he was blubbering outright and I got disgusted and then mad at him and at me and especially at the bookmaker I'd never have a chance to get, because he was too well protected and my weapons were too puny.

"I'll break your goddamn arm if you lie," I said, with my face right up to his. A young, pretty woman walked by just then, looked at Zoot's sweaty face and then at mine, and damn near ran across the street to get away from us.

"It's six-six-eight-two-seven-three-three," he sobbed.

"Repeat it."

"Six-six-eight-two-seven-three-three."

"One more time, and it better come out the same."

"Six-six-eight-two-seven-three-three. Oh, Christ!"

"How do you say it when you phone in the action?"

"Dandelion. I just say the word Dandelion and then I give the bets. I swear, Morgan."

"Wonder what Red Scalotta would say if he knew you gave me that information?" I smiled, and then I let him go when I saw by his eyes that I'd guessed right and he was involved with that particular bookmaker.

He pulled his arm out and sat down on the curb, holding it like it was broken and cursing under his breath as he wiped the tears away.

"How about talking with a vice cop about this?" I said, lighting a fresh cigar while he began rubbing his arm which was probably going numb.

"You're a psycho, Morgan!" he said, looking up.

"You're a real psycho if you think I'd fink on any-body."

"Look, Zoot, you talk to a vice cop like I say, and we'll protect you. You won't get a jacket. But if you don't, I'll personally see that Scalotta gets the word that you gave me the phone number and the code so we could stiff in a bet on the phone clerk. I'll let it be known that you're a paid snitch and when he finds out what you told me you know what? I bet he'll believe it. You ever see what some gunsel like Bernie Zolitch can do to a fink?"

"You're the most rottenest bastard I ever seen," said Zoot, standing up, very shaky, and white as paste.

"Look at it this way, Zoot, you cooperate just this once, we'll take one little pukepot sitting in some phone spot and that'll be all there is to it. We'll make sure we come up with a phony story about how we got the information like we always do to protect an informant, and nobody'll be the wiser. You can go back to your slimy little business and I give you my word I'll never roust you again. Not personally, that is. And you probably know I always keep my word. Course I can't guarantee you some *other* cop won't shag you sometime."

He hesitated for a second and then said, "I'll settle for *you* not rousting me no more, Morgan. Those vice cops I can live with."

"Let's take a ride. How's your arm feeling?"

"Fuck you, Morgan," he said, and I chuckled to my-self and felt a little better about everything. We drove to Central Vice and I found the guy I wanted sitting in the office.

"Why aren't you out taking down some handbook, Charlie?" I said to the young vice cop who was lean-ing dangerously back in a swivel chair with his crepe-soled sneak shoes up on a desk doping the horses on a scratch sheet.

"Hi, Bumper," he grinned, and then recognized Zoot who he himself probably busted a time or two.

"Mr. Lafferty decide to give himself up?" said Charlie Bronski, a husky, square-faced guy with about five years on the Department. I broke him in when he was just out of the academy. I remembered him as a smart aggressive kid, but with humility. Just the kind I liked. You could teach that kind a little something. I wasn't ashamed to say he was Bumper-ized.

Charlie got up and put on a green striped, short-sleeved ivy-league shirt over the shoulder holster which he wore over a white T-shirt.

"Old Zoot here just decided to repent his evil ways, Charlie," I said, glancing at Zoot who looked as sad as anyone I'd ever seen.

"Let's get it over with, Morgan, for chrissake," said Zoot. "And you got to swear you'll keep it confidential."

"Swear, Charlie," I said.

"I swear," said Charlie. "What's this all about?"

"Zoot wants to trade a phone spot to us."

"For what?" asked Charlie.

"For nothing," said Zoot, very impatient. "Just because I'm a good fucking citizen. Now you want the information or not?"

"Okay," Charlie said, and I could tell he was trying to guess how I squeezed Zoot. Having worked with me for a few months, Charlie was familiar with my M.O. I'd always tried to teach him and other young cops that you can't be a varsity letterman when you deal with these barfbags. Or rather, you *could* be, and you'd probably be the one who became captain, or Chief of Police or something, but you can bet there'd always have to be the guys like me on the street to make you look good up there in that ivory tower by keeping the assholes from taking over the city.

"You wanna give us the relay, is that it?" said Charlie, and Zoot nodded, looking a little bit sick.

"*Is* it a relay spot? Are you sure?" asked Charlie.

"I'm not sure of a goddamn thing," Zoot blubbered, rubbing his arm again. "I only came 'cause I can't take this kind of heat. I can't take being rousted and hurt."

Charlie looked at me, and I thought that if this life-long handbook, this ex-con and slimeball started crying, I'd flip. I was filled with loathing for a pukepot like Zoot, not because he snitched, hell, everybody snitches when the twist is good enough. It was this crybaby sniveling stuff that I couldn't take.

"Damn, Zoot!" I finally exploded. "You been a friggin' scammer all your life, fracturing every friggin' law you had nuts enough to crack, and you sit here now acting like a pious nun. If you wanna play your own tune you better damn well learn to dance to it, and right now you're gonna do the friggin' boogaloo, you goddamn hemorrhoid!"

I took a step toward Zoot's chair and he snapped up straight in his seat saying, "Okay, Morgan, okay. Whadda you want? For God's sake I'll tell you what you wanna know! You don't have to get tough!"

"Is the number you phone a relay?" repeated Charlie calmly.

"I think so," Zoot nodded. "Sounds like some goofy broad don't know nothing about the business. I been calling this same broad for six months now. She's probably just some stupid fucking housewife, sitting on a hot seat and taking them bets for somebody she don't even know."

"Usually record them on Formica," Charlie explained to me, "then somebody phones her several times a day and takes the action she wrote down. She can wipe the Formica in case the vice cops come busting down her door. She probably won't even know who pays her or where the phone calls come from."

"Fuck no, she ain't gonna know," said Zoot, looking at me. "This shit's too big, Morgan. It's too goddamn big. You ain't gonna bother nobody by rousting me. You don't understand, Morgan. People *want* us in business. What's a guy get for bookmaking? Even a big guy? A fucking fine. Who does time? You ever see a

book get joint time?" said Zoot to Charlie, who shook
his head. "Fuck no, you ain't and you ain't going to.
Everybody bets with bookies for chrissake and those
that don't, they like some other kind of vice. Give up,
Morgan. You been a cop all these years and you don't
know enough to give up fighting it. You can't save this
rotten world."

"I ain't trying to, Zoot," I said. "I just love the friggin' battle!"

I went down the hall to the coffee room, figuring
that Charlie should be alone with Zoot. Now that I
had played the bad guy, he could play the good guy.
An interrogation never works if it's not private, and
Charlie was a good bullshitter. I had hopes he could
get more out of Zoot because I had him loosened up.
Anytime you get someone making speeches at you,
you have a chance. If he's shaky about one thing, he
might be about something else. I didn't think you
could buy Zoot with money, he was too scared of everything. But being scared of us as well as the mob, he
could be gotten to. Charlie could handle him.

Cruz Segovia was in the coffee room working on his
log. I came in behind him. There was no one else in
the room and Cruz was bent over the table writing in
his log. He was so slim that even in his uniform he
looked like a little boy bent over doing his homework.
His face was still almost the same as when we were in
the academy and except for his gray hair he hadn't
changed much. He was barely five feet eight and sitting there he looked really small.

"*Qué pasó, compadre,*" I said, because he always
said he wished I was Catholic and could have been
the godfather for his last seven kids. His kids considered me their godfather anyway, and he called me
*compadre.*

"*Órale, panzón,*" he said, like a pachuco, which he
put on for me. He spoke beautiful Spanish and could
also read and write Spanish which is rare for a Mexi-

can. He was good with English too, but the barrios of
El Paso Texas died hard, and Cruz had an accent
when he spoke English.

"Where you been hiding out all day?" I said, putting
a dime in the machine and getting Cruz a fresh cup,
no cream and double sugar.

"You bastard," he said. "Where've *I* been hiding.
Communication's been trying to get *you* all day! Don't
you know that funny little box in your car is called a
radio and you're supposed to listen for your calls and
you're even supposed to handle them once in a while?"

"*Chale, chale.* Quit being a sergeant," I said.
"Gimme some slack. I been bouncing in and out of
that black-and-white machine so much I haven't heard
anything."

"You'll be a beat cop all your life," he said, shaking
his head. "You have no use at all for your radio, and if
you didn't have your best friend for a sergeant, your
big ass'd be fired."

"Yeah, but I got him," I grinned, poking him in the
shoulder and making him swear.

"Seriously, Bumper," he said, and he didn't have to
say "seriously" because his large black eyes always
turned down when he was serious. "Seriously, the
skipper asked me to ask you to pay a little more attention to the radio. He heard some of the younger officers complaining about always handling the calls in
your district because you're off the radio walking
around so much."

"Goddamn slick-sleeved rookies," I said, hot as hell,
"they wouldn't know a snake in the grass if one
jumped up and bit them on the dick. You seen these
goddamn rookies nowadays, riding down the friggin'
streets, ogling all the cunt, afraid to put on their hats
because it might ruin their hair styles. Shit, I actually
saw one of these pretty young fuzz sitting in his black-
and-white spraying his hair! I swear, Cruz, most of
these young cats wouldn't know their ass from a burnt
biscuit."

"I know, Bumper," Cruz nodded with sympathy. "And the skipper knows a whole squad of these youngsters couldn't do half the police work you old-timers do. That's why nobody says anything to you. But *hombre*, you have to handle some calls once in a while instead of walking that beat."

"I know," I said, looking at my coffee.

"Just stay on the air a little more."

"Okay, okay, you're the *macho*. You got the *huevos de oro*."

Cruz smiled now that he was through stepping on my meat. He was the only one that ever nagged me or told me what to do. When someone else had ideas along those lines, they'd hit Cruz with them, and if he thought I needed talking to, he'd do it. They figured I'd listen to Cruz.

"Don't forget, *loco*, you're coming to dinner tonight."

"Can you see me forgetting dinner at your pad?"

"You sure Cassie can't come with you?"

"She sure wishes she could. You know Friday's the last day for her at school and they're throwing a little party for her. She *has* to be there."

"I understand," said Cruz. "What day is she actually going up north? She decided yet?"

"Next week she'll be packed and gone."

"I don't know why you don't just take your vacation now and cut out with her. What's the sense of waiting till the end of the month? That vacation pay isn't worth being away from her for a few weeks, is it? She might come to her senses and ask herself why the hell she's marrying a mean old bastard like Bumper Morgan."

I wondered why I didn't tell Cruz that I'd decided to do just that. What the hell was the secret? Friday was going to be my last day. I never cared anything about the vacation pay. Was I really afraid to say it?

"Gonna be strange leaving everything," I muttered to my coffee cup.

"I'm glad for you, Bumper," said Cruz, running his

slim fingers through his heavy gray hair. "If I didn't have all the kids I'd get the hell out too, I swear. I'm glad you're going."

Cruz and me had talked about it lots of times the last few years, ever since Cassie came along and it became inevitable that I'd marry her and probably pull the pin at twenty years instead of staying thirty like Cruz had to do. Now that it was here though, it seemed like we'd never discussed it at all. It was so damn strange.

"Cruz, I'm leaving Friday," I blurted. "I'm going to see Cassie and tell her I'll leave Friday. Why wait till the end of the month?"

"That's fine, 'mano!" Cruz beamed, looking like he'd like to cut loose with a yelp, like he always did when he was drunk.

"I'll tell her today." Now I felt relieved, and drained the last of the coffee as I got up to leave. "And I don't give a damn if I loaf for a month. I'll just take it easy till I feel like starting my new job."

"That's right!" said Cruz, his eyes happy now. "Sit on that big fat *nalgas* for a year if you want to. They want *you* as security chief. They'll wait for you. And you have forty percent coming every month, and Cassie's got a good job, and you still have a good bank account don't you?"

"Hell yes," I answered, walking toward the door. "I never had to spend much money, with my beat and all."

"Shhh," Cruz grinned. "Haven't you heard? We're the new breed of professionals. We don't accept gratuities."

"Who said anything about gratuities? I only take tribute."

Cruz shook his head and said, "*Ahí te huacho,*" which is anglicized slang meaning I'll be seeing, or rather, watching for you.

"*Ahí te huacho,*" I answered.

After I left Cruz I went back to the vice squad office and found Zoot hanging his head, and Charlie downright happy, so I figured Charlie had done all right.

"I'd like to talk to you alone for a minute, Bumper," said Charlie, leading me into the next room and closing the door while Zoot sat there looking miserable.

"He told me lots more than he thinks he did," said Charlie. He was charged up like any good cop should be when he has something worthwhile.

"He thinks you're taking me off his back?" I asked.

"Yeah," Charlie smiled. "Play along. He thinks I'm going to save him from you. Just lay off him for a while, okay, Bumper? He told me he's planning on moving his territory out of the division to Alvarado in a couple of weeks but he has to stay around Figueroa for the time being. I told him I'd talk to you."

"Tell Zoot he doesn't have to worry about old Bumper any more," I said, getting another gas pain. I vowed to myself I'd lay off the soy sauce next time I ate in J-town.

"Yeah, he'll be a problem for the Rampart vice squad then," said Charlie not getting my meaning.

"Want me to take him back to Fig?"

"I'll take him," said Charlie. "I want to talk a little more."

"Do me a favor?"

"Sure, Bumper."

"You think there's any chance of something going down because of what Zoot told you?"

"There's a damn good chance. Zoot half-ass copped that he thinks the broad at the relay spot that takes his action is Reba McClain, and if it is we might be able to swing real good with her."

"How's that?"

"She's Red Scalotta's girlfriend. We took her down in another relay about six months ago and she got probation with a six months' jail sentence hanging. She's a meth head and an ex-con and stir crazy as hell. Kind of a sex thing. She's got a phobia about jails and bull dykes and all that. Real ding-a-ling, but a gorgeous little toadie. We were just talking last week about her and if we could shag her and catch her dirty we might get to Scalotta through her. She's a real shaky bitch. I think she'd turn her mama to stay on the street. You bringing in Zoot with that phone number was a godsend."

"Okay, then I'm really going to ask the favor."

"Sure."

"Take her today or tomorrow at the latest. If she gives you something good, like a back office, take it down on Friday."

"A back office! Jesus, I don't think she'll have that kind of information, Bumper. And hell, Friday is just two days away. Sometimes you stake out for weeks or months to take a back office. Jesus, that's where the book's records are kept. We'd have to get a search warrant and that takes lots of information beforehand. Why Friday?"

"I'm going on vacation. I want to be in on this one, Charlie. I never took a back office. I want it real bad, and it has to be before I go on vacation."

"I'd do it for you, Bumper, if I could, you know that, but Friday's only two days away!"

"Just do police work like I taught you, with balls and brains and some imagination. That's all I ask. Just try, okay?"

"Okay," Charlie said. "I'll give it a try."

Before I left I put on an act for Zoot so he'd think Charlie was his protector. I pretended I was mad at Charlie and Charlie pretended he was going to stop me from any future attempts to stuff Zoot down the goddamn mail chute.

## 6

AFTER I GOT in my car I re-
membered the friendly ass bite Cruz gave me and I
picked up the hand mike and said, "One-X-L-Forty-
five, clear."

"One-X-L-Forty-five, handle this call," said the operator, and I grumbled and wrote the address down.
"Meet One-L-Thirty, Ninth and Broadway."

"One-X-L-Forty-five, roger," I said disgustedly, and
thought, that's what I get for clearing. Probably some
huge crisis like taking a chickenshit theft report from
some fatass stockbroker who got his wallet lifted while
he was reading dirty magazines at the dirty bookstore
on Broadway.

One-X-L-Thirty was a rookie sergeant named Grant
who I didn't know very well. He wore one five-year
hashmark showing he had between five and ten years
on. I'd bet it was a whole lot closer to five. He had a
ruddy, smooth face and a big vocabulary. I never
heard him swear at any rollcall he conducted. I
couldn't trust a policeman who didn't swear once in a
while. You could hardly describe certain things you
see and feelings you have in this job without some
colorful language.

Grant was south of Ninth near Olympic, out of his
car, pacing up and down as I drove up. I knew it was

snobbish but I couldn't call a kid like him "Sergeant."
And I didn't want to be out and out rude so I didn't
call these young sergeants by their last names. I didn't
call them anything. It got awkward sometimes, and I
had to say, "Hey pal," or "Listen bud" when I wanted
to talk to one of them. Grant looked pretty nervous
about something.

"What's up?" I asked, getting out of my car.

"We have a demonstration at the Army Induction
Center."

"So?" I said, looking down the street at a group of
about fifteen marchers picketing the building.

"A lot of draftees go in and out and there could be
trouble. There're some pretty militant-looking types in
that picket line."

"So what're we gonna do?"

"I just called you because I need someone to stand
by and keep them under surveillance. I'm going to talk
to the lieutenant about the advisability of calling a
tactical alert. I'd like you to switch to frequency nine
and keep me advised of any status change."

"Look, pal, this ain't no big thing. I mean, a tactical
alert for fifteen ragtag flower sniffers?"

"You never know what it can turn into."

"Okay," and I sighed, even though I tried not to,
"I'll sit right here."

"Might be a good idea to drive closer. Park across
the street. Close enough to let them see you but far
enough to keep them from trying to bait you."

"Okay, pal," I muttered, as Grant got in his car and
sped toward the station to talk to Lieutenant Hilliard,
who was a cool old head and wouldn't get in a flap
over fifteen peace marchers.

I pulled out in the traffic and a guy in a blue Chev-
vy jumped on his brakes even though he was eighty
feet back and going slow. People get black-and-white
fever when they see a police car and they do idiotic
things trying to be super careful. I've seen them concentrate so hard on one facet of safe driving, like giv-

ing an arm signal, that they bust right through a red light. That's black-and-white fever for you.

The marchers across Broadway caught my eye when two of them, a guy and a girl, were waving for me to come over. They seemed to be just jiving around but I thought I better go over for several reasons. First of all, there might really be something wrong. Second, if I didn't, it looked like hell for a big bad copper to be afraid to approach a group of demonstrators. And third, I had a theory that if enough force could be used fast enough in these confrontations there'd *be* no riot. I'd never seen real force used quick enough yet, and I thought, what the hell, now was my chance to test my theory since I was alone with no sergeants around.

These guys, at least a few of them, two black guys, and one white, bearded scuz in a dirty buckskin vest and yellow headband, looked radical enough to get violent with an overweight middle-aged cop like myself, but I firmly believed that if one of them made the mistake of putting his hands on me and I drove my stick three inches in his esophagus, the others would yell police brutality twice and slink away. Of course I wasn't sure, and I noticed that the recent arrivals swelled their numbers to twenty-three. Only five of them were girls. That many people could stomp me to applesauce without a doubt, but I wasn't really worried, mainly because even though they were fist shaking, most of them looked like middle-class white people just playing at revolution. If you have a few hungry-looking professionals like I figured the white guy in the headband to be, you could have trouble. Some of these could lend their guts to the others and set them off, but he was the only one I saw.

I drove around the block so I didn't have to make an illegal U-turn in front of them, made my illegal U-turn on Olympic, came back and parked in front of the marchers, who ignored me and kept marching and chanting, "Hell no, we won't go." And "Fuck Uncle

Sam, and Auntie Spiro," and several other lewd remarks mostly directed at the President, the governor, and the mayor. A few years ago, if a guy yelled "fuck" in a public place in the presence of women or children, we'd have to drag his ass to jail.

"Hi, Officer, I love you," said one little female peace marcher, a cute blonde about seventeen, wearing two inches of false eyelashes that looked upside-down, and ironed-out shoulder-length hair.

"Hi, honey, I love you too," I smiled back, and leaned against the door of my car. I folded my arms and puffed a cigar until the two who had been waving at me decided to walk my way.

They were whispering now with another woman and finally the shorter girl, who was not exactly a girl, but a woman of about thirty-five, came right up. She was dressed like a teenager with a short yellow mini, violet panty hose, granny glasses, and white lipstick. Her legs were too damned fat and bumpy and she was wearing a theatrical smile with a cold arrogant look beneath it. Up close, she looked like one of the professionals and seemed to be a picket captain. Sometimes a woman, if she's the real thing, can be the detonator much quicker than a man can. This one seemed like the real thing, and I looked her in the eye and smiled while she toyed with a heavy peace medal hanging around her neck. Her eyes said, "You're just a fat harmless cop, not worth my talents, but so far you're all we have here, and I don't know if an old bastard like you is even intelligent enough to know when he's being put down."

That's what I saw in her eyes, and her phony smile, but she said nothing for a few more minutes. Then a car from one of the network stations rolled up and two men got out with a camera and mike.

The interest of the marchers picked up now that they were soon to be on tape, and the chanting grew louder, the gestures more fierce, and the old teenybopper in the yellow dress finally said, "We called you over because you looked very forlorn. Where're the riot troops, or are you all we get today?"

"If you get *me*, baby, you ain't gonna want any more," I smiled through a puff of cigar smoke, pinning her eyeballs, admiring the fact that she didn't bat an eye even though I knew damn well she was expecting the businesslike professional clichés we're trained to give in these situations. I'd bet she was even surprised to see me slouching against my car like this, showing such little respect for this menacing group.

"You're not supposed to smoke in public, are you, Officer?" She smiled, a little less arrogant now. She didn't know what the hell she had here, and was going to take her time about setting the bait.

"Maybe a real policeman ain't supposed to, but this uniform's just a shuck. I rented this ill-fitting clown suit to make an underground movie about this fat cop that steals apples and beats up flower children and old mini-skirted squatty-bodies with socks to match their varicose veins in front of the U.S. Army Induction Center."

Then she lost her smile completely and stormed back to the guy in the headband who was also much older than he first appeared. They whispered and she looked at me as I puffed on the cigar and waved at some of the marchers who were putting me on, most of them just college-age kids having a good time. A couple of them sincerely seemed to like me even though they tossed a few insults to go along with the crowd.

Finally, the guy in the headband came my way shouting encouragement to the line of marchers who were going around and around in a long oval in front of the door, which was being guarded by two men in suits who were not policemen, but probably military personnel. The cameraman was shooting pictures now, and I hid my cigar and sucked in a few inches of gut when he photographed me. The babe in the yellow dress joined the group after passing out some Black

Panther pins and she marched without once looking at me again.

"I hear you don't make like the other cops we've run into in these demonstrations," said the guy with the headband, suddenly standing in front of me and grinning. "The L.A.P.D. abandoning the oh so firm but courteous approach? Are you a new police riot technique? A caricature of a fat pig, a jolly jiveass old cop that we just can't get mad at? Is that it? They figure we couldn't use you for an Establishment symbol? Like you're too fucking comical looking, is that it?"

"Believe it or not, Tonto," I said, "I'm just the neighborhood cop. Not a secret weapon, nothing for lumpy legs to get tight-jawed about. I'm just your local policeman."

He twitched a little bit when I mentioned the broad so I guessed she might be his old lady. I figured they probably taught sociology 1A and 1B in one of the local junior colleges.

"Are you the only swine they're sending?" he asked, smiling not quite so much now which made me very happy. It's hard even for professionals like him to stay with a smirk when he's being rapped at where it hurts. He probably just *loves* everything about her, even the veiny old wheels. I decided, screw it, I was going to take the offensive with these assholes and see where it ended.

"Listen, Cochise," I said, the cigar between my teeth, "I'm the only old pig you're gonna see today. All the young piglets are staying in the pen. So why don't you and old purple pins just take your Che handbooks and cut out. Let these kids have their march with no problems. And take those two dudes with the naturals along with you." I pointed to the two black guys who were standing ten feet away watching us. "There ain't gonna be any more cops here, and there ain't gonna be any trouble."

"You *are* a bit refreshing," he said, trying to grin, but it was a crooked grin. "I was getting awfully sick of those unnatural pseudoprofessionals with their businesslike platitudes, pretending to look right through us when really they wanted to get us in the back room of some police station and beat our fucking heads in. I must say you're refreshing. You're truly a vicious fascist and don't pretend to be anything else."

Just then the mini-skirted broad walked up again. "Is he threatening you, John?" she said in a loud voice, looking over her shoulder, but the guys with the camera and mike were at the other end of the shouting line of marchers.

"Save it till they get to this end," I said, as I now estimated her age to be closer to forty. She was a few years older than he was and the mod camouflage looked downright comical. "Want some bubble gum, little girl?" I said.

"Shut your filthy mouth," he said, taking a step toward me. I was tight now, I wound myself up and was ready. "Stay frosty, Sitting Bull," I smiled. "Here, have a cigar." I offered one of my smokes, but he wheeled and walked away with old lumpy clicking along behind him.

The two black guys hadn't moved. They too were professionals, I was positive now, but they were a different kind. If anything went down, I planned to attack those two right away. They were the ones to worry about. They both wore black plastic jackets and one wore a black cossack hat. He never took his eyes off me. He'd be the very first one I'd go after, I thought. I kept that flaky look, grinning and waving at any kid who gave me the peace sign, but I was getting less and less sure I could handle the situation. There were a couple other guys in the group that might get froggy if someone leaped, and I've seen what only two guys can do if they get you down and put the boots to you, let alone nine or ten.

I hated to admit it but I was beginning to wish Grant would show up with a squad of bluecoats. Still, it was a quiet demonstration, as quiet as these things go, and there was probably nothing to worry about, I thought.

The march continued as it had for a few more minutes, with the young ones yelling slogans, and then headband and mini-skirt came back with six or eight people in tow. These kids were definitely collegiate, wearing flares or bleach-streaked Levis. Some of the boys had muttonchops and moustaches, most had collar-length hair, and two of them were pretty, suntanned girls. They looked friendly enough and I gave them a nod of the head when they stopped in front of me.

One particularly scurvy-looking slimeball walked up, smiled real friendly, and whispered, "You're a filthy, shit-eating pig."

I smiled back and whispered, "Your mother eats bacon."

"How can we start a riot with no riot squad," another said.

"Careful, Scott, he's not just a pig, he's a wild boar, you dig?" said the mini-skirt who was standing behind the kids.

"Maybe *you* could use a little bore, sweetheart, maybe that's your trouble," I said, looking at the guy in the headband, and two of the kids chuckled.

"You seem to be the only Establishment representative we have at the moment, maybe you'd like to rap with us," said Scott, a tall kid with a scrubbed-looking face and a mop of blond hair. He had a cute little baby hanging on his arm and she seemed amused.

"Sure, just fire away," I said, still leaning back, acting relaxed as I puffed. I was actually beginning to *want* to rap with them. One time when I asked some young sergeant if I could take a shot at the "Policeman Bill" program and go talk to a class of high-school kids, he shined me on with a bunch of crap, and I realized then that they wanted those flat-stomached, clear-eyed, handsome young recruiting-poster cops for these jobs. I had my chance now and I liked the idea.

"What's your first name, Officer Morgan?" asked Scott, looking at my nameplate, "and what do you think of street demonstrations?"

Scott was smiling and I could hardly hear him over the yelling as the ring of marchers moved twenty feet closer to us to block the entrance more effectively after the fat bitch in yellow directed them to do it. Several kids mugged at the cameraman and waved "V" signs at him and me. One asshole, older than the others, flipped me the bone and then scowled into the camera.

"That's it, smile and say pig, you pukepot," I mumbled, noticing the two black cossacks were at the other end of the line of marchers talking to purple legs. Then I turned to Scott. "To answer your question, my name's Bumper Morgan and I don't mind demonstrations except that they take us cops away from our beats, and believe me we can't spare the time. Everybody loses when we're not on patrol."

"What do you patrol, the fucking barnyard?" said one little shitbird wearing shades and carrying a poster that showed a white army officer telephoning a black mother about her son being killed in Vietnam. She was shown in a corner of the poster and there was a big white cop clubbing her with an oversized baton.

"That poster doesn't make sense," I said. "It's awful damn lame. You might as well label it, 'Killed by the running dogs of imperialism!' I could do a lot better than that."

"Man, that's *exactly* what I told him," Scott laughed, and offered me a cigarette.

"No thanks," I said, as he and his baby doll lit one. "Now that one's sort of clever," I said, pointing to a sign which said "Today's pigs are tomorrow's porkchops."

None of the other kids had anything to say yet, except the shithead with the poster, who yelled, "Like, what're we doing talking to this fucking fascist lackey?"

"Look," I said, "I ain't gonna lay down and play

dead just because you can say 'fuck' pretty good. I mean nobody's shocked by that cheap shit anymore, so why don't we just talk quiet to each other. I wanna hear what you guys got to say."

"Good idea," said another kid, a black, with a wild natural, wire-rim glasses, and a tiger tooth necklace, who almost had to shout because of the noise. "Tell us why a man would want to be a cop. I mean really. I'm not putting you on, I want to know."

He was woofing me, because he winked at the blond kid, but I thought I'd *tell* them what I liked about it. What the hell, I liked having all these kids crowded around listening to me. Somebody then moved the marchers' line a little north again and I could almost talk in a normal voice.

"Well, I like to take lawbreakers off the street," I began.

"Just a minute," said the black kid, pushing his wire-rims up on his nose. "Please, Officer, no euphemisms. I'm from Watts." Then he purposely lapsed into a Negro drawl and said, "I been known' the PO-lice all mah life." The others laughed and he continued in his own voice. "Talk like a *real* cop and tell us like it is, without any bullshit. You know, use that favorite expression of L.A.P.D.—'asshole,' I believe it is." He smiled again after he said all this and so did I.

"What part of Watts you live in?" I asked.

"One-O-Three and Grape, baby," he answered.

"Okay, I'll talk plainer. I'm a cop because I love to throw assholes in jail, and if possible I like to send them to the joint."

"That's more like it," said the black kid. "Now you're lookin' so good and sounding so fine."

The others applauded and grinned at each other.

"Isn't that kind of a depressing line of work?" asked Scott. "I mean, don't you like to do something *for* someone once in a while instead of *to* them?"

"I figure I do something *for* someone every time I make a good bust. I mean, you figure every real asshole you catch in a dead bang burglary or robbery's tore off probably a hundred people or so before you bring him down. I figure each time I make a pinch I save a hundred more, maybe even some lives. And I'll tell you, most victims are people who can't afford to be victims. People who can afford it have protection and insurance and aren't so vulnerable to all these scummy hemorrhoids. Know what I mean?"

Scott's little girlfriend was busting to throw in her two cents, but three guys popped off at once, and finally Scott's voice drowned out the others. "I'm a law student," he said, "and I intend to be your adversary someday in a courtroom. Tell me, do you really get satisfaction when you send a man away for ten years?"

"Listen, Scott," I said, "in the first place even Eichmann would stand a fifty-fifty chance of not doing ten years nowadays. You got to be a boss crook to pull that kind of time. In fact, you got to work at it to even *get* to state prison. Man, some of the cats I put away, I wouldn't give them ten years, I'd give them a goddamned lobotomy if I could."

I dropped my cigar because these kids had me charged up now. I figured they were starting to respect me a little and I even tried for a minute to hold in my gut but that was uncomfortable, and I gave it up.

"I saw a big article in some magazine a few years ago honoring these cops," I continued. " 'These are not pigs' the article said, and it showed one cop who'd delivered some babies, and one cop who'd rescued some people in a flood, and one cop who was a goddamn boy scout troop leader or something like that. You know, I delivered two babies myself. But we ain't being paid to be midwives or lifeguards or social workers. They got other people to do those jobs. Let's see somebody honor some copper because the guy made thirty good felony pinches a month for ten years and sent a couple hundred guys to San Quentin. Nobody ever gives an award to him. Even his sergeant ain't gonna appreciate that, but he'll get on his ass for not writing a traffic ticket every day because the goddamn city needs the revenue and there's no room in prisons anyway."

I should've been noticing things at about this time. I should've noticed that the guy in the headband and his old lady were staying away from me and so were the two black guys in the plastic jackets. In fact, all the ones I spotted were staying at the other end of the line of marchers who were quieting down and starting to get tired. I should've noticed that the boy, Scott, the other blond kid, and the tall black kid, were closer to me than the others, and so was the cute little twist hanging on Scott's arm and carrying a huge heavy-looking buckskin bag.

I noticed nothing, because for one of the few times in my life I wasn't being a cop. I was a big, funny-looking, blue-suited donkey and I thought I was home-run king belting them out over the fences. The reason was that I was somewhere I'd never been in my life. I was on a soapbox. Not a stage but a soapbox. A stage I could've handled. I can put on the act people want and expect, and I can still keep my eyes open and not get carried away with it, but this goddamned soapbox was something else. I was making speeches, one after another, about things that meant something to me, and all I could see was the loving gaze of my audience, and the sound of my own voice drowned out all the things that I should've been hearing and seeing.

"Maybe police departments should only recruit college graduates," Scott shrugged, coming a step closer.

"Yeah, they want us to solve crimes by these 'scientific methods,' whatever that means. And what do us cops do? We kiss ass and nod our heads and take federal funds to build computers and send cops to college and it all boils down to a cop with sharp eyes and an ability to talk to people who'll get the goddamn job done."

"Don't you think that in the age that's coming, policemen will be obsolete?" Scott's little girlfriend asked the question and she looked so wide-eyed I had to smile.

"I'm afraid not, honey," I said. "As long as there's people, there's gonna be lots of bad ones and greedy ones and weak ones."

"How can you feel that way about people and still care at all about helping them as you say you do when you arrest somebody?" she asked, shaking her head. She smiled sadly, like she felt sorry for me.

"Hell, baby, they ain't much but they're all we got. It's the only game in town!" I figured that was obvious to anybody and I started to wonder if they weren't still a little young. "By the way, are most of you social science and English majors?"

"Why do you say that?" asked the black kid, who was built like a ballplayer.

"The surveys say you are. I'm just asking. Just curious."

"I'm an engineering major," said the blond kid, who was now behind Scott, and then for the first time I was aware how close in on me these certain few were. I was becoming aware how polite they'd been to me. They were all activists and college people and no doubt had statistics and slogans and arguments to throw at me, yet I had it all my way. They just stood there nodding, smiling once in a while, and let me shoot my face off. I knew that something wasn't logical or right, but I was still intrigued with the sound of my own voice and so the fat blue maharishi said, "Anything else about police work you'd like to talk about?"

"Were you at Century City?" asked the little blonde.

"Yeah, I was there, and it wasn't anything like you read in the underground newspapers or on those edited TV tapes."

"It wasn't? I was there," said Scott.

"Well, I'm not gonna deny some people got hurt," I said, looking from one face to another for hostility.

"There was the President of the United States to protect and there were thousands of war protestors out there and I guarantee you that was no bullshit about them having sharpened sticks and bags of shit and broken bottles and big rocks. I bet *I* could kill a guy with a rock."

"You didn't see any needless brutality?"

"What the hell's brutality?" I said. "Most of those bluecoats out there are just kids *your* age. When someone spits in his face, all the goddamn discipline in the world ain't gonna stop him or any normal kid from getting that other cat's teeth prints on his baton. There's times when you just *gotta* play a little catchup. You know what five thousand screaming people look like? Sure, we got some stick time in. Some scumbags, all they respect is force. You just gotta kick ass and collect names. Anybody with any balls woulda whaled on some of those pricks out there." Then I remembered the girl. "Sorry for the four-letter word, miss," I said as a reflex action.

"Prick is a five-letter word," she said, reminding me of the year I was living in.

Then suddenly, the blond kid behind Scott got hostile. "Why do we talk to a pig like this? He talks about helping people. What's he do besides beat their heads in, which he admits? What do you do in the ghettos of Watts for the black people?"

Then a middle-aged guy in a clergyman's collar and a black suit popped through the ring of young people. "I work in the eastside Chicano barrios," he announced. "What do you do for the Mexicans except exploit them?"

"What do *you* do?" I asked, getting uncomfortable at the sudden change of mood here, as several of the marchers joined the others and I was backed up against the car by fifteen or twenty people.

"I fight for the Chicanos. For brown power," said the clergyman.

"You ain't brown," I observed, growing more nervous.

"Inside I'm brown!"

"Take an enema," I mumbled, standing up straight, as I realized that things were wrong, all wrong.

Then I caught a glimpse of the black cossack hat to the left behind two girls who were crowding in to see what the yelling was all about, and I saw a hand flip a peace button at me, good and hard. It hit me in the face, the pin scratching me right under the left eye. The black guy looked at me very cool as I spun around, mad enough to charge right through the crowd.

"You try that again and I'll ding your bells, man," I said, loud enough for him to hear.

"Who?" he said, with a big grin through the moustache and goatee.

"Who, my ass," I said. "You ain't got feet that fit on a limb. I'm talking to *you.*"

"You fat pig," he sneered and turned to the crowd. "He wants to arrest me! You pick out a black, that the way you do it, Mister PO-lice?"

"If anything goes down, I'm getting *you* first," I whispered, putting my left hand on the handle of my stick.

"He wants to arrest me," he repeated, louder now. "What's the charge? Being black? Don't I have any rights?"

"You're gonna get your rites," I muttered. "Your *last* rites."

"I should kill you," he said. "There's fifty braves here and we should kill you for all the brothers and sisters you pigs murdered."

"Get it on, sucker, anytime you're ready," I said with a show of bravado because I was really scared now.

I figured that many people let loose could turn me into a doormat in about three minutes. My breath was coming hard. I tried to keep my jaw from trembling

and my brain working. They weren't going to get me
down on the ground. Not without a gun in my hand. I
decided it wouldn't be that easy to kick *my* brains in. I
made up my mind to start shooting to save myself, and
I decided I'd blow up the two Black Russians, Geroni-
mo, and Purple Legs, not necessarily in that order.

Then a hand reached out and grabbed my necktie,
but it was a breakaway tie, and I didn't go with it
when the hand pulled it into the crowd. At about the
same time the engineering major grabbed my badge,
and I instinctively brought up my right hand, holding
his hand on my chest, backing up until his elbow was
straight. Then I brought my left fist up hard just above
his elbow and he yelped and drew back. Several other
people also drew back at the unmistakable scream of
pain.

"Off the pig! Off the pig!" somebody yelled. "Rip
him off!"

I pulled my baton out and felt the black-and-white
behind me now and they were all screaming and
threatening, even the full-of-shit padre.

I would've jumped in the car on the passenger side
and locked the door but I couldn't. I felt the handle
and it was locked, and the window was rolled up, and
I was afraid that if I fooled around unlocking it, somebody might get his ass up and charge me.

Apparently the people inside the induction center
didn't know a cop was about to get his ticket can-
celled, because nobody came out. I could see the cameraman fighting to get through the crowd which was
spilling out on the street and I had a crazy wish that
he'd make it. That's the final vanity, I guess, but I kind
of wanted him to film Bumper's Last Stand.

For a few seconds it could've gone either way and
then the door to my car opened and hit me in the
back, scaring the shit out of me.

"Get your butt in here, Bumper," said a familiar
voice, which I obeyed. The second I closed the door
something hit the window almost hard enough to

break the glass and several people started kicking at the door and fender of my black-and-white.

"Give me the keys," said Stan Ludlow, who worked Intelligence Division. He was sitting behind the wheel, looking as dapper as always in a dark green suit and mint-colored necktie.

I gave him the keys from my belt and he drove away from the curb as I heard something else clunk off the fender of the car. Four radio cars each containing three Metro officers pulled up at the induction center as we were leaving, and started dispelling the group.

"You're the ugliest rape victim I ever saw," said Stan, turning on Ninth Street and parking behind a plainclothes police car where his partner was waiting.

"What the hell you talking about?"

"Had, man. You just been had."

"I had a feeling something wasn't right," I said, getting sick because I was afraid to hear what I figured he was going to say. "Did they set me up?"

"Did they set you up? No, they didn't have to. You set yourself up! Christ, Bumper, you should know better than to make speeches to groups like that. What the hell made you do it?"

Stan had about fifteen years on the job and was a sergeant, but he was only about forty and except for his gray sideburns he looked lots younger. Still, I felt like a dumb little kid sitting there now. I felt like he was lots older and a damn sight wiser and took the assbite without looking at him.

"How'd you know I was speechmaking, Stan?"

"One of them is one of us," said Stan. "We had one of those guys wired with a mike. We listened to the whole thing, Bumper. We called for the Metro teams because we knew what was going to happen. Damn near didn't get to you quick enough though."

"Who were the leaders?" I was trying to save a grain or two of my pride. "The bitch in the yellow dress and the guru in the headband?"

"Hell no," said Stan, disgustedly. "Their names are
John and Marie French. They're a couple of lames trying to groove with the kids. They're nothing. She's a
self-proclaimed revolutionary from San Pedro and he's
her husband. As a matter of fact he picked up our undercover man and drove him to the demonstration
today when they were sent by the boss. French is
mostly used as errand boy. He drives a VW bus and
picks up everybody that needs a ride to all these peace
marches. He's nothing. Why, did you have them figured for the leaders?"

"Sort of," I mumbled.

"Sort of. What about the two in the Russian hats?"

"Nobody," said Stan. "They hang around all the
time with their Panther buttons and get lots of pussy,
but they're nobody. Just opportunists. Professional
blacks."

"I guess the guy running the show was a tall nice-
looking kid named Scott?" I said, as the lights slowly
turned on.

"Yeah, Scott Hairston. He's from U.C.L.A. His sister
Melba was the little blonde with the peachy ass who
was hanging on his arm. She was the force behind
subversive club chapters starting on her high school
campus when she was still a bubblegummer. Their old
man, Simon Hairston's an attorney and a slippery bastard, and his brother Josh is an old-time activist."

"So the bright-eyed little baby was a goddamn
viper, huh? I guess they've passed me by, Stan."

Stan smiled sympathetically and lit my cigar for me.
"Look, Bumper, these kids've been weaned on this
bullshit. You're just a beginner. Don't feel too bad. But
for God's sake, next time don't start chipping with
them. No speeches, please!"

"I must've sounded like a boob," I said, and I could
feel myself flushing clear to my toes.

"It's not that so much, Bumper, but that little bitch
Melba put you on tape. She always solicits casual

comments from cops. Sometimes she has a concealed hand mike with a wire running up her sleeve down to a box in her handbag. She carrying a big handbag today?"

I didn't have to answer. Stan saw it in the sick look on my face.

"They'll edit your remarks, Bumper. I heard some of them from the mike *our* guy was wearing. Christ, you talked about stick time and putting teeth marks on your baton and kicking ass and collecting names."

"But all that's not how I meant it, Stan."

"That's the way your comments'll be presented—out of context. It'll be printed that way in an underground newspaper or maybe even in a daily if Simon Hairston gets behind it."

"Oooooh," I said, tilting my hat over my eyes and slumping down in my seat.

"Don't have a coronary on me, Bumper," said Stan. "Everything's going to be all right."

"All right? I'll be the laughingstock of the Department!"

"Don't worry, Melba's tapes're going to disappear."

"The undercover man?"

Stan nodded.

"Bless him," I breathed. "Which one was he? Not the kid whose arm I almost broke?"

"No," Stan laughed, "the tall black kid. I'm only telling you because we're going to have to use him as a material witness in a few days anyway, and we'll have to disclose his identity. We got secret indictments on four guys who make pretty good explosives in the basement of a North Hollywood apartment building. He's been working for me since he joined the Department thirteen months ago. We have him enrolled in college. Nice kid. Hell of a basketball player. He can't wait to wear a bluesuit and work a radio car. He's sick of mingling with all these revolutionaries."

"How do you know he can get the tape?"

"He's been practically living in Melba's skivvies for at least six months now. He'll sleep with her tonight and that'll be it."

"Some job," I said.

"He doesn't mind that part of it," Stan chuckled. "He's anxious to see how all his friends react when they find out he's the heat. Says he's been using them as whipping boys and playing the outraged black man role for so long, they probably won't believe it till they actually see him in the blue uniform with that big hateful shield on his chest. And wait'll Melba finds out she's been balling a cop. You can bet she'll keep that a secret."

"Nobody's gonna hear about me then, huh, Stan?"

"I'll erase the tape, Bumper," said Stan, getting out of the car. "You know, in a way it worked out okay. Scott Hairston was expecting a hundred marchers in the next few hours. He didn't want trouble yet. You wrecked his game today."

"See you later, Stan," I said, trying to sound casual, like I wasn't totally humiliated. "Have a cigar, old shoe."

I was wrung out after that caper and even though it was getting late in the afternoon, I jumped on the Harbor Freeway and started driving south, as fast as traffic would permit, with some kind of half-baked idea about looking at the ocean. I was trying to do something which I usually do quite well, controlling my thoughts. It wouldn't do any good at all to stew over what happened, so I was trying to think about something else, maybe food, or Cassie, or how Glenda's jugs looked today—something good. But I was in a dark mood, and nothing good would come, so I decided to think of absolutely nothing which I can also do quite well.

I wheeled back to my beat and called the lieutenant, telling him about the ruckus at the induction center, leaving out all the details of course, and he told me the marchers dispersed very fast and there were only a few cars still at the scene. I knew there'd hardly be any mention of this one, a few TV shots on the six o'clock news and that'd be it. I hung up and got back in my car, hoping the cameraman hadn't caught me smoking the cigar. That's another silly rule, no smoking in public, as if a cop is a Buckingham Palace guard.

## 7

I DROVE AROUND some more, cooling off, looking at my watch every few seconds, wanting this day to end. The noisy chatter on the radio was driving me nuts so I turned it off. Screw the radio, I thought, I never made a good pinch from a radio call. The good busts come from doing what I do best, walking and looking and talking to people.

I had a hell of an attack of indigestion going. I took four antacid tablets from the glove compartment and popped them all but I was still restless, squirming around on the seat. Cassie's three o'clock class would be finished now so I drove up Vermont to Los Angeles City College and parked out front in the red zone even though when I do that I always get a few digs from the kids or from teachers like, "You can do it but we get tickets for it." Today there was nobody in front and I didn't get any bullshit which I don't particularly mind anyway, since nobody including myself really likes authority symbols. I'm always one of the first to get my ass up when the brass tries to restrict my freedom with some idiotic rules.

I climbed the stairs leisurely, admiring the tits on some suntanned, athletic-looking, ponytailed gym teacher. She was in a hurry and took the stairs two at a time, still in her white shorts and sneakers and white

jersey that showed all she had, and it was plenty.
Some of the kids passing me in the halls made all the
usual remarks, calling me Dick Tracy and Sheriff
John, and there were a few giggles about Marlene
somebody holding some pot and then Marlene
squealed and giggled. We didn't used to get snickers
about pot, and that reminded me of the only argument
concerning pot that made any sense to me. Grass, like
booze, breaks the chain and frees the beast, but does it
so much easier and quicker. I've seen it thousands of
times.

Cassie was in her office with the door opened talking to a stringy-haired bubblegummer in a micro-mini
that showed her red-flowered pantygirdle when she
sat down.

"Hi," said Cassie, when she saw me in the doorway.
The girl looked at me and then back at Cassie, wondering what the fuzz was here for.

"We'll just be a minute," said Cassie, still smiling
her clean white smile, and I nodded and walked down
the hall to the water fountain thinking how damn
good she looked in that orange dress. It was one of the
twenty or so that I'd bought her since we met, and she
finally agreed with me that she looked better in hot
colors, even though she thought it was part of any
man's M.O. to like his women in flaming oranges and
reds.

Her hair was drawn back today and either way,
back or down, her hair was beautiful. It was thick
brown, streaked with silver, not gray, but real untouched silver, and her figure was damn good for a
girl her age. She was tanned and looked more like a
gym teacher than a French teacher. She always wore a
size twelve and sometimes could wear a ten in certain
full styles. I wondered if she still looked so good because she played tennis and golf or because she didn't
have any kids when she was married, but then, Cruz's
wife Socorro had a whole squad of kids and though
she was a little overweight she still looked almost as

good as Cassie. Some people just keep it all, I guess, which almost made me self-conscious being with this classy-looking woman when we went places together. I always felt like everyone was thinking, "He must have bread or she'd never be with him." But it was useless to question your luck, you just had to grab on when you had the chance, and I did. And then again, maybe I was one of those guys that's ugly in an attractive sort of way.

"Well?" said Cassie, and I turned my head and saw her standing in the doorway of her office, still smiling at me as I went over her with my eyes. The kid had left.

"That's the prettiest dress you have," I said, and I really meant it. At that moment she'd never looked better, even though some heavy wisps of hair were hanging on her cheeks and her lipstick was almost all gone.

"Why don't you admire my mind instead of my body once in a while like I do yours?" she grinned.

I followed her into the office and stepped close, intending to give her a kiss on the cheek. She surprised me by throwing her arms around my neck and kissing me long and hot, causing me to drop my hat on the floor and get pretty aroused even though we were standing in an open doorway and any minute a hundred people would walk past. When she finally stopped, she had the lazy dazzling look of a passionate woman.

"Shall we sweep everything off that damned desk?" she said in a husky voice, and for a minute or two I thought she would've. Then a bell rang and doors started opening and she laughed and sat down on her desk showing me some very shapely legs and you would never guess those wheels had been spinning for forty odd years. I plopped down in a leather chair, my mouth woolly dry from having that hot body up against me.

"Are you sure you won't come to the party tonight?" she said finally, lighting a cigarette.

"You know how I feel about it, Cassie," I said. "This is *your* night. Your friends and the students want to have you to themselves. I'll have you forever after that."

"Think you can handle me?" she asked, with a grin, and I knew from her grin she meant sexually. We had joked before about how I awoke this in her, which she said had been dormant since her husband left her seven years ago and maybe even before that, from what I knew of the poor crazy guy. He was a teacher like Cassie, but his field was chemistry.

We supposed that some of her nineteen-year-old students, as sex-obsessed as they are these days, might be making love more often than we did, but she didn't see how they could. She said it had never been like this with her, and she never knew it could be so good. Me, I've always appreciated how good it was. As long as I can remember, I've been horny.

"Come by the apartment at eleven," she said. "I'll make sure I'm home by then."

"That's pretty early to leave your friends."

"You don't think I'd sit around drinking with a bunch of educators when I could be learning at home with Officer Morgan, do you?"

"You mean I can teach a teacher?"

"You're one of the tops in your field."

"You have a class tomorrow morning," I reminded her.

"Be there at eleven."

"A lot of these teachers and students that don't have an early class tomorrow are gonna want to jive and woof a lot later than that. I think you ought to stay with them tonight, Cassie. They'd expect you to. You can't disappoint the people on your beat."

"Well, all right," she sighed. "But I won't even see you tomorrow night because I'll be dining with those two trustees. They want to give me one final look, and casually listen to my French to make sure I'm not going to corrupt the already corrupted debs at their institution. I suppose I can't run off and leave *them* either."

"It won't be long till I have you all to myself. Then *I'll* listen to your French and let you corrupt the hell out of me, okay?"

"Did you tell them you're retiring yet?" She asked the question easily, but looked me straight in the eye, waiting, and I got nervous.

"I've told Cruz," I said, "and I got a surprise for you."

"What?"

"I've decided that Friday's gonna be my last day. I'll start my vacation Saturday and finish my time while I'm on vacation. I'll be going with you."

Cassie didn't yell or jump up or look excited or anything, like I thought she would. She just went limp like her muscles relaxed suddenly, and she slipped off the desk and sat down on my lap where there isn't any too much room, and with her arms doubled around the top of my neck she started kissing me on the face and mouth and I saw her eyes were wet and soft like her lips, and next thing I know, I heard a lot of giggling. Eight or ten kids were standing in the hall watching us through the open door, but Cassie didn't seem to hear, or didn't care. I did though because I was sitting there in my bluesuit, being loved up and getting turned on in public.

"Cassie," I gasped, nodding toward the door, and she got up, and calmly shut the door on the kids like she was ready to start again.

I stood and picked up my hat from the floor. "Cassie, this is a school. I'm in uniform."

Cassie started laughing very hard and had to sit down in the chair I'd been in, leaning back, and holding her hands over her face as she laughed. I thought how sexy even her throat was, the throat usually being the first thing to show its age, but Cassie's was sleek.

"I wasn't going to rape you," she said at last, still chuckling between breaths.

"Well, it's just that you teachers are so permissive these days, I thought you might try to do me on the desk like you said."

"Oh, Bumper," she said finally, holding her arms out, and I came over and leaned down and she kissed me eight or ten warm times all over my face.

"I can't even begin to tell you how I feel now that you're really going to do it," she said. "When you said you actually *are* finishing up this Friday, and that you told Cruz Segovia, I just went to pieces. That was relief and joy you saw on my face when I closed the door, Bumper, not passion. Well, maybe a *little* of it was."

"We've been planning all along, Cassie, you act like it was really a shock to you."

"I've had nightmares about it. I've had fantasies awake and asleep of how after I'd gone, and got our apartment in San Francisco, you'd phone me one bitter night and tell me you weren't coming, that you just could never leave your beat."

"Cassie!"

"I haven't told you this before, Bumper, but it's been gnawing at me. Now that you've told Cruz, and it's only two more days, I know it's coming true."

"I'm not married to my goddamn job, Cassie," I said, thinking how little you know about a woman, even one as close as Cassie. "You should've seen what happened to me today. I was flimflammed by a soft-nutted little kid. He made a complete ass out of me. He made me look like a *square*."

Cassie looked interested and amused, the way she always does when I tell her about my job.

"What happened?" she asked, as I pulled out my last cigar and fired it up so I could keep calm when the humiliation swept over me.

"A demonstration at the Army Induction Center. A

kid, a punk-ass kid, conned me and I started blabbing
off about the job. Rapping real honest with him I was,
and I find out later he's a professional revolutionary,
probably a Red or something, and oh, I thought I was
so goddamn hip to it. I been living too much on my
beat, Cassie. Too much being the Man, I guess. Believing I could outsmart any bastard that skated by.
Thinking the only ones I never could really get to
were the organized ones, like the bookmakers and the
big dope dealers. But *sometimes* I could do things that
even hurt *them*. Now there's new ones that've come
along. And they have organization. And I was like a
baby, they handled me so easy."

"What the hell did you *do*, Bumper?"

"Talked. I talked to them straight about things.
About thumping assholes that needed thumping. That
kind of thing. I made *speeches*."

"Know what?" she said, putting her long-fingered
hand on my knee. "Whatever happened out there,
whatever you said, I'll bet wouldn't do you or the Department a damn bit of harm."

"Oh yeah, Cassie? You should've heard me talking
about when the President was here and how we busted up the riot by busting up a skull or three. I was
marvelous."

"Do you know a *gentle* way to break up riots?"

"No, but we're supposed to be professional enough
not to talk to civilians the way we talk in police locker
rooms."

"I'll take Officer Morgan over one of those terribly
wholesome, terribly tiresome TV cops, and I don't
think there's a gentle way to break up riots, so I think
you should stop worrying about the whole thing. Just
think, pretty soon you won't have any of these problems. You'll have a real position, an important one, and
people working under you."

"I got to admit, it gets me pretty excited to think
about it. I bet I can come up with ways to improve
plant security that those guys never dreamed of."

"Of course you can."

"No matter what I do, you pump me up," I smiled. "That's why I wanted you for my girl in spite of all your shortcomings."

"Well, you're my Blue Knight. Do you know you're a knight? You joust and live off the land."

"Yeah, I guess you might say I live off my beat, all right. 'Course I don't do much jousting."

"Just *rousting?*"

"Yeah, I've rousted a couple thousand slimeballs in my time."

"So you're my Blue Knight."

"Wait a minute, kid," I said. "You're only getting a *former* knight if you get me."

"What do you mean, 'if'?"

"It's okay to shuck about me being some kind of hero or something, but when I retire I'm just a has-been."

"Bumper," she said, and laughed a little, and kissed my hand like Glenda did. That was the second woman to kiss my hand today, I thought. "I'm not dazzled by authority symbols. It's really *you* that keeps me kissing your hands." She did it again and I've always thought that having a woman kiss your hands is just almost more than a man can take. "You're going to an important job. You'll be an executive. You have an awful lot to offer, especially to me. In fact, you have so much maybe I should share it."

"I can only handle one woman at a time, baby."

"Remember Nancy Vogler, from the English department?"

"Yeah, you want to share me with her?"

"Silly," she laughed. "Nancy and her husband were married twelve years and they didn't have any children. A couple of years ago they decided to take a boy into their home. He's eleven now."

"They adopted him?"

"No, not exactly. They're foster parents." Cassie's voice became serious. "She said being a foster parent is the most rewarding thing they've ever done. Nancy said they'd almost missed out on knowing what living is and didn't realize it until they got the boy."

Cassie seemed to be searching my face just then. Was she thinking about *my* boy? I'd only mentioned him once to her. Was there something she wanted to know?

"Bumper, after we get married and settled in our home, what would you say to *us* becoming foster parents? Not really adopting a child if you didn't want to, but being foster parents, sharing. You'd be someone for a boy to look up to and learn from."

"A kid! But I never thought about a family!"

"I've been thinking about this for a long time, and after seeing Nancy and hearing about their life, I think about how wonderful it would be for us. We're not old yet, but in ten or fifteen more years when we *are* getting old, there'd be someone else for both of us." She looked in my eyes and then down. "You may think I'm crazy, and I probably am, but I'd like you to give it some thought."

That hit me so hard I didn't know what to say, so I grinned a silly grin, kissed her on the cheek, said, "I'm end of watch in fifteen minutes. Bye, old shoe," and left.

She looked somehow younger and a little sad as she smiled and waved at me when I'd reached the stairway. When I got in my black-and-white I felt awful. I dropped two pills and headed east on Temple and cursed under my breath at every asshole that got in my way in this rush-hour traffic. I couldn't believe it. Leaving the Department after all these years and getting married was change enough, but a kid! Cassie had asked me about my ex-wife one time, just once, right after we started going together. I told her I was divorced and my son was dead and I didn't go into it any further. She never mentioned it again, never talked about kids in that way.

Damn, I thought, I guess every broad in the world

should drop a foal at least once in her life or she'll never be happy. I pushed Cassie's idea out of my mind when I drove into the police building parking lot, down to the lower level where it was dark and fairly cool despite the early spring heat wave. I finished my log, gathered up my ticket books, and headed for the office to leave the log before I took off the uniform. I never wrote traffic tickets but they always issued me the ticket books. Since I made so many good felony pinches they pretty well kept their mouths shut about me not writing tickets, still, they always issued me the books and I always turned them back in just as full. That's the trouble with conformists, they'd never stop giving me those ticket books.

After putting the log in the daywatch basket I jived around with several of the young nightwatch coppers who wanted to know when I was changing to nights for the summer. They knew my M.O. too. Everybody knew it. I hated anyone getting my M.O. down too good like that. The most successful robbers and burglars are the ones who change their M.O.'s. They don't give you a chance to start sticking little colored pins in a map to plot their movements. That reminded me of a salty old cop named Nails Grogan who used to walk Hill Street.

About fifteen years ago, just for the hell of it, he started his own crime wave. He was teed off at some chickenshit lieutenant we had then, named Wall, who used to jump on our meat every night at rollcall because we weren't catching enough burglars. The way Wall figured this was that there were always so many little red pins on the pin maps for nighttime business burglaries, especially around Grogan's beat. Grogan always told me he didn't think Wall ever really read a burglary report and didn't know shit from gravy about what was going on. So a little at a time Nails started changing the pins every night before rollcall, taking the pins out of the area around his beat and sticking them in the east side. After a couple weeks of this,

Wall told the rollcall what a hell of a job Grogan was doing with the burglary problem in his area, and restricted the ass chewing to guys that worked the eastside cars. I was the only one that knew what Grogan did and we got a big laugh out of it until Grogan went too far and pinned a full-blown crime wave on the east side, and Lieutenant Wall had the captain call out the Metro teams to catch the burglars. Finally the whole hoax was exposed when no one could find crime reports to go with all the little pins.

Wall was transferred to the morning watch, which is our graveyard shift, at the old Lincoln Heights jail. He retired from there a few years later. Nails Grogan never got made on that job, but Wall knew who screwed him, I'm sure. Nails was another guy that only lived a few years after he retired. He shot himself. I got a chill thinking about that, shook it off, and headed for the locker room where I took off the bluesuit and changed into my herringbone sport coat, gray slacks, and lemon yellow shirt, no tie. In this town you can usually get by without a tie anywhere you go.

Before I left, I plugged in my shaver and smoothed up a little bit. A couple of the guys were still in the locker room. One of them was an ambitious young bookworm named Wilson, who as usual was reading while sitting on the bench and slipping into his civvies. He was going to college three or four nights a week and always had a textbook tucked away in his police notebook. You'd see him in the coffee room or upstairs in the cafeteria going through it all the time. I'm something of a reader myself but I could never stand the thought of doing it because you had to.

"What're you reading?" I asked Wilson.

"Oh, just some criminal law," said Wilson, a thin youngster with a wide forehead and large blue eyes. He was a probationary policeman, less than a year on the job.

"Studying for sergeant already?" said Hawk, a cocky, square-shouldered kid about Wilson's age, who had two years on, and was going through his badge-heavy period.

"Just taking a few classes."

"You majoring in police science?" I asked.

"No, I'm majoring in government right now. I'm thinking about trying for law school." He didn't look right at me and I didn't think he would. This is something I've gotten used to from the younger cops, especially ones with some education, like Wilson. They don't know how to act when they're with old-timers like me. Some act salty like Hawk, trying to strut with an old beat cop, and it just looks silly. Others act more humble than they usually would, thinking an old lion like me would claw their ass for making an honest mistake out of greenness. Still others, like Wilson, pretty much act like themselves, but like most young people, they think an old fart that's never even made sergeant in twenty years must be nearly illiterate, so they generally restrict all conversation to the basics of police work to spare you, and they generally look embarrassed like Wilson did now, to admit to you that they read books. The generation gap is as bad in this job as it is in any other except for one thing: the hazards of the job shrink it pretty fast. After a few brushes with danger, a kid pretty much loses his innocence, which is what the generation gap is really all about—innocence.

"Answer me a law question," said Hawk, putting on some flared pants. We're too GI to permit muttonchops or big moustaches or he'd surely have them. "If you commit suicide can you be prosecuted for murder?"

"Nobody ever has," Wilson smiled, as Hawk giggled and slipped on a watermelon-colored velvet shirt.

"That's only because of our permissive society," I said, and Wilson glanced at me and grinned.

"What's that book in your locker, Wilson?" I asked, nodding toward a big paperback on the top shelf.

"*Guns of August.*"

"Oh yeah, I read that," I said. "I've read a hundred books about the First World War. Do you like it?"

"I do," he said, looking at me like he discovered the missing link. "I'm reading it for a history course."

"I read T. E. Lawrence's *Seven Pillars of Wisdom* when I was on my First World War kick. Every goddamn word. I had maps and books spread all over my pad. That little runt only weighed in at about a hundred thirty, but thirty pounds of that was brains and forty was balls. He was a boss warrior."

"A loner," Wilson nodded, really looking at me now.

"Right. That's what I dig about him. I would've liked him even better if he hadn't written it all so intimate for everyone to read. But then if he hadn't done that, I'd never have appreciated him. Maybe a guy like that finally gets tired of just enjoying it and *has* to tell it all to figure it all out and see if it means anything in the end."

"Maybe you should write your memoirs when you're through, Bumper," Wilson smiled. "You're as well known around here as Lawrence ever was in Arabia."

"Why don't you major in history?" I said. "If I went to college that'd be my meat. I think after a few courses in criminal law the rest of law school'd be a real drag, torts and contracts and all that bullshit. I could never plow through the dust and cobwebs."

"It's exciting if you like it," said Wilson, and Hawk looked a little ruffled that he was cut out of the conversation so he split.

"Maybe so," I said. "You must've had a few years of college when you came on the Department."

"Two years," Wilson nodded. "Now I'm halfway through my junior year. It takes forever when you're a full-time cop and a part-time student."

"You can tough it out," I said, lighting a cigar and sitting down on the bench, while part of my brain listened to the youngster and the other part was worrying about something else. I had the annoying feeling you get, that can sometimes be scary, that I'd been here with him before and we talked like this, or maybe it was somebody else, and then I thought, yes, that was it, maybe the cowlick in his hair reminded me of Billy, and I got an empty tremor in my stomach.

"How old're you, Wilson?"

"Twenty-six," he said, and a pain stabbed me and made me curse and rub my pot. Billy would've been twenty-six too!

"Hope your stomach holds out when you get my age. Were you in the service?"

"Army," he nodded.

"Vietnam?"

"Yeah," he nodded.

"Did you hate it?" I asked, expecting that all young people hated it.

"I didn't like the *war*. It scared hell out of me, but I didn't mind the *army* as much as I thought I would."

"That's sort of how I felt," I smiled. "I was in the Marine Corps for eight years."

"Korea?"

"No, I'm even older than that," I smiled. "I joined in forty-two, and got out in fifty, then came on the police department."

"You stayed in a long time," he said.

"Too long. The war scared me too, but sometimes peace is just as bad for a military man."

I didn't tell him the truth because it might tune him out, and the truth was that it *did* scare me, the war, but I didn't hate it. I didn't exactly like it, but I didn't hate it. It's fashionable to hate war, I know, and I wanted to hate it, but I never did.

"I swore when I left Vietnam I'd never fire another gun and here I am a cop. Figure that out," said Wilson.

I thought that was something, having him tell *me* that. Suddenly the age difference wasn't there. He was telling me things he probably told his young partners during lonely hours after two a.m. when you're fighting to keep awake or when you're "in the hole" trying to hide your radio car, in some alley where you can doze uncomfortably for an hour, but you never really rest. There's the fear of a sergeant catching you, or there's the radio. What if you *really* fall asleep and a hot call comes out and you miss it?

"Maybe you'll make twenty years without ever firing your gun on duty," I said.

"Have you had to shoot?"

"A few times," I nodded, and he let it drop like he should. It was only civilians who ask you, "What's it feel like to shoot someone?" and all that bullshit which is completely ridiculous, because if you do it in war or you do it as a cop, it doesn't feel like anything. If you do what has to be done, why *should* you feel anything? I never have. After the fear for your own life is past, and the adrenalin slows, nothing. But people generally can't stand truth. It makes a lousy story so I usually give them their clichés.

"You gonna stay on the job after you finish law school?"

"If I ever finish I might leave," he laughed. "But I can't really picture myself ever finishing."

"Maybe you won't want to leave by then. This is a pretty strange kind of job. It's . . . intense. Some guys wouldn't leave if they had a million bucks."

"How about you?"

"Oh, I'm pulling the pin," I said. "I'm almost gone. But the job gets to you. The way you see everyone so exposed and vulnerable. . . . And there's nothing like rolling up a good felon if you really got the instinct."

He looked at me for a moment and then said, "Rogers and I got a good two-eleven suspect last month. They cleared five holdups on this guy. He had a seven-point-six-five-millimeter pistol shoved down the back of his waistband when we stopped him for a traffic ticket. We got hinky because he was sweating and dry-mouthed when he talked to us. It's really something to get a guy like that, especially when you never know how close you came. I mean, he was just sitting there looking from Rogers to me, measuring, thinking about blowing us up. We realized it later, and it made the pinch that much more of a kick."

"That's part of it. You feel more alive. Hey, you talk like you're Bumper-ized and I didn't even break you in."

"We worked together one night, remember?" said Wilson. "My first night out of the academy. I was more scared of you than I was the assholes on the street."

"That's right, we *did* work together. I remember now," I lied.

"Well, I better get moving," said Wilson, and I was disappointed. "Got to get to school. I've got two papers due next week and haven't started them."

"Hang in there, Wilson. Hang tough," I said, as I locked my locker.

I walked to the parking lot and decided to tip a few at my neighborhood pub near Silverlake before going to Cruz's house. The proprietor was an old pal of mine who used to own a decent bar on my beat downtown before he bought this one. He was no longer on my beat of course, but he still bounced for drinks, I guess out of habit. Most bar owners don't pop for too many policemen, because they'll take advantage of it, policemen will, and there'll be so many at your watering hole you'll have to close the goddamn doors. Harry only popped for me and a few detectives he knew real well.

It was five o'clock when I parked my nineteen-fifty-one Ford in front of Harry's. I'd bought the car new and was still driving it. Almost twenty years and I only had a hundred and thirty thousand miles on her, and the same engine. I never went anywhere except at vacation time or sometimes when I'd take a trip to the river to fish. Since I met Cassie I've used the car more than I ever had before, but even with Cassie I seldom went far. We usually went to the movies in Hollywood, or to the Music Center to see light opera, or to the Bowl for a concert which was Cassie's favorite place to go, or to Dodger Stadium which was mine. Often we went out to the Strip to go dancing. Cassie was good. She had all the moves, but she couldn't get the hang of letting her body do it all. With Cassie the mind was always there. One thing I decided I wouldn't get rid of when I left L.A. was my Ford. I wanted to see just how long a car could live if you treated it right.

Harry was alone when I walked in the little knotty-pine tavern which had a pool table, a few sad booths, and a dozen bar stools. The neighborhood business was never very good. It was quiet and cool and dark in there and I was glad.

"Hi, Bumper," he said, drawing a draft beer in a frosted glass for me.

"Evening, Harry," I said, grabbing a handful of pretzels from one of the dishes he had on the bar. Harry's was one of the few joints left where you could actually get something free, like pretzels.

"How's business, Bumper?"

"Mine's always good, Harry," I said, which is what policemen always answer to that question.

"Anything exciting happen on your beat lately?" Harry was about seventy, an ugly little goblin with bony shoulder blades who hopped around behind the bar like a sparrow.

"Let's see," I said, trying to think of some gossip. Since Harry used to own a bar downtown, he knew a lot of the people I knew. "Yeah, remember Frog LaRue?"

"The little hype with the stooped-over walk?"

"That one."

"Yeah," said Harry. "I must've kicked that junkie out of my joint a million times after you said he was dealing dope. Never could figure out why he liked to set up deals in my bar."

"He got his ass shot," I said.

"What'd he do, try to sell somebody powdered sugar in place of the stuff?"

"No, a narco cop nailed him."

"Yeah? Why would anybody shoot Frog? He couldn't hurt nobody but himself."

"Anybody can hurt somebody, Harry," I said. "But in this case it was a mistake. Old Frog always kept a blade on the window sill in any hotel he stayed at. And the window'd be open even in the dead of winter. That was his M.O. If someone came to his door who he thought was cops, Frog'd slit the screen and throw his dope and his outfit right out the window. One night the narcs busted in the pad when they heard from a snitch that Frog was holding, and old Froggy dumped a spoon of junk out the window. He had to slit the screen to do it and when this narc came crashing through the door, his momentum carried him clear across this little room, practically onto Frog's bed. Frog was crouched there with the blade still in his hand. The partner coming through second had his gun drawn and that was it, he put two almost in the ten ring of the goddamn bull's-eye." I put my fist on my chest just to the right of the heart to show where they hit him.

"Hope the poor bastard didn't suffer."

"Lived two days. He told about the knife bit to the detectives and swore how he never would've tried to stab a cop."

"Poor bastard," said Harry.

"At least he died the way he lived. Armload of dope. I heard from one of the dicks that at the last they gave him a good stiff jolt of morphine. Said old Frog laying there with two big holes in his chest actually looked happy at the end."

"Why in the hell don't the state just give dope to these poor bastards like Frog?" said Harry, disgustedly.

"It's the high they crave, not just feeling healthy. They build up such a tolerance you'd have to keep increasing the dose and increasing it until you'd have to give them a fix that'd make a pussycat out of King

Kong. And heroin substitutes don't work with a stone hype. He wants the *real* thing. Pretty soon you'd be giving him doses that'd kill him anyway."

"What the hell, he'd be better off. Some of them probably wouldn't complain."

"Got to agree with you there," I nodded. "Damn straight."

"Wish that bitch'd get here," Harry mumbled, checking the bar clock.

"Who's that?"

"Irma, the goofy barmaid I hired last week. You seen her yet?"

"Don't think so," I said, sipping the beer, so cold it hurt my teeth.

"Sexy little twist," said Harry, "but a kook, you know? She'll steal your eyes out if you let her. But a good body. I'd like to break her open like a shotgun and horsefuck her."

"Thought you told me you were getting too old for that," I said, licking the foam off my upper lip, and finishing the glass, which Harry hurried to refill.

"I am, God knows, but once in a while I get this terrible urge, know what I mean? Sometimes when I'm closing up and I'm alone with her. . . . I ain't stirred the old lady for a couple years, but I swear when I'm with Irma I get the urge like a young stallion. I'm not *that* old, you know. Not by a long shot. But you know how my health's always been. Lately there's been this prostate problem. Still, when I'm around this Irma I'm awful randy. I feel like I could screw anything from a burro to a cowboy boot."

"I'll have to see this wench," I smiled.

"You won't take her away from me, will you, Bumper?"

I thought at first he was kidding and then I saw the desperate look on his face. "No, of course not, Harry."

"I really think I could make it with her, Bumper. I been depressed lately, especially with this prostate, but I could be a man again with Irma."

"Sure, Harry." I'd noticed the change coming over him gradually for the past year. He sometimes forgot to pick up bar money, which was very unusual for him. He mixed up customers' names and sometimes told you things he'd told you the last time he saw you. Mostly that, repeating things. A few of the other regular customers mentioned it when we played pool out of earshot. Harry was getting senile and it was not only sad, it was scary. It made my skin crawl. I wondered how much longer he'd be able to run the joint. I laid a quarter on the bar, and sure enough, he absently picked it up. The first time I ever bought my own drink in Harry's place.

"My old lady can't last much longer, Bumper. I ever tell you that the doctors only give her a year?"

"Yeah, you told me."

"Guy my age can't be alone. This prostate thing, you know I got to stand there and coax for twenty minutes before I can take a leak. And you don't know how lovely it is to be able to sit down and take a nice easy crap. You know, Bumper, a nice easy crap is a thing of beauty."

"Yeah, I guess so."

"I could do all right with a dame like Irma. Make me young again, Irma could."

"Sure."

"You try to go it alone when you get old and you'll be rotting out a coffin liner before you know it. You got to have somebody to keep you alive. If you don't, you might die without even knowing it. Get what I mean?"

"Yeah."

It was so depressing being here with Harry that I decided to split, but one of the local cronies came in.

"Hello, Freddie," I said, as he squinted through six ounces of eyeglasses into the cool darkness.

"Hi, Bumper," said Freddie, recognizing my voice before he got close enough to make me through his half-inch horn-rims. Nobody could ever mistake his twangy voice which could get on your nerves after a bit. Freddie limped over and laid both arthritic hands on the bar knowing I'd bounce for a couple drinks.

"A cold one for Freddie," I said, suddenly afraid that Harry wouldn't even know him. But that was ridiculous, I thought, putting a dollar on the bar, Harry's deterioration was only beginning. I usually bought for the bar when there were enough people in there to make Harry a little coin, trouble is, there were seldom more than three or four customers in Harry's at any one time anymore. I guess everyone runs from a man when he starts to die.

"How's business, Bumper?" asked Freddie, holding the mug in both his hands, fingers like crooked twigs.

"My business's always good, Freddie."

Freddie snuffled and laughed. I stared at Freddie for a few seconds while he drank. My stomach was burning and Harry had me spooked. Freddie suddenly looked ancient too. Christ, he probably was at least sixty-five. I'd never thought about Freddie as an older guy, but suddenly he was. Little old men they were. I had nothing in common with them now.

"Girls keeping you busy lately, Bumper?" Harry winked. He didn't know about Cassie or that I stopped chasing around after I met her.

"Been slowing down a little in that department, Harry," I said.

"Keep at it, Bumper," said Harry, cocking his head to one side and nodding like a bird. "The art of fornication is something you lose if you don't practice it. The eye muscles relax, you get bifocals like Freddie. The love muscles relax, whatta you got?"

"Maybe he *is* getting old, Harry," said Freddie, dropping his empty glass on its side as he tried to hand it to Harry with those twisted hands.

"Old? You kidding?" I said.

"How about you, Freddie?" said Harry. "You ain't got arthritis of the cock, have you? When was the last time you had a piece of ass?"

"About the last time you did," said Freddie sharply.

"Shit, before my Flossie got sick, I used to tear off a chunk every night. Right up till when she got sick, and I was sixty-eight years old then."

"Haw!" said Freddie, spilling some beer over the gnarled fingers. "You ain't been able to do anything but lick it for the past twenty years."

"Yeah?" said Harry, nodding fast now, like a starving little bird at a feed tray. "You know what I did to Irma here one night? Know what?"

"What?"

"I laid her right over the table there. What do you think of that, wise guy?"

"Haw. Haw. Haw," said Freddie who had been a little bit fried when he came in and was really feeling it now.

"All you can do is read about it in those dirty books," said Harry. "Me, I don't read about it, I do it! I threw old Irma right over that bar there and poured her the salami for a half hour!"

"Haw. Haw. Haw," said Freddie. "It'd take you that long to find that shriveled up old cricket dick. Haw. Haw. Haw."

"What's the sense of starting a beef?" I muttered to both of them. I was getting a headache. "Gimme a couple aspirin will you, Harry?" I said, and he shot the grinning Freddie a pissed-off look, and muttering under his breath, brought me a bottle of aspirin and a glass of water.

I shook out three pills and pushed the water away, swallowing the pills with a mouthful of beer. "One more beer," I said, "and then I gotta make it."

"Where you going, Bump? Out to hump?" Harry leered, and winked at Freddie, forgetting he was supposed to be mad as hell.

"Going to a friend's house for dinner."

"Nice slice of tail waiting, huh?" said Harry, nodding again.

"Not tonight. Just having a quiet dinner."

"Quiet dinner," said Freddie. "Haw. Haw. Haw."

"Screw you, Freddie," I said, getting mad for a second as he giggled in his beer. Then I thought, Jesus, I'm getting loony too.

The phone rang and Harry went to the back of the bar to answer it. In a few seconds he was bitching at somebody, and Freddie looked at me, shaking his head.

"Harry's going downhill real fast, Bumper."

"I know he is, so why get him pissed off?"

"I don't mean to," said Freddie. "I just lose my temper with him sometimes, he acts so damned nasty. I heard the doctors're just waiting for Flossie to die. Any day now."

I thought of how she was ten years ago, a fat, tough old broad, full of hell and jokes. She fixed such good cold-cut sandwiches I used to make a dinner out of them at least once a week.

"Harry can't make it without her," said Freddie. "Ever since she went away to the hospital last year he's been getting more and more childish, you noticed?"

I finished my beer and thought, I've *got* to get the hell out of here.

"It happens only to people like Harry and me. When you love somebody and need them so much especially when you're old, and then lose them, that's when it happens to you. It's the most godawful thing that ever could happen to you, when your mind rots like Harry's. Better your body goes like Flossie's. Flossie's the lucky one, you know. You're lucky too. You don't love nobody and you ain't married to nothing but that badge. Nothing can ever touch you, Bumper."

"Yeah, but how about when you get too old to do the job, Freddie? How about then?"

"Well, I never thought about that, Bumper." Freddie tipped the mug and dribbled on his chin. He licked some foam off one knotted knuckle. "Never thought about that, but I'd say you don't have to worry about it. You get a little older and charge around the way you do and somebody's bound to bump you off. It might sound cold, but what the hell, Bumper, look at *that* crazy old bastard." He waved a twisted claw toward Harry still yelling in the phone. "Screwing everything with his imagination and a piece of dead skin. Look at me. What the hell, dying on your beat wouldn't be the worst way to go, would it?"

"Know why I come to this place, Freddie? It's just the most cheerful goddamn drinking establishment in Los Angeles. Yeah, the conversation is stimulating and the atmosphere is very jolly and all."

Harry came back before I could get away from the bar. "Know who that was, Bumper?" he said, his eyes glassy and his cheeks pale. He had acne as a young man and now his putty-colored cheeks looked corroded.

"Who was it," I sighed, "Irma?"

"No, that was the hospital. I spent every cent I had, even with the hospital benefits, and now she's been put in a big ward with a million other old, dying people. And still I got to pay money for one thing or another. You know, when Flossie finally dies there ain't going to be nothing left to bury her. I had to cash in the insurance. How'll I bury old Flossie, Bumper?"

I started to say something to soothe Harry, but I heard sobbing and realized Freddie had started blubbering. Then in a second or two Harry started, so I threw five bucks on the bar for Freddie and Harry to get bombed on, and I got the hell away from those two without even saying good-bye. I've never understood how people can work in mental hospitals and old people's homes and places like that without going nuts. I felt about ready for the squirrel tank right now just being around those two guys for an hour.

**8**

TEN MINUTES LATER I was
driving my Ford north on the Golden State Freeway
and I started getting hungry for Socorro's enchiladas. I
got to Eagle Rock at dusk and parked in front of the
big old two-story house with the neat lawn and flower
gardens on the sides. I was wondering if Socorro
planted vegetables in the back this year, when I saw
Cruz in the living room standing by the front window.
He opened the door and stepped out on the porch,
wearing a brown sport shirt and old brown slacks and
his house slippers. Cruz didn't have to dress up for me,
and I was glad to come here and see everyone comfortable, as though I belonged here, and in a way I
did. Most bachelor cops have someplace like Cruz's
house to go to once in a while. Naturally, you can get
a little ding-a-ling if you live on the beat and don't
ever spend some time with decent people. So you find
a friend or a relative with a family and go there to get
your supply of faith replenished.

I called Cruz my old roomie because when we first
got out of the police academy twenty years ago, I
moved into this big house with him and Socorro. Dolores was a baby, and Esteban a toddler. I took a room
upstairs for over a year and helped them with their
house payments until we were through paying for our

uniforms and guns, and were both financially on our feet. That hadn't been a bad year and I'd never forget Socorro's cooking. She always said she'd rather cook for a man like me who appreciated her talent than a thin little guy like Cruz who never ate much and didn't really appreciate good food. Socorro was a slender girl then, twelve years younger than Cruz, nineteen years old, with two kids already, and the heavy Spanish accent of El Paso which is like that of Mexico itself. They'd had a pretty good life I guess, until Esteban insisted on joining the army and was killed two years ago. They weren't the same after that. They'd never be the same after that.

"How do you feel, *oso?*" said Cruz, as I climbed the concrete stairs to his porch. I grinned because Socorro had first started calling me *"oso"* way back in those days, and even now some of the policemen call me "bear" from Socorro's nickname.

"You hurting, Bumper?" Cruz asked. "I heard those kids gave you some trouble at the demonstration today."

"I'm okay," I answered. "What'd you hear?"

"Just that they pushed you around a little bit. *Hijo la—*. Why does a man your age get involved in that kind of stuff? Why don't you listen to me and just handle your radio calls and let those young coppers handle the militants and do the hotdog police work?"

"I answered a radio call. That's how it started. That's what I get for having that goddamn radio turned on."

"Come on in, you stubborn old bastard," Cruz grinned, holding the wood frame screen door open for me. Where could you see a wood frame screen door these days? It was an old house, but preserved. I loved it here. Cruz and me once sanded down all the woodwork in the living room, even the hardwood floor, and refinished it just as it had been when it was new.

"What're we having?" Cruz asked, brushing back his thick gray-black hair and nodding toward the kitchen.

"Well, let's see," I sniffed. I sniffed again a few times, and then took a great huge whiff. Actually I couldn't tell, because the chile and onion made it hard to differentiate, but I took a guess and pretended I knew.

"*Chile relleno, carnitas* and *cilantro* and onion. And ... let's see ... some enchiladas, some guacamole."

"I give up," Cruz shook his head. "The only thing you left out was rice and beans."

"Well, hell, Cruz, *arroz y frijoles*, that goes without saying."

"An animal's nose."

"Sukie in the kitchen?"

"Yeah, the kids're in the backyard, some of them."

I went through the big formal dining room to the kitchen and saw Socorro, her back to me, ladling out a huge wooden spoonful of rice into two of the bowls that sat on the drainboard. She was naturally a little the worse for wear after twenty years and nine kids, but her hair was as long and black and shiny rich as ever, and though she was twenty pounds heavier, she still was a strong, lively-looking girl with the whitest teeth I'd ever seen. I snuck up behind her and tickled her ribs.

"Ay!" she said, dropping the spoon. "Bumper!"

I gave her a hug from the back while Cruz chuckled and said, "You didn't surprise him, he smelled from the door and knew just what you fixed for him."

"He's not a man, this one," she smiled, "no man ever had a nose like that."

"Just what I told him," said Cruz.

"Sit down, Bumper," said Socorro, waving to the kitchen table, which, big and old as it was, looked lost in the huge kitchen. I'd seen this kitchen when there wasn't a pathway to walk through, the day after Christmas when all the kids were young and I'd brought them toys. Kids and toys literally covered every foot of linoleum and you couldn't even see the floor then.

"Beer, Bumper?" asked Cruz, and opened two cold ones without me answering. We still liked drinking them out of the bottle, both of us, and I almost finished mine without taking it away from my mouth. And Cruz, knowing my M.O. so well, uncapped another one.

"Cruz told me the news, Bumper. I was thrilled to hear it," said Socorro, slicing an onion, her eyes glistening from the fumes.

"About you retiring right away and going with Cassie when she leaves," said Cruz.

"That's good, Bumper," said Socorro. "There's no sense hanging around after Cassie leaves. I was worried about that."

"Sukie was afraid your *puta* would seduce you away from Cassie if she was up in San Francisco and you were down here."

"*Puta?*"

"The beat," said Cruz taking a gulp of the beer. "Socorro always calls it Bumper's *puta.*"

"*Cuidao!*" said Socorro to Cruz. "The children are right outside the window." I could hear them laughing, and Nacho yelled something then, and the girls squealed.

"Since you're leaving, we can talk about her can't we, Bumper?" Cruz laughed. "That beat is a *puta* who seduced you all these years."

Then for the first time I noticed from his grin and his voice that Cruz had had a few before I got there. I looked at Socorro who nodded and said, "Yes, the old *borracho's* been drinking since he got home from work. Wants to celebrate Bumper's last dinner as a bachelor, he says."

"Don't be too rough on him," I grinned. "He doesn't get drunk very often."

"Who's drunk?" said Cruz, indignantly.

"You're on your way, *pendejo,*" said Socorro, and Cruz mumbled in Spanish, and I laughed and finished my beer.

"If it hadn't been for that *puta*, Bumper would've been a captain by now."

"Oh sure," I said, going to the refrigerator and drawing two more beers for Cruz and me. "Want one, Sukie?"

"No thanks," said Socorro, and Cruz burped a couple times.

"Think I'll go outside and see the kids," I said, and then I remembered the presents in the trunk of my car that I had bought Monday after Cruz invited me to dinner.

"Hey, you roughnecks," I said when I stepped out, and Nacho yelled, "Buuuum-per," and swung toward me from a rope looped over the limb of a big oak that covered most of the yard.

"You're getting about big enough to eat hay and pull a wagon, Nacho," I said. Then four of them ran toward me chattering about something, their eyes all sparkling because they knew damn well I'd never come for dinner without bringing them something.

"Where's Dolores?" I asked. She was my favorite now, the oldest after Esteban, and was a picture of what her mother had been. She was a college junior majoring in physics and engaged to a classmate of hers.

"Dolores is out with Gordon, where else?" said Ralph, a chubby ten-year-old, the baby of the family who was a terror, always raising some kind of hell and keeping everyone in an uproar.

"Where's Alice?"

"Over next door playing," said Ralph again, and the four of them, Nacho, Ralph, María, and Marta were all about to bust, and I was enjoying it even though it was a shame to make them go through this.

"Nacho," I said nonchalantly, "would you please take my car keys and get some things out of the trunk?"

"I'll help," shrieked Marta.

"I will," said María, jumping up and down, a little

eleven-year-old dream in a pink dress and pink socks and black patent leather shoes. She was the prettiest and would be heartbreakingly beautiful someday.

"I'll go alone," said Nacho. "I don't need no help."

"The hell you will," said Ralph.

"You watch your language, Rafael," said María, and I had to turn around to keep from busting up at the way Ralph stuck his chubby little fanny out at her.

"Mama," said María. "Ralph did something dirty!"

"Snitch," said Ralph, running to the car with Nacho.

I strolled back into the kitchen still laughing, and Cruz and Socorro both were smiling at me because they knew how much I got a bang out of their kids.

"Take Bumper in the living room, Cruz," said Socorro. "Dinner won't be ready for twenty minutes."

"Come on, Bumper," said Cruz, taking four cold ones out of the refrigerator, and a beer opener. "I don't know why Mexican women get to be tyrants in their old age. They're so nice and obedient when they're young."

"Old age. Huh! Listen to the *viejo*, Bumper," she said, waving a wooden spoon in his direction, as we went in the living room and I flopped in Cruz's favorite chair because he insisted. He pushed the ottoman over and made me put my feet up.

"Damn, Cruz."

"Got to give you extra special treatment tonight, Bumper," he said, opening another beer for me. "You look dog tired, and this may be the last we have you for a long time."

"I'll only be living one hour away by air. You think Cassie and me aren't gonna come to L.A. once in a while? And you think you and Socorro and the kids aren't gonna come see us up there?"

"The whole platoon of us?" he laughed.

"We're gonna see each other plenty, that's for sure," I said, and fought against the down feeling that I was getting because I realized we probably would *not* be seeing each other very often at all.

"Yeah, Bumper," said Cruz, sitting across from me in the other old chair, almost as worn and comfortable as this one. "I was afraid that jealous bitch would never let you go."

"You mean my beat?"

"Right." He took several big gulps on the beer and I thought about how I was going to miss him.

"How come all the philosophizing tonight? Calling my beat a whore and all that?"

"I'm waxing poetic tonight."

"You also been tipping more than a little *cerveza*."

Cruz winked and peeked toward the kitchen where we could hear Socorro banging around. He went to an old mahogany hutch that was just inside the dining room and took a half-empty bottle of mescal out of the bottom cabinet.

"That one have a worm in it?"

"If it did I drank it," he whispered. "Don't want Sukie to see me drinking it. I still have a little trouble with my liver and I'm not supposed to."

"Is that the stuff you bought in San Luis? That time on your vacation?"

"That's it, the end of it."

"You won't need any liver you drink that stuff."

"It's good, Bumper. Here, try a throatful or two."

"Better with salt and lemon."

"Pour it down. You're the big *macho*, damn it. Drink like one."

I took three fiery gulps and a few seconds after they hit bottom I regretted it, and had to drain my bottle of beer while Cruz chuckled and sipped slowly for his turn.

"Damn," I wheezed and then the fire fanned out and my guts uncoiled and I felt good. Then in a few minutes I felt better. That was the medicine my body needed.

"They don't always have salt and lemon lying around down in Mexico," said Cruz handing me back the mescal. "Real Mexicans just mix it with saliva."

"No wonder they're such tough little bastards," I wheezed, taking another gulp, but only one this time, and handing it back.

"How do you feel now, 'mano?" Cruz giggled, and it made me start laughing, his silly little giggle that always started when he was half swacked.

"I feel about half as good as you," I said, and splashed some more beer into the burning pit that was my stomach. But it was a different fire entirely than the one made by the stomach acid, this was a friendly fire, and after it smoldered it felt great.

"Are you hungry?" asked Cruz.

"Ain't I always?"

"You are," he said, "you're hungry for almost everything. Always. I've often wished I was more like you."

"Like me?"

"Always feasting, on *everything*. Too bad it can't go on forever. But it can't. I'm damn glad you're getting out now."

"You're drunk."

"I am. But I know what I'm talking about, 'mano. Cassie was sent to you. I prayed for that." Then Cruz reached in his pocket for the little leather pouch. In it was the string of black carved wooden beads he carried for luck. He squeezed the soft leather and put it away.

"Did those beads really come from Jerusalem?"

"They did, that's no baloney. I got them from a missionary priest for placing first in my school in El Paso. 'First prize in spelling to Cruz Guadalupe Segovia,' the priest said, as he stood in front of the whole school, and I died of happiness that day. I was thirteen, just barely. He got the beads in the Holy Land and they were blessed by Pius XI."

"How many kids did you beat out for the prize?"

"About six entered the contest. There were only seventy-five in the school altogether. I don't think the

other five contestants spoke any English. They
thought the contest would be in Spanish but it wasn't,
so I won."

We both laughed at that. "I never won a thing,
Cruz. You're way ahead of me." It was amazing to
think of a real man like Cruz carrying those wooden
beads. In this day and age!

Then the front door banged open and the living
room was filled with seven yelling kids, only Dolores
being absent that night, and Cruz shook his head and
sat back quietly drinking his beer and Socorro came
into the living room and tried to give me hell for buying all the presents, but you couldn't hear yourself
over the noisy kids.

"Are these real big-league cleats?" asked Nacho as I
adjusted the batting helmet for him and fixed the chin
strap which I knew he'd throw away as soon as the
other kids told him big leaguers don't wear chin
straps.

"Look! Hot pants!" María squealed, holding them
up against her adolescent body. They were sporty,
blue denim with a bib, and patch pockets.

"Hot pants?" Cruz said. "Oh, no!"

"They even wear them to school, Papa. They do.
Ask Bumper!"

"Ask Bumper," Cruz grumbled and drank some
more beer.

The big kids were there then too, Linda, George,
and Alice, all high school teenagers, and naturally I
bought clothes for them. I got George a box of mod-
colored long-sleeved shirts and from the look in his
eyes I guess I couldn't have picked anything better.

After all the kids thanked me a dozen times, Socorro
ordered them to put everything away and called us to
dinner. We sat close together on different kinds of
chairs at the huge rectangular oak table that weighed
a ton. I know because I helped Cruz carry it in here
twelve years ago when there was no telling how many
kids were going to be sitting around it.

The youngest always said the prayers aloud. They crossed themselves and Ralph said grace, and they crossed themselves again and I was drooling because the *chiles rellenos* were on a huge platter right in front of me. The big *chiles* were stuffed with cheese and fried in a light fluffy batter, and before I could help myself, Alice was serving me and my plate was filled before any of those kids took a thing for themselves. Their mother and father never said anything to them, they just did things like that.

"You *do* have *cilantro*," I said, salivating with a vengeance now. I knew I smelled that wonderful spice.

Marta, using her fingers, sprinkled a little extra *cilantro* over my *carnitas* when I said that, and I bit into a soft, handmade, flour tortilla crammed with *carnitas* and Socorro's own *chile* sauce.

"Well, Bumper?" said Cruz after I'd finished half a plateful which took about thirty-five seconds.

I moaned and rolled my eyeballs and everybody laughed because they knew that look so well.

"You see, Marta," said Socorro. "You wouldn't hate to cook so much if you could cook for somebody like Bumper who appreciates your work."

I grinned with a hog happy look, washing down some *chile relleno* and enchilada with three big swigs of cold beer. "Your mother is an artist!"

I finished three helpings of *carnitas*, the tender little chunks of pork which I covered with Socorro's *chile* and *cilantro* and onion. Then, after everyone was finished and there were nine pairs of brown eyes looking at me in wonder, I heaped the last three *chile rellenos* on my plate and rolled one up with the last flour tortilla and the last few bites of *carnitas* left in the bowl, and nine pairs of brown eyes got wider and rounder.

"*Por Dios*, I thought I made enough for twenty," said Socorro.

"You did, you did, Sukie," I said, enjoying being the whole show now, and finishing it in three big bites. "I'm just extra hungry tonight, and you made it extra good, and there's no sense leaving leftovers around to spoil." With that I ate half a *chile relleno* and swallowed some beer and looked around at all the eyes, and Nacho burped and groaned. We all busted up, Ralph especially, who fell off his chair onto the floor holding his stomach and laughing so hard I was afraid he'd get sick. It was a hell of a thing when you think of it, entertaining people by being a damn glutton, just to get attention.

After dinner we cleared the table and I got roped into a game of Scrabble with Alice and Marta and Nacho with the others kibitzing, and all the time I was swilling cold beer with an occasional shot of mescal that Cruz brought out in the open now. By nine o'clock when the kids had to go to bed I was pretty well lubricated.

They all kissed me good night except George and Nacho, who shook hands, and there were no arguments about going to bed, and fifteen minutes later it was still and quiet upstairs. I'd never seen Cruz or Socorro spank any of them. Of course the older ones spanked hell out of the younger ones, I'd seen that often enough. After all, everyone in this world needs a thumping once in a while.

We took the leaf out of the table and replaced the lace tablecloth and the three of us went into the living room. Cruz was pretty well bombed out, and after Socorro complained, he decided not to have another beer. I had a cold one in my right hand, and the last of the mescal in my left.

Cruz sat next to Socorro on the couch and he rubbed his face which was probably numb as hell. He gave her a kiss on the neck.

"Get out of here," she grumbled. "You smell like a stinking wino."

"How can I smell like a wino. I haven't had any wine," said Cruz.

"Remember how we used to sit like this after dinner back in the old days," I said, realizing how much the mescal affected me, because they were both starting to look a little fuzzy.

"Remember how little and skinny Sukie was," said Cruz, poking her arm.

"I'm going to let you have it in a minute," said Socorro, raising her hand which was a raw, worn-out looking hand for a girl her age. She wasn't quite forty years old.

"Sukie was the prettiest girl I'd ever seen," I said.

"I guess she was," said Cruz with a silly grin.

"And still is," I added. "And Cruz was the handsomest guy I ever saw outside of Tyrone Power or maybe Clark Gable."

"You really think Tyrone Power was better looking?" said Cruz, grinning again as Socorro shook her head, and to me he honestly didn't look a bit different now than he ever had, except for the gray hair. Damn him for staying young, I thought.

"Speaking of pretty girls," said Socorro, "let's hear about your new plans with Cassie."

"Well, like I told you, she was gonna go up north to an apartment and get squared away at school. Then after the end of May when Cruz and me have our twenty years, she'd fly back here and we'd get married. Now I've decided to cut it short. I'll work tomorrow and the next day and run my vacation days and days off together to the end of the month when I officially retire. That way I can leave with Cassie, probably Sunday morning or Monday and we'll swing through Las Vegas and get married on the way."

"Oh, Bumper, we wanted to be with you when you get married," said Socorro, looking disappointed.

"What the hell, at our age getting married ain't no big thing," I said.

"We love her, Bumper," said Socorro. "You're lucky, very lucky. She'll be perfect for you."

"What a looker." Cruz winked and tried to whistle, but he was too drunk.

Socorro shook her head and said, *"sinvergüenza,"* and we both laughed at him.

"What're you going to do Friday?" asked Socorro. "Just go into rollcall and stand up and say you're retiring and this is your last day?"

"Nope, I'm just gonna fade away. I'm not telling a soul and I hope you haven't said anything to anyone, Cruz."

"Nothing," said Cruz, and he burped.

"I'm just cutting out like for my regular two days off, then I'm sending a registered letter to Personnel Division and one to the captain. I'll just sign all my retirement papers and mail them in. I can give my badge and I.D. card to Cruz before I leave and have him turn them in for me so I won't have to go back at all."

"You'll have to come back to L.A. for your retirement party," said Cruz. "We're sure as hell going to want to throw a retirement party for you."

"Thanks, Cruz, but I never liked retirement parties anyway. In fact I think they're miserable. I appreciate the thought but no party for me."

"Just think," said Socorro. "To be starting a new life! I wish Cruz could leave the job too."

"You said it," said Cruz, his eyes glassy though he sat up straight. "But with all our kids, I'm a thirty-year man. Thirty years, that's a lifetime. I'll be an old man when I pull the pin."

"Yeah, I guess I'm lucky," I said. "Remember when we were going through the academy, Cruz? We thought we were old men then, running with all those kids twenty-one and twenty-two years old. Here you were thirty-one, the oldest guy in the class, and I was close behind you. Remember Mendez always called us *elefante y ratoncito?*"

"The elephant and the mouse," Cruz giggled.

"The two old men of the class. Thirty years old and I thought I knew something then. Hell, you're still a baby at that age. We were both babies."

"We were babies, *'mano*," said Cruz. "But only because we hadn't been out there yet." Cruz waved his hand toward the streets. "You grow up fast out there and learn too much. It's no damn good for a man to learn as much as you learn out there. It ruins the way you think about things, and the way you feel. There're certain things you should believe and if you stay out there for twenty years you can't believe them anymore. That's not good."

"You still believe them, don't you, Cruz?" I asked, and Socorro looked at us like we were two raving drunks, which we probably were, but we understood, Cruz and me.

"I still believe them, Bumper, because I want to. And I have Sukie and the kids. I can come home, and then the other isn't real. You've had no one to go to. Thank God for Cassie."

"I've got to go fix school lunches. Excuse me, Bumper," said Socorro, and she gave us that shake of the head which meant, it's time to leave the drunken cops to their talk. But Cruz hardly ever got drunk, and she didn't really begrudge him, even though he had trouble with his liver.

"I never could tell you how glad we were when you first brought Cassie here for dinner, Bumper. Socorro and me, we stayed awake in bed that night and talked about it and how God must've sent her, even though you don't believe in God."

"I believe in the *gods*, you know that," I grinned, gulping the beer after I took the last sip of the mescal.

"There's only one God, goddamnit," said Cruz.

"Even your God has three faces, goddamnit," I said, and gave him a glance over the top of my beer bottle, making him laugh.

"Bumper, I'm trying to talk to you seriously." And his eyes turned down at the corners like always. I couldn't woof him anymore when his eyes did that.

"Okay."

"Cassie's the answer to a prayer."

"Why did you waste all your prayers on me?"

"Why do you think, *pendejo*? You're my brother, *mi hermano*."

That made me put the beer down, and I straightened up and looked at his big eyes. Cruz was struggling with the fog of the mescal and beer because he wanted to tell me something. I wondered how in hell he had ever made the Department physical. He was barely five-eight in his bare feet, and he was so damn skinny. He'd never gained a pound, but outside of Esteban, he had the finest-looking face you would ever see.

"I didn't know you thought that much about Cassie and me."

"Of course I did. After all, I prayed her here for you. Don't you see what you were heading for? You're fifty years old, Bumper. You and some of the other old beat cops've been the *machos* of the streets all these years, but Lord, I could just see you duking it out with some young stud or chasing somebody out there and all of a sudden just lying down on that street to die. You realize how many of our classmates had heart attacks already?"

"Part of being a policeman," I shrugged.

"Not to mention some asshole blowing you up," said Cruz. "You remember Driscoll? He had a heart attack just last month and he's not nearly as fat as you, and a few years younger, and I'll bet he never does anything harder than lift a pencil. Like you today, all alone, facing a mob, like a rookie! What the hell, Bumper, you think I want to be a pallbearer for a guy two hundred and eighty pounds?"

"Two seventy-five."

"When Cassie came, I said, 'Thank God, now Bumper's got a chance.' I worried though. I knew you were smart enough to see how much woman you had, but I was afraid that *puta* had too strong a grip on you."

"Was it *you* that kept getting me assigned to the north end districts all the time? Lieutenant Hilliard keep telling me it was a mistake every time I bitched about it."

"Yeah, I did it. I tried to get you away from your beat, but I gave up. You just kept coming back down anyway and that meant nobody was patrolling the north end, so I didn't accomplish anything. I can guess what it was to you, being *el campeón* out there, having people look at you the way they do on your beat."

"Yeah, well it isn't so much," I said, nervously fidgeting with the empty bottle.

"You know what happens to old cops who stay around the streets too long."

"What?" I said, and the enchilada caught me and bit into the inside of my gut.

"They get too old to do police work and they become *characters*. That's what I'd hate to see. You just becoming an old character, and maybe getting yourself hurt bad out there before you realize you're too old. Just too old."

"I'm not that old yet. Damn it, Cruz!"

"No, not for civilian life. You have lots of good years ahead of you. But for a warrior, it's time to quit, 'mano. I was worried about her going up there and you coming along in a few weeks. I was afraid the *puta* would get you alone when Cassie wasn't there. I'm so damn glad you're leaving with Cassie."

"So am I, Cruz," I said, lowering my voice like I was afraid to let myself hear it. "You're right. I've half thought of these things. You're right. I think I'd blow my brains out if I ever got as lonely as some I've seen, like some of those people on my beat, homeless wandering people, that don't belong anywhere. . . ."

"That's it, Bumper. There's no place for a man alone, not really. You can get along without love when you're young and strong. Some guys can, guys like you. Me, I never could. And nobody can get along without it when he gets old. You shouldn't be afraid to love, 'mano."

"Am I, Cruz?" I asked, chewing two tablets because

a mailed fist was beating on my guts from the inside. "Is that why I feel so unsure of myself now that I'm leaving? Is that it?"

I could hear Socorro humming as she made lunches for the entire tribe. She would write each one's name on his lunch sack and put it in the refrigerator.

"Remember when we were together in the old days? You and me and Socorro and the two kids? And how you hardly ever spoke about your previous life even when you were drunk? You only said a little about your brother Clem who was dead, and your wife who'd left you. But you really told us more, much more about your brother. Sometimes you called him in your sleep. But mostly you called someone else."

I was rocking back now, holding my guts which were throbbing, and all the tablets in my pocket wouldn't help.

"You never told us about your boy. I always felt bad that you never told *me* about him, because of how close we are. You only told me about him in your sleep."

"What did I say?"

"You'd call 'Billy,' and you'd say things to him. Sometimes you'd cry, and I'd have to go in and pick up your covers and pillow from the floor and cover you up because you'd throw them clear off the bed."

"I never dreamed about him, never!"

"How else would I know, *'mano*?" he said softly. "We used to talk a lot about it, Socorro and me, and we used to worry about a man who'd loved a brother and a son like you had. We wondered if you'd be afraid to love again. It happens. But when you get old, you've got to. You've *got* to."

"But you're safe if you *don't*, Cruz!" I said, flinching from the pain. Cruz was looking at the floor, not used to talking to me like this, and he didn't notice my agony.

"You're safe, Bumper, in one way. But in the way

that counts, you're in danger. Your soul is in danger if you don't love."

"Did you believe that when Esteban was killed? Did you?"

Cruz looked up at me, and his eyes got even softer than normal and turned way down at the corners because he was being most serious. His heavy lashes blinked twice and he sighed, "Yes. Even after Esteban, and even though he was the oldest and you always feel a little something extra for the firstborn. Even after Esteban was killed I felt this to be the truth. After the grief, I knew it was God's truth. I believed it, even then."

"I think I'll get a cup of coffee. I have a stomachache. Maybe something warm...."

Cruz smiled, and leaned back in his chair. Socorro was finishing the last of the lunches and I chatted with her while we warmed up the coffee. The stomachache started to fade a little.

I drank the coffee and thought about what Cruz said which made sense, and yet, every time you get tied up to people something happens and that cord is cut, and I mean really cut with a bloody sword.

"Shall we go in and see how the old boy's doing?"

"Oh sure, Sukie," I said, putting my arm around her shoulder. Cruz was stretched out on the couch snoring.

"That's his drinking sleep. We'll never wake him up," she said. "Maybe I just better get his pillow and a blanket."

"He shouldn't be sleeping on the couch," I said. "It's drafty in this big living room." I went over to him and knelt down.

"What're you going to do?"

"Put him to bed," I said, picking him up in my arms.

"Bumper, you'll rupture yourself."

"He's light as a baby," I said, and he *was* surprisingly light. "Why the hell don't you make him eat more?" I said, following Socorro up the stairs.

"You know he doesn't like to eat. Let me help you, Bumper."

"Just lead the way, Mama. I can handle him just fine."

When we got in their bedroom I wasn't even breathing hard and I laid him on the bed, on the sheets. She had already pulled back the covers. Cruz was rattling and wheezing now and we both laughed.

"He snores awful," she said as I looked at the little squirt.

"He's the only *real* friend I ever made in twenty years. I know millions of people and I see them and eat with them and I'll miss things about all of them, but it won't be like something inside is gone, like with Cruz."

"Now you'll have Cassie. You'll be ten times closer with her." She held my hand then. Both her hands were tough and hard.

"You sound like your old man."

"We talk about you a lot."

"Good night," I said, kissing her on the cheek. "Cassie and me are coming by before we leave to say goodbye to all of you."

"Good night, Bumper."

"Good night, old shoe," I said to Cruz in a loud voice and he snorted and blew and I chuckled and descended the stairs. I let myself out after turning out the hall light and locking the door.

When I went to bed that night I started getting scared and didn't know why. I wished Cassie was with me. After I went to sleep I slept very well and didn't dream.

# Thursday,
# the Second Day

## 9

THE NEXT MORNING I
worked on my badge for five minutes, and my boondockers were glistening. I was kind of disappointed
when Lieutenant Hilliard didn't have an inspection, I
was looking so good. Cruz looked awful. He sat at the
front table with Lieutenant Hilliard and did a bad job
of reading off the crimes. Once or twice he looked at
me and rolled his eyes which were really sad this
morning because he was so hung over. After rollcall I
got a chance to talk to him for a minute.

"You look a little *crudo*," I said, trying not to smile.

"What a bastard you are," he moaned.

"It wasn't the mescal. I think you swallowed the
worm."

"A complete bastard."

"Can you meet me at noon? I wanna buy you
lunch."

"Don't even talk about it," he groaned, and I had to
laugh.

"Okay, but save me your lunch hour tomorrow. And
pick out the best, most expensive place in town. Somewhere that doesn't bounce for bluecoats. That's where
we're going for my last meal as a cop."

"You're actually going to *pay* for a meal on duty?"

"It'll be a first," I grinned, and he smiled but he acted like it hurt to grin.

"*Ahí te haucho*," I said, heading for the car.

"Don't forget you have court this afternoon, *'mano*," he said, always nagging me.

Before getting into my black-and-white I looked it over. It's always good to pull out the back seat before you leave, in case some innocent rookie on the night-watch let one of his sneaky prisoners stash his gun down there, or a condom full of heroin, or a goddamn hand grenade. It takes so long to make a policeman out of some of these kids, nothing would surprise me. But then I reminded myself what it was like to be twenty-two. They're right in the middle of growing up, these babies, and it's awful tough growing up in that bluecoat as twenty-two-year-old Establishment symbols. Still, it chills my nuts the way they stumble around like civilians for five years or so, and let people flimflam them. Someday, I thought, I'll probably find a dead midget jammed down there behind the friggin' seat.

As soon as I hit the bricks and started cruising I began thinking about the case I had this afternoon. It was a preliminary hearing on a guy named Landry and the dicks had filed on him for being an ex-con with a gun, and also filed one count of possession of marijuana. I didn't figure to have any problems with the case. I'd busted him in January after I'd gotten information on this gunsel from a snitch named Knobby Booker, who worked for me from time to time, and I went to a hotel room on East Sixth Street on some phony pretext I couldn't completely remember until I reread the arrest report. I busted Landry in his room while he was taking a nap in the middle of the afternoon. He had about two lids of pot in a sandwich bag in a drawer by his bed to give him guts when he pulled a robbery, and a fully loaded U.S. Army forty-five automatic under his mattress. He damned near went for it when I came through the door, and I al-

most blew him up when he started for it. In fact, it
was a Mexican standoff for a few seconds, him with
his hand an inch or so under the mattress, and me
crouching and coming to the bed, my six-inch Smith
aimed at his upper lip, and warning about what I was
going to do if he didn't pull his hand out very very
slow, and he did.

Landry had gotten out on five thousand dollars' bail
which some old broad put up for him. He'd been a
half-assed bit actor on TV and movies a few years
back, and was somewhat of a gigolo with old women.
He jumped bail and was rearrested in Denver and
extradited, and the arrest was now four months old.
I didn't remember all the details, but of course I
would read the arrest report and be up on it before I
testified. The main thing of course was to hold him to
answer at the prelim without revealing my informant
Knobby Booker, or without even letting anyone know
I *had* an informant. It wasn't too hard if you knew
how.

It was getting hot and smoggy and I was already
starting to sweat in the armpits. I glanced over at an
old billboard on Olive Street which said, "Don't start a
boy on a life of crime by leaving your keys in the car,"
and I snorted and farted a couple of times in disgust.
It's the goddamn do-gooder P.R. men, who dream up
slogans like that to make everybody but the criminals
feel guilty, who'll drive all *real* cops out of this business one of these days.

As I pulled to the curb opposite the Grand Central
Market, a wino staggering down Broadway sucking on
a short dog saw me, spun around, fell on his ass,
dropped his bottle, and got up as though nothing happened. He started walking away from the short dog,
which was rolling around on the sidewalk spilling
sweet lucy all over the pavement.

"Pick up the dog, you jerk," I called to him. "I ain't
gonna bust you."

"Thanks, Bumper," he said sheepishly and picked

up the bottle. He waved, and hustled back down Broadway, a greasy black coat flapping around his skinny hips.

I tried to remember where I knew him from. Of course I knew him from the beat, but he wasn't just a wino face. There was something else. Then I saw through the gauntness and grime and recognized him and smiled because these days it always felt good to remember and prove to yourself that your memory is as sharp as ever.

They called him Beans. The real name I couldn't recall even though I'd had it printed up on a fancy certificate. He almost caused me to slug another policeman about ten years ago and I'd never come close to doing that before or since.

The policeman was Herb Slovin and he finally got his ass canned. Herb was fired for capping for a bail bondsman and had a nice thing going until they caught him. He was working vice and was telling everybody he busted to patronize Laswell Brothers Bail Bonds, and Slim Laswell was kicking back a few bucks to Herb for each one he sent. That's considered to be as bad as stealing, and the Department bounced his ass in a hurry after he was caught. He would've gone behind something else though if it hadn't been that. He was a hulking, cruel bastard and so horny he'd mount a cage if he thought there was a canary in there. I figured sooner or later he'd fall for broads or brutality.

It was Beans that almost caused me and Herb to tangle. Herb hated the drunk wagon. "Niggers and white garbage," he'd repeat over and over when something made him mad which was most of the time. And he called the wagon job "the N.H.I. detail." When you asked him what that stood for he'd say "No Humans Involved," and then he let out with that donkey bray of his. We were working the wagon one night and got a call on Beans because he was spread-eagled prone across San Pedro Street blocking two lanes of traffic, out cold. He'd puked and wet all over himself and didn't even wake up when we dragged him to the wagon and flipped him in on the floor. There was no problem. We both wore gloves like most wagon cops, and there were only two other winos inside. About ten minutes later when we were on East Sixth Street, we heard a ruckus in the back and had to stop the wagon and go back there and keep the other two winos from kicking hell out of Beans who woke up and was fighting mad for maybe the first time in his life. I'd busted him ten or twenty times for drunk and never had any trouble with him. You seldom have to hassle a stone wino like Beans.

They quieted down as soon as Herb opened the back door and threatened to tear their heads off, and I was just getting back in the wagon when Beans, sitting by the door, said, "Fuck you, you skin-headed jack-ass!" I cracked up laughing because Herb was bald, and with his long face and big yellow teeth and the way he brayed when he laughed, he *did* look like a skin-headed jackass.

Herb though, growled something, and snatched Beans right off the bench, out of the wagon into the street, and started belting him back and forth across the face with his big gloved hand. I realized from the thuds that they were sap gloves and Beans's face was already busted open and bleeding before I could pull Herb away and push him back, causing him to fall on his ass.

"You son of a bitch," he said, looking at me with a combination of surprise and blood red anger. He almost said it like a question he was so surprised.

"He's a wino, man," I answered, and that should've been enough for any cop, especially a veteran like Herb who had twelve years on the job at that time and knew that you don't beat up defenseless winos no matter what kind of trouble they give you. That was one of the first things we learned in the old days from the beat cops who broke us in. When a man takes a swing at you or actually hits you, you have the right to kick ass, that goes without saying. It doesn't have to be tit for tat, and if some asshole gives you tit, you tat his goddamn teeth down his throat. That way, you'll save some other cop from being slugged by the same puke-pot if he learns his lesson from you.

But every real cop also knows you don't beat up winos. Even if they swing at you or actually hit you. Chances are it'll be a puny little swing and you can just handcuff him and throw him in jail. Cops know very well how many fellow policemen develop drinking problems themselves, and there's always the thought in the back of your mind that there on the sidewalk, but for the gods, sleeps old Bumper Morgan.

Anyway, Herb had violated a cop's code by beating up the wino and he knew it, which probably saved us a hell of a good go right there on East Sixth Street. And I'm not at all sure it might not've ended up by me getting my chubby face changed around by those sap gloves because Herb was an ex-wrestler and a very tough bastard.

"Don't you ever try that again," he said to me, as we put Beans back inside and locked the door.

"I won't, if you never beat up a drunk when you're working with me," I answered casually, but I was tense and coiled, ready to go, even thinking about un-snapping my holster because Herb looked damned dangerous at that moment, and you never know when an armed man might do something crazy. He was one of those creeps that carried an untraceable hideout gun and bragged how if he ever killed somebody he shouldn't have, he'd plant the gun on the corpse and claim self-defense. The mood was interrupted by a radio call just then, and I rogered it and we finished the night in silence. The next night Herb asked to go back to a radio car because him and me had a "person-ality conflict."

Shortly after that Herb went to vice and got fired, and I forgot all about that incident until about a year later on Main Street, when I ran into Beans again. That night I got into a battle with two guys I'd watched pull a pigeon drop on some old man. I'd stood inside a pawnshop and watched them through binoculars while they flimflammed him out of five hundred bucks.

They were bad young dudes, and the bigger of the two, a block-faced slob with an eighteen-inch neck was giving me a pretty good go, even though I'd already cracked two of his ribs with my stick. I couldn't finish him because the other one kept jumping on my back, kicking and biting, until I ran backward and slammed into a car and a brick wall, with him between me and the object. I did this twice and he kept hanging on and then somebody from the crowd of about twenty assholes who were gathered around enjoying the fight barreled in and tackled the little one and held him on the sidewalk until I could finish the big one by slapping him across the Adam's apple with the stick.

The other one gave up right then and I cuffed the two of them together and saw that my helper was old Beans the wino, sitting there throwing up, and bleeding from a cut eye where the little dude clawed him. I gave Beans a double sawbuck for that, and took him to a doctor, and I had the Captain's adjutant print up a beautiful certificate commending Beans for his good citizenship. Of course, I lied and said Beans was some respectable businessman who saw the fight and came to my aid. I couldn't tell them he was a down-and-out wino or they might not have done it. It was nicely framed and had Beans's real name on it, which I couldn't for the life of me remember now. I presented it to him the next time I found him bombed on East Sixth Street and he really seemed to like it.

As I remembered all this, I felt like calling him back and asking him if he still had it, but I figured he probably sold the frame for enough to buy a short dog, and used the certificate to plug the holes in his shoe. It's always best not to ask too many questions of people or to get to know them too well. You save yourself disappointment that way. Anyway, Beans was half a block away now, staggering down the street cradling the wine bottle under his greasy coat.

I took down my sunglasses which I keep stashed behind the visor in my car and settled down to cruise and watch the streets and relax even though I was too restless to really relax. I decided not to wait, but to cruise over to the school and see Cassie, who would be coming in early like she always did on Thursdays. She'd feel like I did, like everything she did these last days at school would be for the last time. But at least she knew she'd be doing similar things in another school.

I parked out front and got a few raspberries from students for parking my black-and-white in the no parking zone, but I'd be damned if I'd walk clear from the faculty lot. Cassie wasn't in her office when I got there, but it was unlocked so I sat at her desk and waited.

The desk was exactly like the woman who manned it: smart and tidy, interesting and feminine. She had an odd-shaped ceramic ashtray on one side of the desk which she'd picked up in some junk store in west L.A. There was a small, delicately painted oriental vase that held a bunch of dying violets which Cassie would replace first thing after she arrived. Under the plastic cover on the desk blotter Cassie had a screwy selection of pictures of people she admired, mostly French poets. Cassie was long on poetry and tried to get me going on haiku for a while, but I finally convinced her I don't have the right kind of imagination for poetry. My reading is limited to history and to new ways of doing police work. I liked one poem Cassie showed me about wooly lambs and shepherds and wild killer dogs. I understood that one all right.

The door opened and Cassie and another teacher, a

curvy little chicken in a hot pink mini, came giggling through the door.

"Oh!" said the young broad. "Who are you?" the blue uniform shocked her. I was sitting back in Cassie's comfortable leather-padded desk chair.

"I am the Pretty Good Shepherd," I said, puffing on my cigar and smiling at Cassie.

"Whatever that means," said Cassie, shaking her head, putting down a load of books, and kissing me on the cheek much to the surprise of her friend.

"You must be Cassie's fiancé," the friend laughed as it suddenly hit her. "I'm Maggie Carson."

"Pleased to meet you, Maggie. I'm Bumper Morgan," I said, always happy to meet a woman, especially a young one, who shakes hands, and with a firm friendly grip.

"I've heard about Cassie's policeman friend, but it surprised me, seeing that uniform so suddenly."

"We've all got our skeletons rattling, Maggie," I said. "Tell me, what've you done that makes you jump at the sight of the fuzz?"

"All right, Bumper," Cassie smiled. I was standing now, and she had me by the arm.

"I'll leave you two alone," said Maggie, with a sly wink, just as she'd seen and heard it in a thousand corny love movies.

"Nice kid," I said, after Maggie closed the door and I kissed Cassie four or five times.

"I missed you last night," said Cassie, standing there pressed up against me, smelling good and looking good in her yellow sleeveless dress. Her arms were red tan, her hair down, touching her shoulders.

"Your dinner date tonight still on?"

"Afraid so," she murmured.

"After tomorrow we'll have all the time we want together."

"Think we'll ever have all the time we want?"

"You'll get sick of seeing me hanging around the pad."

"Never happen. Besides, you'll be busy launching that new career."

"I'm more worried about the other career."

"Which one?"

"Being the kind of husband you think I'll be. I wonder if I'll be really good for you."

"Bumper!" she said, stepping back and looking to see if I meant it, and I tried a lopsided grin.

I kissed her then, as tenderly as I could, and held her. "I didn't mean it the way it came out."

"I know. I'm just a very insecure old dame."

I could've kicked my ass for blurting out something that I knew would hurt her. It was like I wanted to hurt her a little for being the best thing that ever happened, for saving me from becoming a pitiful old man trying to do a young man's work, and doing brass balls police work was definitely a young man's work. I never could've been an inside man. Never a jailer, or a desk officer, or a supply man handing out weapons to guys doing the real police work. Cassie was saving me from that nightmare. I was getting out while I was still a man alive, with lots of good years ahead. And with somebody to care about. I got a vicious gas pain just then, and I wished I wasn't standing there with Cassie so I could pop a bubble breaker.

"I guess *I'm* the silly one," said Cassie.

"If you only knew how bad I want out, Cassie, you'd stop worrying." I patted her back like I was burping her when really I was wishing I could burp myself. I could feel the bubble getting bigger and floating up in my stomach.

"All right, Bumper Morgan," she said. "Now what day are we actually leaving Los Angeles? I mean actually? As man and wife. We've got a million things to do."

"Wait till tomorrow night, me proud beauty," I answered. "Tomorrow night when we have some time to talk and to celebrate. Tomorrow night we make all the plans while having a wonderful dinner somewhere."

"In my apartment."

"Okay."

"With some wonderful champagne."

"I'll supply it."

"Police discount?"

"Naturally. My last one."

"And we celebrate tomorrow being the last day you'll ever have to put on that uniform and risk your neck for a lot of people who don't appreciate it."

"Last day I risk my neck," I nodded. "But I never did risk it for anyone but myself. I had some fun these twenty years, Cassie."

"I know it."

"Even though sometimes it's a rotten job I wouldn't wish on anyone, still, I had good times. And any risks were for Bumper Morgan."

"Yes, love."

"So get your heart-shaped fanny in gear and get your day's work done. I still got almost two days of police work left to do." I stepped away from her and picked up my hat and cigar.

"Coming by this afternoon?"

"Tomorrow."

"Tonight," she said. "I'll get away before midnight. Come to my apartment at midnight."

"Let's get some sleep tonight, baby. Tomorrow's the last day for us both on our jobs. Let's make it a good one."

"I don't like my job as well since you charged into my life, do you know that?"

"Whadda you mean?"

"The academic life. I was one of the students who never left school. I loved waddling around with a gaggle of eggheads, and then *you* had to come along so, so . . . I don't know. And now nothing seems the same."

"Come on down, kid, I like your earthy side better."

"I want you to come tonight," she said, looking me dead in the eye.

"I'd rather be with you tonight than with anyone in the world, you know that, but I really ought to go by Abd's Harem and say good-bye to my friends there. And there're a few other places."

"You mustn't disappoint people," she smiled.

"You should try not to," I said, heating up from the way she looked me in the eye just then.

"It's getting tough to make love to you lately."

"A couple more days."

"See you tomorrow," she sighed. "I think I'll jump you here in my office when I get my hands on you."

"On duty?" I frowned, and put my hat on, tipping it at a jaunty angle because, let's face it, you feel pretty good when a woman like Cassie's quivering to get you in bed.

"Good-bye, Bumper," she smiled sadly.

"Later, kid. See you later."

As soon as I cleared after leaving Cassie I got a radio call.

"One-X-L-Forty-five, One-X-L-Forty-five," said the female communications operator, "see the man at the hotel, four-twenty-five South Main, about a possible d.b."

"One-X-L-Forty-five, roger," I said, thinking this will be my last dead body call.

An old one-legged guy with all the earmarks of a reformed alky was standing in the doorway of the fleabag hotel.

"You called?" I said, after parking the black-and-white in front and taking the stick from the holder on the door and slipping it through the ring on my belt.

"Yeah. I'm Poochie the elevator boy," said the old man. "I think a guy might be dead upstairs."

"What the hell made you think so?" I said sarcastically, as we started up the stairs and I smelled the d.b. from here. The floorboards were torn up and I could see the ground underneath.

The old guy hopped up the stairs pretty quick on his one crutch without ever stopping to rest. There were about twenty steps up to the second floor where the smell could drop you and would, except that most of the tenants were bums and winos whose senses, all of them, had been killed or numbed. I almost expected the second story to have a dirt floor, the place was so crummy.

"I ain't seen this guy in number two-twelve for oh, maybe a week," said Poochie, who had a face like an ax, with a toothless puckered mouth.

"Can't you smell him?"

"No," he said, looking at me with surprise. "Can you?"

"Never mind," I said, turning right in the hallway. "Don't bother telling me where two-twelve is, I could find it with my eyes closed. Get me some coffee."

"Cream and sugar?"

"No, I mean dry coffee, right out of the can. And a frying pan."

"Okay," he said, without asking dumb questions, conditioned by fifty years of being bossed around by cops. I held a handkerchief over my nose, and opened a window in the hallway which led out on the fire escape in the alley. I stuck my head out but it didn't help, I could still smell him.

After a long two minutes Poochie came hopping back on his crutch with a frying pan and the coffee.

"Hope there's a hot plate in here," I said, suddenly thinking there might not be, though lots of the transient hotels had them, especially in the rooms used by the semipermanent boarders.

"He's got one," nodded Poochie, handing me the passkey. The key turned but the door wouldn't budge.

"I coulda told you it wouldn't open. That's why I called you. Scared old man, Herky is. He keeps a bolt on the door whenever he's inside. I already tried to get in."

"Move back."

"Going to break it?"

"Got any other suggestions?" I said, the handkerchief over my face, breathing through my mouth.

"No, I think I can smell him now."

I booted the door right beside the lock and it crashed open, ripping the jamb loose. One rusty hinge tore free and the door dangled there by the bottom hinge.

"Yeah, he's dead," said Poochie, looking at Herky who had been dead for maybe five days, swollen and steamy in this unventilated room which not only had a hot plate, but a small gas heater that was raging on an eighty-five degree day.

"Can I look at him?" said Poochie, standing next to the bed, examining Herky's bloated stomach and rotting face. His eyelids were gone and the eyes stared silver and dull at the elevator boy who grinned toothlessly and clucked at the maggots on Herky's face and swollen sex organs.

I ran across the room and banged on the frame until I got the window open. Flies were crawling all over the glass, leaving wet tracks in the condensation. Then I ran to the hot plate, lit it, and threw the frying pan on the burner. I dumped the whole can of coffee on the frying pan, but the elevator boy was enjoying himself so much he didn't seem to mind my extravagance with his coffee. In a few minutes the coffee was burning, and a pungent smoky odor was filling the room, almost neutralizing the odor of Herky.

"You don't mind if I look at him?" asked Poochie again.

"Knock yourself out, pal," I answered, going for the door.

"Been dead a while hasn't he?"

"Little while longer and he'd have gone clear through the mattress."

I walked to the pay phone at the end of the hall on the second floor. "Come with me, pal," I called, figuring he'd roll old Herky soon as my back was turned. It's bad enough getting rolled when you're alive.

I put a dime in the pay phone and dialed operator.

"Police department," I said, then waited for my dime to return as she rang the station. The dime didn't come. I looked hard at Poochie who turned away, very innocently.

"Someone stuffed the goddamn chute," I said. "Some asshole's gonna get my dime when he pulls the stuffing out later."

"Bunch of thieves around here, Officer," said Poochie, all puckered and a little chalkier than before.

I called the dicks and asked for one to come down and take the death report, then I hung up and lit a cigar, not that I really wanted one, but any smell would do at the moment.

"Is it true they explode like a bomb after a while?"

"What?"

"Stiffs. Like old Herky."

"Yeah, he'd've been all over your wallpaper pretty soon."

"Damn," said the elevator boy, grinning big and showing lots of gums, upper and lower. "Some of these guys like Herky got lots of dough hidden around," he said, winking at me.

"Yeah, well let's let him keep it. He's had it this long."

"Oh, I didn't mean we should take it."

"Course not."

"It's just that these coroner guys, they get to steal anything they find laying around."

"How long's old Herky been living here?" I asked, not bothering to find out his whole name. I'd let the detective worry about the report.

"Off and on, over five years I know of. All alone. Never even had no friends. Nobody. Just laid up there in that room sucking up the sneaky pete. Used to drink a gallon a day. I think he lived off his social security. Pay his rent, eat a little, drink a little. I never could do it myself. That's why I'm elevator boy. Can't make it on that social security."

"You ever talk to him?"

"Yeah, he never had nothing to say though. No family. Never been married. No relatives to speak of. Really alone, you know? I got me eight kids spread all over this damn country. I can go sponge off one of them ever' once in a while. Never gonna see old Poochie like that." He winked and tapped his chest with a bony thumb. "Guys like old Herky, they don't care about nobody and nobody cares about them. They check out of this world grabbing their throat and staring around a lonely hotel room. Those're the guys that swell up and pop all over your walls. Guys like old Herky." The elevator boy thought about old Herky popping, and he broke out in a snuffling croupy laugh because that was just funny as hell.

I hung around the lobby waiting for the detective to arrive and relieve me of caring for the body. While I was waiting I started examining both sides of the staircase walls. It was the old kind with a scalloped molding about seven feet up, and at the first landing there were dirty finger streaks below the molding while the rest of the wall on both sides was uniformly dirty, but unsmudged. I walked to the landing and reached up on the ledge, feeling a toilet-paper-wrapped bundle. I opened it and found a complete outfit: eyedropper, hypodermic needle, a piece of heavy thread, burned spoon, and razor blade.

I broke the eye dropper, bent the needle, and threw the hype kit in the trash can behind the rickety desk in the lobby.

"What's that?" asked the elevator boy.

"A fit."

"A hype's outfit?"

"Yeah."

"How'd you know it was there?"

"Elementary, my dear Poochie."

"That's pretty goddamn good."

The detective came in carrying a clipboard full of death reports. He was one of the newer ones, a young collegiate-looking type. I didn't know him. I talked to

him for a few minutes and the elevator boy took him
back to the body.

"Never catch old Poochie going it alone," he called
to me with his gums showing. "Never gonna catch old
Poochie busting like a balloon and plastered to your
wallpaper."

"Good for you, Poochie," I nodded, taking a big
breath out on the sidewalk, thinking I could still smell
the dead body. I imagined that his odor was clinging
to my clothes and I goosed the black-and-white, ripping off some rubber in my hurry to get away from
that room.

I drove around for a while and started wondering
what I should work on. I thought about the hotel burglar again and wondered if I could find Link Owens, a
good little hotel creeper, who might be able to tell me
something about this guy that'd been hitting us so
hard. All hotel burglars know each other. Sometimes
you see so many of them hanging around the lobbies
of the better hotels, it looks like a thieves' convention.
Then I got the code-two call to go to the station.

**10**

         CODE TWO MEANS hurry up, and whenever policemen get that call to go to the station they start worrying about things. I've had a hundred partners tell me that: "What did I do wrong? Am I in trouble? Did something happen to the old lady? The kids?" I never had such thoughts, of course. A code-two call to go to the station just meant to me that they had some special shit detail they needed a man for, and mine happened to be the car they picked.

When I got to the watch commander's office, Lieutenant Hilliard was sitting at his desk reading the morning editorials, his millions of wrinkles deeper than usual, looking as mean as he always did when he read the cop-baiting letters to the editor and editorial cartoons which snipe at cops. He never stopped reading them though, and scowling all the way.

"Hi, Bumper," he said, glancing up. "One of the vice officers wants you in his office. Something about a bookmaker you turned for them?"

"Oh yeah, one of my snitches gave him some information yesterday. Guess Charlie Bronski needs to talk to me some more."

"Going to take down a bookie, Bumper?" Hilliard grinned. He was a hell of a copper in his day. He wore seven service stripes on his left forearm, each one signifying five years' service. His thin hands were knobby and covered with bulging blue veins. He had trouble with bone deterioration now, and walked with a cane.

"I'm a patrol officer. Can't be doing vice work. No time."

"If you've got something going with Bronski, go ahead and work on it. Vice caper or not, it's all police work. Besides, I've never seen many uniformed policemen tear off a bookmaker. That's about the only kind of pinch you've never made for me, Bumper."

"We'll see what we can do, Lieutenant," I smiled, and left him there, scowling at the editorials again, an old man that should've pulled the pin years ago. Now he'd been here too long. He couldn't leave or he'd die. And he couldn't do the work anymore, so he just sat and talked police work to other guys like him who believed police work meant throwing lots of bad guys in jail and that all your other duties were just incidental. The young officers were afraid to get close to the watch commander's office when he was in there. I've seen rookies call a sergeant out into the hall to have him approve a report so they wouldn't have to take it to Lieutenant Hilliard. He demanded excellence, especially on reports. Nobody's ever asked that of the young cops who were TV babies, not in all their lives. So he was generally avoided by the men he commanded.

Charlie Bronski was in his office with two other vice officers when I entered.

"What's up, Charlie?" I asked.

"We had some unbelievable luck, Bumper. We ran the phone number and it comes back to an apartment on Hobart near Eighth Street, and Red Scalotta hangs around Eighth Street quite a bit when he's not at his restaurant on Wilshire. I'm betting that phone number you squeezed out of Zoot goes right into Reba McClain's pad just like I hoped. She always stays close by Red, but never *too* close. Red's been married happily for thirty years and has a daughter in Stanford and a son in medical school. Salt of the earth, that asshole is."

"Gave nine thousand last year to two separate churches in Beverly Hills," said one of the other vice officers, who looked like a wild young head with his collar-length hair, and beard, and floppy hat with peace and pot buttons all over it. He wore a cruddy denim shirt cut off at the shoulders and looked like a typical Main Street fruit hustler.

"And God returns it a hundredfold," said the other vice officer, Nick Papalous, a melancholy-looking guy, with small white teeth. Nick had a big Zapata moustache, sideburns, and wore orange-flowered flares. I'd worked with Nick several times before he went to vice. He was a good cop for being so young.

"You seemed pretty hot on taking a book, Bumper, so I thought I'd see if you wanted to go with us. This isn't going to be a back office, but it might lead to one, thanks to your friend Zoot. What do you say, want to come?"

"Do I have to change to civvies?"

"Not if you don't want to. Nick and Fuzzy here are going to take the door down. You and me could stiff in the call from the pay phone at the corner. Your uniform wouldn't get in the way."

"Okay, let's go," I said, anxious for a little action, glad I didn't have to take the uniform off. "Never went on a vice raid before. Do we have to circumcise our watches and all that?"

"I'll do the door," Nick grinned. "Fuzzy'll watch out the window and keep an eyeball on you and Bumper down at the pay phone on the corner. When you get the bet stiffed, Fuzzy'll see your signal and give me the okay and down goes the door."

"Kind of touch kicking, ain't it, Nick, in those crepe-soled, sneak-and-peek shoes you guys wear?"

"Damn straight, Bumper," Nick smiled. "I could sure use those size-twelve boondockers of yours."

"Thirteens," I said.

"Wish I could take down the door," said Fuzzy. "Nothing I like better than John Wayne-ing a god-damn door."

"Tell Bumper why you can't, Fuzzy," Nick grinned.

"Got a sprained ankle and a pulled hamstring," said Fuzzy, taking a few limping steps to show me. "I was off duty for two weeks."

"Tell Bumper how it happened," said Nick, still grinning.

"Freakin' fruit," said Fuzzy, pulling off the wide-brimmed hat and throwing back his long blond hair. "We got a vice complaint about this fruit down at the main library, hangs around out back and really comes on strong with every young guy he sees."

"Fat mother," said Charlie. "Almost as heavy as you, Bumper. And strong."

"Damn!" said Fuzzy, shaking his head, looking serious even though Nick was still grinning. "You shoulda seen the arms on that animal! Anyway, I get picked to operate him, naturally.'"

" 'Cause you're so pretty, Fuzzy," said Charlie.

"Yeah, anyway, I go out there, about two in the af-ternoon, and hang around a little bit, and sure enough, there he is standing by that scrub oak tree and I don't know which one's the freakin' tree for a couple min-utes, he's so wide. And I swear I never saw a hornier fruit in my life 'cause I just walked up and said, 'Hi.' That's all, I swear."

"Come on, Fuzzy, you winked at him," said Charlie, winking at me.

"You asshole," said Fuzzy. "I swear I just said, 'Hi, Brucie,' or something like that, and this mother grabbed me. Grabbed me! In a bear hug! He pinned my arms! I was shocked, I tell you! Then he starts bouncing me up and down against his fat belly, say-ing, 'You're so cute. You're so cute. You're so cute.'"

Then Fuzzy stood up and started bouncing up and down with his arms up against his sides and his head bobbing. "Like this I was," said Fuzzy. "Like a goddamn rag doll bouncing, and I said, 'Y-y-y-you're u-u-u-under a-a-a-arrest,' and he stopped loving me and said, 'What?' and I said, 'YOU'RE UNDER ARREST, YOU FAT ZOMBIE!' And he threw me. Threw me! And I rolled down the hill and crashed into the concrete steps. And you know what happens then? My partner here lets him get away. He claims he couldn't catch the asshole and the guy couldn't run no faster than a pregnant alligator. My brave partner!"

"Fuzzy really wants that guy bad," Charlie grinned. "I tried to catch him, honest, Fuzzy." Then to me, "I think Fuzzy fell in love. He wanted the fat boy's phone number."

"Yuk!" said Fuzzy, getting a chill as he thought about it. "We got a warrant for that prick for battery on a police officer. Wait'll I get him. I'll get that prick in a choke hold and lobotomize him!"

"By the way, what's the signal you use for crashing in the pad?" I asked.

"We always give it this," said Charlie, pumping his closed fist up and down.

"Double time," I smiled. "Hey, that takes me back to my old infantry days." I felt good now, getting to do something a little different. Maybe I should've tried working vice, I thought, but no, I've had lots more action and lots more variety on my beat. That's where it's at. That's where it's really at.

"Reba must have some fine, fine pussy," said Fuzzy, puffing on a slim cigar and cocking his head at Charlie. I could tell by the smell it was a ten- or fifteen-center. I'd quit smoking first, I thought.

"She's been with Red a few years now," said Nick to Fuzzy. "Wait'll you meet her. Those mug shots don't do her justice. Good-looking snake."

"You cold-blooded vice cops don't care how good-looking a broad is," I said, needling Charlie. "All a broad is to you is a booking number. I'll bet when some fine-looking whore thinking you're a trick lays down and spreads her legs, you just drop that cold badge right on top of her."

"Right on her bare tummy," said Nick. "But I'll bet Reba has more than a nice tight pussy. A guy like Scalotta could have a million broads. She must give extra good head or something."

"That's what I need, a little skull," said Fuzzy, leaning back in a swivel chair, his soft-soled shoes propped up on a desk. He was a pink-faced kid above the beard, not a day over twenty-four, I'd guess.

"A *little* skull'd be the first you ever had, Fuzzy," said Nick.

"Ha!" said Fuzzy, the cigar clenched in his teeth. "I used to have this Chinese girlfriend that was a go-go dancer. . . ."

"Come on, Fuzzy," said Charlie, "let's not start those lies about all the puss you got when you worked Hollywood. Fuzzy's laid every toadie on Sunset Boulevard three times."

"I can tell you yellow is mellow," Fuzzy leered. "This chick wouldn't ball nobody but me. She used to wet her pants playing with the hair on my chest." Fuzzy stood up then, and flexed his bicep.

Nick, always a man of few words, said, "Siddown, fruitbait."

"Anyway, Reba ain't just a good head job," said Charlie. "That's not why Scalotta keeps her. He's a leather freak and likes to savage a broad. Dresses her up in animal skins and whales the shit out of her."

"I never really believed those rumors," said Nick.

"No shit?" said Fuzzy, really interested now.

"We had a snitch tell us about it one time," said Charlie. "The snitch said Red Scalotta digs dykes and whips and Reba's his favorite. The snitch told us it's the only way Red can get it up anymore."

"He *is* an old guy," said Fuzzy seriously. "At least fifty, I think."

"Reba's a stone psycho, I tell you," said Charlie.

"Remember when we busted her, Nick? How she kept talking all the way to jail about the bull daggers and how they'd chase her around the goddamn jail cell before she could get bailed out."

"That broad got dealt a bum hand," said Nick.

"Ain't got a full deck even now," Charlie agreed.

"She's scared of butches and yet she puts on dyke shows for Red Scalotta?" said Fuzzy, his bearded baby face split by a grin as he pictured it.

"Let's get it over with," said Charlie. "Then we can spend the rest of the day shooting pool in a nice cool beer bar, listening to Fuzzy's stories about all those Hollywood groupies."

Nick and Fuzzy took one vice car and I rode with Charlie in another one. It's always possible there could be more than one in the pad, and they wanted room for prisoners.

"Groovy machine, Charlie," I said, looking over the vice car which was new and air-conditioned. It was gold with mags, a stick, and slicks on the back. The police radio was concealed inside the glove compartment.

"It's not bad," said Charlie, "especially the air conditioning. Ever see air conditioning in a police car, Bumper?"

"Not the ones I drive, Charlie," I said, firing up a cigar, and Charlie tore through the gears to show me the car had some life to it.

"Vice is lots of fun, Bumper, but you know, some of the best times were when I walked with you on your beat."

"How long'd you work with me, Charlie, couple months?"

"About three months. Remember, we got that burglar that night? The guy that read the obituaries?"

"Oh yeah," I said, not remembering that it was Charlie who'd been with me. When they have you breaking in rookies, they all kind of merge in your memory, and you don't remember them very well as individuals.

"Remember? We were shaking this guy just outside the Indian beer bar near Third, and you noticed the obituary column folded up in his shirt pocket? Then you told me about how some burglars read the obituaries and then burgle the pads of the dead people after the funeral when chances are there's nobody going to be there for a while."

"I remember," I said, blowing a cloud of smoke at the windshield, thinking how the widow or widower usually stays with a relative for a while. Rotten M.O., I can't stand grave robbing. Seems like your victim ought to have some kind of chance.

"We got a commendation for that pinch, Bumper."

"We did? I can't remember."

"Of course I got one only because I was with you. That guy burgled ten or fifteen pads like that. Remember? I was so green I couldn't understand why he carried a pair of socks in his back pocket and I asked you if many of these transient types carried a change of socks with them. Then you showed me the stretch marks in the socks from his fingers and explained how they wear them for gloves so's not to leave prints. You never put me down even when I asked something that dumb."

"I always liked guys to ask questions," I said, beginning to wish Charlie'd shut up.

"Hey, Charlie," I said, to change the subject, "if we take a good phone spot today, what're the chances it could lead to something big?"

"You mean like a back office?"

"Yeah."

"Almost no chance at all. How come you're so damned anxious to take a back?"

"I don't know. I'm leaving the job soon and I never really took a big crook like Red Scalotta. I'd just like to nail one."

"Christ, I never took anyone as big as Scalotta either. And what do you mean, you're leaving? Pulling the pin?"

"One of these days."

"I just can't picture you retiring."

"*You're* leaving after twenty years aren't you?"

"Yeah, but not *you.*"

"Let's forget about it," I said, and Charlie looked at me for a minute and then opened the glove compartment and turned to frequency six for two-way communication with the others.

"One-Victor-One to One-Victor-Two," said Charlie.

"One-Victor-Two, go," said Nick.

"One-Victor-One, I think it's best to park behind on the next street east, that's Harvard," said Charlie. "If anybody happens to be looking they wouldn't see you go in through the parking area in the rear."

"Okay, Charlie," said Nick, and in a few minutes we were there. Eighth Street is all commercial buildings with several bars and restaurants, and the residential north-south streets are lined with apartment buildings. We gave them a chance to get to the walkway on the second floor of the apartment house, and Charlie drove about two hundred feet south of Eighth on Harvard. We walked one block to the public telephone on the southwest corner at Hobart. After a couple of minutes, Fuzzy leaned over a wrought iron railing on the second floor and waved.

"Let's get it on, Bumper," said Charlie, dropping in a dime. Charlie hung up after a second. "Busy."

"Zoot give you the code and all that?"

"Twenty-eight for Dandelion is the code," Charlie nodded. "This is a relay phone spot. If it was a relay call-back we might have some problems."

"What's the difference?" I asked, standing behind the phone booth so someone looking out of the apartment wouldn't see the bluesuit.

"A call-back is where the bettor or the handbook like Zoot calls the relay, that's like I'm going to do now. Then every fifteen minutes or so, the back office calls the relay and gets the bettor's number and calls the bettor himself. I think we'd have a poor chance with that kind of setup because back office clerks are sharper than some dummy sitting on the hot seat at a phone spot. Last time we took Reba McClain it was a regular relay spot where the bettor calls her and she writes the bets on a Formica board and then the back office calls every so often and she reads off the bets and wipes the Formica clean. It's better for us that way because we always try to get some physical evidence if we can move quick enough."

"The Formica?"

"Yeah," Charlie nodded. "Some guys kick in the door and throw something at the guy on the hot seat to distract him so he can't wipe the bets off. I've seen cops throw a tennis ball in the guy's face."

"Why not a baseball?"

"That's not a bad idea. You'd make a good vice cop, Bumper."

"Either way the person at the phone spot doesn't know the phone number or address of the back office?" I asked.

"Hell no. That's why I was telling you the chances are nil."

Charlie dropped the dime in again and again hung it up.

"Must be doing a good business," I said.

"Red Scalotta's relay spots always do real good," said Charlie. "I know personally of two Superior Court judges that bet with him."

"Probably some cops too," I said.

"Righteous," he nodded. "Everybody's got vices."

"Whadda you call that gimmick where the phone goes to another pad?"

"A tap out," said Charlie. "Sometimes you bust in an empty room and see nothing but a phone jack and a wire running out a window, and by the time you trace the wire down to the right apartment, the guy in the

relay spot's long gone. Uusually with a tap out, there's
some kind of alarm hooked up so he knows when you
crash in the decoy pad. Then there's a toggle relay,
where a call can be laid off to another phone line. Like
for instance the back office clerk dials the relay spot
where the toggle switch is and he doesn't hang up.
Then the bettor calls the relay and the back can take
the action himself. All these gimmicks have disadvan-
tages though. One of the main ones is that bettors
don't like call-back setups. Most bettors are working
stiffs and maybe on their coffee breaks they only have
a few minutes to get in to their bookie, and they don't
have ten or fifteen minutes to kill waiting for call-
backs and all that crap. The regular relay spot with
some guy or maybe some housewife earning a little
extra bread by sitting on the hot seat is still the most
convenient way for the book to operate."

"You get many broads at these phone spots?"

"We sure do. We get them in fronts and backs. That
is, we get them in the relay phone spots as well as
back offices. We hear Red Scalotta's organization pays
a front clerk a hundred fifty a week and a back clerk
three hundred a week. That's a good wage for a
woman, considering it's tax free. A front clerk might
have to go to jail once in a while but it ain't no big
thing to her. The organization bails them out and pays
all legal fees. Then they go right back to work. Hardly
any judge is going to send someone to county jail for
bookmaking, especially if she's female. And they'll
never send anyone to state prison. I know a guy in the
south end of town with over eighty bookmaking arrests. He's still in business."

"Sounds like a good business."

"It's a joke, Bumper. I don't know why I stay at it, I
mean trying to nail them. We hear Red Scalotta's back
offices gross from one to two million a year. And he
probably has at least three backs going. That's a lot of
bread even though he only nets eleven to sixteen per-

cent of that. And when we take down these agents and convict them, they get a two-hundred-and-fifty-dollar fine. It's a sick joke."

"You ever get Red Scalotta himself?"

"Never. Red'll stay away from the back offices. He's got someone who takes care of everything. Once in a while we can take a front and on rare occasions a back and that's about all we can hope for. Well, let's try to duke our bet in again."

Charlie dropped in his dime and dailed the number. Then he looked excited and I knew someone answered.

"Hello," said Charlie, "this is twenty-eight for Dandelion. Give me number four in the second, five across. Give me a two-dollar, four-horse round robin in the second. The number two horse to the number four in the third to the number six in the fourth to number seven in the fifth."

Then Charlie stiffed in a few more bets for races at the local track, Hollywood Park, which is understood, unless you specify an Eastern track. Midway through the conversation, Charlie leaned out the phone booth and pumped his fist at Fuzzy, who disappeared inside the apartment building. Charlie motioned to me and I took off my hat and squeezed into the hot phone booth with him. He grinned and held the phone away from his ear, near mine.

I heard the crash over the phone, and the terrified woman scream and a second later Nick's voice came over the line and said, "Hello, sweetheart, would you care for a round robin or a three-horse parley today?"

Charlie chuckled and hung up the phone and we hopped back in the vice car and drove to the apartment house, parking in front.

When we got to the second floor, Fuzzy was smooth talking an irate landlady who was complaining about the fractured door which Nick was propping shut for privacy. A good-looking, dark-haired girl was sitting on the couch inside the apartment crying her eyes out.

"Hi, Reba," Charlie grinned as we walked in and looked around.

"Hello, Mister Bronski," she wailed, drenching the second of two handkerchiefs she held in her hands.

"The judge warned you last time, Reba," said Charlie. "This'll make your third bookmaking case. He told you you'd get those six months he suspended. You might even get a consecutive sentence on top of it."

"Please, Mister Bronski," she wailed, throwing herself face down on the couch and sobbing so hard the whole couch shook.

She was wearing a very smart jersey blouse and skirt, and a matching blue scarf was tied around her black hair. Her fair legs had a very light spattering of freckles on them. She was a fine-looking girl, very Irish.

Charlie took me in the frilly sweet-smelling bedroom where the phone was. Reba had smeared half the bets off a twelve-by-eighteen chalkboard, but the other bets were untouched. A wet cloth was on the floor where the board was dropped along with the phone.

"I'll bet she wet her pants again this time," said Charlie, still grinning as he examined the numbers and x's on the chalkboard which told the track, race, handicap position, and how much to win, place or show. The bettor's identification was written beside the bets. I noticed that K.L. placed one hell of a lot of bets, probably just before Charlie called.

"We're going to squeeze the shit out of her," Charlie whispered. "You think Zoot was shaky, wait'll you hear this broad. A real ding-a-ling."

"Go ahead," Nick was saying to someone on the phone when we came back in the living room. Fuzzy was nodding politely to the landlady and locking her out by closing the broken door and putting a chair in front of it.

"Right. Got it," said Nick, hanging up. A minute later the phone rang again.

"Hello," said Nick. "Right. Go ahead." Every few seconds he mumbled, "Yeah," as he wrote down bets. "Got it." He hung up.

"Nick's taking some bets mainly to fuck up Scalotta," Charlie explained to me. "Some of these guys might hit, or they might hear Reba got knocked over, and then they'll claim they placed their bet and there'll be no way to prove they didn't, so the book'll have to pay off or lose the customers. That's where we get most of our tips, from disgruntled bettors. It isn't too often a handbook like Zoot Lafferty comes dancing in, anxious to turn his bread and butter."

"Mister Bronski, can I talk to you?" Reba sobbed, as Nick and then Fuzzy answered the phone and took the bets.

"Let's go in the other room," said Charlie, and we followed Reba back into the bedroom where she sat down on the soft, king-sized bed and wiped away the wet mascara.

"I got no time for bullshit, Reba," said Charlie. "You're in no position to make deals. We got you by the curlies."

"I know, Mister Bronski," she said, taking deep breaths. "I ain't gonna bullshit you. I wanna work with you. I swear I'll do anything. But please don't let me get this third case. That Judge Bowers is a bastard. He told me if I violated my probation, he'd put me in. Please, Mister Bronski, you don't know what it's like there. I couldn't do six months. I couldn't even do six days. I'd kill myself."

"You want to work for me? What could you do?"

"Anything. I know a phone number. Two numbers. You could take two other places just like this one. I'll give you the numbers."

"How do you know them?"

"I ain't dumb, Mister Bronski. I listen and I learn

things. When they're drunk or high they talk to me, just like all men."

"You mean Red Scalotta and his friends?"

"Please, Mister Bronski, I'll give you the numbers, but you can't take me to jail."

"That's not good enough, Reba," said Charlie, sitting down in a violet-colored satin chair next to a messy dressing table. He lit a cigarette as Reba glanced from Charlie to me, her forehead wrinkled, chewing her lip. "That's not near good enough," said Charlie.

"Whadda you want, Mister Bronski? I'll do anything you say."

"I want the back," said Charlie easily.

"What?"

"I want one of Red's back offices. That's all. Keep your phone spots. If we take too much right away it'll burn you and I want you to keep working for Red. But I want his back office. I think you can help me."

"Oh God, Mister Bronski. Oh Mother of God, I don't know about things like that, I swear. How would I know? I'm just answering phones here. How would I know?"

"You're Red's girlfriend."

"Red has other girlfriends!"

"You're his *special* girlfriend. And you're smart. You listen."

"I don't know things like that, Mister Bronski. I swear to God and His Mother. I'd tell you if I knew."

"Have a cigarette," said Charlie, and pushed one into Reba's trembling hand. I lit it for her and she glanced up like a trapped little rabbit, choked on the smoke, then took a deep breath, and inhaled down the right pipe. Charlie let her smoke for a few seconds. He had her ready to break, which is what you want, and you shouldn't wait, but she was obviously a ding-a-ling and you had to improvise when your subject is batty. He was letting her unwind, letting her get back a little confidence. Just for a minute.

"You wouldn't protect Red Scalotta if it meant your ass going to jail, would you, Reba?"

"Hell no, Mister Bronski, I wouldn't protect my mother if it meant that."

"Remember when I busted you before? Remember how we talked about those big hairy bull dykes you meet in jail? Remember how scared you were? Did any of them bother you?"

"Yes."

"Did you sleep in jail?"

"No, they bailed me out."

"What about after you get your six months, Reba? Then you have to sleep in jail. Did you see any dildoes in jail?"

"What's that?"

"Phony dicks."

"I hate those things," she shuddered.

"How would you like to wake up in the middle of the night with two big bull dykes working on you? And what's more, how would you feel if you really started *liking* it? It happens all the time to girls in jail. Pretty soon you're a stone butch, and then you might as well cut off that pretty hair, and strap down those big tits, because you're not a woman anymore. Then you can lay up in those butch pads with a bunch of bull daggers and a pack of smelly house cats and drop pills and shoot junk because you can't stand yourself."

"Why're you doing this to me, Mister Bronski?" said Reba, starting to sob again. She dropped the cigarette on the carpet and I picked it up and snuffed it. "Why do men like to hurt? You all hurt!"

"Does Red hurt you?" asked Charlie calmly, sweating a little as he lit another cigarette with the butt of the last one.

"Yes! He hurts!" she yelled, and Fuzzy stuck his head in the door to see what the shouting was about, but Charlie motioned him away while Reba sobbed.

"Does he make you do terrible things?" asked Charlie, and she was too hysterical to see he was talking to her like she was ten years old.

"Yes, the bastard! The freaky bastard. He hurts me! He likes to hurt! That fucking old freak!"

"I'll bet he makes you do things with bull daggers," said Charlie, glancing at me, and I realized I broke him in right. He wasn't a guy to only stick it in halfway.

"He *makes* me do it, Mister Bronski," said Reba. "I don't enjoy it, I swear I don't. I hate to do it with a woman. I wasn't raised like that. It's a terrible sin to do those things."

"I'll bet you don't like taking action for him either. You hate sitting on this hot seat answering the phones, don't you?"

"I *do* hate it, Mister Bronski. I *do* hate it. He's so goddamn cheap. He just won't give me money for anything. He makes me always work for it. I have to do those things with them two or three nights a week. And I have to sit here in this goddamn room and answer those goddamn phones and every minute I know some cop might be ready to break down the door and take me to jail. Oh, please help me, Mister Bronski."

"Stop protecting him then," said Charlie.

"He'll kill me, Mister Bronski," said Reba, and her pretty violet eyes were wide and round and her nostrils were flared, and you could smell the fear on her.

"He won't kill you, Reba," said Charlie soothingly. "You won't get a jacket. He'll never know you told me. We'll make it look like someone else told."

"No one else *knows*," she whispered, and her face was dead white.

"We'll work it out, Reba. Stop worrying, we know how to protect people that help us. We'll make it look like someone else set it up. I promise you, he'll never know you told."

"Tell me you swear to God you'll protect me."

"I swear to God I'll protect you."

"Tell me you swear to God I won't go to jail."

"We've got to book you, Reba. But you know Red'll bail you out in an hour. When your case comes up I'll personally go to Judge Bowers and you won't go to jail behind that probation violation."

"Are you a hundred percent sure?"

"I'm almost a hundred percent sure, Reba. Look, I'll talk for you myself. Judges are always ready to give people another chance, you know that."

"But that Judge Bowers is a bastard!"

"I'm a hundred percent sure, Reba. We can fix it."

"You got another cigarette?"

"Let's talk first. I can't waste any more time."

"If he finds out, I'm dead. My blood'll be on you."

"Where's the back?"

"I only know because I heard Red one night. It was after he'd had his dirty fun with me and a girl named Josie that he brought with him. She was as sick and filthy as Red. And he brought another guy with him, a Jew named Aaron something."

"Bald-headed guy, small, glasses and a gray moustache?"

"Yeah, that's him," said Reba.

"I know of him," said Charlie, and now he was squirming around on the velvet chair, because he had the scent, and I was starting to get it too, even though I didn't know who in the hell Aaron was.

"Anyway, this guy Aaron just watched Josie and me for a while and when Red got in bed with us, he told Aaron to go out in the living room and have a drink. Red was high as a kite that night, but at least he wasn't mean. He didn't hurt me. Can I please have that cigarette, Mister Bronski?"

"Here," said Charlie, and his hand wasn't quite as steady, which is okay, because that showed that good information could still excite him.

"Tastes good," said Reba, dragging hard on the cigarette. "Afterwards, Red called a cab for Josie and sent her home, and him and Aaron started talking and I stayed in the bedroom. I was supposed to be asleep, but like I say, I'm not dumb, Mister Bronski, and I always listen and try to learn things.

"Aaron kept talking about the 'laundry,' and at first I didn't get it even though I knew that Red was getting ready to move out of his back offices. And even though I never saw it, or any other back office, I knew about them from talking to bookie agents and people in the business. Aaron was worrying about the door to the laundry and I figured there was something about the office door being too close to the laundry door, and Aaron tried to argue Red into putting another door in the back near an alley, but Red thought it would be too suspicious.

"That was all I heard, and then one day, when Red was taking me to his club for dinner, he said he had to stop by to pick up some cleaning and he parks by this place near Sixth and Kenmore, and he goes in a side door and comes out after a few minutes and says his suits weren't ready. Then I noticed the sign on the window. It was a Chinese laundry." Reba took two huge drags, blowing one through her nose as she drew on the second one.

"You're a smart girl, Reba," said Charlie.

"I ain't guaranteeing this is the right laundry, Mister Bronski. In fact, I ain't even sure the laundry they were talking about had anything to do with the back office. I just *think* it did."

"I think you're right," said Charlie.

"You got to protect me, Mister Bronski. I got to live with him, and if he knows, I'll die. I'll die in a bad way, a *real* bad way, Mister Bronski. He told me once what he did to a girl that finked on him. It was thirty years ago, and he talked about it like it was yesterday, how she screamed and screamed. It was so awful it made me cry. You got to protect me!"

"I will, Reba. I promise. Do you know the address of the laundry?"

"I know," she nodded. "There were some offices or something on the second floor, maybe like some business offices, and there was a third floor but nothing on the windows in the third floor."

"Good girl, Reba," Charlie said, taking out his pad and pencil for the first time, now that he didn't have to worry about his writing breaking the flow of the interrogation.

"Charlie, give me your keys," I said. "I better get back on patrol."

"Okay, Bumper, glad you could come." Charlie flipped me the keys. "Leave them under the visor. You know where we park?"

"Yeah, I'll see you later."

"I'll let you know what happens, Bumper."

"See you, Charlie. So long, kid," I said to Reba.

"Bye," she said, wiggling her fingers at me like a little girl.

## 11

It was okay driving back to the Glass House in the vice car because of the air conditioning. Some of the new black-and-whites had it, but I hadn't seen any yet. I turned on the radio and switched to a quiet music station and lit a cigar. I saw the temperature on the sign at a bank and it said eighty-two degrees. It felt hotter than that. It seemed awfully muggy.

After I crossed the Harbor Freeway I passed a large real estate office and smiled as I remembered how I cleaned them out of business machines one time. I had a snitch tell me that someone in the office bought several office machines from some burglar, but the snitch didn't know who bought them or even who the burglar was. I strolled in the office one day during their lunch hour when almost everyone was out and told them I was making security checks for a burglary prevention program the police department was sponsoring. A cute little office girl with a snappy fanny took me all around the place and I checked their doors and windows and she helped me write down the serial numbers of every machine in the place so that the police department would have a record if they were ever stolen. Then as soon as I got back to the station, I phoned Sacramento and gave them the numbers and found that thirteen of the nineteen machines had been stolen in various burglaries around the greater Los Angeles area. I went back with the burglary dicks and impounded them along with the office manager. IBM electric typewriters are just about the hottest thing going right now. Most of the machines are sold by the thieves to "legitimate" businessmen who, like everyone else, can't pass up a good buy.

It was getting close to lunch time and I parked the vice car at the police building and picked up my black-and-white, trying to decide where to have lunch. Olvera Street was out, because I'd had Mexican food with Cruz and Socorro last night. I thought about Chinatown, but I'd been there Tuesday, and I was just about ready to go to a good hamburger joint I know of when I thought about Odell Bacon. I hadn't had any bar-b-que for a while, so I headed south on Central Avenue to the Newton Street area and the more I thought about some bar-b-que the better it sounded and I started salivating.

I saw a Negro woman get off a bus and walk down a residential block from Central Avenue and I turned on that street for no reason, to get over to Avalon. Then I saw a black guy on the porch of a whitewashed frame house. He was watching the woman and almost got up from where he was sitting until he saw the black-and-white. Then he pretended to be looking at the sky and sat back, a little too cool, and I passed by and made a casual turn at the next block and then stomped down hard and gave her hell until I got to the first street north. Then I turned east again, south on Central, and finally made the whole block, deciding to come up the same street again. It was an old scam around here for purse snatchers to find a house where no one was home and sit on the stoop of the house near a bus stop, like they lived at the pad, and when a broad walked by, to run out, grab the purse, and then cut through the yard to the next street where a car would be stashed. Most black women around here don't carry

purses. They carry their money in their bras out of
necessity, so you don't see that scam used too much
anymore, but I would've bet this guy was using it now.
And this woman had a big brown leather purse. You
just don't get suspicious of a guy when he approaches
you from the porch of a house in your own neighborhood.

I saw the woman in mid-block and I saw the guy
walking behind her pretty fast, I got overanxious and
pushed a little too hard on the accelerator, instead of
gliding along the curb, and the guy turned around,
saw me, and cut to his right through some houses. I
knew there'd be no sense going after him. He hadn't
done anything yet, and besides, he'd lay up in some
backyard like these guys always do and I'd never find
him. I just went on to Odell Bacon's Bar-b-que, and
when I passed the woman I glanced over and smiled,
and she smiled back at me, a pleasant-looking old ewe.
There were white sheep and black sheep and there
were wild dogs and a few Pretty Good Shepherds.
There'd be one sheep herder less after tomorrow, I
thought.

I could smell the smoky meat a hundred yards
away. They cooked it in three huge old-fashioned
brick ovens. Odell and his brother Nate were both behind the counter when I walked in. They wore sparkling white cook's uniforms and hats and aprons even
though they served the counter and watched the register and didn't have to do the cooking anymore. The
place hadn't started to fill up for lunch yet. Only a few
white people ate there, because they're afraid to come
down here into what is considered the ghetto, and
right now there were only a couple customers in the
place and I was the only paddy. Everyone in South
L.A. knew about Bacon's Bar-b-que though. It was the
best soul food and bar-b-que restaurant in town.

"Hey, Bumper," said Nate, spotting me first. "What's
happenin', man?" He was the youngest, about forty,

coffee brown. He had well-muscled arms from working construction for years before he came in as Odell's
partner.

"Nothin' to it, Nate," I grinned. "Hi, Odell."

"Aw right, Bumper," said Odell, and smiled big. He
was a round-faced fat man. "I'm aw right. Where you
been? Ain't seen you lately."

"Slowing down," I said. "Don't get around much
these days."

"That'll be the day," Nate laughed. "When ol'
Bumper can't git it on, it ain't worth gittin'."

"Some gumbo today, Bumper?" asked Odell.

"No, think I'll have me some ribs," I said, thinking
the gumbo did sound good, but the generous way
these guys made it, stuffed full of chicken and crab, it
might spoil me for the bar-b-que and my system was
braced for the tangy down-home sauce that was their
specialty, the like of which I'd never had anywhere
else.

"Guess who I saw yestiday, Bumper?" said Odell, as
he boxed up some chicken and a hot plate of beef,
French fries, and okra for a take-out customer.

"Who's that?"

"That ponk you tossed in jail that time, 'member?
That guy that went upside ol' Nate's head over a argument about paying his bill, and you was just comin'
through the door and you rattled his bones but good.
'Member?"

"Oh yeah, I remember. Sneed was his name.
Smelled like dogshit."

"That's the one," Nate nodded. "Didn't want him as
a customer no how. Dirty clothes, dirty body, dirty
mouf."

"Lucky you didn't get gangrene when that prick hit
you, Nate," I said.

"Ponk-ass bastard," said Nate, remembering the
punch that put him out for almost five minutes. "He
come in the other day. I recognized him right off, and

I tol' him to git his ass out or I'd call Bumper. He musta 'membered the name, 'cause he got his ass out wif oney a few cuss words."

"He remembered me, huh?" I grinned as Odell set down a cold glass of water, and poured me a cup of coffee without asking. They knew of course that I didn't work Newton Street Station and they only bounced for the Newton Street patrol car in the area, but after that Sneed fight, they always fed *me* free too, and in fact, always tried to get me to come more often. But I didn't like to take advantage. Before that, I used to come and pay half price like any uniformed cop could do.

"Here come the noonday rush," said Nate, and I heard car doors slam and a dozen black people talking and laughing came in and took the large booths in the front. I figured them for teachers. There was a high school and two grade schools close by and the place was pretty full by the time Nate put my plate in front of me. Only it wasn't a plate, it was a platter. It was always the same. I'd ask for ribs, and I'd get ribs, a double portion, and a heap of beef, oozing with bar-b-que sauce, and some delicious fresh bread that was made next door, and an ice-cream scoop of whipped butter. I'd sop the bread in the bar-b-que and either Nate or Odell would ladle fresh hot bar-b-que on the platter all during the meal. With it I had a huge cold mound of delicious slaw, and only a few fries because there wasn't much room for anything else. There just was no fat on Odell's beef. He was too proud to permit it, because he was almost sixty years old and hadn't learned the ways of cutting corners and chiseling.

After I got over the first joy of remembering exactly how delicious the beef was, one of the waitresses started helping at the counter because Odell and Nate were swamped. She was a buxom girl, maybe thirty-five, a little bronzer than Nate, with a modest natural hairdo, which I like, not a way-out phony Afro. Her waist was very small for her size and the boobs soared out over a flat stomach. She knew I was admiring her and didn't seem to mind, and as always, a good-looking woman close by made the meal perfect.

"Her name's Trudy," said Odell, winking at me, when the waitress went to the far end of the counter. His wink and grin meant she was fair game and not married or anything. I used to date another of his waitresses once in a while, a plump, dusky girl named Wilma who was a thirty-two-year-old grandmother. She finally left Odell's and got married for the fourth time. I really enjoyed being with her. I taught her the swim and the jerk and the boogaloo when they first came out. I learned them from my Madeleine Carroll girlfriend.

"Thanks, Odell," I said. "Maybe next time I come in I'll take a table in her section."

"Anythin' funny happen lately, Bumper?" asked Nate after he passed some orders through to the kitchen.

"Not lately. . . . Let's see, did I ever tell you about the big dude I stopped for busting a stop sign out front of your place?"

"Naw, tell us," said Odell, stopping with a plate in his hand.

"Well, like I say, this guy blew the stop sign and I chased him and brought him down at Forty-first. He's a giant, six-feet-seven maybe, heavier than me. All muscle. I ran a make on him over the radio while I'm writing a ticket. Turns out there's a traffic warrant for his arrest."

"Damn," said Nate, all ears now. "You had to fight him?"

"When I tell him there's this warrant he says, 'Too bad, man. I just ain't going to jail.' Just that cool he said it. Then he steps back like he's ready."

"Goddamn," said Odell.

"So then it just comes to me, this idea. I walk over to the police car and pick up the radio and say in a loud voice, 'One-X-L-Forty-five requesting an ambulance at Forty-first and Avalon.' The big dude, he looks around and says, 'What's the ambulance for?' I say, 'That's for you, asshole, if you don't get in that car.'

"So he gets in the car and halfway to jail he starts chuckling, then pretty soon he really busts up. 'Man,' he says, 'you really flimflammed my ass. This is the first time I ever laughed my way to jail.'"

"Gud-damn, Bumper," said Odell. "You're somethin' else. Gud-damn." Then they both went off laughing to wait on customers.

I finished the rest of the meat, picked the bones, and sopped up the last of the bread, but I wasn't happy now. In fact, it was depressing there with a crowd of people and the waitresses rushing around and dishes clattering, so I said good-bye to Nate and Odell. Naturally, I couldn't tip them even though they personally served me, so I gave two bucks to Nate and said, "Give it to Trudy. Tell her it's an advance tip for the good service she's gonna give me next time when I take a table in her section."

"I'll tell her, Bumper," Nate grinned as I waved and burped and walked out the door.

As I was trying to read the temperature again over a savings and loan office, the time flashed on the marquee. It was one-thirty, which is the time afternoon court always convenes. It dawned on me that I'd forgotten I had to be at a preliminary hearing this afternoon!

I cursed and stomped on it, heading for the new municipal court annex on Sunset, near the Old Mission Plaza, and then I slowed down and thought, what the hell, this is the last time I'll ever go to court on duty. I may get called back to testify after I'm retired, but this'll be the last time *on duty* as a working cop, and I'd never been late to court in twenty years. So what the hell, I slowed down and cruised leisurely to the court building.

I passed one of the Indian bars on Main Street, and saw two drunken braves about to duke it out as they headed for the alley in back, pushing and yelling at each other. I knew lots of Payutes and Apaches and others from a dozen Southwest tribes, because so many of them ended up downtown here on my beat. But it was depressing being with them. They were so defeated, those that ended up on Main Street, and I was glad to see them in a fistfight once in a while. At least that proved they could strike back a little bit, at something, even if it was at another drunken tribal brother. Once they hit my beat they were usually finished, or maybe long before they arrived here. They'd become winos, and many of the women, fat five-dollar whores. You wanted to pick them up, shake them out, send them somewhere, in some direction, but there didn't seem to be anywhere an Indian wanted to go. They were hopeless, forlorn people. One old beat cop told me they could break your heart if you let them.

I saw a Gypsy family walking to a rusty old Pontiac in a parking lot near Third and Main. The mother was a stooped-over hag, filthy, with dangling earrings, a peasant blouse, and a full red skirt hanging lopsided below her knees. The man walked in front of her. He was four inches shorter and skinny, about my age. A very dark unshaven face turned my way, and I recognized him. He used to hang around downtown and work with a Gypsy dame on pigeon drops and once in a while a Jamaican switch. The broad was probably his old lady, but I couldn't remember the face just now. There were three kids following: a dirty, beautiful teenage girl dressed like her mother, a ragtag little boy of ten or so, and a curly-haired little doll of four who was dressed like mama also.

I wondered what kind of scam they were working on now, and I tried to think of his name and couldn't, and I wondered if he'd remember me. As late as I was for court, I pulled to the curb.

"Hey, just a minute," I called.

"What, what, what?" said the man. "Officer, what's the problem? What's the problem? Gypsy boy. I'm just a Gypsy boy. You know me don't you, Officer? I talked with you before, ain't I? We was just shopping, Officer. Me and my babies and my babies' mother."

"Where're your packages?" I asked, and he squinted from the bright sunshine and peered into the car from the passenger side. His family all stood like a row of quail, and watched me.

"We didn't see nothing we liked, Officer. We ain't got much money. Got to shop careful." He talked with his hands, hips, all his muscles, especially those dozen or so that moved the mobile face, in expressions of hope and despair and honesty. Oh, what honesty.

"What's your name?"

"Marcos. Ben Marcos."

"Related to George Adams?"

"Sure. He was my cousin, God rest him."

I laughed out loud then, because every Gypsy I'd ever talked to in twenty years claimed he was cousin to the late Gypsy king.

"I know you don't I, Officer?" he asked, smiling then, because I had laughed, and I didn't want to leave because I enjoyed hearing the peculiar lilt to the Gypsy speech, and I enjoyed looking at his unwashed children who were exceptionally beautiful, and I wondered for the hundredth time whether a Gypsy could ever be honest after centuries of living under a code which praised deceit and trickery and theft from all but other Gypsies. Then I was sad because I'd always wanted to really know the Gypsies. That would be the hardest friendship I would ever make, but I had it on my list of things to accomplish before I die. I knew a clan leader named Frank Serna, and once I went to his home in Lincoln Heights and ate dinner with a houseful of his relatives, but of course they didn't talk about things they usually talked about, and I could tell by all the nervous jokes that having an outsider and especially a cop in the house was a very strange thing for the clan. Still, Frank asked me back, and when I had time I was going to work on breaking into the inner circle and making them trust me a little because there were

Gypsy secrets I wanted to know. But I could never hope to do it without being a cop, because they'd only let me know them if they first thought I could do them some good, because all Gypsies lived in constant running warfare with cops. It was too late now, because I would *not* be a cop, and I would *never* get to learn the Gypsy secrets.

"We can go now, Officer?" said the Gypsy, holding his hands clasped together, in a prayerful gesture. "It's very hot for my babies' mama here in the sun."

I looked at the Gypsy woman then, looked at her face and she was *not* a hag, and not as old as I first thought. She stood much taller now and glared at me because her man was licking my boots and I saw that she had once been as pretty as her daughter, and I thought of how I had so often been accused of seeing good things in all women, even ones who were ugly to my partners, and I guessed it was true, that I exaggerated the beauty of all women I knew or ever saw. I wondered about that, and I was wallowing in depression now.

"Please, sir. Can we go now?" he said, the sweat running down the creases in his face, and on his unwashed neck.

"Go your way, Gypsy," I said, and dug out from the curb, and in a few minutes I was parked and walking in the court building.

THE BLUE KNIGHT

## 12

"BEEN WAITING FOR YOU, Bumper," said the robbery detective, a wrinkled old-timer named Miles. He had been a robbery detective even before I came on the job and was one of the last to still wear a wide-brimmed felt hat. They used to be called the "hat squad," and the wide felt hat was their trademark, but of course in recent years no one in Los Angeles wore hats like that. Miles was a stubborn old bastard though, he still wore his, and a wide-shouldered, too-big suit coat with two six-inch guns, one on each hip, because he was an old robbery detective and the hat squad legend demanded it and other policemen expected it.

"Sorry I'm late, Miles," I said.

"That's okay, the case just got sent out to Division Forty-two. Can you handle this by yourself? I got another prelim in Forty-three and a couple of rookie arresting officers for witnesses. If I ain't in there to tell this young D.A. how to put on his case, we might lose it."

"Sure, I'll handle it. Am I the only witness?"

"You and the hotel manager."

"Got the evidence?"

"Yeah, here it is." Miles pulled a large manila envelope out of his cheap plastic briefcase and I recog-

nized the evidence tag I had stuck on there months
ago when I made the arrest.

"The gun's in there and two clips."

"Too bad you couldn't file a robbery."

"Yeah, well like I explained to you right after that
caper, we were lucky to get what we did."

"You filed an eleven-five-thirty too, didn't you?"

"Oh yeah. Here's the pot, I almost forgot." Miles
reached back in the briefcase and pulled out an ana-
lyzed-evidence envelope with my seal on it that contained the marijuana with the chemist's written analysis on the package.

"How many jobs you figure this guy for?"

"I think I told you four, didn't I?"

"Yeah."

"Now we think he done six. Two in Rampart and
four here in Central."

"It's a shame you couldn't make him on at least one
robbery."

"You're telling me. I had him in a regular show-up
and I had a few private mug-shot show-ups, and I
talked and coaxed and damn near threatened my victims and witnesses and the closest I could ever come
was one old broad that said he *looked* like the bandit."

"Scumbag really did a good job with the makeup,
huh?"

"Did a hell of a job," Miles nodded. "Remember, he
was an actor for a while and he did a hell of a good
job with paint and putty. But shit, the M.O. was identical, the way he took mom and dad markets. Always
asked for a case of some kind of beer they were short
of and when they went in the back for the beer, boom,
he pulled the forty-five automatic and took the place
down."

"He ever get violent?"

"Not in the jobs in Central. I found out later he pis-
tol-whipped a guy in one of the Rampart jobs. Some
seventy-year-old grocery clerk decided he was Wyatt
Earp and tried to go for some fucked-up old thirty-

two he had stashed under the counter. Landry really laid him open. Three times across the eyes with the forty-five. He blinded him. Old guy's still in the hospital."

"His P.O. going to violate him?"

"This asshole has a rabbit's foot. He finished his parole two weeks before you busted him. Ain't that something else? Two weeks!"

"Well, I better get in there," I said. "Some of these deputy D.A.'s get panicky when you're not holding their hands. You get a special D.A. for this one?"

"No. It's a dead bang case. You got him cold. Shouldn't be any search and seizure problems at all. And even though we know this guy's a good robber, we ain't got nothing on him today but some low-grade felonies, ex-con with a gun and possession of pot."

"Can't we send him back to the joint with his record?"

"We're going to try. I'll stop in the courtroom soon as I can. If you finish before me, let me know if you held him to answer."

"You got doubts I'll hold him?" I grinned, and headed for the courtroom, feeling very strange as I had all day. The last time I wore a bluesuit into a courtroom, I thought.

This courtroom was almost empty. There were only three people in the audience, two older women, probably the kind that come downtown and watch criminal trials for fun, and a youngish guy in a business suit who was obviously a witness and looked disgusted as hell about being here. Since these courtrooms are for preliminary hearings only, there was no jury box, just the judge's bench and witness box, the counsel tables, the clerk's desk, and a small desk near the railing for the bailiff.

At least I'll be through hassling with this legal machinery, I thought, which cops tend to think is designed by a bunch of neurotics because it seems to go a hundred miles past the point where any sane man would've stopped. After a felony complaint is filed, the defendant is arraigned and then has a preliminary hearing which amounts to a trial. This takes the place of a grand jury indictment and it's held to see if there's good enough cause to bind him over to superior court for trial, and then he's arraigned again in superior court, and later has a trial. Except that in between there're a couple of hearings to set aside what you've done already. In capital cases there's a separate trial for guilt and another for penalty, so that's why celebrated California cases drag on for years until they cost so much that everybody gives up or lets the guy cop to a lesser included offense.

We have a very diligent bunch of young public defenders around here who, being on a monthly salary and not having to run from one good paying client to another, will drive you up a wall defending a chickenshit burglary like it was the Sacco-Vanzetti trial. The D.A.'s office has millions of very fine crimes to choose from and won't issue a felony complaint unless they're pretty damned sure they can get a conviction. But then, there aren't that many real felony convictions, because courts and prisons are so overcrowded. A misdemeanor plea is accepted lots of times even from guys with heavyweight priors.

All this would make Los Angeles a frustrating place to be a cop if it weren't for the fact that the West in general is not controlled by the political clubhouse, owing to the fact that our towns are so sprawling and young. This means that in my twenty years I could bust *any* deserving son of a bitch, and I never got bumrapped except once when I booked an obnoxious French diplomat for drunk driving after he badmouthed me. I later denied to my bosses that he told me of his diplomatic immunity.

But in spite of all the bitching by policemen there's one thing you can't deny: it's still the best system going, and even if it's rough on a cop, who the hell would want to walk a beat in Moscow or Madrid, or anywhere in between? We gripe for sympathy but most of us know that a cop's never going to be loved by people in general, and I say if you got to have lots of love, join the fire department.

I started listening a little bit to the preliminary hearing that was going on. The defendant was a tall, nice-looking guy named John Trafford, about twenty-seven years old, and his pretty woman, probably his wife, was in the courtroom. He kept turning and making courageous gestures in her direction which wasn't particularly impressing Judge Martha Redford, a tough, severe-looking old girl who I had always found to be a fair judge, both to the people and the defense. There was a fag testifying that this clean-cut-looking young chap had picked him up in a gay bar and gone to the fag's pad, where after an undescribed sex act the young defendant, who the fag called Tommy, had damn near cut his head off with a kitchen knife. And then he ransacked the fruit's pad and stole three hundred blood-soaked dollars which were found in his pocket by two uniformed coppers who shagged him downtown to Fifth and Main where he later illegally parked his car.

The defense counsel was badgering the fruit, an effeminate little man about forty years old, who owned a photography studio, and the fruit wasn't without sympathy for the defendant as he glanced nervously at his friend "Tommy," and I thought this was darkly humorous and typical. Weak people need people so much they'd forgive anything. I didn't think the defense counsel was succeeding too well in trying to minimize the thing as just another fruitroll, since the hospital record showed massive transfusions and a hundred or so sutures needed to close up the neck wounds of the fruit.

The young defendant turned around again and shot a long sad glance at pretty little mama who looked brave, and after Judge Redford held him to answer on the charges of attempted murder and robbery, his lawyer tried to con her into a bail reduction because the guy had never been busted before except once for wife beating.

Judge Redford looked at the defendant then, staring at his handsome face and calm eyes, and I could tell she wasn't listening to the deputy D.A. who was opposing the bail reduction and recounting the savagery of the cutting. She was just looking at the young dude and he was looking at her. His blond hair was neatly trimmed and he wore a subdued pin-striped suit.

Then she denied the motion for bail reduction, leaving the huge bail on this guy and I was sure she saw what I saw in his face. He was one to be reckoned with. You could see the confidence and intelligence in his icy expression. And power. There's real power you can feel when it's in a guy like this and it even gave me a chill. You can call him a psychopath or say that he's evil, but whatever he is, he's the deadly Enemy, and I wondered how many other times his acts ended in blood. Maybe it was him that ripped the black whore they dug out of a garbage pile on Seventh Street last month, I thought.

You've got to respect the power to harm in a guy like him, and you've got to be scared by it. It sure as hell scared Her Honor, and after she refused to lower the bail he smiled a charming boyish smile at her and she turned away. Then he looked at his teary wife again and smiled at her, and then he felt me watching and I caught his eye and felt *myself* smiling, and my look was saying: I know you. I know you very well. He looked at me calmly for a few seconds, then his eyes sort of glazed over and the deputy led him out of court. Now that I knew he hung around downtown, I thought, I'd be watching for that boy on my beat.

The judge left the bench and the deputy D.A., a youngster whose muttonchops and moustache didn't fit, started reading the complaint to get ready for my case.

Timothy Landry, my defendant, was led in by a

deputy sheriff. A deputy public defender was handling the case since Landry was not employed, even
though Miles figured he'd stolen ten thousand or so.

He was a craggy-looking guy, forty-four years old,
with long, dyed black hair that was probably really
gray, and a sallow face that on some guys never seems
to get rosy again after they do some time in the joint.
He had the look of an ex-con all over him. His bit
movie parts were mostly westerns, a few years back,
right after he got out of Folsom.

"Okay, Officer," said the young D.A., "where's the
investigator?"

"He's busy in another court. I'm Morgan, the arresting officer. I'm handling the whole thing. Dead bang
case. You shouldn't have any problems."

He probably had only a few months' experience.
They stick these deputy D.A.'s in the preliminary
hearings to give them instant courtroom experience
handling several cases a day, and I figured this one
hadn't been here more than a couple months. I'd never
seen him before and I spent lots of time in court because I made so many felony pinches.

"Where's the other witness?" asked the D.A., and for
the first time I looked around the courtroom and spotted Homer Downey, who I'd almost forgotten was
subpoenaed in this case. I didn't bother talking with
him to make sure he knew what he'd be called on to
testify to, because his part in it was so insignificant
you almost didn't need him at all, except as probable
cause for me going in the hotel room on an arrest warrant.

"Let's see," muttered the D.A. after he'd talked to
Downey for a few minutes. He sat down at the counsel table reading the complaint and running his long
fingers through his mop of brown hair. The public defender looked like a well-trimmed ivy-leaguer, and the
D.A., who's theoretically the law and order guy, was
mod. He even wore round granny glasses.

"Downey's the hotel manager?"

"Right," I said as the D.A. read my arrest report.

"On January thirty-first, you went to the Orchid Hotel at eight-two-seven East Sixth Street as part of your routine duties?"

"Right. I was making a check of the lobby to roust any winos that might've been hanging around. There were two sleeping it off in the lobby and I woke them up intending to book them when all of a sudden one of them runs up the stairs, and I suddenly felt I had more than a plain drunk so I ordered the other one to stay put and I chased the first one. He turned down the hall to the right on the third floor and I heard a door close and was almost positive he ran into room three-nineteen."

"Could you say if the man you chased was the defendant?"

"Couldn't say. He was tall and wore dark clothes. That fleabag joint is dark even in the daytime, and he was always one landing ahead of me."

"So what did you do?"

"I came back down the stairs, and found the first guy gone. I went to the manager, Homer Downey, and asked him who was living in room three-nineteen, and he showed me the name Timothy Landry on the register, and I used the pay telephone in the lobby and ran a warrant check through R and I and came up with a fifty-two dollar traffic warrant for Timothy Landry, eight-twenty-seven East Sixth Street. Then I asked the manager for his key in case Landry wouldn't open up and I went up to three-nineteen to serve the warrant on him."

"At this time you thought the guy that ran in the room was Landry?"

"Sure," I said, serious as hell.

I congratulated myself as the D.A. continued going over the complaint because that wasn't a bad story now that I went back over it again. I mean I felt I could've done better, but it wasn't bad. The truth was that a half hour before I went in Landry's room I'd

promised Knobby Booker twenty bucks if he turned
something good for me, and he told me he tricked
with a whore the night before in the Orchid Hotel and
that he knew her pretty good and she told him she just
laid a guy across the hall and had seen a gun under his
pillow while he was pouring her the pork.

With that information I'd gone in the hotel through
the empty lobby to the manager's room and looked at
his register, after which I'd gotten the passkey and
gone straight to Landry's room where I went in and
caught him with the gun and the pot. But there was no
way I could tell the truth and accomplish two things:
protecting Knobby, and convicting a no-good dangerous scumbag that should be back in the joint. I
thought my story was very good.

"Okay, so then you knew there was a guy living in
the room and he had a traffic warrant out for his arrest, and you had reason to believe he ran from you
and was in fact hiding in his room?"

"Correct. So I took the passkey and went to the
room and knocked twice and said, 'Police officer.' "

"You got a response?"

"Just like it says in my arrest report, counsel. A male
voice said, 'What is it?' and I said, 'Police officer, are
you Timothy Landry?' He said, 'Yeah, what do you
want?' and I said, 'Open the door, I have a warrant for
your arrest.' "

"Did you tell him what the warrant was for?"

"Right, I said a traffic warrant."

"What did he do?"

"Nothing. I heard the window open and knew there
was a fire escape on that side of the building, and figuring he was going to escape, I used the passkey and
opened the door."

"Where was he?"

"Sitting on the bed by the window, his hand under
the mattress. I could see what appeared to be a blue
steel gun barrel protruding a half inch from the mattress near his hand, and I drew my gun and made him

stand up where I could see from the doorway that it *was* a gun. I handcuffed the defendant and at this time informed him he was under arrest. Then in plain view on the dresser I saw the waxed-paper sandwich bag with the pot in it. A few minutes later, Homer Downey came up the stairs, and joined me in the defendant's room and that was it."

"Beautiful probable cause," the D.A. smiled. "And real lucky police work."

"Real luck," I nodded seriously. "Fifty percent of good police work is just that, good luck."

"We shouldn't have a damn bit of trouble with Chimel or any other search and seizure cases. The contraband narcotics was in plain view, the gun was in plain view, and you got in the room legally attempting to serve a warrant. You announced your presence and demanded admittance. No problem with eight-forty-four of the penal code."

"Right."

"You only entered when you felt the man whom you held a warrant for was escaping?"

"I didn't hold the warrant," I reminded him. "I only knew about the existence of the warrant."

"Same thing. Afterwards, this guy jumped bail and was rearrested recently?"

"Right."

"Dead bang case."

"Right."

After the public defender was finished talking with Landry he surprised me by going to the rear of the courtroom and reading my arrest report and talking with Homer Downey, a twitchy little chipmunk who'd been manager of the Orchid for quite a few years. I'd spoken to Homer on maybe a half-dozen occasions, usually like in this case, to look at the register or to get the passkey.

After what seemed like an unreasonably long time, I leaned over to the D.A. sitting next to me at the counsel table. "Hey, I thought Homer was the people's witness. He's grinning at the P.D. like he's a witness for the defense."

"Don't worry about it," said the D.A. "Let him have his fun. That public defender's been doing this job for exactly two months. He's an eager beaver."

"How long you been going it?"

"Four months," said the D.A., stroking his moustache, and we both laughed.

The P.D. came back to the counsel table and sat with Landry, who was dressed in an open-throat, big-collared, brown silk shirt, and tight chocolate pants. Then I saw an old skunk come in the courtroom. She had hair dyed like his, and baggy pantyhose and a short skirt that looked ridiculous on a woman her age, and I would've bet she was one of his girlfriends, maybe even the one he jumped bail on, who was ready to forgive. I was sure she was his baby when he turned around and her painted old kisser wrinkled in a smile. Landry looked straight ahead, and the bailiff in the court was not as relaxed as he usually was with an in-custody felony prisoner sitting at the counsel table. He too figured Landry for a bad son of a bitch, you could tell.

Landry smoothed his hair back twice and then seldom moved for the rest of the hearing.

Judge Redford took the bench again and we all quieted down and came to order.

"Is your true name Timothy G. Landry?" she asked the defendant, who was standing with the public defender.

"Yes, Your Honor."

Then she went into the monotonous reading of the rights even though they'd been read to Landry a hundred times by a hundred cops and a dozen other judges, and she explained the legal proceeding to him which *he* could have explained to *her*, and I looked at the clock, and finally, she tucked a wisp of straight gray hair behind her black horn-rimmed glasses and said, "Proceed."

She was a judge I always liked. I remembered once in a case where I'd busted three professional auto thieves in a hot Buick, she'd commended me in court. I'd stopped these guys cruising on North Broadway through Chinatown and I knew, *knew* something was wrong with them and something wrong with the car when I noticed the *rear* license plate was bug-spattered, but the license, the registration, the guy's driver's license, everything checked out. But I felt it and I knew. And then I looked at the identification tag, the metal tag on the door post with the spot-welded rivets, and I stuck my fingernail under it and one guy tried to split, and only stopped when I drew the six-inch and aimed at his back and yelled, "Freeze, asshole, or name your beneficiary."

Then I found that the tag was not spot-welded on, but was glued, and I pulled it off and later the detectives made the car as a Long Beach stolen. Judge Redford said it was good police work on my part.

The D.A. was ready to call his first witness, who was Homer Downey, and who the D.A. needed to verify the fact that he rented the room to Landry, in case Landry later at trial decided to say he was just spending the day in a friend's pad and didn't know how the gun and pot got in there. But the P.D. said, "Your Honor, I would move at this time to exclude all witnesses who are not presently being called upon to testify."

I expected that. P.D.'s always exclude all witnesses. I think it's the policy of their office. Sometimes it works pretty well for them, when witnesses are getting together on a story, but usually it's just a waste of time.

"Your Honor, I have only two witnesses," said the D.A., standing up. "Mr. Homer Downey and Officer Morgan the arresting officer, who is acting as my investigating officer. I would request that he be permitted to remain in the courtroom."

"The investigating officer will be permitted to re-

main, Mr. Jeffries," she said to the public defender.
"That doesn't leave anyone we can exclude, does it?"

Jeffries, the public defender, blushed because he
hadn't enough savvy to look over the reports to see
how many witnesses there were, and the D.A. and I
smiled, and the D.A. was getting ready to call old
Homer when the P.D. said, "Your Honor, I ask that if
the arresting officer is acting as the district attorney's
investigating officer in this case, that he be instructed
to testify first, even if it's out of order, and that the
other witness be excluded."

The D.A. with his two months' extra courtroom experience chuckled out loud at that one. "I have no objection, Your Honor," he said.

"Let's get on with it, then," said the judge, who was
getting impatient, and I thought maybe the air-conditioner wasn't working right because it was getting
close in there.

She said, "Will the district attorney please have his
other witness rise?"

After Downey was excluded and told to wait in the
hall the D.A. finally said, "People call Officer Morgan,"
and I walked to the witness stand and the court clerk,
a very pleasant woman about the judge's age, said,
"Do you solemnly swear in the case now pending before this court to tell the truth, the whole truth, and
nothing but the truth, so help you God?"

And I looked at her with my professional witness
face and said, "Yes, I do."

That was something I'd never completely understood. In cases where I wasn't forced to embellish, I
always said, "I do," and in cases where I was fabricat-
ing most of the probable cause, I always made it more
emphatic and said, "Yes, I do." I couldn't really explain that. It wasn't that I felt guilty when I fabricat-
ed, because I didn't feel guilty, because if I hadn't fab-
ricated, many many times, there were people who
would have been victimized and suffered because I
wouldn't have sent half the guys to the joint that I sent

over the years. Like they say, most of the testimony by all witnesses in a criminal case is just lyin' and denyin'. In fact everyone expects the *defense* witnesses to "testilie" and would be surprised if they didn't.

"Take the stand and state your name, please," said the clerk.

"William A. Morgan, M-O-R-G-A-N."

"What is your occupation and assignment?" asked the D.A.

"I'm a police officer for the City of Los Angeles assigned to Central Division."

"Were you so employed on January thirty-first of this year?"

"Yes, sir."

"On that day did you have occasion to go to the address of eight-twenty-seven East Sixth Street?"

"Yes, sir."

"At about what time of the day or night was that?"

"About one-fifteen p.m."

"Will you explain your purpose for being at that location?"

"I was checking for drunks who often loiter and sleep in the lobby of the Orchid Hotel, and do damage to the furniture in the lobby."

"I see. Is this lobby open to the public?"

"Yes, it is."

"Had you made drunk arrests there in the past?"

"Yes, I had. Although usually, I just sent the drunks on their way, my purpose being mainly to protect the premises from damage."

"I see," said the D.A., and my baby blues were getting wider and rounder and I was polishing my halo. I worked hard on courtroom demeanor, and when I was a young cop, I used to practice in front of a mirror. I had been told lots of times that jurors had told deputy D.A.'s that the reason they convicted a defendant was that Officer Morgan was so *sincere* and honest-looking.

Then I explained how I chased the guy up the stairs and saw him run in room three-nineteen, and how nat-

urally I was suspicious then, and I told how Homer
showed me the register and I read Timothy Landry's
name. I phoned R and I and gave them Landry's name
and discovered there was a traffic warrant out for his
arrest, and I believed he was the man who had run in
three-nineteen. I wasn't worried about what Homer
would say, because I *did* go to his door to get the passkey of course, and I *did* ask to see the register, and as
far as Homer knew about the rest of it, it was the gos-
pel.

When I got to the part about me knocking on the
door and Landry answering and telling me he was
Timothy Landry, I was afraid Landry was going to fly
right out of his chair. That was his first indication I
was embellishing the story a bit, and the part about
the window opening could have been true, but the
bastard snorted so loud when I said the gun was sticking out from under the mattress, that the P.D. had to
poke him in the ribs and the judge shot him a sharp
look.

I was sweating a little at that point because I was
pissed off that a recent case made illegal the search of
the premises pursuant to an arrest. Before this, I
could've almost told the whole truth, because I
would've been entitled to search the whole goddamn
room which only made good sense. Who in the hell
would waste four hours getting a search warrant when
you didn't have anything definite to begin with, and
couldn't get one issued in the first place?

So I told them how the green leafy substance resembling marijuana was in plain view on the dresser, and
Landry rolled his eyes up and smacked his lips in disgust because I got the pot out of a shoe box stashed in
the closet. The P.D. didn't bother taking me on *voir
dire* for my opinion that the green leafy substance was
pot, because I guessed he figured I'd made a thousand
narcotics arrests, which I had.

In fact, the P.D. was so nice to me I should've been

warned. The D.A. introduced the gun and the pot and the P.D. stipulated to the chemical analysis of the marijuana, and the D.A. introduced the gun as people's exhibit number one and the pot as people's number two. The P.D. never objected to anything on direct examination and my halo grew and grew until I must've looked like a bluesuited monk, with my bald spot and all. The P.D. never opened his mouth until the judge said, "Cross," and nodded toward him.

"Just a few questions, Officer Morgan," he smiled. He looked about twenty-five years old. He had a very friendly smile.

"Do you recall the name on the hotel register?"

"Objection, Your Honor," said the D.A. "What name, what are we . . ."

The judge waved the D.A. down, not bothering to sustain the objection as the P.D. said, "I'll rephrase the question, Your Honor. Officer, when you chased this man up the stairs and then returned to the manager's apartment did you look at the name on the register or did you ask Mr. Downey who lived there?"

"I asked for the register."

"Did you read the name?"

"Yes, sir."

"What was the name?"

"As I've testified, sir, it was the defendant's name, Timothy G. Landry."

"Did you then ask Mr. Downey the name of the man in three-nineteen?"

"I don't remember if I did or not. Probably not, since I read the name for myself."

"What was the warrant for, Officer? What violation?"

"It was a vehicle code violation, counsel. Twenty-one four-fifty-three-A, and failure to appear on that traffic violation."

"And it had his address on it?"

"Yes, sir."

"Did you make mention of the warrant number and the issuing court and the total bail and so forth on your police report?"

"Yes, sir, it's there in the report," I said, leaning forward just a little, just a hint. Leaning was a sincere gesture, I always felt.

Actually it was two hours after I arrested Landry that I discovered the traffic warrant. In fact, it was when I was getting ready to compose a plausible arrest report, and the discovery of a traffic warrant made me come up with this story.

"So you called into the office and found out that Timothy G. Landry of that address had a traffic warrant out for his arrest?"

"Yes, sir."

"Did you use Mr. Downey's phone?"

"No, sir, I used the pay phone in the hall."

"Why didn't you use Mr. Downey's phone? You could've saved a dime." The P.D. smiled again.

"If you dial operator and ask for the police you get your dime back anyway, counsel. I didn't want to bother Mr. Downey further, so I went out in the hall and used the pay phone."

"I see. Then you went back upstairs with the key Mr. Downey gave you?"

"Yes, sir."

"You knocked and announced yourself and made sure the voice inside was Timothy Landry, for whom you had knowledge that a warrant existed?"

"Yes, sir. The male voice said he was Timothy Landry. Or rather he said yes when I asked if he was Timothy Landry." I turned just a little toward the judge, nodding my head ever so slightly when I said this. Landry again rolled his eyeballs and slumped down in his seat at that one.

"Then when you heard the window opening and feared your traffic warrant suspect might escape down the fire escape, you forced entry?"

"I used the passkey."

"Yes, and you saw Mr. Landry on the edge of the bed as though getting ready to go out the window?"

"Yes, that's right."

"And you saw a metal object protruding from under the mattress?"

"I saw a blue metal object that I was sure was a gun barrel, counsel," I corrected him, gently.

"And you glanced to your right and there in plain view was the object marked people's two, the sandwich bag containing several grams of marijuana?"

"Yes, sir."

"I have no further questions of this witness," said the P.D., and now I was starting to worry a little, because he just went over everything as though he were the D.A. on direct examination. He just made our case stronger by giving me a chance to tell it again.

What the hell? I thought, as the judge said, "You may step down."

I sat back at the counsel table and the D.A. shrugged at my questioning look.

"Call your next witness," said the judge, taking a sip of water, as the bailiff got Homer Downey from the hall. Homer slouched up to the stand, so skinny the crotch of his pants was around his knees. He wore a dirty white shirt for the occasion and a frayed necktie and the dandruff all over his thin brown hair was even visible from the counsel table. His complexion was as yellow and bumpy as cheese pizza.

He gave his name, the address of the Orchid Hotel, and said he had been managing the place for three years. Then the D.A. asked him if I contacted him on the day of the arrest and looked at his register and borrowed his passkey, and if some ten minutes later did he come to the defendant's room and see me with the defendant under arrest, and how long had the defendant lived there, and did he rent the room to the defendant and only the defendant, and did all the events testified to occur in the city and county of Los Angeles, and Homer was a fairly good talker and a

good witness, also very sincere, and was finished in a
few minutes.

When direct examination was finished the public
defender stood up and started pacing like in the Perry
Mason shows and the judge said, "Sit down, counsel,"
and he apologized and sat down like in a real courtroom, where witnesses are only approached by lawyers when permission is given by the judge and where
theatrical stuff is out of the question.

"Mister Downey, when Officer Morgan came to
your door on the day in question, you've testified that
he asked to see your register, is that right?"

"Yes."

"Did he ask you who lived in three-nineteen?"

"Nope, just asked to see the register."

"Do you remember whose name appeared on the
register?"

"Sure. His." Downey pointed at Landry, who stared
back at him.

"By him, do you mean the defendant in this case?
The man on my right?"

"Yes."

"And what's his name?"

"Timothy C. Landowne."

"Would you repeat that name, please, and spell it?"

My heart started beating hard then, and the sweat
broke out and I said to myself, "Oh no, oh no!"

"Timothy C. Landowne. T-I-M . . ."

"Spell the last name please," the P.D. smiled and I
got sick.

"Landowne. L-A-N-D-O-W-N-E."

"And the middle initial was C as in Charlie?"

"Yes, sir."

"Are you sure?"

"Sure I'm sure. He's been staying at the hotel for
four, five months now. And he even stayed a couple
months last year."

"Did you ever see the name Timothy G. Landry on
any hotel records? That's L-A-N-D-R-Y?"

"No."

"Did you ever see the name anywhere?"

"No."

I could feel the D.A. next to me stiffen as he finally started to catch on.

"Did you at any time tell Officer Morgan that the man in three-nineteen was named Timothy G. Landry?"

"No, because that's not his name as far as I know, and I never heard that name before today."

"Thank you, Mister Downey," said the public defender, and I could feel Landry, grinning with his big shark teeth, and I was trying hard to come up with a story to get out of this. I knew at that moment, and admitted to myself finally and forever, that I should've been wearing my glasses before this, and could no longer do police work or anything else without them, and if I hadn't been so stupid and had my glasses on, I would've seen that the name on that register was a half-assed attempt at an alias on the part of Landry, and even though the traffic warrant was as good as gold and really belonged to him, I couldn't possibly have got the right information from R and I by giving the computer the wrong name. And the judge would be sure of that in a minute because the judge would have the defendant's make sheet. And even as I was thinking it she looked at me and whispered to the court clerk who handed her a copy of the make sheet and nowhere in his record did it show he used an alias of Landowne. So I was trapped, and then Homer nailed the coffin tight.

"What did the officer do after you gave him the key?"

"He went out the door and up the stairs."

"How do you know he went up the stairs?"

"The door was open just a crack. I put my slippers on in a hurry because I wanted to go up there too so's not to miss the action. I thought something might happen, you know, an arrest and all."

"You remember my talking to you just before this hearing and asking you a few questions, Mister Downey?"

"Yes, sir."

"Do you remember my asking you about the officer using the pay phone in the lobby to call the police station?"

"Yes, sir," he said, and I had a foul taste in my mouth and I was full of gas and had branding iron indigestion pains and no pills for them.

"Do you remember what you said about the phone?"

"Yes, sir, that it didn't work. It'd been out of order for a week and I'd called the phone company, and in fact I was mad because I thought maybe they came the night before when I was out because they promised to come, and I tried it that morning just before the officer came and it was still broke. Buzzed real crazy when you dropped a dime in."

"Did you drop a dime in that morning?"

"Yes, sir. I tried to use it to call the phone company and it didn't matter if I dialed or not, it made noises so I used my own phone."

"You could *not* call out on that phone?"

"Oh no, sir."

"I suppose the phone company would have a record of your request and when they finally fixed the phone?"

"Objection, Your Honor," said the D.A. weakly. "Calls for a conclusion."

"Sustained," said the judge, looking only at me now, and I looked at Homer just for something to do with my eyes.

"Did you go upstairs behind the officer?" asked the P.D. again, and now the D.A. had slumped in his chair and was tapping with a pencil, and I'd passed the point of nervous breathing and sweat. Now I was cold and thinking, thinking about how to get out of this and what I would say if they recalled me to the stand, if either of them recalled me, and I thought the defense might call me because I was *their* witness now, they owned me.

"I went upstairs a little bit after the officer."

"What did you see when you got up there?"

"The officer was standing outside Mister Landowne's room and like listening at the door. He had his hat in his hand and his ear was pressed up to the door."

"Did he appear to see you, or rather, to look in your direction?"

"No, he had his back to my end of the hall and I decided to peek from around the corner, because I didn't know what he was up to and maybe there'd be a big shoot-out or something, and I could run back down the stairs if something dangerous happened."

"Did you hear him knock on the door?"

"No, he didn't knock."

"Objection," said the D.A. "The witness was asked . . ."

"All right," said the judge, holding her hand up again as the D.A. sat back down.

"Did you ever *hear* the officer knock?" the judge asked the witness.

"No, sir," said Homer to the judge, and I heard a few snickers from the rear of the court, and I thanked the gods that there were only a few spectators and none of them were cops.

"Did the officer say anything while you were there observing?" asked the P.D.

"Nothing."

"How long did you watch him?"

"Two, three minutes, maybe longer. He knelt down and tried to peek in the keyhole, but I had them all plugged two years ago because of hotel creepers and peeping toms."

"Did you . . . strike that, did the officer say anything that you could hear while you were climbing the stairway?"

"I never heard him say nothing," said Homer, looking bewildered as hell, and noticing from my face that something was sure as hell wrong and I was very unhappy.

"Then what did he do?"

"Used the key. Opened the door."

"In what way? Quickly?"

"I would say careful. He like turned the key slow and careful, and then he pulled out his pistol and then he seemed to get the bolt turned, and he kicked open the door and jumped in the room with the gun out front."

"Could you hear any conversation then?"

"Oh yeah," he giggled, through gapped, brown-stained teeth. "The officer yelled something to Mister Landowne."

"What did he say? His *exact* words if you remember."

"He said, 'Freeze asshole, you move and you're wallpaper.'"

I heard all three spectators laugh at that one, but the judge didn't think it was funny and neither did the D.A., who looked almost as sick as I figured I looked.

"Did you go in the room?"

"Yes, sir, for a second."

"Did you see anything unusual about the room?"

"No. The officer told me to get out and go back to my room so I did."

"Did you notice if anything was on the dresser?"

"I didn't notice."

"Did you hear any other conversation between the officer and the defendant?"

"No."

"Nothing at all?"

"The officer warned him about something."

"What did he say?"

"It was about Mister Landowne not trying anything funny, something like that. I was walking out."

"What did he say?"

"Well, it's something else not exactly decent."

"We're grown up. What did he say?"

"He said, 'You get out of that chair and I'll shove this gun so far up your ass there'll be shit on the grips.' That's what he said. I'm sorry." Homer turned red and giggled nervously and shrugged at me.

"The defendant was sitting in a chair?"

"Yes."

"Was it his own gun the officer was talking about?"

"Objection," said the D.A.

"I'll rephrase that," said the P.D. "Was the officer holding his own gun in his hand at that time?"

"Yes, sir."

"Did you see the other gun at that time?"

"No, I never saw no other gun."

The P.D. hesitated for a long, deadly silent minute and chewed on the tip of his pencil, and I almost sighed out loud when he said, "I have no further questions," even though it was much too late to feel relieved.

"I have a question," said Judge Redford, and she pushed her glasses up over a hump on her thin nose and said, "Mister Downey, did you happen to go into the lobby any time that morning *before* the officer arrived?"

"No."

"You never went out or looked out into the lobby area?"

"Well, only when the officer drove up in front. I saw the police car parked in front, and I was curious and I started out the door and then I saw the officer climbing the front steps of the hotel and I went back inside to put a shirt and shoes on so's to look presentable in case he needed some help from me."

"Did you look into the lobby?"

"Well, yes, it's right in front of my door, ma'am."

"Who was in the lobby?"

"Why, nobody."

"Could you see the entire lobby? All the chairs? Everywhere in the lobby area?"

"Why sure. My front door opens right on the lobby and it's not very big."

"Think carefully. Did you see two men sleeping anywhere near the lobby area?"

"There was nobody there, Judge."

"And where was the officer when you were looking into the empty lobby?"

"Coming in the front door, ma'am. A couple seconds later he came to my door and asked about the room and looked at the register like I said."

My brain was burning up now like the rest of me, and I had an idiotic story ready when they recalled me about how I'd come in the lobby once and then got out and come in again when Homer saw me and thought it was the first entry. And I was prepared to swear the phone worked, because what the hell, anything was possible with telephone problems. And even if that bony-assed, dirty little sneak followed me up the stairs, maybe I could convince them I called to Landry *before* Downey got up there, and what the hell, Downey didn't know if the marijuana was on the dresser or in the closet, and I was trying to tell myself everything would be all right so I could keep the big-eyed honest look on my kisser because I needed it now if ever in my life.

I was waiting to be recalled and I was ready even though my right knee trembled and made me mad as hell, and then the judge said to the public defender and the D.A., "Will counsel please approach the bench?"

Then I knew it was all over and Landry was making noises and I could feel the shark grin as his head was turned toward me. I just stared straight ahead like a zombie and wondered if I'd walk out of this courtroom in handcuffs for perjury, because anybody in the world could see that dumb shit Homer Downey was telling the stone truth and didn't even know what the P.D. was doing to me.

When they came back to the table after talking with the judge, the D.A. smiled woodenly at me and whispered, "It was the name on the register. When the public defender realized that Homer didn't know Landry's real name, he asked him about the register. It was the register that opened it all up for him. She's going to dismiss the case. I don't know what to advise you, Officer. I've never had anything like this happen before. Maybe I should call my office and ask what to do if . . ."

"Would you care to offer a motion to dismiss, Mister Jeffries?" asked the judge to the public defender, who jumped to his feet and did just that, and then she dismissed the case, and I hardly heard Landry chuckling all over the place and I knew he was shaking hands with that baby-faced little python that defended him. Then Landry leaned over the public defender and said, "Thanks, stupid," to me, but the P.D. told him to cool it. Then the bailiff had his hand on my shoulder and said, "Judge Redford would like to see you in her chambers," and I saw the judge had left the bench and I walked like a toy soldier toward the open door. In a few seconds I was standing in the middle of this room, and facing a desk where the judge sat looking toward the wall which was lined with bookcases full of law books. She was taking deep breaths and thinking of what to say.

"Sit down," she said, finally, and I did. I dropped my hat on the floor and was afraid to stoop down to pick it up I was so dizzy.

"In all my years on the bench I've never had that happen. Not like that. I'd like to know why you did it."

"I want to tell you the truth," I said and my mouth was leathery. I had trouble forming the words. My lips popped from the dryness every time I opened my mouth. I had seen nervous suspects like that thousands of times when I had them good and dirty, and they knew I had them.

"Maybe I should advise you of your constitutional rights before you tell me anything," said the judge, and she took off her glasses and the bump on her nose was more prominent. She was a homely woman and looked smaller here in her office, but she looked stronger too, and aged.

"The hell with my rights!" I said suddenly. "I don't give a damn about my rights, I want to tell you the truth."

"But I intend to have the district attorney's office issue a perjury complaint against you. I'm going to have that hotel register brought in, and the phone company's repairman will be subpoenaed and so will Mister Downey of course, and I think you'll be convicted."

"Don't you even care about what I've got to say?" I was getting mad now as well as scared, and I could feel the tears coming to my eyes, and I hadn't felt anything like this since I couldn't remember when.

"What can you say? What can anyone say? I'm awfully disappointed. I'm sickened in fact." She rubbed her eyes at the corners for a second and I was busting and couldn't hold on.

"*You're* disappointed? *You're* sickened? What the hell do you think I'm feeling at this minute? I feel like you got a blowtorch on the inside of my guts and you won't turn it off and it'll never be turned off, that's what I feel, Your Honor. Now can I tell the God's truth? Will you at least let me tell it?"

"Go ahead," she said, and lit a cigarette and leaned back in the padded chair and watched me.

"Well, I have this snitch, Your Honor. And I've got to protect my informants, you know that. For his own personal safety, and so he can continue to give me information. And the way things are going in court nowadays with everyone so nervous about the defendant's rights, I'm afraid to even mention confidential informants like I used to, and I'm afraid to try to get a search warrant because the judges are so damn hinky they call damn near every informant a material witness, even when he's not. So in recent years I've started . . . exploring ways around."

"You've started lying."

"Yes, I've started lying! What the hell, I'd hardly ever convict any of these crooks if I didn't lie at least a little bit. You know what the search and seizure and arrest rules are like nowadays."

"Go on."

Then I told her how the arrest went down, exactly how it went down, and how I later got the idea about the traffic warrant when I found out he had one. And when I was finished, she smoked for a good two minutes and didn't say a word. Her cheeks were eroded and looked like they were hacked out of a rocky cliff. She was a strong old woman from another century as she sat there and showed me her profile and finally she said, "I've seen witnesses lie thousands of times. I guess every defendant lies to a greater or lesser degree and most defense witnesses stretch hell out of the truth, and of course I've seen police officers lie about probable cause. There's the old hackneyed story about feeling what appeared to be an offensive weapon like a knife in the defendant's pocket and reaching inside to retrieve the knife and finding it to be a stick of marijuana. That one's been told so many times by so many cops it makes judges want to vomit. And of course there's the furtive movement like the defendant is shoving something under the seat of the car. That's always good probable cause for a search, and likewise that's overdone. Sure, I've heard officers lie before, but nothing is black and white in this world and there are degrees of truth and untruth, and like many other judges who feel police officers cannot possibly protect the public these days, I've given officers the benefit of the doubt in probable cause situations. I never really believed a Los Angeles policeman would *completely* falsify his entire testimony as you've done today. That's why I feel sickened by it."

"I didn't falsify it all. He had the gun. It *was* under the mattress. He *had* the marijuana. I just lied about where I found it. Your Honor, he's an active bandit. The robbery dicks figure him for six robberies. He's beaten an old man and blinded him. He's . . ."

She held up her hand and said, "I didn't figure he was using that gun to stir his soup with, Officer Morgan. He has the look of a dangerous man about him."

"You could see it too!" I said. "Well . . ."

"Nothing," she interrupted. "That means nothing. The higher courts have given us difficult law, but by God, it's the law!"

"Your Honor," I said slowly. And then the tears filled my eyes and there was nothing I could do. "I'm not afraid of losing my pension. I've done nineteen years and over eleven months and I'm leaving the Department after tomorrow, and officially retiring in a few weeks, but I'm not afraid of losing the money. That's not why I'm asking, why I'm *begging* you to give me a chance. And it's not that I'm afraid to face a perjury charge and go to jail, because you can't be a crybaby in this world. But, Judge, there are people, policemen, and other people, people on my beat who think I'm something special. I'm one of the ones they really look up to, you know? I'm not just a character, I'm a hell of a cop!"

"I know you are," she said. "I've noticed you in my courtroom many times."

"You have?" Of course I'd been in her courtroom as a witness before, but I figured all bluecoats looked the same to blackrobes. "Don't get down on us, Judge Redford. Some coppers don't lie at all, and others only lie a little like you said. Only a few like me would do what I did."

"Why?"

"Because I care, Your Honor, goddamnit. Other

cops put in their nine hours and go home to their families twenty miles from town and that's it, but guys like me, why I got nobody and I want nobody. I do my living on my beat. And I've got things inside me that make me do these things against my better judgment. That proves I'm dumber than the dumbest moron on my beat."

"You're not dumb. You're a clever witness. A very clever witness."

"I never lied that much before, Judge. I just thought I could get away with it. I just couldn't read that name right on that hotel register. If I could've read that name right on the register I never would've been able to pull off that traffic warrant story and I wouldn't've tried it. And I probably wouldn't be in this fix, and the reason I couldn't really see that name and only assumed it must've been Landry is because I'm fifty years old and far-sighted, and too stubborn to wear my glasses, and kidding myself that I'm thirty and doing a young man's job when I can't cut it anymore. I'm going out though, Judge. This clinches it if I ever had any doubts. Tomorrow's my last day. A knight. Yesterday somebody called me a Blue Knight. Why do people say such things? They make you think you're really something and so you got to win a battle every time out. Why should *I* care if Landry walks out of here? What's it to *me*? Why do they *call* you a knight?"

She looked at me then and put the cigarette out and I'd never in my life begged anyone for anything, and never licked anyone's boots. I was glad she was a woman because it wasn't quite so bad to be licking a woman's boots, not *quite* so bad, and my stomach wasn't only burning now, it was hurting in spasms, like a big fist was pounding inside in a jerky rhythm. I thought I'd double over from the pain in a few minutes.

"Officer Morgan, you fully agree don't you that we can call off the whole damn game and crawl back in primeval muck if the orderers, the enforcers of the

law, begin to operate outside it? You understand that
there could be no civilization, don't you? You know,
don't you, that I as well as many other judges am terribly aware of the overwhelming numbers of criminals
on those streets whom you policemen must protect us
from? You cannot always do it and there are times
when you are handcuffed by court decisions that presume the goodness of people past all logical presump-
tion. But don't you think there are judges, and yes,
even defense attorneys, who sympathize with you?
Can't you see that you, you policemen of all people,
must be more than you are? You must be patient and
above all, honest. Can't you see if you go outside the
law regardless of how absurd it seems, in the name of
enforcing it, that we're all doomed? Can you see these
things?"

"Yes. Yes, I know, but old Knobby Booker doesn't
know. And if I had to name him as my snitch he might
get a rat jacket and somebody might rip him off. . . ."
And now my voice was breaking and I could hardly
see her because it was all over and I knew I'd be taken
out of this courtroom and over to the county jail.
"When you're alone out there on that beat, Your
Honor, and everyone knows you're the Man. . . . The
way they look at you . . . and how it feels when they
say, 'You're the champ, Bumper. You're a warlord.
You're a Knight, a Blue Knight. . . .'" And then I could
say no more and said no more that day to that woman.

The silence was buzzing in my ears and finally she
said, "Officer Morgan, I'm requesting that the deputy
district attorney say nothing of your perjured testimony in his report to his office. I'm also going to request
the public defender, the bailiff, the court reporter and
the clerk, not to reveal what happened in there today.
I want you to leave now so I can wonder if I've done
the right thing. We'll never forget this, but we'll take
no further action."

I couldn't believe it. I sat for a second, paralyzed,
and then I stood up and wiped my eyes and walked

toward the door and stopped and didn't even think to thank her, and looked around, but she was turned in her chair and watching the book stacks again. When I walked through the courtroom, the public defender and the district attorney were talking quietly and both of them glanced at me. I could feel them look at me, but I went straight for the door, holding my stomach, and waiting for the cramps to subside so I could think.

I stepped into the hall and remembered vaguely that the gun and narcotics evidence were still in the courtroom, and then thought the hell with it, I had to get out in the car and drive with the breeze in my face before the blood surging through my skull blew the top of my head off.

I went straight for Elysian Park around the back side, got out of the car, filled my pockets with acid eaters from the glove compartment, and climbed the hill behind the reservoir. I could smell eucalyptus, and the dirt was dry and loose under my shoes. The hill was steeper than I thought and I was sweating pretty good after just a few minutes of walking. Then I saw two park peepers. One had binoculars to see the show better. They were watching the road down below where couples sit in their cars at any hour of the day or night under the trees and make love.

"Get outta my park, you barfbags," I said, and they turned around and saw me standing above them. They both were middle-aged guys. One of them, with fish-belly pale skin, wore orange checkered pants and a yellow turtleneck and had the binoculars up to his face. When I spoke he dropped them and bolted through the brush. The other guy looked indignant and started walking stiff-legged away like a cocky little terrier, but when I took a few steps toward him, cursing and growling, he started running too, and I picked up the binoculars and threw them at him, but missed and they bounced off a tree and fell in the brush. Then I climbed the hill clear to the top and even though it was smoggy, the view was pretty good.

By the time I flopped on the grass and took off my Sam Browne and my hat, the stomach cramps were all but gone. I fell asleep almost right away and slept an hour there on the cool grass.

## 13

WHEN I WOKE UP, the world tasted horrible and I popped an acid eater just to freshen my mouth. I laid there on my back for a while and looked up at a bluejay scampering around on a branch.

"Did you shit in my mouth?" I said, and then wondered what I'd been dreaming about because I was sweaty even though it was fairly cool here. A breeze blowing over me felt wonderful. I saw by my watch it was after four and I hated to get up but of course I had to. I sat up, tucked in my shirt, strapped on the Sam Browne and combed back my hair which was tough to do, it was so wild and wiry. And I thought, I'll be glad when it all falls out and then I won't have to screw around with it anymore. It was hell sometimes when even your hair wouldn't obey you. When you had no control over anything, even your goddamn hair. Maybe I should use hair spray, I thought, like these pretty young cops nowadays. Maybe while I still had some hair I should get those fifteen-dollar haircuts and ride around in a radio car all day, spraying my hair instead of booking these scumbags, and then I could stay out of trouble, then no judge could throw me in jail for perjury, and disgrace me, and ruin everything I've done for twenty years, and ruin everything they all think about me, all of them, the people on the beat.

One more day and it's over, thank Christ, I thought, and half stumbled down the hill to my car because I still wasn't completely awake.

"One-X-L-Forty-five, One-X-L-Forty-five, come in," said the communications operator, a few seconds after I started the car. She sounded exasperated as hell, so I guess she'd deen trying to get me. Probably a major crisis, like a stolen bicycle, I thought.

"One-X-L-Forty-five, go," I said disgustedly into the mike.

"One-X-L-Forty-five, meet the plainclothes officer at the southeast corner of Beverly and Vermont in Rampart Division. This call has been approved by your watch commander."

I rogered the call and wondered what was going on and then despite how rotten I felt, how disgusted with everything and everybody, and mostly this miserable crummy job, despite all that, my heart started beating a little bit harder, and I got a sort of happy feeling bubbling around inside me because I knew it had to be Charlie Bronski. Charlie must have something, and next thing I knew I was driving huckety-buck over Temple, slicing through the heavy traffic and then bombing it down Vermont, and I spotted Charlie in a parking lot near a market. He was standing beside his car looking hot and tired and mad, but I knew he had something or he'd never call me out of my division like this.

"About time, Bumper," said Charlie. "I been trying to reach you on the radio for half an hour. They told me you left court a long time ago."

"Been out for investigation, Charlie. Too big to talk about."

"Wonder what *that* means," Charlie smiled, with his broken-toothed, Slavic, hard-looking grin. "I got something so good you won't believe it."

"You busted Red Scalotta!"

"No, no, you're dreaming," he laughed. "But I got the search warrant for the back that Reba told us about."

"How'd you do it so fast?"

"I don't actually have it yet. I'll have it in fifteen minutes when Nick and Fuzzy and the Administrative Vice team get here. Nick just talked to me on the radio. Him and Fuzzy just left the Hall of Justice. They got the warrant and the Ad Vice team is on the way to assist."

"How the hell did you do it, Charlie?" I asked, and now I'd forgotten the judge, and the humiliation, and the misery, and Charlie and me were grinning at each other because we were both on the scent. And when a real cop gets on it, there's nothing else he can think about. Nothing.

"After we left Reba I couldn't wait to get started on this thing. We went to that laundry over near Sixth and Kenmore. Actually, it's a modern dry cleaning and laundry establishment. They do the work on the premises and it's pretty damned big. The building's on the corner and takes in the whole ground floor, and I even saw employees going up to the second floor where they have storage or something. I watched from across the street with binoculars and Fuzzy prowled around the back alley and found the door Reba said Aaron was talking about."

"Who in the hell *is* Aaron, Charlie?"

"He's Scalotta's think man. Aaron Fishman. He's an accountant and a shrewd organizer and he's got everything it takes but guts, so he's a number two man to Scalotta. I never saw the guy, I only heard about him from Ad Vice and Intelligence. Soon as Reba described that little Jew I knew who she was talking about. He's Scalotta's link with the back offices. He protects Red's interests and hires the back clerks and keeps things moving. Dick Reemey at Intelligence says he doesn't think Red could operate without Aaron Fishman. Red's drifting away from the business more and more, getting in with the Hollywood crowd. Anyway, Fuzzy, who's a nosy bastard, went in the door to the laundry and found a stairway that was locked, and a door down. He went down and found a basement and an old vented furnace and a trash box, and he started sifting through and found a few adding machine tapes all ending in five's and zero's, and he even found a few charred pieces of owe sheets and a half-burned scratch sheet. I'll bet Aaron would set fire to his clerk if he knew he was that careless."

Charlie chuckled for a minute and I lit a cigar and looked at my watch.

"Don't worry about the time, Bumper, the back office clerks don't leave until an hour or so past the last post. He's got to stay and figure his tops."

"Tops?"

"Top sheets. This shows each agent's code and lists his bettors and how much was won and lost."

"Wonder how Zoot Lafferty did today?" I laughed.

"Handbooks like Zoot get ten percent hot or cold, win or lose," said Charlie. "Anyway, Fuzzy found a little evidence to corroborate Reba, and then came the most unbelievable tremendous piece of luck I ever had in this job. He's crawling around down there in the basement like a rat, picking up burned residue, and next thing he sees is a big ugly guy standing stone still in the dark corner of the basement. Fuzzy almost shit his pants and he didn't have a gun or anything because you don't really need weapons when you're working books. Next thing, this guy comes toward him like the creature from the black lagoon and Fuzzy said the door was behind the guy and just as he's thinking about rushing him with his head down and trying to bowl him over on his ass, the giant starts talking in a little-boy voice and says, 'Hello, my name is Bobby. Do you know how to fix electric trains?'

"And next thing Fuzzy knows this guy leads him to a little room in the back where there's a bed and a table and Fuzzy has to find a track break in a little electric train set that Bobby's got on his table, and all the time the guy's standing there, his head damn near touching the top of the doorway he's so big, and making sure Fuzzy fixes it."

"Well, what . . ."

"Lemme finish," Charlie laughed. "Anyway, Fuzzy gets the train fixed and the big ox starts banging Fuzzy on the back and shoulders out of sheer joy, almost knocking Fuzzy's bridgework loose, and Fuzzy finds out this moron is the cleanup man, evidently some retarded relative of the owner of the building, and he lives there in the basement and does the windows and floors and everything in the place.

"There're some offices on the second floor with a completely different stairway, Fuzzy discovers, and this locked door is the only way up to this part of the third floor except for the fire escape in back and the ladder's up and chained in place. This giant, Bobby, says that the third floor is all storage space for one of the offices on the second floor except for 'Miss Terry's place,' and then he starts telling Fuzzy how he likes Miss Terry and how she brings him pies and good things to eat every day, so Fuzzy starts pumping him and Bobby tells him how he hardly ever goes in Miss Terry's place, but he washes the windows once in a while and sometimes helps her with something. And with Fuzzy prodding, he tells about the wooden racks where all the little yellow cards are with the numbers. Those're the ABC professional-type markers of course, and he tells about the adding machine, two adding machines, in fact, and when Fuzzy shows him the burned National Daily Reporter, Bobby says, yeah, those are always there. In short, he completely describes an elite bookmaking office right up to the way papers are bundled and filed."

"You used this Bobby for your informant on the search warrant affidavit?"

"Yeah. I didn't have to mention anything about Reba. According to the affidavit, we got the warrant solely on the basis of this informant Bobby and our own corroborative findings."

"You'll have to use the poor guy in court?"

"He'll certainly have to be named," said Charlie.

"How old a guy is he?"

"I don't know, fifty, fifty-five."

"Think they'll hurt him?"

"Why should they? He doesn't even know what he's doing. They can see that. They just fucked up, that's all. Why should they hurt a dummy?"

"Because they're slimeballs."

"Well, you never know," Charlie shrugged. "They might. Anyway, we got the warrant, Bumper. By God, I kept my promise to you."

"Thanks, Charlie. Nobody could've done better. You got anybody staked on the place?"

"Milburn. He works in our office. We'll just end up busting the broad, Terry. According to the dummy she's the only one ever comes in there except once in a while a man comes in, he said. He couldn't remember what the man looked like. This is Thursday. Should be a lot of paper in that back office. If we get enough of the records we can hurt them, Bumper."

"A two-hundred-and-fifty-dollar fine?" I sniffed.

"If we get the right records we can put Internal Revenue on them. They can tax ten percent of gross for the year. And they can go back as far as five years. That hurts, Bumper. That hurts even a guy as big as Red Scalotta, but it's tough to pull it off."

"How're you going in?"

"We first decided to use Bobby. We can use subterfuge to get in if we can convince the court that we have information that this organization will attempt to destroy records. Hell, they all do that. Fuzzy thought about using Bobby to bang on the lower door to the inside stairway and call Terry and have Terry open the door which she can buzz open. We could tell Bobby it's a game or something, but Nick and Milburn voted us down. They thought when we charged through the door and up the steps through the office door and got Terry by the ass, old Bobby might decide to end the game. If he stopped playing I imagine he'd be no more dangerous than a brahma bull. Anyway, Nick and Milburn were afraid we'd have to hurt the dummy so they voted us down."

"So how'll you do it?"

"We borrowed a black policewoman from Southwest Detectives. We got her in a blue dungaree apron suit like the black babes that work pressing downstairs. She's going to knock on the downstairs door and start yelling something unintelligible in a way-out suede dialect, and hope Terry buzzes her in. Then she's going to walk up the steps and blab something about a fire in the basement and get as close to Terry as she can, and we hope she can get right inside and get her down on the floor and sit on her because me and Nick'll be charging up that door right behind her. The Administrative Vice team'll follow in a few minutes and help us out since they're the experts on a back-office operation. You know, I only took one back office before so this'll be something for me too."

"Where'll I be?"

"Well, we got to hide you with your bluesuit, naturally, so you can hang around out back, near the alley behind the solid wood fence on the west side. After we take the place I'll open the back window and call you and you can come on in and see the fruits of your labor with Zoot Lafferty."

"What'll you do about getting by your star witness?"

"The dummy? Oh, Fuzzy got stuck with that job since he's Bobby's best pal," Charlie chuckled. "Before any of us even get in position Fuzzy's going in to get Bobby and walk him down the street to the drugstore for an ice cream sundae."

"One-Victor-One to Two, come in," said a voice over frequency six.

"That's Milburn at the back office," said Charlie, hurrying to the radio.

"Go, Lem," said Charlie over the mike.

"Listen, Charlie," said Milburn. "A guy just went in that doorway outside. It's possible he could've turned left into the laundry, I couldn't tell, but I think he made a right to the office stairway."

"What's he look like, Lem?" asked Charlie.

"Caucasian, fifty-five to sixty, five-six, hundred fifty, bald, moustache, glasses. Dressed good. I think he parked one block north and walked down because I saw a white Cad circle the block twice and there was a bald guy driving and looking around like maybe for heat."

"Okay, Lem, we'll be there pretty quick," said Charlie, hanging up the mike, red-faced and nodding at me without saying anything.

"Fishman," I said.

"Son of a bitch," said Charlie. "Son of a bitch. He's there!"

Then Charlie got on the mike and called Nick and the others, having trouble keeping his voice low and modulated in his excitement, and it was affecting me and my heart started beating. Charlie told them to hurry it up and asked their estimated time of arrival.

"Our E.T.A. is five minutes," said Nick over the radio.

"Jesus, Bumper, we got a chance to take the office and Aaron Fishman at the same time! That weasely little cocksucker hasn't been busted since the depression days!"

I was still happy as hell for Charlie, but looking at it realistically, what the hell was there to scream about? They had an idiot for an informant, and I didn't want to throw cold water, but I knew damn well the search warrant stood a good chance of being traversed, especially if Bobby was brought into court as a material witness and they saw his I.Q. was less than par golf. And if it wasn't traversed, and they convicted the clerk and Fishman, what the hell would happen to them, a two-hundred-fifty-dollar fine? Fishman probably had four times that much in his pants pocket right now. And I wasn't any too thrilled about I.R.S. pulling off a big case and hitting them in the bankbook, but even if they did, what would it mean? That Scalotta couldn't buy a new whip every time he had parties with sick little girls like Reba? Or maybe Aaron Fishman would have to drive his Cad for two years without getting a new one? I couldn't see anything to get ecstatic about when I considered it all. In fact, I was feeling lower by the minute, and madder. I prayed Red Scalotta would show up there too and maybe try to resist arrest, even though my common sense told me nothing like that would ever happen, but if it did . . .

"There should be something there to destroy the important records," said Charlie, puffing on a cigarette and dancing around impatiently waiting for Nick and the others to drive up.

"You mean like flash paper? I've heard of that," I said.

"They sometimes use that, but mostly in fronts," said Charlie. "You touch a flame or a cigarette to it and it goes up in one big flash and leaves no residue. They also got this dissolving paper. You drop it in water and it dissolves with no residue you can put under a microscope. But sometimes in backs they have some type of small furnace they keep charged where they can throw the real important stuff. Where the hell is that Nick?"

"Right here, Charlie," I said, as the vice car sped across the parking lot. Nick and Fuzzy and the Negro policewoman were inside and another car was following with the two guys from Administrative Vice.

Everybody was wetting their pants when they found out Aaron Fishman was in there, and I marveled at vice officers, how they can get excited about something that is so disappointing, and depressing, and meaningless, when you thought about it. And then Charlie hurriedly explained to the Ad Vice guys what a uniformed cop was doing there, saying it start-

ed out as my caper. I knew one of the Ad Vice officers
from when he used to work Central Patrol and we
jawed and made plans for another five minutes, and finally piled into the cars.

We turned north on Catalina from Sixth Street before getting to Kenmore and then turned west and
came down Kenmore from the north. The north side of
Sixth Street is all apartment buildings and to the south
is the Miracle Mile, Wilshire Boulevard. Sixth Street
itself is mostly commercial buildings. Everybody
parked to the north because the windows were painted on the top floor of the building on this side. It was
the blind side, and after a few minutes everybody got
ready when Fuzzy was seen through binoculars skip-
ping down the sidewalk with Bobby, who even from
this distance looked like Gargantua. With the giant
gone the stronghold wasn't quite so impregnable.

In a few minutes they were all hustling down the
sidewalk and I circled around the block on foot and
came in behind the wooden fence and I was alone and
sweating in the sunshine, wondering why the hell I
wanted this so bad, and how the organization would
get back on its feet, and another of Red's back offices
would just take as much of the action as it could until
a new back could be set up, and Aaron would get his
new Cad in two years. And he and Red would be free
to enjoy it all and maybe someone like me would be
laying up in the county jail for perjury in the special
tank where they keep policemen accused of crimes,
because a policeman put in with the regular pukepots
would live probably about one hour at best.

This job didn't make sense. How could I have told
myself for twenty years that it made any sense at all?
How could I charge around that beat, a big blue stupid clown, and pretend that anything made any sense
at all? Judge Redford *should've* put me in jail, I
thought. My brain was boiling in the sunshine, the
sweat running in my eyes and burning. That would've

been a consistent kind of lunacy at least. What the hell are we doing here like this?

Then suddenly I couldn't stand it there alone, my big ass only partly hidden by the fence, and I walked out in the alley and over to the fire escape of the old building. The iron ladder was chained up like an ancient fearsome drawbridge. A breach of fire regulation to chain it up, I thought, and I looked around for something to stand on, and spotted a trash can by the fence which I emptied and turned upside down under the ladder. And then in a minute I was dangling there like a fat sweaty baboon, tearing my pants on the concrete wall, scuffing my shoes, panting, and finally sobbing, because I couldn't get my ass up there on a window ledge where I could climb over the railing on the second floor.

I fell back once, clear to the alley below. I fell hard on my shoulder, and thought if I'd been able to read that hotel register I'd never have been humiliated like that, and I thought of how I was of no value whatever to this operation which was in itself of no value because if I couldn't catch Red Scalotta and Aaron Fishman by the rules, then they would put *me* in jail. And I sat on my ass there in the alley, panting, my hands red and sore and my shoulder hurting, and I thought then, if I go to the dungeon and Fishman goes free, then *I'm* the scumbag and *he's* the Blue Knight, and I wondered how he would look in my uniform.

Then I looked up at that ladder and vowed that I'd die here in this alley if I didn't climb that fire escape. I got back on the trash can and jumped up, grabbing the metal ladder and feeling it drop a little until the chain caught it. Then I shinnied up the wall again, gasping and sobbing out loud, the sweat like vinegar in my eyes, and got one foot up and had to stop and try to breathe in the heat. I almost let go and thought how that would make sense too if I fell head first now onto the garbage can and broke my fat neck. Then I took a huge breath and knew if I didn't make it now I never would make it, and I heaved my carcass up, up, and then I was sitting on the window ledge and surprisingly enough I still had my hat on and I hadn't lost my gun. I was perched there on the ledge in a pile of birdshit, and a fat gray pigeon sat on the fire escape railing over me. He cooed and looked at me gasping and grimacing and wondered if I was dangerous.

"Get outta here, you little prick," I whispered, when he crapped on my shoulder. I swung my hat at him and he squawked and flew away.

Then I dragged myself up carefully, keeping most of my weight on the window ledge, and I was on the railing and then I climbed over and was on the first landing of the fire escape where I had to rest for a minute because I was dizzy. I looked at my watch and saw that the policewoman should be about ready to try her flimflam now, so, dizzy or not, I climbed the second iron ladder.

It was steep and long to the third floor, one of those almost vertical iron ladders like on a ship, with round iron hand railings. I climbed as quietly as I could, taking long deep breaths. Then I was at the top and was glad I wouldn't have to make the steep descent back down. I should be walking out through the back office if everything went right. When Charlie opened the back door to call to me, I'd be standing right here watching the door instead of crouched in some alley. And if I heard any doors breaking, or any action at all, I'd kick in the back door here, and maybe I'd be the first one inside the place, and maybe I'd do something else that could land me in jail, but the way I felt this moment, maybe it would be worth it because twenty years didn't mean a goddamn thing when Scalotta and Fishman could wear *my* uniform and I could wear jail denims with striped patch pockets and lay up there in the cop's tank at the county jail.

Then I heard a crash and I knew the scam hadn't worked because this was a door breaking far away,

way down below, which meant they'd had to break in
that first door, run up those steps clear to the third
floor and break in the other door, and then I found
myself kicking on the back door which I didn't know
was steel reinforced with a heavy bar across it. It
wouldn't go, and at that moment I didn't know how
sturdy they had made it and I thought it was a regular
door and I was almost crying as I kicked it because I
couldn't even take down a door anymore and I
couldn't do *anything* anymore. But I kicked, and
kicked, and finally I went to the window on the left
and kicked right through it, cutting my leg. I broke
out the glass with my hands and I lost my hat and cut
my forehead on the glass and was raging and yelling
something I couldn't remember when I stormed
through that room and saw the terrified young woman
and the trembling bald little man by the doorway,
their arms full of boxes. They looked at me for a second and then the woman started screaming and the
man went out the door, turned right and headed for
the fire escape with me after him. He threw the bar
off the steel door and was back out on the fire escape,
a big cardboard box in his arms crammed with cards
and papers, and he stopped on the landing and saw
how steep that ladder was. He was holding tight to the
heavy box and he turned his back to the ladder and
gripped the box and was going to try to back down
the iron stairs when I grabbed him with my bloody
hands and he yelled at me as two pigeons flew in our
faces with a whir and rattle of wings.

"Let me go!" he said, the little greenish sacs under
his eyes bulging. "You ape, let me go!"

And then I don't know if I just let him go or if I put
pressure against him. I honestly don't know, but it
doesn't really make any difference, because pulling
away from me like he was, and holding that box like
Midas's gold, I knew exactly what would happen if I
just suddenly did what he was asking.

So I don't know for sure if I shoved him or if I just

released him, but as I said, the result would've been the same, and at this moment in my life it was the only thing that made the slightest bit of sense, the only thing I could do for any of it to make any sense at all. He would never wear my bluesuit, never, if I only did what he was asking. My heart was thumping like the pigeon's wing, and I just let go and dropped my bleeding hands to my sides.

He pitched backward then, and the weight of the box against his chest made him fall head first, clattering down the iron ladder like an anchor being dropped. He was screaming and the box had broken open and markers and papers were flying and sailing and tumbling through the air. It *did* sound like an anchor chain feeding out, the way he clattered down. On the landing below where he stopped, I saw his dentures on the first rung of the ladder not broken, and his glasses on the landing, broken, and the cardboard box on top of him so you could hardly see the little man doubled over beneath it. He was quiet for a second and then started whimpering, and finally sounded like a pigeon cooing.

"What happened, Bumper?" asked Charlie, running out on the fire escape, out of breath.

"Did you get all the right records, Charlie?"

"Oh my God, what happened?"

"He fell."

"Is he dead?"

"I don't think so, Charlie. He's making a lot of noises."

"I better call for an ambulance," said Charlie. "You better stay here."

"I intend to," I said, and stood there resting against the railing for five minutes watching Fishman. During this time, Nick and Charlie went down and unfolded him and mopped at his face and bald head, which was broken with huge lacerations.

Charlie and me left the others there and drove slowly in the wake of the screaming ambulance which was taking Fishman to Central Receiving Hospital.

"How bad is your leg cut?" asked Charlie, seeing the blood, a purple wine color when it soaks through a policeman's blue uniform.

"Not bad, Charlie," I said, dabbing at the cuts on my hands.

"Your face doesn't look bad. Little cut over your eye."

"I feel fine."

"There was a room across from the back office," said Charlie. "We found a gas-fed burn oven in there. It was fired up and vented through the roof. They would've got to it if you hadn't crashed through the window. I'm thankful you did it, Bumper. You saved everything for us."

"Glad I could help."

"Did Fishman try to fight you or anything?"

"He struggled a little. He just fell."

"I hope the little asshole dies. I'm thinking what he means to the organization and what he is, and I hope the little asshole dies, so help me God. You know, I thought you pushed him for a minute. I thought you did it and I was glad."

"He just fell, Charlie."

"Here we are, let's get you cleaned up," said Charlie, parking on the Sixth Street side of Central Receiving where a doctor was going into the ambulance that carried Fishman. The doctor came out in a few seconds and waved them on to General Hospital where there are better surgical facilities.

"How's he look, Doctor?" asked Charlie, as we walked through the emergency entrance.

"Not good," said the doctor.

"Think he'll die?" asked Charlie.

"I don't know. If he doesn't, he may wish he had."

The cut on my leg took a few stitches but the ones on my hands and face weren't bad and just took cleaning and a little germ killer. It was almost seven o'clock when I finished my reports telling how Fishman jerked out of my grasp and how I got cut.

When I left, Charlie was dictating his arrest report to a typist.

"Well, I'll be going now, Charlie," I said, and he stopped his dictation and stood up and walked with me a little way down the hall and looked for a second like he was going to shake hands with me.

"Thanks, Bumper, for everything. This is the best vice pinch I've ever been in on. We got more of their records than I could've dreamed of."

"Thanks for cutting me in on it, Charlie."

"It was *your* caper."

"Wonder how Fishman's doing?" I said, getting a sharp pain and feeling a bubble forming. I popped two tablets.

"Fuzzy called out there about a half hour ago. Couldn't find out much. I'll tell you one thing, I'll bet Red Scalotta has to get a new accountant and business advisor. I'll bet Fishman'll have trouble adding two-digit numbers after this."

"Well, maybe it worked out right."

"Right? It was more than that. For the first time in years I feel like maybe there *is* some justice in the world, and even though they fuck over you and rub it in your face and fuck over the law itself, well, now for the first time I feel like maybe there's other hands in it, and these hands'll give you some justice. I feel like the hand of God pushed that man down those stairs."

"The hand of God, huh? Yeah, well I'll be seeing you, Charlie. Hang in there, old shoe."

"See you, Bumper," said Charlie Bronski, his square face lit up, eyes crinkled, the broken tooth showing.

The locker room was empty when I got there, and after I sat down on the bench and started unlacing my boondockers, I suddenly realized how sore I was. Not the cuts from the glass, that was nothing. But my shoulder where I fell in that alley, and my arms and back from dangling there on that fire escape, when I couldn't do what any young cop could do—pull my ass up six feet in the air. And my hands were blistered and raw from hanging there and from clawing at the concrete wall trying to get that boost. Even my ass was sore, deep inside, the muscles of both cheeks, from kicking against that steel reinforced door and bouncing off it like a tennis ball, or maybe in my case like a lumpy medicine ball. I was very very sore all over.

In fifteen minutes I'd gotten into my sport coat and slacks, and combed my hair as best I could, which just means rearranging what resembles a bad wiring job, and slipped on my loafers, and was driving out of the parking lot in my Ford. The gas pains were gone, and no indigestion. Then I thought of Aaron Fishman again, folded over, his gouged head twisted under the puny little body with the big cardboard box on top. But I stopped that nonsense right there, and said, no, no, you won't haunt my sleep because it doesn't matter a bit that I made you fall. I was just the instrument of some force in this world that, when the time is right, screws over almost every man, good or bad, rich or poor, and usually does it just when the man can bear it least.

## 14

IT WAS DARK NOW, and the spring night, and the cool breeze, even the smog, all tasted good to me. I rolled the windows down to suck up the air, and jumped on the Hollywood Freeway, thinking how good it would be at Abd's Harem with a bunch of happy Arabs.

Hollywood was going pretty good for a Thursday night, Sunset and Hollywood Boulevards both being jammed with cars, mostly young people, teeny boppers who've literally taken over Hollywood at night. The place has lost the real glamour of the forties and early fifties. It's a kid's town now, and except for a million hippies, fruits and servicemen, that's about all you see around the Strip and the main thoroughfares. It's a very depressing place for that reason. The clubs are mostly bottomless skin houses and psychedelic joints, but there're still some places you can go, some excellent places to eat.

I'd come to know Yasser Hafiz and the others some ten or twelve years ago when I was walking my beat on Main Street. One night at about two a.m., I spotted a paddy hustler taking a guy up the back stairs of the Marlowe Hotel, a sleazy Main Street puke hole used by whores and fruits and paddy hustlers. I was alone because my partner, a piss-poor excuse for a cop named Syd Bacon, was laying up in a hotel room knocking a chunk off some bubble-assed taxi dancer he was going with. He was supposed to meet me back on the beat at one-thirty but never showed up.

I hurried around the front of the hotel that night and went up the other stairway and hid behind the deserted clerk's desk, and when the paddy hustler and his victim came that way down the hall, I jumped inside the small closet at the desk. I was just in time because the paddy hustler's two partners came out of a room two doors down and across the hall.

They were whispering, and one of them faded down the front stairway to watch the street. The second walked behind the desk, turned the lamp on and pretended to be reading a newspaper he carried with him. They were black of course. Paddy hustling was always a Negro flimflam and that's where the name came from, but lately I've seen white hustlers using this scam on other paddies.

"Say, brother," said the hustler who was with the paddy. I left the door open a crack and saw the paddy was a well-dressed young guy, bombed out of his skull, weaving around where he stood, trying hard to brush his thick black hair out of his eyes. He'd lost his necktie somewhere, and his white dress shirt was stained from booze and unbuttoned.

"Wha's happenin', blood?" said the desk clerk, putting down his paper.

"Alice in tonight?" said the first one, acting as the procurer. He was the bigger of the two, a very dark-skinned guy, tall and fairly young.

"Yeah, she's breathin' fire tonight," said the other one. He was young too. "Ain't had no man yet and that bitch is a nymphomaniac!"

"Really," said the procurer. "Really."

"Let's go, I'm ready," said the paddy, and I noticed his Middle East accent.

"Jist a minute, man," said his companion. "That whore is fine pussy, but she is a stone thief, man. You better leave the wallet with the desk clerk."

"Yeah, I kin put it in the safe," said the bored-look-ing guy behind the desk. "Never tell when that whore might talk you into a all-night ride and then rob your ass when you falls asleep."

"Right, brother," said the procurer.

The paddy shrugged and took out his wallet, put-ting it on the desk.

"Better leave the wristwatch and ring, too," warned the desk clerk.

"Thank you," the paddy nodded, obeying the desk clerk, who removed an envelope from under the counter, which he had put there for the valuables.

"Kin I have my five dollars now?" asked the first man. "And the clerk'll take the five for Alice and three for the room."

"All right," said the paddy, unsteadily counting out thirteen dollars for the two men.

"Now you go on in number two-thirty-seven there," said the desk clerk, pointing to the room where the first one had come out. "I'll buzz Alice's room and she be in there in 'bout five minutes. And baby, you better hold on 'cause she move like a steam drill."

The paddy smiled nervously and staggered down the hall, opening the door and disappearing inside.

"Ready, blood?" grinned the desk clerk.

"Le's go," said the big one, chuckling as the clerk turned off the lamp.

I'd come out of the closet without them seeing, and stood at the desk now, with my Smith pointed at the right eyeball of the desk clerk. "Want a room for the night, gentlemen?" I said. "Our accommodations ain't fancy, but it's clean and we can offer two very square meals a day."

The procurer was the first to recover, and he was trying to decide whether to run or try something more dangerous. Paddy hustlers didn't usually carry guns, but they often carried blades or crude saps of some kind. I aimed at *his* eyeball to quiet down his busy mind. "Freeze, or name your beneficiary," I said.

"Hey, Officer, wha's happenin'?" said the desk clerk with a big grin showing lots of gold. "Where you come from?"

"Down the chimney. Now get your asses over there and spread-eagle on the wall!"

"Sheee-it, this is a humbug, we ain't done nothin'," said the procurer.

"Shit fuck," grumbled the desk clerk.

This was in the days when we still believed in wall searches, before so damn many policemen got shot or thumped by guys who practiced coming out of that spread-eagled position. I abandoned it a few days before the Department did, and I put hot suspects on their knees or bellies. But at this time I was still using the wall search.

"Move your legs back, desk clerk!" I said to the smaller one, who was being cute, barely leaning forward. He only shuffled his feet a few inches so I kicked him hard behind the right knee and he screamed and did what I told him. The scream brought the paddy out.

"Is something wrong?" asked the paddy who was half-undressed, trying to look sober as possible.

"I'm saving you from being flimflammed, asshole," I said. "Get your clothes on and come out here." He just stood there gaping. Then I yelled, "Get dressed, stupid!" my gun in my left hand still pointing at the spread-eagled paddy hustlers, and my handcuffs in my right hand getting ready to cuff the two hustlers together, and my eyes drilling the dipshit victim who stood there getting ready to ask more dumb questions. I didn't see or hear the third paddy hustler, a big bull of a kid, who'd crept up the front stairway when he heard the ruckus. If he'd been an experienced hustler instead of a youngster he'd have left the other two and gone his way. But being inexperienced, he was loyal to his partners, and just as I was getting ready to kick the paddy in the ass to get him moving, two hundred

pounds falls on my back and I'm on the floor fighting
for my gun and my life with all three hustlers.

"Git the gun, Tyrone!" yelled the desk clerk to the
kid. "Jist git the *gun!*"

The procurer was cursing and hitting me in the face,
head, and neck, anywhere he could, and the desk clerk
was working on my ribs while I tried to protect myself
with my left arm. All my thoughts were on the right
arm, and hand, and the gun in the hand, which the kid
was prying on with both his strong hands. For a few
seconds everything was quiet, except for the moans
and breathing and muffled swearing of the four of us,
and then the kid was winning and almost had the gun
worked loose when I heard a godawful Arab war cry
and the paddy cracked the desk clerk over the head
with a heavy metal ashtray.

Then the paddy was swinging it with both hands
and I ducked my head, catching a glancing blow on
the shoulder that made me yelp and which left a
bruise as big as your fist. The fourth or fifth swing
caught the procurer in the eyes and he was done, laying there holding his bleeding face and yelling,
"YOW, YOW, YOW," like somebody cut his nuts off.

The kid lost his stomach at this point and said, "Aw
right, aw right, aw right," raising his hands to surrender and scooting back on his ass with his hands in the
air until he backed against the wall.

I was so sick and trembling I could've vomited and I
was ready to kill all three of them, except that the desk
clerk and the procurer looked half-dead already. The
kid was untouched.

"Stand up," I said to the kid, and when he did, I put
my gun in the holster, reached for my beavertail, and
sapped him across the left collarbone. That started
him yelling and bitching, and he didn't stop until we
got him to the hospital, which made me completely
disgusted. Up until then I had some respect for him
because he was loyal to his friends and had enough
guts to jump a cop who had a gun in his hand. But

when he couldn't suffer in silence, he lost my respect. I figured this kind of crybaby'd probably make a complaint against me for police brutality or something, but he never did.

"What can I do, sir?" asked the paddy after I had the three hustlers halfway on their feet. I was trying to stay on mine as I leaned against the desk and covered them with the gun. This time I kept my eyes open.

"Go downstairs and put a dime in the pay phone and dial operator," I panted, still not sure how sober he was, even though he damn near decapitated all of us. "Ask for the police and tell them an officer needs assistance at the Marlowe Hotel, Fifth and Main."

"Marlowe Hotel," said the paddy. "Yes, sir."

I never found out what he said over the phone, but he must've laid it on pretty good because in three minutes I had patrol units, vice cops, felony cars, and even some dicks who rolled from the station. There were more cops than tenants at the Marlowe and the street out front was lined with radio cars, their red lights glowing clear to Sixth Street.

The paddy turned out to be Yasser's oldest son, Abd, the one the Harem was named for, and that was how I got to know them. Abd stayed with me for several hours that night while I made my reports, and he seemed like a pretty good guy after he had a dozen cups of coffee and sobered up. He had a very bad recollection of the whole thing when we went to court against the paddy hustlers, and he ended up testifying to what I told him happened before we went in the courtroom. That part about saving my ass, he never did remember, and when I drove him home to Hollywood after work that night, in gratitude for what he did for me, he took me in the house, woke up his father, mother, uncle, and three of his brothers to introduce me and tell them that I saved him from being robbed and killed by three bandits. Of course he never told them the whole truth about how the thing went down in a whorehouse, but that was okay with me,

and since he really thought *I* saved *him* instead of the
other way around, and since he really enjoyed having
been saved even though it didn't happen, and making
me the family hero, what the hell, I let him tell it the
way he believed it happened so as not to disappoint
them.

It was about that time that Yasser and his clan had
moved here from New York where they had a small
restaurant. They had pooled every cent they could lay
hands on to buy the joint in Hollywood, liquor license
and all, and had it remodeled and ready to open. We
sat in Yasser's kitchen that night, all of us, drinking
*arak* and wine, and then beer, and we all got pretty
zonked except Abd who was sick, and I picked out the
name for the new restaurant.

It's a corny name, I know, but I was drunk when I
picked it and I could've done better. But by then I was
such a hero to them they wouldn't have changed it for
anything. They insisted on me being a kind of perma-
nent guest of Abd's Harem. I couldn't pay for a thing
in there and that's why I didn't come as often as I
wanted to.

I drove in the parking lot in back of Abd's Harem
instead of having the parking lot attendant handle the
Ford, and I came in through the kitchen.

"*Al-salām 'alaykum, Baba*," I said to Yasser Hafiz
Hammad, a squat, completely bald old man with a
heavy gray moustache, who had his back to me as
he mixed up a huge metal bowlful of *kibbi* with
clean powerful hands which he dipped often in ice
water so the *kibbi* wouldn't stick to them.

"Bumper! *Wa-'alaykum al-salām*," he grinned
through the great moustache. He hugged me with his
arms, keeping his hands free, and kissed me on the
mouth. That was something I couldn't get over about
Arabs. They didn't usually kiss women in greeting,
only men.

"Where the hell you keep yourself, Bumper?" he

said, dipping a spoon in the raw *kibbi* for me to sample it. "We don't see you much no more."

"Delicious, *Baba*," I said.

"Yes, but is it ber-fect?"

"It's ber-fect, *Bubba*."

"You hungry, eh, Bumper?" he said, returning to the *kibbi* and making me some little round balls which he knew I'd eat raw. I liked raw *kibbi* every bit as good as baked, and *kibbi* with yogurt even better.

"You making *labaneeyee* tonight, *Baba*?"

"Sure, Bumper. Damn right. What else you want? *Sfeeha*? *Bamee*? Anything you want. We got lots of dish tonight. Bunch of Lebanese and Syrian guys in the banquet room. Ten entrées they order special. Son of a bitch, I cook all goddamn day. When I get rest, I coming out and have a goddamn glass of *arak* with you, okay?"

"Okay, *Baba*," I said, finishing the *kibbi* and watching Yasser work. He kneaded the ground lamb and cracked wheat and the onion and cinnamon and spices, after dipping his hands in the ice water to keep the mixture pliable. This *kibbi* was well stuffed with pine nuts and the meat was cooked in butter and braised. When Yasser got it all ready he spread the *kibbi* over the bottom of a metal pan and the *kibbi* stuffing over the top of that, and another layer of *kibbi* on top of that. He cut the whole pan into little diamond shapes and then baked it. Now I couldn't decide whether to have the *kibbi* with yogurt or the baked *kibbi*. What the hell, I'll have them both, I thought. I was pretty hungry now.

"Look, Bumper," said Yasser Hafiz, pointing to the little footballs of *kibbi* he'd been working on all day. He'd pressed hollows into the center and stuffed them with lamb stuffing and was cooking them in a yogurt sauce.

Yeah, I'll have both, I thought. I decided to go in and start on some appetizers. I was more than hungry all of a sudden and not quite so tired, and all I could think of was the wonderful food of Abd's Harem.

Inside, I spotted Ahmed right away, and he grinned and waved me to a table near the small dance area where one of his dancers could shove her belly in my face. Ahmed was tall for an Arab, about thirty years old, the youngest of Yasser's sons, and had lived in the States since he was a kid. He'd lost a lot of the Arab ways and didn't kiss me like his father and his uncles did, when the uncles were here helping wait tables or cooking on a busy weekend night.

"Glad you could come tonight, Bumper," said Ahmed with a hint of a New York accent, since his family had lived there several years before coming to Los Angeles. When he talked to the regular customers though, he put on a Middle East accent for show.

"Think I'll have some appetizers, Ahmed. I'm hungry tonight."

"Good, Bumper, good," said Ahmed, his dark eyes crinkling at the corners when he grinned. "We like to see you eat." He clapped his hands for a good-looking, red-haired waitress in a harem girl's outfit, and she came over to the table.

Abd's Harem was like all Middle East restaurants, but bigger than most. There were Saracen shields on the walls, and scimitars, and imitation Persian tapestries, and the booths and tables were dark and heavy, leather-padded, and studded with hammered bronzework. Soothing Arab music drifted through the place from several hidden speakers.

"Bring Bumper some lamb tongue, Barbara. What else would you like, Bumper?"

"A little *humos tahini*, Ahmed."

"Right. *Humos* too, Barbara."

Barbara smiled at me and said, "A drink, Bumper?"

"All right, I'll have *arak*."

"If you'll excuse me, Bumper," said Ahmed, "I've got to take care of the banquet room for the next hour. Then I'll join you and we'll have a drink together."

"Go head on, kid," I nodded. "Looks like you're gonna have a nice crowd."

"Business is great, Bumper. Wait'll you see our new belly dancer."

I nodded and winked as Ahmed hurried toward the banquet room to take care of the roomful of Arabs. I could hear them from where I sat, proposing toasts and laughing. They seemed pretty well lubricated for so early in the evening.

The appetizers were already prepared and the waitress was back to my table in a few minutes with the little slices of lamb's tongue, boiled and peeled and seasoned with garlic and salt, and a good-sized dish of *humos*, which makes the greatest dip in the world. She gave me more *humos* than any of the paying customers get, and a large heap of the round flat pieces of warm Syrian bread covered with a napkin. I dipped into the *humos* right away with a large chunk of the Syrian bread and almost moaned out loud it was so delicious. I could taste the sesame seeds even though they were ground into the creamy blend of garbanzo beans, and I poured olive oil all over it, and dipped lots of oil up in my bread. I could also taste the clove and crushed garlic and almost forgot the lamb tongue I was enjoying the *humos* so much.

"Here's your *arak*, Bumper," said Barbara, bringing me the drink and another dish of *humos* a little smaller than the first. "Yasser says not to let you ruin your dinner with the tongue and *humos*."

"No chance, kid," I said, after swallowing a huge mouthful of tongue and bread. I gulped some *arak* so I could talk. "Tell *Baba* I'm as hungry as a tribe of Bedouins and I'll eat out his whole kitchen if he's not careful."

"And as horny as a herd of goats?"

"Yeah, tell him that too," I chuckled. That was a standing joke between Yasser and Ahmed and me that all the girls had heard.

Now that the starvation phase was over I started to

feel pain in my leg and shoulder. I poured some water into the clear *arak*, turning it milky. I glanced around to make sure no one could see and I loosened up my belt and smiled to myself as I smelled the food all through the place. I nibbled now, and tried not to be such a crude bastard, and I sipped my *arak*, getting three refills from Barbara who was a fast and good waitress. Then the pain started to go away.

I saw Ahmed running between kitchen, bar, and banquet room, and I thought that Yasser was lucky to have such good kids. All his sons had done well, and now the last one was staying in the business with him. The Arab music drifted slowly through the place and mingled with the food smell, and I was feeling damn warm now. In about an hour the band would be here, a three-piece Armenian group who played exotic music for the belly dancer that I was anxious to see. Ahmed really knew his dancers.

"Everything okay, Bumper?" Ahmed called in an Arab accent since other customers were around.

"Okay," I grinned, and he hurried past on one of his trips to the kitchen.

I was starting to sway with the sensual drums and I was feeling much better, admiring the rugs hanging on the walls, and other Arabian Nights decorations like water pipes that kids used now for smoking dope, and the swords up high enough on the walls so some drunk couldn't grab them and start his own dance. Abd's Harem was a very good place, I thought. Really an oasis in the middle of a tacky, noisy part of Hollywood which was generally so phony I couldn't stand it.

I noticed that Khalid, one of Yasser's brothers, was helping in the bar tonight. I figured as soon as he saw me I'd get another big hairy kiss.

"Ready, Bumper?" said Barbara, smiling pretty, and padding quietly up to my table with a huge tray on a food cart.

"Yeah, yeah," I said, looking at the dishes of baked

*kibbi, kibbi* with yogurt, stuffed grape leaves and a small skewer of shish kebab.

"Yasser said to save room for dessert, Bumper," said Barbara as she left me there. I could think of nothing at times like these, except the table in front of me, and I waged a tough fight against myself to eat slowly and savor it, especially the grape leaves which were a surprise for me, because Yasser doesn't make them all the time. I could taste the mint, fragrant and tangy in the yogurt that I ladled over the grape leaves, pregnant with lamb and rice, succulent parsley, and spices. Yasser added just the right amount of lemon juice for my taste.

After a while, Barbara returned and smiled at me as I sat sipping my wine, at peace with the world.

"Some pastry, Bumper? *Baklawa?*"

"Oh no, Barbara," I said, holding my hand up weakly. "Too rich. No *baklawa*, no."

"All right," she laughed. "Yasser has something special for you. Did you save a little room?"

"Oh no," I said painfully, as she took away the cartload of empty plates.

Arabs are so friendly and hospitable, and they like so much to see me eat, I would've hated to do something horrible like upchucking all his hard work. My belly was bulging so much I had to move the chair back two inches, and my shirt was straining to pop open. I thought of Fatstuff in the old "Smilin' Jack" cartoon strip and remembered how I used to laugh at the poor bastard always popping his buttons, when I was young and slim.

A few minutes later Barbara came back with an oversized sherbet glass.

"*Moosh moosh!*" I said. "I haven't had *moosh moosh* for a year."

Barbara smiled and said, "Yasser says that Allah sent you tonight because Yasser made your favorite dessert today and thought about you."

"*Moosh moosh!*" I said as Barbara left me, and I

scooped up a mouthful and let it lay there on my tongue, tasting the sweet apricot and lemon rind, and remembering how Yasser's wife, Yasmine, blended the apricot and lemon rind and sugar, and folded the apricot purée into the whipped cream before it was chilled. They all knew it was my very favorite. So I ended up having two more cups of *moosh moosh* and then I was really through. Barbara cleared the table for the last time and Ahmed and Yasser both joined me for ten minutes.

There's an Arab prayer which translates something like, "Give me a good digestion, Lord, and something to digest." It was the only prayer I ever heard that I thought made a lot of sense, and I thought that if I believed in God I wouldn't lay around begging from Him and mumbling a lot of phony promises. This particular Arab prayer said all I'd say to Him, and all I'd expect of Him, so even though I didn't believe, I said it before and after I ate dinner in Abd's Harem. Sometimes I even said it at other times. Sometimes even at home I said it.

When the Armenians arrived, I was happy to see the *oud* player was old Mr. Kamian. He didn't often play at Abd's Harem anymore. His grandsons Berge and George were with him, and anyone could see they were his grandsons, all three being tall, thin, with hawk noses and dark-rimmed blazing eyes. Berge would play the violin and George, the youngest, a boy not yet twenty, would play the *darbuka* drums. It was just a job to the two young ones. They were good musicians, but it was old Kamian I would hear as he plucked and stroked those *oud* strings with the quill of an eagle feather. It's a lute-like instrument and has no frets like a guitar. Yet the old man's fingers knew exactly where to dance on that *oud* neck, so fast it was hard to believe. It gave me goose bumps and made it hard to swallow when I saw that old man's slender, brittle-looking fingers dart over those twelve strings.

Once I was there in the afternoon when they were

rehearsing new dancers, and old Kamian was telling Armenian tales to Berge's children. I sat there hidden behind a beaded curtain and heard Kamian tell about the fiery horses of Armenia, and pomegranates full of pearls and rubies, and about Hazaran-Bulbul, the magic nightingale of a thousand songs. He made me feel like a kid that day listening to him, and ever since, when I hear him play the *oud*, I could almost climb aboard one of those fiery horses.

Another time when I was here late at night listening to Mr. Kamian play, his oldest son Leon sat with me drinking scotch and told me the story of his father, how he was the only survivor of a large family which totaled, cousins and all, half of a village that was massacred by Turkish soldiers. Mr. Kamian was fifteen years old then, and his body was left in a big ditch with those of his parents, brothers, sisters, everyone in his entire world.

"The thing that saved him that day was the *smell* of death," said Leon, who spoke five languages, English with only a slight accent, and like all Armenians, loved to tell stories. "As he lay there, my father wanted to be dead with the others. It wasn't the sight or idea of death that made him drag himself up and out of that ditch, it was the smell of rotting bodies which at last was the only unbearable thing, and which drove him to the road and away from his village forever.

"For almost a year he wandered, his only possession an *oud* which he rescued from a plundered farmhouse. One night when he was huddling alone in the wilderness like Cain, feeling like the only human being left on earth, he became very angry that God would let this happen, and like the child he was, he *demanded* a sign from Him, and he waited and listened in the darkness, but he heard only the wind howling across the Russian steppes. Then he wondered how he could ever have believed in a God who would let this happen to Armenia, His tiny Christian island in a sea of Islam. There was no sign, so he strummed the *oud* and sang brave songs into the wind all that night.

"The very next night the boy was wandering through a village much like his had been, and of course he passed hundreds of starving refugees on the road. He took off from the road to find a place to sleep in the trees where someone wouldn't kill him just to steal the *oud*. There in the woods he saw a black sinister shape rising from the ground, and the first thing the boy thought was that it was a *dev*, one of those fearsome Armenian ogres his *nany* used to tell him about. He raised the flimsy *oud* like it was an ax and prepared to defend himself. Then the dark form took shape and spoke to him in Armenian from beneath a ragged cloak, 'Please, do you have something to eat?'

"The boy saw a child in the moonlight, covered with sores, stomach bloated, barely able to walk. Her teeth were loose, eyes and gums crusted, and a recently broken nose made it hard for her to breathe. He examined her face and saw that at no time could that face have been more than homely, but now it was truly awful. He spoke to her a few moments and found she was thirteen years old, a wandering refugee, and he remembered the proud and vain demand he had made of God the night before. He began to laugh then, and suddenly felt stronger. He couldn't stop laughing and the laughter filled him with strength. It alarmed the girl, and he saw it, and finally he said, 'The God of Armenians has a sense of humor. How can you doubt someone with a sense of humor like His? You're to come with me, my little *dev*.'

"'What do you want of me, sir?' she asked, very frightened now.

"'What do I want of you?' he answered softly. 'Look at you. What do you have to offer? Everything has been taken from you and everything has been done to you. What could anyone in the world possibly want of you now? Can you think of what it is, the thing I want?'

"'No, sir.'

"'There is only one thing left. To *love* you, of course. We're good for no more than this. Now come with me. We're going to find *our* Armenia.'

"She went with the half-starved, wild-eyed boy. They survived together and wandered to the Black Sea, somehow got passage, and crossed on foot through Europe, through the war and fighting, ever westward to the Atlantic, working, having children. Finally, in 1927, they and five children, having roamed half the world, arrived in New York, and from force of habit more than anything, kept wandering west, picking up jobs along the way until they reached the Pacific Ocean. Then my mother said, 'This is as far as we go. This ocean is too big.' And they stopped, had four more children, sixty-one grandchildren, and so far, ten great-grandchildren, more than forty with the Kamian name that would not die in the ditch in Armenia. Most of his sons and grandsons have done well, and he still likes to come here sometimes once a week and play his *oud* for a few people who understand."

So that was the story of old Kamian, and I didn't doubt any of it, because I've known a lot of tough bastards in my time that could've pulled off something like that, but the thing that amazed me, that I couldn't really understand, is how he could've taken the little girl with him that night. I mean he could've helped her, sure. But he purposely *gave* himself to her that night. After what he'd already been through, he up and *gave* himself to somebody! That was the most incredible thing about Mr. Kamian, that, and how the hell his fingers knew exactly where to go on that *oud* when there were no frets to guide them.

"You eat plenty, Bumper?" asked Yasser, who came to the table with Ahmed, and I responded by giving him a fatcat grin and patting him on the hand, and whispering *"shukran"* in a way that you would know meant thanks without knowing Arabic.

"Maybe you'll convert me, feeding me like that. Maybe I'll become a Moslem," I added.

"What you do during Ramadan when you must fast?" laughed Yasser.

"You see how *big* Abd's kids?" said Yasser, lifting his apron to reach for his wallet, and laying some snapshots on me that I pretended I could see.

"Yeah, handsome kids," I said, hoping the old man wouldn't start showing me all his grandkids. He had about thirty of them, and like all Arabs, was crazy about children.

Ahmed spoke in Arabic that had to do with the banquet room, and Yasser seemed to remember something.

"Scoose me, Bumper," said the old boy, "I come back later, but I got things in the kitchen."

"Sure, *Baba*," I said, and Ahmed smiled as he watched his father strut back to the kitchen, the proud patriarch of a large family, and the head of a very good business, which Abd's Harem certainly was.

"How old is your father now?"

"Seventy-five," said Ahmed. "Looks good, doesn't he?"

"Damn good. Tell me, can he still eat like he used to, say ten, fifteen years ago?"

"He eats pretty well," Ahmed laughed. "But no, not like he used to. He used to eat like you, Bumper. It was a joy to watch him eat. He says food doesn't taste quite the same anymore."

I started getting gas pains, but didn't pop a tablet because it would be rude for Ahmed to see me do that after I'd just finished such a first-rate dinner.

"It'd be a terrible thing for your appetite to go," I said. "That'd be almost as bad as being castrated."

"Then I never want to get *that* old, Bumper," Ahmed laughed, with the strength and confidence of only thirty years on this earth. "Of course there's a third thing, remember, your digestion? Got to have that, too."

"Oh yeah," I said. "Got to have digestion or appetite ain't worth a damn."

Just then the lights dimmed, and a bluish spot danced around the small bandstand as the drums started first. Then I was amazed to see Laila Hammad run out to the floor, in a gold-and-white belly dancer's costume, and the music picked up as she stood there, chestnut hair hanging down over her boobs, fingers writhing, and working the *zils*, those little golden finger cymbals, hips swaying as George's hands beat a blood-heating rhythm on the *darbuka*. Ahmed grinned at me as I admired her strong golden thighs.

"How do you like our new dancer?"

"Laila's your dancer?"

"Wait'll you see her," said Ahmed, and it was true, she really was something. There was art to the dancing, not just lusty gyrations, and though I'm no judge of belly dancing, even I could see it.

"How old is she now?" I said to Ahmed, watching her mobile stomach, and the luxurious chestnut hair, which was all her own, and now hung down her back and then streamed over her wonderful-looking boobs.

"She's nineteen," said Ahmed, and I was very happy to see how good-looking she'd turned out.

Laila had worked as a waitress here for a few years, even when she was much too young to be doing it, but she always looked older, and her father, Khalil Hammad, was a cousin of Yasser's, who lingered for years with cancer, running up tremendous hospital bills before he finally died. Laila was a smart, hard-working girl, and helped support her three younger sisters. Ahmed once told me Laila never really knew her mother, an American broad who left them when they were little kids. I'd heard Laila was working in a bank the last couple years and doing okay.

You could really see the Arab blood in Laila now, in the sensual face, the nose a little too prominent but just suiting her, and in the wide full mouth, and glittering brown eyes. No wonder they were passionate people, I thought, with faces like that. Yes, Laila was a jewel, like a fine half-Arab mare with enough American blood to give good height and those terrific thighs. I wondered if Ahmed had anything going with her. Then Laila started "sprinkling salt" as the Arabs say. She revolved slowly on the ball of one bare foot, jerking a hip to each beat of the *darbuka*. And if there'd been a small bag of salt tied to the throbbing hip, she would've made a perfect ring of salt on the floor around her. It's a hot, graceful move, not hard at all. I do it myself to hard-rock music.

When Laila was finished with her dance and ran off the floor and the applause died down I said, "She's beautiful, Ahmed. Why don't you con her into marrying you?"

"Not interested," said Ahmed, shaking his head. He leaned over the table and took a sip of wine before speaking. "There's rumors, Bumper. Laila's supposed to be whoring."

"I can't believe that," I said, remembering her again as a teenage waitress who couldn't even put her lipstick on straight.

"She left her bank job over a year ago. Started belly dancing professionally. You never knew her when she was a real little tot. I remember when she was three years old and her aunts and uncles taught her to dance. She was the cutest thing you ever saw. She was a smart little girl."

"Where did you hear she was tricking?"

"In this business you hear all about the dancers," said Ahmed. "You know, she's one of the few belly dancers in town that's really an Arab, or rather, half-Arab. She's no cheapie, but she goes to bed with guys if they can pay the tariff. I hear she gets two hundred a night."

"Laila's had a pretty tough life, Ahmed," I said. "She had to raise little sisters. She never had time to be a kid herself."

"Look, I'm not blaming her, Bumper. What the hell, I'm an American. I'm not like the old folks who wait around on the morning after the wedding to make sure there's blood on the bridal sheets. But I have to admit that whoring bothers me. I'm just not that Americanized, I guess. I used to think maybe when Laila got old enough . . . well, it's too late now. I shouldn't have been so damn busy these last few years. I let her get away and now . . . it's just too late."

Ahmed ordered me another drink, then excused himself, saying he'd be back in a little while. I was starting to feel depressed all of a sudden. I wasn't sure if the talk about Laila set it off or what, but I thought about her selling her ass to these wealthy Hollywood creeps. Then I thought about Freddie and Harry, and Poochie and Herky, and Timothy G. for goddamn Landry, but that was *too* depressing to think about. Suddenly for no reason I thought about Esteban Segovia and how I used to worry that he really would become a priest like he wanted to be when he returned from Vietnam, instead of a dentist like I always wanted him to be. That dead boy was about Laila's age when he left. Babies. Nobody should die a baby.

All right, Bumper, I said to myself, let's settle down to some serious drinking. I called Barbara over and ordered a double scotch on the rocks even though I'd mixed my drinks too much and had already more than enough.

After my third scotch I heard a honey-dipped voice say, "Hi, Bumper."

"Laila!" I made a feeble attempt at getting up, as she sat down at my table, looking smooth and cool in a modest white dress, her hair tied back and hanging down one side, her face and arms the color of a golden olive.

"Ahmed told me you were here, Bumper," she smiled, and I lit her cigarette, liberated women be damned, and called Barbara over to get her a drink.

"Can I buy you a drink, kid?" I asked. "It's good to see you all grown up, a big girl and all, looking so damn gorgeous."

She ordered a bourbon and water and laughed at

me, and I knew for sure I was pretty close to being
wiped out. I decided to turn it off after I finished the
scotch I held in my hand.

"I was grown up last time you saw me, Bumper,"
she said, grinning at my clownish attempts to act
sober. "All men appreciate your womanhood better
when they see your bare belly moving for them."

I thought about what Ahmed had told me, and
though it didn't bother me like it did Ahmed, I was
sorry she had to do it, or that she *thought* she had to
do it.

"You mean that slick little belly was moving for ol'
Bumper?" I said, trying to kid her like I used to, but
my brain wasn't working right.

"Sure, for you. Aren't you the hero of this whole
damned family?"

"Well how do you like dancing for a living?"

"It's as crummy as you'd expect."

"Why do you do it?"

"You ever try supporting two sisters on a bank tell-
er's wage?"

"Bullshit," I said too loud, one elbow slipping out
from under me. "Don't give me that crybaby stuff. A
dish like you, why you could marry any rich guy you
wanted."

"Wrong, Bumper. I could screw any rich guy I
wanted. And get paid damn well for it."

"I wish you wouldn't talk like that, Laila."

"You old bear," she laughed, as I rubbed my face
which had no feeling whatever. "I know Ahmed told
you I'm a whore. It just shames the hell out of these
Arabs. You know how subtle they are. Yasser hinted
around the other day that maybe I should change my
name now that I'm show biz. Hammad's too ordinary,
he said. Maybe something more American. They're as
subtle as a boot in the ass. How about Feinberg or
Goldstein, Bumper? I'll bet they wouldn't mind if I
called myself Laila Feinberg. That'd explain my being

a whore to the other Arabs, wouldn't it? They could start a rumor that my mother was a Jew."

"What the hell're you telling *me* all this for?" I said, suddenly getting mad. "Go to a priest or a headshrinker, or go to the goddamn mosque and talk to the Prophet, why don't you? I had enough problems laid on me today. Now you?"

"Will you drive me home, Bumper? I do want to talk to you."

"How many more performances you got to go?" I asked, not sure I could stay upright in my chair if I had another drink.

"I'm through. Marsha's taking my next one for me. I've told Ahmed I'm getting cramps."

I found Ahmed and said good-bye while Laila waited for me in the parking lot. I tipped Barbara fifteen bucks, then I staggered into the kitchen, thanked Yasser, and kissed him on the big moustache while he hugged me and made me promise to come to his house in the next few weeks.

Laila was in the parking lot doing her best to ignore two well-dressed drunks in a black Lincoln. When they saw me staggering across the parking lot in their direction the driver stomped on it, laid a patch of rubber, and got the hell out.

"Lord, I don't blame them," Laila laughed. "You look wild and dangerous, Bumper. How'd you get those scratches on your face?"

"My Ford's right over there," I said, walking like Frankenstein's monster so I could stay on a straight course.

"The same old car? Oh, Bumper." She laughed like a kid and she put my arm around her and steered me to my Ford, but around to the passenger side. Then she patted my pockets, found my keys, got them, pushed me in, and closed the door behind me.

"Light-fingered broad," I mumbled. "You ever been a hugger-mugger?"

"What was that, Bumper?" she said, getting behind the wheel and cranking her up.

"Nothing, nothing," I mumbled, rubbing my face again.

I dozed while Laila drove. She turned the radio on and hummed, and she had a pretty good voice too. In fact, it put me to sleep, and she had to shake me awake when we got to her pad.

"I'm going to pour you some muddy Turkish coffee and we're going to talk," she said, helping me out of the Ford, and for a second the sidewalk came up in my eyes, but I closed them and stood there and everything righted itself.

"Ready to try the steps, Bumper?"

"As I'll ever be, kid."

"Let's get it on," she said, my arm around her wide shoulders, and she guided me up. She was a big strong girl. Ahmed was nuts, I thought. She'd make a hell of a wife for him or *any* young guy.

It took some doing but we reached the third floor of her apartment building, a very posh place, which was actually three L-shaped buildings scattered around two Olympic-sized pools. Mostly catered to swinging singles which reminded me of the younger sisters.

"The girls home?" I asked.

"I live alone during the school year, Bumper. Nadia lives in the dorm at U.S.C. She's a freshman. Dalal boards at Ramona Convent. She'll be going to college next year."

"Ramona Convent? I thought you were a Moslem."

"I'm nothing."

We got in the apartment and Laila guided me past the soft couch, which looked pretty good to sleep on, and dumped me in a straight-backed kitchen chair after taking off my sport coat and hanging it in a closet.

"You even wear a gun off duty?" she asked as she ladled out some coffee and ran some water from the tap.

"Yeah," I said, not knowing what she was talking

about for a minute, I was so used to the gun. "This job makes you a coward. I don't even go out without it in this town anymore, except to Harry's bar or somewhere in the neighborhood."

"If I saw all the things you have, maybe I'd be afraid to go out without one too," she shrugged.

I didn't know I was dozing again until I smelled Laila there shaking me awake, a tiny cup of Turkish coffee thick and dark on a saucer in front of me. I smelled her sweetness and then I felt her cool hand again and then I saw her wide mouth smiling.

"Maybe I should spoon it down your throat till you get sober."

"I'm okay," I said, rubbing my face and head.

I drank the coffee as fast as I could even though it scalded my mouth and throat. Then she poured me another, and I excused myself, went to the head, took a leak, washed my face in cold water, and combed my hair. I was still bombed when I came back, but at least I wasn't a zombie.

Laila must've figured I was in good enough shape. "Let me turn on some music, Bumper, then we can talk."

"Okay." I finished the second cup almost as fast as the first and poured myself a third.

The soft stirring song of an Arab girl singer filled the room for a second and then Laila turned down the volume. It's a wailing kind of plaintive sound, almost like a chant at times, but it gets to you, at least it did to me, and I always conjured up mental pictures of the Temple of Karnak, and Giza, and the streets of Damascus, and a picture I once saw of a Bedouin on a pink granite cliff in the blinding sun looking out over the Valley of the Kings. I saw in his face that he knew more about history, even though he was probably illiterate, than I ever would, and I promised myself I'd go there to die when I got old. If I ever did *get* old, that is.

"I still like the old music," Laila smiled, nodding to-

ward the stereo set. "Most people don't like it. I can
put on something else if you want."

"Don't touch it," I said, and Laila looked in my eyes
and seemed glad.

"I need your help, Bumper."

"Okay, what is it?"

"I want you to talk to my probation officer for me."

"You're on probation? What for?"

"Prostitution. The Hollywood vice cops got three of
us in January. I pleaded guilty and was put on probation."

"Whadda you want me to do?"

"I wasn't given *summary* probation like my lousy
thousand-dollar lawyer promised. I got a tough judge
and I have to report to a P.O. for two years. I want to
go somewhere and I need permission."

"Where you going?"

"Somewhere to have a baby. I want to go somewhere, have my baby, adopt it out, and come back."

She saw the 'Why me? Why in the hell me?' look in
my eyes.

"Bumper, I need you for this. I don't want my sisters
to know anything. Nothing, you hear? They'd only
want to raise the baby and for God's sake, it's hard
enough making it in this filthy world when you know
who the hell your two parents are and have them to
raise you. I've got a plan and you're the only one my
whole damned tribe would listen to without question.
They trust you completely. I want you to tell Yasser
and Ahmed and all of them that you don't think I
should be dancing for a living, and that you have a
friend in New Orleans who has a good-paying office
job for me. And then tell the same thing to my P.O.
and convince her it's the truth. Then I'll disappear for
seven or eight months and come back and tell everyone I didn't like the job or something. They'll all get
mad as blazes but that'll be it."

"Where the hell you going?"

"What's it matter?" she shrugged. "Anywhere to have the kid and farm it out. To New Orleans. Wherever."

"You're not joining the coat hanger corps are you?"

"An abortion?" she laughed. "No, I figure when you make a mistake you should have the guts to at least see it through. I won't shove it down a garbage disposal. I was raised an Arab and I can't change."

"You got any money?"

"I've got thirteen thousand in a bank account. I'd like you to handle it for me and see that the girls have enough to get them through the summer while they're living here in my apartment. If everything goes right I'll be back for a New Year's Eve party with just you and me and the best bottle of scotch money can buy."

"Will you have enough to live on?" I asked, knowing where she got the thirteen thousand.

"I've got enough," she nodded.

"Listen, goddamn it, don't lie to me. I'm not gonna get involved if you're off somewhere selling your ass in a strange town with a foal kicking around in your belly."

"I wouldn't take any chances," she said, looking deep in my eyes again. "I swear it. I've got enough in another account to live damn well for the whole time I'll be gone. I'll show you my bankbooks. And I can afford to have the kid in a good hospital. A private room if I want it."

"Wow!" I said, getting up, light-headed and dizzy. I stood for a second and shuffled into the living room, dropping on the couch and laying back. I noticed that the red hose on Laila's crystal and gold narghile was uncoiled. Those pipes are fine decorator items but they never work right unless you stuff all the fittings with rags like Laila's was. I often smoked mint-flavored Turkish tobacco with Yasser. Laila smoked hashish. There was a black-and-white mosaic inlaid box setting next to the narghile. The lid was open and it was half full of hash, very high-grade, expensive, shoe-leather hash, pressed into dark flat sheets like the sole of your shoe.

Laila let me alone and cleared the kitchen table. What a hell of a time. First the decision to retire. And after I told Cassie, everything seemed right. And then Cassie wants a kid! And a goddamn pack of baby Bolsheviks make an ass out of me. Humiliate me! Then perjury, for chrissake. I felt like someone was putting out cigars on the inside of my belly, which was so hard and swollen I couldn't see my knees unless I sat up straight. But at least I got a back office, even if I did almost die in the pigeon shit.

"What a day," I said when Laila came in and sat down on the end of the couch.

"I'm sorry I asked you, Bumper."

"No, no, don't say that. I'll do it. I'll help you."

She didn't say anything, but she got up and came over and sat on the floor next to me, her eyes wet, and I'll be a son of a bitch if she didn't kiss my hand!

Laila got up then, and without saying anything, took my shoes off, and I let her lift my legs up and put them on the couch. I felt like a beached walrus laying there like that, but I was still swacked. In fact, I felt drunker now laying down, and I was afraid the room would start spinning, so I wanted to start talking. "I had a miserable goddamn day."

"Tell me about it, Bumper," said Laila, sitting there on the floor next to me and putting her cool hand on my hot forehead as I loosened my belt. I knew I was gone for the night. I was in no shape to get up, let alone drive home. I squirmed around until my sore shoulder was settled against a cushion.

"Your face and hands are cut and your body's hurting."

"Guess I can sleep here, huh?"

"Of course. How'd you get hurt?"

"Slipped and fell off a fire escape. Whadda you think about me retiring, Laila?"

"Retiring? Don't be ridiculous. You're too full of hell."

"I'm in my forties, goddamnit. No, I might as well level with you. I'll be fifty this month. Imagine that. When I was born Warren G. Harding was a new President!"

"You're too alive. Forget about it. It's too silly to think about."

"I was sworn in on my thirtieth birthday, Laila. Know that?"

"Tell me about it," she said, stroking my cheek now, and I felt so damn comfortable I could've died.

"You weren't even born then. That's how long I been a cop."

"Why'd you become a cop?"

"Oh, I don't know."

"Well, what did you do *before* you became a cop?"

"I was in the Marine Corps over eight years."

"Tell me about it."

"I wanted to get away from the hometown, I guess. There was nobody left except a few cousins and one aunt. My brother Clem and me were raised by our grandmother, and after she died, Clem took care of me. He was a ripper, that bastard. Bigger than me, but didn't look anything like me. A handsome dog. Loved his food and drink and women. He owned his own gas station and just before Pearl Harbor, in November it was, he got killed when a truck tire blew up and he fell back into the grease pit. My brother Clem died in a filthy grease pit, killed by a goddamn tire! It was ridiculous. There was nobody else I gave a damn about so I joined the Corps. Guys actually *joined* in those days, believe it or not. I got wounded twice, once in Saipan and then in the knees at Iwo, and it almost kept me off the Department. I had to flimflam the shit out of that police surgeon. You know what? I didn't hate war. I mean, why not admit it? I didn't hate it."

"Weren't you ever afraid?"

"Sure, but there's something about danger I like,

and fighting was something I could do. I found that
out right away and after the war I shipped over for
another hitch and never did go back to Indiana. What
the hell, I never had much there anyway. Billy was
there with me and I had a job I liked."

"Who's Billy?"

"He was my son," I said, and I heard the air-conditioner going and I knew it was cool, because Laila
looked so crisp and fresh, and yet my back was soaked
and the sweat was pouring down my face and slipping
beneath my collar.

"I never knew you were married, Bumper."

"It was a hundred years ago."

"Where's your wife?"

"I don't know. Missouri, I think. Or dead maybe. It's
been so long. She was a girl I met in San Diego, a farm
girl. Lots of them around out here on the coast during
the war. They drifted out to find defense work, and
some of them boozed it too much. Verna was a pale,
skinny little thing. I was back in San Diego from my
first trip over. I had my chest full of ribbons and had a
cane because my first hit was in the thigh. That's one
reason my legs aren't worth a shit today, I guess. I
picked her up in a bar and slept with her that night
and then I started coming by whenever I got liberty
and next thing you know, before I ship out, she says
she's knocked up. I had the feeling so many guys get,
that they're gonna get bumped off, that their number's
up, so we got drunk one night and I took her to a justice of the peace in Arizona and married her. She got
an allotment and wrote me all the time and I didn't
think too much about her till I got hit the second time
and went home for good. And there she was, with my
frail, sickly Billy. William's my real name, did you
know that?"

"No, I didn't."

"So anyway, I screwed up, but just like you said,
Laila, there was no sense anybody else suffering for it
so I took Verna and Billy and we got a decent place to

stay in Oceanside, and I thought, what the hell, this is a pretty fair life. So I reenlisted for another hitch and before long I was up for master sergeant. I could take Verna okay. I mean I gotta give her credit, after Billy came she quit boozing and kept a decent house. She was just a poor dumb farm girl but she treated me and Billy like champs, I have to admit. I was lucky and got to stay with Headquarters Company, Base, for five years, and Billy was to me, like . . . I don't know, standing on a granite cliff and watching all the world from the Beginning until Now, and for the first time there was a reason for it all. You understand?"

"Yes, I think so."

"You won't believe this, but when he was barely four years old he printed a valentine card for me. He could print and read at four years old, I swear it. He asked his mother how to make the words and then he composed it himself. It said, 'Dad. I love you. Love, Billy Morgan.' Just barely four years old. Can you believe that?"

"Yes, I believe you, Bumper."

"But like I said, he was a sickly boy like his mother, and even now when I tell you about him, I can't picture him. I put him away mentally, and it's not possible to picture how he looked, even if I try. You know, I read where only schizophrenics can control subconscious thought, and maybe I'm schizoid, I don't doubt it. But I can do it. Sometimes when I'm asleep and I see a shadow in a dream and the shadow is a little boy wearing glasses, or he has a cowlick sticking up in the back, I wake up. I sit straight up in my bed, wide awake. I *cannot* picture him either awake or asleep. You're smart to adopt out your kid, Laila."

"When did he die?"

"When he was just five. Right after his birthday, in fact. And it shouldn't have surprised me really. He was anemic and he had pneumonia twice as a baby, but still, it *was* a surprise, you know? Even though he was sick so long, it *was* a surprise, and after that,

Verna seemed dead too. She told me a few weeks after we buried him that she was going home to Missouri and I thought it was a good idea so I gave her all the money I had and I never saw her again.

"After she left, I started drinking pretty good, and once, on weekend liberty, I came to L.A. and got so drunk I somehow ended up at El Toro Marine Base with a bunch of other drunken jarheads instead of at Camp Pendleton where I was stationed. The M.P.'s at the gate let the other drunks through, but of course my pass was wrong, so they stopped me. I was mean drunk then, and confused as hell, and I ended up swinging on the two M.P.'s.

"I can hardly remember late that night in the El Toro brig. All I really recall was two brig guards, one black guy and one white guy, wearing khaki pants and skivvy shirts, dragging me off the floor of the cell and taking me in the head where they worked me over with billies and then to the showers to wash off the blood. I remember holding onto the faucets with my head in the sink for protection, and the billies landing on my arms and ribs and kidneys and the back of my head. That was the first time my nose was ever broken."

Laila was still stroking my face and listening. Her hands felt cool and good.

"After that, they gave me a special courtmartial, and after all the M.P.'s testified, my defense counsel brought out a platoon or so of character witnesses, and even some civilians, wives of the marines who lived near Verna and Billy and me. They all talked about me, and Billy, and how extra smart and polite he was. Then the doctor who treated me in the brig testified as a defense witness that I was unbalanced at the time of the fight and not responsible for my actions, even though he had no psychiatric training. My defense counsel got away with it and when it was over I didn't get any brig time. I just got busted to buck sergeant.

"Is it hot in here, Laila?"

"No, Bumper," she said, stroking my cheek with the back of her fingers.

"Well, anyway, I took my discharge in the spring of nineteen-fifty and fooled around a year and finally joined the Los Angeles Police Department."

"Why did you do it, Bumper? The police force?"

"I don't know. I was good at fighting. I guess that's why. I thought about going back in the Corps when Korea broke out, and then I read something that said, 'Policemen are soldiers who act alone,' and I figured that was the only thing I hated about the military, that you couldn't act alone very much. And as a cop I could do it all myself, so I became a cop."

"You never heard from Verna?" asked Laila quietly, and suddenly I was cold and damp and getting chills laying there.

"About six years after I came on the job I got a letter from a lawyer in Joplin. I don't know how he found me. He said she'd filed for divorce and after that I got the final papers. I paid his fee and sent her about five hundred I'd saved, to get her started. I always hoped maybe she found some nice working stiff and went back to the farm life. She was one who couldn't make it by herself. She'd have to love somebody and then of course she'd have to suffer when something took them away from her, or maybe when they left on their own. She'd never learn you gotta suffer *alone* in this world. I never knew for sure what happened to her. I didn't try to find out because I'd probably just discover she was a wino and a streetwalking whore and I'd rather think otherwise."

"Bumper?"

"What?"

"Please take my bed tonight. Go in and shower and take my bed. You're dripping wet and you'll get sick if you stay here on the couch."

"I'll be okay. You should see some of the places I've slept. Just give me a blanket."

"Please."

She began trying to lift me and that almost made me laugh out loud. She was a strong girl, but no woman was about to raise Bumper Morgan, two hundred and seventy-five pounds anytime, and almost three hundred this night with all of me cold dead weight from the booze.

"Okay, okay," I grumbled, and found I wasn't too drunk when I stood up. I made my way to her bedroom, stripped, and jumped in the shower, turning it on cold at the end. When I was through I dried in her bath towel which smelled like woman, took the wet gauze bandage off my leg, and felt better than I had all day. I rinsed my mouth with toothpaste, examined my meat-red face and red-webbed eyes, and climbed in her bed naked, which is the only way to sleep, winter or summer.

The bed smelled like her too, or rather it smelled like woman, since all women are pretty much the same to me. They all smell and feel the same. It's the essence of womanhood, that's the thing I need.

I was dozing when Laila came in and tiptoed to the shower and it seemed like seconds later when she was sitting on the bed in a sheer white nightgown whispering to me. I smelled lilac, and then woman, and I came to with her velvet mouth all over my face.

"What the hell?" I mumbled, sitting up.

"I touched you tonight," said Laila. "You told me things. Maybe for the first time in years, Bumper, I've really touched another person!" She put her hand on my bare shoulder.

"Yeah, well that's enough touching for one night," I said, disgusted with myself for telling her all those personal things, and I took her hand off my shoulder. Now I'd have to fly back to L.A. in a couple of weeks to set this thing up with Laila and her family. Everyone was complicating my life lately.

"Bumper," she said, drawing her feet up under her and laughing pretty damn jolly for this time of night. "Bumper, you're wonderful. You're a wonderful old panda. A big blue-nosed panda. Do you know your nose is blue?"

"Yeah, it gets that way when I drink too much," I said, figuring she'd been smoking hash, able to see right through the nightie at her skin which was now exactly the color of apricots. "I had too many blood vessels busted too many times there on my nose."

"I want to get under the covers with you, Bumper."

"Look, kid," I said. "You don't owe me a goddamn thing. I'll be glad to help you flimflam your family."

"You've let me touch you, Bumper," she said, and the warm wide velvet mouth was on me again, my neck and cheek, and all that chestnut hair was covering me until I almost couldn't think about how ridiculous this was.

"Goddamnit," I said, holding her off. "This is a sickening thing you're doing. I knew you since you were a little girl. Damn it, kid, I'm an old bag of guts and you're still just a little girl to me. This is unnatural!"

"Don't call me kid. And don't try to stop me from having you."

"*Having* me? You're just impressed by cops. I'm a father symbol. Lots of young girls feel like that about cops."

"I hate cops," she answered, her boobs wobbling against my arms, which were getting tired. "It's you I want because you're more man than I've ever had my hands on."

"Yeah, I'm about six cubic yards," I said, very shaky.

"That's not what I meant," she said, her hands going over me, and she was kissing me again and I was doing everything I could to avoid the pleasures of a thousand and one nights.

"Listen, I couldn't if I wanted to," I groaned. "You're just too young, I just couldn't do it with a kid like you."

"Want to bet?"

"Don't, Laila."

"How can a man be so aware and be so square," she

smiled, standing up and slipping off the nightie.

"It's just the bluesuit," I said with a voice gone hoarse and squeaky. "I probably look pretty sharp to you in my uniform."

Laila busted up then, falling on the bed and rolling on her stomach, laughing for a good minute. I smiled weakly, staring at her apricot ass and those thunder thighs, thinking it was over. But after she stopped laughing she smiled at me softer than ever, whispered in Arabic, and crept under the sheet.

# Friday,
# the Last Day

## 15

I WOKE UP FRIDAY morning with a terrible hangover. Laila was sprawled half on top of me, a big smooth naked doe, which was the reason I woke up. After living so many years alone I don't like sleeping with anyone. Cassie, who I made love to maybe a hundred times, had never slept with me, not all night. We'd have to get twin beds, Cassie and me. I just can't stand to be too close to anybody for too long.

Laila didn't wake up and I took my clothes into the living room and dressed, leaving a note that said I'd get in touch in a week or so, to work out the details of handling her bank account and dumping a load of snow on Yasser and the family.

Before I left I crept back into the bedroom to look at her this last time. She was sprawled on her stomach, sleek and beautiful.

"*Salām*, Laila," I whispered. "A thousand *salāms*, little girl."

I very carefully made my way down the stairs of Laila's apartment house to my car parked in front, and I felt a little better when I got out on the road with the window down driving onto the Hollywood Freeway on a windy, not too smoggy day.

Then I thought for a few minutes about how it had been with Laila and I was ashamed because I always prided myself on being something more than the thousands of ugly old slimeballs you see in Hollywood with beautiful young babies like her. She did it because she was grateful and neurotic and confused and I took advantage. I'd always picked on someone my own size all my life, and now I was no better than any other horny old fart.

I went home and had a cold shower and a shave and I felt more or less human after some aspirin and three cups of coffee that started the heartburn going for the day. I wondered if after a few months of retirement my stomach might begin to rebuild itself, and who knows, maybe I'd have digestive peace.

I got to the Glass House a half hour early and by the time I shined my black high-top shoes, buffed the Sam Browne, hit the badge with some rouge and a cloth, I was sweating a little and feeling much improved. I put on a fresh uniform since the one from yesterday was covered with blood and birdshit. When I pinned on the gleaming shield and slid the scarred baton through the chrome ring on my Sam Browne I felt even better.

At rollcall Cruz was sitting as usual with the watch commander, Lieutenant Hilliard, at the table in front of the room, and Cruz glanced at me several times like he expected me to get up and make a grand announcement that this was my last day. Of course I didn't, and he looked a little disappointed. I hated to disappoint anyone, especially Cruz, but I wasn't going out with a trumpet blare. I really wanted Lieutenant Hilliard to hold an inspection this morning, my last one, and he did. He limped down the line and said my boondockers and my shield looked like a million bucks and he wished some of the young cops looked half as sharp. After inspection I drank a quart or so from the water fountain and I felt better yet.

I meant to speak to Cruz about our lunch date, but Lieutenant Hilliard was talking to him so I went out to the car, and decided to call him later. I fired up the black-and-white, put my baton in the holder on the door, tore off the paper on my writing pad, replaced the old hot sheet, checked the back seat for dead midgets, and drove out of the station. It was really unbelievable. The *last time*.

After hitting the bricks, I cleared over the air, even though I worried that I'd get a burglary report or some other chickenshit call before I could get something in my stomach. I couldn't stand the idea of anything heavy just now so I turned south on San Pedro and headed for the dairy, which was a very good place to go for hangover cures, at least it always was for me. It was more than a dairy, it was the plant and home office for a dairy that sold all over Southern California, and they made very good specialty products like cottage cheese and buttermilk and yogurt, all of which are wonderful for hangovers if you're not too far gone. I waved at the gate guard, got passed into the plant, and parked in front of the employee's store, which wasn't opened yet.

I saw one of the guys I knew behind the counter setting up the cash register and I knocked on the window.

"Hi, Bumper," he smiled, a young guy, with deep-set green eyes and a mop of black hair. "What do you need?"

"Plasma, pal," I said, "but I'll settle for yogurt."

"Sure. Come on in, Bumper," he laughed, and I passed through, heading for the tall glass door to the cold room where the yogurt was kept. I took two yogurts from the shelf, and he gave me a plastic spoon when I put them on the counter.

"That all you're having, Bumper?" he asked, as I shook my head and lifted the lid and spooned out a half pint of blueberry which I finished in three or four gulps and followed with a lime. And finally, what the hell, I thought, I grabbed another, French apple, and ate it while the guy counted his money and said something to me once or twice which I nodded at, and I smiled through a mouthful of cool creamy yogurt that was coating my stomach, soothing me, and making me well.

"Never saw anyone put away yogurt like that, Bumper," he said after I finished.

I couldn't remember this young guy's name, and wished like hell they wore their names on the gray work uniform because I always like to make a little small talk and call someone by name when he's feeding me. It's the least you can do.

"Could I have some buttermilk?" I asked, after he threw the empty yogurt containers in a gleaming trash can behind the counter. The whole place sparkled, being a dairy, and it smelled clean, and was nice and cool.

"Why sure, Bumper," he said, leaving the counter and coming back with a pint of cold buttermilk. Most of the older guys around the dairy wouldn't bring me a pint container, and here I was dying of thirst from the booze. Rather than say anything I just tipped it up and poured it down, only swallowing three times to make him realize his mistake.

"Guess I should've brought you a quart, huh?" he said after I put the milk carton down and licked my lips.

I smiled and shrugged and he went in the back, returning with a quart.

"Thanks, pal," I said. "I'm pretty thirsty today." I tipped the quart up and let it flow thick and delicious into my mouth, and then I started swallowing, but not like before, more slowly. When I finished it I was really fit again. I was well. I could do anything now.

"Take a quart with you?" he said. "Would you like more yogurt or some cottage cheese?"

"No thanks," I said. I don't believe in being a hog like some cops I've worked with. "Gotta get back to the streets. Friday mornings get pretty busy sometimes."

I really should've talked a while. I knew I should,

but I just didn't feel like it. It was the first time this
guy ever served me so I said the thing that all policemen say when they're ninety percent sure what the answer will be.

"How much do I owe you?"

"Don't mention it," he said, shaking his head. "Come
see us anytime, Bumper."

While driving out the main gate of the dairy, I fired
up a fresh cigar which I knew couldn't possibly give
me indigestion because my stomach was so well coated I could eat tin cans and not notice.

Then I realized that was the last time I'd ever make
my dairy stop. Damn, I thought, everything I do today
will be for the last time. Then I suddenly started hoping I'd get some routine calls like a burglary report or
maybe a family dispute which I usually hated referee-
ing. I wouldn't even mind writing a traffic ticket
today.

It would've been something, I thought, really something to have stayed on the job after my twenty years.
You have your pension in the bag then, and you own
your own mortgage, having bought and paid for them
with twenty years' service. Regardless of what you
ever do or don't do you have a forty percent pension
the rest of your life, from the moment you leave the
Department. Whether you're fired for pushing a slimeball down the fire escape, or whether you're booked
for lying in court to put a scumbag where he ought to
be, or whether you bust your stick over the hairy little
skull of some college drat who's tearing at your badge
and carrying a tape recorder at a demonstration, no
matter what you do, they got to pay you that pension.
If they have to, they'll mail those checks to you at San
Quentin. Nobody can take your pension away. Knowing that might make police work even a little *more*
fun, I thought. It might give you just a little more
push, make you a little more aggressive. I would've
liked to have done police work knowing that I owned
my own mortgage.

As I was cruising I picked a voice out of the radio chatter. It was the girl with the cutest and sexiest voice I ever heard. She was on frequency thirteen today, and she had her own style of communicating. She didn't just come on the horn and answer with clipped phrases and impersonal "rogers." Her voice would rise and fall like a song, and getting even a traffic accident call from her, which patrol policemen hate worst because they're so tedious, was somehow not quite so bad. She must've been hot for some cop in unit Four-L-Nine because her voice came in soft and husky and sent a shiver through me when she said, "Foah-L-Ninah, rrrrrrraj-ahh!"

Now that's the way to roger a call, I thought. I was driving nowhere at all, just touring the beat, looking at people I knew and ones I didn't know, trying not to think of all the things I'd never do out here. I was trading them for things I'd *rather* do, things any sane man would rather do, like be with Cassie and start my new career and live a civilized normal life. Funny I should think of it as *civilized,* that kind of life. That was one of the reasons I'd always wanted to go to North Africa to die.

I always figured kind of vaguely that if somebody didn't knock me off and I lasted say thirty years, I'd pull the pin then because I could never do my kind of police work past sixty. I really thought I could last that long though. I thought that if I cut down on the groceries and the drinking and the cigars, maybe I could last out here on the streets until I was sixty. Then I'd have learned almost all there was to learn here. I'd know all the secrets I always wanted to know and I'd hop a jet and go to the Valley of the Kings and look out there from a pink granite cliff and see where all civilization started, and maybe if I stayed there long enough and didn't get drunk and fall off a pyramid, or get stomped to death by a runaway camel, or ventilated by a Yankee-hating Arab, maybe if I lasted there long enough, I'd find out the last thing I wanted

to know: whether *civilization* was worth the candle
after all.

Then I thought of what Cruz would say if I ever got
drunk enough to tell him about this. He'd say,
"'*Mano*, let yourself love, and give yourself away.
You'll get your answer. You don't need a sphinx or a
pink granite cliff."

"Hi, Bumper," a voice yelled, and I turned from the
glare of the morning sun and saw Percy opening his
pawnshop.

"Hi, Percy," I yelled back, and slowed down to
wave. He was a rare animal, an honest pawnbroker.
He ran hypes and other thieves out of his shop if he
even suspected they had something hot. And he always demanded good identification from a customer
pawning something. He was an *honest* pawnbroker, a
rare animal.

I remembered the time Percy gave me his traffic
ticket to take care of because this was the first one
he'd ever gotten. It was for jaywalking. He didn't own
a car. He hated them and took a bus to the shop every
day. I just couldn't disillusion old Percy by letting him
know that I couldn't fix a ticket, so I took it and paid it
for him. It's practically impossible to fix a ticket anymore in this town. You have to know the judge or the
City Attorney. Lawyers take care of each other of
course, but a cop can't fix a ticket. Anyway, I paid it,
and Percy thought I fixed it and wasn't disappointed.
He thought I was a hell of a big man.

Another black-and-white cruised past me going
south. The cop driving, a curly-haired kid named Nelson, waved, and I nodded back. He almost rear-ended
a car stopped at the red light because he was looking
at some chick in hot pants going into an office building. He was a typical young cop, I thought. Thinking
of pussy instead of police work. And just like all these
cats, Nelson loved talking about it. I think they all
love talking about it these days more than they love
doing it. That gave me a royal pain in the ass. I guess

I've had more than my share in my time. I've had some good stuff for an ugly guy, but by Maggie's muff, I never talked about screwing a dame, not with anybody. In my day, a guy was unmanly if he did that. But your day is over after this day, I reminded myself, and swung south on Grand.

Then I heard a Central car get a report call at one of the big downtown hotels and I knew the hotel burglar had hit again. I'd give just about anything, I thought, to catch that guy today. That'd be like quitting after your last home run, like Ted Williams. A home run your last time up. That'd be something. I cruised around for twenty minutes and then drove to the hotel and parked behind the black-and-white that got the call. I sat there in my car smoking a cigar and waited another fifteen minutes until Clarence Evans came out. He was a fifteen-year cop, a tall stringbean who I used to play handball with before my ankles got so bad.

We had some good games. It's especially fun to play when you're working nightwatch and you get up to the academy about one a.m. after you finish work, and play three hard fast games and take a steam bath. Except Evans didn't like the steam bath, being so skinny. We always took a half case of beer with us and drank it up after we showered. He was one of the first Negroes I worked with as a partner when L.A.P.D. became completely integrated several years ago. He was a good copper and he liked working with me even though he knew I always preferred working alone. On nightwatch it's comforting sometimes to have someone riding shotgun or walking beside you. So I worked with him and lots of other guys even though I would've rather had a one-man beat or an "L" car that you work alone, "L" for lonesome. But I worked with him because I never could disappoint anyone that wanted to work with me that bad, and it made the handball playing more convenient.

Then I saw Clarence coming out of the hotel carrying his report notebook. He grinned at me, came walking light-footed over to my car, opened the door and sat down.

"What's happening, Bumper?"

"Just curious if the hotel creeper hit again, Clarence."

"Took three rooms on the fifth floor and two on the fourth floor," he nodded.

"The people asleep?"

"In four of them. In the other one, they were down in the bar."

"That means he hit before two a.m."

"Right."

"I can't figure this guy," I said, popping an antacid tablet. "Usually he works in the daytime but sometimes in the early evening. Now he's hitting during the night when they're in and when they're not in. I never heard of a hotel burglar as squirrelly as this guy."

"Maybe that's it," said Evans. "A squirrel. Didn't he try to hurt a kid on one job?"

"A teddy bear. He stabbed hell out of a big teddy bear. It was all covered with a blanket and looked like a kid sleeping."

"That cat's a squirrel," said Evans.

"That would explain why the other hotel burglars don't know anything," I said, puffing on the cigar and thinking. "I never did think he was a pro, just a lucky amateur."

"A lucky looney," said Evans. "You talked to all your snitches?" He knew my M.O. from working with me. He knew I had informants, but like everyone else he didn't know how many, or that I paid the good ones.

"I talked to just about everyone I know. I talked to a hotel burglar who told me he'd already been approached by three detectives and that he'd tell us if he knew anything, because this guy is bringing so much heat on all the hotels he'd like to see us get him."

"Well, Bumper, if anybody lucks onto the guy I'm betting you will," said Evans, putting on his hat and getting out of the car.

"Police are baffled but an arrest is imminent," I winked, and started the car. It was going to be a very hot day.

I was given a report call at Pershing Square, an injury report. Probably some pensioner fell off his soapbox and was trying to figure how he could say there was a crack in the sidewalk and sue the city. I ignored the call for a few minutes and let her assign it to another unit. I didn't like to do that. I always believed you should handle the calls given to you, but damn it, I only had the rest of the day and that was it, and I thought about Oliver Horn and wondered why I hadn't thought about him before. I couldn't waste time on the report call so I let the other unit handle it and headed for the barbershop on Fourth Street.

Oliver was sitting on a chair on the sidewalk in front of the shop. His ever-present broom was across his lap, and he was dozing in the sunshine.

He was the last guy in the world you would ever want to die and come back looking like. Oliver was built like a walrus with one arm cut off above the elbow. It was done maybe forty years ago by probably the worst surgeon in the world. The skin just flapped over and hung there. He had orange hair and a big white belly covered with orange hair. He long ago gave up trying to keep his pants up, and usually they barely gripped him below the gut so that his belly button was always popping out at you. His shoelaces were untied and destroyed from stepping on them because it was too hard to tie them one-handed, and he had a huge lump on his chin. It looked like if you squeezed it, it'd break a window. But Oliver was surprisingly clever. He swept out the barbershop and two or three businesses on this part of Fourth Street, including a bar called Raymond's where quite a few ex-cons hung out. It was close to the big hotels and a good place to scam on the rich tourists. Oliver didn't miss anything and had given me some very good information over the years.

"You awake, Oliver?" I asked.

He opened one blue-veined eyelid. "Bumper, how's it wi'choo?"

"Okay, Oliver. Gonna be a hot one again today."

"Yeah, I'm gettin' sticky. Let's go in the shop."

"Don't have time. Listen, I was just wondering, you heard about this burglar that's been ripping us downtown here in all the big hotels for the past couple months?"

"No, ain't heard nothin'."

"Well, this guy ain't no ordinary hotel thief. I mean he probably ain't none of the guys you ordinarily see around Raymond's, but he might be a guy that you would *sometimes* see there. What the hell, even a ding-a-ling has a drink once in a while, and Raymond's is convenient when you're getting ready to rape about ten rooms across the street."

"He a ding-a-ling?"

"Yeah."

"What's he look like?"

"I don't know."

"How can I find him then, Bumper?"

"I don't know, Oliver. I'm just having hunches now. I think the guy's done burglaries before. I mean he knows how to shim doors and all that. And like I say, he's a little dingy. I think he's gonna stab somebody before too long. He carries a blade. A *long* blade, because he went clear through a mattress with it."

"Why'd he stab a mattress?"

"He was trying to kill a teddy bear."

"You been drinkin', Bumper?"

I smiled, and then I wondered what the hell I was doing here because I didn't know enough about the burglar to give a snitch something to work with. I was grabbing at any straw in the wind so I could hit a home run before walking off the field for the last time.

Absolutely pathetic and sickening, I thought, ashamed of myself.

"Here's five bucks," I said to Oliver. "Get yourself a steak."

"Jeez, Bumper," he said, "I ain't done nothin' for it."

"The guy carries a long-bladed knife and he's a psycho and lately he takes these hotels at any goddamn hour of the day or night. He just might go to Raymond's for a drink sometime. He just might use the rest room while you're cleaning up and maybe he'll be tempted to look at some of the stuff in his pockets to see what he stole. Or maybe he'll be sitting at the bar and he'll pull a pretty out of his pocket that he just snatched at the hotel, or maybe one of these sharp hotel burglars that hangs out at Raymond's will know something, or say something, and you're always around there. Maybe anything."

"Sure, Bumper, I'll call you right away I hear anything at all. Right away, Bumper. And you get any more clues you let me know, hey, Bumper?"

"Sure, Oliver, I'll get you a good one from my clues closet."

"Hey, that's aw right," Oliver hooted. He had no teeth in front, upper or lower. For a long time he had one upper tooth in front.

"Be seeing you, Oliver."

"Hey, Bumper, wait a minute. You ain't told me no funny cop stories in a long time. How 'bout a story?"

"I think you heard them all."

"Come on, Bumper."

"Well, let's see. I told you about the seventy-five-year-old nympho I busted over on Main that night?"

"Yeah, yeah," he hooted, "tell me that one again. That's a good one."

"I gotta go, Oliver, honest. But say, did I ever tell you about the time I caught the couple in the back seat up there in Elysian Park in one of those maker's acres?"

"No, tell me, Bumper."

"Well, I shined my light in there and here's these two down on the seat, the old boy throwing the knockwurst to his girlfriend, and this young partner I'm with says, 'What're you doing there?' And the guy gives the answer ninety percent of the guys do when you catch them in that position: 'Nothing, Officer.'"

"Yeah, yeah," said Oliver, his shaggy head bobbing.

"So I say to the guy, 'Well, if *you* ain't doing anything, move over there and hold my flashlight and lemme see what *I* can do.'"

"Whoooo, that's funny," said Oliver. "Whoooo, Bumper."

He was laughing so hard he hardly saw me go, and I left him there holding his big hard belly and laughing in the sunshine.

I thought about telling Oliver to call Central Detectives instead of me, because I wouldn't be here after today, but what the hell, then I'd have to tell him *why* I wouldn't be here, and I couldn't take another person telling me why I should or should not retire. If Oliver ever called, somebody'd tell him I was gone, and the information would eventually get to the dicks. So what the hell, I thought, pulling back into the traffic and breathing exhaust fumes. It would've been really something though, to get that burglar on this last day. Really something.

I looked at my watch and thought Cassie should be at school now, so I drove to City College and parked out front. I wondered why I didn't feel guilty about Laïla. I guess I figured it wasn't really my fault.

Cassie was alone in the office when I got there. I closed the door, flipped my hat on a chair, walked over, and felt that same old amazement I've felt a thousand times over how well a woman fits in your arms, and how soft they feel.

"Thought about you all night," she said after I kissed her a dozen times or so. "Had a miserable evening. Couple of bores."

"You thought about me all night, huh?"

"Honestly, I did." She kissed me again. "I still have this awful feeling something's going to happen."

"Every guy that ever went into battle has that feeling."

"Is that what our marriage is going to be, a battle?"

"If it is, you'll win, baby. I'll surrender."

"Wait'll I get you tonight," she whispered. "You'll surrender all right."

"That green dress is gorgeous."

"But you still like hot colors better?"

"Of course."

"After we get married I'll wear nothing but reds and oranges and yellows. . . ."

"You ready to talk?"

"Sure, what is it?"

"Cruz gave me a talking-to—about you."

"Oh?"

"He thinks you're the greatest thing that ever happened to me."

"Go on," she smiled.

"Well . . ."

"Yes?"

"Damn it, I can't go on. Not in broad daylight with no drink in me. . . ."

"What did you talk about, silly?"

"About you. No, it was more about me. About things I need and things I'm afraid of. Twenty years he's my friend and suddenly I find out he's a damned intellectual."

"What do you need? What're you afraid of? I can't believe you've ever been afraid of anything."

"He knows me better than you know me."

"That makes me sad. I don't want anyone knowing you better than I do. Tell me what you talked about."

"I don't have time right now," I said, feeling a gas bubble forming. Then I lied and said, "I'm on the way to a call. I just had to stop for a minute. I'll tell you all about it tonight. I'll be at your pad at seven-thirty. We're going out to dinner, okay?"

"Okay."

"Then we'll curl up on your couch with a good bottle of wine."

"Sounds wonderful," she smiled, that clean, hot, female smile that made me kiss her.

"See you tonight," I whispered.

"Tonight," she gasped, and I realized I was crushing her. She stood in the doorway and watched me all the way down the stairs.

I got back in the car and dropped two of each kind of pill and grabbed a handful from the glove compartment and shoved them in my pants pockets for later.

As I drove back on the familiar streets of the beat I wondered why I couldn't talk to Cassie like I wanted. If you're going to marry someone you should be able to tell her almost anything about yourself that she has a right to know.

I pulled over at a phone booth then and called Cruz at the station. Lieutenant Hilliard answered and in a couple seconds I heard Cruz's soft voice, "Sergeant Segovia?" He said it like a question.

"Hello, Sergeant Segovia, this is future former Officer Morgan, what the hell you doing besides pushing a pencil and shuffling paper?"

"What're you doing besides ignoring your radio calls?"

"I'm just cruising around this miserable beat thinking how great it'll be not to have to do it anymore. You decided where you want me to take you for lunch?"

"You don't have to take me anywhere."

"Look, goddamnit, we're going to some nice place, so if you won't pick it, I will."

"Okay, take me to Seymour's."

"On my beat? Oh, for chrissake. Look, you just meet me at Seymour's at eleven-thirty. Have a cup of coffee but don't eat a damn thing because we're going to a place I know in Beverly Hills."

"That's a long way from your beat, all right."

"I'll pick you up at Seymour's."

"Okay, *'mano, ahí te huacho.*"

I chuckled after I hung up at that Mexican slang because *watching* for me is exactly what Cruz always
did when you stop and think about it. Most people
say, "I'll be seeing you," because that's what they do,
but Cruz, he always watched for me. It felt good to
have old sad-eye watching for me.

## 16

I GOT BACK IN my car and cruised down Main Street, by the parking lot at the rear of the Pink Dragon. I was so sick of pushing this pile of iron around that I stopped to watch some guys in the parking lot.

There were three of them and they were up to something. I parked the car and backed up until the building hid me. I got out and walked to the corner of the building, took my hat off, and peeked around the corner and across the lot.

A skinny hype in a long-sleeved blue shirt was talking to another brown-shirted one. There was a third one with them, a little T-shirt who stood a few steps away. Suddenly Blue-shirt nodded to Brown-shirt, who walked up and gave something to little T-shirt, who gave Brown-shirt something back, and they all hustled off in different directions. Little T-shirt was walking toward me. He was looking back over his shoulder for cops, and walking right into me. I didn't feel like messing around with a narco bust but this was too easy. I stepped in the hotel doorway and when T-shirt walked past, squinting into the sun, I reached out, grabbed him by the arm, and jerked him inside. He was just a boy, scared as hell. I shoved him face forward into the wall, and grabbed the hip pocket of his denims.

"What've you got, boy? Bennies or reds? Or maybe you're an acid freak?"

"Hey, lemme go!" he yelled.

I took the bennies out of his pocket. There were six rolls, five in a roll, held together by a rubber band. The day of ten-benny rolls was killed by inflation.

"How much did they make you pay, kid?" I asked, keeping a good grip on his arm. He didn't look so short up close, but he was skinny, with lots of brown hair, and young, too young to be downtown scoring pills in the middle of the morning.

"I paid seven dollars. But I won't ever do it again if you'll lemme go. Please lemme go."

"Put your hands behind you, kid," I said, unsnapping my handcuff case.

"What're you doing? Please don't put those on me. I won't hurt you or anything."

"I'm not afraid of you hurting me," I laughed, chewing on a wet cigar stump that I finally threw away. "It's just that my wheels are gone and my ass is too big to be chasing you all over these streets." I snapped on one cuff and brought his palms together behind his back and clicked on the other, taking them up snug.

"How much you say you paid for the pills?"

"Seven dollars. I won't never do it again if you'll lemme go, I swear." He was dancing around, nervous and scared, and he stepped on my right toe, scuffing up the shine.

"Careful, damn it."

"Oh, I'm sorry. Please lemme go. I didn't mean to step on you."

"Those cats charged you way too much for the pills," I said, as I led him to the radio car.

"I know you won't believe me but it's the first time I ever bought them. I don't know *what* the hell they cost."

"Sure it is."

"See, I knew you wouldn't believe me. You cops don't believe nobody."

"You know all about cops, do you?"

"I been arrested before. I know you cops. You all act the same."

"You must be a hell of a heavyweight desperado. Got a ten-page rap sheet, I bet. What've you been busted for?"

"Running away. Twice. And you don't have to put me down."

"How old are you?"

"Fourteen."

"In the car," I said, opening the front door. "And don't lean back on the cuffs or they'll tighten."

"You don't have to worry, I won't jump out," he said as I fastened the seat belt over his lap.

"I ain't worrying, kid."

"I got a name. It's Tilden," he said, his square chin jutting way out.

"Mine's Morgan."

"My first name's Tom."

"Mine's Bumper."

"Where're you taking me?"

"To Juvenile Narcotics."

"You gonna book me?"

"Of course."

"What could I expect," he said, nodding his head disgustedly. "How could I ever expect a cop to act like a human being."

"You shouldn't even expect a human being to act like a human being. You'll just get disappointed."

I turned the key and heard the click-click of a dead battery. Stone-cold dead without warning.

"Hang loose, kid," I said, getting out of the car.

"Where could I go?" he yelled, as I lifted the hood to see if someone had torn the wires out. That happens once in a while when you leave your black-and-white somewhere that you can't keep an eye on it. It looked okay though. I wondered if something was wrong with the alternator. A call box was less than fifty feet down the sidewalk so I moseyed to it, turning around several times to keep an eye on my little prisoner. I called in and asked for a garage man with a set of booster cables and was told to stand by for about twenty minutes and somebody'd get out to me. I thought about calling a sergeant since they carry booster cables in their cars, but I decided not to. What the hell, why be in a rush today? What was there to prove now? To anyone? To myself?

Then I started getting a little hungry because there was a small diner across the street and I could smell bacon and ham. The odor was blowing through the duct in the front of the place over the cooking stoves. The more I sniffed the hungrier I got, and I looked at my watch and thought, what the hell. I went back and unstrapped the kid.

"What's up? Where we going?"

"Across the street."

"What for? We taking a bus to your station or something?"

"No, we gotta wait for the garage man. We're going across the street so I can eat."

"You can't take me in there looking like this," said the kid, as I led him across the street. His naturally rosy cheeks were lobster-red now. "Take the handcuffs off."

"Not a chance. I could never catch a young antelope like you."

"I swear I won't run."

"I know you won't, with your hands cuffed behind you and me holding the chain."

"I'll die if you take me in there like a dog on a leash in front of all those people."

"Ain't nobody in there you know, kid. And anybody that might be in there's been in chains himself, probably. Nothing to be embarrassed about."

"I could sue you for this."

"Oh *could* you?" I said, holding the door and shoving him inside.

There were only three counter customers, two con guys, and a wino drinking coffee. They glanced up for a second and nobody even noticed the kid was cuffed. I pointed toward a table at the rear.

"Got no waitress this early, Bumper," said T-Bone, the proprietor, a huge Frenchman who wore a white chef's hat and a T-shirt, and white pants. I'd never seen him in anything else.

"We need a table, T-Bone," I said, pointing to the kid's handcuffs.

"Okay," said T-Bone. "What'll you have?"

"I'm not too hungry. Maybe a couple over-easy eggs and some bacon, and a few pieces of toast. And oh, maybe some hash browns. Glass of tomato juice. Some coffee. And whatever the kid wants."

"What'll you have, boy?" asked T-Bone, resting his huge hairy hands on the counter and grinning at the boy, with one gold and one silver front tooth. I wondered for the first time where in hell he got a silver crown like that. Funny I never thought of that before. T-Bone wasn't a man you talked to. He only used his voice when it was necessary. He just fed people with as few words as possible.

"How can I eat anything?" said the kid. "All chained up like a convict or something." His eyes were filling up and he looked awful young just then.

"I'm gonna unlock them," I said. "Now what the hell you want? T-Bone ain't got all day."

"I don't know what I want."

"Give him a couple fried eggs straight up, some bacon, and a glass of milk. You want hash browns, kid?"

"I guess so."

"Give him some orange juice too, and an order of toast. Make it a double order of toast. And some jam."

T-Bone nodded and scooped a handful of eggs from a bowl by the stove. He held four eggs in that big hand and cracked all four eggs one at a time without using the other hand. The kid was watching it.

"He's got some talent, hey, kid?"

"Yeah. You said you were taking these off."

"Get up and turn around," I said, and when he did I unlocked the right cuff and fastened it around the chrome leg of the table so he could sit there with one hand free.

"Is this what you call taking them off?" he said. "Now I'm like an organ grinder's monkey on a chain!"

"Where'd you ever see an organ grinder? There ain't been any grinders around here for years."

"I saw them on old TV movies. And that's what I look like."

"Okay, okay, quit chipping your teeth. You complain more than any kid I ever saw. You oughtta be glad to be getting some breakfast. I bet you didn't eat a thing at home this morning."

"I wasn't even *at* home this morning."

"Where'd you spend the night?"

He brushed back several locks of hair from his eyes with a dirty right hand. "I spent part of the night sleeping in one of those all-night movies till some creepy guy woke me up with his cruddy hand on my knee. Then I got the hell outta there. I slept for a little while in a chair in some hotel that was open just down the street."

"You run away from home?"

"No, I just didn't feel like sleeping at the pad last night. My sis wasn't home and I just didn't feel like sitting around by myself."

"You live with your sister?"

"Yeah."

"Where's your parents?"

"Ain't got none."

"How old's your sister?"

"Twenty-two."

"Just you and her, huh?"

"Naw, there's always somebody around. Right now

it's a stud named Slim. Big Blue always got somebody around."

"That's what you call your sister? Big Blue?"

"She used to be a dancer, kind of. In a bar. Topless. She went by that name. Now she's getting too fat in the ass so she's hustling drinks at the Chinese Garden over on Western. You know the joint?"

"Yeah, I know it."

"Anyway, she always says soon as she loses thirty pounds she's going back to dancing which is a laugh because her ass is getting wider by the day. She likes to be called Big Blue so even *I* started calling her that. She got this phony dyed-black hair, see. It's almost blue."

"She oughtta wash your clothes for you once in a while. That shirt looks like a grease rag."

"That's 'cause I was working on a car with my next door neighbor yesterday. I didn't get a chance to change it." He looked offended by that crack. "I wear clothes clean as anybody. And I even wash them and iron them myself."

"That's the best way to be," I said, reaching over and unlocking the left cuff.

"You're taking them off?"

"Yeah. Go in the bathroom and wash your face and hands and arms. And your neck."

"You sure I won't go out the window?"

"Ain't no window in that john," I said. "And comb that mop outta your face so somebody can see what the hell you look like."

"Ain't got a comb."

"Here's mine," I said, giving him the pocket comb.

T-Bone handed me the glasses of juice, the coffee, and the milk while the kid was gone, and the bacon smell was all over the place now. I was wishing I'd asked for a double order of bacon even though I knew T-Bone would give me an extra big helping.

I was sipping the coffee when the kid came back in. He was looking a hundred percent better even though his neck was still dirty. At least his hair was slicked back and his face and arms up to the elbow were nice and clean. He wasn't a handsome kid, his face was too tough and craggy, but he had fine eyes, full of life, and he looked you right in your eye when he talked to you. That's what I liked best about him.

"There's your orange juice," I said.

"Here's your comb."

"Keep it. I don't even know why I carry it. I can't do anything with this patch of wires I got. I'll be glad when I get bald."

"Yeah, you couldn't look no worse if you was bald," he said, examining my hair.

"Drink your orange juice, kid."

We both drank our juice and T-Bone said, "Here, Bumper," and handed a tray across the counter, but before I could get up the kid was on his feet and grabbed the tray and laid everything out on the table like he knew what he was doing.

"Hey, you even know what side to put the knife and fork on," I said.

"Sure. I been a busboy. I done all kinds of work in my time."

"How old you say you are?"

"Fourteen. Well, almost fourteen. I'll be fourteen next October."

When he'd finished he sat down and started putting away the chow like he was as hungry as I thought he was. I threw one of my eggs on his plate when I saw two weren't going to do him, and I gave him a slice of my toast. He was a first-class eater. That was something else I liked about him.

While he was finishing the last of the toast and jam, I went to the door and looked across the street. A garage attendant was replacing my battery. He saw me and waved that it was okay. I waved back and went back inside to finish my coffee.

"You get enough to eat?" I asked.

"Yeah, thanks."

"You sure you don't want another side of bacon and a loaf or two of bread?"

"I don't get breakfasts like that too often," he grinned.

When we were getting ready to leave I tried to pay T-Bone.

"From you? No, Bumper."

"Well, for the kid's chow, then." I tried to make him take a few bucks.

"No, Bumper. You don't pay nothin'."

"Thanks, T-Bone. Be seeing you," I said, and he raised a huge hand covered with black hair, and smiled gold and silver. And I almost wanted to ask him about the silver crown because it was the last time I'd have a chance.

"You gonna put the bracelets back on?" asked the boy, as I lit a cigar and patted my stomach and took a deep sniff of morning smog.

"You promise you won't run?"

"I swear. I hate those damn things on my wrists. You feel so helpless, like a little baby."

"Okay, let's get in the car," I said, trotting across the street with him to get out of the way of the traffic.

"How many times you come downtown to score?" I asked before starting the car.

"I never been downtown alone before. I swear. And I didn't even hitchhike. I took a bus. I was even gonna take a bus back to Echo Park. I didn't wanna run into cops with the pills in my pocket."

"How long you been dropping bennies?"

"About three months. And I only tried them a couple times. A kid I know told me I could come down here and almost any guy hanging around could get them for me. I don't know why I did it."

"How many tubes you sniff a day?"

"I ain't a gluehead. It makes guys crazy. And I never sniffed paint, neither."

Then I started looking at this kid, really looking at him. Usually my brain records only necessary things about arrestees, but now I found myself looking really close and listening for lies. That's something else you can't tell the judge, that you'd bet your instinct against a polygraph. I *knew* this boy wasn't lying. But then, I seemed to be wrong about everything lately.

"I'm gonna book you and release you to your sister. That okay with you?"

"You ain't gonna send me to Juvenile Hall?"

"No. You wanna go there?"

"Christ, no. I gotta be free. I was scared you was gonna lock me up. Thanks. Thanks a lot. I just gotta be free. I couldn't stand being inside a place like that with everybody telling you what to do."

"If I ever see you downtown scoring pills again, I'll make sure you go to the Hall."

The kid took a deep breath. "You'll never see me again, I swear. Unless you come out around Echo Park."

"As a matter of fact, I don't live too far from there."

"Yeah? I got customers in Silverlake and all around Echo Park. Where do you live?"

"Not far from Bobby's drive-in. You know where that is? All the kids hang around there."

"Sure I do. I work with this old guy who's got this pickup truck and equipment. Why don't you let us do your yard? We do front and back, rake, trim, weed and everything for eight bucks."

"That's not too bad. How much you get yourself?"

"Four bucks. I do all the work. The old guy just flops in the shade somewhere till I'm through. But I need him because of the truck and stuff."

This kid had me so interested I suddenly realized we were just sitting there. I put the cigar in my teeth and turned the key. She fired right up and I pulled out in the traffic. But I couldn't get my mind off this boy.

"Whadda you do for fun? You play ball or anything?"

"No, I like swimming. I'm the best swimmer in my class, but I don't go out for the team."

"Why not?"

"I'm too busy with girls. Look." The boy took out his wallet and showed me his pictures. I glanced at them while turning on Pico, three shiny little faces that all looked the same to me.

"Pretty nice," I said, handing the pictures back.

"*Real* nice," said the kid with a wink.

"You look pretty athletic. Why don't you play baseball? That used to be my game."

"I like sports I can do by myself."

"Don't you have any buddies?"

"No, I'm more of a ladies' man."

"I know what you mean, but you can't go through this world by yourself. You should have some friends."

"I don't need nobody."

"What grade you in?"

"Eighth. I'll sure be glad to get the hell out of junior high. It's a ghoul school."

"How you gonna pass if you cut classes like this?"

"I don't ditch too often, and I'm pretty smart in school, believe it or not. I just felt rotten last night. Sometimes when you're alone a lot you get feeling rotten and you just wanna go out where there's some people. I figured, where am I gonna find lots of people? Downtown, right? So I came downtown. Then this morning I felt more rotten from sleeping in the creepy movie so I looked around and saw these two guys and asked them where I could get some bennies and they sold them to me. I really wanted to get high, but swear to God, I only dropped bennies a couple times before. And one lousy time I dropped a red devil and a rainbow with some guys at school, and that's all the dope I ever took. I don't really dig it, Officer. Sometimes I drink a little beer."

"I'm a beer man myself, and you can call me Bumper."

"Listen, Bumper, I meant it about doing your yard work. I'm a hell of a good worker. The old man ain't no good, but I just stick him away in a corner somewheres and you should see me go. You won't be sorry if you hire us."

"Well, I don't really have a yard myself. I live in this apartment building, but I kind of assist the manager and he's always letting the damn place go to hell. It's mostly planted in ivy and ice plant and junipers that he lets get pretty seedy-looking. Not too much lawn except little squares of grass in front of the downstairs apartments."

"You should see me pull weeds, Bumper. I'd have that ice plant looking alive and green in no time. And I know how to take care of junipers. You gotta trim them a little, kind of shape them. I can make a juniper look soft and trim as a virgin's puss. How about getting us the account? I could maybe give you a couple bucks kickback."

"Maybe I'll do that."

"Sure. When we get to the police station, I'll write out the old man's name and phone number for you. You just call him when you want us to come. One of these days I'm getting some business cards printed up. It impresses hell out of people when you drop a business card on them. I figure we'll double our business with a little advertising and some business cards."

"I wouldn't be surprised."

"This the place?" The kid looked up at the old brown brick station. I parked in the back.

"This is the place," I said. "Pretty damned dreary, huh?"

"It gives me the creepies."

"The office is upstairs," I said, leading him up and inside, where I found one of the Juvenile Narcotics officers eating lunch.

"Hi, Bumper," he said.

"What's happening, man," I answered, not able to think of his name. "Got a kid with some bennies. No big thing. I'll book him and pencil out a quick arrest report."

"Worthwhile for me talking to him?"

"Naw, just a little score. First time, he claims. I'll take care of it. When should I cite him back in?"

"Make it Tuesday. We're pretty well up to the ass in cite-ins."

"Okay," I said, and nodded to another plainclothes officer who came in and started talking to the first one.

"Stay put, kid," I said to the boy and went to the head. After I came out, I went to the soft drink machine and got myself a Coke and one for the boy. When I came back in he was looking at me kind of funny.

"Here's a Coke," I said, and we went in another office which was empty. I got a booking form and an arrest report and got ready to start writing.

He was still looking at me with a little smile on his face.

"What's wrong?" I said.

"Nothing."

"What're you grinning at?"

"Oh, was I grinning? I was just thinking about what those two cops out there said when you went to the john."

"What'd they say?"

"Oh, how you was some kind of cop."

"Yeah," I mumbled as I put my initial on a couple of the bennies so I could recognize them if the case went to court. I knew it wouldn't though. I was going to request that the investigator just counsel and release him.

"You and your sister're gonna have to come in Tuesday morning and talk to an investigator?"

"What for?"

"So he can decide if he ought to C-and-R you, or send you to court."

"What's C and R? Crush and rupture?"

"Hey, that's pretty good," I chuckled. He was a spunky little bastard. I was starting to feel kind of proud of him. "C and R means counsel and release.

They almost always counsel and release a kid the first time he's busted instead of sending him to juvenile court."

"I told you I been busted twice for running away. This ain't my first fall."

"Don't worry about it. They're not gonna send you to court."

"How do you know?"

"They'll do what I ask."

"Those juvies said you was really some kind of cop. No wonder I got nailed so fast."

"You were no challenge," I said, putting the bennies in an evidence envelope and sealing it.

"I guess not. Don't forget to lemme give you the old guy's name and phone number for the yard work. Who you live with? Wife and kids?"

"I live alone."

"Yeah?"

"Yeah."

"I might be able to give you a special price on the yardwork. You know, you being a cop and all."

"Thanks, but you should charge your full price, son."

"You said baseball was your game, Bumper?"

"Yeah, that's right." I stopped writing for a minute because the boy seemed excited and was talking so much.

"You like the Dodgers?"

"Yeah, sure."

"I always wanted to learn about baseball. Maury Wills is a Dodger, ain't he?"

"Yeah."

"I'd like to go to a Dodger game sometime and see Maury Wills."

"You never been to a big league game?"

"Never been. Know what? There's this guy down the street. Old fat fart, maybe even older than you, and fatter even. He takes his kid to the school yard across the street all day Saturday and Sunday and hits fly balls to him. They go to a game practically every week during baseball season."

"Yeah?"

"Yeah, and know what the best part of it is?"

"What?"

"All that exercise is really good for the old man. That kid's doing him a *favor* by playing ball with him."

"I better call your sister," I said, suddenly getting a gas bubble and a burning pain at the same time. I was also getting a little light-headed from the heat and because there were ideas trying to break through the front of my skull, but I thought it was better to leave them lay right now. The boy gave me the number and I dialed it.

"No answer, kid," I said, hanging up the phone.

"Christ, you gotta put me in Juvenile Hall if you don't find her?"

"Yeah, I do."

"You can't just drop me at the pad?"

"I can't."

"Damn. Call Ruby's Playhouse on Normandie. That joint opens early and Slim likes to hang out there sometimes. Damn, not the Hall!"

I got Ruby's Playhouse on the phone and asked for Sarah Tilden, which he said was her name.

"Big Blue," said the boy. "Ask for Big Blue."

"I wanna talk to Big Blue," I said, and then the bartender knew who I was talking about.

A slurred young voice said, "Yeah, who's this?"

"This is Officer Morgan, Los Angeles Police, Miss Tilden. I've arrested your brother downtown for possession of dangerous drugs. He had some pills on him. I'd like you to drive down to thirteen-thirty Georgia Street and pick him up. That's just south of Pico Boulevard and west of Figueroa." After I finished there was a silence on the line for a minute and then she said, "Well, that does it. Tell the little son of a bitch to get himself a lawyer. I'm through."

I let her go on with the griping a little longer and then I said, "Look, Miss Tilden, you'll have to come pick him up and then you'll have to come back here Tuesday morning and talk to an investigator. Maybe they can give you some advice."

"What happens if I don't come pick him up?" she said.

"I'd have to put him in Juvenile Hall and I don't think you'd want that. I don't think it would be good for him."

"Look, Officer," she said. "I wanna do what's right. But maybe you people could help me somehow. I'm a young woman, too goddamn young to be saddled with a kid his age. I can't raise a kid. It's too hard for me. I got a lousy job. Nobody should expect me to raise a kid brother. I been turned down for welfare even, how do you like that? If I was some nigger they'd gimme all the goddamn welfare I wanted. Look, maybe it would be best if you *did* put him in Juvenile Hall. Maybe it would be best for him. It's *him* I'm thinking of, you see. Or maybe you could put him in one of those foster homes. Not like a criminal, but someplace where somebody with lots of time can watch over him and see that he goes to school."

"Lady, I'm just the arresting officer and my job is to get him home right now. You can talk about all this crap to the juvenile investigator Tuesday morning, but I want you down here in fifteen minutes to take him home. You understand me?"

"Okay, okay, I understand you," she said. "Is it all right if I send a family friend?"

"Who is it?"

"It's Tommy's uncle. His name's Jake Pauley. He'll bring Tommy home."

"I guess it'll be okay."

After I hung up, the kid was looking at me with a lopsided smile. "How'd you like Big Blue?"

"Fine," I said, filling in the boxes on the arrest report. I was sorry I had called her in front of the kid, but I wasn't expecting all that bitching about coming to get him.

"She don't *want* me, does she?"

"She's sending your uncle to pick you up."

"I ain't got no uncle."

"Somebody named Jake Pauley."

"Hah! Old Jake baby? Hah! He's some uncle."

"Who's he? One of her friends?"

"They're friendly all right. She was shacked up with him before we moved in with Slim. I guess she's going back to Jake. Jesus, Slim'll cut Jake wide, deep, and often."

"You move around a lot, do you?"

"*Do* we? I been in seven different schools. Seven! But, I guess it's the same old story. You probably hear it all the time."

"Yeah, I hear it all the time."

I tried to get going on the report again and he let me write for a while but before I could finish he said, "Yeah, I been meaning to go to a Dodger game. I'd be willing to pay the way if I could get somebody with a little baseball savvy to go with me."

Now in addition to the gas and the indigestion, I had a headache, and I sat back with the booking slip finished and looked at him and let the thoughts come to the front of my skull, and of course it was clear as water that the gods conspire against men, because here was this boy. On my last day. Two days after Cassie first brought up the thing that's caused me a dozen indigestion attacks. And for a minute I was excited as hell and had to stand up and pace across the room and look out the window.

Here it is, I thought. Here's the thing that puts it all away for good. I fought an impulse to call Cassie and tell her about him, and another impulse to call his sister back and tell her not to bother sending Jake baby, and then I felt dizzy on top of the headache. I looked down at my shield and without willing it I reached down and touched it and my sweaty finger left a mark on the brass part which this morning had been polished to the luster of gold. The finger mark turned a tarnished orange before my eyes, and I thought about trading my gold and silver shield for a little tinny retirement badge that you can show to old men in bars to prove what you used to be, and which could never be polished to a luster that would reflect sunlight like a mirror.

Then the excitement I'd felt for a moment began to fade and was replaced with a kind of fear that grew and almost smothered me until I got hold of myself. This was too much. This was all *much* too much. Cassie was one terrible responsibility, but I needed her. Cruz told me. Socorro told me. The elevator boy in the death room of the hotel told me. The old blubbering drunks in Harry's bar told me. I needed her. Yes, maybe, but I didn't need this other kind of responsibility. I didn't need *this* kind of cross. Not me. I walked into the other room where the juvenile officer was sitting.

"Listen, pal," I said. "This kid in here is waiting for his uncle. I explained the arrest to his sister and cited her back. I gotta meet a guy downtown and I'm late. How about taking care of him for me and I'll finish my reports later."

"Sure, Bumper. I'll take care of it," he said, and I wondered how calm I looked.

"Okay, kid, be seeing you," I said, passing through the room where the boy sat. "Hang in there, now."

"Where you going, Bumper?"

"Gotta hit the streets, kid," I said, trying to grin. "There's crime to crush."

"Yeah? Here's the phone number. I wrote it down on a piece of paper for you. Don't forget to call us."

"Yeah, well, I was thinking, my landlord is a cheap bastard. I don't think he'd ever go for eight bucks. I think you'd be better off not doing his place anyway. He probably wouldn't pay you on time or anything."

"That's okay. Give me your address, we'll come by

and give you a special price. Remember, I can kick back a couple bucks."

"No, it wouldn't work out. See you around, huh?"

"How 'bout us getting together for a ball game, Bumper? I'll buy us a couple of box seats."

"I don't think so. I'm kind of giving up on the Dodgers."

"Wait a minute," he said, jumping to his feet. "We'll do your gardening for four dollars, Bumper. Imagine that! Four dollars! We'll work maybe three hours. You can't beat that."

"Sorry, kid," I said, scuttling for the door like a fat crab.

"Why did you ever mention it then? Why did you ever say 'maybe'?"

I can't help you, boy, I thought. I don't have what you need.

"Goddamn you!" he yelled after me, and his voice broke. "You're just a cop! Nothing but a goddamn cop!"

I got back in the car feeling like someone kicked me in the belly and I headed back downtown. I looked at my watch and groaned, wondering when this day would end.

At the corner of Pico and Figueroa I saw a blind man with a red-tipped cane getting ready to board a bus. Some do-gooder in a mod suit was grabbing the blind man's elbow and aiming him, and finally the blind man said something to the meddler and made his own way.

"That's telling him, Blinky," I said under my breath. "You got to do for yourself in this world or they'll beat you down. The gods are strong, lonesome bastards and *you* got to be too."

## 17

AT ELEVEN-FIFTEEN I was parking in front of Seymour's to met Cruz. His car was there but I looked in the window and he wasn't at the counter. I wondered where he could be. Then I looked down the block and saw three black-and-whites, two detective cars, and an ambulance.

Being off the air with the kid I hadn't heard a call come out, and I walked down there and made my way through a crowd of people that was forming on the sidewalk around the drugstore. Just like everybody else, I was curious.

"What's happening, Clarence?" I said to Evans, who was standing in front of the door.

"Didn't you hear, Bumper?" said Evans, and he was sweating and looked sick, his coffee-brown face working nervously every-which way, and he kept looking around everywhere but at me.

"Hear what?"

"There was a holdup. A cop walked in and got shot," said a humpbacked shine man in a sailor's hat, looking up at me with an idiotic smile.

My heart dropped and I felt the sick feeling all policemen get when you hear that another policeman was shot.

"Who?" I asked, worrying that it might've been that young bookworm, Wilson.

"It was a sergeant," said the hunchback.

I looked toward Seymour's then and I felt the blood rush to my head.

"Let me in there, Clarence," I said.

"Now, Bumper. No one's allowed in there and you can't do anything. . . ."

I shoved Evans aside and pushed on the swinging aluminum doors, which were bolted.

"Bumper, please," said Evans, but I pulled away from him and slammed my foot against the center of the two doors, driving the bolt out of the aluminum casing.

The doors flew open with a crash and I was inside and running through a checkstand toward the rear of the big drugstore. It seemed like the store was a mile long and I ran blind and light-headed, knocking a dozen hair spray cans off a shelf when I barreled around a row of display counters toward the popping flashbulbs and the dozen plainclothesmen who were huddled in groups at the back of the store.

The only uniformed officer was Lieutenant Hilliard and it seemed like I ran for fifteen minutes to cover the eighty feet to the pharmacy counter where Cruz Segovia lay dead.

"What the hell . . ." said a red-faced detective I could barely see through a watery mist as I knelt beside Cruz, who looked like a very young boy sprawled there on his back, his hat and gun on the floor beside him and a frothy blood puddle like a scarlet halo fanning out around him from a through-and-through head shot. There was one red glistening bullet hole to the left of his nose and one in his chest which was surrounded by wine-purple bloodstains on the blue uniform. His eyes were open and he was looking right at me. The corneas were not yet dull or cloudy and the eyes were turned down at the corners, those large eyes more serious and sad than ever I'd seen them, and I knelt beside him in his blood and whispered, "'*Mano!* '*Mano!* '*Mano!* Oh, Cruz!*"

"Bumper, get the hell out of here," said the bald detective, grabbing my arm, and I looked up at him, seeing a very familiar face, but still I couldn't recognize him.

"Let him go, Leecher. We got enough pictures," said another plainclothesman, older, who was talking to Lieutenant Hilliard. He was one I should know too, I thought. It was so strange. I couldn't remember any of their names, except my lieutenant, who was in uniform.

Cruz looked at me so serious I couldn't bear it. And I reached in his pocket for the little leather pouch with the beads.

"You mustn't take anything from him," Lieutenant Hilliard said in my ear with his hand on my shoulder. "Only the coroner can do that, Bumper."

"His beads," I muttered. "He won them because he was the only one who could spell English words. I don't want them to know he carries beads like a nun."

"Okay, Bumper, okay," said Lieutenant Hilliard, patting my shoulder, and I took the pouch. Then I saw the box of cheap cigars spilled on the floor by his hand. And there was a ten-dollar bill there on the floor.

"Give me that blanket," I said to a young ambulance attendant who was standing there beside his stretcher, white in the face, smoking a cigarette.

He looked at me and then at the detectives.

"Give me that goddamn blanket," I said, and he handed the folded-up blanket to me, which I covered Cruz with after I closed his eyes so he couldn't look at me like that. "*Ahí te huacho,*" I whispered. "I'll be watching for you, '*mano.*" Then I was on my feet and heading toward the door, gulping for breath.

"Bumper," Lieutenant Hilliard called, running painfully on his bad right leg and holding his hip.

I stopped before I got to the door.

"Will you go tell his wife?"

"He came in here to buy me a going-away present," I said, feeling a suffocating pressure in my chest.

"You were his best friend. You should tell her."

"He wanted to buy me a box of cigars," I said, grabbing him by the bony shoulder. "Damn him, I'd never smoke those cheap cigars. Damn him!"

"All right, Bumper. Go to the station. Don't try to work anymore today. You go on home. We'll take care of the notification. You take care of yourself."

I nodded and hurried out the door, looking at Clarence Evans but not understanding what he said to me. I got in the car and drove up Main Street, tearing my collar open to breathe, and thought about Cruz lying frail and naked and unprotected there in the morgue and thinking how they'd desecrate him, how they'd stick that turkey skewer in him for the liver temperature, and how they'd put a metal rod in the hole in his face for the bullet angle, and I was so damned glad I'd closed his eyes so he wouldn't be watching all that.

"You see, Cruz," I said, driving over Fourth Street with no idea where I was going. "You see? You almost had me convinced, but you were all wrong. I was right."

"You shouldn't be afraid to love, 'mano," Cruz answered, and I slammed on my brakes when I heard him and I almost slid through the red light. Someone leaned on his horn and yelled at me.

"You're safe, Bumper, in one way," said Cruz in his gentle voice, "but in the way that counts, you're in danger. Your soul is in danger if you don't love."

I started when the light was green but I could hardly see.

"Did you believe that when Esteban was killed? Did you?"

"Yes, I knew it was the God's truth," he said, and his sad eyes turned down at the corners and this time I *did* blow a red light and I heard tires squeal and I

turned right going the wrong way on Main Street and
everyone was honking horns at me but I kept going to
the next block and then turned left with the flow of
traffic.

"Don't look at me with those goddamn turned-down
eyes!" I yelled, my heart thudding like the pigeon's
wing. "You're wrong, you foolish little man. Look at
Socorro. Look at your children. Don't you see now,
you're wrong? Damn those eyes!"

Then I pulled into an alley west of Broadway and
got out of the car because I suddenly couldn't see at
all now and I began to vomit. I threw it all up, all of it.
Someone in a delivery truck stopped and said something but I waved him off and heaved and heaved it
all away.

Then I got back in the car and the shock was wearing off. I drove to a pay phone and called Cassie before she left her office. I crowded in that phone booth
doubled over by stomach cramps and I don't really
know everything I said to her except that Cruz was
dead and I wouldn't be going with her. Not now, not
ever. And then there was lots of crying on the other
end of the line and talking back and forth that didn't
make any sense, and finally I heard myself say, "Yes,
yes, Cassie. You go on. Yes, maybe I'll feel different
later. Yes. Yes. Yes. Yes. You go on. Maybe I'll see you
there in San Francisco. Maybe someday I'll feel different. Yes."

I was back in my car driving, and I knew I'd have to
go to Socorro tonight and help her. I wanted to bury
Cruz as soon as possible and I hoped she would want
to. And now, gradually at first, and then more quickly,
I felt as though a tremendous weight was lifted from
my shoulders and there was no sense analyzing it, but
there it was. I felt somehow light and free like when I
first started on my beat. "There's nothing left now but
the *puta*. But she's not a *puta*, *'mano*, she's not!" I said,
lying to both of us for the last time. "You couldn't tell
a whore from a bewitching lady. I'll keep her as long

as I can, Cruz, and when I can't keep her anymore she'll go to somebody that can. You can't blame her for that. That's the way the world is made." And Cruz didn't answer my lie and I didn't see his eyes. He was gone. He was like Herky now, nothing more.

I began thinking of all the wandering people: Indians, Gypsies, Armenians, the Bedouin on that cliff where I'd never go, and now I knew the Bedouin saw nothing more than sand out there in that valley.

And as I thought these things I turned to my left and I was staring into the mouth of the Pink Dragon. I passed the Dragon by and drove on toward the station, but the further I drove, the more the anger welled up in me, and the anger mixed with the freedom I felt, so that for a while I felt like the most vigorous and powerful man on earth, a real *macho*, Cruz would've said. I turned around and headed back to the Dragon. This was the day for the Dragon to die, I thought. I could make Marvin fight me, and the others would help him. But no one could stand up to me and at last I'd destroy the Dragon.

Then I glanced down at my shield and saw that the smog had made the badge hideous. It was tarnished, and smeared with a drop of Cruz's blood. I stopped in front of Rollo's and went inside.

"Give it a fast buff, Rollo. I'm in a hurry."

"You know there ain't a single blemish on this badge," Rollo sighed.

"Just shine the goddamn badge."

He glanced up with his faded eyes, then at my trousers, at my wet bloody knees, and he bent silently over the wheel.

"There you are, Bumper," he said when he finished it.

I held the badge by the pin and hurried outside.

"Be careful, Bumper," he called. "Please be careful."

Passing by Rollo's store front I saw the distorted reflection in the folds of the plastic sun covering. I watched the reflection and had to laugh at the grotesque fat policeman who held the four-inch glittering shield in front of him as he lumbered to his car. The dark blue uniform was dripping sweat and the fat policeman opened the burning white door and squeezed his big stomach behind the wheel.

He settled in his saddle seat and jammed the nightstick under the seat cushion next to him, pointed forward.

Then he fastened his shield to his chest and urged the machine westward. The sun reflecting off the hood blinded him for a moment, but he flipped down the visor and drove west to the Pink Dragon.

"Now I'll kill the Dragon and drink its blood," said the comic blue policeman. "In the *front* door, down the Dragon's throat."

I laughed out loud at him because he was good for no more than this. He was disgusting and pathetic and he couldn't help himself. He needed no one. He sickened me. He only needed glory.

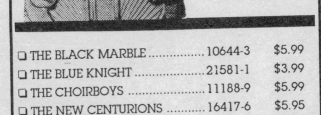

"Stuart Hopen's *Warp Angel* is perhaps the strangest science fiction novel I've ever read—wondrously strange. This story of the rediscovery of love and faith in a decadent future has more compelling ideas and images in the first few chapters than you'll find in a dozen ordinary SF novels. From the opening scene at a party held among wrecked starships to the final struggle on a planet where time has been bent out of shape, *Warp Angel* takes you places no other novel ever even approached.

"What else can I say. I think it's the most original and at the same time accessible SF I've read in years."

"It deserves to be a bestseller."

—Lawrence Watt-Evans, author of *The Misenchanted Sword*

"Riveting, action-driven... Hopen skillfully combines elements of space opera, cleverly drawn battle scenes, and metaphysical speculations on the power of faith—all without pausing a single step in a story line of unrelenting action. Great entertainment for fans of military SF and an excellent first effort from a writer to watch."

—*Booklist*

"Stuart Hopen has taken all the best elements of space action/adventure writing, dressed them for a Sister of Mercy vid, and then set them all spinning on their ears."

—S.N. Lewitt, author of *Blind Justice*

"Hopen's first novel features a strong, dedicated female protagonist and a well-imagined, dystopic far-future setting. Combining elements of space opera, action-adventure, and hard SF, this [is a] tightly crafted story of revenge and redemption.

—*Library Journal*

"Stuart Hopen has unexpectedly subtle ideas and a talent for wildly imaginative events with surprising resolutions. This should be the start of a distinguished career."

—Wilhelmina Baird, author of *Crash Course*

"Hopen reveals himself to be a subtle and impressive thinker, as well as inventive and enjoyable yarn-spinner."

—*St. Louis Post Dispatch*

# $\text{W}$arp
# $\text{A}$ngel

## STUART
## HOPEN

TOR ®

A TOM DOHERTY ASSOCIATES BOOK
NEW YORK

This is a work of fiction. All the characters and events portrayed in this book are either products of the author's imagination or are used fictitiously.

WARP ANGEL

Copyright © 1995 by Stuart Hopen

Cover art by Gary Ruddell

A Tor Book
Published by Tom Doherty Associates, Inc.
175 Fifth Avenue
New York, NY 10010

Tor Books on the World Wide Web:
http://www.tor.com

Tor® is a registered trademark of Tom Doherty Associates, Inc.

ISBN: 0-812-53653-3
Library of Congress Card Catalog Number 95-2061

First edition: May 1995
First mass market edition: November 1996

Printed in the United States of America

0  9  8  7  6  5  4  3  2  1

The author gratefully acknowledges the efforts, guidance, and contributions of Lawrence Watt-Evans and Greg Cox.

# Warp
# Angel

# 1

## THE FALL

**A** beautiful woman wandered into a graveyard of angels.

Collapsed cruisers and destroyed freight vessels littered the canyon in a panorama of rusting fuselages, struts, and frames. Once these great ships could race faster than light, could dart into folds in the universe, shrug off substance and spread measureless wings—but then mankind discovered an unexpected, insidious danger: warp travel was gradually eroding the structure of time and space itself.

For the past two hundred years, warp travel had been banned.

A huge cracked support beam threw shadows shaped like broken wings across the woman's almost bare back. Once a great pilot, Amelia Strados didn't fly anymore either.

A wild streak of white ran through her hair. She chose

neither to dye nor rejuvenate it. Her nose was slightly too long—just slightly—but she left it as it was and never lacked for admirers. Her cerulean blue eyes obviously had been genetically engineered, but that was done without her consent, two generations before.

She followed the sound of distant music, casually crossing a trail of glittering shattered windshields and silicon chips. Oxidized dust, the last iron from Earth, blew on the wind and stung Amelia's cheeks.

Nearby, at a clearing in the rubble, a crowd paraded ceremoniously toward the largest of the old ships. The party was just beginning. Bright, freshly painted nihilistic designs decorated the great ship's flanks. Nostalgic melodies leaked from rust holes across the ten-mile hull.

As Amelia crossed the gangplank to the old ship, she surveyed the scene below. The most prominent citizens of the Draconian system milled about at ground level: prancing fish who farmed the deep sea; chrome-skinned machine builders; and compound-eyed bodyguards who saw the world through 360-degree kaleidoscopes. Each wore a costume reflecting his craft, a kind of free advertising. A trapper wore elegant furs with the heads of animals still attached. He spoke to a Health Care worker, who wore a necklace of sharpened scalpels above her bare breasts. Weapons flashed occasionally, trade squabbles lighting up the crowd. Everyone was celebrating liberty.

The Earthlings who originally colonized the Draconian system came here seeking freedom. No one is quite certain what they were seeking freedom from—but to this day, there are no laws and no governments. The system had been named with fierce irony.

Generally, in the absence of law and currency, goods could only be obtained by pledging fealty to powerful commercial organizations, called "bodies" or "bods" in the local vernacular. The bods provided protection, shelter, clothing, food, amusements . . . everything. Those who did not belong to the bods had to depend on force of arms to sustain themselves. They had to barter at outrageously inflated values. That was the price of independence.

Amelia was the only unincorp invited, and she wore an outfit of scanty diaphanous scarves that were polarized, so they changed color and opacity as she moved. She would have preferred dressing more modestly for the evening. Forty years old, she didn't like displaying the way age had taken some of the firmness from her flesh. Yet the current fashions of the Draconian system tended to be revealing. Better to show how well she had preserved herself than invite conjecture by covering up.

Inside the antique warpship, smoke stained the air with stimulants. Amelia caught the ice-and-clove scent of cadmadine and the honey smell of cannabis. Thick bundles of wire hung like wreaths, decorated by printed circuit chips and fragments of machinery. Stars shone through man-sized rust holes in the ceiling.

A reptilian humanoid greeted Amelia with a hiss, and he thrust forward a scaled, web-fingered hand. He was Olagy, the prime director of the Slavers Bod. Like many of the guests, he was a flamboyant product of microsurgery and chromosome splicing, trying to break with tradition, even on the genetic level. His gait betrayed years in ankle irons. He had once been a slave.

"Welcome to our party," Olagy said. "Enjoy your freedom. Use it to excess. Do what you will." Then he proffered a glass of foaming amber liquid. "Try some champagne?"

"You're joking?"

"Not at all. This is real champagne. We found some crates in an old cargo hold."

Amelia accepted a handblown glass crafted from old photographs especially for the occasion. The drink was a legendary symbol to a long decadent culture. Real champagne hadn't been tasted in the Draconian system in two hundred years—ever since the gutting of the warships permanently severed ties to Earth. With a dramatic flourish, she took a sip.

It tasted bitter; vinegary and vile. Amelia put on a false, polite smile, pretending to like it for a moment. Then she set the glass down and walked away. She could not hide her disappointment.

"Everyone else is drinking it!" shouted Olagy.

Amelia glanced around at the other guests. They seemed giddy, playing with the refuse on the floor—ancient ballistic pistols or flanges from self-repairing mechanisms, curious remnants of a non-slave culture. Some were running their fingers through mounds of discarded coins. The jingling amused them.

Amelia found it hard to believe that the tiny bits of round metal at her feet once symbolized value. What did their mass-produced designs have to offer? Why did these miniature portraits of old Draconian pioneers provoke such melancholy? Was there some hidden meaning to the cryptic geometries and bas-relief frills? Monetary systems had been abolished long ago. The coins had no value now, not even as curiosities. Neither did the old guns, nor the self-repairing mechanisms that occasionally jerked with postmortem spasms. The concept of antique value, like all antiques, had become a thing of the past.

Amelia felt the vast, uncrossable distance between her world and the world of her ancestors.

A young, fair-haired mercenary, his weapons on display, swaggered boldly up to Amelia. He said, "Place like this—cramped, smoky, pistols all over the place, everyone trying to get into your pockets . . . place like this a rich woman shouldn't come alone." He was barely more than a boy. Too young, too pretty, and too dangerous.

Amelia tried to turn away, but the boy caught her shoulder.

"I'm Chev Carson. You may have heard of me. I'm the

fastest-rising member in the Merc Bod. I'll be your body-guard tonight. I'll stick real close. No charge.''

"No thanks," said Amelia.

He looked like an angel, with soft curly blond hair, but his eyes were full of blue cruelty. He wore a low-slung belt decorated with holographic icons of immeasurable depth. It was obvious that the religious imagery meant nothing to him, for the belt had been hung in a position that drew attention to the boy's loins.

"You know, there's people here getting drunk for the first time ever. They get real unpredictable. They're like cocked guns. You should be afraid!"

"I'm afraid you're an idiot!"

Chev reached for a conveniently handy gun. He toyed with the trigger, deciding what to do. In a momentary lapse, Amelia had forgotten how to deal with boys. She had forgotten how impulsive and violent they could be. Trying to look calm, she now regretted leaving her armed escorts back at her flier.

"Do you think you can always get what you want by frightening people?" Amelia asked.

"Yeah," said Chev Carson. "There was only one girl in my life who ever paid attention to me. She always said I terrified her. She was a hit." His hand lingered on the gun.

A member of the Morticians Bod approached the couple with slow, even steps. He was the only one in the room unbothered by the aura of imminent disaster. He seemed drawn to it.

"Carson is not to blame for this rude behavior," said the mortician. "Mercs can't handle liquor."

"I'm not. I can't," said Chev. He turned his attention to ancient statuettes of cherubim that adorned the trimmings on the corridor. He began shooting off the wings.

"Chev's profession allows little opportunity to drink," continued the mortician, his face showing no emotion.

Pale, grey, waxy makeup covered his complexion. "And Chev has fallen victim to the uneasiness of this place. We all feel it. Because of the rust. Rust is a symbol of death."

"Everything is a symbol of death to you," said Amelia, and Chev laughed.

"This place also reminds us that beautiful things fall into ruin," said the mortician, casting a measured glance at Amelia.

Chev belched up a bolus of air that stank of liquor and vinegar. He leveled his gun at Amelia's head. A red targeting dot appeared on her brow.

She opened her mouth, about to protest, when the sky burst into fire.

The night was glittering brightly through the rust holes; suddenly it had become a dazzling canopy of opal.

Chev now stared drunkenly upward. It looked as if a fireworks display had started. Amelia sucked in the smoky air, gasping, amazed she hadn't been shot.

She took the opportunity to bolt. She started a stampede. All the other guests followed, rushing to see the fireworks. Wild, uninhibited laughter, like children's laughter, echoed through faded velvet hallways.

Amelia put the crowd between her and Chev. Once outside, she whistled for her slaves. A contingent of armed, muscular bodyguards hustled from Amelia's cruiser. She waited until they surrounded her, then started to walk back with them, toward the cruiser.

The crowd was roaring. Amelia caught the faint smell of fried air. The rumble of battle cruisers breaking the sound barrier made her pause. Lasers were hissing high over her head.

It was not a fireworks display erupting across the sky, but rather a dogfight. Four small ships weaved beautiful colors in all directions, light filtered through precious jewels. Light from the killing end of the spectrum.

The dogfight held Amelia's attention. She recognized

the make of three of the warships: Ruinators. They flew in formation, bearing the logos of the Slavers Bod. Their funneled engine housings cut entropy with a variation of pyramid power. Very effective fighting machines.

The fourth ship, the Ruinator's quarry, looked strange; some kind of highly customized variation of a very old model—Wanderers, they were called, one of the earliest one-seat fighters.

Useless ornaments adorned the Wanderer's frame. Though the ornaments had been brightly polished, they still looked like junk. Heavy chrome lions crossed paws on the prow, just above a set of brass ram's horns. Crystal globes dangled freely on chains underneath the wing struts. Shocking red fins placed haphazardly across the fuselage contributed nothing to aerodynamics. It should have been a rattletrap, yet somehow it managed to evade the Ruinators.

The Wanderer jerked across the sky at irregular speeds that would vary suddenly, anywhere from 1,100 to 4,000 knots. Amelia couldn't tell if the engines were malfunctioning, or if the haphazard pace was deliberate, to make the ship a difficult target.

One of the Ruinators scored a hit, though not a serious one. Sparks flew from the Wanderer's hull. The Ruinators jetted in closer.

"Great, huh?" said Olagy, addressing the crowd. "The Ruinators, they cost plenty. I bet that guy they're chasing won't get away! I bet one thousand slaves!"

Amelia studied the sky battle. Despite the clear advantage the Ruinators held, both in number and in firepower, they had not scored any crippling blows.

"I'll take that bet, Olagy," she said.

Suddenly the Wanderer bled airspeed, dropping straight down, trapping the Ruinators in a treacherous overshoot. They zoomed past. When it bobbed back up, the Wanderer faced three sets of afterburners, in a perfect kill position. It could pick off any of the Ruinators at will. A strategically placed series of light stabs from the Wanderer amputated a pair of geometrically variable wings from the rearmost Ruinator. Crippled, the Ruinator dropped, pure dead weight. It hit the ground spinning, raising giant fans of oxidized dust among the ruins. The amputated wings sailed gracefully on their own, past the horizon.

Amelia couldn't repress a grin. "Well done, well done," she commented, shading her eyes from the glare. She sensed that the Wanderer's pilot was a woman, luring her opponents into recklessness by feigning vulnerability. A woman's tactics. Almost as good as I used to do, she thought.

The remaining two Ruinators snap-rolled and peeled in opposite directions, maneuvering to catch the Wanderer within a prong formation.

The Wanderer snapped into an eight-g bat turn, lofting to a face-to-face kill position with one of the Ruinators. It was a nervy and dangerous move: a gamble on having faster reflexes than the Ruinator. It was a gamble that paid off, as the Wanderer unleashed a quick burst of fractured rainbows. Despite its age, the Wanderer had very modern guns. The Ruinator's nose erupted like a volcano.

Dead, the Ruinator turned ninety degrees, then tumbled from the sky with a sudden rush of shrieking air. Globes of melted metal rained into its wake.

The other Ruinator was forced to swerve and barely avoided impact.

The Wanderer was not such a bad ship after all. That old model had spawned countless imitations. Even the Ruinators followed the same basic design.

The second Ruinator pulled back, sobered and cautious. Its pilot planned to strike from a distance, taking advantage of his ship's advanced weaponry.

The Wanderer looped, rolled, and weaved among the rusting hulks, no longer making any pretense about its capacity for speed or its maneuvering abilities. The brass ram's horns bellowed as the ship accelerated. The chains whipped around and rattled.

With manual aiming nearly impossible, the Ruinator engaged its computerized targeting system. Fine beams of red light established a grid across the sky. A great flaming net spread in all directions, with the Ruinator in the center.

The Wanderer's ornamentation, that elaborate, shining, absurd-looking mess, took hit after hit. A flash of force sheared off one of the ram's horns. Fins flew loose. The chains went whistling free. And yet the Wanderer's flight pattern showed no signs of injury. Amelia began to understand. The ship's decorations were a disguise suggesting foolish and easy prey. And more. The absurd façade decoyed fire away from vital areas.

The Wanderer ejected clumps of tinsel through its ballast tubes. The tinsel drifted, deflecting the ruby grid vectors. The fire net tore open, causing the Ruinator's shots to go wild. The onlookers scrambled.

While the Ruinator's targeting system choked on tinsel, the Wanderer climbed to pure vertical, then looped around at ten g's, a maneuver called a St. Angelo Immelmann. It carried nasty risks for c-spine fractures, but it proved to be another astute combat decision. After scoring two severe hits on the underbelly of the Ruinator, the Wanderer swerved out of the way. Plumes of smoke flowed from both impact sites.

The Ruinator swung into hard pursuit. With a burst of power, it gained on the Wanderer. The smoke plumes thinned into translucent threads as the Ruinator's speed increased. The distance between the two ships narrowed.

The Ruinator hung dangerously close now. The Wanderer weaved and dodged, trying to lead its pursuer to wreckage against jutting frames and useless cannons in a rusting maze.

The Ruinator's pilot steered a course that showed no regard for caution.

"He must be severely wounded. He flies like he has nothing to lose," Amelia commented.

Olagy grunted.

The Ruinator let loose a volley of bright flashes. Half of the Wanderer's left tail fin split into fragments. The Ruinator was too close to avoid flying into the tail debris, which immediately skittered harmlessly over his windshield.

Wobbling, but holding the air, the Wanderer left a wide trail of smoke. Seriously crippled, it careened toward the party ship. Then the Wanderer escaped into one of the biggest rust holes, disappearing inside the ancient hulk.

The Ruinator followed into ruin.

The great hulk shook. The crowd heard sounds of internal battle: the small ships crashing through decayed decks and firing at one another. Trapped echoes rumbled. Smoke poured out of the rust holes in streams that blotted out the stars. The stink of various carbon compounds spread with the smoke.

A loud growl began to shake the hulk. Suddenly, a fireball blew out the hulk's two-mile posterior. Not far from the point of the explosion, the Wanderer shot out through the vistaview—a huge window built along the observation decks for warp tourists. The window fell apart on impact, with a high-pitched whine and a treble shower of sound. Transparent metal musically ricocheted off the surrounding junkyard ships.

The Wanderer skidded to a halt at the fringe of the crowd.

"Is anyone hurt?" asked the woman wearing the scalpels.

"No," shouted Olagy, not bothering to check.

A few party guests crept forward to inspect the wreckage. Heat was radiating from the scab-textured sides of the

Wanderer. Cracked engines hissed and sprayed scalding oil, anointing the hood of the fallen spacecraft.

The pilot—a woman, as Amelia had surmised—crawled out through a jagged opening.

Foreign-looking, almond-shaped eyes smoldered beneath the shadows of the pilot's helmet. Amber star bursts on the green irises surrounded her adrenaline-bloated pupils. The stiff collar of her flight suit had been zipped all the way up to her jawline. A rough-hewn cloth covered every part of her body except her face and the lower part of her right leg. The sharp white point of a snapped tibia had torn the fabric when it pierced her shin. At her side, the leg lay twisted awkwardly. The exposed bone shined bright as polished metal. Blood dripped from the girl's leg wound and fuel bled from her ship. Both gathered in puddles, not quite mixing; red globes bobbing in amber depths.

The pilot's features contorted with pain. She might have been pretty under other circumstances, possibly. It was too hard to tell.

"Three thousand slaves to anyone who kills her!" shouted Olagy.

Chev Carson lunged forward, his gun already unholstered.

"Don't shoot!" shouted Amelia.

"Why not?" asked Chev. "What do I care if you win your bet?"

"Don't shoot! You'll ignite the spilled fuel and kill us all!"

Amelia was right. He couldn't use the gun. Whipping around, searching for a knife, he moved swiftly, but the booze upset his equilibrium. His body wasn't equal to the demands he was making on it. Fumbling for a blade, he sliced his thumb. Then he sucked on the cut, hoping he hadn't accidently poisoned himself, lethally or otherwise. The crowd started laughing. Chev turned, his third rotation in less than a minute, trying to see what was so funny. Thumb still in his mouth, he lost his balance and tumbled forward. As he fell into the puddle, blood and fuel splashed.

The fallen pilot reached through her shattered windshield, groping for something. Finally a pistol had come to hand.

A number of mercs and bodyguards pushed their way through the crowd, their blades glinting.

The fallen pilot fired her gun. Not at any particular target, but straight up into the air. She held the pistol high, its light beam stabbing up to heaven. As she waved her hand, the beam swayed from side to side with an almost hypnotic rhythm, like a magic wand of infinite size.

The mercs resheathed their blades. They dared not kill her. If she died, her gun would fall. The beam would ignite the fuel, and the ensuing fireball would incinerate everything within a half-mile radius.

The crowd began to creep backward, slowly.

Only Amelia stepped forward. "Trust me," she said. "I bet heavily on you tonight. I saved your life a moment ago. You can trust me."

"You saved your own life, too," said the pilot. She seemed totally self-contained. Her face was a mask, a shell.

"You'll never get out of here alone," said Amelia. "You'll bleed to death . . . soon . . . if you just sit there."

The pilot thrust her arm forward to show how rigidly she could hold it. "Look at the light, reaching all the way up to God. I don't waver. I can slow my heart and hold my blood in my veins, and I can still keep alert. I can go on like this for days if I must. And if I die, I won't die alone!"

"You don't want to die."

"I'm not afraid."

"You are a survivor. I knew that about you just watching the way you fly. If you want to live, you are going to have to have faith in me. Faith is a gamble, girl, but gambling has its own rewards. Faith is better than certain death."

The pilot scanned the crowd. Despite her bravado, small tremors afflicted her arm. "All right," she said.

"I swear you can trust me." Amelia snapped her fingers, and her slaves came forward. "Carry her to the ship," Amelia commanded.

"I don't have any choice," said the pilot. "I must go with you. But I won't be carried by slaves." She snapped off the light beam, but the gun muzzle still glowed white hot. *"You!* You give me your hand!"

Amelia approached the wreckage. She hoisted the girl to her feet. Amelia's slaves, weapons out, parted the crowd.

Leaning on Amelia for support, the girl hobbled slowly past the vinegar-scented revelers.

Amelia had never seen anyone dressed as modestly as this girl, in opaque, formless clothing. She felt nearly naked holding the girl at her side. They were both out in the open, painfully displayed and exposed.

Assassins scurried for good positions, jostling the onlookers. The girl watched the spaces in the crowd, the openings between onlookers' limbs. Suddenly she fired her still-hot pistol at a mercenary who had taken cover behind a row of bare knees. A shower of sizzling brains erupted from inside the crowd and the merc slumped forward.

Two more mercs jumped into the clearing, only to be cut down by Amelia's bodyguard slaves.

As Amelia and the girl drew closer to Amelia's craft, the crowd rolled in closer, like an onrushing tide, covering the cleared path behind them. Would-be assassins shoved against reckless onlookers, each competing for the best views. The air stunk of musk and barbecue smoke.

As Amelia and the pilot mounted the steps to the escape craft, gunlight flashed on all sides. Without hesitation, Amelia's slaves threw themselves around her as a living—though not for long—shield. Amelia hurried the girl through the doorway.

"Some of your slaves are wounded out there, still alive," said the girl as the cabin door closed down behind her. "We can't leave them."

"Someone with an eye for value will pick them up," said Amelia. "They were good slaves, and well worth more than the cost of a little medical care." She snapped her fingers, and the slave in the cockpit revved the engines.

"Let me handle liftoff," said the girl. "We're under fire. Slaves' reflexes are worthless. So is their judgment. I can get us out of here."

"You're in no condition."

"With God's help . . ."

The girl passed out. She was right, though.

Amelia pushed her slave pilot aside and took the controls herself.

She sailed through a volley of pistol fire that erupted from the crowd. Fortunately, the handguns weren't strong enough to pierce the shielding on her cruiser.

It was good to fly again. Ultrasonic vapor trailed from her wingtips as she pushed the ragged envelope of the Summer World. The ineffectual light of the handguns chased her all the way into space.

The headquarters of the Slavers Bod dominated the skyline of the Summer World, the Draconian system's center of commerce. Shaped like a giant statue of Bacchus, the edifice boasted of the awesome amount of manpower that had gone into its construction. A reddish brown patina, the color of dried blood, darkened in the folds of the robe and the ringlets of the beard, where the work had been more hazardous.

Dissa Banach viewed the towers of bods great and small

through a round window in the wine god's dilated pupil. He loved the blistering city. He loved its heat and its status, even though he lived in perpetual air-conditioning. Velvet robes kept him warm and hid his scars.

Dissa tried to affect an air of nobility, but his posture was hunched and his manner crude. Beneath those perfumed velvets, his massively muscled body rippled with steroid and surgical enhancements.

He left the giant stone eye, a bubble-shaped solarium, and crossed an odorless corridor.

Dissa found Olagy basking in a marble tub permanently installed in the center of his office. Slaves poured oils and liquors into the bathwater. A pretty girl slave manicured Olagy's talons, while a pretty boy slave massaged his scales.

Olagy cradled his head and moaned, "The Ruinators ruined my party. They were part of a campaign nobody told me about. I'm supposed to be conducting all the offensive actions around here! Who runs this outfit anyway?"

Olagy looked up and saw Dissa filling the doorway.

Dissa said, "Here is the story, Olagy. Your party crasher committed repeated acts of sabotage against the bod over the last few months. Totally unprovoked acts, I might add." Dissa fanned away the pungent steam from Olagy's bath. "We spotted her. We gave chase. Our actions were appropriate under the circumstances." Dissa chose his words carefully now—he didn't want to minimize the urgency in stopping the girl. At the same time, Dissa didn't want to reveal the full extent of the girl's raids, which had been an embarrassment to the enforcement arm of the bod. "She has caused certain isolated losses that could be considered significant."

"Uh-huh . . ." muttered Olagy, thinking of the one thousand slaves he had lost to Amelia Strados.

"I have a plan to terminate this girl, who has been a pest to both of us."

"It better be good," shouted Olagy. "She's holed up with the wealthiest unincorp in the system. Amelia Strados lives on an asteroid. Her place is a fortress."

"A lone assassin could get through," said Dissa. "I suggest Chev Carson."

"*Carson!* That's the dumbest idea I ever heard. She made a fool out of him at the party. Everyone saw it."

"So much the better. Carson has truly outstanding skills. A superb specimen who partied just a little too hard. He'll do anything to recapture his reputation, to avenge the insult to his pride."

"The guy's incompetent. It's the dumbest idea I ever heard. I swear, lately I get blue in the face repeating myself."

Suddenly Olagy made a sound like a hiccough cracking in his throat. His eyes bulged, and he slid into the bathwater. His head floated, slightly bobbing on the surface of the water, as if held buoyant by his bugged-out dead eyes.

A twin of Olagy peeked out from behind a curtain, holding a still glowing handgun. Years before, Olagy had decided he couldn't keep up with himself, so he had had a clone made. No more inclined to servitude than the original, the clone cloned himself. It seemed as if he had been born with the idea. As new clones were made, each proved equally lazy—slaves, so to speak, to their genes. Clones made clones, and after a while, Olagy had lost track of how many times he had been replicated. The duplicates began to battle among themselves for identity, like parents and children.

"I agree completely with your plan," hissed the new Olagy. "I grant you full authority to carry it out." Implicit in the grant was a plea for alliance.

"Thank you, Olagy." Dissa bowed ceremoniously.

The new Olagy watched the slaves pull his dead reflection from the bathwater; then he undressed and mounted the bathtub like a throne, luxuriating in the liquors and oils, and in the blood that might as well be his own.

As Dissa departed, he wondered if the original Olagy still survived somewhere. Not that he cared.


The Strados asteroid drifted through space in and out of the shadows of worlds.

Pure cast zirconia formed the outer walls and columns of the mansion, as well as the perimeter battlements. Dense collections of diamond mirrors reflected the wild and silver crags of the surrounding mass. The estate itself was all but invisible from a distance. Up close, the crystal architecture would seem to unfold from the agitated vistas of rock and stars. Its jeweled vectors, a melange of palatial styles, surmounted the island in space.

Amelia's great-grandfather had built this diamond castle. He built it to last forever. He wanted walls that would withstand enemy cannon fire. He wanted a monument for selected eyes only, a perfect blend of security and spectacle. The same penchant for paranoia and ostentation motivated the family in all of their dealings over succeeding generations.

Because of the asteroid's irregular shape and elliptical orbit, the estate sometimes fell out of the path of sunlight. Night would fall without warning.

In the largest guest room on the starboard side of the mansion, the rescued girl lay sweat-soaked and feverish under silken sheets. Her wandering was finished for a time.

A complex aluminum traction held her broken leg suspended above the bed. Magnetic field generators hummed around the cast to enhance the healing of the bone.

Amelia peeled back the sheets. She could not help but

take note of the astonishing tone of the girl's muscles. Touching the left deltoid ever so lightly, Amelia tested its firmness. A warrior's sinews.

Suddenly the girl's eyes blinked open. They glared, full of questions, devoid of trust. Suspicion burned for an instant, hotter than the girl's fever. Then weakness got the better of her, and heat resealed her eyelids.

Amelia ran a cool wet sponge over the rescued girl's forehead and thought, She must suppose I want a warrior slave—or an amusement. Why am I doing this? If she had the strength, she'd throttle me and head for the stars.

Amelia continued the sponge bath. She had risked far more for this undeserving stranger than she had ever risked for any friend, or lover, or family. Perhaps some late-blooming inbred predisposition toward altruism was manifesting itself, despite Amelia's Draconian upbringing. Or perhaps simple curiosity had led Amelia to discover a unique form of self-satisfaction—helping others. She would try anything once. The element of risk added sport to the matter.

Amelia felt heat radiating from the girl's hard muscles—muscles shaped by life-and-death struggles. The fever would not stop rising. The rescued girl was in terrible danger. And so was Amelia.


Heavy cloud banks shrouded the Autumn World. From space, the misted planet glowed at the outermost periphery with a thin, multicolored aura.

Down below, on the planet's surface, in vast forests, leaves perpetually changed color, a never-ending fall. Only one city rose above the rainbow wilderness. It was built by a cult of fortune-tellers, priests, self-styled witches, and other mystics, who conducted their affairs as an enormous commune. They called their city Dante, and had designed it around a series of ascending and descending circles. All of the system knew that Autumners were crazy, mist-mad, or high on God.

As Chev brought his craft in for a landing, he gripped the controls so hard the muscles in his forearms burned. He scouted the mists. He hated landing in fog, guided only by a distant red glare.

His knuckles whitened, his veins bulged as he maneuvered his flier down to a dangerous landing on a narrow cobblestone street. The locals distrusted technology and made no accommodations for aircraft.

Chev hated the Autumn World. He hated the mind readers, who were almost impossible to hit. He hated losing the privacy of his own skull every time he turned a corner. And he hated the mists, which were rumored to contain small quantities of free-floating hallucinogens.

To make things worse, he had been assigned to hunt a fellow mercenary here, someone he had once considered a friend. Hunting his own kind was a dangerous and distasteful business, the lowest kind of scut work. Doing it on the Autumn World was even worse. Chev never thought he'd be the one to take the fall.

As Chev opened his ship's hatchway, tendrils of thick fog rolled in. Outside, visibility was so poor, he nearly stumbled while descending the landing plank.

Chev was forced to navigate the street by groping for tactile landmarks on sculpted buildings. He made a left turn when he felt a monkey straddling a skull. The intricacy of the façades surprised him. It rivaled bod craftsmanship.

The cultists in their black uniforms passed by, interrupting their usual blank stares to shoot disapproving glances at Chev. These people did not welcome outsiders—except new recruits. Chev, decked out in weapons, clearly had not come to Dante for religious reasons.

* * *

Chev's quarry was hiding out in a fortune-teller's shop in the city's psychic district. Chev followed a tip that brought him to a pink cloud of pastel light suspended in the fog. As he got closer, he saw an organically illuminated sign at the center of the pink cloud. Glass letters filled with live glowing insects boasted:

SOLUTIONS TO EVERY PROBLEM

Chev groped for the doorway to the fortune-teller's shop. Finding it, he stepped inside.

The shop smelled like an old bible. Low-burning lamps, faintly smelling of whale oil, lit the foyer. An old crone softly singing to herself laid tarot cards atop an iron table. The metallic snapping of cards kept rhythm with her quiet song. She wore a heavy, formless cape that hinted of grossly misshapen contours. Chev looked at her and grunted. He held a low opinion of people who tamper with their genes for shock value.

Then Chev began to search the shop. First he opened a spider-filled closet. Peering behind a tattered curtain, he found only a pile of nonhuman bones.

"What do you want?" asked the crone.

"I'm looking for a friend," answered Chev. "A mercenary named Alex Fable."

A noise startled Chev. He fired a ray blast, scorching a row of crumbling books on a shelf. Crablike creatures scuttled to safety amid a shower of burning paper motes.

"You lie," hissed the crone. "You seek a man but you are not his friend."

"How'd you guess? Are you psychic or something?" Chev kicked open the lid of a coffin-sized box. He steadied his gun. A beast with long claws looked up pathetically at him, its fur dotted with small festering sores. It shivered inside the box.

Chev turned away, disgusted, still on guard. There was danger nearby.

"Well, I sure used to be Fable's friend." This much was true. Chev remembered feeling depressed one night after a particularly unpleasant kill. Since most mercs consider conscience a sign of weakness and efforts at consolation to be in poor taste, all his bod brothers were avoiding him. All except Fable, who took him aside and talked to him for hours. Fable rambled on and on about stupid, meaningless topics. For some reason it made Chev feel better. That was really the only social contact they had ever had. They were friends, sort of.

"It's not my fault Fable tried to beat the Gunsmiths Bod," said Chev.

"Most mercenaries avoid the Autumn World," said the crone. "They're afraid of meeting their former victims. Ghosts walk the streets, or so it is said."

Chev kicked over a wicker basket. A severed head, eyes and lips sewn shut, tumbled out.

The danger was closer now.

Chev tried to spread his gaze as close to 180 degrees as possible, shoving his peripheral vision into near clarity. He snorted to get the smell of burning paper out of his nose.

"Tell me," he asked, "is there really a solution to every problem?"

"Oh yes," replied the crone, "whether we like it or not."

A large hairy hand snapped forward from inside the crone's cloaks. The hairy hand held a gun, the nozzle pointing at Chev's forehead. The crone looked absurd with a muscular third arm extending from her chest.

"Fable? Hiding under skirts? You've really changed," said Chev.

"Your coming here was foreseen," said the crone, smiling toothlessly.

A muffled voice inside the crone's cloaks said, "I don't want to kill you. I always liked you."

Chev said, "I always liked you, too. So I'll be straight up with you. The gun won't work. It's in range of my jammer. Maybe I could have bought some extra time or gained some advantage by acting scared or something. But I'm letting you know up front—your gun won't work."

Fable squeezed the trigger. The gun threw green sparks and screeched, but it would not fire. For some reason, Fable kept pulling the trigger, as if he could get it to work by wishing.

Chev shook his head condescendingly. He'd warned Fable, but Fable wasted a full fifteen seconds fiddling with the gun anyway.

Then Fable lunged out through the flaps of the crone's cloaks. He'd lost weight, which made his nose look larger and his eyes smaller. Looking more rat-faced than ever, he held two long polished knives, one in each hand.

Instinctively, Chev peeled off a shot from his pistol on the off chance that Fable might not be wearing a jammer. No such luck. A quick sideways knife slash drew a weeping red line across Chev's arm.

Chev wasn't usually that slow. Something had dulled his battle responses. Conscience? Supposedly, conscience had largely been bred out of the warrior castes. However, his tutors had warned him that momentary relapses might occur from time to time. "If this happens, let yourself revert to reflex," they cautioned. "Let your muscles think for you." Chev shifted into reflex mode, action without thought.

Chev stomped hard on his left heel, cracking the plastic cover, releasing an olive-colored corrosive gas. Fable's knives pitted and withered away. The gas was poisonous as hell, but Chev could breathe it because of self-adjusting antitoxins in his bloodstream. Chev hoped that Fable had not taken a dose of antitoxin within the last twenty-four hours, so this grim business would be over with minimal physical contact. Fable retreated, clearly well dosed with active antitoxin, alive and angling for escape. The crone keeled over, though. Her disgusting little pets tumbled off the shelves and dropped from the rafters as poisonous wisps fanned over the foyer.

Chev pulled an empty leather-bound sword handle from his belt of rainbows. With a twist, he shook loose a liter of potent, frothing acid. Then he flicked on a stasis field and froze the splatter in midair.

Fable responded by producing his own acid blade, wincing at the stink as the acid sprayed out. He tested the weightless weapon, slicing the air. The blade hissed. Ripples shivered across its length. Fable wiped the sweat from his brow. "Acid sword's a nasty piece of work."

Both men assumed formal postures. They held their weapons as if in midcut, rigid as photographs for nearly a minute in silence. Each dared the other to make the first move.

The thin blades wafted slightly with the hesitant opening feints. Each stroke left a wake of warmed air. Effervescent currents bubbled along the cutting edges.

Chev and Fable cautiously inched toward each other. If their blades should touch, the stasis fields would breach and the acid would splatter. The weapon suited Chev well. It took nerve and skill. It took stupidity, too—considering the odds that both combatants would end up dead or maimed.

Fable went on the offensive, swinging his frothing sword like a battle-ax. It effortlessly cut through all solid matter in its path. Bookshelves tumbled as the swordsmen stabbed at each other. Chunks of severed animal limbs flew with charred pages and bits of old bone.

Chev jumped on top of the iron table, which rang like a bell. He danced around, clowning, shaking his hips at Fable, spinning his blade like a baton, scattering the crone's tarot cards with his footwork, flaunting his superior skills.

He took a slice from Fable's shoulder.

Fable screamed. Desperate, bleeding, enraged, Fable swung at Chev and missed. Then he aimed at the table instead and lopped off an iron leg. Chev fell on his ass as the table tumbled. Vibrations hummed up Chev's spine and made his teeth buzz.

Fable blew his temporary advantage by chickening on a stab. Knowing he'd stalled just a little too long, he tried to keep Chev from getting to his feet by telegraphing a vertical cut. Chev grinned at the crude attack—all bluster and bluff. Chev jumped up and parried with the mere threat of touching blades. The swords cackled with every hint of closeness.

They fanned acid-warmed air at each other. The action of the duel was interrupted occasionally by a series of formal halts.

"This ain't a fair fight!" shouted Fable as he froze his slash. "You really need work this bad? I tell you we should head out to Winter and go pirate. With what we know, we could live like prime directors among the unincorps. What do you say? Who needs this shit anyway?"

Fable was talking to a reflex. Chev stroked the fringes of Fable's sword, and a small globe of acid tore loose. It landed on Fable's knuckles, turning three of them to bubbling broth. Fable howled, switched hands, and grazed Chev's stasis field with his weapon. A fine acid mist sprayed over Chev's thigh. The fabric evaporated. A rash of blisters and blood beads spread where the acid had fallen.

"That's the way it is with an acid duel," said Chev, seemingly unbothered by the wound. He was mentally turning down the volume on the pain and savoring the rush of adrenaline and endorphins. "You got to take your burns. If you try to walk away unmarked, you lose."

The bottomless rainbows of Chev's holographic belt shined through the poison-misted air, its scenes of the afterlife full of morbid implications.

Slowly, Fable was maneuvering his way over to a blue porcelain vase where a single rose drooped. Water will make an acid sword explode. He had no other chance for survival.

Chev's blade rhythmically slashed the air, spreading its sulfurous bouquet. He took a sudden stab, and an inch of ear flew from Fable's head, fringed in sizzling blood. Incited by the pain, Fable grabbed the blue vase and pitched the contents—rancid water and a dying flower—in Chev's direction. Chev dodged.

The blades tore the air in wild succession, narrowly avoiding one another, like the whirling of meshed fans. Stroke, counterstroke, feint. Sweat fogged the room.

Chev executed a series of rapid gestures, as if he were signing his name in warm currents. He hummed a popular tune softly. Fable gave up ground, intimidated by the formality of Chev's assault.

Chev repeated the series stroke for stroke. Fable inched involuntarily toward a corner.

As Chev began the third repetition, Fable slashed into Chev's combat space, anticipating the trajectory of Chev's next cut. But this time, Chev reversed the pattern of his gestures, grazing Fable's sword on the inside edge.

The blades touched with an electrical blast. The fields breached, blowing off a bolus of smoke. The acid sprayed. All sizzle and hiss; a sudden searing rain.

Chev twisted violently and curled like a fetus to protect his face as he hit the ground. A sprinkle of acid splashed his back, fried its way through his shirt. He braced for the flare of pain. In fast-forming black-rimmed holes across the wooden floor, droplets gurgled.

Chev turned to face his opponent—but Fable no longer had a face. The dying renegade lay on the ground, hyperventilating in agonized moans. He cursed through corroding teeth on a lipless smile.

With a single stroke, Chev hacked off Fable's head and his hands. He took off the hands only because they got in the way at the last moment, raised to ward off the blow.

Chev stumbled through the door. Blood rolled down his spine in warm, slow streams. Blisters swelled on his hand, his thighs, his back. His brain burned. His stomach knotted. He had acid indigestion. He tried, but he could not rechannel his misery. Weirdly, it was the way he felt the night Fable had comforted him long ago. Chev wished he could talk to Fable one more time. He wanted to apologize. But what would he say? "I didn't mean to kill you. I lose my head sometimes. You know what that's like."

Chev started to laugh. He laughed until he realized he was lost in the fog.

He groped, trying to find the rows of architecture that could guide him back to his ship. He couldn't find contact with anything tactile. He shouted and listened for echoes, but either the fog muffled them or he had wandered too far astray from the buildings. Though he stomped his feet in frustration, his footsteps made no sound. The street was smooth, soft. Where were the cobblestones?

He broke into a run through absolute silence, choking on white, tasteless mists. He started to panic. All of his senses had been heightened through a lifetime of discipline. He was programmed to constantly monitor his surroundings for signs of danger. But now the fog, like a suffocating blanket, had separated him from the tangible world. Sensory deprivation was unbearable to Chev.

"Help me!" he shouted. "If anyone can hear me— help me!"

The mists in front of Chev began to curdle. Chev caught Fable's death scent: the freshly emptied bladder, the beginning of decay. Fable's headless form began to take shape. It waved handless arms that spurted smoke at the wrists. With wild arm gestures, Fable seemed to be signaling a warning. Did the apparition care about revenge? Could it harm Chev? Did it even want to harm him? The ghost seemed preoccupied with its frustrated attempts at communication.

Yet Chev felt a cold flush of terror. He wasn't so much afraid of what the ghost might do. He worried about what it might tell. He had no desire to hear advice from a stiff. Death should end life. This was one of his most cherished beliefs, death without end, life without consequence.

Chev fired off a volley of lights, trying to drive the vision away. Distantly he heard the breaking of glass, the patter of falling stone chips hidden by the fog. It sounded as if he had hit one of the storefronts, nothing else. The ghost continued its dance, unaffected by the laser. The stub of its neck muscles twisted from side to side, as if shaking its absent head. It seemed to be signaling a *no*.

No to what?

The ghostly arms swept the ether, a charade conveying nothing. Perhaps some malice remained in Fable, perhaps that's all the apparition was—Fable's disembodied malice come to bring a message Chev did not want to hear. The secrets of hell, the secrets of paradise, the secrets of whatever. But no message came forth, for want of a head and hands. Fable's image drifted like a virus, a snippet of data, unable to connect to a greater source that would give it meaning.

Chev took a deep breath. Relaxed, he said, "Forget about it, Fable. Just get on going to wherever you're going."

A strange noise emanated from the ghost. It sounded like a word, almost. A bubble of gastric air squeezed through the lips of the severed esophagus. It sounded like the word *love*, but it was such a rude report, it could have been a burp or a fart.

"What am I supposed to do?" asked Chev.

The ghost retreated, its smoke beginning to unweave.

Chev pursued, thinking, When he was dead, I wished he would come back. When he comes back, I want him gone. When he goes, I follow. I must be getting psycho.

A series of smoke ruptures began to tear the ghost apart, as though the effort of producing the single word had been too much for it. The contours of the vision bled like watercolors into sheets of mist. Chev dove into the last traces of Fable's smoke, chasing the riddle of the belch. But Fable had vanished, smoke lost in smoke.

Chev's eyes were burning. He comprehended nothing of what had just occurred, but the ghost's strange word had provoked feelings he couldn't rechannel. He had killed Fable with a reflex action. Why should he blame himself for actions he couldn't control? His whole life had been a reflex. The burning of his eyes was a reflex, as was the single tear produced by the burning. Tears were a reflex he wasn't supposed to have.

Then Chev heard the sound of the communicator in his flier. The soft ringing began to restore Chev's sense of reality. He followed the muffled sound that seeped through the fog, for he had nothing else to follow.

He was able to make contact with his craft. The solidity of its frame, the creak of its hinges as he opened the door, made him feel awake again. He decided he'd been hallucinating. The ghost's word meant nothing anymore, just dream gibberish, but the word lingered on in his thoughts.

Chev had arrived at his craft just in time to take a call from Dissa Banach.

"I have need of your services," Dissa's voice crackled. The fog disturbed the transmission.

"Yes?" Chev couldn't concentrate. *Love.* People didn't talk about *love* anymore.

"The girl from the party . . . I want her . . ."

*Love* was a mistrusted word. Ambiguous. Archaic.

". . . terminated. Defunct. Discontinued. Dead. I want her dead!"

Chev wanted a drink. But drink is suicide for a merc who can't hold his liquor.

# 2

## THE CLOUD GARDEN

From a round kitchen window, Amelia watched the sunrise edge over her asteroid. No daylight had shined for over a week, yet Amelia did not miss it. Despite the fact that it wasn't really "morning," Amelia associated the light with routine beginnings and missed opportunities, a response conditioned by planetside living. The artificial atmosphere colored the days a dull beige. She preferred the purple of night and the silver of stars.

After changing her clothes more than a dozen times, Amelia finally decided to wear a cotton robe embroidered with birds. The girl she had rescued was finally awake and would be here soon. Amelia hoped images of flight would put the girl at ease. The robe was the only modest attire in the house, something that had belonged to Amelia's mother.

While waiting in the kitchen, Amelia stirred a pot of

cloned herbs, ginseng, cinnamon, and a potent cocoa descendant called verbilamide. Amelia's chief security officer, Dawson, appeared, escorting the girl. A cyborg, he held her tightly in a brass, robotic grip. A group of armed slaves followed, keeping close guard. Wearing simple khakis and a fringed kerchief over her head, the rescued girl hobbled along. Her leg was still casted. Guns surrounded her.

The girl glowered at Amelia.

"Leave us alone for a moment," said Amelia to Dawson.

"No way! She's much too dangerous."

"She is not a prisoner."

"You are wrong, Amelia. Dead wrong. But I am only a slave, and I'll do what you say, as always." Dawson managed a grimace through what Amelia called his "iron mustache"—the wire and grillwork that replaced the upper lip he had lost in an acid duel.

Amelia dismissed him and his entourage of slaves with a wave of her hand.

"What do you want of me?" asked the girl.

Amelia poured herself a cup of the broth. "I don't want anything. I am trying to help you."

"Why?"

"I like the way you fly. I guess I built up sympathies betting on you. That's all." Amelia took a sip. "Really."

The combination of stimulants cleared her head.

Suddenly a mugdub scampered over the kitchen counter. It looked like a little ball of mud or shit with five legs and splay toes. A disgusting evolutionary quirk had taken the mugdub out of the food chain. Unfit to eat, unfit to even touch, mugdubs thrived, unthreatened by predators. Survival of the unfittest.

Amelia screamed. "Oh, kill it quickly!"

The girl hurled a fork at the mugdub. Just barely missing, the fork buried itself, quivering, in the wall. The mugdub scurried away, leaving a small trail of brown splay-toed footprints.

"Why did you let it get away? They breed like mad and are a source of infection."

The girl shrugged, making almost no effort to conceal a smirk.

Amelia felt her temper rising, but she kept herself under control. Gaining the girl's confidence had become a challenge.

"Come out to my cloud garden," said Amelia. "We both need to calm down."

Amelia loosened the bolt on an enormous frosted-glass door.

Miniature clouds effloresced across the terrace, a fallen fragment of summer sky beneath the drab artificial atmosphere. Amelia gathered a handful of powder. As she spread the powder over the tiny clouds, seeding them, they plumped up, floating three to seven feet above the ground.

The girl smiled as the clouds grew fluffy, and she seemed a little less tired, a little less pained. The clouds were lovely.

Amelia said, "You take pity on mugdubs, but you don't hesitate to shoot down slavers. I don't understand your values, girl."

"The slavers took my husband."

"That is terrible," said Amelia, trying to be agreeable. The loss of a particular man, though, seemed not so great a tragedy.

"I tried to get him back. I wrote letters. I talked to all the bureaucrats. The bod ignored me. Then I tried war. I know a lot about how to make war. Too much."

"I see," said Amelia. The girl was scanning the garden for escape routes.

"It was not right they should ignore me like that. I

made them pay. I have a special hatred for slavery. I am descended from a race of freed slaves."

"I wouldn't have guessed. Your skin is so pale. I don't see any trace of African ancestry."

"Because I am a Jew."

Amelia fell quiet. The answer embarrassed her and she didn't know why. A moment earlier, she had felt a kinship with the girl, a camaraderie of flight. Abruptly, the kinship was gone, the differences between them insurmountable. A long silence afterward made Amelia feel even more embarrassed. She lifted new handfuls of seeding powder and casually scattered them over the clouds to keep her hands occupied while she rummaged for the smallest bit of polite conversation. The rescued girl just stared.

At last Amelia said, "By the way, what is your name?"

"I have been known by many names, but once I was mostly called Magen. You can call me Magen. It means 'star' or 'shield' in my language."

Amelia continued to seed the clouds absentmindedly while the girl talked. The garden slowly bruised and began to rumble because she had added too much seed.

"Let's go inside," said Amelia. "I am getting cold."

Night fell like a hatchet.

In a vineyard not far from the mansion, Dawson watched the skies for stars that moved and stars that flared. He rubbed the mosaic of circuitry along his chin, and the gears in his wrist whirred softly. Another attack was coming. He could feel it in the few natural bones he had left. Computer enhancements of his cerebral cortex confirmed the probability.

He caught sight of Amelia strolling across the compound toward him. He shouted at her, signaling for her to go back to the house. With her usual stubbornness, she kept on coming. What the hell was she doing? His organic parts were getting too old to put up with Amelia's whims. Even his machine parts were getting too old. As she approached, the antenna attached to Dawson's auditory canal began to quiver. The perimeter observation towers were reporting three new ships with slaver markings, which had managed to get past the first line of defenses.

Dawson rushed toward Amelia, grabbed her, and pulled her behind the shelter of a vine-covered wall. He knocked her to the ground.

"Stay down," Dawson insisted.

"What is going on?"

"For once, do what I tell you. We have been attacked several times over the last few days. Slavers Bod vessels, mostly. Some Merc Bod. Even some unincorp hirelings."

A squadron of attack craft roared overhead, flying in perfect fingertip formation. Jeweled light strafed a flower bed. Small fires broke out. Long-petaled orchid hybrids curled and danced and crisped.

"Why didn't you tell me?"

"I don't like to see you worried. It gives you wrinkles," said Dawson.

"Who is in charge here?"

"How do you want me to behave, like a slave or like a friend?"

"A friend. Always a friend. I trust no one else in the universe. Friends shouldn't keep secrets from one another. Agreed?" She always consulted Dawson. Sometimes it seemed his wisdom was infinite.

"What is it you require?"

"I have a question for you. Why have I never met a Jew before?"

Dawson grinned through his iron mustache. "You got some Jew blood in you. Not much. Dates back to Earth days. Your father told me one night when he was drunk."

Amelia's eyes widened. Her lips parted slightly and she

touched her neck defensively. "You should have told me!"

"It was better kept a secret. Most Jews in the Draconian system were wiped out years ago. The Health Care Bod identified them as the source of a plague on the Summer World. The bods claimed that the unique genetic structure of Jews bred the virus."

"You were afraid I would catch it from that girl?"

"Hell, no! It wasn't true. The funny thing, it was a Jew who first hit on the idea—a doctor named Abraham Sidney. He recanted very quickly, but the bods shut him up. But you know, to this day, they still try to hide behind Sidney's initial findings whenever the subject arises. They had lots of evidence refuting the theory, but they suppressed it. Justifying themselves, they said action had to be taken quickly without doubt or conscience. The Jewish extermination initiative drew attention away from the Health Care Bod's failure to contain the plague in the first place.

"What's more, the Jewish community had more or less operated independently of the bods. Not really like unincorps. They worked more together. Most of the prime directors were really glad to have an excuse to have their economic model 'vanish' from the system."

As Dawson finished speaking, a terrible beauty filled the sky, spacecraft rolling and weaving beneath multicolored electric arcs.

"No wonder the girl is so untrusting," said Amelia.

"More than just 'untrusting.' She's served time in the Merc Bod and gathered quite a reputation. She's been a foot soldier. She's even fought in the arenas. I've known lots of people like her. Killing becomes instinctive, a solution for every problem. You look at them the wrong way, and you're dead."

"You should have warned me."

"I did."

Amelia looked over at the mansion. She saw Magen lingering by the window, a shadow of tension. No doubt the girl was watching the aerial battle. No doubt she wanted to be part of it.

"You know, six years ago someone assassinated the corporate heads who ordered the Jewish extermination. I'll bet it was your friend up there."

"Impossible. Six years ago she would have been about twelve years old."

Dawson grinned as he looked up. A series of blasts was tearing up the sky. The precision flight patterns of the invading vessels made them easy targets. It almost seemed they were flying into the mansion's defense fire.

Smoking fragments of falling metal fell in a steady rain.

The security force began to clean up fallen pieces from the battle: shattered shatterproof glass, broken pistons, ropes of intestines. Even Amelia was appalled at the waste of life and machinery.

"Double the guard," shouted Dawson to a nearby soldier. "We don't want to get caught with our pants down again!"

"No need, sir," replied the young man. "We've drifted into a dense asteroid belt. No kind of warcraft could possibly get through. Should hold us secure for ten, possibly twelve hours."

Dawson unbuckled a strap around his metal biceps. He flipped open a hinged compartment in his robot arm and pulled out a flask. "One good belt deserves another," he said, and took a swig. The hard, hot kick of fermentation made him wince, and the skin on his forehead tugged at islands of corrugated wiring scattered over his bald pate. Then Dawson waved the flask in front of the young soldier. "You want a hit?"

"No thanks. I never drink on the job."

As the soldier walked away, the rainbows of his holographic belt glittered amid the scattered, dying flames of the burning flowers.

* * *

A ghost had admonished Chev to love. So Chev pondered the advice and considered the things he loved. He loved food and consumed large quantities without getting fat because of his rapid metabolism and constant exercise. He loved thinking about women. Not being with them—but thinking about them. Most of all, he loved his work. He loved the challenge of mastering new and exotic weaponry. He loved the artistry and terror of dueling. And he loved outwitting tradition-bound strategists like Dawson.

Chev had slipped through the asteroid's defense systems by pretending to crash, a raindrop in a storm of flaming and smoking warships. His craft had appeared to be totaled when it landed, though most of the external damage had been done before he took off. After he crawled from the wreckage, he had no trouble losing himself amid Amelia's security force.

Crossing the manicured lawn in front of the mansion, falling into the routine of troop movement as if he belonged, Chev felt grateful to the pilots who had died to give him cover for his landing. He smelled them cooking in their cockpits. He had never flown with braver men. You can't top slaves for courage.

A pale glow began to crackle up around the mansion. Sealed up for bedtime. Chev smirked. An energy shield around the house provided some level of protection for the occupants, but it also kept the home troops at a distance.

He walked around to the rear of the estate where a young girl stood guard. Blond hair spilled out from her silver helmet. She would not have been pretty, even if her face hadn't been mangled in too many bare-knuckle brawls. She wore a pissed-off expression. She must have lost the weekly lottery, pulling the worst watch duty of all, right in front of the exhaust ports of the sanitation and energy exchange system. Not even the lowliest of sewer slaves could stand the nauseating stink. Chev could hear the tough-looking girl cursing to herself.

A black river of fuel flowed through the mansion's bowels. The processors of the sanitation and energy-exchange system stripped down to basic carbons all organic garbage: silks that had fallen out of fashion, uneaten bits of pastry, stained cotton bedsheets, vinyl high heels, vomit, shit, and blood. The treated sludge reeked of the basest parts of living matter. It reeked of entropy and rot. The main exchange unit had to be located outside of the energy shield, otherwise the stink would quickly build up inside the house when the containment web was activated for the night. Pipes from the processor led into the mansion to disposal units located at convenient points.

The compressors were grinding. They sloshed and rumbled.

Chev strolled up to the girl; he murmured a greeting. She looked hard at him. He could tell by the way she studied him that she thought he was handsome. She smiled, but her smile dropped abruptly. He was too handsome, and she would have recognized his face if she had ever seen it before. She started to shout a warning to the night watch, but Chev's hand shot forward and caught the warning in the middle of her throat.

She tried to squeeze the warning out anyway. As the muscles in her lungs constricted, Chev could feel an urgent bubble of sound trying to push past his fingers. Only a pathetic hiss escaped. Her trachea crunched. Chev relaxed his grip.

He shook out his acid sword and hacked through a four-foot-diameter pipe. Thick black oil sprayed in all directions. Ocher clouds of vile gas rose up from the muck.

Chev had conditioned himself to enjoy the stink. He thought of fecund ground and orifices and sex. Slowly he hoisted a ninety-three-pound severed section of pipe and shoved it aside. Then he climbed into the system. With brass knuckles he punched through the blades of a guillotine door, which opened into a large sludge tunnel under the fire tubes. As he crawled past, he felt as if he were being baked. Fortunately, the temperatures in the conversion chambers were not quite hot enough to ignite his clothes. He was soaked in combustible sludge.

He slipped into the yawning, dripping main conduit. A gust of warm air felt cool to him. Degraded sludge flowed in slow but strong currents. He lifted tiny pools of black oil in his hands and let them dribble through his fingers like coins.

Occasionally, yellow toxic diamonds bubbled up in the effervescent tar, a by-product of malfunctioning pressure valves. Chev wallowed in wasted wealth. He sloshed like an otter along the wet walls of this private place, amid the rudest parts of silks, flowers, wines, and blood.

It made him feel rich.

Filthy rich.


Amelia stirred uneasily in a light sleep when the pipes rumbled.

The door opened just a crack. A shaft of light fell across her left hand and breast. The muffled thumping of Magen's cast beat across the carpet. Amelia tossed briefly beneath her sheets, but it wasn't the sounds that woke her—it was the palpable presence of fear.

"Wake up," rasped a voice.

Amelia's eyes fluttered. Dimly, she could make out Magen's form, a silhouette, umber on black in the darkness.

"What are you doing in my room?" Amelia asked. Instantly she regretted her sharp tone. As her eyes adjusted to the light, she saw wildness tugging against restraint in the girl's features: brow furrowed, eyes wide, lips tight. Magen leaned on her cane and wore an ill-fitting, unflattering jumpsuit made of cotton.

"The time has come I go on my way," said Magen.

"Impossible. The house is sealed for the night."

Magen said nothing at first. She began to pace, leaning on her cane for support. Then she tossed the cane aside, though she was still unsteady, and continued pacing. "I am in danger here," Magen said at last.

"No. Really, no. I wouldn't harm you. My men wouldn't harm you. You see how we've been fighting off the slavers' forces."

"I don't like you should be in danger for me."

"There's no real danger."

"And I don't like I should be in your debt."

Amelia felt suddenly desperate to have this strange girl out of her room. She tried to will her away, but the girl kept pacing. The more Amelia willed, the more the rescued girl seemed determined to stay, entrenched, like a tick under the skin. Amelia thought, Perhaps she suspects a plot, or wants a hostage in case there's trouble. Who could tell what this girl's motives were? She was mystery itself.

"You need to sleep. We both need sleep. You can leave whenever we both wake up, when the shields come down. There is nothing to fear."

"I am used to fear. I don't mind it so much."

"OK. Wrong word. Why don't you just go back to sleep?"

Amelia couldn't think straight. She started to panic. She had gambled too much on this girl, this much too strange rescued girl. She wanted to dive for the panic button that would instantly summon Dawson—but she sensed that any sudden movement might prove fatal.

"I need something to calm me down," said Amelia, turning toward a bedside table on which rested a statue of an angel. She opened a drawer in the bedside table very, very slowly. She held the drawer open for a moment so the girl could see clearly that no weapons lay inside. Then Amelia produced an elaborately decorated bottle half-filled with blue fluid. Cadmadine. "You should drink some. It is very relaxing."

"What do you care if I relax?"

"You're starting to frighten me." Amelia uncorked the bottle and took a belt of the blue fluid. Immediately her tensions unbundled, her thoughts crystallized, her fear vanished.

Magen eyed Amelia with suspicion. "You don't need to be afraid of me as long as you are telling the truth and don't try to attack me. Why are you so afraid so suddenly . . ."

"Dawson said you killed the corporate heads who were responsible for the Health Care Bod's Jewish extermination campaign."

"They deserved to die."

"You killed all of them—by yourself?"

"Not all of them. There was one I didn't kill."

The girl leaned forward, almost losing her balance. "Maybe you are afraid because you feel what I feel. A sense of dread. A warning, I think. God has ways to warn without using words, I think."

"I don't feel anything." A blue pleasantness rolled down Amelia's spine.

"How can you not feel it?" Magen retrieved her cane and increased the tempo of her pacing.

"You know, I am not without contacts in the Slavers Bod. Perhaps I can arrange a meeting between you and Olagy."

The pacing stopped.

Amelia continued. "I still wield considerable influence in the system. Perhaps I can even pressure the bod into releasing your husband."

"You can do this?"

"I am quite certain I can."

Magen believed her, Amelia could tell. She wasn't lying, either, but cadmadine was notorious for filling one with an overinflated sense of self-importance. Anyway, for the time being Amelia had made herself valuable to Magen, at least until the house shields were turned off.

"I can call due some old favors," said Amelia. The seductive calming smell of cadmadine spices seeped from the uncorked bottle. "At least it is worth a try." Then she proffered the bottle to Magen. "This will help you sleep. It will make the time go faster. After all I have done for you, haven't you learned to trust me?"

Amelia rose and stepped away from her bed. She wore an airy translucent gown that seemed to glow with its own light, romanticizing Amelia's nakedness underneath with a silky haze. The drug made her bold, and she waved the bottle, spreading its bouquet.

"Thank you but no." Magen pushed the bottle away.

"Trust me. This is what you need more than anything right now. It has no residual effects. You are completely safe in my house behind an impenetrable shield. I will be insulted if you don't join me in a drink."

Amelia thrust the bottle forward.

Magen took it from her hands, then paused. She understood the protocols and courtesies of the streets, and of the bods. But she didn't understand people like Amelia—upper-echelon unincorps. Holding the bottle of cadmadine, Magen tried to measure the cultural differences between the two of them, and the potential gravity of the alleged insult. She sniffed the rim of the bottle.

The cadmadine smelled of sky and freedom and light. It smelled of nutmeg and clove and ice. It smelled of dreams. Magen took a hesitant sip. The wondrous taste surprised her. She took a more solid swig. Then another.

"I trust you, I do," said Magen, smiling crookedly. "There is a parable among my people about God sending angels in human disguise, and about the fools who refuse to recognize them."

"I'm no angel."

"Shalom."

"What?"

"Shalom. It means peace. It also means hello, good-bye. Good night."

Magen hobbled into the darkened hallway alone. She had only felt relaxed once or twice since childhood, and never to this degree. Her cast banged and dragged over the carpet, her anchor in a sea of ether. Everything she saw or heard or touched delighted her: the casual pink wallpaper, the vaulted ceilings, the beat of her heart, the hum and gurgle of the sanitation energy-exchange system, the smell of cadmadine lingering in her nostrils. All things in creation bore the imprint of God's handiwork.

A random black smudge in the corridor caught her attention. At first she didn't know why it fascinated her. Tiny whorls stirred in a black cloud of vagueness. Ebony drops seeped down, leaving black degraded trails. She stared for time out of time. The image metamorphosed, a Rorschach kaleidoscope; it became a bird, a face, a running dog, a dead octopus. Finally, she realized it was a handprint and it smelled like shit.

She tried to turn on the hall lights, but they would not work. In the semi-light, she saw a trail of oily footprints headed up the corridor.

Slowly, through her drug-induced haze, she came to the conclusion that someone had crawled up through the sludge pipes.

Magen headed back to Amelia's bedroom. The initial

euphoria of the cadmadine had faded quickly, leaving an aching numbness, like many limbic-system relaxants.

After a vigorous shaking, Amelia awoke muttering curses.

"There is an assassin in the house."

"Impossible."

"Trust me."

Amelia reached for the panic button by her bed. She pounded on it, waited.

No response.

She pounded again.

Nothing.

"I need a weapon," said Magen. "A gun, a knife, a vase I can break to put a blade on the cane. Anything." Her hands knotted nervously.

"Are you all right?"

"Fine. Just fine. Too fine."

Magen started swiftly across the room, almost losing her balance. The sound of the cast banging on the carpet penetrated the blue haze drawn across her cerebral cortex. Finding she couldn't walk without making noise, she got on her hands and knees and crawled. Amelia followed, also crawling, believing it was a prudent thing to do, not really appreciating the reason.

Magen crawled through the half-light, out of the room. She felt numb in her eyes, her groin, her soul—as devoid of feeling as hair or fingernails. She felt totally calm, except that she felt a little twinge of guilt for taking the drug. The act of crawling made things worse. Her mind floated in a blue puddle. Never before had she felt so vulnerable. A lifetime of training undone with a single, foolish act of trust.

Amelia screamed. In the darkness, in the hallway, she had crawled over Dawson's unconscious, bleeding body. His severed robotic limbs lay scattered nearby, sparking.

Her scream drew an immediate volley of laser fire from the foyer below. The blue flashes illuminated Amelia's profile, her hair floating like smoke from accumulated static electricity. The white streak, lighter than the other strands, rose slightly higher. Her nightgown glowed over her trembling breasts. Then the gunlight stopped.

Magen realized the assassin was deliberately trying to avoid hitting Amelia. Why? Was he in her employ? Magen didn't think so—she thought herself a better judge of people—but the blue haze muddled her thoughts and reminded her of recent folly.

Progressively larger fragments of Dawson littered the ascending steps on the spiral staircase. Apparently he had fought all the way up, losing more and more of himself as his defense capacities diminished.

Frantically, Magen searched Dawson's still-breathing torso for a weapon. The assassin had stripped the gun belts. The utility chambers were broken and empty.

Amelia crossed into a shaft of clear starlight, grabbing for a smoldering metal arm. She lingered too long, a clean and obvious target, but no shooting ensued. Magen's suspicions flared again, but she hesitantly dismissed them again. Complicity with the assassin seemed unlikely. Perhaps he was saving her for hostage value.

Amelia achieved a tenuous hold on the severed limb and pulled it toward her by loose wires. She unstrapped a panel over the dented wrist. Out tumbled a deactivated acid sword.

"You were right about angels coming sometimes," whispered Amelia.

"Shit," said Magen. She could not hide her disappointment. "This is a bad weapon. I don't like it. I never liked it. Too much skill is needed. My hands are dead."

"At least you have something. Back there you were asking for a vase or something. Well, here is something. You can do it. Yes. Yes. You can do it. Go do it, girl. Do it. Do it." Amelia's eyes started to glaze, a weird psychotropic response induced by a mixture of panic and cadmadine.

Magen took a deep breath. "Peace, Amelia."

Chev lurked below the staircase. He didn't want to betray his position. He had no way of knowing whether or not Magen had a gun. She clearly had the advantageous position, with altitude.

He was getting nervous. He had waited too long for her to make her play. Soon the house shields would shut down. The security force would storm the mansion at the first hint of a break in routine. He tried to jockey for a clear shot through the spaces in the spiral banister.

Then he caught a glimpse of Amelia's softly glowing gown fluttering at the top of the stairs. It floated over firm thighs, stepping slowly. A pair of bare feet, lit by the gown's glow, descended with spectral grace.

He heard Magen's cast banging out a quick tattoo across the corridor above.

"Strados! Get out of the way!" yelled Chev. "I always liked you. I don't want to hurt you—but one way or another, I'm going to nail that bitch!"

The glowing gown continued its downward course, undaunted, as relaxed as death. Another ghost suggesting love, this time with soft breasts and hair like smoke. Chev watched, almost hypnotized, but he didn't lose track of the pounding cast upstairs. The ghostly feet, lit by the glow of the gown, continued ever so slowly, bravely, in the line of fire—a sharp contrast to the frantic pounding of the cast.

The moment the glowing gown reached the bottom of the staircase, Chev lurched forward to shove Amelia out of the way. The smell of the woman's perfume startled him. It was too strong, too plebeian. Catching the vaguest sniff of sulfur, he pulled backward immediately, just as an acid sword splattered open. A sideways fan slash cut through his gun and sliced off the tip of his right forefinger. Had the blow fallen just a little faster, a little surer, it would have split open his chest.

Magen was wearing the glowing gown. She had used the acid sword to cut the cast off her leg. Unsteady, she was squinting to see in the half-light, trying to mask her grogginess.

Chev sidestepped the next two clumsy slashes. He sucked on the ragged end of his wounded finger and spat out a dollop of blood. No time to slap an adhesive on the wound, though he would have welcomed the painkillers. He pulled out his own acid sword and splashed out its blade. Acid and blood froze together in the stasis field.

With a quick thrust into her combat space, Chev tested her responses, reading her disorientation with a glance. Her dulled senses made him wary. So much of a traditional acid duel depended on bluff and reaction to bluff. So much depended on the opponent's level of fear. A drugged opponent, pumped full of artificial courage, could be more dangerous than a cautious opponent, no matter how skilled. An acid duel was mostly a matter of nerve.

He danced a semicircle around her with short steps, toes classically pointed forward. He tried to play for an advantage with subtle moves. He toyed with her, gently brushing his blade against hers with mock tenderness. A fine burning mist of acid sprayed onto her forearms. Her skin fried away, leaving nerves exposed.

She stopped cursing the blue fog in her mind. It provided a small hedge against the pain.

She fought on automatic. Muscles and nerves performed according to years of programming. She feinted to the left, forcing a retreating counterswing of Chev's torso; then she caught him with a snap kick to the kidney. The kick should have been devastating, but it lacked power.

Chev grunted at the stab of organ pain, but he kept on slashing, seemingly unfazed.

Though almost healed, her recently broken leg still gave her difficulty. The kick had left her unstable. She fell back against delicately latticed glass doors, shifting her weight just in time to keep from crashing through. Chev attacked, his weightless saber aimed at her neck. She did a full-body retreat, arching her spine with a swift motion that snapped her through the glass and lattices she had just avoided. Soprano thunder filled her bleeding ears. Raining glass trilled.

She hit the hard terrace of the cloud garden. Her glowing gown was now in tatters and full of bloating red stains.

Chev stepped through the demolished doors. He stalked her. His weapon swung back and forth as steadily as a pendulum. She was on her knees. Dead meat in an acid duel.

To gain a second, Magen pitched her sword at Chev. The splatter blade twisted wildly as it flew, like a kite without a tail. Chev sidestepped into a cumulus hedge to avoid the sword.

Magen ripped open a bag of cloud seed and cast the powder in a floating haze toward Chev. He sneezed. The tiny clouds around him instantly darkened. Chev frantically tossed his sword aside as a miniature storm broke out around him. On contact with rain, the burning blade exploded.

Acid splashed on Chev's leg, hot beads eating instantly through fabric, skin, and muscle. The air smelled of ozone and sulfur. Chev paused for a minute to shake the acid from a black spot sizzling on his hand. Then, enraged, he grabbed a bag full of seeding powder and flung it around with such force that the bag ripped open. Clouds spilled onto clouds. The floating thunderheads mottled and rolled out in all directions.

Filaments of miniature lightning flashed down on

Magen. Everywhere she turned, sprigs of numbness shocked her. Chev leaped furrows of storm clouds in his path. He kneed her in the belly, and when she bent forward, he drummed hammer blows on her back.

He gloried in the sound of her pained grunts, and the smell of her blood overcrowding the smell of her weird perfume. Never before had he taken such joy at a victim's expense. He always enjoyed winning—true enough, but sadism was unprofessional.

Chev found himself caught up in emotions he had never experienced before in battle. A wild delirium shook him. This was payback for humiliating him, for tarnishing his reputation, and for making him lose over a month's worth of job time.

He laughed when she fell. On the terrace, below cloud level, the toy lightning struck her highest places, her forehead, her hips, her knees.

With a flick of his wrist, Chev activated a pulley mechanism that slid a dagger into his palm. Preparing to cut her throat, he stooped to embrace his fallen adversary. She lay beneath a blanket of storm, aglow with filaments of bolts.

"Stop!" shouted Amelia. Wearing Magen's simple oversized cottons, she crossed onto the terrace scattering handfuls of counterreactive to the cloud seeds. "I'll double in value the fee from Olagy if you spare her life. You should check with your superiors before you turn me down." The storm subsided in Amelia's wake.

Chev froze. "No!" he shouted. But the blade dallied at Magen's carotid.

"Triple."

"I have my professional pride to think of. My bosses would be pissed if I blew a chance like this." The blade moved but drew only a small bead of blood as Magen sighed unconsciously. Amelia knew he was bargaining.

"What do you want?"

"You," said Chev.

The proposition stunned Amelia, and it flattered her. She looked him up and down. Despite his hair being soaked in sanitation sludge, and despite the stink that made her gag, he seemed much more attractive than he did the night of the party. Maybe because his muscles were pumped up from the fight. Maybe because he was sober now. Maybe it was the way his eyes burned, fiercely alert.

The house shield would hold for at least another two hours, and she knew he could take her if he really wanted her so badly. Lower-caste liaisons had been rare in Amelia's past, but not totally unpleasant. This one would not be so bad, if he took a bath first.

"I agree," Amelia said. A fine wet mist rained out of the garden.

"For marriage," said Chev.

His new proposition stunned her even more, but flattered her less. Now she understood. The young upstart was a fortune hunter.

"No."

Chev waved the knife. Unconscious, Magen moaned.

"One night," said Amelia. "But it will be a grand night, I promise."

"At least a year," he demanded.

"One night!" But now she smiled on the verge of giddy laughter. The cadmadine she had taken earlier numbed her to the seriousness of the situation.

The two of them bargained, and began to enjoy the contest in the wet mist, their clothes soaked and sticking to their skin.

# 3

## THE STALKING WIND

Daylight woke Magen and filled the cloud garden with glorious rainbows. Her eyes ached. She still wore Amelia's gown, which no longer glowed. Designed for darkness, it seemed tawdry and lurid in the light, especially in the way it revealed her cuts and bruises.

She grunted herself upright. Being alive amazed her, and she uttered a grateful prayer, making certain that her lips moved even though she produced no sound.

Then Magen crossed through the demolished doors and entered the mansion. The light of the blazing rainbows revealed the beheaded corpses of a dozen of Amelia's elite guardsmen.

The fighting had roused a nest of mugdubs. Tiny splay-toed footprints covered the fine upholstery. The little shit balls ran amok, occasionally colliding and splattering against one another.

Magen found the clothes she had exchanged with Amelia. They were littered in progression up the stairs and across the inside corridor, mingled with Chev's clothes and Dawson's limbs. The discarded clothes described a path to Amelia's bedroom.

Magen pressed her ear to the locked door and heard sighs and moans, and the rhythmic creaking of the wooden bed frame. She debated forcing open the door— but the sounds were obvious expressions of intense consensual sex and a rapidly approaching shared orgasm.

Magen dressed and covered her head with a towel, wrapping it like a turban. A short way up the corridor, she found Dawson. He propelled himself across the carpet by using his chin for leverage. The image was so pathetic, and made such a mockery of human will, Magen understood why Chev had spared Dawson; not as an act of mercy, but as a contemptuous prank.

"Would you like some help?" Magen asked.

"Now, what the hell makes you think that?" replied Dawson.


When Amelia heard the buzz of the house shields shutting down, she looked out the window of the bedroom and saw the rainbows glittering below. Soon the morning patrol would march into the house, and she would be forced to make a decision about how to deal with the intruder. She rose naked from beneath silken sheets. Warm clots of the intruder's seed rolled in surprising quantities down the inside of her thigh. The sensation made her ovaries tingle.

She walked across the room with a lightness in her step that had not been there in years. She had never been one to overreact to, or romanticize, a good fuck, but her liaison with Chev had resulted in a startling communion, and it had stirred her in unexpected ways. Even though his technique lacked sophistication, he was amazingly adept at interpreting her body signals, maybe because of his combat training. The moment they joined, it became obvious they shared a common sense of adventure and hedonism, a common longing and loneliness, a common void.

His youth had been an unexpected treat. Undeniably, youth was an aphrodisiac.

She looked at herself in the mirror. The wild streak of white hair suddenly lost its exotic appeal. A badge of age. Crow's feet, sags, wrinkles, the effects of gravity on her breasts and buttocks, the slight bulging of her belly, the increase in distance between her iliac crests; all of these things had not existed the day before.

Chev emerged from an adjoining bathroom. She could tell he was thinking about her, about the way he had reduced her to a helpless blob of pleasure. His smile bloated with ego. He sported an enormous, flushed erection.

"This room smells like a whorehouse in summer," he said.

Amelia felt her cheeks heating with sudden shame and anger. She had not been seduced, she reminded herself. She had been blackmailed into bed. No matter how fine a fuck he was, this stranger had invaded her house, slain her guards, and threatened her friends.

Amelia, raging, lifted the winged angel statuette. She started to hurl it at Chev, but changed her mind mid-arm-swing, and sent it flying in the direction of the mirror instead. The wings struck first, crashing loudly and breaking. Cobwebs fanned out from the point of impact, spreading across the reflective surface, multiplying images of Amelia's nudity. As the mirror fell apart, the images collapsed into cubism.

"Get out!" Amelia shouted. "Get the hell out of my room!"

"Why? What did I do wrong?"

She pushed him out into the corridor and slammed the door behind him.

Chev found himself surrounded by Amelia's morning patrol. The elite troops instantly snapped into battle stance in unison with military precision. Their brass buttons sparkled, their faces were emotionless masks. The nozzles of their light guns leveled at Chev.

Chev smiled his usual arrogant smirk. It looked stupid, and he knew it. He stood there naked, smelling of scented moisturizing soap, his erection rapidly wilting.

Inside her room, Amelia combed her perfumed hair. She looked at her face in a fragment of mirror and applied makeup a little more heavily than usual, then calmly dressed herself in a stylish outfit made with fur and golden lamé. She listened to the sound of boots marching down the stairs. Some heavy dragged object bumped on every step. She waited until these sounds reached the bottom of the spiral staircase.

Now, looking radiant and fully in control, wary of showing any sign of weakness to the slaves, Amelia descended the stairs with the regal slowness and elegant airs Magen had imitated so well the night before.

Amelia even maintained her composure when she found an uncountable number of mugdubs scampering wildly and fornicating over her costly furniture. She stepped over the headless guards, whose bodies were still multicolored with bruises even after the rainbows outside had faded. She found a modest chair that had been spared brown stains, sat down, took a breath, and began to calculate the amount of resources it would take to effect repairs.

"What should I do with *him?*" asked the captain of the first watch.

"I don't know," said Amelia.

"Do you want us to kill him?"

"I don't know."

"Do you want us to torture him a little while you make up your mind?"

She stared at the soldier's impassive face, trying to decide if he was being serious or impertinent.

"Bring the intruder to me," she said.

Chev was still naked when they brought him before Amelia, and she enjoyed the psychological advantage that clothing, particularly costly clothing, gave her. The presence of rampaging mugdubs slightly diminished the pomp of Amelia's court. Her armed guards brandished their weapons threateningly at Chev. They were nervous, and itching to kill him. Too many of their peers lay in blood and excrement on the floor. And they were afraid of him, even naked.

"Get rid of the corpses," said Amelia. She was buying time, trying to make up her mind.

The soldiers began hauling away the dead, without ceremony.

"You know," said Chev, "I could have taken anything I wanted. You. Your friend. Any number of trinkets worth more than I make in a year. I could have taken them and been gone out the tubes, and no one would have stopped me." His hand snapped forward and he caught a leaping mugdub in midair. He squeezed it, letting shit and small greasy organs dribble between his fingers to the ground. Amelia averted her eyes.

"I stuck around for you. I did nothing to hurt you. The opposite, I thought."

"Surely you don't really think I will marry you. Why did you stay? Most women in my position would have had you shot by now. Why did you take the chance?"

. Looking bitter, he said, "Ever since I met you, things have gone wrong for me. I felt bad about myself like I never felt before. I thought croaking that bitch who crashed Olagy's party would set things right. That's what I thought right up to the point where I beat her and I had her down at knifepoint. Then I saw you, and I remembered, it wasn't really the bitch who messed me up that night—you messed me up, right from the start. It was you. I tried to be friendly. I tried to give you a friendly warning, and you wanted to show off how fucking clever you could be. The bitch was fighting for her life—but you insulted me just to draw blood. I was drunk and defenseless and trying to be friendly, and you got off on putting me down."

"I am used to saying whatever I like to whomever I like, or don't like. Your behavior was atrocious that night."

"You liked me better when I was going to croak your friend?"

"So you revenged my insult in bed?"

He thought maybe he shouldn't have mouthed off to her. The verbal jab had wounded an unguarded area.

"I wanted you to like me." Though he was full of feints and bluster, he was probably telling the truth. He wasn't taking revenge, he was rewriting his own personal history. He was fleshing it out.

She folded her arms across her chest. A flush reddened underneath her makeup. She dug the tips of her toes into the bloody, stained carpet. She was mulling over his response. She would feel sorry, very sorry for killing him, but it would probably be cathartic for her.

"You're right about one thing," she announced. "You spared my life. I feel obligated to return the favor."

"I know that everything I did before was wrong." This did not sound like an apology anymore. He was being self-righteous. "I should have thought things through—but I am not that kind of person. I never know what I'm going to do until after it is done."

"I'm the same way," said Amelia. Without thinking things through, she kissed him.

* * *

"I don't understand Amelia at all, why she does what she does," said Magen. She carried Dawson, only a head and torso, cradling him like a child made of iron, sweating with the effort. There was bile on his breath, and strong odors of polychlorides and hormones seeping from his open sockets.

"Did you know Amelia had sex with the man who almost killed both of us?"

Dawson let out a slow exasperated sigh. A distant look obscured his expression. "Well, I am not surprised. No. Not at all." He thought about it. "Nope, no surprise." Despite his denials, his voice betrayed at least some failure of expectation, if not true surprise.

Inside his modest room, decorated with hanging weaponry, she laid him down beside his collected limbs on a patchwork quilt spread over a polished bronze bed. A lukewarm bowl of soup waited, full of vegetables and dismembered parts of a native animal crossbred and gene-spliced for centuries until it vaguely tasted like Earth chicken. Magen propped up Dawson's head with one hand and brought a spoonful of the tepid broth to his dried lips with the other. He sucked at it, dribbling a little on his rug-burned chin.

"I know Amelia too well after all these years," he said at last. "She likes to make problems for herself. It's a disease of the wealthy, keeps them from getting bored. That's mostly why she rescued you. Sure as hell wasn't out of the goodness of her heart."

"I see." She raised an eyebrow. The explanation satisfied her. She dipped for another spoonful of broth.

"Amelia pushes her luck to its limits, then escapes by using her assets, her sexuality, or her charm. She is damn charming. She thinks she can get away with anything because she has a special gift for making people like her."

"I know. I like her."

"I do too." He said it almost reluctantly. He had lived with liking her for too long.

"Where can I find someone to put you back together?"

"Don't bother. I'll summon him after a while. I need to sleep first."

She drew up another spoonful of soup. It was getting cooler. Flakes of fat were crystallizing on the surface. She brought the spoon to his lips, and he sucked in the soup.

Dawson surmised that Magen was only helping him because he was visibly incapable of harming her, and he was profoundly pathetic—yet her present kindness made him regret his earlier lack of courtesy. He felt too ashamed of it to bring up the subject, even to make an apology. Dawson was only a slave—despite his long relationship with Amelia and the enormous amount of trust she placed in him. As a slave, he owned nothing he could give to Magen as a token of friendship. He could not even offer a handshake. The only thing he had to share was a secret.

He said, "I am going to give you some very good advice about Amelia. Don't trust her. I mean, she won't double-cross you or anything, but she is completely unreliable. Don't depend on her for anything."

Unnerved by this counsel, Magen accidently plunged her elbow into the bowl of soup, tilting it, splashing broth in Dawson's face. He sputtered, spraying broth and saliva.

She wiped his face, then dabbed his copper chest plate. He blinked his eyes clear, and saw her teeth set on edge. The advice he had offered as a gift upset her terribly.

"What did Amelia promise you?"

"She said she could get my husband free. She said she had power and people owed her favors. You see, this is my best hope, the only hope I have had in a very long time.

Amelia made a promise to me. Do you think she will not keep it?"

"I don't know," said Dawson bitterly. "She might end up keeping her word. You never can tell. She will lavish fortunes on complete strangers. She will risk life, limb, and honor for complete strangers. That's what she's like. She'll go to bed with a complete stranger while she leaves an old friend helpless and in pieces. Yeah, she might keep her promise."

The arrangements for a meeting with Olagy proved more difficult than Amelia anticipated. She had a major connection in the upper echelons of the bod, a former lover named Chadwick Hubbel; however, reaching him was not easy. After their stormy breakup years before, she had lost contact with him. She knew only that he held prime managerial responsibility for the public-relations division. He was always very good at "relating." She wasn't even sure of his exact title, except that it had "vice" in it.

To contact him, she had to slowly work her way through several layers of complicated bureaucracy. The bod staffed the lower-level positions in its organization with slaves. Each could perform only a limited number of routine tasks—usually tasks associated with collecting receivables and harassing debtors. The system confounded creditors, and insured that only the most persistent and clever callers could get through to the bod's directors. The slaves handled their limited duties with surprising efficiency.

For external purposes, all mistakes made by the bod were blamed on the people occupying the lower-level positions. When occasional important messages were lost, the lower-level bureaucrats received the usual disciplinary measures—torture, or death, or both, depending on the severity of the mistake. These measures usually appeased anyone offended by a lower-level bureaucrat.

Because the lower-level bureaucrats were trained to respond with memorized statements, which would be triggered by key buzzwords, an unusual request could not be processed. Amelia's request for the freedom of a single slave was unusual in the extreme, and it wrought utter confusion. After several attempts at communication, Amelia got fed up with listening to gelding voices speaking with flat affect. She threatened war. The lower-level bureaucrats in the public-relations division switched her over to the lower-level bureaucrats in the military division. She found herself talking to a slave who had been trained to recite threats of retaliation in a very convincing psychotic voice.

"Do you realize to whom you are speaking?" shouted Amelia.

The line went dead, but within an hour, she received a call from a higher-ranking bod official, a young man who spoke in pleasant tones and who sounded sincere in his desire to help. Amelia had uttered one of the key password phrases that allowed her access to the next level of the bureaucracy.

Amelia discussed her problem in great detail. The official put her in touch with several other bod officials who sounded equally sincere. After a while, getting nothing but sincerity, Amelia noticed that a number of sentences were being repeated with no change in intonation. Although the middle level of management had been trained to perform a wider variety of tasks, and, although they believed themselves to be in control, they were just mere slaves who had little or no comprehension of the words they were repeating. Amelia tested a number of key phrases on them, and found, eventually, that cleverly worded insults gained her access to the next echelon.

After that, she progressed rapidly through the remaining levels. She learned how to trigger responses. She learned how to cut corners through this intricate verbal maze.

Eventually she reached Hubbel. The phone call from Amelia genuinely surprised him, until he realized she had called to ask for a favor. He surprised her in return by being cordial.

"The matter interests me," he said, "mainly for personal reasons. It presents a splendid opportunity to embarrass Dissa Banach. I don't know if I can help you, but I will certainly try." He spoke to her as he might a business associate. His voice revealed no hint of resentment, and no hint of warmth, as if whatever had occurred between them had been trivial. His friendly manner actually piqued her, as he knew it would.

The meeting between Olagy, Amelia, and Magen took place one week later. Requiring neutral territory, the parties selected the ruins of a pre-Draconian failed colony located in the forests of the Autumn World.

The dead city had been designed around towers of mirror, some of which remained standing with randomly placed windows reflecting the patchwork colors of the surrounding trees. Other towers had toppled in the unrelenting forest, like broken prisms spilling patchwork views of a tattered landscape.

Under the shade of a ruptured ten-story church, Olagy's personal slaves worked busily to prepare an elaborate feast. A wide assortment of rare delicacies lay shining upon silver or jeweled trays. The aroma of seared sugars, citrus, meats, and recombinant spices filled the air. Hubbel, who had spent years apprenticing in psychophysiology, selected an array of foods that would subtly influence the negotiation process—hard-to-digest items that clogged the digestive system and dulled the mind.

Hummingbirds gene-spliced with oranges. Fish wrapped in candied orchids. Embryo soup.

The meal boasted of the bod's wealth and resources. Such dishes were also the staple of the pampered few. Amelia would appreciate them and put down anyone who didn't. The meal would accentuate the caste differences between Amelia and her new companions. After this dinner, the opposition would be divided, intimidated, sated, and dulled.

Olagy snatched bits and pieces of food from the table. He came mostly for show, and sat quietly daydreaming reptilian fantasies while a slave rubbed his scales.

Amelia's craft was arriving. As it descended vertically, autumn leaves blew in all directions. Finally, the ship came to a lopsided rest upon a cushion of treetops. Amelia gracefully disembarked, strolling down a spiral ramp that wound to catch each step. A temperate autumn wind seemed to follow her, the wind of a perpetually lost summer and a never-to-be winter. She was the closest thing to royalty in the Draconian system, directly descended from Hadly Strados, the eccentric genius who developed faster-than-light travel. One of the most awe-inspiring men who had ever lived, Hadley Strados freed mankind from the confines of the Milky Way and nearly destroyed the universe in the process.

The extraordinary genes of Hadley Strados had been tempered over the centuries until they took the form of Amelia. The eyes, the mouth, the breasts, the rump. Nothing could compare to them.

Hubbel sighed to himself.

Chev Carson and Dawson emerged from the topmost exit hatch. Armed troops dressed in purple and brass clamored out of the other exit hatches, then shimmied down rope ladders to the leaf-covered ground. The troops split into twin phalanxes, one led by Chev, the other by

Dawson. In unison, they formed a prong around the negotiation table.

Both Amelia and Olagy had invested heavily in a peace bond to insure that the proceedings would be conducted amicably. The surety sent from the Insurance Bod relayed his annoyance at Amelia's troops by bowing and posturing obsequiously, exaggerating his manners as a show of insolence. In contrast to Amelia's troops, the Slavers Bod officials carried no visible weapons, brought no soldiers. Although peace bonds were frequently broken on the pretense of technical violations, and although there were no formal mechanisms for enforcing the bonds in the absence of law, a show of arms when a peace bond had been placed was considered to be in poor taste.

"How unlike Amelia," observed Hubbel, "to breach etiquette. Chev Carson's influence, no doubt."

Wearing flexible armor, and decked out with guns, knives, and grenades, Magen took her place at the negotiation table. She refused to sit until Amelia's troops fell into tactical positions.

Amelia approached the table. She traded cryptic, nostalgic smiles with Hubbel, and she murmured greetings to Olagy. She thought Hubbel had aged well. Wrinkles and sags around his eyes gave his face a kindly, wise expression, though the parenthetical creases around his smile were too deep now, and he looked as if he had gotten them in a knife fight. His spine had stayed straight. He had kept most of his hair.

Amelia greeted Olagy courteously. He returned the greeting with a dull stare.

"How do you know you are dealing with the real Olagy?" Dawson called to Amelia, from behind a stand of oaks.

Olagy responded, "Everyone asks that question these

days. I am bored with having to prove myself." He clapped his webbed hands.

A porter rolled out a silver cart on which rested twenty-four severed heads, each with identical reptilian features. Olagy shooed flies away from the riper display mountings.

"Here you have it," said Olagy. "All of my clones are dead."

"I'm convinced," said Amelia, averting her eyes and gesturing dismissal toward the cart.

A drumroll sounded. Out of the forest marched a procession of unarmed, slack-faced, naked slaves. They prostrated themselves at the sound of a trumpet blast, forming a carpet of flesh.

Dissa Banach made his entrance, striding over the backs of the flattened slaves. He wore shoes fitted with six-inch spikes, sharp enough to pierce bone. The slaves beneath him did not even flinch, not at the crunching sounds of punctured skulls, not at the warmth of blood flowing downhill, not at the sucking hiss of chest wounds. Glassy-eyed, they submitted to death and worse beneath Dissa's piercing tread. They showed no sign of objection, other than an occasional grunt.

"It is a horrible spectacle," muttered Hubbel, "but awesome." Amelia smiled halfheartedly, trying to be polite, trying not to show how much the display upset her.

Blood had glued leaves to Dissa's legs all the way up to his thighs. He said, as he came stomping toward Magen, "I always insist on the red-carpet treatment!" The spikes on his shoes scraped across ancient sidewalk beneath the leaves.

"You're not eating. I hope I haven't spoiled your appetite."

"The laws of my religion forbid all this food," said Magen, glaring.

Hubbel slapped himself on the forehead. "I'm so

sorry," he said. "This is my fault. Tell us what you want to eat, and I shall send for it at once."

"I didn't come to eat. I want my husband returned to me."

"Perhaps we can arrange for a substitute," suggested Dissa.

"I want only my husband. No one else will do."

"A very quaint notion," said Hubbel, "but consider your position. Although your attacks have proved irksome, you cannot hope to prevail against the full armed might of the most powerful bod in the system. You must realize that, I'm sure. Your anachronistic ideas about sex were born of an age when beauty was rare and bestowed by chance. Fidelity carried epidemiological imperatives. Some vestiges of ancient feelings may surface from time to time . . ." Hubbel stole a glance at Amelia. ". . . but if you cling to them, they will kill you. We are trying to reach a compromise."

"No compromise," said Magen. "I am not like you. Maybe once I was, but I am not anymore. You are taught never to hold one mate. You share many partners, find beauty in anyone and take pleasure with everyone. My husband and I found the old ways were better. The old Earth ways. When I pledged myself to him, and to him alone, I found . . . such beauty. Two souls turned only to each other, trying to be one. It is worse than death to be away from him. You cannot know what I feel."

Hubbel leaned forward, resting his chin on a bridge of fingers, suddenly fascinated by the opportunity to observe firsthand a phenomenon he had only read about in old texts. He said, "Conventional wisdom holds that limiting your mating options leads to unhappiness. Even when romance was in vogue, people were fickle. Even the most ardent of loves were fragile, death taking the best of them.

Love is unwise—as best illustrated by your present circumstances.''

"Give him back or I fight you forever!" Blood rushed to her face.

"She is ridiculous," said Dissa. "You can't deal with her."

"My husband is dead. Why do you not admit it? Why do you prolong this? Let us just get on with our fighting."

Dawson tensed, clearly afraid the girl was about to open fire. She was losing control.

"We aren't certain where he is. That's the truth," said Hubbel. "Tracking a single slave through our channels is far more difficult than you imagine. Every minute, all over the Draconian system, millions of slaves are bought, stolen, bartered, born, or buried. Nonetheless, we have devoted the bod's extensive resources to the problem. You must provide us with a full description of him and his background. I am curious as to what kind of man inspires such devotion in a woman."

"He is an ordinary man," said Magen, settling back in her chair. Just thinking about her husband seemed to calm her. "His name is Adam Greene. He is a bible scholar who brought me back to my people and the God of my ancestors.''

Hubbel scanned her body language, her eye movements. He had been trained to spot symptoms of lying. He deduced that most of what she said was true, but not all of it.

"Women turn to God when the devil is done with them," said Dissa Banach.

"You are disrupting this conference," said Hubbel, trembling slightly as he turned to face Dissa. "I think you should leave!"

"I haven't eaten yet, and I'm hungry," said Dissa.

Hubbel turned to Olagy, and said, "I think you should

order him to leave. We won't make any progress as long as he's here."

"Yes, yes," muttered Olagy, who was preoccupied with trying to lick loose a bit of syrupy fruit glued to one of his molars. "Dissa, go away, leave us alone."

Dissa glared. "We don't need public relations! All we need is fear!" He rose up from the table. Magen rose up as well. She seized Dissa by the shoulders suddenly, and before he had time to respond, she planted a kiss on his cheek and said, "God watch over you and grant you wisdom."

He wiped aside the wet spot with the back of his hand, disgust twisting his features. He stormed away into the shadows of the forest, his spikes clanking.

Hubbel turned his attentions to Magen. "You are a rather extraordinary woman. Alone and with limited resources, you've done noticeable damage to our operations. I cannot believe that an extraordinary woman can be satisfied with an ordinary man."

Magen looked down the table. She rubbed her forehead and took a deep breath of humid air. She looked Hubbel in the eye. "When I was a child, a horrible creature came into my room and told me to run for my life. I didn't even recognize that it was my mother—splashed with acid. From the sewers of the Summer World, I watched my entire village dissolve. My parents, my big sister, my uncles, my cousins, my friends. For one year I did not leave the sewers. I had no company but mugdubs. I swore no one would ever take me like my village was taken. So I pledge myself to the Mercenary Bod. My whole life I have done nothing for anyone but take lives. In the battlefields, in the shadows, doing assassin work. You think I am so special because I can do so much killing, so much smashing. But this is not special to me. Adam took me away from killing. I love him because he is ordinary." Her eyes burned. Love and desperation welled up in her. She gripped her hands together and they shook as if she were wrestling with herself. Voice cracking, she said, "I love him because he is *nothing* like me!"

A single tear rolled down Hubbel's cheek. He said, "Your story moved me. I'm sorry." He wiped away the tear. "That was very unprofessional of me."

"Very professional, if you ask me," said Dawson, folding his arms across his chest. "And I bet that entire scene with Dissa was prearranged, too."

Amelia nodded. She knew Hubbel well. He kept his passions under tight rein, and only showed emotion when it suited his purposes.

Hubbel ignored Dawson's remarks. He said, "I will do everything in my power to find and free your husband. I promise this, but my promise is not unconditional. You must suspend all hostile actions against our bod during the interim period."

"If I stop fighting, you will stop looking. When you give me my husband back, I will stop fighting. Not until," said Magen coyly, settling back in her chair.

"But you are asking us to do a difficult, expensive task for you. How can we accomplish our mutual goal if the bod's resources are tied up with defending against your attacks?"

"If I stop fighting, you will think I've lost resolve. You will try to think up ambushes and tricks. No. Some beasts you can trust. Some you must give them sugar. And some beasts must be whipped to make them do the right thing."

"You are making a big mistake."

"Maybe yes. Maybe no."

Their business finished, the parties strategically withdrew from the table. The surety sat nibbling nervously at his mustache, patiently watching his clock as the slavers vanished into the patchwork wilderness. Chattering squirrels immediately fell upon the cold uneaten dinner, while crows and other carrion eaters attended to the corpses of the slaves who had laid down their lives beneath Dissa's spikes.

Amelia turned to Magen and asked, "Why did you kiss Dissa Banach? It was a beautiful gesture in some ways, foolish and disgusting in others. Don't get me wrong. I found it quaint. This religion thing of yours—does it tell you to love your enemies, too?"

"I picked his pocket," said Magen. She produced a handful of small items culled from Dissa's coat: an appointment book full of scrawled notations, a fingerblade, a key ring, a pornographic hologram. "I learned how to pick pockets from the street unincorps. That was before I joined the Merc Bod. I used to be good at picking pockets."

"It looks like you still are."

"Not so good as I used to be. He picked my pocket, too."

Leading Amelia's entourage, Dawson glanced cautiously around and cocked his hand blaster.

The surety remained in his chair. The sun began to set.

Magen tensed, she heard something. A faint hum. A click.

Amelia lay a reassuring hand on Magen's shoulder. "It's only the wind," she said smiling, as a gentle autumn breeze played across her hair.

Magen shoved Amelia violently to the ground, then dove for cover herself. A powerful blast of wind roared over the two women, sucking breath from their lips. The leaves scattered into swirling smears of color.

The twilight sky above boiled and darkened. Tattered clouds whipped around like epileptic spirits. The wind roared in bass. Tornado tendrils stabbed into various parts of the forest, sucking up leaves, animals, troopers—anything that got in their way.

Chev found the strength to hold his ground momentarily. The storm's suction grabbed at him. Flying leaves slapped his cheeks. He stripped off his shirt, twisted it into a cord, and tied himself tightly to the trunk of a sycamore. Secure, he fired off a round into the accelerating wind, aiming at blurred forms: leaves, limbs, and other objects gathered into the folds of the building storm. The sudden storm had not arisen naturally, he was sure. He stole a glance in the direction of the surety, ready to register a protest. The chair was empty, and the stand of trees behind the chair showed an increased percentage of red leaves.

Chev hurled a volley of concussion bombs into the roaring air, with the hope that the blasts would disrupt the weather patterns. The wind caught the bombs and threw them back. When the bombs detonated overhead, huge branches exploded loose and the debris disappeared into leaf cluttered slip streams.

Stripped of its branches, the tree that held Chev quivered violently in the wind. It rattled.

Flying objects carried by a banner of storm turned 180 degrees and shot back toward Chev. He cut himself loose from his tree and dove for the ground. His fingers scrambled for a handhold. The wind yanked his hair and pressured his face into a fish-lipped frown. His popping ears threatened to burst.

Inching his way across the root-choked ground, Chev found the spot where Amelia had fallen. She sobbed uncontrollably, her chest heaving, her hands covering her face, as if she were trying to keep the wind from vacuuming out her breath. Chev tried to calm her down, but she couldn't hear him over the roaring storm. He stopped trying to communicate with words and covered her with his weight while grabbing hold of the sturdiest roots he could find. Amelia kept crying.

Dawson was searching for Amelia in the mad haze of leaves, dust, and flying objects, when he spotted something else—a shadow dancing in the eye of the storm. He looked harder, enhancing the image on his retina with computer overlays. It amazed him.

The entire storm poured from a cylindrical flying mechanism not much larger than ten feet in circumference and fifteen feet in height. Superheated rotating ratchets at the core of the mechanism spun wet warm air in a steady sweep into the chilled, foggy atmosphere of the Autumn World. Mist swirled in to fill the resulting vacuum, encircling the tower of warm updraft. As hot and cold air clashed, the upper levels of fog organized themselves into storm cells.

Dawson guessed that the device was self-sustaining, powered by the storm it had created. He coughed. It was getting impossible to breathe without filling his throat with dirt.

A dome of scattered leaves rode over the storm's eye, sucked upward by low pressure. Satellite probes, guided by laser and microwaves, were orbiting the main mechanism. They shifted position to aim jets of wind current. Thin red vectors swept across the vista.

Dawson fired several shots at the device, illuminating it with startling laser clarity. Some of the shots narrowly missed. The storm retaliated, blowing branches in Dawson's direction. The branches targeted him, then dropped in a heap. He vanished from sight, lost under the woodpile.

Magen stepped away from a sheltering stand of trees and took a shot at the device. A sudden blast of wind sent her skidding across the concrete street, which had been covered by leaves but was now stripped bare. She rolled with the wind, getting scraped and bruised. All around her, miles of drenched branches swayed back and forth, undulating like ocean waves.

Great tree trunks cracked and split open.

The forest reeked of sap and ozone.

Using her hand blaster, Magen punched footholds three feet deep in the concrete. She anchored herself, standing upright, then took aim. Animal parts, stones, branches, and clumps of dirt hurtled toward her. She shot most of the flying debris in midair and managed to dodge most of what slipped past her gunfire—but more objects flew at her. The winds blew so hard she could barely breathe. Her eyes were only half-open. Weird g-forces tugged at her, making her heart skip beats.

The storm's black chaos, its shrieks and howls, made it seem like something alive. Membranes of wind rose and fell. The clouds and mists and drafts shared an interactive relationship that fed each other's fury. Storm cells reproduced in undulating erotic rhythms, then coalesced. The beast not only hungered, it grew, it evolved.

On their bed of roots, Chev and Amelia trembled against the powerful suction. Chev's fingers were raw; his muscles were their only anchor. Amelia clung desperately to him, trying to contribute whatever gravity she could, but she felt insignificant. She felt unbound in space, weightless. It seemed she would fly away, but for the man who lay on top of her shaking and moaning with effort while the wind lacerated him.

The storm was everywhere: all-powerful, self-sustaining, and terrifying in its random treatment of the creatures trapped within its cloaks. The winds lifted some of the animals gently into the air and set them down safely miles away, sometimes in branches, or on beds of leaves. Other animals were grabbed violently, their limbs torn off or their eyes sucked out. A mile above the ground, a pitifully small human form gyrated frantically. Amelia couldn't tell if the soldier was still alive, if his form was animated by wind or by terror.

The sky churned, swirled, erupting with thunderbolts. Funnel clouds rose in curious intertwining helix formations.

Wind burned Magen's skin and chilled her bones. She said a prayer into the storm. The wind seemed to suck the words from her lips. Then the tail end of the jet stream passed. There was another moment's calm while the storm held its breath to change direction. This time as the wind current turned, it blew out the mirrored windows of the ruins and gathered the shattered glass. Roaring clouds of shrapnel flew directly at Magen. Abandoning her footholds, she charged back to the stand of trees. As she ran, bits of flying glass sheared through her clothing.

She dove for cover behind the stand of trees. The wind slammed into the trunks and branches, ripping away layers of bark. Glass, splinters, and wood chips sprayed like confetti. Magen hugged the wet ground as the vibrating air, full of fragments, flew over her, millions of tiny crystal blades.

In the space of a breath, Magen stood and fired at the mechanical heart of the storm. It was only a shadow surrounded by swirling veils, a ghost of an image. She aimed more by instinct than by sight, reaching for a center in the chaos. In a moment of calm, she knew exactly where to shoot. Her gun flared.

She nicked the machine. It spun wildly and crashed into an ancient tower of glass; then it wobbled around, trying to right itself. As the winds began to disperse, and as friction weakened the percolating storm cells, Magen fired again, sure of herself. This time she scored a direct hit, shearing the rotaries in midair. The mechanism broke into three parts and scattered.

The dark dervish clouds began to unwind, visibly turning to mist as the wind slowed. Heavy ancient relics began to rain out of the sky, along with leaves, branches, and bits of mirror.

The helix whirlwinds surrendered, falling apart. The multiple membranes of the eye wall dissolved and the remnants collapsed into one another. Squall lines became unbruised and billowed upward. The sky began to fill with soft pastel colors against the night, diffuse refractions of starlight shining in dull rainbows as the mist gathered. The endless cover of knitting fog, lit by occasional flashes of light, made it seem as if the atmosphere were trying to mend the terrible rifts wrought by the storm. It was glorious to watch the storm end and the sky fix itself.

Magen found herself standing in the center of an enormous star-burst shape on the ground etched by a wind shear. Wringing chilled water from her hair, she shivered. The howl and whistle of dying winds sounded almost like silence compared to the roar that had preceded them. Her ears were clearing. After a while, she could even hear the soft rustle of leaves in the dissipating gusts.

Covered by mud and sap, Amelia and Chev untangled their embrace and rose up from their bed of roots.

Dawson slowly tore himself from the pile of fallen branches that had covered him. He began to search the perimeter for their craft, or whatever was left of it.

# 4

## THE BUTCHER

Amelia sat alone in the cloud garden, watching the cumulus fulminate with half-glazed eyes. Small rainbows encircled the stars shining through the mist. She absently toyed with her multilayered diaphanous robe.

Magen wore a jacket of leather and silver, and a matching kerchief on her head. A small goatskin bag dangled from her shoulder. Magen had dressed for travel.

"I have come to say good-bye and to ask a favor," said Magen.

"How can I help you?"

"I need a ship."

"Of course. And you're so certain I'll grant the favor, you're saying good-bye in advance?"

"Yes, and thank you for everything."

Amelia stood and paced. She resented being taken for

granted, but more than that, she resented being found so predictable. "Where are you going?"

"It is best if you do not know."

Amelia caught her hand. "Perhaps I will grant one last favor for you. There is something I want in return, though. I don't know how to say this. I think . . . I think I am in love."

"Chev?"

"I think so. But I am not sure. I don't know anyone else to ask about this. Usually I take my questions to Dawson, but what would a slave know about love? What is love? How do you identify love? The old books say you can tell at a glance, at the moment you meet. But when I first met Chev, I felt nothing—absolutely nothing. He was beneath contempt."

"I did not like Chev either, not very much, when we first met."

"But what about your husband? Did you love him the first time you saw him?"

Magen shifted her gaze from Amelia to rows of billowing cumulus miniatures. Her tone grew distant and her eyes narrowed. She muttered, "I thought I was going to kill him."

Amelia shivered. "Take a ship. Leave."

The first time Magen saw the man she would later marry, she was looking through the crosshairs on the sniper scope of a high-power rifle.

Although Magen's husband had been sold into slavery under the name Adam Greene, his real name was Adam Hirsch. At the time of his capture, he had been traveling incognito. The pseudonym had been necessary, for a tremendous bounty had been placed on his head by a coalition of bods.

Magen herself had once tried to collect that bounty.

She crouched on a carpet more lush with fungus than fabric, on the third floor of a derelict hotel. The poorly lit room stank of yeasty piss. Mugdubs rolled in a corner, their footprint motifs played over the interior like an ugly wallpaper pattern.

The room overlooked a vast, open-air unincorp marketplace. Magen primed her laser rifle. Peering through the gun's sniper scope, she scanned the crowd around the trade stalls below. She passed over a fat man with a ring in his nose coupling with a courtesan under her gene-spliced peacock feathers. She shifted her focus, saw a child, a street unincorp, torturing a mange-riddled dog. Then a pumped-up steroid mutant came into view—he was smashing a food vendor's cart.

A commanding voice began to boom out from some point she could not immediately identify. The bystanders slowly turned away from their various transactions and listened. The babble of voices began to hush.

That was when she spotted him.

Adam Hirsch stood almost seven feet tall. Even under the cover of loose-fitted dark clothing, the solid bulk of his muscle was unmistakable. A dark beard bubbled down his chest. His curly hair winged out around his ears. Magen found him uniquely handsome, despite the odd black hat he wore and the wire-rim glasses. He had the intense, blue-eyed gaze and high forehead of an intellectual. Men who were handsome on the raw force of their personality, without any genetic engineering, were extremely rare. This man's genuineness, and his undeniable power, stirred something primitive in Magen. She felt as if she were confronting a mountain. She regretted having to kill him.

She assessed her murderous options. With a fine, nearly invisible beam, she could gun down Hirsch undetected—however, the scope's optic overlays confirmed that Hirsch was wearing heavy shielding that would deflect any finely honed beam. She could punch through the shielding at this distance with a heavier beam setting, but that would cut a red vector straight to her location. The market below offered no escape routes. A strange crowd had gathered to hear Hirsch speak—unwashed unincorp artisans, prostitutes, pirates, and a surprising number of bod middle-level managers who had come to trade pilfered goods for items they could not obtain owing to fiscal cutbacks.

The crowd was ten times larger than she had expected. They were enthusiastically cheering Hirsch. Hookers, pirates, middle managers. They all loved him.

Adam Hirsch's heavily armed bodyguards mingled with the crowd outside the hotel, patrolling the perimeters around the trade stalls. Magen spotted them easily. Then she searched for the group of mercenaries who had allegedly been hired to maintain order for the gathering, and to lay down cover fire for Magen's escape. But she couldn't find them. She wondered if they were even there.

Magen rummaged through a chamois backpack and pulled up a tarnished Luger. The gun had been pressed into her hands by her dying mother. Having no time to pass on teachings, morals, or values, her mother passed on a legacy of death. Ammunition for the unspeakably rare and ancient weapon had been hard to come by. The bullets had to be custom crafted on the Winter World. Ballistic weaponry had become a largely overlooked technology in the system. It was sort of a lingering taboo, too earthly, too simple. And yet the old gun suggested many possible solutions for her present problem. If she could get close enough, she could fire from inside the crowd. Hirsch's diffusion shield would not stop a metal projectile. The bullet's trajectory would be invisible. She could fire and lose herself in the ensuing melee.

The weapon felt old and dusty in her grip.

She headed down to crowd level, descending a vomit-stained staircase that creaked and wobbled under her weight. Magen had to force the front door open, for the crowd had swollen and surrounded the hotel.

All exits from the market were choked off.

She tried to squeeze through the multitude, then gave up. Her gun remained holstered inside her leather jacket. She looked for the disguised mercs who were supposed to have kept people away. Either they had never showed up, or they had become intimidated by the size and eagerness of the throng. Or perhaps the mercs, too, had been caught up in the speaker's spell.

For an hour, Hirsch spoke through a bullhorn, advocating the establishment of government to control the bods. Magen understood very little of what he said. She had trouble hearing over the murmurs and cheers. But Hirsch impressed her with his command of the crowd.

He said, "Using sophisticated psychological manipulations, the bods have created two categories of slaves. There are slaves who know they are slaves, and there is everyone else—the slaves who don't know what they are. It is time to stop hating yourselves." He repeated the last simple phrase over and over. "It is time to stop hating yourselves."

That phrase struck a common chord in the disparate crowd. Almost all of them had been raised in bods that promoted self-contempt as part of the corporate culture. Individual egos were subverted to further company goals. For a moment, everyone assembled threw off self-hatred and cheered. Even Magen was cheering.

She knew that it would be difficult, very difficult, to kill this man. She stopped listening to his voice, and turned her attention to scheming.

For the next two weeks, Magen followed Adam Hirsch, taking note of his habits, listening to his speeches. During all that time, not one opportunity for a clean hit presented itself—at least, no opportunity she couldn't rationalize away.

Then she discovered one gaping breach in his security system. He placed an inordinate amount of faith in an aged hermit named Papa Russia, a butcher and a cook. The old man prepared all of Hirsch's meals.

One morning Magen followed Papa Russia from Hirsch's hotel room. The trail led through unincorporated dark alleys to the outskirts of the city, to the wet, mushroom-infested jungle that sprawled under the shadow of Summer City's towers.

She landed her aircraft, pulping the ground with blasts from her retro rockets. The landing raised clouds of spores.

She planned to survey the old man's operations and to put poison on his cookware or in his spices. She had just the right kind of poison—something very slow-acting, so slow that even if the old man sampled his preparations while he was cooking, he would still live long enough to deliver the meal to Hirsch.

The air hung wet, scented with mildew. Magen climbed from her craft, then hacked away some spongy undergrowth. She heard something heavy stumbling through the brush.

Suddenly a large, primitive-looking bull ambled in front of her. It was looking for grass, or whatever it ate. Its slippery hooves beat a skittish tattoo on the slime-covered remnants of an old tile floor that lay beneath the fungus. Magen instinctively reached for a weapon; there were so many to choose from——lining her pockets, strapped to her limbs and body hollows. She opted for something sharp and noiseless, something that wouldn't flash. Though the bull presented no danger, and no sport, she killed it anyway. Something about this place made her nervous, very nervous.

As she explored further, she found the collapsing ruins of a long-abandoned development community. Despite the decay, despite the blue-green patina of moss covering what was left of apartment façades, there was no mistaking the distinctive patterns of acid damage.

Magen had stumbled onto the ruins of the old Jewish Quarter of the Summer World. She could dimly make out the shapes of mezuzahs on the doorframes.

The place had never shed its reputation for plague, and the city had realigned its borders to exclude the imagined contagion. An electric tingle shivered through Magen's spine.

She ran down the streets of the ghost town, occasionally seeing vaguely recognizable buildings that set off a chain of overwhelming, mixed emotions. Before the pogrom, she had been very happy as a child. This was the only place she had ever known happiness, but she could not access any happy memories without conjuring memories of terror.

Old skulls peered at her from beneath layers of moist fungus along the street.

Suddenly two flashes of blue light stabbed her. One blast seared her shoulder; the other cut her left thigh, throwing her to the moss-wet ground. A red targeting dot fluttered over her heart. She had foolishly let her guard down in a moment of emotional weakness. She had let the old man get the drop on her.

He surprised her again, this time by not firing. He let her know how accurately his handgun was aimed, as a warning, but he did not pull the trigger. It made no sense to her, letting an armed stranger linger in your sights.

"Throw aside all of your weapons," said Papa Russia.

Magen tossed aside a token handgun and a dagger to appease him.

"Why did you come here?" he demanded.

Magen said nothing. She was in too much pain to come up with a credible lie.

"I could have killed you easy, you know it."

"Thank you for letting me live."

"Maybe I am crazy to do that. You must tell me the truth. What are you after here? I warn you, I am not afraid to kill. I let you live because I have too much blood on my hands already. I do not like to kill, but if I have to . . ."

She blurted out the truth. "This was my home when I was a child." She said it reluctantly, particularly with the red dot dancing over her heart. She rarely revealed her background. She had intentionally forgotten most of what she knew about her heritage. She knew this much—it placed her in constant jeopardy. It made people distrust her, fear her, and sometimes, hate her.

"You are a Jew?" he asked incredulously.

"Yes."

She told her story, saying nothing of her present assignment. Papa Russia interrogated her at great length. The red dot fluttered over her heart as the old man's hand shook with slight parkinsonian tremors. He pressed her on a number of details about her childhood. He spoke strange words and gauged her reactions. He asked her about the atrocities.

She answered all of his questions honestly—but she had trouble looking him in the eye. She'd never seen such drastic, undoctored effects of old age, except in photographs. The wrinkles, the odors, the random loss of hair and teeth revolted her. She knew she was risking her life by avoiding his gaze, but she couldn't help herself.

He lowered the gun and shut off the targeting mechanism. At this close range, she could kill him instantly in a dozen different ways—but he seemed to have settled down. He wasn't threatening her anymore, and if she killed him, her plan for poisoning Hirsch would be blown.

He said, "I have some wine with me. It will help your pain."

"I have these," said Magen, pulling out two anesthetic adhesives.

Papa Russia shook his head. "Those only increase the chance of infection in this heat, and they are highly carcinogenic. They are made to get you through a fight, and to hell with you after that. I know. I used to be a doctor with the bods."

She took the wine.

"Can you walk?"

She nodded. "It is only pain."

They walked a short distance to a farmhouse, little more than portions of prefab houses shoved together and hammered loosely in place. Chickens clucked. Their claws clattered atop the tin-gabled roof. The windows had been taken from the synagogue, stained-glass murals depicting scenes from Exodus.

"You want something to eat?" asked the old man.

"It is not necessary."

"You want a sandwich? I got good sandwiches. And I got a pickle."

"Well, I am getting hungry."

Inside, the farmhouse was dark except for muted points of color shining through the story of Moses. Papa Russia began to light candles on a row of antique menorahs, some partially dissolved with blue-green acid scars. He found a roll of gauze.

He crossed over to her side and held out his hands. She offered her wounded thigh to him. He disinfected it with some primitive, stinking liquid, and began to wrap the gauze.

"I think I knew your parents. If they are who I think, they used to live downstairs from my cousin Yoshe. God rest his soul. I am glad I did not kill you. There are not many Jews in the Draconian system, and very, very few young pretty girls. You got a boy?"

"From time to time."

He shot her a disapproving look. "You should marry."

He went over to his icebox, and pulled out some meat wrapped in rumpled plastic. "I have lived here all alone twelve years," he said. "You are my first guest."

"Were there no other survivors?"

"Yes. A fair number. There are hidden ghettos in the unincorp sections of this world. The braver souls fled to the Spring World, where they live with no technology."

"Why do you live all alone?"

A look of great sadness misted the old man's eyes. For a moment, he seemed withdrawn, deep in thought. She thought he was getting ready to confide something to her. He was lonely, not truly a hermit by nature.

"This is my home," he said, at last. But it didn't ring true. They didn't want him, she thought.

He cut two slices of yellow bread, and threw them together with a leaf of lettuce, a pickle, some tomato slices, and a coat of mustard. He handed the sandwich to her as if it were an heirloom.

She smiled and took a large bite, but immediately spat it out. She couldn't help herself. The meat was stringy and it had a primitive, greasy taste, thickly bovine and gamy. It was undisguised heavy animal muscle—the most horrible thing she had ever tasted.

"You're not used to eating kosher food," he said. "You like better bioengineered meat. I grant you—it is more tender, and more . . . gentle . . . in taste. But it is unclean. The great summer plague they blamed on us, it came from gene-spliced cattle. Did you know that?"

"No," said Magen. She felt sick to her stomach.

"When I was younger, I was like you. I ate the meat of the bods, and I must confess, I liked it. I liked it too much. But it is an abomination before God the way they cross-breed species."

His reference to God was the first she'd heard since the massacre. She had vivid recollections of an all-powerful fairy-tale father figure who watched everything in the universe all at once. She had imagined him sitting in a great hall of video screens. Her parents told her to trust in God with his infinite wisdom and his supernatural powers. They told her God would protect her and watch over her. After the great pogrom, she stopped trusting God. It came as no surprise to her when she discovered that religion had fallen out of vogue all over the system.

Papa Russia continued, "Let me explain something very difficult to understand. I did not understand it when I was your age, and I have suffered greatly for not understanding. Suffered very greatly.

"Listen to me. However you grew up—whatever you believe—you are a Jew, and God demands you live like a Jew. That means you must give up certain things. You must behave a certain way. You must follow certain laws."

Magen said, "I don't understand 'laws.' "

"Laws are like what you call protocols. Prescribed actions. These laws are not easy to follow. Our ancestors called themselves the 'Chosen People.' Not because they thought they were better than anyone else. The legends say they did not want to be chosen—at first. They stood under a mountain to receive the laws, Mount Sinai, it was called, on Earth. The great books tell us to read the passage literally—that God lifted the mountain into the air, held it above the heads of our ancestors, and told them that if they did not accept the laws, the mountain would be dropped."

"You expect me to believe this?"

"It doesn't matter what you believe. Only what you do. If you obey the laws, belief will follow. Sometimes our people have not obeyed the laws, over the course of our fifteen-thousand-year history. When they forget the laws, then comes the troubles. Like here. There were many Jews violating the laws here. Not keeping the sabbath. Eating the unclean meat. That's what confused me."

Suddenly he grew silent.

"What do you mean?"

"I was very confused when I was young." He seemed eager to stop talking, for a change, embarrassed at having been caught babbling like an old man.

They walked through a wing of the house decorated with plaster death masks. The old man had taken as many as he could from the corpses littering the streets. He had no other way to keep a record of the dead. Magen scanned the walls. All of the plaster faces seemed both familiar and strange.

Papa Russia poured her a glass of sweet cherry wine. They sat on the veranda for an hour. The wine on an empty stomach went straight to her head. She forgot completely about her mission until the old man said that it was time for the slaughter.

He had a dinner to prepare and a cow to kill.

He busily set to work sharpening a long metal knife, screwing up his eyes to check for nicks along the blade. "The knife must be perfectly sharp according to the laws of God," he said. "An imperfect blade makes an imperfect cut, which might pain the animal. The slaughter must be painless—it is a sign of respect for God's creation that you wish to eat. The laws of kashruth are the most blessed and merciful laws of killing in the universe."

Magen let out a sarcastic grunt. Now he was talking about killing—something she understood almost perfectly. "If you want a flawless cut, and a perfect blade, why not use a laser? If you really want to be fast, painless . . ."

"Because that is too easy. If you respect the animal, you must take the extra time to sharpen the blade yourself, to check it for flaws. You must not take the easy way. Does this make sense to you? Nicely honed steel can cut as fast—maybe faster—than a laser. Believe me."

She nodded, and picked up the knife, testing its weight, eyeing the rainbows dancing along its edge. She found his arguments for steel compelling in their own way, and felt a kinship with the old man. But she wondered—did the kinship stem from her distant and largely unknown heritage? Or did they have only one thing in common—killing?

She watched, not even flinching, as he cut the cow's throat. He used a single swift slash that severed the trachea, the esophagus, the vagus nerves, the carotid artery, and the jugular vein. The cow died instantly, spouting a geyser of blood. Digestive juices, gore, and knots of chewed grass spewed out of the neck wound. The old man muttered prayers. He checked the organs for purity and examined tissue samples under a microscope to insure the absence of chromosomal engineering.

When he was done preparing the meat, he walked back to the kitchen in the farmhouse and set to work chopping vegetables with the same care and respect he had shown the cow.

Magen wandered across the veranda while Papa Russia was fixing the meal. She pulled yellowed books down off a shelf. Though they were written in a language she couldn't understand, the dry smell of the aged paper and the odd shapes of a melted, mirror-image alphabet made her shiver.

Her assignment grew distant, even repugnant to her. She considered going unincorp and staying in this green and private place forever—or at least until she could work through all the feelings that were tearing her apart.

She strayed into another room. More death masks covered the walls. Each face in this room differed only slightly from the one beside it, chronicling a gradual deterioration. Magen realized it was the face of Papa Russia, a self-portrait of the aging process. There was a great deal of emotional pain visibly struggling across the replicated features. It seemed as if pain had wrought as much damage as the passage of time. She traced the old man's history across the wall, from youth to obsolescence and back again. This time the earliest mask struck a chord of recognition. She knew that face from somewhere. The memory nagged at her through the wine. Then she shrugged off the feeling as some irrelevant childhood association, or an artificial recollection manufactured by studying the multiple variations of his sad face.

She went back on the veranda, headed for the kitchen. The sun beat hard on her hair. Her wounds ached. Dizziness gathered in her throat.

Strapped behind her thigh, she kept a small vial of nerve toxin. She pulled it loose and held it to the light like a purple gem. The slow, painful death it would produce seemed somehow grossly inappropriate for Adam Hirsch. She thought about killing him up close, with steel, as a sign of respect. But that would not be possible. Poison. There was no other way.

She stood in the kitchen door, waiting for the old man to finish his preparations, holding the purple vial in the hollow of her hand.

When the dinner was ready, the old man gathered it into pots and boxes. Papa Russia turned his back for a moment, and Magen emptied her vial into the soup.

She helped him carry the meal out to his flier. The two of them kept staring at each other as they walked past acid-burned buildings and bone-filled streets under the sun. Being out in the open seemed to have suddenly changed the way they regarded one another.

At the edge of the ruins, Papa Russia found his bull where Magen had killed it. He knelt by the animal's corpse, and retrieved Magen's blade extending from the base of its neck. His eyes accused her.

"Why did you do this?"

"He frightened me."

"Do not lie to me, girl. You do not frighten so easy."

He studied her face. "Why did you come here?" Suddenly he saw her in a different light—not as a lost kinsman returned to the fold. He saw the coldness in her eyes, and he saw the hardened muscles of a warrior straining against her clothing. "Why did you come here?"

"I told you."

"You came looking for me."

"No. I just came looking. What is so special about you that I should come looking for you?" Her stance shifted.

The old man began to shake, suddenly realizing the danger he had been in all along. He mopped his brow with a cotton kerchief. "You are going to kill me?"

She studied him. "I do not kill for no reason. I do not like it."

"What about the bull?"

"I had my reasons. It was this place. It upset me."

Papa Russia closed his eyes and held them closed as if expecting an explosion. A full minute later, he opened them.

Magen hadn't moved. His shoulders quivered as he sucked air. "You are not going to kill me?"

"No."

"Thank God. I am just being a foolish old man. I have been rude to you, I think. Can you forgive me?"

"Yes. I do not think you are so foolish. I expect people to be afraid of me. I worry when they are not."

"That is no way for a young girl to be. Would you like to come with me to dinner? There is someone I would like you to meet. You will like him. And there is much you can learn from him."

She paused, afraid to refuse—half-certain she had botched her scheme over this stupid business with the bull.

"I do not like your cooking very much," she said.

"Oh. Oh yes." The old man glanced at the pots and boxes they were both carrying. "You don't have to eat it. But come with me and meet my friend. You will like him. And you don't have to eat my cooking."

She accepted the offer, figuring she had nothing to lose. The old man was too full of God and ideals to have any guile. He had set no traps, she felt certain. Having established a satisfactory excuse for not eating, she could sit back and be a spectator at dinner. She could make small talk and flirt with Adam Hirsch. The poison would not take effect for two weeks.

Magen steered Papa Russia's lightweight craft through the city. Her daredevil approach to flying unnerved him no end, particularly when she insisted on fooling with her makeup in the rearview mirror while traveling at high speeds.

"You are pretty enough already!" shouted Papa Russia.

Her sudden concern for appearances had nothing to do with vanity. She applied touches of highlights and color to deemphasize the severity of her features, and to defrost her uncaring gaze. She pulled off the elastics that kept her hair bound in a tight assassin's knot. Her sun-tinted mane fell loosely around her shoulders. It was beautiful hair.

"You should keep your head covered when you go to meet Adam," said Papa Russia. He found a faded, rumpled old hat jammed underneath the backseat of the flier. He handed it to her. "Wear this."

To humor him, she put on the hat. At every opportunity, when the old man looked away, or covered his eyes to avoid dealing with the way Magen drove, she discretely shed her remaining weapons.

The old man shouted directions to Adam's Summer headquarters. She knew the way well, but pretended she didn't.

The flier jetted into the unincorp section of town. The buildings lacked the flourishes, advertising, arches, and statuary that adorned bod-built structures. Instead, the architecture was unrelentingly functional, all rectangles and prefab, painted only by accumulations of graffiti.

Magen swooped down to a landing and bounced on impact with the road. Rubber wheels screeched.

Hirsch's followers were patrolling the perimeters. They eyed Magen suspiciously.

The guard at the front door would not let her in.

"That's fine," said Magen. She turned to Papa Russia. "I will meet your friend some other time."

Papa Russia said to the guard, "She is all right. She is a friend. And she is a Jew, believe it or not. I want to introduce her to Adam. She is a Jew."

The guard, who wore a cross around his neck, seemed unpersuaded.

They searched her electronically and manually. Even divested of her weapons, she was not trusted. She felt hopelessly out of her element, and regretted coming along. She hoped she could bluff her way through the rest of the evening, but already she had her doubts. Playacting was not one of her strong points, nor was dealing with people outside of a combat or bod social context. She felt naked without her weapons, and ridiculous with Papa Russia's smashed hat on her head. At least it made her look less threatening.

"She is all right," insisted Papa Russia, just as the magnetic frisk device stopped buzzing.

The guard let her pass. Magen carried in Papa Russia's heavy iron pots piled one on top of another, with the highest pot just under her chin. She found the smell almost unbearable. Her arms began to ache, particularly around her wounded shoulder.

Papa Russia led her down a papyrus-colored corridor. A malfunctioning air-conditioner hissed. The air hung wet and artificially cold, smelling of chilled mildew.

She heard a baritone voice at the far end of the hall making strange sounds. As she drew closer, she recognized the sounds as a kind of singing. Note clusters repeated without regard to any coherent structure, driven only by the meter of a foreign prose. The music was as basic and potent as the taste of Papa Russia's kosher meat.

She started walking faster, struggling with the fragments of a memory. Abruptly, the music stopped. As Hirsch prepared to leave his room, his shadow fell through the doorway and spilled out into the corridor. It looked like the shadow of a ghost, with a tombstone-shaped head and massive shoulders.

Hirsch stepped out into the yellow light wearing a prayer shawl wrapped over his head like a hood. Dark leather straps bound one small black box to the center of his forehead, and a second black box to the inside of his left arm. A rush of memories took Magen completely by surprise. Standing in the corridor, Adam Hirsch brought to mind the image of her father at prayer just before sunset.

The pots slipped out from her grasp. The poisoned dinner spilled out over a well-worn, deeply stained rug.

The guards rushed inside at the sound of clattering metal. They berated Magen, their anger fueled by hunger. A wall of shouting men surrounded her. They gestured with weapons in their hands, punctuating their curses with unspoken threats. Unarmed, she felt helpless.

"Leave her alone!" shouted Adam. "It was an accident. It is nothing to get so upset about. It was only a meal!" His voice boomed over the din.

Magen burst into tears. An effigy of her father had rescued her. She found herself on the cusp of emotions long repressed and subverted to the business of survival.

After a few moments of conversation with Adam Hirsch, Magen felt as if she had known him for years. His voice was hypnotic, perhaps purposefully so.

She told him about her fights in the sewers under the besieged ghetto. She told him about picking the pockets of Summer tourists, and about her life in the bods. They talked all night.

Magen fell asleep on the couch. When she awoke, she decided she would not—could not—kill Adam Hirsch.

She failed to report to her bod that afternoon. Within a week, she had gone unincorp.

Adam made arrangements for Magen's housing. She moved into the refurbished dormitory where most of Adam's followers lived. The building had been vacated by a defunct toymaker's bod following a long and ruinous bankruptcy war. Commercial slogans and odd pictures of baby-faced animals appeared through tattered wallpaper, sharply contrasting with the icons and religious figurines that formed the new decor. All the tenants followed one religion or another. They had all gone unincorp to promote Adam's political movement, yet most of them seemed more interested in prayer than politics.

The amount of time her neighbors spent reading their sacred texts astounded Magen. The writings were unbelievably ancient. Generally, due to the intense proliferation of data in the system, most Draconians treated anything older than thirteen weeks as obsolete. Nonetheless, around the complex, the old Earth religions seemed most favored. There were many Hindus, Buddhists, Muslims, and Christians, but the greatest number were Universalists. Adam had recruited heavily among the theistic minority in the system, and he promoted new theologies to forge his disparate followers into a kind of unity.

Adam visited the compound frequently and held interfaith discussions. In one of the larger basements, he lectured to a group of newcomers, which included Magen.

He began by discussing changes in the laws of physics during recent recorded history—particularly the astounding changes brought about by warp travel.

"These changes," he argued, "should force men to new conclusions about the nature of God. To build on a biblical metaphor, if man has been made in God's image, then God is a living entity made of both spirit and substance. As with all living things, God's spirit is inextricably and interchangeably bound to his physical manifestation, which is the universe. Changes in the order of physical reality force me to the conclusion that God is changing as well. I believe that God is evolving. I believe that God has always been evolving. Perhaps the creation of the universe is one of the prime achievements of his evolutionary process.

"Identifying God as an evolving entity seems to be the only solution to the many questions that troubled me all my life. Questions such as: Why are there so many different religions? Why is it important for people to have free will? Why does God bother with the upkeep of the universe? What is in it for him?

"But if you consider that God is evolving, the format of creation makes sense. God created a universe in which all living things have free will so that the natural order would be in a constant state of flux, unprogrammed, wild, sometimes chaotic, alternatively hideous and beautiful—a universe shaping itself of its own accord—to catalogue possibilities. This senseless universe seems to have been designed by a perfect being for one purpose. So that God can explore his potential over eternity. So that the all-knowing can learn."

Adam further postulated that part of God's evolutionary process was dependent on prayer—the prayers of a vast complement of competing, perhaps even contradictory religions. He argued that no single set of beliefs, no matter how comprehensive or cogent, could explain all the endless mysteries of God. Acceptance of mystery for its own sake was not good enough anymore. God was trying to understand himself. Adam suggested that prayer was part of an ongoing feedback and negative feedback system. He urged that prayer was meant to be far more than a simple act of adoration.

Using Adam's rationale, rabbis began to reinterpret

the ancient Hebrew maxim that man was not meant to learn from nature, but rather to rise above it.

Adam's Christian followers espoused new theories about God's motives for becoming flesh.

Adam's Hindu followers found a new rationale for their belief that a soul cannot join Brahman until it has advanced through trial, setback, and growth.

There were still many quarrels with the concept, though, in all quarters. The notion flew in the face of the concept that God is immutable, sacred to many religions. Adam pointed out that in a changing universe, even perfection is relative, and God must change in order to remain the same. The paradox appealed to many of the younger generation, but the elders found it glib, and dissatisfying.

In another era, Adam might have been burned at the stake for suggesting that perfection had room for improvement, but he argued that anything is possible for an omnipotent being. Draconian theologians became fascinated by the proposition. Atheism was still the dominant belief mode in Draconian society, and a framework for interfaith cooperation was desirable for political reasons. In this context, the differences between faiths began to appear less and less significant.

There had been a much earlier attempt to join all religions together through the Universalist Church back on Earth. It had failed miserably, creating new dogmas rather than reconciling old, and setting off decades of holy war. Adam's movement was the first opportunity in centuries to reverse the trend of moral entropy that had gripped the system since the banning of warp travel.

Adam's followers shared a common goal in addition to their somewhat similar values, but the popular acceptance of Adam Hirsch's ideas—be they heresy or revelation—owed more to his personal charisma than anything else.

Magen shared a room with a woman named Elsa, who

sang litanies off-key and hung the walls with holographic depictions of Golgotha. After a few days of listening to Elsa's preaching, Magen confronted Adam. She asked, "Do you really believe this business about God evolving and needing all kinds of prayers? Or is it just an excuse to bring people together?" The question had been the subject of much debate and conjecture on the compound.

"Who can say what God is, or what he is doing? With God, anything is possible."

"Then why don't you pray like a Christian sometimes, or like a Muslim?"

"Because I am a Jew. All faiths play a part in God's plan, but I am a Jew. The heart cannot do the work of the liver, not even on a part-time basis."

"You have me very confused about where you want me to live, Adam. When I was a child, the Jews lived with Jews and the non-Jews lived with the non-Jews. My father said that was the way things should be. Was he wrong?"

"You can learn from the other religions around you. We are short of housing right now. Perhaps things will change when the movement gathers more followers. Where you live is fine—it is better than most unincorp facilities, don't you think? Would you rather go back to your bod?"

"They took better care of me."

"Did they really?"

"In some ways. Adam, why can't I live with you?"

He took her hand. "If you stay with me, it will always be less comfortable than life with the bods. Always."

"I don't mind if we are together."

He suddenly seemed to notice her hand in his and lifted it to his lips. She fascinated him. He admired her will, her courage, and her strength. Though not beautiful in the classic sense, her face was interesting; he admired her chutzpah in not having it doctored. Magen had become a challenge to Adam. She represented the Draconian tragedy, the loss of roots, the absence of values. If he could find a way to change her, then perhaps he could change the entire system.

He wanted her to change and he knew there were many ways to bring about rapid and long-lasting fundamental changes in the behavior patterns of individuals. One way was through religion. Adam did his best to reintroduce Magen to Jewish life. It was slow, difficult work. She hated kosher food, and she hated going to temple because she had to sit away from Adam. Another way to change people was through love. They spent more and more time together. The interactions of these two extremely dissimilar spirits began to produce strange and intense romantic harmonies.

One night, Adam asked Magen to dine alone with him at his apartment in the unincorp sector. Sensing something auspicious in the invitation, Magen dressed herself in the most seductive fashions she could find: a sheer, tight-fitting outfit trimmed with frills and leather.

His eyes widened when he opened the door to greet her. At first she felt flattered, but as the evening wore on, there was no mistaking his shock and dismay. He avoided looking at her and kept unusually quiet.

She finally asked, "Did I do something wrong?"

"Your clothes. It is not right to bare so much of your body. A woman should be more modest."

"You don't like to see my body?"

He looked into her eyes, showing he wasn't intimidated. "You are an attractive woman. That isn't the point."

She edged closer. "Adam, I want to lie with you tonight. I have wanted you so much for so very long. I can't wait any longer. You want me, too. I know it."

He nodded, smiling. "But we are not married. It goes against the laws."

She laughed. "The laws. That's all you ever talk about,

Adam. That's all you ever think about. Why should God, the great, all-knowing, evolving spirit of the universe, care at all if I lie with you with no marriage? Why should he care?"

"The special commandments—mitzvahs—are constant reminders of the holiness of life, so that every moment you exercise some kind of self-control. Free will is God's greatest gift. God wants you to celebrate your ability to make choices every moment, so that you never forget your own worth. You would be surprised at how easily people forget the value of life."

"No, I wouldn't," she said bitterly.

Adam stared at the city's spires shining in the distance, reminding him of how the bods offered technological solutions to every problem. He saw the central headquarters of the Slavers Bod, literally painted in the blood of its workers. "You know what runs the system, don't you? Death worship. Slavery. Terror. I can't understand how so much evil is embraced."

"With so much wrong in the universe, why should God prohibit small pleasures?" She put her arms around him.

"Perhaps because God knows how weak people are," he answered. "He wants to keep them busy with little things, trivial prohibitions, so they will be too busy for major mischief."

"But why should he care about things so unimportant?"

"All throughout the system, you can see that people will do whatever they can get away with—and they always test to see just how much that is. If you draw the line at marriage and the mikvah, you will have a lot less adultery."

He still had not answered her question, at least not to her satisfaction—but Adam had taken the discussion outside of her range, and veered off on one of his philosophical discussions. She couldn't outword him, so she shifted the conversation.

"I think I could limit myself to just one man, if he were very special, like you."

"Are you saying you would marry me?"

"I think it is something I would like to try."

"Marriage is not something you try. You make a decision, and you live with it."

"All right, then."

"All right what?"

"I will marry you." She nestled closer to him.

He paused, more than a little embarrassed. He wanted to escape from the moment without making her lose face. "I don't know, Magen. When you show up dressed like this, I think you are not ready to accept my ways. You will not fit in with the Jewish community. Your soul, I fear, still belongs to the bods."

She shook her head, exasperated. "Why do you go on and on about this? I said I would marry you."

"I haven't asked you yet."

"So what do I have to do to get you to ask?"

"I don't know. I was going to ask you to marry me. Not tonight, but soon. Then you show up dressed like this and I fear there will be problems between us."

She laughed. "I think it is silly to change your mind because you don't like my clothes. You're just making excuses because you are nervous. If you don't like what I wear, I'll take it off." She began to undress, laughing harder.

"No . . . No . . ." he said.

He mulled over the situation. He had hoped to gradually reintroduce her to Jewish customs and traditions, buying time to assess how she would acclimate. But she had forced the issue. She seemed jubilant and cocky. How could she understand that marriage is not approached as casually as a bod liaison?

If he refused her awkward proposal, he risked losing her. She would retreat strategically. He wanted to hand her a list of requirements about keeping the Sabbath, washing in the mikvah, observing the kosher laws—a thousand things that wouldn't have to be discussed at all if Magen had been raised as a Jew. But if he sought assurances for marriage, she would read the gesture in military terms. She would eventually view their marriage as capitulation.

He had to make a choice. Now.

"Magen, will you marry me?" he asked.

Over the weeks that followed, Magen surprised Adam. She forced herself to eat only kosher food, and she covered her head with a kerchief, and she said prayers to a God she doubted. Sometimes she told him she thought his customs were stupid, but she performed them anyway. Observance gave her a rhythm to her life. She did what Adam told her to do, and the more she did, the less she questioned.

The wedding was to be held on the Summer World. Magen was anxious to marry and be done with it. The long tedious business of preparation, of invitations, of endless parties and meetings with Adam's family wore on her. This was strictly Adam's show. She had no desire to share the moment with any of the people she had grown up with, which meant that during the most significant moment of her life, she would be surrounded entirely by strangers.

Papa Russia sent his best wishes, but also his regrets. He said that he could not attend the wedding. He gave no reason.

Though she had only spoken to Papa Russia three or four times since their initial meeting, Magen felt a small, independent claim to friendship with the old man. His refusal to attend her wedding disappointed her. Then it depressed her. Then it began to irritate her.

A week before the wedding, Magen had a vivid, terrible nightmare. Time became displaced. Commandos wearing stiff, acid-resistant canvas suits lumbered across her sight. The stink of dissolving mortar and humanity filled the air. She found herself in the middle of the Summer Pogrom—but she wasn't a child this time. Full-grown and armed, she fought back. All of the weapons she had mastered during her days with the Merc Bod came magically to hand. Clumsy in their stiff suits, the genocidal army fell before her assault. Laser shuriken burned through the glass visors over their eyes. With steel vibraswords, she hacked off limbs. But no matter how many she killed, the walls of the ghetto continued to dissolve. Rivers of melted flesh hissed through the gutters. She couldn't stop the slaughter, not even in her dreams. Even with all she had become, she couldn't stop the slaughter. She could only match it.

Knee-deep in gore, Magen saw Papa Russia wandering through the streets. A dazed look clouded his eyes.

"Come over here," she shouted, "I'll protect you."

But he wouldn't come. She beckoned and pleaded, afraid that any minute he'd melt away. He wouldn't listen, yet somehow, miraculously, none of the flying jets of acid touched him.

"Why won't you come over to me?" she demanded.

"I am very confused," he said. Not far from where he was standing, a bull broke loose from its pen and charged into the streets. Papa Russia began to follow the bull. A knife appeared in the old man's left hand. "I was very confused. When I was young, I was very confused."

He slit the bull's throat. He pulled out a seemingly endless chain of knotted entrails, which he then examined under a microscope. He kept pulling on the entrails, and after a while, they ceased to be bovine. There were human entrails roped around his arms.

She awoke full of anger, enraged that Papa Russia would not come to her wedding. Her fingers clenched in tight fists. A splash of cold water and deep breathing calmed her down a little. When she thought more about it, she understood the reasons for his refusal. They had nothing to do with her.

And she remembered where she had seen his face before, the face of Papa Russia as a young man, hung on the wall, preserved in the plaster of a death mask.

Magen snuck away without waking Elsa. She flew past the borders of the city with the windshield of her cruiser wide open. Warm air blew in her face.

She brought the cruiser to a jerky landing, and ran out across the acid-stained ruins of her childhood. At night, she could feel the surreal tingle of haunted ground. Ghosts seemed to be gathering around, making the place feel more like Autumn than Summer. She wished the bones littering the streets would reassemble themselves and walk beside her and give her some assurance that what she planned to do was right. She needed greater counsel than the tingling in the air. With only a few weeks of rudimentary moral teaching to guide her, Magen found herself confronting a dense and imponderable ethical dilemma.

The bones lay still, blue-green with acid and mold. Perhaps that was their counsel, the sadness of their silence.

She did not make a sound as she entered Papa Russia's house. Quiet as an assassin, she paused at the foot of his bed, studying his face. He tossed from side to side in his sleep, moaning, his forehead beaded with sweat. His sleep was light and troubled, but he did not rouse until she seized him by the drool-stained collar of his pajamas. She dragged him to the ground.

"What do you want from me?" he sputtered.

"I know you, Doctor. Abraham Sidney. It was you who gave the bods the excuse to begin the slaughter. You pig! You stupid pig!"

Papa Russia coughed and cleared his throat of phlegm.

"Abraham Sidney died a long time ago. He died in the massacre. Take my word for it. He is dead."

"You don't fool me."

"I hate Abraham Sidney more than any man. But even if he were not dead, and if he were here now, I would spare his life so that he could have even more time to repent." He said it with a twinkle in his eye, as if it were a joke, as if he could charm her out of killing him.

She was not amused.

"I have been hunting you for so long, I cannot believe I didn't know you at once. But I know you now, and I am certain. There is no point in trying to lie your way out of this. You are about to die."

He turned pale and a loose cluster of wrinkles on his jowls began to quiver. "I knew Abraham Sidney. He did not mean to cause death and destruction. When he came up with his theory about Jews causing the plague, he thought he had made a remarkable discovery. He was a scientist who got caught up in a single problem. He never really thought about what would come from his theories. When he said that the Jews were the source of the plague virus, he believed it. He was trying to help all humanity, I think. Perhaps his judgment was a little tainted by self-hatred—but he didn't know that. All bod workers are made to hate themselves and what they are. Abraham Sidney hated himself a lot then. If he were still alive, he'd hate himself even more now. He was not a very good Jew, not a very good person, and most of all—he was not a very good scientist."

Magen felt a sudden stab of pity for the old man, one of the only friends she had ever known. He was the man who had started her personal transformation, and he was the man who had brought her to Adam. The softness of age made him seem helpless. Looking at the flesh gathering in folds and pouches under his chin, she thought of acid victims.

She unsheathed a long silver blade. "If you wish, I will kill you as you kill your cows. Out of mercy. Out of respect. You must die, but I don't want you should feel any pain." She tightened her grip on his collar.

Papa Russia shuddered. What she said was horrible, blasphemous in ways she couldn't know. And he suddenly realized that the ancient laws of slaughter had as much to do with easing the conscience of the butcher as easing the passing of the slaughtered. The sight of the knife gleaming before him snapped him to attention. He read indecision in her eyes. He knew her weaknesses.

"Listen to me," he said. "However you were raised, whatever you believe, you are still a Jew. You must behave in a certain way, you must obey certain laws. Under our laws, it takes a court of twenty-three men to pass a judgment of death. It must be proven that the crime was deliberate and done with malice, and this can only be proven by having at least two witnesses who actually heard the accused say he was going to commit the crime. The two witnesses must have warned him not to commit the crime, and they must have quoted specific portions of the Scripture to him. If you are so sure I am Abraham Sidney, take me to a rabbinic court to stand trial."

"You think you should escape punishment just because of some old protocols that make no sense! No! I have heard enough!"

She seized a shock of his white hair and pulled back his head so that his Adam's apple protruded. He gasped in her face, and his breath smelled like old blood.

"Wait!" he shouted. "Turning away from the law was Abraham Sidney's mistake. Kill me, and you are the same as he. And you are not the same. You want to turn away from killing. You want to embrace the laws. This is a test for you. A test from God. Do you want to be a killer? Or do you want to be a Jew? You cannot be both. God has been testing you a long time to see what you really want. He even used me to test you once before. It is true. I knew you put poison in Adam's food. I am not so much of an old blind fool as you think. I knew you were going to show mercy at the last minute. I knew it!''

The warrior in her took it as an insult, a suggestion of weakness. She knew he was trying to manipulate her. "You are wrong. When I dropped the poisoned meal, it was an accident! I would have killed him. He startled me, is what happened. He was saved by a coincidence." She tugged at Papa Russia's hair, raised the knife.

"Then don't marry him!"

The knife slashed downward, flashing blue glints of reflected starlight. Just as the razored point touched the old man's jugular vein, the knife came to an abrupt halt—a very flashy show of skill. Then Magen tossed the knife aside.

"You see," said Papa Russia, "it was not coincidence. Go ahead and marry the boy. You just proved to me that you would not have killed him no matter what." He smiled as if it were a game. "You have been tested, Magen. I am not Abraham Sidney."

Anxious to leave Amelia's asteroid, Magen hurriedly packed. She had little to take with her, except some new clothes and some toiletries that Amelia had given as gifts, and a small charm she had been wearing around her neck when she crashed. In golden letters, it spelled "life" in Hebrew. Papa Russia had given it to her the day he died. He said that it was a good-luck charm, but it hadn't brought him much luck. Perhaps he gave it to her out of spite for turning him in.

Papa Russia's trial took place in the ruins of the old Jewish ghetto. Citing ancient precedents that held that the

Talmudic prohibitions against capital punishment do not apply to perpetrators of genocide, the court sentenced Papa Russia to face a firing squad of wide-beam laser rifles. In the course of the execution, four months after Magen's wedding, a square mile of the surrounding forest vanished under the heavy blue light barrage. Not a trace of Papa Russia remained. It was as if they had dropped a mountain on him.

Adam Hirsch was later captured by low-level slavers. Not realizing his true identity, or the enormous bounty on his head, they bartered him away for a month's worth of provisions on one of the moons of Autumn.

Magen dressed for travel, slipping on a flexible flak jacket, tying knives to her ankles, strapping holsters under her arms. As she hung the necklace with the golden charm, she wondered if her saving Papa Russia had indeed been a test, as the old butcher claimed. She felt that somehow it had been a test—but for what purpose? Even though she had spared him, Papa Russia died anyway. His death both saddened and relieved her.

And despite her having passed that test without killing him, she was forced to return to war anyway. For Adam's sake, she had to regenerate the parts of her personality he fought so hard to subdue.

So why did God submit her struggling spirit to such a cruel test of will when the end results were the same? Perhaps Adam was right when he said that God is unknowable, even to God.

Even if these separate events, the sparing of Papa Russia and the selling of Adam Hirsch, were not linked by Divine strategy, they were linked in Magen's mind by trick of human perception.

# 5

## FREE SLAVES

**R**epresentatives from all the bods gathered in the ruins of the Halls of Justice to negotiate their trade accords. The building had once been a courthouse. No one bothered to remove the marble statues of blinded women who held scales in dimly lit corners. The symbols caused no offense, for law had not been abolished through violence or revolution. It had simply complicated itself out of existence.

For centuries before the law collapsed, jurists had struggled to accommodate multiple subcultures that sprang up as a result of severing the ties to Earth. The process was accelerated by the increasing mental and physical specialization required to maintain the burgeoning technology of Draconian society. Judges soon found that a warrior's notion of fairness differed drastically from an accountant's. To achieve an illusion of equity, the law became increasingly academic, abstract, and at times, surreal.

The bod prime directors came to the conclusion that they didn't need laws for stability in their dealings. Production of even the simplest of commodities had become enormously sophisticated. Competition between bods wasn't feasible. Only dedicated resources could muster the required economies of scale. In order to be cost-effective, goods had to be produced in huge quantities. Accordingly, they had to be sold in huge quantities to guaranteed markets. Absolute economic dependence on one another forged much greater bonds between the bods than the law ever had with its contracts and treaties. Given that absolute dependence, trade negotiations were mostly a matter of formality, like the seduction rituals of long-married couples.

In the absence of currency, the Draconian tradesmen measured value in creative ways. Frequently, they based their assessments on units of commonly needed goods. For comparative values, sometimes they used narcotics. Sometimes they used tons of grain. Mostly, though, they bought, sold, haggled, wagered, and bartered using slaves as the coin of the realm. Ironically, they called this place and this process "the Free Market."

There were slaves on display everywhere in the Free Market. Long, naked parades followed young executives who pulled on chains like purse strings. Some slaves stayed frozen in poses for use as furniture. Some scarred curiosities, with their pain centers surgically removed, offered their faces as ashtrays.

The slaves of Earth antiquity owed their status to the artifice of law. Their owners held property rights. In the totally free Draconian society, ownership welled from a much deeper source—the breaking of the will.

Magen circulated through the crowd, pausing occasionally to eavesdrop, catching only fragments of transactions. She had changed her hair color, her eye color, the shape of her nose. She had padded her breasts with plastic explosives. Dressed like a captain of the Mercenary Bod, she was hardly in disguise at all.

There were people she knew from her days in the bod mingling among the traders. Former acquaintances, friends, rivals, even a former lover failed to recognize her. She wondered if she had really changed so very much. Familiar sensations all around her tugged at her with familiar temptations, like the smell of sweet narcotic smoke and aphrodisiac colognes. Clouds of steam from roasting shellfish hawked by vendors in the crowds made her hungry. She found beauty in the glitter of gun cartridges worn as jewelry and in the subsonic murmur of relaxation subliminals piped in over the sound system under the familiar beat of a bod anthem. Had she really changed?

Armed guards patrolled the premises, their holobadges flashing authority with prismatic colors. Hawkers worked the crowd. During live demonstrations, slaves mutilated themselves on command. The onlookers were encouraged to shout out their own suggestions—did they want to see an eye gouged out? A limb hacked off? A tongue bitten through?

A bloodied chorus line was carving Olagy's motto with razors across their chests in large weeping letters: "Where there is no will, there is a way."

To insure that no slave would ever break conditioning again, the way Olagy had, through years of slow burning hatred and rage, Olagy promoted new methods for inducing subservience. He used combinations of psychosurgery, behavioral modification, and potent neurotropics, as well as old-fashioned torture. The bod had produced a new subclass that would do anything, even the unspeakable, on command.

In desperation, Magen had conceived a mad plan, one with little chance of bringing about reunion with her husband—but one that brought her a measure of hope. She found a goal to occupy her time, which otherwise would be empty as death. Her private war continued, but the objective shifted from harassing the Slavers Bod to freeing as many slaves as possible. She held, as an article of faith, the belief that Adam would someday be among the slaves she freed, and that he would somehow find his way back to her.

Adam would probably disapprove of her present course. He hated violence. But what else could she do? She felt lonelier than she had ever felt before. She was used to being alone, but in the past, she never had anything to compare solitude against.

Even if she could find a bod to recorporate her, she could not slip back into the bod lifestyle. Neither could she find contentment living in one of the hidden Jewish ghettos of the Summer World without Adam by her side.

She returned to war, picking it up again, like a bad habit.

Magen glided toward the main slave pen, which served as a kind of gigantic purse for loose human change, frequently drawn upon during the course of active trading. She expected a dungeon with bars—something she could blast away. And she expected to find obedient slaves that could be herded like cattle. Instead she found a brightly lit showroom, where catatonic slaves posed like mannequins in diorama scenes depicting Draconian life. Stiffened ship workers stood locked in the act of hauling up nets full of plastic fish from a resin sea. A sculptor at work seemed as much a statue as his creation. Younglings sat in a mock kid-care classroom, trapped under the tutelage of a slave nanny. Diamond miners aimed their picks at a rhinestone-studded wall, while across from them, doll-like courtesans held open their paralyzed loins—smiles frozen on their faces. High fashion armbands graced each motionless wrist with decorative inventory bar codes. Deep trances had slowed their metabolic rates to a near halt, so they could be maintained with only a sparse amount of food, until the time for delivery.

Magen searched for Adam among the models. As she moved from scene to scene, dead eyes stared back at her, a gallery of extinguished lamps.

Some of the displays showed signs of neglect: slaves sinking into contractures, eyelashes and fingernails growing in long fluted patterns, unabraded due to total lack of activity. Exceptionally plump, blood-bloated mosquitoes stalked the showroom, emboldened by feasting without interference for countless bug generations.

How could she move these human timbers? What would she do with them afterward?

Magen hung close to a diorama display that depicted a battle scene. By the light of animated explosions glowing on the cloth backdrop, she carefully inspected the living mannequins. When no one was looking, she stepped up on to the platform. Quickly, she unholstered one of her guns, and rested a foot on a prostrate comatose slave who was supposed to be a dead soldier. She took aim at the head of an opposing mannequin. There Magen froze. How easily she had stepped back into her former life.

Magen's respiratory rate decreased and her heart rate kept pace. She felt confident she could keep rigid for hours, if need be. From this vantage point, she hoped to discover the code or method for reviving the slaves.

As the first hour passed, commerce in the Free Market began to accelerate. Slaves were being awakened constantly. Each would climb down from his or her frozen moment, returning to true Draconian life under the charge of a new master. But Magen couldn't figure out how it was being done. She listened carefully. The guards invoked no special words. Although it was hard to get a good view of each transaction without frank eye movements, she concluded that no secret hand gestures had been used to rouse the slaves. What was the signal? Could it be some pungent scent? Or a dermal patch full of stimulants? Did the inventory bracelet hold the key?

Frustration was making Magen tense. The bright lights began to bother her eyes, but she held them open, wide and glassy. The gun weighed down her hand. She regretted stepping out into the open this way. Tactically, it had been stupid. She had expected quick, easy answers. Instead, she got nothing. She could still handle the discomfort of being motionless, but she wasn't as confident about how long she could endure. The tendons in her wrist were torturing her. She hadn't let herself get soft—not at all. But she'd fallen out of strict bod discipline routines. She hoped her hands wouldn't start to tremble.

By now, a great crowd had gathered around the war diorama. Magen couldn't step down. She couldn't even move. Posed as she was, with a live weapon in her hand, she'd be shot immediately if she gave anyone cause to be suspicious.

She wondered what had prompted her to begin her campaign in the Free Market. This was the least likely place to find Adam. If Adam were still in the Free Market, Hubbel would have been able to find him quickly. And this was the hardest place to steal slaves. All exits were closely guarded, all departures carefully inventoried. Magen realized she had chosen the Free Market for the worst of reasons: for revenge—or suicide.

She quieted her thoughts. She assured herself that the crowds would soon thin and she could slip away. Or perhaps someone would trade for her. She would have an easier time hijacking an order of slaves once she got past the exits.

As her mind relaxed, her respiratory rhythms subconsciously synchronized with the slow and steady breathing of thousands of slaves in the showroom. She stared fixedly at the glassy-eyed toy soldiers around her, noticing, for the first time, slow gestures of speech without sound, glacial winks, and hand signals. Hints of communication seemed to be passing among the frozen slaves.

Did symptoms of will persist like the itch of an amputated leg?

Magen wondered if there was some way to join in this chorus—perhaps to learn the revival code directly from the slaves themselves. But she was too afraid to make any sound—even the softest whisper. Too many speculators crowded the diorama now, pinching her thighs, blowing spicy cadmadine smoke in her face. Guards were weaving regular patrols through the displays.

After three motionless hours, studying the situation, Magen finally figured out the key to waking the slaves. The guards flashed their holo-badges before giving commands. The prismatic glare signaled obedience. The insight came too late. Frozen in place, Magen could not snare a badge. The crowd did not thin as the hours passed, but rather, it swelled.

A contingent from the Mercenary Bod—Magen's former bod—encircled the war diorama. She panicked inside, but kept her pose. Gaudy purple cowls, bound in place by silver headbands, marked the two mercenaries in front as elite assassins, a man and a woman. Both wore matching ribbon blades, both held the rank of vice-general director.

The woman had been an undeclared rival to Magen within the bod. Verna Cruise. She possessed a surgically overwrought beauty, which Magen had always found repulsive, though her bod brothers disagreed. How quickly she had risen in rank since Magen's absence, aided, no doubt, by her formidable skills, her brutal wit, her aggressive passions.

The male, Marcus Darien, didn't know Magen as well as Verna—but he was just as likely to penetrate the disguise. He carefully studied reports of bod members who went unincorp, and held responsibility for allocating the resources to hunt them down.

The other five mercenaries were combat jocks, scantily clad to show off their sinewy bulk. Leather thongs strapped their weapons in place.

The two vice-general directors took an instant interest in Magen. Verna gripped her by the deltoid muscles and squeezed hard. She tested the abdominals with a push, then ran a discriminating hand up the back of Magen's leg, all the way to the gluteus muscles. No doubt Magen's muscle tone had attracted their attention, and held their interest. It was rare to see a broad range of exercised muscle groups on a slave. Were they suspicious? Perhaps they were only bargain hunting. AWOL bod-trained experts frequently turned up in the slave market as merchandise.

"I want this one," said Verna, pointing to Magen.

"We'll take the entire display," Marcus shouted to the guards.

The rainbow light of a holo-badge flashed in Magen's face. She resurrected on cue, shaking off her pose. Slavers Bod officials stripped the weapons and costumes from the slaves before they left the display. The props were not part of the package. They dressed Magen in a simple white robe, which marked her as departing goods.

Magen felt relieved to be moving again, as she followed the twenty-five other slaves down to the trading floor. Together they marched toward the exit scanners. Magen wasn't wearing the proper inventory bar codes—but she doubted that an overcharge to the Mercenary Bod would set off any alarms.

She passed through the scanning portals without incident.

Slavers Bod personnel kept the flow of human commerce in motion. Long lines of slaves marched out, most with a stiff-limbed gait from prolonged comatose posturing. The guards let nothing break the precision of crowd movement. That was their art, a necessary and practical art, what with armies of newly acquired slaves to move out. They performed their art with unshakable, mime-like smiles.

Guards conducted the merc contingent and their new slaves outside. From there, they boarded a tram, which carried them to the loading platforms. During the short, bumpy, open-air ride, Magen angled herself to jump from the tram. Escape was imperative. If she let herself be taken back to the Merc Bod dormitories, someone was bound to recognize her, once her makeup and hair dye washed off.

The opportunity to jump from the tram never came. The five combat jocks kept her hemmed in. They casually bared sensitive nerve clusters to the other newly purchased slaves, as if daring them to act—but showed greater modesty toward Magen. They seemed nonchalant around her, on the surface—but kept her surrounded.

The tram carrying the Merc Bod contingent converged with other trams; then all queued up in neat rows. They screeched to choreographed halts, one after another. The tram occupants disembarked in timed waves.

Thirty-foot neon archways lit the entrance to the loading platforms. These led to a honeycomb of long tunnels, a kind of drive-through spaceport, strictly for pickup and delivery.

A rumbling, densely packed mob squeezed into the terminal. Even if the opportunity for a clean, quick strike presented itself, Magen would never be able to force her way through the crush of people.

Hydraulic cattle elevators, built to hold hundreds at a time, hissed upward to the topmost loading deck. Magen found herself delivered into a huge tunnel. Recycled broken spaceships buttressed the interior ceiling, an inverted reef strewn with half-melted or crumbled wings of Ruinators, Obliterators, Herpes Hellcats, Jonah Transports, Wanderers, and even an occasional warpship. The wreckage hung as a warning to the incoming pilots: keep moving.

Slavers Bod guards hustled the arriving slaves onto timed conveyor belts. When they reached the departure gates, the slaves were carefully divided into segregated queues, sorted by owner.

The transport ships were loading and leaving in precise ten-minute intervals. Some with exceptionally large slave orders were given as long as twenty minutes, a concession to buying power—provided they adhered to strict loading protocols.

Across from Magen's group, separated by a ten-foot space, a cluster of slaves prepared to leave. Plump masters, wearing shawls and crowns of blue flowers, stood patiently, waiting for their ship. The sweet scent of flowers made Magen wish she had been bought by them—the Horticulture Bod, or the Perfumers Bod, or whoever they were. Escape would have been no problem.

As the groups broke into lines for departure, the aisles required for segregation afforded plenty of room for a hasty dash. But now the combat jocks had fallen to the rear of the procession. The two vice-general directors flanked Magen. The shift in position seemed deliberate.

With only a few minutes before the arrival of the transport ship, Magen pondered her best course of action. Verna, to her right, carried a wide assortment of weapons. She let the guns dangle close to Magen, tempting her. Was it a trick to make Magen abandon her ruse?

A transport ship bearing Merc Bod logos gently coasted into the station, retros hissing. As soon as it aligned its course into the channel gate, its engines shut off to keep the tunnels free of exhaust. Slaves pushed the ship the rest of the way down the neon-accented loading aisles.

The hatchway to the ship snapped open. Verna Cruise ordered the slaves to embark.

Pretending to stumble, Magen fell against Verna. With a quick, darting motion, Magen snaked a laser derringer out of a shoulder harness and brought it to a halt under Verna's chin.

Verna had moved just as quickly, in reciprocal coordination, pulling a second pistol from a holster on her thigh. The two women finished their maneuvers facing each other, in mirror-image poses—each with a gun nozzle pressed to the chin.

Marcus and the combat jocks strutted around them, guns drawn, but Verna motioned them to stand aside.

"Magen," shouted Verna. "This is a surprise. I would have never recognized you under all that gunk—but your style is unmistakable."

"I have you hostage," said Magen.

"You wouldn't dare shoot. I can pull the trigger with my last nerve synapse."

"I can do the same. We have each other hostage."

"Don't be silly. How will you ever escape?"

The two women stared at each other. Verna's skin shined like plastic under the neon lights, seamless, with no visible pores. But she was starting to sweat with the gun pressed to her chin.

"Go ahead and shoot," said Magen. "I am not afraid of death."

"Nor I. It is dying that bothers me."

"I don't want I should hurt you. Why don't you just let me go?" This wasn't an appeal to friendship. The two women had always been too closely matched in skills, and too intent on similar goals to be real friends. It came across as a plea for mercy. Bad mistake.

"All right, Magen. Just drop the gun and I'll deliver you."

"What do you mean? Deliver me where?"

"Nowhere. Just slice out your liver." Verna began to laugh.

Verna's free hand wriggled down toward a sheathed blade. Magen caught her. While the two women wrestled for the knife, pulling closer, pistols still in place, Verna danced a graceful vertical kick to the side of Magen's face. The pepsin smell of bootwax spiced the heavy blow. It was an impressive move, but Magen held her gun in place. Behind her, the combat jocks huddled into a blockade. They intended to keep Magen from escaping while giving Verna a chance to perform.

Blood began to fill Magen's eyes and roll down her cheeks like scarlet tears. Pain stabbed her neck every time she moved. She couldn't tell if she had injured muscle or bone or spinal cord.

"You've gotten better since I've left," said Magen at last.

"No, you've gotten worse."

"I think some part of me is afraid to strike an officer. Maybe that's why I don't want to hurt you. Funny how old habits don't die."

Absorbed in watching the two women, the merc contingent had stalled the loading procedures for the entire terminal. The ship behind the merc transport was blowing horns and flashing lights. The skies were beginning to crowd with approaching ships flying in holding patterns. New groups of departing slaves continued to unload, and the platform mob grew denser around the small arena flanked by combat jocks.

A potbellied Slavers Bod guard strode onto the loading deck, shouting demands.

Marcus called to Verna, "This has gone on long enough. We have higher priorities."

Verna said, "Marcus will shoot us both if we keep him stalled."

The time for bluff and threat was quickly passing. The two women regarded each other warily, their lives tied together by mutual threat. Magen did not want to shoot, and she read a reflection of her own hesitancy in Verna's eyes. They had caught each other in a game neither could win. Each would have to share the other's fate—if their skills were truly equal.

Magen pulled the trigger. It felt like opening fire on herself.

Both women had fired at the same time, necks twisting at the same time; faces jerking out of the path of laser light. An oozing burn bubbled across Verna's cheek. She had been a little slow.

As the beams shot upward, guns responded to guns automatically, a stampede of trigger fingers around the platform. Random flashes of light erupted within the crowd.

Verna and Magen hit the ground together, then coiled into a wrestling knot.

Verna launched her hands. Magen executed a series of blocks, deflecting a symphony of hand thrusts and finger stabs. Then she threw her forehead into Verna's smile.

Intent on her combat, lost in her art, Magen found that she had missed this. She had dedicated her life to fighting, and it came to her more easily than prayer, more easily than love. The smell of bootwax brought back memories of cadet chores and combat practice. This fight seemed like the games she and Verna had played while growing up, as if it were simple combat for its own sake, without consequence. And then she remembered what was at stake. "We've never fought to the death, before," said Magen, not realizing how obvious her observation had been until the words were out of her mouth.

"Too bad. Then we wouldn't have to do it now."

Marcus began to try to kick Magen loose. Three combat jocks joined in, forming a kicking gauntlet, but their thrusts lacked Marcus's precision. They hit Verna as often as they hit Magen.

Magen peeled herself loose from Verna and lunged toward the slave guard. One of the combat jocks swiveled forward to block her, but she hit his eyes with the heels of her palms and his groin with her knee.

In two quick paces, she caught up to the Slavers Bod guard, latched on to his wrist, and spun him. Her elbow crooked around his neck. He shielded her from the entire Merc Bod contingent.

As Magen retreated, the guard started to hyperventilate, his feet shuffling as if doing a hanged man's dance. "Don't worry," she said to her hostage. "The mercs won't risk harming you on your own bod's turf." She angled to lose herself in the crowd of waiting slaves.

Marcus started to squint, even before he raised his pistol. Magen took that as a cue to drop the guard and roll for cover. A bright red beam split the guard diagonally across his pot belly. As arteries opened, it looked as if the beam were splattering into liquid on impact.

Dodging ray blasts, Magen rolled toward the body of the guard, scooping up his holo-badge from the spilled abdominal stew in which it had fallen.

She waved the holo-badge at the crowd of slaves in the adjacent aisle. She called, "Over here, over here. Come at once."

En masse, the slaves abandoned their flowered masters and marched to Magen's command.

The captains of the flowery bod paced after their slaves patiently, more like concerned parents than Draconian masters. They shouted unheeded commands with eerie calm; but the two groups of slaves meshed like an evenly shuffled deck of cards. Densely packed bodies pressed everyone into captivity—mercs, flowery captains, and both parcels of slaves.

A cadre of Slavers Bod guards stormed onto the loading deck, flashing jeweled rifles with acid bayonets, prepared to clear the source of traffic congestion, no matter what it took.

The flowery captains calmly stated their requirements

to the Merc Bod officers, who shouted back insults. But neither party could move.

Swiftly, using inventory scanners, the Slavers Bod guards re-sorted the slaves into their appropriate groups. Verna screamed threats of high-level retaliation, but the Slavers Bod guards ignored her, secure behind a ring of primed lasers. Loading of the flower ship and the merc ship proceeded swiftly.

Magen left with the flower slaves, having swiped one of their armbands while caught in the crush. With the sweet smell of perfume in her nostrils, she resisted the urge to look back at Verna while crossing the loading gate. Gloating would accomplish nothing.

Magen did not learn that she had cast her fate with the Cadmadine Bod until she surprised the flowery captains in deep space. They offered little resistance. Throughout the entire hijacking, they stayed calm, very calm.


Magen drifted from world to world, camping in the wilds, and sleeping in the blackness between stars. Her activities had grown more ambitious. Yet the more successful her raids became, the more pathetic they seemed. She catalogued her failures. A great number of slaves had been led out of bondage, but for what?

In the cockpit of a fighter ship, Magen pulled down a star chart and surveyed multicolored pins that marked off her most recent raids. A cargo of newly liberated slaves filled the storage compartments behind her. Muscle-bound steroid brutes were shuffling back and forth, disrupting the gyroscopic balance of the small craft. She could feel the flight pattern waffling under her. Some scholarly slaves were reciting physics texts they did not understand to one another. She knew from past experience that the scholars were especially vulnerable when set free. They usually starved to death while spouting esoteric information to uninterested passersby. At least the steroid brutes had the good sense to seek new masters.

Magen wondered about where she would take this latest group of slaves. She searched the star charts. The Autumn World caught her attention. She had heard the rumors about hallucinogens in the atmosphere, and ghosts haunting the rainbow forests. Such legends would help her by keeping away the merc and bod patrols.

She took the shipment of slaves to Autumn.

On approach to the planet, Magen spotted a stretch of forest ablaze with wild fire. Dense black smoke blanketed the area for miles around. The area appealed to her. She welcomed the smog cover for as long as it would last, and landed a short distance away. To her surprise, the air smelled sweet and primeval, despite the carbon billows spreading over the sky.

Following her commands, the freed slaves set to work, digging deep trenches so that the nearby fire would not spread to their new home. In the days that followed, they built roughhewn log cabins, and planted crops with excellent results.

Magen brought new slaves in greater numbers. The community flourished.

There was no discord of any description. The life led by the rescued slaves seemed idyllic, apart from the fact that they took no independent actions at all. Their entire daily routines had been preordained by Magen. Many of the newer slaves, the products of more intense conditioning, would not even eat, except on command. She even had to tell them when to be tired, so they would not work themselves to death.

Magen found, to her dismay, that even the most functional of the slaves, even the warriors, the encyclopedias, the cunning conversationalists, all of them, had something broken deep inside. With glassy eyes and blunt affects, they gathered to recite the prayers Magen had taught them. She had expected prayer to set them free, but prayer had no effect on them at all. Their Seder had an odd pathos.

No one quarreled, no one killed, no one coveted. Not even the coming of the Messiah could bring such absolute peace. Magen would have done anything for a show of insubordination.

One night, Magen returned from an overlong sojourn in space. Lumps of molten metal sprouted like tumors on her damaged cruiser. The bods had upped the security on their slave shipments, and she had met with unexpected, heavy resistance. Her past raids had been too successful.

She flew in low, skimming the treetops; then she crashed. Magen stumbled from her ship, burns on her arms. Hair dye ran down her cheeks and tasted inky in her mouth. Her kidneys throbbed with the pain of organ bruises.

She found her slave community in a state of virtual standstill. Some slaves had frozen into comatose statuary with the completion of the most recently appointed tasks, while others were caught in loops of behavior patterns.

Magen stumbled past a woman doing laundry. The clothes in her tub had long been scrubbed into thready fragments. Her hands had swollen close to bursting.

"Stop! Stop right now!" commanded Magen.

The slave woman looked up from the work that had occupied her for the past thirty-six hours.

"How beautiful you look tonight, Magen," said the slave, with a smile that almost looked genuine.

"Thank you," said Magen; then she burst out in edgy laughter. For just a moment, she had been genuinely flattered by the compliment she had programmed the week before.

Magen felt suddenly dizzy, weak from exhaustion and loss of blood. Once she had refused the assistance of slaves, but her pride had been eroded along with her illusions. Surrounded by servants, she felt more and more like a master.

After six months of ruling as an absolute monarch, Magen began to doubt that her slaves could ever be rehabilitated. How can you force someone to be free? Perhaps it was not will that distinguished man from the beasts, but rather plasticity—a near infinite ability to absorb programming. Perhaps choice was not the foundation of the universe, but rather, slavery.

Her fingers snapped. Commands barked out. A group of slaves shook themselves out of immobility and carried Magen to her simple bed.

Magen awoke the next morning, feeling menstrual and mean-spirited. Walking with a cane for support, she inspected her frozen village. The population stood among the fallen leaves, their faces lit by the distant flickering of the great forest fire. Flesh without spirit, the opposite of ghosts.

Magen's failures overwhelmed her, made her feel disgusted and spiteful. She lashed out with her cane at a slave lying on the ground, scattering leaves and dust with the stroke.

"Get up," Magen demanded.

Sluggishly, the steroid-inflated male, three times her size, rose to his feet.

"Don't do what I say," she said. "Don't ever obey my commands."

The slave stared curiously, uncertain whether or not to remain standing.

"Now dance," said Magen.

The slave shuffled his feet and swayed his hands absurdly.

Magen rapped him across the knees with her cane. "I told you not to do what I say."

The slave's eyes widened in confusion and protest. Magen laughed. The huge brute could waste her with a single blow if he had the will. Instead he simply stood there, paralyzed.

"Why aren't you dancing?" she asked.

"You told me not to obey you."

"And you obeyed?"

The slave began to dance again. The cane struck his knees again. This continued for almost an hour.

Burning with fever, too sick for slave raiding, and too disheartened, Magen lingered in the Autumn village inventing cruel pranks to play on her worshipers. She riddled her commands with contradictions, paradoxes, and ambiguities:

"Clean the windows until they are dirty."

"Remember to forget your duties."

"Don't do what you are supposed to do."

"Make nothingness."

She made them wear foolish-looking hats and capes. She made them sing nonsense songs, off-key.

Sometimes she punished them for obeying her, other times she rewarded them. It was arbitrary. If they were going to treat her like God, then by God, she would treat them the way God treats man.

As she sat sipping a warm, pungent tea brewed with Autumn leaves, her slaves moaned around her, groping with new confusion over her latest commands. The foolishness of the slaves made all of Magen's obsessions seem foolish. Why had she started this crusade? For a man, a slave at that. A lost, hopelessly irredeemable slave. Adam's face abstracted in her mind. Her quest no longer seemed to be connected to any individual, and yet it was no less important to her.

The slaves became increasingly neurotic. All along the rows of crude log houses, slaves spun in circles, repeating unobeyable commands like mantras. Some developed facial tics. Others became incontinent. One had a seizure. As long as they would allow themselves to be preoccupied with undoable commands, as long as they would allow Magen to tie comical hats to their heads and purple streamers to their asses, as long as they would be content to obey, Magen would be content to take revenge upon them. Since she was as willful as the slaves were will-less, it seemed they would eventually destroy each other.

The forest fires continued to rage in the distance, far longer than Magen had ever expected. The village had grown too large to evacuate. What would she do if a stray spark set off an inferno? Still, she chose not to move. The dark folds of smoke provided security, even though they made the days drab and grey. And she found the natural force less threatening than her enemies, for no particular reason.

Beneath the odorless, smoke-filled skies, the crops lay stillborn in their furrows. The wells began to run dry. Thirst and hunger aggravated Magen's health problems, which kept her out of battle. She devoted her energies solely to planning new challenges for her subjects. She gave her slaves no peace, neither the luxury to loaf, nor the dignity of labor.

The fire seemed more and more dangerous, though it had not spread in all this time. The dryness of the village increased its flammability. The smoke cloud had become a constant warning.

Then the wind shifted.

Expecting a storm of sparks, Magen ordered all of the slaves to stay outdoors. They cleared a wide area, so that they would have a safe haven, even if all the buildings burned. For hours they watched smoke drift across the sky.

But the fire never came. It kept to its own territory like a caged beast.

This miracle bewildered Magen. She wondered what she had done to deserve it, but she thanked God anyway. Then she began to wonder if it was truly a miracle, or if some dark purpose lay behind the fire.

Magen overheard some slaves jabbering about a stand of trees in the Autumn forest that were ablaze without being consumed. At first Magen shrugged it off. But the reports continued, and the fire in the distance never dimmed, though the fuel in that stretch of wood should have been exhausted long ago. Now she wondered if the legends of Autumn were true. Hallucinogens in the mist? Ghosts? Perhaps this fire was a phantom echo of some remote event, a ghost with no more substance or power than the other ghosts reputed to roam the Autumn World.

Magen took her cane and a gun and stumbled into the wilderness, determined to inspect for the first time the strange fire that had been a neighbor for so long. The slaves could not lie. The symbol was too specific to be coincidental. The prospect of being a new Moses to a new nation of slaves made her laugh. She laughed as she followed the distant lights, laughed a ragged laughter interrupted by frequent coughing.

The light grew brighter as Magen wandered farther away from the village.

Glaring shafts of light, full of sparkling motes, stabbed suddenly through the spaces between the trees and lit the forest like a crown. Magen had never seen such light before—light that seemed to seep directly into the brain without interruption by the eyes. The trees seemed to burn, but only with light. Magen pressed forward, overcome with curiosity, still laughing at delusions of grandeur she knew had no merit.

She stopped laughing when she passed the next line of trees. A wall of heat crisped her hair. She closed her eyes to avoid the vision. Smoke stung her nostrils and set off another bout of coughing that produced gobs of foul-tasting phlegm. She coughed until she nearly vomited. She stepped back and opened her eyes again.

Sheets of flame enveloped a ring of towering elms. Though Magen could feel the heat from twenty paces away, the trees defied consumption. Against the brilliance, the leaves faded to transparency, showing their veins. Unsinged, they rustled softly under the crackling of fire.

Magen fell to her knees, about to burst into prayer, but she saw people in the fire—forms scattered amid the dark network of branches. Some seemed to dangle in the air like meat hung up for smoking. Others seemed like souls floating in rapture.

An old woman curled in a backbreaking posture, in the shimmering blue core of the fire. Her fingernails and eyelashes rolled out in long fluting patterns, like those of the Free Market slaves who never moved. A turbaned black man lay peaceful as a mummy, his features flaccid.

Leaning upon her cane, Magen strained her eyes to decipher the shapes in the glare. She could not understand why this holy image was riddled with aspects of slavery. Autumn ghosts? Hallucinations? The vision had drawn her this far by appealing to her illusions. Now it mocked her with them.

The sound of rustling silk made Magen turn. The most beautiful woman she had ever seen approached, wearing white scarves that seemed to float in the air. Magen felt ugly and crude wearing cutoff fatigues, and ammo for jewelry. The beautiful woman had the kind of facial symmetry and angularity that the bone cutters of Summer emulated, but she also had a startling uniqueness to her face and a subtle lack of perfection that only occurs with the random linkage of chromosomes. Fragile. So feminine. Her hair hung like a white cape across her back. Her eyes, fringed by transparent lashes, were as blue as the core of the fire. Everything about the woman fit Magen's conceptions of an angel, everything except the trident symbol she wore around her neck. The talisman identified her as a Universalist, a member of a missionary sect that attempted to embrace all religions by focusing on the power of raw belief.

"This is the Council of Autumn," said the beautiful woman. "My name is Veil."

Magen tossed her gun aside, to show she had no hostile intent, and as a gesture of surrender to superior forces. Language, symbolic or otherwise, was not needed at this point. She knew what she was dealing with.

"You are psychics," Magen said.

"The most powerful in the system." No pride showed in the response.

"I did not mean to disturb you."

"You have disturbed us, terribly. We are most sensitive. Have you any idea how deeply you torment your slaves?"

"They don't seem to mind."

"We know you are bitter, but you must stop these atrocities. Slaves cannot help being slaves. You cannot restore their will any more than you can restore breath to a corpse. God has reclaimed some part of their souls. Leave the slaves in peace."

Magen studied the flames and the figures within the flames who looked so much like slaves themselves. "They are in a trance?"

"We share the trance."

"You have so much power. Perhaps you could find a way to make the slaves well again."

"Don't you understand? Slaves cannot be freed. They can only be given to different masters."

Magen threw up her hands. "I am so tired. I know this is stupid, what I do, but I don't know what else I should do. If I give up on Adam, he is lost."

"He is lost anyway."

"Even lost, he is all I have."

"Find a better cause. God has greater purposes in mind for you."

Magen nodded. She was spent, and she could not stand being open to inspection like this—nearly blinded by the light, unable to plot attack or escape, her thoughts as transparent as a butterfly under a bulb.

"We knew of your husband's works, his teachings. Adam Hirsch was a great man with a great dream."

Magen stiffened at the invocation of her husband's true name. It seemed she would be allowed no secrets here.

"If you wish to honor him, you will turn your talents toward his goals."

"I never understood them."

"I studied your husband's writings extensively. I believe I understand them. I can tell you this—he would never condone your present course of action."

Magen said nothing, but shot a sudden blast of resentment toward the young psychic.

"I am sorry you hate me," said Veil. "I am only trying to help those pathetic creatures you so sorely abuse. I am not your enemy, Magen Hirsch."

"Only because I don't know how to fight you!"

Magen turned her back on the vision of the burning forest. She hobbled home slowly, kicking leaves in frustration. She was still in denial about losing Adam, but she resigned herself to change. Or at least to try to change. Really, she had no choice in the matter.

When she returned to the village, she was astounded to find a group of slaves at work in a field. A young girl weeded the soil. A red-haired male guided a plow pulled by a harnessed slave, who was naked except for his cone and streamers. Other slaves were planting seeds. Puffy lids squeezed on their glazed eyes. Their muscles were loose and stringy. God knows when they last saw sleep.

"What are you doing?" Magen asked.

"Tending the land. You need food. You're wasting away," said the red-haired man. His neck cocked to one side, as if he had trouble supporting his head.

Magen leaned forward, curious. "Who told you to do this? The Council of Autumn?"

"I'm doing what you want." He gripped the leather handles of the plow and guided the blade through the soil.

"This is not what I told you to do."

"Mistress, you weren't saying what you wanted. I thought about what you told me to do for a very long time. I was very confused. When you left, I did what you wanted. I will always do what you want."

Magen rubbed her chin. In her absence, the slaves had figured a way out of her riddles, an excuse to return to their zombielike chores. They looked ridiculous. The girl kept tugging at weeds in the ground, though the weeds were the stronger of the two.

"Yes, yes, of course," said Magen. "I have wronged you and I am so very sorry. Soon I will give you a new mistress. She has great wealth and power, and she knows how to care for slaves. She can rule you better. I don't know that you can be happy, but you will be better off with Amelia than with me."

"I had to think for a very long time, a very long time about what you wanted," said the slave.

"I know, I know. I did evil to you and I am sorry, but it is over now. You can stop what you are doing and get some sleep."

"I had to think."

"I said you should get some rest!" shouted Magen.

The red-haired man let go of the plow. He tramped a short way over the furrows he had dug, then he stopped short in the dirt. He looked confused.

"Get some rest," said Magen, taking a gentler tone. "You have earned it. That is an order."

"No," said the slave.

Magen smiled.

* * *

When Hubbel requested a meeting with Amelia, she invited him to dine on the asteroid.

She prepared his favorite dish.

As they sat by the cloud garden, with the meal steaming in front of them, Amelia thought that it seemed a shame to cut the brittle shell of the aquatic crustacean she had boiled for the occasion. It shined with a metallic blue luster derived from a remote housefly ancestor. She cut the pretty shell anyway and scooped out a generous helping of abdominal jelly, which she offered to Hubbel.

"Do you want some guts?" she asked.

Hubbel shook his head. "Just a few of the eyes, please."

Amelia scraped bunches of compound-eye segments loose from the central orb. They bounced onto Hubbel's plate like olives.

"I have a problem. A very serious problem. Your friend, Magen Hirsch." He paused, waiting for a response. Amelia looked at him, impassive and perplexed by the pause. He continued, "Yes, I know her real name. I know who her husband is, too. Dissa Banach doesn't know, but I do."

"I don't know what you are talking about."

"Hmmm. Maybe you don't. Adam Hirsch is a notorious renegade with an enormous bounty placed on his head by a coalition of bods. Apparently, he was captured and traded into slavery while traveling under a false name. All in all, I think the unincorps who caught him got a month's worth of provisions—only a fraction of his true worth."

"So he wasn't really a gentle bible scholar."

"From what I hear, he was a heretic. Many of his former followers consider his disappearance to be a kind of divine retribution. Do you know about the Council of Autumn?"

Amelia shook her head.

"Hmmm. I'll tell you about them. The Council of Autumn is a group of aberrants who have some outstanding mental abilities. Some of them read thoughts. Occasionally, they can predict the future. I suspect they have developed a sensitivity to Draconian time distortions. We've known about them for a long time, even approached them about the possibilities of working together. The bod owns a few of its own psychics—all males. We tried to interest the council in a breeding joint venture. We could have made a fortune in the genetic futures market. They refused us. Religious fanatics, most of them, absolutely no business sense. They could be the bringers of a new age, the next step in the evolution of humanity—if they had the right kind of promoters."

"I don't think I would like knowing the future."

"Well, we wish we had known the future when we first met the council members. We let them live, even though they refused us. Big mistake. We didn't think they would be a problem. They never used to have any interest in Draconian affairs. Most of their time was spent zoned out in a communal trance, oblivious."

"Sounds nice."

"Contemplating God."

"God." She couldn't think of anything else to say.

"Most of them are Universalists. Maybe there's merit to what they say about trying to follow every known faith. Certainly covers all the bases for the hereafter. I'd be interested in joining their church if they weren't all celibate. Utter fanatics. We should have destroyed them when we had the chance.

"Your friend Magen did something that impressed

them. She found a way to undo slave conditioning in certain of our most popular product lines.''

"That is impressive.''

"Yes. I trust you will keep this information to yourself. You understand that damage that would result if people lost faith in their slaves.''

"Of course.''

"We don't know how she does it. Not yet. We're working on it. We'll find out eventually, and find a way to program around it. But in the meantime, Magen has stepped up her activities against us. With the support of the Council of Autumn, the effects have been devastating. Substantial decreases in our productivity margins. Actually, all of the bods have been hurt, our economies are so interdependent.''

Amelia smiled. "You want me to betray Magen.''

"Actually, I want you to help her. To be more specific, I want you to help me to help her. In return for a small amount of assistance, I am willing to supply you with ten thousand new slaves at no cost.''

"Free slaves? That's a laugh. Why do you think you have to throw in so many incentives to get me to help my friend?'' She let the question hang.

He said nothing, knowing the question was meant to be rhetorical.

"You're trying to set Magen up for some kind of trap.'' She said it as if she had some sly insight.

Hubbel grasped Amelia firmly by the shoulders. He looked her in the eye, a penetrating gaze full of old intimate knowledge.

"I know you so well, Amelia. It makes me ache in my heart and in my balls when I think of how well I know you. No matter what I said, you would suspect me of plotting to trap your friend. I've thrown in the added 'incentives,' as you call them, so that you will hear me out, so that you will not dismiss my plan as a trap—which is exactly what would happen if there was nothing in this for you.''

"So why do you want to help Magen?''

"She is only interested in one thing, right? Her husband. If she gets her husband back, she will leave our bod alone. Am I right?''

"I think so—depending on what shape he is in. I can't claim to know Magen very well.''

"I am fairly certain that Magen's husband is still alive and not terribly molested. Perhaps those rehabilitation techniques might work on him.''

"So why doesn't the bod turn him over?''

"Well, that's what I would do if I ran the bod. But I don't. For all intents and purposes, Dissa Banach runs the bod these days and Dissa Banach is the only one who knows where to find Magen's husband.''

"I don't understand.''

"Under ordinary circumstances, the major bod divisions are more or less autonomous, reporting to Olagy, which is the same as reporting to no one. By creating a state of war, your friend has aided her greatest enemy. Military imperatives control, and all division heads must now report to Dissa, who is in charge of armed forces. Because of my early involvement in this affair, Dissa has characterized the entire problem as a public-relations failure. My credibility in the bod has been greatly damaged.''

"I'm beginning to see what you want.''

"As long as Magen poses a substantial threat, Dissa Banach remains in control of the most powerful bod in the system. Covertly, he located and secured Magen's husband. I don't know where he is being held. Most likely, I won't be able to find out.''

"So what do I need to do, to get the sanctions lifted and all those slaves?''

"Tell Magen you learned that Dissa is keeping her husband captive. Let her know that her husband is not with the other slaves. Tell her that if she wants her husband, she will have to deal with Dissa directly. I will be working on a way to make the confrontation possible. Only don't tell her that I am your source. Dissa has spies among her followers. If he finds out that I am plotting against him, he'll have me excorporated—in one manner or another."

"How should I say I came by this information?"

"I'm sure you can come up with something credible. You have great gifts for fabrication."

"There is just one problem . . . one very basic problem . . ."

"You still don't trust me. Amelia, I offer Magen the one chance that exists to find her husband. I am her only hope, but I can do nothing if you have no faith in me."

"Chadwick, I have no idea where Magen is."

# 6

---

## THE TRAP

At dawn, Magen hit the envelope of the Autumn World with a bump and felt friction warming the ship's hull. The stubby trapezoid wings of her craft cut ribbons of clarity in the haze. Flecks of paint peeled loose along the edges of newly acquired laser scars. The port cannons, already warm, began to blush from the friction. She was coming in too fast.

Suddenly the slave village spread before her. Magen skimmed the rooftops, avoiding wooden tridents mounted high on wooden poles; then she brought the ship down gently for a vertical landing.

As the ship settled on a bed of leaves, Magen climbed out, then walked around to the rear of the ship and flipped open the back hatchway. The cargo of hijacked slaves stumbled out to their new lives, blinking at the brightness of the rising sun. When their eyes readjusted, they gaped at the humble cottages, and at the mounted tridents.

A Universalist church had been built during Magen's absence. The elaborate arches of the building made it seem very old, though it was very new. On the eastern wall of the church, a stained-glass portrayal of Zeus arm in arm with Krishna and Buddha glowed with inner light. The figures were huge, visible even from a great distance. The boundless dedication of the slaves never ceased to amaze Magen. Some of the façades showed the beginnings of elaborate friezes depicting a variety of scenes from various religions. The intricate detail showed the handiwork of newly liberated artisans conditioned to work almost constantly. A life-sized portrait of Christ, carved in bas-relief on newly cut wood, wept tears of sap. From his right hand sprouted thin branches hung with miniature autumnal leaves.

Soon the new slaves would be baptized and consecrated to all of the known Gods—if they had no objections. That was part of the bargain Magen struck with the Council of Autumn. Magen did not care which face of God the freed slaves worshiped, or if they worshiped them all, as the Universalists preached. Judaism discouraged, rather than sought, converts, or so Adam had told her. Magen had other priorities for her harvest of souls.

She slipped off her infrared goggles and took in the new day. Engine oil dripped in gobs from her hair. Trident-shaped shadows rolled over her as she walked toward the cottages.

This particular raid had been uncommonly bloody. Deviating from her usual routines, she pursued a military target. She wanted to update her arsenal and reap some well-trained battle techs for assistants. She didn't need precognition to anticipate a reprimand from the council over the body count. Fine. Next raid she would go back to scavenging the Accountants Bod or the Artists Bod, or some other easy pickings.

Magen came upon two shadows, standing at the edge of the village. One of the shadows moved like a warrior, but with a slow and easy pace. The other looked ominously familiar.

Magen slid a pistol into each hand.

Amelia stepped into the light, smiling and throwing wide her arms. "Magen! How good to see you."

"What the hell are you doing here?" Fresh from battle, the smell of fuel explosions and vaporized fat still clinging to her skin, she was on edge.

"Isn't it obvious?" Amelia put her hands on her hips in an exaggerated show of indignation. "We came to see you. I was expecting a warmer welcome."

Magen stood her ground. "I did not expect to ever see you again, Amelia. You surprised me. I did not think I was so easy to find."

"Chev got the location of your camp from your arms dealers on the Winter World. Don't worry. I don't think they'll be so quick to share the information with the bods."

"How did they find out?"

"When will you stop being so suspicious? We came here at great risk to bring you news of your husband."

"News? What is this news?"

"I would have told you right away if you had been friendlier."

Magen lowered the guns.

"I'm too tired to tell you now. Much too tired. Perhaps after I rest and get a good meal in me I'll be in the mood to talk."

"Amelia, you can't do this to me. It is not right."

"No, I'm much too tired and you will have to wait."

Magen shook her head slowly and let out an exasperated sigh. Chev looked away, embarrassed.

Amelia refused to sleep in the dormitories, where newly freed slaves shared an immense open space. Flaunting the still undisclosed secret information, Amelia blackmailed Magen into surrendering her single-room bungalow.

Before settling into their new quarters, Amelia and Chev washed together under a small waterfall in the forest.

"You looked awful this afternoon," said Amelia. "That's what hurt our credibility. You looked like dishonest scum. I have a lot staked on this venture. I can't afford to have you ruin my chances."

"It wasn't my fault!" said Chev. In fact, Chev had not looked awful. He seemed to have grown taller over the past two years. Taller, stronger, and more mature.

"You don't know anything, Chev," said Amelia, scrubbing her hair vigorously, particularly around the widening white streak—as if she could clean it away with shampoo.

That night, they ate a native Autumn fish fried with berries. Chev wore a cream-colored suit and a wire tie. Amelia wore silk, her hair elaborately braided. She looked like an empress.

Sitting in neat rows, thousands of greasy-lipped villagers sucked threads of meat from comb-shaped fish vertebrae. Despite their numbers, the villagers were eerily quiet and well behaved.

Magen glanced around nervously, obviously expecting another person.

Chev stiffened abruptly, his eyes focused on a floating white sheet across the hall. Amelia squinted, trying to make out the approaching form. Seeing that it was a woman, she slapped Chev's arm with the back of her hand, but it didn't break his gaze. His eyes stayed fixed on the strangely dressed woman. He looked alert and wary, the same expression he wore when dueling with acid.

Inappropriate behavior from Chev came as no surprise, but Veil returned his looks with equal intensity. By the time Veil reached the table, Magen was squirming with embarrassment. Veil slowly crossed over to Chev and placed her hand on his cheek. There was a kind of recognition showing in both their eyes.

"You two know each other?" asked Amelia sharply.

Veil remembered herself and pulled her hand away as if it had been burned. "I'm sorry," said Veil. "I have seen this man before in visions. I needed to check to see if he was real. Sometimes I have trouble telling the visions from reality. I am sorry."

"Veil is psychic," said Magen.

"What are you so angry about?" Chev said to Amelia, anticipating her mood.

Amelia shook her head. She didn't know. She had sampled old Earth love on a whim, and now she had to deal with old Earth jealousy. She just glared, her lips gathered.

Veil took her seat.

Magen said to Amelia, "Tell me about my husband now." She was eager for an answer, but she also wanted to break the awkwardness of the moment.

"Not a moment before I finish eating," snapped Amelia.

"Aw, lay off it," urged Chev.

"No."

"Amelia, I have been patient," said Magen. "This afternoon, I let you play your games on me. It is not right you should keep me in suspense so long."

"I will do as I please, and on my own terms," said Amelia. "I owe you nothing, Magen Hirsch, while you, on the other hand, owe me a great deal."

The rest of the meal proceeded in silence. Amelia

looked lovely as she ate slowly. Chev didn't seem to notice. He kept stealing glances at Veil, trying not to be obvious in a way that was painfully obvious.

Veil made a show of ignoring Chev, too much of a show.

Magen waited patiently for Amelia to finish. When the last sliver of fish was washed down by the last drop of ale, Magen asked, "What do you know about my husband?"

Amelia replied nonchalantly, "He is alive and unharmed. Dissa Banach is holding a prisoner within the Slavers Bod."

"Who told you this?"

"A very close friend of mine—Dissa's current paramour."

Magen turned to Veil for confirmation. Veil shifted a quick look at Amelia, then back to Magen, and hesitantly shook her head.

Magen sank into herself, she hung her face into her arms. Her shoulders heaved with deep breaths that could be laughter or sobbing.

"Go away, Amelia, just go away," said Magen.

Amelia rose, keeping her composure. "We'll talk again in the morning." With a cock of her head, she beckoned Chev. Thousands of eyes followed them as they slowly trekked to the exit.

Outside Chev leaned close to Amelia and whispered, "Go back in and tell her the truth."

"I can't."

Amelia's fingers trembled. She fumbled through her pockets and found a tattered cadmadine reefer and a jeweled lighter. She broke off the unsmokable portion of the reefer, jammed the good part between her lips, and lit up. The smoke was blue in the moonlight. It smelled like clove and ice.

"I would have pulled it off if it hadn't been for that girl. I will get her for this. I will."

* * *

From the moment Chev first spotted Veil in the dining hall, he became fixated on her. At first it was an amusement, a diversion from the dreariness of the awful village on the awful planet. He persisted in his obsessions even after he learned that she had taken an oath of celibacy. Even the most pathetic and odious forms of entertainment were preferable to boredom. Raw egotism provoked fantasies about Veil returning his affections.

Using sophisticated bod surveillance techniques, he followed Veil through the Autumn forests all day. She didn't seem to notice him. Apparently, she failed to read his thoughts, though they were often loud and crude. Why didn't she sense him?

He watched her pick flowers and tend to the village children. He watched her eating and praying.

He read frustrated romantic urging into her every gesture; when she looked in his direction, when she looked away, when she seemed happy, when she seemed sad, and when she seemed impassive.

Two years had passed since Fable's ghost gave Chev its cryptic advice. Like most of the inhabitants of the Draconian system, Chev knew very little of matters outside his specialty, which was combat. And so he knew nothing of love, but the more he learned about it, through life with Amelia, the more love seemed like combat.

In this form of combat called love, Chev found himself hopelessly disadvantaged. Youth and firm flesh had given him a strategic advantage over Amelia in the beginning of their relationship. He used to be able to subdue Amelia with ecstasy whenever they disagreed. But now Amelia had built up defenses to his best moves. An old master of a wide array of romantic weapons, she outclassed him now. With deadly skill, she used teasing, ego manipulation, guilt, and other armaments Chev did not know how to handle.

Yet Chev could not leave Amelia. He had nowhere else to go. He no longer fit into Draconian society. He maintained all his skills, but the bods would have nothing to do with him. That left unincorp life or pirate gangs—two alternatives well below his accustomed standard of living. Circumstances bound him to Amelia. His fantasies about Veil provided him an escape of sorts.

In many ways, Veil was a good choice for a fantasy. Not just because of her beauty, and power, and grace. She was untouchable. Unobtainable. Absolutely safe.

In late afternoon, Veil walked to the sector of woods occupied by the Council of Autumn. She parted the walls of mental illusion, and disappeared inside the fire. There she stayed until twilight.

When Veil walked back into the forest, Chev stalked her through shadows, his passions growing. She seemed apprehensive. Had he finally grown too bold in his pursuit? If she knew she was being followed, why did she not call out for help? Why didn't she head for the village rather than the most secluded part of the woods? She seemed so vulnerable, her robes fluttering in the dying light, like a moth who had learned to avoid the flame, but who now had no sense of direction. The fluttering robes made a whispering music distinct from the rustling of the leaves.

Chev caught the scent of something honeyed and exotic lingering in her trail. Possibly perfume. She must know he was there. She must. What did she expect him to do, alone in the dark, in the far, distant part of the forest? He didn't even know what he would do.

His heart began to race. The smell of her trail grew stronger. Was it perfume? He thought of peeling off her robes. He tried to imagine the shape and texture of her breasts, the softness of her skin. The smell grew stronger still. He was closer than he should be.

He visualized the smoothness of her belly, the pinkness

of her nipples. Surely she heard his thoughts now. In the far distant part of the woods. He didn't care if she heard. This was an invitation, wasn't it? He didn't know what he would do. He just didn't know. But she might know.

She stopped suddenly and turned, a white shadow in the rainbow forest.

Alone, she stepped into a wreath of twilight illumination. Fresh tears dribbled out of her eyes. Gutters of dry salt lined her cheeks. She had been crying for some time. Maybe all day.

Chev expected to see acquiescence in her eyes, or at least doubt and shame. He would not have been surprised to see terror. But the expression on her face was unreadable.

She breathed slowly and deeply, from the abdomen. Standing rigidly straight, she was pulling herself under control, reining her emotions, her doubts. No desire shone in her eyes. No invitation.

She stabbed Chev telepathically. He felt mental energy bands combing his thoughts until she found something ugly and buried deep in his subconscious. She let him catch the smallest glimpse of it. Then, with perfect control, she let it drop back into the sewers of his mind before he could fix it in memory.

While she was in his mind, he shared a tiny fragment of her thoughts, pure and abstract as music. Unbound by desire. She shared this secret with him for less time than a drop of dream—just to show him how wrong he had been about her.

Her gaze was a weapon that could shrivel his soul, if she wished. She looked through and beyond Chev, beyond the woods, beyond the moment.

The power. The absolute self-control. The blazing eyes. Chev almost fell to his knees in reverence, but power and purity seemed somehow incongruent with her tears.

"I won't hurt you," he said.

"That is not true. You are about to hurt me very much. You are about to destroy me."

"I won't lay a hand on you."

"Count on it."

"I won't even come near you."

"It isn't that. You are about to tell me something that will ruin any chance of happiness that I might ever have. But if you don't tell me, the consequences will be far worse, affecting the fate of the entire Draconian system. I have been trying to decide what to do all day. I knew you were coming, but I didn't know when. I didn't think it would be so soon. I don't think I'm ready."

"I'll go."

"No." She trembled. The decision was made. A reflex. Veil was pathologically unselfish. She should have foreseen it. Chev made the hard moment even harder with his angelic face and his ugly thoughts. "Go ahead," said Veil. "Tell me."

Chev scratched his head. He couldn't imagine what he could say that would be so important. He thought a moment longer, then blurted out, "I love you."

She laughed, suddenly relieved. "You don't even know what the word means."

"I suppose you are right," he sighed, resigned and disappointed at her indifference. "I don't know what else to say."

The two of them stared at each other as the forest grew darker. They said nothing for a time. A lone animal howled in the distance, breaking the silence.

"Maybe you were wrong," said Chev.

"Maybe."

"Maybe I do love you."

"I'm very sorry if you do."

Another long and awkward silence followed. Veil and Chev stood ghastly still, waiting for something momentous to happen. Leaves swirled around them. Nothing more.

"All right," said Veil at last, "I can go. I was wrong. You have nothing for me. It is over. We both can leave this place." She took in a deep suck of air. She seemed enormously relieved.

"I'm sorry," said Chev, alarmed at suddenly becoming insignificant. "Maybe if you gave me a few more minutes . . ."

"No. I have had enough."

"Let me go with you. Maybe I will think of it later."

She turned her back and began to walk away.

Chev opened his mouth to shout at her, but he changed his mind. He settled into the leaves and sat like a man in a bathtub. He was flattered when this near perfect woman elevated him to a position of importance, and he took it hard when she dismissed him. He took it as an insult. Defensively, he began to find fault with her. She was wrong about the moment. She was wrong to warn Magen about listening to Amelia. He reckoned Veil couldn't read minds or see the future near so well as she pretended. She was wrong, wrong as hell about him.

"I am not wrong," said Veil. She had come back without making a sound. "Amelia lied."

Chev took a moment to recover from this intrusion into his thoughts. He rose up from the leaves.

"So you care about what I think?"

"I care about what happens to Magen."

"Well, some of what Amelia said was a lie, but not all of it. She was tricked into lying. Amelia doesn't always use her head. She was tricked. But Amelia has a solid lead on Magen's husband. For real. I'll tell you why you didn't know that Amelia had this solid good lead. You thought that because she said one wrong thing, then everything she says is false. But that is not the way it is. No matter what, Amelia would never do anything to hurt Magen."

"I don't believe that. But I see you believe it."

"It wasn't Amelia's idea to lie. It was Chadwick Hubbel's. That's who fed her the lies and the information. I know Hubbel is a slime, but he's wired to the right sources. He told us where to find your camp. He promised Amelia all kinds of rewards for being a messenger. And that is all Amelia had to do, spill the data and not mention Hubbel. She was going to keep her word—but she was also going to volunteer me for backup. That wasn't part of her deal with Hubbel. It was an extra—for Magen's protection. Amelia was going to volunteer her own. You didn't give her the chance."

"She should have told us the truth."

"Hubbel told her to keep his name out of it. I don't really see how it makes a difference one way or the other. I think Hubbel just miscalculated."

"I am quite certain that there was no miscalculation. The information from Hubbel leads into a trap."

"I don't think so. I really don't. You should hear me out on this score. Maybe I don't see into the future, and maybe I can't read minds, but I know a lot about fighting and a lot about traps. I have thought this one through, all the way through. Have faith in me."

She smiled cryptically. "I don't have to rely on faith when I deal with people. I know what is true and what isn't."

"If it is a trap, then I am going down, too. Amelia asked me to cover Magen, and I said I would. That's no small protection. I'm one of the best in the merc business. Maybe the very best. I was getting really big in the bod. Getting it up there, you know what I mean."

"I believe you. Why do you take such chances for Magen?"

"Magen's all right. She's a good fighter. A damn good fighter. I have to respect that."

"But why do you risk your life for her?"

He paused. He thought he had answered her question. "Magen's all right and Amelia asked me to. She would have sent Dawson, too—her security chief—but someone had to keep watch over the mansion. You see, Amelia's not so bad."

"You love Amelia?"

That word again. Did he detect a note of jealousy? "You said yourself I don't know what the word means."

"She really meant no harm?"

"Really."

"You are telling the truth."

"Yeah. Hubbel had this inside information. He told us how we could snatch Dissa Banach. Now, maybe Hubbel figured Amelia's bluff would be spotted. Maybe it is a double bluff, but I don't think so. Amelia can be damn convincing when she lies, and Hubbel knows it. And he gave us a setup that looks risky as hell on the surface—not really the kind of setup anyone would use for a trap. No, it is the kind of setup you go into fully armed and wired. A place where there are all kinds of unpredictable factors. In nonbod territory. Not the kind of place you'd want to lay a trap. The Pickpockets' Ball."

Veil looked lost for a moment, out of her element, vulnerable, when trying to assess the strange milieu of traps and lies that Chev inhabited. She knew only that he was telling her the truth as he heard it. She couldn't tell if someone was lying to Chev, or why.

He put his hand on her shoulder, instinctively, to establish rapport. She pulled away and broke into a cold sweat. "What is the Pickpockets' Ball?"

"It is like a contest played by pirates and trade thieves and unincorps. Once a year on the Winter World, everyone dresses up with lots of jewelry and crowds into a big room. The point is, you steal whatever you can and you try to hold on to what you have. Sort of an excuse to squeeze up close to strangers and grab at them."

"Hubbel is lying. I don't believe Dissa Banach would ever go to this contest. Not on the Winter World, where they shoot bod officers on sight. I have looked into his mind. He is too cautious."

"Hubbel says Banach goes there to keep himself fit. It sharpens his edge, sort of. I dunno. I can see it. I'd do something like that if I got stuck running a bod bureaucracy. If I wanted to keep my edge, I would. It is probably something only a combat jock would understand. You learn to get off on fear. It makes you more dangerous. Yeah, I would do it if I was him."

"These things are so alien to my ways. I do not understand them. They are so . . . ugly . . . so . . ."

"Exciting?"

"Ugly . . . I don't know. Maybe I have misjudged you. There is so much I don't understand. I would have thought Banach would be more careful."

"He is plenty careful. He goes in disguise, of course. And he cheats. He brings a psychic named Ivor with him. Ivor not only acts as a bodyguard, he guides Dissa through the crowds. I hear Dissa exits with quite a nice haul every year. Makes the outing more than just a little cost-effective."

"Ivor Purse?"

"You know him? Hubbel says he is the most powerful psychic in the system."

"I am the most powerful psychic in the system."

"You know Purse?"

"I know of him. I will tell you that this affair sounds more and more like a trap. I believe you are quite sincere. I appreciate your candor and your courage. Still, I sense something ominous and untold in this intelligence delivered via Hubbel. I intend to warn Magen away from your expedition."

"You are wrong."

"My instincts seldom fail me."

"But we're not talking about you right now, I mean,

your well-being. We're talking about what is important to Magen. Look at it this way—all year long Dissa Banach surrounds himself with troops. He secures himself behind the tightest security web in the system. All year long no one can lay a finger on him. This is our one shot at him with no troops around, no radar nets, no pursuit shooters, no chases through bod-controlled space. No warning systems to deal with but Ivor Purse—but the council can blindside him, right?"

"I don't know if the council will agree."

"What about you? I mean, we have me and Magen. And you, if you'll help. Between the three of us, it should not be impossible to take out Dissa Banach."

Chev could feel Veil's eyes tracing the ridges of defined muscle and protruding veins along his bare arms. She studied a scar on his neck. A mental probe flashed out, this one hitting deeper than the last. She took a sip of his spirit, tasted how dangerous it was. Then she retreated inside herself. She stood absolutely still, like a gorgeous statue, waiting for the future.

"Well?" said Chev.

Veil said nothing. She was gone. Her flesh stood in the forest, eyes wide open, but no one was home.

"Hey!" yelled Chev. "Don't do this to me."

He waited. A sullen wind lightly stirred Veil's platinum hair. She didn't seem to notice when a wayward wisp tangled on her eyelashes.

He shouted again and got no response, so he kissed her. The softness of her lips astounded him. Soft, almost insubstantial lips. Like kissing a flower. He found some wetness on those soft lips and a shock went through his spine. She still didn't notice him. He pulled away, afraid to touch her again. He waited for another ten minutes. She blinked, waking from her trance.

"Well, did you learn anything?" he asked.

Veil looked sad, distant as a dreamer. As if talking to herself, she said, "I have a decision to make after all." Then she tasted something strange and tart on her lips.

For the next few days, Veil seemed particularly aloof—lost in her own thoughts or in the thoughts of others. Dark circles formed under her eyes. She lost weight.

Amelia suspected something sinister behind Veil's strange behavior. Not a conscious malice—even Amelia knew Veil was incapable of harmful intent. But Amelia feared that Veil was wrestling with long-repressed and once-defeated demons.

Amelia feared that she and Chev would become the center of Veil's unresolved conflicts.

Over the course of the next week, Amelia had a series of nightmares. Horrible, vivid, frequently sexual nightmares in which all five senses were engaged, nightmares that could not be distinguished from waking reality.

A malignant, presence began to manifest itself. Something invisible that hid behind curtains of dream, a shadow over her consciousness. She fled from the shadow, over dreamscapes the color of bone, over hills the texture of wet mushrooms. But the shadow, or malignancy, or presence—whatever it was—seemed imbued within the total surroundings. Hidden, but hidden everywhere: it haunted the ceilings of sleep, and glinted on blue razor-edged branches in dream forests. It followed her through dust roads to nowhere, down dream wells. It probed out morbid fantasies she could never confess to anyone. She felt its eyes—or whatever it used to watch—gazing upon her.

Amelia had rarely had nightmares before. When she was very young, she mastered her dreams, delighting in irrational defenses against irrational dangers. She hated losing control of any situation, ever, though the cost had been a lifetime of light, fragile sleep.

But now her dreams had drifted beyond her control. It was as if she had fallen into someone else's dreams, as if she were enveloped in a dominant, incomprehensible consciousness. The intruder seemed omnipotent, capable of limitless manipulations of this intangible medium.

Amelia could no longer conjure defenses at will or block out unpleasantries. When she resisted the entity's probing, it punished her. She would dream of her flesh decaying in the grave, her throat melting to slime, the smell of putrefaction strong and real in her nose. Or she would dream of cancers erupting through the walls of her abdomen. All efforts at resistance were met with unassailable force.

For Amelia, wakefulness became an unbearable trial of exhaustion. One rough morning, Amelia awoke feeling as if her insides had turned to slate. Chev was talking to her, but his words did not register. She mumbled a reply that Chev couldn't understand, but he feigned communication, grunting sympathetically. He started talking again—but stopped when he realized she wasn't listening. He strode over to the bed and whipped aside the covers. Grasping Amelia's shoulders firmly, he jerked her upright in the bed and thrust his face in front of hers. Their noses were touching. He shouted loudly enough to penetrate her daze. "Do you know what your problem is? It's that blue shit you take! It's the blue shit, Amelia!"

"No," she muttered. "It isn't the problem. It is the solution."

"If you keep this up, you're going to become addicted."

"I don't care."

She began to increase her intake, but not even massive doses of cadmadine could bring peace to Amelia's sleep.

Like Veil, Amelia lost weight, and she became jittery. It seemed as if the two women shared a common affliction, possibly each other.

Perhaps Amelia would have been more frightened by this plague of nightmares if she were not certain of their etiology. She concluded that Veil had subconsciously invaded her dreams. Amelia believed that in sleep, some tortured portion of Veil's psyche roamed free to share its woe. Veil meant no harm, but Amelia was quite certain that the young psychic harbored poisons.

Weak, delirious, and sleep-deprived, there was not much left to Amelia's spirit but her contrariness. Low as she was, Amelia refused to succumb to the likes of Veil.

Amelia resolved that no one was going to drive her insane or to the grave—no one except maybe Amelia herself. She was determined to somehow get the better of Veil, her undeclared rival.

On a Sunday night, Amelia settled down for sleep laughing to herself. She pulled the covers over her face like the walls of a womb, and she folded her forearms over her eyes. The position was uncomfortable, but she lay still. She had no power left for anything, no more reserves. She drifted into unconsciousness, ready to face her oppressor. Tonight she set a trap with the one mental weapon left at her disposal.

Sleep rolled over her, a sea of numbness, a foaming broth mixing the real with the imagined and the transmuted. Old conversations replayed with unresolved conflicts, silent rooms, sighs, breaths, heartbeats. Undulating geometries roamed her mind, impossible harmonies of sound and color swirled into dream stuff. She lay in wait in the miasma. After a time unknown in the twilight, she found herself in a familiar but long-lost room, a place from her childhood, a memory long untouched. Her mother's bedroom. Her father had let that portion of the mansion fall into ruin after her mother's death.

She could not recall directly the details of the room, not consciously, but as she explored the elegant geometries of this recaptured, re-remembered dream space, everything seemed correct—the blue weave of the carpet, the echoes amplified by marble walls, the sunken triangular foyer, the embroidered armchairs, the closets hung with perfumed silks, furs, and sashes, the glass double doors leading to . . .

No. Amelia did not want to leave the room. This was a place of strength for her. Her mother still lingered here. The smell of her bath oils. Strands of her black hair. The outline of her form pressed into wrinkled bedsheets. A ghost inside a room inside a dream. Amelia sat down in her mother's chair, waiting for her adversary. She stared at the ceiling. She felt comfortable on this echo of a time-lost chair, and yet the sensations of her bones weighing into long-destroyed velveteen cushions seemed unreal and otherworldly, unlike anything experienced in dreams or in drugs. It was as if she had tumbled into a consciousness deeper than sleep, deeper than dreams, deeper than life. The consciousness of nonconsciousness. Perhaps the consciousness of death. Was that the reason she felt the palpable nearness of her mother? The thought of death provoked no special dread. If this was death, it wasn't so bad. Certainly not what she had expected, but still not so bad. The re-creation of things vanished, the nearness of dead loved ones. Soon she would walk out the door, probe the necroscape, and discover what eternity had to offer. Soon. But for the time being the unreal chair felt comfortable.

Then a sudden panic squeezed her abdomen and a cold sweat poured down her back. It was a sort of dream worry that gives seed to night terrors.

The presence of her mother, which had hung in the air so warm and reassuring, was gone—suddenly replaced by the breath of corruption, the smell of worm fodder and grave shit. An unbearable agony gripped Amelia as though her bones were being ground to powder with living nerves still connected. She screamed. First she screamed for her mother. Receiving no answer, she screamed for Jesus. She had never put any kind of credence in deity legends before. But the sudden agony was too much for her. Much too horrible to be anything but Hell. And her long days of suffering, surrounded by Universalist churches and hymns and the council and Veil and Veil and Veil—all these things made Amelia scream for Jesus as loudly as she could. The pain continued. She babbled phrases she picked up from the ex-slaves in the village, as if the words were infused with magic.

She pleaded for Jesus and Zeus and God, and all the other figures on the windows of the Universalist church. She felt that she was alone, but her agony did not abate. Nerves roasting, sheets of pain. Pain like rain. She tried magical words she didn't understand. Nothing. Nothingness.

Dead. Too late. Death without oblivion. Death without release.

No loved ones to embrace.

But she was not alone.

She shared the room with someone or something. Not her mother, but something that had disguised itself as her mother, draping itself insidiously in shawls, perfumes, and other snippets of sensation culled from Amelia's memory. Amelia called out for God and the disguises dropped away—just for an instant. The room began dissolving, shards of a fading wall hung against infinite darkness. Amelia caught just the briefest glimpse of a sickly, androgynous thing. The dream invader was fleeing the room fragments, fleeing the dream. The creature's face was sexless, betraying the worst traits of both genders, cold, yet weak, cruel, aggressive, frightened and corrupted by self-denial, and preoccupied with death. High cheekbones, blond and pale like Veil and just as fragile-looking. Vaulting eyebrows, sunken cheeks, like Veil with a change of hormones and three weeks in the grave. Just the briefest glimpse of a thing that wasn't a whole creature in any event—it was an escaped thought, a virus of ectoplasm, a ragged bit of soul, as insubstantial as a guess.

Then it was gone, fleeing the cadmadine withdrawal pains that it shared as deeply as it had shared Amelia's dreams. Her trap. Her weakness and her weapon. Cadmadine withdrawal.

Free at last from her dream intruder, free of all dreams and thoughts, Amelia lapsed into a fathomless sleep. Exhaustion being the best and truest anesthesia, Amelia slept through the tail end of withdrawal. She slept through the night and beyond.

Amelia put on a dress appropriate for going to church, a high-collared, loosely flowing silk weave trimmed with snippets of lace and velvet, tied at the waist with a studded sash. She put her hair up. Too much makeup made her complexion look chalky and unreal. Still, it was better than the greyish natural pallor she had developed. She looked weird, but intimidating.

The time had come to confront Veil.

Amelia charged out into the dazzling sunlight. Storming through the village lanes, she demanded an audience with Veil. She barked out orders to the ex-slaves she encountered, and they ran, on reflex, to summon their priestess.

Amelia found Veil seated on a hillside reading to a group of children. As Amelia approached, Veil looked up from her worn copy of the Bhagavad Gita.

"Keep out of my dreams!" Amelia demanded.

Veil regarded her for a moment, a quick scan from head to toe. A chill wind blew. Then Veil rose reluctantly from her seat on the ground, seeming as light and fragile as the dry leaves around her. Veil looked weary; the circles under her eyes had puffed into prominent crescent moons. Bitterly, and with some hint of disgust that she tried to disguise, she said, "I wish I could keep out of your dreams."

"You admit it?"

"Admit what?"

"You have been prying into my dreams."

"I cannot help but hear what you choose to broadcast. I can ease your pain, if you wish."

"Fuck that idea."

"You don't need to be rude. You are the one torment-ing me with your horrible, loud, blaring dreams." She shuddered as if a swift, harsh torment had touched her. A tear rolled down her cheek. Perhaps she cried for Amelia or perhaps she cried for herself. Amelia couldn't tell, but she softened, overwhelmed by an instant of pity for Veil, so powerful and yet so frail.

"Listen, I apologize. You don't really mean harm, I can tell. But this business has to stop before it destroys both of us." She paused to let the need for cooperation sink in. "I will tell you what is happening. There is a side to you that you cannot control. That is human nature, Veil. Believe it or not, you are human. You may not consciously mean to hurt me, but . . ."

Veil brushed aside her tears, cheeks flushing. "I don't want this psychology business discussed in front of the chil-dren."

The children, who hadn't been paying attention up to this point, suddenly pricked up their ears to catch every word of what they weren't supposed to hear.

Gently, but insistently, Veil continued, "You may take whatever comfort you wish from not being in control of your actions, but don't project your own lack of control onto me."

"What is this? Are you saying you don't have a sub-conscious mind?"

"It is just an excuse to sin. If you give yourself excuses, then you will sin. It is that simple."

"I don't need excuses."

"There is the will to do good or the will to do evil. Nothing else. These fabrications of conscious and unconscious mind are only metaphors to explain away God. They are ancient heresies that blinded man to his own soul—much to blame for the way sin has spread like a disease all over the system. I won't have you spouting such dangerous ideas in front of the children."

Amelia folded her arms across her breasts. She had encountered a wall. So much for the gentle approach. She had greatly underestimated Veil's capacity for rationalization. Pacing circles around Veil and the children, Amelia decided that subtlety wouldn't work and neither would rhetoric. Amelia had to attack directly.

"You can't shut me out that easily, girl!" said Amelia. "No more than I can shut you out. Do you understand? You are going to have to deal with me in one form or another. Maybe you can fool other people with your lofty cant about God and his bullshit—but you cannot fool me."

"You don't even understand what I am trying to tell you," said Veil. "You don't even understand the word *sin*, at least not in the ancient sense."

Amelia shrugged. "I have seen your other side, girl. I have seen the sick, withered, vicious thing that drives you, the castrated, diseased . . ."

"Enough!" A threat lurked in the tone.

"Go ahead! Hit me with everything you have. Hit me with all the castrated, diseased power you have. I know you, girl. I have seen what you carry inside. You carry something that hates life and everything that goes with life. A dark, demented, sexless . . ."

"That was not me!"

"It was a part of you. Oh, you try to hide it. You hide it so well from everyone but me. You busy yourself drawing pus from the boils of half-wits. You give food to the lazy and the maimed. You ram your fairy tales down the throats of unfortunates who lack the wit and will to resist. But I know you. A death worshiper, that's what you are. You can't stand your own life, so you remake death into something attractive. Something more salable. You call death 'Heaven,' then you worship it. You are so overwhelmed by death, you call it God. You can dismiss psychology if you want, Veil, but there's a lot more going on in your head than you realize, more than you want to admit. You know what I mean." Then, casually, Amelia added, "I suspect that you always have to wonder if the so-called shameful thoughts you are hearing are yours or someone else's."

Veil's eyes widened. Amelia had drawn blood.

The children giggled, for no apparent reason.

Now tears flowed freely down Veil's cheeks. "I'm sorry, so sorry . . ." She stared at the ground.

Amelia straightened, willing to accept Veil's surrender. "I accept your apology." Taking a step forward, Amelia couldn't resist a subtle gloat. "I regret that I was forced to use such drastic means to make you confront the problem. There was no other way, girl. Look to yourself and keep out of my dreams."

Veil kept on crying. The children stirred restlessly. Amelia almost felt ashamed of gloating. When Veil could finally speak, she said, "I wasn't apologizing. I am sorry you are so lost, Amelia. I wish I were able to help you, but I am powerless, and you are in grave danger for your soul and your life. I have witnessed your nightmares, though I did not cause them. I know who did."

"You. Yourself."

"You won't believe me, but I know."

"All right, tell me."

"It was someone not human. A great and fearful force. All-powerful—almost. A sick, withered, vicious thing—to use your words. This force opposes God in all his works. It hides in plain sight, like the way it hid in your dream, wrapping itself in familiar things. It tempts mankind away from the light. Recognition of this force was universal on Earth. Nearly every religion has its own name for it—the lying mind, the serpent, the Christians called it Lucifer, the Jews Satan, the Muslims called it Iblis, the Buddhists Mara. The Devil was in your dreams. He has you by the throat."

Amelia laughed, nervously.

Veil continued, "I think the Devil knows you are close to death, and you are ripe for either salvation or damnation. You are teetering on the edge of the void. For some reason I cannot guess, you are special to God, Amelia. He made an extra effort for you last night, to drive out the Devil. That is a miracle I know you don't appreciate."

Amelia pursed her lips. Veil's strange, unexpected compliment made her pause. "Special to God? Me?"

"I think so. And that makes you even more prone to attack from Satan. You have a choice to make, the clearest choice in the world. God or Satan."

Determined not to be manipulated by flattery, Amelia rejected the whole notion. Absurd. One all-powerful, all-seeing entity was hard enough to accept. Two was out of the question.

"No, Veil, it was not the Devil. It could feel what I felt. I chased whoever it was away by subjecting it to my cadmadine withdrawal. It ran from pain, a very animal, a very flesh-linked response. Whatever it was, it felt pain. Couldn't have been an ethereal being. I may not know much about your God and his menagerie, but I can recognize human suffering."

"You called out for God. That's why it ran. You don't

realize how lucky you are, Amelia, how much God loves you. You were in Hell, trapped by the Devil. You called out to God and he chased the Devil away. He gave you a second chance. A warning. A taste of Hell and a taste of salvation. That doesn't happen very often. It is beautiful, Amelia. You have been blessed and you don't even know it. Your aura is so dark, tainted by your sins, by your contempt of God. You accuse me of being diseased—but you are the one who is dying. Killing yourself with sin and poison and hatred and lust and envy. Yet rotten as you are, God heard you calling him and he pulled you out of Hell. It is one of the most beautiful things I have ever heard, and you don't even appreciate it. You don't even believe it."

Amelia stiffened.

Veil continued, "You are ready to march back into Hell, on a moment's notice. And blame me. You always blame other people for the things you do to yourself."

Amelia smiled, a strange, uncontrolled, lopsided smile, full of flash insight and hostility. It was an ambushed smile. "Why . . . you clever little bitch . . . you . . ."

"Come along children, come along. . . ." Veil gathered her flock with outstretched arms. Her sleeves flapped in the wind as she hustled the children away from Amelia.

"You clever little bitch . . ." Amelia said to the air, knowing she would be heard.

Amelia kept repeating the phrase "you clever little bitch" as she strolled back to her bungalow. She found Veil's characterization of the universe unnerving. Was it possible? A duel between two all-powerful entities, each vying for a harvest of souls. Amelia liked the idea that her own soul was a jewel of great worth. She found evidence of cosmic struggle in her renewed craving for cadmadine, and in her slowly emerging desires to resist. She found evidence in her mixed feelings toward Veil. She found evidence in the misbehaving children of slaves defying their parents in the streets of the village. She found evidence in her own despair.

"You clever little bitch . . ." Amelia muttered, her perspectives on reality altered for a time.

# 7

## THE PICKPOCKETS' BALL

While Amelia rested in bed, still sick and chronically weak, Veil flew across space in a midsized craft with Chev and Magen aboard.

Amelia feared the bitter cold of the Winter World. She feared leaving Chev and Veil alone with one another, but she feared the cold even more.

As Veil surmised, Amelia was ripe for either damnation or conversion, and Amelia might have further pondered the possibility of being caught in a tug-of-war between God and the Devil, if Veil had stayed around and provoked further discussion. But Veil was bound for the Pickpockets' Ball, nominated by the council to be their sole representative.

The night that Veil departed, the nightmares departed.

* * *

The craft was spacious, fitted with luxury options. The gorgeous interior was marred by only a slight amount of damage when Magen liberated it from the Accountants Bod. A few indelible blood spots stained the pilot's cabin. Blobs of metal, patinaed in flame licks, hung like bulbous fruit on bare portions of the inner frame.

Chloroform rebreathers freshened the air. Small fountains, cooled by the vacuum of space, added a pleasant smell and a hint of spring to the contained atmosphere.

Despite the ample room aboard, Magen felt claustrophobic, trapped between Chev and Veil and their unresolved conflicts. She retired to her room and began to prepare herself for the ball. She wove three flexible blow darts and a thin, transparent tube into her hair; then she covered her head with a fringed cap beaded with baby emeralds. To better blend with the expected crowd, she applied makeup in the gaudy, provocative fashion of pirate and unincorp women. Orange lips. Gold-leaf eye shadow.

It took almost twenty minutes to squeeze into an impossibly tight mother-of-pearl lamé costume. The fabric was thin, but tough as leather. She had not worn the outfit in years. Once on, it was comfortable enough, and did not restrict her movements. Although shamefully immodest, it wouldn't desensitize her to contact, as heavier clothing would.

Then Magen popped open the lock of a small carrying case, heavy with her past. Piece by piece, she unwrapped the jewelry she had accumulated during her days with the bod. Valuable necklaces, bracelets, rings, earrings, sashes, scarabs, broaches, all delicately packed in clumps of scented tissue. Next, she opened a cask of gems volunteered by Amelia. The difference between the two collections was immediately obvious. Magen's jewels tended to be larger, and the fashions seemed dated, garish. Amelia's pieces were beautiful in timeless ways, with fluted or filigreed settings that perfectly matched the stones. Magen couldn't believe that Amelia considered these "throwaway" items.

Magen and Chev would have to put both collections at risk to gain admittance to the ball. She didn't care about losing any of her own jewelry, though once the trinkets had seemed very important to her. Gems seemed trivial compared to her greater loss.

She began to adorn herself with baubles, setting aside certain gender-neutral ornaments for Chev.

When all of the jewelry had been hung, snapped, pinned, and placed, Magen adorned herself with weapons. A spring derringer under each armpit, a belt of shuriken, all placed as carefully as she had placed the gems. She filed her nails to razor points and blew away the dust. Then she walked out to the antechamber where Veil and Chev sat.

"You almost died," said Chev.

"What?" Magen tensed.

"I mean, I did not recognize you. I thought we had a stowaway or something. You almost died."

"This is who I used to be."

"You look like a killer whore."

Veil said, "That is not a very nice thing to say." But she was obviously just as disconcerted by Magen's transformation.

Magen stood in the passageway, studying Chev.

"So what is your problem, killer whore?"

"You almost died," said Magen.

"Seems like more has changed than just your clothes," said Chev.

When they reached the Winter World, Chev snapped mirrored goggles over his eyes. The wind carried sharp bits of crystalline grit, which tapped constantly on his lenses from the moment he stepped outside. Snow crunched under his footsteps.

He circled an ancient building the locals called the Temple of Ice, where pickpockets from all over the system were beginning to gather. Ice obscured most of the original architecture, flowing in sheets across the walls, hanging from ramparts and cornices in menacing patterns. Claws of ice, daggers of ice, gargoyles of ice.

Only the vast dome on top and the front entrance had been spared the onslaught of ice. Polished by the abrasive wind for centuries, the dome reflected the clear night sky full of stars and arcing lights of arriving spacecraft. The building looked like a cage, topped by a ball of displaced cosmos.

Periodically, Chev could hear Veil check in on him telepathically. She had been scanning the new arrivals. Not a single thought among them about Magen or her small party. Still, Chev felt more and more uneasy as he conducted his routine surveillance of the icebound building.

Only one way in. Only one way out. This was a trap. Obviously it was a trap. And yet Chev had sorted through all the angles. He doubted seriously that Hubbel and Banach could reach any concord or form any alliance. Bod brothers or not, those two hated each other. But one thing kept troubling Chev. Why had Hubbel insisted that Amelia keep his name out of the information conveyed to Magen? Perhaps he figured that Magen would discredit any data coming from Hubbel. That explanation made some sense, but wasn't completely satisfying. Did Hubbel really think Amelia would fool Veil? Or the council? Was it a lie meant to be spotted as a lie, a double bluff? Why did Hubbel want his involvement kept a secret? Or not kept a secret? Or whatever?

As Chev completed his circle around the cage of ice, he

heard an old shale-oil generator puffing as it strained to work in the bitter cold. It powered a jammer field, which was needed to neutralize all energy-based weapons. With transceivers nestled in evenly spaced niches chiseled into the ice, the jammer field buzzed. It was absolutely essential. Tempers tended to run hot at the ball. The jammers disarmed most of the heavier forms of weaponry—lasers, even acid swords. Energy-based weapons would cause a bloodbath in these tight quarters.

Chev continued on around. The wind whipped his face. His lips began to crack and bleed. Pink saliva crackled around his mouth. Now the sounds of the generator were barely audible. He had a fine view of the pathway leading up to the front entrance.

The incoming pickpockets strolled leisurely, clouds of breath streaming from their mouths, opulent furs wrapped around their bodies, concealing the bounty underneath. They kept a safe distance from one another until they were forced to squeeze through the doors.

Veil's voice whispered directly into Chev's cerebral cortex. The intense intimacy of her voice in his mind made him ache. He remembered the stolen kiss.

She informed him that Dissa Banach and Ivor Purse had broken the Winter envelope and were about to make landfall.

Chev jerked his head skyward. The night was now thick with arriving spacecraft; yet among the descending armor, he could pick out Banach's craft almost immediately, despite the absence of bod markings. Ornamental chains ran the length of the fuselage, leading up to a metal masthead cast in the image of an abused woman. Iron hooks pierced the cheeks of the masthead, anchoring undulating chains. The woman's mouth was forced open in the shape of an O.

When the ship landed, the gangplank slid out of the open mouth, like a rigid tongue.

Magen, who had been circling counterclockwise from

Chev's beat, now emerged around the other side of the building.

Telepathing to both of them, Veil confirmed the target.

Chev unzipped a furred pocket and extracted a spring pistol—a small handgun powered by a compressed metal coil that spat dermal darts. If he got close enough to Banach, he could anesthetize him with a shot to the cheek and drag him away while Magen dealt with Ivor. Veil assured them that she would keep Ivor blocked and ignorant.

Dissa Banach and Ivor Purse descended the gangplank. Dissa's heavy furs bristled on his enormous frame, making it appear as if he had doubled his bulk. Ivor wore tight-fitting, glittery thermal plastics. He was thin and graceful. Feline, he moved like a dancer.

Both men wore masks of solid gold. Clever. Valuable enough to meet at least a third of the minimum stakes to get them through the door, but hard to filch. Right under their noses—damned hard to filch.

The spring pistol would be of no use. Chev holstered it. He extracted a long-nosed customized syringe that could penetrate the furs. He weighed it in his hand. He thought-signaled to Veil, who relayed the message to Magen.

Chev and Magen began to close in. They walked in tandem swiftly, but not betraying any urgency. Dissa and Ivor strode thirty paces ahead, following the pathway to the Temple of Ice.

The incoming revelers began to choke the icy path. Chev found himself blocked by some slow-moving new arrivals. He tried to weave around them, but they refused to get out of his way. As Chev pressed for ground, one of them bumped him hard—a butt bump from a saucily shaken hip. Chev nearly fell. His heels screeched as he caught himself. Dissa and Ivor shot a backward glance in his direction, but lost interest when they saw him stumbling on the ice. There was no hint of recognition. Furs and goggles covered Chev's face.

Chev tried making excuses to himself about being weighted down by furs and disadvantaged by the cold—but he knew he was seriously out of shape.

Dissa and Ivor moved closer to the entrance. If they got inside, the entire maneuver would become hopelessly complicated. Chev quickened his pace. He kept his balance. Gripping the syringe tightly, he eased through a press of revelers who blocked his path. He surged up six feet behind Dissa. Magen stepped slightly ahead, ready to pounce on Ivor.

At this close range, Chev could sense enormous energies radiating from Ivor, but Ivor seemed oblivious of the approaching threat. This simple show of Veil's abilities made Chev's mouth go dry.

Chev paced within striking distance of Dissa Banach. He prepared to drive the needle home. Magen waited. She jerked her head almost imperceptibly, signaling Chev to attack.

Chev just stood there with an absurd, confounded expression showing through the furs, a foolish frown on his lips. His hands were empty.

Back along the path, one of the pickpockets lay anesthetized on the ice.

Magen stared angrily at Chev.

Embarrassed, Chev held up his empty hands and shrugged sheepishly.

Ivor and Dissa proceeded leisurely through the door to the Pickpockets' Ball, vanishing inside the Temple of Ice.

Chev and Magen followed, falling into line with the other ingoing revelers. The crowd coagulated as they approached the entrance. En masse, they squeezed through.

Chev and Magen found themselves in a spacious area where the air was warm and thick with exhalations. A num-

ber of pendants and shuriken had already been plucked
off them.

The assembled pickpockets were shucking off their
furs and peeling off their gloves. Jewels and knives glittered on the undraped bodies.

Magen passed a girl of not more than fourteen who
had covered her hands and lips with cephalopod suction
cups. With sticky fingers, tonight was her night. Her escort,
an even younger male, was naked except for sapphires em-
bedded in his skin.

Some of the more defensive players wore venomous insects disguised as scarabs, their glittering green armor
resembling semiprecious metals.

A grey-bearded pirate proudly tested new neural connections especially installed for the occasion—opening
and closing a set of bird talons affixed to his abdominal
wall.

Some wore bits of alarm webbing over or under their
garments.

The unincorp crowd made lavish use of biotechnology,
frequently to hideous effect, like stripes of reptile scales
against stripes of fur against stripes of flesh. One steroid
brute had plastered frog skin all over his cheeks. The bods
had overused gene splicing for industrial purposes, and
the unincorps overused it cosmetically. They scrambled
their chromosomes to assert their individuality, indifferent to the risks of cancer and sterility. They prized their
own uniqueness above all else. That was why they lived outside the bods in the first place. That was why they armored
themselves like crustaceans and hung bird bills over their
noses.

The din of conversation was sprinkled with leopard
growls, barking, cawing, and the voices of turtles. The
human race was splintering—every man was a species unto
himself.

Guarding the row of doors that led to the main ball-room, a team of heavily armed locals scrutinized the entry stakes on the new arrivals. As Chev and Magen presented themselves for admission, the eyes of one of the team members bugged out with jeweler's glass implants. He looked like a fish as he examined the contestants.

Many of the contestants were turned away. Those who refused to leave were knifed or shot down with crossbows on the spot. The disenfranchised inhabitants of the Winter World regarded the Pickpockets' Ball with almost religious zeal. This was their one night of glory and release, and they would not tolerate any breach of their protocols.

Magen and Chev had managed to retain enough of their booty to gain entrance. They pushed through the swinging doors into the main ballroom.

Magen scanned the crowd for Dissa. A soft glow lit the room, something like candlelight. She couldn't find any sign of him amid the bangles, feathers, flesh, and knives. Partyers bumped into her. Some flashed lecherous smiles. Magen felt a series of tugs on her costume as she navigated the ballroom. Her necklaces were gone. The broaches vanished. If she didn't start paying attention to the sport of the moment, she would lose everything. Already, she had lost sight of Chev.

The roar of the crowd sounded more like a jungle than a gathering of humans. Magen doubted that the roar represented any kind of communication, or even attempts at communication. It was too loud, too animal. The only social interaction under the dome was pilferage. Bits and pieces of value rapidly changed hands and passed through the crowd, exchanges of material goods instead of information: the language of larceny.

Magen called out mentally to Veil. It felt good to reestablish the link between them; it broke the overwhelming sense of isolation Magen felt. She let Veil guide her.

Magen began to recoup her losses along the way,

snatching chains of gold, strings of pearls, broaches, and pendants. And rings. She liked rings. Moving through a sea of hands, she continued to incur some losses. Rude tugs pulled at her. Someone ripped out an earring, splitting her earlobe in bleeding flaps. Some of the pickpockets showed more finesse, with gentle, almost intangible taps. Magen managed to pick up at least as much as she was losing, hitting a kind of equilibrium.

From atop a raised dais at the north end of the hall, a phalanx of winter locals trained crossbows on the crowd, a modest attempt to keep the chaos under control. Murders would be tolerated, even confined brawls, but any suggestion of rioting would be dealt with harshly.

As the room became more crowded, Magen detected subtle smells of death in the air, an undercurrent of blood and bile floating under the smells of sweat and perfume.

The Winter World ushers were tapping out the empty-pocketed losers and signaling them to leave. Every now and then, they would drag away a corpse.

Magen stumbled across the young boy she had seen earlier, the naked youth with the sapphires. He was alone now, and dead on the floor with all the gems plucked from his body.

Telepathing directions, Veil led Magen to Dissa. Simultaneously, she guided Chev to the same point. Magen sensed the beginnings of mental fatigue in Veil, a subtle drop in her energy level, a loss of volume in her cerebral voice.

Magen assessed the situation, plotting a new approach to seizing Dissa. His furs gone, he wore a net of tight, finely linked chain mail. If she could get close enough, there was a chance she could slide one of the smaller syringe needles through the mesh of links. She relayed plans to Chev via Veil, even though they stood not five feet apart. No chance of being heard in there. He maneuvered into position.

Magen sashayed past Dissa Banach, openly flashing her

jewels and charms. The display held an implicit invitation. She played it that she was wide open, vulnerable.

Dissa seemed not to recognize her, but he saw through her pose. Nonetheless, he seemed intrigued. He shot a glance toward Ivor, who nodded him on. Dissa glided through the crowd, inclining in Magen's direction. Magen flashed a mental salute to Veil, thanking her and complimenting her on keeping Ivor blocked so well.

Dissa was so close now that Magen could smell his desire. He was aroused, she was certain, not by her body but by her jewelry. His strong hand brushed over Magen's breast, snatching a broach, unpinning it with a single motion. He swept prizes off her without tearing the fabric of her clothing.

He was good, but as he withdrew, she culled a handful of earrings he had stored in his hip pocket, his pickings from earlier in the evening, worth far more than the broach. He made another pass at her, groping for the earrings. She turned away from him, coyly, a half-turn. He pressed closer. He didn't like to lose.

They plucked small trinkets from one another's bodies in a tango of theft. His chain mail put him at a certain disadvantage; it stiffened his movements, and it desensitized him to her prying fingers. She let him stay close. She teased him by exposing one of Amelia's most alluring pendants—but she kept it just beyond his grasp. While he chased her offerings, she let a small syringe slide into her hand.

Chev pulled up behind Dissa.

Ivor watched Dissa and Magen duelling like pickpockets. He seemed unconcerned, standing limp-wristed and at ease.

She dangled the pendant again, a laser gem in an art-deco setting. It glittered with auburn points of angry light. As he grabbed for the bait, the golden cheek of his mask made cold contact with her face.

With a fluid motion, she thrust the syringe upward.

Dissa caught Magen by the wrist and held her fast. The needle tarried in the air, below Dissa's right pectoral muscle.

Now that she had made her move, he recognized her. He saw past the veneer of makeup and cosmetic surgery. He said something to her she couldn't make out over the roar of the revelers. With his free hand, he pulled a knife. She scrambled frantically with her free hand for a weapon, but all the weapons within her limited range of motion had been plucked off by the crowd.

Chev tackled Dissa. The two men exchanged a quick volley of forceful blows. Their fists fell with such visible power, Magen imagined the smack of bone and muscle colliding, even though the surrounding sea of noise absorbed the actual sounds.

Tangled together, a knot of limbs, Chev and Dissa rolled across the floor. They had knives out, sweeping at one another. Both men bled heavily. The onlookers dodged the blades and cleared a small arena on the ground.

Magen caught a soft message from Veil, who was fading fast. Veil was trying to persevere, but her thought signals were brittle. She relayed Chev's new plan. He would try to pull off Dissa's golden mask, or cut a hole in his chain mail. He wanted Magen to hit Dissa with a blow dart the moment skin was exposed.

She quickly unweaved a hollow tube from a lock of hair under her cap. She pulled free a dart and loaded the tube, placing it between her dry lips. She circled around the brawling men. Dissa had not forgotten about her. He tried to throw a kick in her direction, but she stayed just beyond his reach.

Chev's hands lunged for the mask. He planted his fingers firmly on the shining cheeks and pulled as hard as he could. Instead of resisting, Dissa threw his weight into the yank, propelling his head forward, riding Chev's own strength. The mask hit Chev's forehead with a terrible impact. Magen heard the mask ringing, even above the roar of the crowd, a single vibrating, golden note.

Dissa disentangled himself quickly and spun around to face Magen. Chev lay on the ground, limp, his forehead bruised and mottled, his perfect nose flattened. Magen heard a gasp, a tone of mental anguish inside her mind; then Veil disappeared. Magen was alone, facing Dissa.

To everyone's surprise, Chev struggled to sit upright. Teetering at the waist, he pulled back his arm, knife in hand. Dissa wheeled about, hit him with a snap kick under the chin. The blow shot Chev backward into the crowd. A cluster of onlookers collapsed on top of him, and he disappeared under a wave of falling bodies.

Magen used the split-second respite to blend into the crowd. She tried to reestablish contact with Veil, stretching her thoughts beyond the top of the dome, to the skies. She met silence. What had happened to Veil? Exhaustion? Or had she dropped her shields just low enough for Ivor to spot her? Had Ivor and Veil clashed on their ethereal plane? Or was there something else?

Magen broke into a cold sweat. Without Veil protecting her, Magen would be exposed, her thoughts open to Ivor, her strategies conveyed to Dissa the moment she formed them. Her throat dried. She couldn't bring her breathing under control, and her heart raced.

She shoved her way through the crowd, trying to veer toward the walls. Anything to limit the angles of attack. She felt tugs of nibbling fingertips as she lost various items of value. She was too preoccupied to play the game.

When she reached the wall, she paused for a moment. She leaned upon an ancient bronze plaque, supporting her weight on one hand. Metal upraised letters pressed into the softness of her wet palms. The hideous cold of the world outside bled through the concrete walls and the metal plaque. When she withdrew her hand, she saw Hebrew letters imprinted on her skin. Mirror-image Hebrew letters. Scanning the plaques, she found they covered the entire length of the wall. Row after row, Jewish names written in Hebrew letters, each accompanied by a date. The names of the dead. Memorial plaques.

Her eyes drifted upward from the plaques to the great dome and saw, for the first time, a gigantic engraving of a Star of David.

She realized that the Temple of Ice had once been a literal temple. Behind the bowmen on the dais, she could make out the ruins of an empty ark, its portals decorated by sculpted lions and dense layers of graffiti. On an upper balcony, where women once sat segregated from the men during services, scantily clad pickpockets now rubbed against one another, searching for something of value.

Finding herself in a temple, a once holy place so badly desecrated, filled her with despair. The ancient Jews who had settled here must have been brave and powerful and wealthy to raise such a sanctuary in so bleak a wilderness. How had their strength served them? Was it wasted in the impossible cold? What had happened to their community? Had they been wiped out, or assimilated into the pirates and unincorps? Were the bowmen on the dais their descendants?

She looked upward in prayer and saw again the huge star on the inside of the dome, undiminished in its grandeur, out of reach of the graffiti artisans. It comforted her a little. What a beautiful temple it must have been. Perhaps the Jews who had built it migrated to less hostile worlds. Perhaps they were her ancestors. Or Adam's. There on the killing ground, she had only the cold names of dead kindred spirits to stand beside her. She decided to head for the exit. Time to abort this insane, suicidal venture. She no longer held any hope for success. She had come ill prepared, vulnerable, open, and unable to breach Dissa's defenses. She resolved to head for the exit. She would try to capture Dissa another day.

"Don't give up."

Magen heard a voice in her mind. It sounded like Veil, but it didn't feel like Veil.

"Ivor?"

"No, it is me, Veil. Trust me. Dissa is circling the exits. He's waiting for you to bolt. It is an ambush."

Who was this whispering in her mind beside the names of the dead? Angel or devil?

"It is really me," said the mental voice. "I am really Veil. Ivor thinks such wicked thoughts. Violent. Hideous. I couldn't take it anymore, but I am rested now and I feel better. You must have faith, Magen." Then, impatiently, she added, "Do you really have a choice?"

Twenty feet away, Dissa's golden mask glittered in between spaces in the crowd. None of her weapons could harm him. The blades would catch on the chain mail. The spring guns didn't have enough force to penetrate his protection. Anyway, they had been lifted.

"I will guide you to a weapon," whispered the voice of Veil. "Seventy degrees to your right, see the boy with the red cape? Tap his right breast pocket."

"Veil, is it really you?"

"Have faith."

Magen took off after the boy. She pressed up beside him, felt a rigid tube in his top pocket, then lifted it.

She angled through the crowd, trying to keep as many people as possible between her and Dissa. She tried to figure out what kind of weapon she had acquired. It looked something like a pen, a single tube with a single cartridge inside with a crude trigger mechanism at the top. She suspected it was some kind of ballistic weapon, a one-shot, something primitive and ancient like her old Luger. With a weapon like this, something that could only kill or maim, there was no way she could take Dissa alive. Her one hope for survival would end all hope of ever finding Adam.

She cursed the weapon, cursed the choice it placed in her hands, cursed her foul luck. As she cursed, the weapon vanished from her fingertips, as if she had wished it away.

"The girl in the feather bodice," whispered Veil's voice, "she has it."

Magen gave chase. The crowd had begun to thin a little. With the losers tagged out, the level of activity increased to a frantic pace. Only the most skilled pickpockets remained.

The bounty picked from the losers sparkled abundantly as gems moved from pocket to pocket amid the players who were still left. Fortunes were made and fortunes were lost with the flick of a wrist. Goods were changing hands so quickly now that everyone left in the room was a winner—just for a moment.

Magen brushed against the girl in the feathered bodice. It took three probes, but she recovered the weapon. Veil had been right.

Then Veil screamed a warning, a high-pitched cerebral note. Magen ducked just in time to avoid a knife ambush from Dissa. She ducked under the cover of the crowd again.

The warning reassured Magen that she was being watched over by Veil. She paused for a moment, scrutinizing the tubular mechanism. Another warning sounded in her brain.

Magen spied Dissa's golden face cruising toward her.

She steadied the weapon. One shot. One chance. Losing Adam forever. Losing her life. Dissa charged forward, transparent knife blades gripped in each hand. One chance, one shot.

Magen's fingers faltered on the trigger. She froze. The

weapon was raised, poised to kill, but she couldn't bring herself to fire.

Veil's voice screamed in her mind, "Kill him, kill him, kill him . . ."

Magen wheeled around, just in time to avoid Dissa's attack slash. The blade cut deep into her left biceps.

Before he had time to cut her again, and before she had time to re-aim, an eddy of revelers flowed between them.

She took a moment to slit open her left sleeve and slap a dermal adhesive on the wound. She couldn't afford to lose blood. While she ministered to her injury, trinkets flew from her body. Someone managed to scarf up the weapon as well.

Veil's voice steered Magen toward the culprit again.

"Get the weapon, keep it, kill Dissa." She wasn't sure if it was Veil who was telling her these things, or her own instincts.

This time it was harder to get the weapon back. Magen's left hand went numb. In her rush, she had botched the dermal patching, and a dark hematoma spread under the cloned adhesive tissue. She could feel the opposite walls of the wound sucking on one another.

Magen finally managed to grab the tube away from a blond pirate, largely because she had been willing to sacrifice two bracelets and a dagger. She held the weapon.

"Keep it, kill Dissa," said the voice inside her head.

Roaming the ballroom, she lost the weapon again. She had clutched it too hard, made it look too valuable. Someone pulled it right out of her fingertips.

The voice helped her get it back.

She lost it again in an undertow of fingers.

Rummaging through velvet pockets, she got it back.

She lost it.

She got it back.

She fought the pulling tide.

The voice in her head screamed, "You're letting it slip away on purpose. Hold on to it, kill Dissa. Hold on to it. Kill. Forget Adam. Forget Adam. Don't even think about Adam. Don't even think his name. Don't even think about someone you can't name. Don't even think . . ."

Magen pulled out of a wave of bodies about twenty feet behind Dissa. He had his back to her. With one hand, he carried Ivor aloft, gripping the psychic's tunic. Ivor's feet frantically trod air. Clearly, Dissa was furious at Ivor for his ineffectual performance against Veil.

Magen closed in. For an instant, she could feel Veil's will clashing against Ivor, grating, whining in the air, like neurofeedback. She caught just the faintest trace of a warning squeal—Ivor to Dissa, or Veil to Magen, she couldn't tell. She closed in, uncertain of the range of her weapon. One shot. One chance.

Dissa spun around without breaking stride and without dropping Ivor. He let loose a dagger. Magen fired her one shot as the dagger slammed into her right shoulder.

A small round hole appeared in the forehead of Dissa's mask. He fell backward. His spine flopped around on the deck of the desecrated temple. Amazingly, he wasn't dead.

The seizure action of his spine eased up. Signaling frantically to Magen, Dissa pointed to his mouth. Teetering on the edge of life, a bullet in his brain, he wanted to tell Magen something. He had one secret to share before passing on. He was frantic about it, insistent. She raced to his side.

She knew what he wanted to say. He wanted to tell her how to find Adam. What else could it be? Staring God in the face, he wanted to atone. He was saying something. She couldn't hear over the crowd noise, but she could feel his breath blowing through his mouth hole. She struggled to pry off the golden mask; perhaps she could read his lips.

As she worked on the straps, she praised God, awed that even Dissa Banach could repent. Tears filled her eyes and rolled down her cheeks, gathering silver flake. She pulled loose the tiny buckles as quickly as she could. Both hands were clumsy now from her wounds.

Before she could finish, one of the Winter ushers tapped her on her wounded shoulder. He motioned for her to leave. She held up a single finger, her eyes begging to stay just for a moment longer. The usher shook his head, motioning over to the dais where bowmen stood beside the ruined ark of the covenant.

"You will have to leave," she read on his lips, "you have lost everything."

A gust of tremors swept over Dissa Banach's body and a great relaxation emptied his bladder.

# 8

## A CHAT WITH THE DEVIL

A great bell sounded. It was the only sound in the world—pealing over the outer reaches of Chev's awareness. It rang loud and clear. It rang like pain.

Then, in the center of the ringing, there was a scream. A woman was screaming in terror and despair. Veil was screaming inside his head, screaming for help.

Unsteadily, tentatively, he hauled himself upright and searched the crowded horizons for an escape route. He caught sight of Dissa Banach lying dead on the ballroom floor. This was no time to gloat—Veil was in trouble.

The mental scream sounded again, and Chev pushed through the crowd. He paused briefly in the outer lobby to retrieve his furs, then charged into the cold outside.

The snow was deep and dry. Veil was still calling to him. Not Magen. Not anybody else. She was calling to him. His mouth began to crook in a half-conscious, self-satisfied smirk, but his lips immediately retreated into a neutral expression as pain from his broken nose rebounded across his face.

Thinking of Veil spurred him on. Boots pounding, he trudged through the snow. The air burned his throat, and cracked open chapped fissures on his lips. He couldn't breathe through his nose, yet he found power and balance thinking of Veil in danger and coming to her rescue.

Even at this level of frenzy, it would take him ten to fifteen minutes to reach the ship.

*Fine.*

Chev was out of the way for the time being.

*Magen.*

Ivor Purse turned his attention to Magen.

In the outer lobby of the Temple of Ice, Magen was patching the knife wound on her shoulder, slapping on a thick dermal patch. Then she rummaged through stacks of furs, searching for her own coat. For a moment, she considered walking out with nothing but her slim garments and letting the wind numb her to all her pain.

She found her coat buried at the bottom of the stack. She felt eyes upon her and became suddenly self-conscious of being almost naked. Self-conscious and ashamed. Out of habit, out of instinct, she held the coat to the light and scanned the seams for signs of tampering. Five viper beetles scuttled out of the sleeves. For a dangerous moment, she paused to admire their shimmering beauty, their green metallic armor wrought in intricate designs. Their barbed legs combed gently through forests of fur. Jewelry for the world to come.

She dropped the coat, plucked a slender dart from under her cap, then carefully impaled the bugs with the sharp tip. One by one, they crunched and leaked venom.

Had someone targeted her for a hit? The bugs could have been coincidental; there were enough of them crawling around in the crowd. Or perhaps the danger had not ended with Dissa's death. Perhaps she had walked into a trap after all.

After completing a slow, careful inspection, she donned her furs and headed outside. The feeling of being watched stayed with her.

Outside, she had to face the snow plane, dry and white as her despair. The locals shuffled about. Guns strapped to their shoulders, most of them were smoking tobacco as they policed the grounds.

There were three hills around the Temple of Ice, describing a triangle. They could have been man-made hills. Clusters of spaceships sat parked at the base of the hills, on ground level, following the triangle like an ornamental picket fence.

The sun had risen an hour ago and glare on the snow made it difficult to approximate the distance to the three hills. They were well out of range of ballistic weaponry, but not out of range of lasers. Magen thought she could make out nests of assassins at the peak of each hill. Paranoia, perhaps. Or perhaps despair. She had nothing to go on—odd crooked shadows, glints of colored light that could be sun on snow or sun on jeweled muzzles.

Magen lingered close to the Temple of Ice, venturing to the point she imagined to be the outermost fringes of the jammer field. She felt eyes upon her, perhaps eyes that peered through sniper scopes. Standing absolutely still, on the rim of safety, she dared her unseen observers to open fire. Perhaps the jammer field would be strong enough to dissolve any light shots. Perhaps it wouldn't. She yelled taunts. She just wanted to know if someone was out there, watching her.

Nothing happened.

She could not tarry forever on the edge of the jammer field. The snow plane was the avenue of departure. To death. Or to deliverance. The snow plane shined white and expansive and inviting. It reminded her of heaven in some obscure way, heaven surrounded by snipers.

She had no weapons left, except for the blow gun and darts under her hood. Despite the eloquence of her despair, she was not prepared to march into the crosshairs of a sniper scope, real or imagined—at least not until she found a weapon that had some range to it.

She ducked back into the temple lobby.

A local girl about Magen's height ambled past, a bored, mean look on her face, a double holster strapped around her waist. Magen whistled the girl down and offered her luxuriant furs and the cap of baby emeralds in exchange for a hand laser and something modest to keep warm. It was a deal heavily weighted in favor of the local girl, apart from the fact that Magen was dressing her as a decoy.

"I dunno . . ." the girl muttered, her eyes sequined with transplanted fish scales, her fingertips and lips stained blue and amber from cadmadine and tobacco. The deal was too good to be true. "Gimme a minute. . . ."

Magen's conscience nagged at her. The girl had never done Magen any harm. Why should she go to death in Magen's place?

Why? Because it was the only way out of this trap. The locals wouldn't pay any attention to a lone offworlder shot down on the snow plane—but one of their own was a different matter. They would storm the hills and Magen could escape in the confusion. If, by chance, there were no killers waiting on the hills, then the girl would be richer by one fine fur coat and a cap of baby emeralds. The girl might end up with the better end of the bargain, and Magen had no other way to escape.

Voices nagged at her inside her head. One voice told her to face her fate on the snow, even if it meant death. It told her to spare the girl. But the voice of her conscience sounded so much like the voice of the Devil, she chose to disregard it. She chose survival at any cost. Maybe the assassins weren't real anyway.

In the end, greed got the better of the girl. She donned Magen's cap and furs and headed outside. Magen followed at a stalker's distance. The voices in her head had grown silent. The local girl paused at the fringes of the jammer field, just for a moment, and shot a backward glance at Magen. The girl's sequined eyes shone listless, despite their glitter, indifferent, jaded.

Magen felt suddenly sorry for the girl dressed as a decoy. The voice of Magen's conscience had grown silent, and there was nothing left to rebel against. She felt a deep, impenetrable regret.

"Don't go!" shouted Magen.

"You want to back out of our deal?"

"Yes."

"Too late."

The girl spun around. Slowly, she ventured onto the snow plane, swaying her hips in mockery, stumbling occasionally from intoxication. She crossed the dazzling white from one end to the other.

No lights flashed. No one died.

The girl crossed under the hills and continued beyond. By this time, Chev had reached the waiting spaceship.

Ivor Purse was about to turn his focus away from Magen and back to Chev when Chadwick Hubbel laid a hand gently on his shoulder. Hubbel said, "Tell the men on the hills to monitor Hirsch and Carson and to interrupt if there's a material change in their positions. Then take a five-minute break, so you don't burn yourself out."

Ivor's eyes rolled back for another half-minute; then he slackened his shoulders. He had been performing incredible mental feats all night long. He was tired. The cold ate at him despite the state-of-the-art heaters in Hubbel's ship. It had been a very long night. He would have dropped from exhaustion before now if it hadn't been for the stimulants and the naked thrill of synergistic artistry he and Hubbel shared when they toyed with lesser beings.

He took particular delight in fooling Veil, in keeping her blocked for most of the evening and feeding her contrived sense impressions. Ivor enjoyed masquerading as the voice of Magen's conscience, as the ghost of Amelia's mother when he invaded Amelia's dreams, and most of all, he loved masquerading as Veil.

Ivor had the power. Hubbel provided genius and subtlety to the game.

At last Ivor had ended his years of false loyalty to Dissa Banach. He felt relieved and free just to have Hubbel close by. The two of them had grown up together, friends ever since they shared the attentions of a common nanny in bod kid-care. They were bod kin in the profoundest sense. Ivor had been Hubbel's man all along. His woman, too. Not that Hubbel ever had any sexual interest in his own gender. Ever the transvestite, Ivor kept at hand a wardrobe of woman slaves, stunning creatures he could inhabit whenever the mood was right.

When reconnoitering in Amelia's dreams, Ivor couldn't resist the temptation to pick her subconscious for erotic tips on pleasing Hubbel. Amelia had been one of Hubbel's favorites—Ivor could tell by the way he went out of his way to keep her protected. Ivor grew jealous at the way Hubbel had insured that Amelia would be too sick to come to the Winter World. Amelia was to be spared any danger, while Ivor was thrust in the thick of it.

So far, Hubbel's scheme had been working well. With calculated false signals, Ivor and Hubbel had tricked Magen into killing Dissa Banach. That was step one. They had almost succeeded at step two, which was killing Magen. Ivor had almost convinced her to step out of the jammer field, into the gun sights of the snipers waiting atop the hills. But he and Hubbel had miscalculated the girl's instincts, her natural paranoia and contrariness.

Well, they both were tired and entitled to make a few mistakes.

"She was very close to suicidal ideation back there," said Ivor, sniffing the cologne rising from Hubbel's furs. "I think we should tell her the truth about her husband. I think that would push her over the edge. She'll do our work for us."

Hubbel shook his head. "It seems part of her pathology to find cause for hope where others would be inclined to give up. She is too volatile right now. The truth could drive her over the edge, as you say, or it could create a monster."

Hubbel handed Ivor three small pills that looked like teddy bear eyes. Ivor let them dissolve on his tongue, tasting the salt from Hubbel's palm with the bitter medicinal tang. Hubbel popped three pills into his own mouth and chewed them.

*Chev.*

Chev clambered up the side ladder of the spacecraft. He paused for a moment to check his weaponry before charging inside, but he caught the sight of his smeared nose reflected on the gleaming friction sheath. He couldn't stand the thought of looking less than handsome in front of Veil, even when rescuing her. Firmly gripping the cracked perpendicular plate of his nose, he tugged it back into a warped approximation of its prior position. Dried clots broke loose. Blood gushed from his nostrils. With no time left for vanity, he pulled open the airlock and slid through the narrow passage.

Slowly, he manipulated the last door separating him from Veil. Noiselessly, it opened.

Inside, it was absolutely quiet.

Chev stalked through the cramped corridors, through the oppressive silence. Wary of announcing his presence, he made no sound himself, even though there were no visible signs of violence within the craft. A shiver crept up

Chev's nerve endings. He could not shake the oppressive chill of winter.

Veil's cabin door stood ajar, opened just a crack. He cautiously approached. Veil's scents drifted down the hall, the smell of bleach on her linens, the unperfumed detergents she used to cleanse her skin, and more—the acid smell of female terror. He could hear her breathing rapidly. He could almost hear her heart pounding.

He kicked open the door and wheeled inside, gripping a gun in one hand and a knife in the other. Veil screamed.

Chev spun around, searching the room. They were alone. Veil stopped screaming.

She sat cross-legged on the ground, covered with tiny tridents. She had wrapped Universalist rosaries around her head until it looked as if she were wearing a veil of thorns. She trembled like a fever victim, and the beads clattered softly.

"The Devil," she said.

'Where?''

"There!" She pointed to a cluster of the darkness in the corner. Chev pitched his knife in that direction. It struck hard wood with a resonating note.

"No Devil in there," he said.

"There," she said, this time pointing to his forehead.

He grinned, hit the side of his head in burlesque, as if to knock the Devil out through his left ear. "No Devil in there either."

"Don't make fun of me," said Veil. "This is real. The devil is real, nearby. He is very close to Magen right now, very close to you. I don't know why I didn't see it before."

"Calm down. I am here now. I won't let anyone hurt you."

"I don't need your kind of shelter. Go away. Go find Magen. She is the one who needs your help. She is in terrible danger."

"No. Everything is all right. Dissa Banach is dead. I saw his corpse. Our mission here is a success."

"We weren't supposed to kill him."

He stopped and thought a moment. After two years of living free and unincorp, he still measured success in merc terms. The winner is the one who walks away, and the loser is the one left lying in a bed of piss. But Veil was right, and he remembered, with a touch of embarrassment, that their mission had nothing to do with assassination.

"Where's Magen? In what way is she in trouble?"

Veil closed her eyes and tried to concentrate. She strained herself, eyelids gathering in tight wrinkled bunches. Beads of sweat shined beneath the tangle of tridents obscuring her face. When she opened her eyes, they were full of astonishment. "I don't know."

"I'll see if I can find her."

"Don't go." The words came clearly, in beautiful seductive tones, not from her lips, but directly into Chev's brain. Confused, he turned and looked into her eyes.

"I'll stay if you want," said Chev.

"Magen needs you." Veil's beads continued to clatter from her trembling.

"All right, then."

"Magen needs you, but I want you." Again, not from her lips. "Listen to me—don't listen to me."

He smiled. He sat down beside her and took her hand into his. "You're confused, that's all."

She tried to pull her hand away, but he held it fast.

He continued, "You just don't want to admit how bad you're scared. That's OK. You need me more than Magen does. Magen can take care of herself."

Veil's hand was growing slippery with sweat. The more she wriggled, the wetter their contact. It sent waves of thrill through Chev's glands.

"The Devil," hissed Veil.

Ivor smiled. He liked this masquerade. He liked parading in horns and terrifying virgins. Just as he was starting to savor the seduction, Hubbel shook him. The snipers on the hill had lost sight of Magen Hirsch.

Ivor was irritated at having to drop, even for a moment, this wickedly delicious amusement—but he disengaged from Chev's consciousness and scanned the snow for Magen. He found her quickly, but he couldn't place her. The entire visual field was white. There were no definite tactile sensations; overwhelming cold and numbness. Cold stabbing through the cheap unincorp thermal coat. Nothing but cold and white.

Ivor said, "I think she's burrowing through the snow."

"What's she planning?" asked Hubbel.

"Shit! Her thoughts are all gibberish. No language I've ever heard. Either she's decompensating, or she's deliberately trying to block me out."

"She's probably thinking in Hebrew. Shit! She's on to you, Ivor. You laid it on too thick when she spotted the snipers."

"That was your fault."

"No. You weren't listening to my directions. I say we abort the rest of the operation. It hasn't been a total failure. At least Dissa is dead. Let's head home."

"Not yet. Please."

"We blew it. Too risky now."

"I'm having too much fun. Anyway, how is it risky? We're okay here, Chad. She can't find us, you know—how would she pick this ship out from all the others? Besides, the snipers will nail her. She's all alone out there, in the snow. Nothing but a handgun, probably local make without much punch. I can keep Chev and Veil 'occupied.' Where's the risk?"

Hubbel smiled indulgently. "You know me. I prefer the conservative approach."

"Just because Dissa is gone doesn't mean that you'll

get promoted. Bringing back the girl's corpse will clinch it, though. That's what we came for in the first place. We're only half-done."

Hubbel grunted. He knew it was useless to argue with Ivor at this point. Ivor had become fixated. He didn't care about Magen Hirsch, or Hubbel's advancement in the bod. He was after Veil.

Hubbel retreated up to the viewscreens to keep visual contact with the snipers.

Ivor slipped back into Chev.

By this time Veil had managed to get her hand loose from Chev's grip. She crammed herself into a corner and hugged her legs to her chest. Chev sat on the floor, directly in front of her. He kept a safe distance away. She had stung him with a mental bolt to make him release her hand. He kept her cornered, though. No way around him.

They seemed so very alone. Chev was trying to make sense of all the mixed signals he had been getting from Veil. Her strange responses to him when they first met, her willingness to come to the Winter World with him, the way Amelia took ill beset by bad dreams, blaming Veil, and the whisperings in his mind, the soft seductive urging that might be subconscious pleas for attention.

The mental bolt she had used to slap him when he wouldn't let go—it hadn't been so bad. She was capable of much worse. It was as if she didn't really want to hurt him. As she sat huddled in her corner, shaking from head to toe, she seemed at war with unseen enemies. He guessed she was at war with herself, torn between the urging of flesh and the demands of her beliefs. He wanted to believe she was at war with herself over him.

"You really like me, don't you?" he asked.

"I don't believe in lying." A new wave of tremors shook her. "I do like you. I don't know why." Then she seemed to calm down. She felt trapped by Chev, and confession seemed to ease her struggles.

Ivor rejoiced. He couldn't have asked for a better answer for his purposes.

Amid Ivor's jubilation, he suddenly found himself shaken back into his actual surroundings, Hubbel pushing at his shoulders.

"What is your problem?" asked Ivor, his eyes slitting open.

"I have lost contact with the southeast hilltop. Can't raise anything on the video screens. Even reconnoitered outside and saw some blue flashes."

"The snipers are dead," said Ivor, matter-of-factly.

"Let's get the fuck out of here."

"I knew they were dead. Trust me, Chad. I will decide when we need to get the fuck out of here. I will let you know the minute any real danger threatens."

"Just don't get too distracted."

"I am in complete control." Ivor ate another teddy bear eye; then he returned to monitoring Chev.

"Maybe you think I'm handsome?" asked Chev.

Veil looked him right between his eyes. "Not so much with your nose broken."

"I'll have it fixed for you, any way you like it. I think you're beautiful. Even like this. I haven't changed what I said, you know, about loving you. Here's what I think, OK. I think you love me back. Your feelings are buried deep. I really think so. I guess you don't realize it, but you keep giving me these signals. . . ." He inched closer.

She looked away from him, her eyes settling on the patch of darkness where the knife had been thrown. "Don't touch me again. I swear next time I will do serious damage to you. I don't want to . . . but . . ."

"I want you," whispered Ivor, softly, very softly, almost subliminally, more to himself than to Chev. "You won't hurt me. I won't hurt you. We won't hurt each other."

Chev moved closer, slowly.

"I want you," Ivor whispered in perfect imitation of

Veil's cerebral voice. Then he worried he might be getting too bold, too obvious. The way things were going, he almost didn't have to say anything else to get his way.

She took a deep breath, prepared to strike. Chev braced. He knew she might hurt him, but at least she wouldn't kill him. He grabbed her hand again. Veil tensed, then tossed a spear of pure anguish at him.

His grip stayed firm. He smiled. No pain at all. "You don't know yourself. You don't know what you want," he said.

Ivor had deflected the mental bolt.

Veil knew at once that she hadn't hurt Chev, but she didn't know why. She tried to strike at him again. It didn't work; his smile lingered on his lips.

Amazed, disbelief spread over her features. Her blue eyes widened as she struck again and again with no results. She kept striking instinctively, with ineffectual blows, like a cornered, declawed cat.

Chev maintained his grip on her hand. Her bones were light and fragile, her flesh so soft.

"Why didn't you hurt me?" Chev asked.

"I tried," she said incredulously, "I really tried."

"You see, sometimes you just don't understand what you really want. I'm not going to hurt you. I want to make you feel good." Satisfied he could act with impunity, he crowded closer to her.

She trembled, moaned. He snaked his arm around her. He said, "Let me warm you. Let me hold you. Let me give you strength. You see, I just want you to feel good."

"Yes, yes," whispered Ivor. "Yes, yes, yes . . ."

Chev mistook Veil's trembling for passion, and unwound her layers of beads and tridents. Slowly, he exposed her face, wet with perspiration, then her neck, cords tensed, then one shoulder. He couldn't resist her any longer.

He leaned forward and pressed his lips to her fabulous

neck and traced a bulging vein with the tip of his tongue. He followed the trail of pulsing life all the way to her earlobe. She did not resist. She only trembled the way she had been trembling all night long. He took that as consent to continue, peeling back her robes with brazen familiarity.

He fell into the pattern of disrobing that had become routine between him and Amelia, until the sight of Veil's breasts startled him out of the routine. The linens Veil wore were so loose and formless, they obscured the contours of her shape. Chev had always assumed Veil's breasts would be full and ample, like Amelia's. But Veil's breasts were small. At first he was disappointed, but he couldn't take his eyes off her breasts. And when he looked at her face, her hands, her hair, her nipples, he realized how beautifully she was made, how all of her parts fit together to form an ethereal image of light and feminine fragility. He became fiercely aroused staring at her small breasts that were nothing like Amelia's. He cupped his hand over her nipples and felt that they were stiff. And he felt her tremble.

He had gone past any semblance of self-control, an animal cooking in a hormone stew. He expected her to stop fighting her instincts, to surrender to him. He waited.

She only trembled. Instead of reaching out to him, she seemed more withdrawn. Her eyes misted, making him feel base and undeserving.

"Don't stop, don't stop," whispered Ivor, as if Chev had the power to stop.

"God has abandoned me," gasped Veil.

Chev breathed a long, despairing sigh. She was still going on and on about this God business of hers. God, he couldn't understand it.

Peeling off his shirt, he felt waves of dry, oppressive heat on his skin, the ship's climate controls straining against winter. Weighted by his hologrammed belt, Chev's pants hit the ground. Carefully, he unwrapped the tongs of his scrotal shield and flung it aside. It landed near the knife, clattering in the Devil-haunted shadows.

He told himself, There is no stopping now. If she can see the future, she knows what will happen next. He took her face into his hands. Surrounding her mouth with his own, he took a deep taste.

She choked as she pulled away, wiping crusts of dried blood from her lips.

"I'm sorry," he said. Her undergarments twisted in his fingers as he jerked them loose.

Ivor nestled closer, trying to sample Chev's desire.

Ivor felt a slap across his face. Hubbel had to hit him hard to bring him back to awareness.

Ivor responded with a hypnotic stab at Hubbel's genitals that brought excruciating pain. Hubbel fell to his knees, screaming.

"Don't disturb me again," hissed Ivor. "Do I make myself clear?"

"The north hill is under attack," gasped Hubbel. "I can see it clearly from the portholes."

"Was under attack. Don't worry, she didn't get any prisoners. The snipers are all dead. We are still safe. Let me be the judge of the proper time to panic."

"Ivor, you're becoming obsessed."

"If you interrupt again, Chad, you will be very sorry. On the other hand, if you don't interrupt anymore, I will find some suitable reward for your patience. Stay cool. Be brave. Have faith."

Ivor returned to Chev's thoughts just in time. Veil was saying, "If you love me, as you say, please . . . don't . . ."

Ivor whispered, "I need to be conquered. I need someone strong to reach the inner me. I need someone strong inside of me."

Chev pulled her naked body next to his. The sensations astounded him, skin on skin, silk on silk.

"If you love me . . ." she repeated.

"This is the only way I can reach you," Chev said. "There's a part of you calling out to me. It is like you keep it locked up and it wants to be set free. This is the only way you can be free, Veil. I wish you wouldn't make it so difficult. I wish you'd stop fighting yourself . . . and I wish you would reach out to me. Can't you feel how bad I need you?"

Veil closed her eyes. "The Devil," she said.

"No," Chev insisted. "Cut out this bullshit. It is not the Devil in you. It is your own self."

Veil grabbed at the trident rosaries on the floor. Holding bunches in each hand, she struck at Chev. Strings of beads whipped his face. Veil's eyes rolled back into her head. Babbling indistinct phrases about the Devil and salvation, she lashed out in terror at Chev's embrace. But he held tight. He was so very strong and she was so very weak, unexpectedly stripped of her defenses.

Seeing the hopelessness of her situation, she gave up. She knew she couldn't win this battle on the physical plane, so she sank deep into herself. Even if God would not grant her rescue, he would provide a balm. Absolute terror gave rise to a profoundly deep spiritual trance. Veil entered hidden realms of being, plunging all the way to the bottom of memories, to pre-life. Instead of finding the void she expected, she found God. An untainted shaft of light shone upon her. A golden glow entered her body. God had not abandoned her after all, and his rapture shook her nervous system. Light shot through her mind, her body, and her soul, thunderous light illuminating tunnels in the hidden realms of being. Sanctifying light. God made her his vessel and let loose his power. And she knew the ecstasy of being one with God. And she felt his power as streams of prayer spun from her lips. This glorious contact. And she knew that God was not a casual observer, not a benign ruler of a laissez-faire universe. He shared his power with his faithful, his vessels.

The power of God was inside Veil, moving inside her. God cared. God loved her after all. And there was a great blister of fire that burst and raptured. And a river of light. She saw the Devil screaming before her, screaming as he fled from Chev's body. The Devil was on fire. Through a mask of flame, Veil saw her own face, in agony. The Devil had stolen her face, to mock her. But he was leaving, now. He could not stand the power of the Lord, which had been sifted through Veil.

And then it was over.

She opened her eyes to find Chev moaning on the ground a few feet away from her. He shivered, from the cold or from shock. His eyes were dull and exhausted. One of the rosaries had caught on his ear and the trident tangled in his hair. He would recover momentarily. It seemed that all was well: she had not harmed him, and he had not harmed her. It wasn't his fault, not entirely. Chev had been possessed by the Devil, but he was free now. Saved, now. They had both been saved from the Devil.

Veil had exorcised him.


Chadwick Hubbel glanced nervously from the phosphorescent video screen on the console of the ship to the windows and the snow outside. He watched the last remaining hill, the final stronghold of his retained snipers. No obvious signs of battle appeared. No lasers flashed. He could only see the hill and the indistinct forms on top. The wind smeared the sky with snow.

Hubbel hadn't really expected to see gunfire on this last hill. Magen had failed to take a prisoner during the last two engagements, on the other hills. Without a prisoner, someone to interrogate, she wouldn't be able to pinpoint his location. She would be far more cautious in her approach to the last hill.

Hubbel knew he could not rely on his snipers to keep

quiet, especially this far from the Summer World, with the option of going unincorp only a few feet away. Staring down the barrel of Magen's gun, they'd reveal all; perhaps they would even escort her to his doorstep.

So Hubbel watched the hill, even though he took no comfort in his vigil. Blue flashes would signal danger, but the absence of flashes did not guarantee safety. He was desperate to flee the Winter World. Direct confrontation was not Hubbel's style. Unfortunately, he feared retaliation from Ivor more than he feared Magen. Trapped between two fears, he tried to calm himself down. He rummaged through his catalogue of psychological tricks to clear his own head. He couldn't. He feared he would worry his ulcer to the point of perforation.

Faith. Ivor was capable of near omniscience at times, as long as he didn't let his odd obsessions get the better of him.

Hubbel listened to the drone of the heat controls. He watched the hill and saw nothing but the action of the wind and the blurring of the snow. The hill seemed quiet and empty. The white nothingness frightened him now. All of his faith in Ivor vanished in a single moment of watching wind sweep snow. A dull ache glowed slightly to the left of his navel.

Cold air suddenly cut through waves of artificially dry heat. The chilled current breathed over Hubbel's scalp and constricted his hair follicles. He shuddered.

What had chilled the air? Was it a momentary lapse in the climate controls? A power outage? A faulty circuit? Was it a prank played by Ivor to test his faith?

Hubbel knew what the current of cold air meant. A breach in the ship's security, a hatchway or porthole pried open long enough to let an intruder climb in.

He waited for a moment. He strained his ears, but heard no sounds. He decided he couldn't trust Ivor any longer. Ivor had been too intent on a matter that had nothing to do with their mission. He was too preoccupied with competing with Veil.

Scampering down the hatchway, Hubbel armed his handgun. He let go of his faith in Ivor and felt liberated.

Hubbel found Ivor sitting upright, his eyes closed. His face mirrored Veil's—the high cheekbones, the delicate nose, the pale skin, the silken, platinum hair. He could have been Veil's brother. Ivor breathed regularly, but with a harsh rasp on inspiration. At peace, his androgynous face seemed drained of masculinity. He looked almost exactly like Veil, now. Perhaps that was the reason for his sexual preoccupation with her. Perhaps that was why he despised her.

Hubbel sternly shook Ivor and got no response. He slapped Ivor hard. A thin stream of blood-tinged vomitus trickled out of Ivor's nostril. Hubbel pried open Ivor's eyelids. The pupils were blown.

Ivor was still breathing, but the rasp was probably aspiration pneumonia. Cerebral death was probable. Clearly, this wasn't Magen Hirsch's doing. She could never have gotten this close to Ivor without being detected. No, this was something Veil had done. He had warned Ivor about toying with Veil.

Hubbel couldn't tell how long Ivor had been braindead. He had no way of knowing how long the ship had been unguarded. He scrambled for the intercom, found the microphone, and calmly began to broadcast through the overhead speakers.

"Magen Hirsch, I know you are on board," Hubbel said. "You are angry, I know, but I have something to offer as an alternative to a showdown. I know where to find your husband. I will trade that information for my life."

"I don't believe you." Magen's voice echoed through the cabin.

Where was she? In the shadows? In the walls?

"I tried to find your husband, but Dissa kept him hidden from me, from the entire bod. I didn't know where he was until last night, I swear to you. Dissa was trying to tell you with his dying breath. You couldn't hear what he was saying, but Ivor read his mind. Ivor told me. I will tell you in exchange for your promise to let me go free. Do we have a deal?"

"Maybe. It depends on what you say."

"Uh-uh. I have to have your word up front."

"You want I should trade you something when I don't know what I am getting?"

"You won't be happy with what I have to say. Your husband is alive, but I expect you will be angry about where Dissa put him. I have to have your promise. I have nothing else to offer."

"I give you two promises. One, I don't hurt you now if you tell. Two, if you lie, I hunt you down later."

"Fair enough. Dissa sent your husband to Abaddon."

"You are a lying bastard and I am going to kill you anyway."

"You gave your word."

"You think to send me someplace I can't ever come back from. I see through your tricks."

"You gave your word. I gave you the truth, ugly as it is."

A long silence followed. Then the echoes said, "This is what Dissa Banach tried to tell me?"

"Yes. For revenge." Try as he might, Hubbel could not hold back a chuckle. He shut his eyes, expecting her anger to explode, expecting the chuckle to cost him his life. He debated peeling off a shot in the direction of the echoes, but he decided against it. Better to take his chances with the bargain he had struck than to risk renegotiation.

He stood motionless, waiting, afraid to do anything that would startle Magen, or further provoke her. He did not even move after he felt a second blast of cold air in his face, a token of her going out. It could have been a trick, a ploy to make him give up an unsuspected advantage, to lure him into the open. He stood like a statue, listening to the rasp of Ivor's breathing until Ivor's windpipe finally occluded and no sounds followed.

# 9

## THE DAY OF ATONEMENT

All the way back to the Autumn World, Veil sat in a well-lit corner, an enigmatic smile on her face. She felt closer to God and all of his manifestations than she had ever felt before. Traveling through a void, she was awash in God's love, embraced as part of his plan, no longer alone and groping in the darkness for clues to verify the tenets of her faith. She thanked God for emerging from his hiding place to save her, an actual rescue, not an opiate of faith.

She found meaning in the simple wonders around her: the chromatics of reflected starlight playing across her linens, the reassurance of warmth in her fingertips, the music of three lives breathing, the darkness outside the ship's portholes, granulated with light for the benefit of man, to guide the way. Space travel seemed miraculous to her—floating in a bubble, wrapped in a fragile skin of steel. It would not take much to burst this bubble, a wayward meteorite, an undetected flaw in the friction sheath. And yet the ship endured. It crossed between points of gravity, defying the void. The ship was wondrously made.

Chev sulked in a corner. Veil wanted to take him aside, to preach the good words to him, to let him know he was loved and forgiven—but she couldn't tell if the time was right. She resisted the temptation to look into his thoughts, partially out of respect for his privacy, partially out of fear of what she might find lurking beneath his dark mood. If she waited, the time would come. Someday, he would be ready to talk to her about God. She was certain the right time would come.

She wondered about her earlier premonitions, the flash insights that warned her about Chev. Why had they not come to pass?

She came to the conclusion that God does not fix the destinies of men like a primitive computer program. God does not ordain the future, nor does he control it; rather, as the future unfolds, it unfolds into God. The Devil had brought her to the brink of disaster, trying to make her renounce the light. But instead of making her faith falter, it made her faith grow. Like Isaac under the knife, she was spared and given a new covenant.

The disasters she had foreseen for herself were merely landmarks, points along a dangerous road where she could steer her own course. She had the power to avert those disasters now; all it took was faith.

Then she felt Magen's despair. It drifted over her consciousness like a thunderhead. Veil felt Magen touch her shoulder.

Before Magen could speak, Veil asked, "How can I help you?"

"Chadwick Hubbel told me that Adam is on Abaddon. Can you tell me if it is true?"

Veil ventured a look in the future. It was all grey. The future had vanished. She looked harder and could see nothing, not even grey now, not even black. Not even emptiness. At first Veil panicked, a dead end in her future sight. Perhaps her death was near after all. But she calmed herself quickly, remembering her recent rapture. There were explanations other than death. Perhaps the future had been jolted by her change of destiny on the Winter World. Perhaps it was in a state of chaos and not yet congealed. Or perhaps she had lost her future sight all together. Perhaps that was the price of freedom— uncertainty.

Or perhaps this absence of vision was Abaddon. Little was known about Abaddon. It was said to be a planet or a moon, but no one was sure. No one had ever returned. And it yielded no data. They couldn't even measure it from afar. In the telescope, it appeared as a grey smear in space. Probes vanished within its depths. Even the council could not penetrate its mysteries. It wasn't a black hole. They didn't know what it was. Perhaps the nothingness Veil had seen was Abaddon. She couldn't say for certain, but it seemed credible.

Veil said, "I believe Hubbel was telling the truth."

Chev turned to Veil and asked, "Do you realize where you are sending Magen? She will go any place where you say she can find her husband. You know her."

Before Veil could respond, Magen interrupted, "What is so terrible if I go to Abaddon?"

"Do you know what you're in for?"

"No one does. There are stories. I heard them too. But no one really knows about Abaddon."

"That isn't so," Chev said. "There are some factions of the bods that come and go all the time. Dawson has been to Abaddon. That's where they rewired his brain. There used to be a slave-processing plant there, where they did the worst kinds of flesh and nerve manipulations. Dawson said that everyone on Abaddon is crazy. Everything there is unreal, like something out of a nightmare. He couldn't even process most of what he saw.

"Dawson told this one story about someone who got shot through the heart by one of the guards. The guy wouldn't die. His hair fell out, his skin blackened and shriveled, his teeth and eyes fell out, but he still didn't die. They cut off his head to put him out of his misery, but the head didn't die either. They set him on fire, and he kept on screaming. The fire wouldn't burn him up. The flames kept on crackling and the guy kept on screaming. Then they tried to put out the fire, but they couldn't."

"Yes, yes. I've heard things like that. This story is stupid. I don't believe it at all."

"I didn't either. But Dawson played a tape of it from his memory circuits. It is true. Ask Amelia. So if your husband is on Abaddon, you should forget him. Better dead—really dead—than on Abaddon. Dawson said Abaddon is Hell. Nothing there but misery and suffering."

Magen wore a deep, thoughtful expression. "If Adam is suffering, that is all the more reason I should go to him."

"I should have never spoken," said Veil. "I fear I have done something wrong."

"What else could you do? Lie? It is not your way," said Magen.

Veil blushed. She hadn't realized that she told an untruth until that moment. Not that it was entirely untrue. She said that she believed Hubbel, and that was true enough—except for the implications. Believing that Adam was alive on Abaddon was better than believing that her own death was near. She wanted to believe that Magen and her husband would somehow be reunited.

Something had happened to Veil on the Winter World. Something had changed her. The failure of her powers of future sight instilled a need for optimism, a need to believe that the future she could no longer divine would be better than the present. And this need had tricked her into a lie. A small lie. A grey lie, but one with potentially disastrous consequences.

Veil said slowly, "I told you I believed Hubbel. I did. That was my mistake. My belief was not based on anything special, Magen. I haven't any visions. I haven't read his mind. The truth is, I don't know anything about how to find your husband."

Magen raised an eyebrow. "Veil, you don't expect me to believe this now. Don't worry about putting me in danger. I can handle the danger."

"I was telling the truth."

"Which time?"

Veil burst into tears.

Chev pointed a rigid finger in Magen's face. "You're a rare bitch," he said.

Magen replied, "I am sorry if I hurt your feelings, Veil. I am just trying to decide what to do."

Chev started to put his arm around Veil for comfort, but he held himself back. He bowed his head.

"I am so sorry," said Veil. "I have so many feelings I never felt before. Good feelings, happy feelings. But I am confused. I don't even know why I am crying." Carefully, Veil collected herself and her thoughts. "I have made some mistakes, Magen. I am exhausted, though I may not seem it. My spirit buoys, and this gives the illusion of energy. Over the past days, I have spent my resources in your service—so do not blame me overmuch if I stumble and waver now. I don't seem to be able to see the future, right now. I can't even read minds, I am so tired."

Magen looked away, tense strands of muscle strumming along her jaw. "I am just so angry about this Abaddon business, I don't think about what I say. I am tired too."

"I don't know whether or not your husband was sent to

Abaddon. The council doesn't know either, and can't find out. If I have put you on the course to Abaddon by carelessly speaking, I am sorry. I did not mean that result. On reflection, I think you should not go there. I wouldn't trust any intelligence delivered by Hubbel."

"He was too afraid to lie."

"It might have been an act. He lies well."

Magen folded her arms across her chest. "Maybe I cannot read minds—but I know my enemies, probably better than I know my friends. Hubbel wasn't lying."

Veil continued, "Your best destiny lies on the Autumn World, continuing the fight against slavery. Not on Abaddon. Slavery is the worst of all blasphemies. Even the council didn't realize that until you showed them. We must continue to oppose Olagy and his machinery. How can we if you go to Abaddon? Perhaps this fight will not bring your husband back—but it is the right thing to do. I say this without the benefit of future sight. In this counsel, I am groping as all people grope, guided only by moral sense and friendship."

"I grope too. I have to do this thing."

"Magen, don't you realize that this is exactly what Hubbel wants. The council will never be able to carry on the fight against slavery without you."

"I am not fighting for the council. I only do this for Adam."

"No one among our ranks has the skill to replace you. It comes to this, Magen—do you want to be part of something worthy and moral, or do you want to go to Hell?"

Magen shuddered, and that was her answer.

Chev pounded a fist into the interior hull, to attract attention. The walls buzzed. He said, "Magen's not so great as you're making out. Lots of people could do a better job. I'm just speaking as a professional. I could do a better job."

"You don't understand, Chev," said Veil, trying to dismiss him.

"I'm better than she is, you know."

"I don't want to argue about who is better. Stop being petty and full of pride, for once, Chev."

He cast her a wounded look. "I was saying I'd take her place, if it is really that important to you. I'm better than she is—why don't you want me?"

Veil looked startled.

Magen started to laugh. "Don't you understand, Chev? Veil was saying these things mostly to talk me from going to Abaddon. She does this out of friendship, I think. She doesn't need someone like you around. Besides, Amelia would never agree."

"Fuck Amelia. I'm not her slave."

"It seems we will need someone, since Magen is determined to leave. I never expected you to volunteer. Why, Chev? Why would you want to do such a thing?"

Chev's lips tightened. "I just want you happy," he said. Veil stepped to one side, so that she could catch his gaze. He threw up his hands defensively, hiding his face. "Please, don't look into my mind. Please . . ."

"I couldn't, even if I wanted to." Now he stopped looking away from her and met her eyes. Veil looked at Chev carefully, truly seeing him for the first time since they had entered the ship. His face had changed profoundly; more than just the red-rimmed exhaustion in his eyes, more than the broken, blood-caked nose. He seemed almost a different person. No hint of the old lusts when he returned her gaze; they had been replaced by a look of sincere concern. What had wrought this amazing change? Was it the exorcism she had performed? Had she driven out all of this man's devils?

Veil wondered why she had not seen the change in him sooner. She cleared her throat, blinking. "I would be honored if you would fight for our cause."

Magen's eyes narrowed. "I'll tell you what he is really after, Veil."

Veil said, "It doesn't matter to me why a person chooses a moral course of action. I think he really means well."

"I do."


Amelia missed Chev far more than she expected. Something about his being in danger made him more precious. And jealousy over Veil worried her, too. What a bitter yet exciting sensation jealousy proved to be.

Over the passing days, Amelia had prepared for Chev's return. Their bags were packed, and waiting by the door. She applied less makeup than usual; she didn't need as much. She managed to shrug off the last vestiges of cadmadine addiction and exercised herself firm enough to slip into something very scanty, but she resisted the urge to be obvious. There was a chill in the air. And suppose Chev didn't survive the mission? She didn't want to be left standing half-naked in front of Veil and Magen and all of those slaves, a weeping spectacle of grief and unfulfilled desire. Instead, she tugged on one of her old black leather outfits, something suitable for either seduction, travel, or mourning—whatever the occasion would require when the ship returned from the Winter World.

When she heard the free slaves chattering excitedly, she went outside. Though her bags were heavy and cumbersome, she took them with her, so that there would be no reason to ever return to this dreary bungalow. The time had come to depart this primitive place and return to the comforts of technology.

In the distance, she heard the caterwaul of a rocket landing. The eager flow of free slaves rushing to meet their priestess swept Amelia through the alleys of the village.

By the time Amelia reached the runway, Chev was

jumping from the bottom rung of the deplaning ladder. Magen and Veil lingered above him, hesitating to climb down, obviously keeping their distance from the imminent reunion, trying hard not to look like spectators. The gathered throng of free slaves was less polite.

Amelia broke into a large smile, relieved that she had not been widowed. She expected to see reciprocal joy in Chev, but he wore a fixed, blank expression. Not an expression of disinterest, or boredom, but rather a show of intense concentration masquerading as distraction. The kind of look men don to show off how well they can tolerate pain. He was hiding something, some wound or guilty secret.

"The mission didn't go well, I take it. Dissa escaped you?"

"He's dead. It didn't go well at all."

"Let's not spoil this moment," said Amelia. "You can tell me the details once we're in space. I am anxious to be gone from this planet."

"I'm not leaving."

"We've been here long enough. Our purpose has been served, regardless of the outcome for Magen. Let's go."

Chev cleared his throat. But even with his throat clear, he couldn't speak. Amelia waited. After several grunts, false starts, Chev said, "Magen is going to Abaddon. I am staying here, to take her place."

Amelia stood stunned and disbelieving. After a moment to digest the news, she said, "I don't know which of you is the greater fool."

"Don't ask me to explain. You wouldn't understand."

"I understand very well. Something happened between you and Veil." A tremor shook through Amelia's face. She was determined not to cry over Chev. There was too large an audience around: hundreds of wide-eyed slaves, and Magen. And Veil.

"It isn't what you think."

"What is it then? This God nonsense?"

"No. Not that. I just have to do this. I have to help Veil."

"Why?"

He stared at her, warily, for a full minute, as if the word had been an exposed dagger. Amelia gritted her teeth. "I know why." She glanced off in the distance, to where Veil stood, scarves, linens, and pale hair flapping around her young form. She couldn't believe that a perpetual challenge would interest Chev as much as perpetual gratification. Chev was a creature of appetite. But it seemed the sport of the matter appealed to him more, for the moment. How could Amelia hope to compete with this young, unreachable beauty?

"Not that. I don't even want to touch her. Not ever again. I don't want to touch anyone." There was a hint of disgust in his voice. He shivered.

What was wrong? She couldn't fathom the motivations for his sudden change, couldn't read past his lack of expression. This was not the man she knew.

"She's controlling you. Using her mind powers to bend you to her own purposes."

"I made this choice on my own."

"You wouldn't know if she was controlling you or not. She might not even know it."

Suddenly his hand was at her throat, so fast she hadn't seen it. He gently stroked the blood vessels pulsing there, a gesture of affection, or a threat. "I wish she were forcing me to this. Maybe that would make it easier. If she tried to force me, I'd let her force me. It doesn't matter why I'm doing this. So stop asking."

She had hit a tender spot. Up to this point, she'd felt helpless and disadvantaged before him, taken by surprise. For the first time in their relationship, she couldn't outmaneuver him. But she had hit upon a weakness here. A secret he was keeping. Something he didn't even want to think about. The reason behind the decision. That was what he was dodging. That was the reason he tried to cut the discussion short. The reason why. Why he would give up Amelia. Why he would take up Magen's fight. Why he would swear to never touch Veil again. *Why.*

Amelia looked him in the eye, even though his fingers were still at her throat. "You're not staying here because you prefer her to me, right?"

He nodded sullenly.

"This isn't a contest for your love. You really meant it when you said you never wanted to touch her again. Am I right?"

He nodded again.

"Where did you touch her the first time?"

His eyes widened. He looked trapped. His grip tightened on her neck.

"Go ahead. Kill me."

He released her throat.

"Do you want to tell me about it? This secret you're hiding."

"I can't talk about it. I can't even think it."

"If you don't tell me, she will. She never lies."

"Don't go to her. Please."

"Where did you touch her? How many times? I want details." Then cold, painful realization slid into her chest. She felt stabbed by the psychic resonance of his infidelity. "You fucked her."

"No."

"You did. I can see it in your eyes. I can feel it in my heart. I am too close to you, Chev. I know."

"No." His voice sounded weak, frightened, unconvincing.

"I'll kill her."

He grabbed her hands and squeezed. Then he drew her close, his arms trapping her body against his. His desperate muscles threatened her with their strength. He took a nervous glance in Veil's direction, hoping that she was still unable to read minds—whether from exhaustion, as she claimed . . . or perhaps because of what he had done. He wanted to keep it a secret, this terrible thing. But he couldn't. Amelia was forcing the issue. She had tricked him and caught him in his own lies. Confession would be the only way to protect Veil from Amelia's questions. He whispered into her imprisoned ear. "Don't tell anyone. Don't even think it. She doesn't know."

"What is this bullshit?"

"I thought it would be beautiful. I thought she wanted me. But she didn't. She really didn't. It was horrible. She went into some kind of trance when I did it." Ever so softly, he said, "I raped her. While she was tranced out. I raped her. She didn't want me after all. Blotted it all out . . . doesn't even know it happened."

Veil was now surrounded by adoring subjects. She was smiling and greeting them, apparently distracted from the turmoil playing out between Amelia and Chev.

Amelia struggled up through Chev's iron grip to put her hands to his face. "Let's just get out of here," she said. "Give me a chance to put my thoughts together. We need to talk, we need many long talks to sort this out. This is not the place—with all these people around."

"No more words, Amelia. I have to stay. It's like I belong to Veil, now. I have to make up for what I have done. If I don't stay here to make it up to her, I'll slit my throat, I swear." He meant it. Maybe not tonight, but sometime soon. He would kill himself if she found a way to hold on to him; and if the mood hit him under the wrong circumstances, he would kill her, too.

"You're going to be miserable here."

"And everywhere."

She looked at the ground. "I can't live on this planet any longer. But we can still see each other now and then. It doesn't matter that much to me about what you did. It hurts, but it doesn't matter. I forgive you—if you didn't enjoy it too much."

"I love you, Amelia. Strange word. It doesn't always mean sex. I love Veil, too." He looked off toward Veil again. The way he regarded her pained Amelia. No desire. Nothing but innocent adoration, like what the slaves showed. Lust would have been easier to take.

"Maybe we shouldn't see each other," said Chev.

"Maybe."

"I don't think we should."

"That's it, then."

"That's it."

Amelia tried to make a show of strength with an artificial, oddly twisted smile.

"It is a bitch," said Chev.

Amelia's eyes rolled back, her cheeks flushed. She screamed something at Chev, a long, drawn-out string of words. Incomprehensible. She was screaming so loudly the sounds were shredding in her throat. She whipped her white-streaked hair from side to side, as motes of spittle sprayed from her mouth. Her feet stomped in rapid succession. Her heels drummed. She threw wild kicks. Blood was dripping from her fists, where her long fingernails dug into the palms of her hands.

The crowd stared dumbly at Amelia.

Chev effortlessly blocked the kicks and punches she threw at him. A blood vessel burst in the white of her left eye, surrounding the unnatural blue iris with scarlet.

Flushed, breathing in heavy snorts, she clawed at Chev's face. She seemed to be in the throes of a seizure. Her face shriveled from crying, eyes squeezed tight, her jaw clenched, her teeth grinding.

Magen broke from her idle observance of this odd spectacle and snapped to attention. She sprang to Amelia's side, tried to talk to her for a moment, then gave up. She grabbed Amelia and dragged her across the carpet of leaves. All the way, Amelia screamed, spat, howled, bit, scratched, kicked, cried, and cursed.

As tremors of rage passed from Amelia, she found herself alone in Magen's bungalow. Sensory impressions reordered, clarified. It was like the passage of sleep into wakefulness, though Amelia had been conscious the entire time.

So she would have to let Chev pass out of her life. She would give him to Veil. An act of charity. She was so bighearted, so magnanimous. She hoped Veil would appreciate her charity.

After a while, she stopped feeling pain—but a kind of misery clung to her spirit, a sadness that had the consistency of magnetic glue.

She sat in a wooden, cushionless chair by the window for three more hours. All along the arm of the chair, fresh green shoots grew from the dead wood. The trees of Autumn never seemed to die, even when chopped down. Tiny leaves on the new shoots had already begun their moribund recoloration. Amelia stroked the rows of unripe branches on the arm of the chair as if they were cat fur.

She watched stone-faced slaves outside, going about their chores, hauling timbers, cracking boulders, shoveling pathways through the leaves, distributing snacks, weaving intricate patterns of autumn colors on manual looms, transporting the sick, slaughtering animals, singing atonal hymns, forging tools, digging graves, and carving tombstones. They worked constantly, past the point of exhaustion, never laughing, never talking to each other, except about work or to exchange canned chatter about the greatness of God. Amelia felt like the freed slaves, broken in spirit and repaired the wrong way.

As Amelia stared out the window, her focus shifted from the wandering free slaves outside to her own translucent reflection on the glass. The white of one eye was still red from the burst blood vessel. She looked like a mournful demon.

The image of Magen's face became superimposed over the image of Amelia's. Magen tapped on the glass. Wearily, Amelia rose to let her in.

"I would have thought you'd be gone by now," said Amelia.

"I wanted to be sure you are all right."

Amelia said nothing. She let silence hang between them like acid suspended in a sword, a weapon and a shield. She could maintain the silence indefinitely. Magen waited patiently, politely, trying to decipher Amelia's silence. After a while, the meaning was plain enough, though Amelia's features expressed no emotions, conveyed no messages.

Magen turned to go, but she paused at the door. "This has turned out badly for you. I don't know what it is I have done that you should be so angry at me. Whatever it is, I am sorry. Shalom, Amelia."

"I am not angry at anyone in particular. I am just angry. I have lost the one thing I truly cared about. The one thing that gave me pleasure. I have lost him."

"I know what it means to lose everything."

"Don't compare yourself to me, girl. We have nothing in common. You are used to having nothing. I am not."

"I don't say we are alike. I am not like you at all. When I want something, I don't just complain. But because you are not like me does not mean you are so unique. Just because you lose everything, you are not unique. God gives us everything—and he always takes it away. Little by little, he strips away what we have. Our happiness, our loves, and in the end, our lives. He strips them all away, bit by bit. My husband used to say that God does this to us to make us stronger. If you don't find a way to get stronger when God takes something away from you, then God will do no more favors for you. If you don't help God grow, then God has no more use for you and no more gifts to give."

"I don't have much use for this advice. I don't care to hear preaching."

"I thought maybe I could help you. My husband was very smart. He used to have to comfort people who had terrible sorrows, real sorrows. Women with dead children, men who lost their sight. Things like that. When I lost my husband, I remembered his words."

Amelia asked, "What could this God of yours possibly give me that would be greater than love, my only love, my pretty boy? What could he possibly give me that would make up for such a loss?"

Magen thought a moment. "The chance to grow."

The answer was so easy. Amelia could see how it would appeal to simple minds and simple hearts. We get stripped of everything we value, we grow, and when we are done growing, we go back to the source of our sorrow. Amelia looked beyond the window, beyond the freed souls working outside, beyond the darkness. She stood up. "Oh God, Oh God." Amelia tapped her foot. "Oh God, Oh God." She broke into laughter, ugly, sarcastic laughter.

"What is so funny?"

"You trying to comfort me. You. It seems that all my misfortunes began with you. Just because I saved your life on a whim. On a bet."

On the airfield, Magen prepared for liftoff. The turbo fans mounted on the aft side of her craft beat up clouds of leaves. Amelia dived into the leaf storm and scampered up the ship's side ladder. She pounded on the Plexiglas hatch, screaming.

Magen popped open the hatch. Grabbing Amelia by the shoulders, she dragged her inside. Magen kicked the hatch window shut, her ears popping as it vacuum-sealed.

Liftoff slammed Amelia to the carpet. Magen busied herself with the guidance systems, setting trajectory and plotting a course. The ship's engines bellowed as long as there was air to convey sound. Inside the steering compartment, it wasn't quiet enough for conversation until they broke past the envelope and settled into inertial drift.

"Why did you want to come aboard?" asked Magen. "You know where I am headed. Do you want to go to Abaddon? I could use a good wing man."

"I want you to take me home. I would rather not have to ride with Chev."

Magen nodded.

"Chev raped Veil," said Amelia.

"No, he didn't." Magen seemed weary of everything but her own problem.

"He says he did. He says it happened while she was in a trance. He said she doesn't even know about it."

Magen rubbed her eyes. She looked pained, but she said, "Who knows what is true?"

"Why aren't you angry?"

"Who says I am not angry?" shouted Magen. She grabbed Amelia by the arm, suddenly. "You thought I would go back and kill Chev for raping Veil?"

"Something like that," said Amelia defensively, gently trying to free herself from Magen's grasp. "I need to do something extreme. Kill Chev. Kill myself. Go to Abaddon. I haven't decided yet. I haven't felt so bad in a very long time, not since the night I ran off to join the Air Force Bod. Desperate. In need of change."

"There are many reasons I don't kill Chev." Magen grabbed Amelia's other arm. "For one, I have more important things to do. For second, it will not be so easy. For next, he is taking my place when no one else would. For next, he is my friend. And for last, if he has done wrong, he is trying to atone, I think." She released Amelia as she finished her list.

"Atone? What's that?"

"Atonement. An old word. If you do something bad you can't fix, you do something bad to yourself."

"Chev is staying with Veil to hurt himself?"

"I think so."

"That's why you're not going to kill him?"

"At least I understand better why he is staying."

"I wish I did."

A dim amber light filled the cabin. The spacecraft had been designed as a one-man fighter. Amelia shifted her weight uneasily in the cramped space, then took a deep suck of the thick, wet air as if she were dragging on a cigarette.

"Love is shit, Magen. You think it is real one minute, and then it is gone, and maybe it was never real. Love is just shit."

"I'm going to Hell for love," said Magen.

"Perhaps I will go to Abaddon with you."

"I didn't mean it, earlier."

"You did. You were trying to exploit my depression."

"I said I could use a good wing man. You would not be good."

"Bod-trained."

"You're out of practice."

"I've kept up my skills over the years," said Amelia, lying.

Magen shrugged. "You can come with me if you like, if you think you can really handle it. I would be glad for the help."

"Well, maybe."

Amelia turned toward the hatch window and wiped away a haze of condensation. When she looked out, she saw, in the far distance, a grey cyanotic smear haunting the space between two stars. Abaddon was closer than she expected, maybe two days away straight travel time, not counting the detour to her asteroid.

Amelia floated up to the upper levels of the cabin and pulled down the view pipe. Under telescopics, the image of Abaddon was even stranger, like a tear in the vacuum. Neither reflective nor effulgent, it seemed devoid of light, and yet, somehow, its grey shroud contrasted against the grey of space. Its color was like a knife wound in the eye. Yet she found herself being drawn to Abaddon, the most forbidden sphere. Its frescoes of chaos offered comfort in their lack of meaning. As with every taboo, there lurked a seductive promise of a new kind of excitement.

She zoomed in on an area of indistinct movement, something like a flickering across the miasma. The suggestion of vague forms made her increase the telescopics and switch on computerized image enhancers. Even with the view pipe on full power, the images were hazy and translucent. Ships of ancient design were navigating the mist currents, churning the atmosphere into whirlpools in their wake.

Amelia caught glimpses of obsolete docking satellites and support craft running relays through a spiral-shaped hole in the mist.

Suddenly, two modern ships appeared in the view pipe. The two modern ships tried to sail past the museum pieces.

A dogfight erupted. She was afraid to watch. The old ships moved so much faster than their modernized opponents. It was too mysterious for Amelia. Old ships buzzing around like hummingbirds, yet spewing engine parts as they flew, littering space with bits of deteriorated machinery.

She pushed the optical systems as far as they would go, beyond their maximum limits, and jockeyed the computer for greater magnification.

Behind the windshields of the modern crafts she saw something terrifying. It was like everything she hated about the Autumn World—the auguries, the ghosts, the visions, the blurring of past and future. Only this was worse. Much worse.

She swore she would do everything she could to stay away from Abaddon, and she would try to talk Magen out of going there. But she knew that no matter how much she protested and girded her will, it wouldn't do any good. She would never be able to sway Magen from her mission. She knew for certain. She had seen Magen through the view pipe, flying and fighting over the mists of Abaddon. Unmistakably, despite the graininess of the image in the view pipe, it was Magen.

And she had seen herself, flying nearby.

She couldn't understand what force compelled her to do favors for Magen, again and again. Was it the tug of blood ties, though ancient and diluted? This strange Jewishness thing. Was the preordained flight to Abaddon another aspect of the contest for Amelia's soul between God and the Devil? Veil's invisible creatures. Which of them stood to profit most from a detour to Hell?

Amelia returned to the flight cabin. "I'll fly with you," she said, since she had no choice in the matter anyway.

"Why?"

"Out of despair, I don't know. On a whim. To prove to Chev that I can atone better than he can."

"Atone for what?"

"I don't know. I don't really understand the word, but if Chev can do it, so can I."

During the flight to Abaddon, the two women planned the assault together. They plotted an approach near the spiral of atmospheric darkness. Magen superimposed imaginary flight lines on Abaddon's mists by drawing on the window with a grease pencil. The only discernible shipping activity moved in and out of that spiral, indicating that it was some kind of clearing, or access point. The area was also heavily guarded by those ships, the old ships, the fast ships, the ghost ships. Amelia suggested trying to use

the fog, or mist, or whatever it was, to some tactical advantage, to cover a sneak approach.

Magen and Amelia made several stops along the way to
Abaddon: twice for rest; once for food; once to hijack a
second one-seater fighting ship.

The craft they stole was respectable, but not outstanding. Most of its guts still carried warranties from various
bods, but the ancillary systems were generics, probably
custom-tooled at the whim of a middle manager caught in
a cost-containment crunch.

Magen let Amelia take the better of the two ships. Amelia took the gift for granted, without trifling over polite expressions of gratitude. After all, she had saved Magen's life
more than once, and lavished her with gifts worth far more
than this simple fighter. Later, when Amelia saw the grey
horizon of the hell world looming beneath her, she decided it didn't matter what she was flying. She was doomed.

The grey scud coating Abaddon wasn't really vapor.
Amelia couldn't figure out what the hell it was. Up close,
Abaddon's atmosphere showed as a visual blur, as if the
world had been caught in the act of orbiting, contrary to
its reputation. Abaddon was supposed to stay anchored to
a fixed spot in the sky, never showing any signs of astral
motion. The blur seemed to glow, but it didn't feel like
light upon Amelia's retinas. It felt like some weary, disenfranchised imitation of light, sluggish and speed-retarded.

Computer analysis of the grey stuff turned out statisti-
cal gibberish, and the circuits began to steam. Amelia shut
down the probes for fear they'd burn themselves out.

Magen's craft dipped a wing, rolled, angled its nose,
and dropped. Amelia followed, flying in reciprocal formation.

The two women hit the grey stuff at reduced speeds,
and slammed into resistance of an unidentifiable nature.
It wasn't atmospheric or magnetic turbulence. It wasn't

anything solid or electrical. Yet no matter how much fuel they pumped into their afterburners, no matter how they cocked their flaps, they could not descend past the blur.

A hard oscillation shimmied through Amelia's craft as she slammed into the grey. Her wings hummed in vibrato. G-forces whipped through the cabin. The buckles of her leg-restraint garters cut into her thighs. Her craft skipped across the unyielding surface tension, each bounce pealing cymbal crashes inside the cockpit. She retreated.

Magen assaulted the stuff with her usual stubborn determination, but she fared no better than Amelia. When she finally gave up, and her craft rose to vertical, there were cracks running through her undercarriage. Some of the racks had been torn loose, and the paint had been wiped away in swatches that looked like wire-brush work.

Magen chucked their original flight plan without even consulting Amelia. She shot toward the dark spiral, and Amelia followed.

They approached the spiral opening, the only hole in Abaddon's impenetrable shell.

Suddenly, ground artillery began picking off small, nonessential pieces of Amelia's craft. The shots hit with exacting precision. A radio antenna was slagged. A rack was sniped free, one support strut at a time. Two bulging bombs on the undercarriage were sliced loose by a single blue castrating stroke. Amelia broke into a cold sweat. The old hide casing on her joystick became slippery in her hand, coated by a viscous film of rehydrated leather. She felt the creep of each nanosecond. Searching the sky for Magen's craft, she saw only empty space. She tried to raise Magen on the ship's radio, but picked up on broadcast gibberish, eerie frequency shrieks.

She was little more than a toy in the air, a source of amusement for incomprehensible enemies. They could shoot her down at any time, now.

Suddenly a staccato flash of laser zips burned bubbling

black letters onto the outside surface of her plastic windshield. The message was clear and simple:

TURN BACK.

She didn't understand how it could be done by anyone—writing on her windshield while she was flying at Mach two. Maybe it was Veil's all-powerful spook—God, or Zeus, or Jesus, whatever his name was. Maybe this was the word from on high. Turn back.

So that's what she did. She turned back. She took the writing on her windshield as a clear sign of permission. Somehow she had been shown mercy on Abaddon. Maybe this atonement thing worked after all.

For some reason, Magen had not been spared. Maybe she hadn't atoned enough. Her word. Her concept, but somehow it didn't seem to work for her. Maybe she had been too eager, too aggressive, too stubborn to see that she had taken on superior forces.

Amelia hit her speed brakes and barrel-rolled into retreat. Her ship passed through airspace occupied by a bogie, but it offered no resistance. Perhaps it had crumbled on contact, or perhaps it was only a hologram after all. Amelia accelerated as fast as she could. This time she was turning back. Going home.


Adam Hirsch was alive, or so he thought, but there were many on Abaddon who had died, but who were not at rest, who believed they were still alive. Like Syckle, who shared the dusty front office of the exploratory station with Adam.

Syckle had once been a master, but he died a slave. A retrovirus took him shortly after he arrived on Abaddon.

Syckle sat in a green plastic swivel chair. He propped his feet upon the table. His toes were so rotten that most had autoamputated, and the ones remaining hung by threads of gristle. A papery yellow light washed over the room, its source uncertain. Both of Syckle's eye sockets were empty, yet these holes of his behaved as if they could see, remembering the action of light, even though they no longer had the proper equipment to register vision. His empty nose sniffed the air, as if searching the dusty quarters for companionship. He still wore his favorite shirt, a red, collarless tangle of threads held together by the seams of many zippered pockets. A few blond hairs hovered over his sloughing scalp. He talked, waved his arms, got up and hunted for water now and then. Sometimes the master and sometimes the slave. Time was the problem. Syckle was animated by a network of nerves that did not know when they were: synapses displaced in time.

Time had long been the problem on Abaddon. Time had been a problem all over the Draconian system. Temporal ecological imbalances left worlds that rotated and orbited, yet the seasons never changed. Distances were often warped, making interplanetary travel within the system weirdly easy. These anomalies had all been caused by the traffic of the warpships bringing settlers from Earth centuries ago.

Of all the planets in the system, Abaddon showed the most damage. Time collected in eddies and pools on Abaddon. It could race, or creep. Taking a piss could consume a year. Distances had no meaning. A room could become as large as a continent. Mirages of yesterdays and tomorrows would flicker on the hillsides. The dead did not even know when to lie down. So hideous were the results of time anomalies here, the inhabitants of the Draconian system were able to agree for once on a single moral point—warp travel had to cease.

Abaddon had been the spaceport. The antique immigration turnstiles where Adam's ancestors once crossed were still standing in the shell of an old building not far from the exploratory station. Every now and then, Adam saw mirages of new arrivals haunting the check-in counters, dressed in odd costumes, colored by the soil of a distant home.

"Fetch me my . . ." shouted Syckle, the final words of his command slurring on a tongue turned to mush.

Adam had come to this—sharing a room with a rotting dead man, whose commands would have to be obeyed sooner or later. Even though Syckle was a slave, and a dead slave at that, commands were commands.

Adam remembered the ancient Jewish folktales about the nature of the afterlife. It was said that the present ceases to exist and the experiences of a lifetime merge into a single experience of simultaneity that lasts forever. Sins melded into mitzvahs, joys melded into pain. Abaddon was like that sometimes. Abaddon was like death.

Adam had committed terrible blasphemies, and God had condemned him to Hell.

Suddenly the yellow papery light turned gold and crimson. It flickered and strobed. Adam looked out of the window up to the sky, up to the spiral hole that was the only way in and out of Abaddon. Normally it looked like a whirling patch of night, black and dotted with stars, turning very slowly. But now it was red, colored by battle lights.

The reflected glow of lasers flickered over the ramparts of the four steel towers that held the hole open. Millions of slaves had labored over the course of fifty years to build those towers. Bones littered the beacon coils. Temporal mirages of suffering slaves haunted the iron base. To those who lived on Abaddon, nothing was more important than those towers.

All along the seven-mile length of the spiral hole, strobing lights changed colors. Battling ships darted from one end of the rotating blades of serrated darkness to the other.

The spires of the four towers leaned toward the spiral. Each tower held a primal black hole, small enough to be surrounded by a stasis field. The spiral and the black holes balanced one another, singularities pressing against singularities. The result was an opening from Hell into the real universe.

Adam could almost see energy wave patterns swirling out of the towers. Who could be fighting out there? Adam prayed that the battling ships were only time mirages. But they weren't. Wayward laser shots were chipping bits off the huge ceramic disks covering the magnets on the yard-arms of the towers. It would take very little violence to disrupt their delicate balance.

The primal black holes nestled in their stasis fields behind an insulated mesh. A central syncshaft turned according to constantly changing, constantly recomputed logarithms. The gravitational tug ratios could shift dramatically at times, but these mechanisms were sensitive to such sporadic changes. The status quo was maintained by keeping the tug ratios in a constant state of flux. On an as-needed basis, determined by the central processing chips, the rotors would be dampened by a mathematical lullaby so that the towers wouldn't shake to wreckage at every change of signal frequency. The entire mechanism functioned on an assumption of uninterrupted peace. If any one of the towers became damaged, the spiral hole would close and there would be no way to reopen it.

Adam held his breath. The lights were getting brighter. The battle was getting closer.

Suddenly, a single fighter ship dashed through the hole.

The fool. The damned fool. Adam raced out of the offices, screaming, waving his arms. He tried to shout warnings to the ship, knowing he could not be heard. The damned fool. Didn't the pilot know how delicate the towers were—and the consequences if their complex mechanisms sustained even the least bit of damage?

The damned fool kept firing anyway at phantoms, images from the past. Adam kept shouting and waving.

The battle seemed to be taking place in the present. It was hard to tell. The battle centered around the towers, and the four towers were generally a constant on the landscape. Still, it might be some future event.

Adam's warnings were useless. The worst happened. The very worst.

The invader flew directly into the path of the signal beam, trying to avoid an arc of laser light a hundred years old. A wingtip tore loose.

The ship banged into the eastern tower, then skidded down the outer edge of a spire, raising a wake of sparks. Latticed wiring burned loose and wound into the main axles. The rotors groaned and slammed to a halt.

One by one, the spin boxes shut down, going blank in the same sequence as they once crunched numerical values.

The spiral hole in the sky closed, its circumference pulling in suddenly, like a pupil confronting the sun.

Abaddon was sealed again. Sealed so tightly, not even a prayer could escape.

The invading ship crashed somewhere in the unreal distance.

The damned fool.

This was it, the final punishment. No hope of reprieve ever. No escape from Hell.

Every word of Adam's old speeches rang in his memory. He recanted everything he had written. It humiliated him. How could he presume to question the nature of God?

Adam pondered his miseries. They were grotesque and absurd, and yet somehow a fitting punishment for the grotesque and absurd theories he had propagated about God. Adam recanted his blasphemies. God trying to evolve. Man influencing God. His mistake—he saw now—was in trying to determine what God was, rather than what God demanded.

And worse. He had tried to use God's name to accomplish his own ends. He manipulated his fellow men with visions of God that appealed to the human ego.

Adam had once preached the notion that mankind could shape the course of God's growth—each person contributing a tiny share—like the minute influence of a single DNA molecule in a single cell upon the course of the larger creature it inhabits. Adam's ideas cast the universe as a splatter painting rather than a grand design. He had slandered God by overextending a metaphor. Evolution was adaptation to an environment. Why would God need to adapt to anything?

Adam was never certain if he truly believed that strange theology, but it played well. And he had grand goals. Fine intentions. The Draconian system needed reformation. Adam thought he could bring about a great moral revolution. What arrogance!

God needing to grow! Man influencing God! Folly! He remembered the prohibitions of the Mishnah: It is forbidden to contemplate what is below, what is above, what was before time, and what will be after.

Adam walked over to his desk in the main office and extracted from the drawers a long bundle of papers. There were complex calculations scrawled in Hebrew letters, which were numbers as well. Adam's equations were based on numerology and folklore more than anything else. He was trying to read a pattern into Abaddon's time labyrinths. He tried to weigh the flight of days, assign values to the spread of minutes. He tried to discover correlations between places and degrees of time distortion.

Adam was trying to find the Day of Atonement.

# 10

## A BANQUET OF WEEDS

The day before his first mission, Veil took Chev to the city of Dante. They visited open-air markets and listened to fortune-tellers; some were more accurate than others, according to Veil. They passed by quaint displays of unicorn skulls, and drug boutiques rich with the smell of cadmadine oils.

Under pastel banks of torch-lit fog, mystics and pseudomystics conducted their commerce, hawking incantations, prayers, theories about the colors that butterflies see, pamphlets explaining the mysteries of God, handwritten prophecies, and other forms of esoterica.

A cultist pushed a wheeled cart over the cobblestones, distributing food to his fellows. Steam rose from the cart, and the smell of freshly fried vegetables and melted cheese mingled with the fog. The smell, richly spiced with tarragon and savory, enticed Veil. Her stomach growled. She pulled Chev over to the cart.

"Will you share some of your food with outsiders?" asked Veil. "We have nothing to trade but gratitude."

"I am not supposed to," said the cultist, a thin boy, good intentions and weakness evident in his voice. He scanned the odd pair, Chev in his khakis and holsters and Veil in her robes. His eyes kept returning to Veil, though he could not meet her gaze.

"If I am seen, I'll be out of the cult. I'll starve. I got no way to get offworld."

"I will make certain no one sees you," said Veil.

"I can't. This is holy food."

"We are God's creatures and hungry." It was hard to refuse Veil anything.

The cultist sighed deeply and flipped open a panel flap on his cart. He extracted two fist-sized bread pockets filled near to bursting with oily vegetables and webs of melted cheese. Surrendering the handouts, he cautioned, "This is holy food. It must not touch the ground."

Chev took cautious nibbles, turning the bread pocket carefully, maintaining a steady balance. Veil tried to imitate Chev's method, but her fingers were too clumsy and she couldn't eat fast enough. The oil began to seep into the bread, making it more friable.

"I can do it. I can do it. I can manage," said Veil, trying to convince the cultist and herself.

A glob of stuffing breached the side of the pocket. Veil propped up two fingers to cage it.

"Don't let the food fall." The cultist broke into a sweat.

"Don't worry," said Veil. She took a deep breath, studying the meal like a puzzle. An errant cluster of eggplant slid through her fingers.

Chev's hands were full of his own meal, but he twisted sharply and kicked the eggplant into Veil's robe. The vegetable hung in an unsightly splatter on the crisp, otherwise flawlessly white silk.

"I'm sorry," said Chev. The oil and vegetable juices were already bleeding into the fabric.

"It was that or the ground," said Veil, not bothering to wipe the stain, her entire attention focused on the crisis in her hands. The bread was disintegrating. "Ooh, this is impossible."

Chev stuffed the remainder of his food into his mouth, bloating his cheeks. He put his hands around Veil's hands, encasing them and the collapsing sandwich.

"Thank you," said Veil.

Chev said something incomprehensible, his mouth still overstuffed. Veil began to eat from the bowl formed by two pairs of hands.

Chev held Veil's hands until she finished eating.

The cultist, soaked in nervous sweat, let out a weak sigh.

Later, as if in reward for his services, Veil handed Chev the battle plans given to her by the Council of Autumn. Uncanny material, written in a rambling, dreamlike prose, with surprising details about Olagy's security systems and troop movements. Aerial tactics were listed in advance; including some snap decisions that would be made in battle. No wonder Magen had been able to shake the economic foundation of the Draconian system.

When Veil escorted Chev to the airfield, she seemed buoyant, filled with excitement at having a new warrior for her cause. All along the way, Chev took deep breaths, forcing himself into rigid control, a sort of combat posture he constantly maintained around Veil. Chev feared her, as a child fears a strict parent, or the dark, or a ghost.

As Chev prepared to leave, Veil said, "The others want to wish you luck, too."

"What others?"

Then he spied a group of slaves peering at him from a

thicket of shadows. Veil smiled, inviting them over with a hand gesture. The slaves shyly gathered around Chev, their eyes gaping—not their usual glassy stares. They wore curious, amazed expressions. Some hesitantly touched the bright gold buttons of Chev's leather flight coat.

"Get them away from me," said Chev.

"They won't harm you," said Veil.

"All right."

Veil was stroking the stringy hair of an emaciated girl. Suddenly, a swarm of cretinous parasites crawled from their nesting places under the girl's scalp and attached themselves to the skin of Veil's hand. She did not recoil. Calmly, Veil lifted the hand up to the moonlight. Purple blisters, full of bugs, dotted her knuckles and palms. She called for a needle. One by one, she teased the bugs from their carbuncled berths. Because she allowed the slaves to remain pressed up against her, every bug she removed was instantly replaced.

"I think the Autumn World makes people insane!" said Chev.

"So they say all throughout the system," replied Veil. "And it is true, in a way. But Summer is just as insane. Summer is Draconia's flesh and Autumn is its soul. Flesh and soul are always at odds, each thinking the other mad." Chev thought he detected a note of sadness, a repressed sigh, an admission of inner turmoil. Then she added, "Summer says we have hallucinogens in the fog. We say they have aphrodisiacs in the water."

Veil and Chev laughed. For some reason, she seemed happy around him, and that made things easier.

Veil lifted a child with one arm to wave good-bye to Chev. She extended her free arm, inviting an embrace. He couldn't pass on the opportunity for contact, even though it yielded only a brief passionless hug. The adult slaves huddled around them.

As Chev was climbing up to the hatch of his ship, the bugs began to attack his cheeks.

He gripped his visionary battle plans, and thought about the power entrusted to him. The bugs pulsing under his skin no longer seemed vile. Instead they carried a humble beauty, jewels of poverty, connecting him to Veil, the slaves, and the Council of Autumn.

Adam awoke to find his head cradled in his arms. His back ached. He had fallen asleep seated at a dusty old writing table. A muscle spasmed painfully at the back of his neck.

Syckle had vanished, presumably lured off somewhere by the fireworks outside, or the vibrations humming through the air. Strobing lights shined through the window, as if from lightning. Adam looked up from the desktop. The papers he had been working on stuck to his bare forearms.

A time storm ripped across the surface of Abaddon. Chronostreams collided and reversed, their ecologies upset by the closure of the hole in the sky. At the epicenter of the time storm, the tragic fall of the energy towers replayed across the sky. Again and again, the showers of sparks, the arcs of lasers, the collision of the intruding craft. The planet itself seemed preoccupied with the event, displaying endless repetitions like a visual mantra.

He heard the wail of dissolving hours.

Ten feet away from Adam's window, a blond-haired boy watched the skies. He wore the blue-grey costume of a novice shuttle pilot freshly promoted in the Air Force Bod. His lips were trembling. Overwhelmed at being trapped beneath the grey dome, the despised scud, he unholstered his laser pistol, pressed the nozzle to his temple, and pulled the trigger. The blast looked like a spray of vomit exploding from his head, full of pink-tinged brain mush and blond-fringed rags of scalp, all riding a core of red

lightning. As the boy fell, he splashed into a stream of reversed time, and the vomit spray sucked itself back into his
head. The burn hole on his temple sealed. Then his arm
spastically snapped back up, repositioning the gun, and he
blew his brains out again. The boy would never be able to
stop killing himself. His eyes kept rolling up and down
with the rhythms of his suicide, like the eyes of a toy doll.
There was no escaping from Abaddon, not even in death.

Jet fighters took to the air. Even people who didn't
know how to fly were jumping into planes and taking off.
They would do anything to escape.

Images of planes from past, present, and future
crossed one another in flight. Waves of wings beat over
clouds of smoke and fire. Lasers were firing at the grey
dome. The skies glittered with shining wings and swords of
light and crystal canopies. It seemed as if the entire population was trying to take flight, all at once. One of the pan-
icking young pilots took off so quickly, he collided with
himself in a moment of chronofeedback.

In the midst of the chaos, trying to convince himself
that Abaddon was no different from Earth, or the Summer
World, or anywhere, Adam tried to pray. He wanted to
show that he loved God and God's commandments, no
matter how terrible his afflictions. This life was a cloak of
illusions, a disguise wrapped around an incomprehensible
core. Adam remembered the words of his teachers, that
the only way to bring meaning to chaos was through the
laws laid down at Sinai, the halakah, the complex matrix of
deeds that transformed the chore of living into an act of
worship. He wanted to demonstrate his repentance.

And yet, Adam lacked the proper tools for Jewish worship. Perhaps that was part of his punishment. No holy
books. No tallith. No t'fillin. No minyan. No temple. No
Shabbat. No family. No community. No home. How could
he be a Jew in a vacuum?

When Adam first arrived on Abaddon, he found small

mitzvahs he could perform. He tended a small garden of seminutritious weeds so that he could have something ko-sher to eat. He cultivated hope in much the same way, be-cause optimism is a sign of respect for the wisdom of God's choices. He found ways to help his fellow slaves, and even showed kindness to his masters.

Now Abaddon was sealed. No one could escape that grey shell of impenetrable time. How could Adam con-tinue to hope?

Outside the exploratory station, crushed airships rained from the skies. Flaming, broken wings streaked downward.

Over the hill, two hastily formed coalitions were bat-tling over a food storage bin. Adam sat at a worm-eaten, splintering rolltop desk. He picked up a pencil and started jotting down notes about the destruction of the energy tower, peppering his objective observations with specula-tions about Abaddon's chronoecology. Even though he knew his masters would never call for this report, he was obliged to finish writing it. He remained obedient to the unretracted order.

Billows of smoke rolled toward the exploratory station and soon obscured Adam's view of the battles raging out-side. A dingy yellow film began to coat the windowpanes. Adam could hear shouts and whining weapons, sometimes playing in reverse like the voices of demons. Men were dying out there, or rather they were doing what passed for dying on Abaddon.

As the night wore on, food battles intensified. Wayward laser beams poked holes in the walls and windowpanes. Snakes of smoke writhed through. Adam covered his nose and mouth with rags to keep from breathing the smoke, for it stank of laser kills, a noxious odor heavy with aerosol fragments of DNA.

Adam looked up from his work. He stared out into the vistas of smoke, trying to read the patterns playing across his line of sight. The indistinct form of a soldier emerged from the haze, at first only a silhouette, a shadow accumulating detail as it drew closer. A metal flak jacket glittered on the form. A flash of laser reflected off a goggled helmet. He thought about trying to get away from the approaching soldier—but choosing an escape route required too much will. He sat very still, hoping to be ignored. The shadow ran elegantly, chased by other shadows. More laser lines slammed through the walls. The running soldier was drawing fire in Adam's direction. Still, Adam did not try to flee. He watched the warriors outside perform their ugly dances.

Suddenly the smoke was parted by a wet, red explosion. A blast of light had ripped open a human body. A volley of white projectiles tore uneven holes in the windowpanes. The projectiles ricocheted, then clattered like dice on the wooden floor. When they came to rest, Adam saw they were teeth.

Now only one soldier remained in the field of smoke. There was something familiar about the soldier's stride, an echo of confidence and anger, a glide of effortless coordination, and a hint of sexuality. It was a female soldier. She reminded him very much of someone he knew, someone from long ago, from a distant other life.

Adam stood up from his desk to get a better view.

The closer the woman soldier got, the more striking the resemblance became.

Magen.

He couldn't believe his eyes. Surely this was too much of a coincidence, absurd and improbable. And yet who else would be crazy enough to invade Abaddon?

What would he do if it were really Magen?

It couldn't be Magen. The image had to be some kind of wish-fulfillment fantasy. A Rorschach Magen. Of course he saw Magen in the running form. He thought about her all the time and saw her in all things. In dreams, he chased her shadow through the corridors of their old home. While exploring the plains of Abaddon for his masters, he rehearsed reunions with Magen he never expected would come to pass. In part he blamed her for his present circumstances and sometimes would rage in phantom arguments with her inside his own mind, but he was still the victim of the obsessive love he'd felt for her from the very beginning. That woman, that beguiling, dangerous, forbidden fruit. He loved her, and hated her, and craved her, and prayed for their reunion, and in the same breath prayed to never see her again. He felt every kind of deep emotion a man could feel for a woman who wasn't there. In the course of his constant pondering about her, she achieved the weight of legend in his mind.

Could it really be her? How should he act? Like the slave that he was, or should he pretend to be something more? He had come to think of his broken spirit as a puzzle to occupy the time between now and death, an issue between Adam and God that Adam would have to work out by himself. He couldn't stand the thought of Magen finding him like this. Broken. A slave.

The door of the exploratory station swung open, and the woman walked in amid a wave of foul-smelling smoke. Her nose was broken, her lips painted luridly with her own blood. Her eyes had changed color since the last time he saw her, and she had aged much more than he had. But he recognized her.

Magen. Undeniably Magen. If nothing else, he could tell it was her by the way she stared at him.

"Thank God I have found you," she said, after a long silence.

He stood very still, trying to decide what to do. His choices were simple. Give her the ugly truth, tell her that he had been turned into a slave and grovel at her feet. Or opt for theatrics. He could pretend to be a real man with a real soul. He didn't know what to do.

They stared at each other a long time, shaking their heads in disbelief.

"I told them you were alive," she said. "Everyone said I was crazy, but I knew in my heart."

"You are crazy. You have no idea what you have done to yourself."

"I know, Adam. I have been on Abaddon for a while. I can't say how long. Maybe a week. It is so hard to say. I tell time by my smell. I haven't even changed clothes since I landed." She laughed. "My odor is terrible. I think I smell like a week."

"I wish I could say I was happy to see you. I am, in a way—but Abaddon is a wretched place to be. I can't take happiness from anything that will bring you misery."

"It is worth it for this moment."

She crossed over to where he stood. He felt her eyes probing his soot-smeared flesh, his labor-pumped muscles, his rags. Her gaze finally met his sleep-deprived, time-tortured eyes.

"How long has it been?"

"Five years, Adam."

He shook his head. "I didn't think it would be so long. It is impossible to judge time on this world. I thought maybe it has only been nine months. Maybe less."

"It seemed much more than five years to me, Adam. It seemed a lifetime."

"Maybe five years for you, maybe less than a year for me. Time passes differently here."

She took his hand, just for a second. The two of them tested what contact would be like. He felt her blood lubricating the space between their skin. She pulled back suddenly, blushing.

"I know it has been a long time and you have been through much. So have I. Maybe I have not been so good a wife to you as I should have been, and you have many reasons to be angry with me. But I have gone through so much hardship to get here. You can't even imagine what I have been through."

"I am not angry," said Adam.

"You don't look so bad." She forced a smile. "I was expecting so much worse. I have been with slaves, too much, these five years. You don't look so bad for a slave."

What could he say to her? She had come so far and endured so much, or so she said, and he didn't doubt her. Finding a mental cripple at the end of her quest seemed too shabby a reward.

"I am not a slave."

He lied to her. He couldn't stand the thought of her treating him like a slave. Somehow he would have to maintain an illusion of will to support the lie. He believed he could do it. The slavers had not broken him completely, as they had the others. And he understood the nature of Abaddon, which Magen did not. Perhaps Adam could hide his infirmities behind the vagaries of this place. Maybe he could fool her indefinitely, if no one gave him any direct orders.

"How is it that you are not a slave?"

He lowered his head toward the ground. "I had to trade my identity so they would not give me brain drugs. I gave them my name, my real name, in return for my soul. I had to let them know my mind was of some value to them, so they wouldn't kill it. On Abaddon, they needed someone who understood physics to make reports. That's why I am here, because of physics." He told the story convincingly because he did not have to lie. He had managed to rescue some of his will from total obliteration. Still, he was too ashamed to tell her how much damage had been done before they sent him to Abaddon.

"What do you know of physics? You have to be in a bod to learn such things."

"I used to read a lot of books. Anything I could get my hands on. Even books on obsolete sciences like economics, sociology, philosophy. I used to memorize the names of stars that can't be seen from here. I don't know why. Once I studied some outdated physics."

"You have been lucky, then."

"No."

"All right, Adam, you have not been lucky if you think so. But I am grateful to God that I have found you and you don't look so bad and you are not a slave. They have not cut you in body or brain."

He was afraid of conversation, afraid that he might reveal his crippled state. He said nothing.

"I have changed, Adam."

He inspected her the way she had inspected him. Two lightweight rifles hung from slings, one over each shoulder. He counted three holstered handguns. Too many knives to count. A belt of grenades. His eyes began to tarry on her breasts and hips. He tried to force his eyes to the ground, but they stayed on her body. Primitive lusts swept through his torso. Animal lusts, slave lusts. Magen deserved better than that.

"Tomorrow, we find a way out of this mess," she said unconvincingly, trying to get him to talk.

He started to tell her there was no way out of the mess, but he held his tongue. It was too much like something a slave would say, even though it was true.

"I have some food," said Magen. She slipped the rifles off her shoulders, then pulled loose the knapsack strapped to her back. From inside, she extracted a portion of pink meat wrapped in cellophane. She offered the meat to him, but he pushed her hand away.

As his hand touched her knuckles, he was overwhelmed by hungers that had nothing to do with food. Her cheeks flushed pink under the soot. He wanted to grab her, but he fought back the urge.

"The food isn't kosher," said Adam.

"You should eat it anyway. You will need strength."

Adam shuddered. Magen's entreaty hit him with the full force of an order, and he was compelled to obey. Despite the revulsion sieging through his nerves, he found himself reaching for the pink slab of flesh. He took the bag into his hands, felt the meat sliding on grease under the cellophane.

"All right, all right, don't eat it if it makes you so unhappy," said Magen. "You have something better to eat?"

Adam walked over to his bed and pulled his mattress to one side. He wanted to give her a kiss, but instead, he offered a handful of weeds.

She sniffed the stems, then skeptically took a small taste. "I can't live on this," she said.

"You do as you wish."

"We are talking about life and death here, Adam. God doesn't want I should starve to stay kosher."

"These plants have kept me alive."

Magen took the weeds from Adam's hands and stuffed them into her mouth.

"You must eat slowly. They are hard to digest."

She glared, but she continued eating. The situation struck Adam as weirdly ironic. Unknowingly, she had bowed to the influence of a slave.

"I don't think I will get very much strength from this meal . . ." she said. A tear began to pool in the corner of her eye, very slowly. Her tear continued to grow, eventually gaining enough weight to amble down her cheek. Clicking noises came from the base of her throat. A long, drawn-out hiss separated each click. She was talking, too slowly to be understood. Magen had settled into a stream of retarded time. A look of desperation froze on her face, as if caught inadvertently on a snapshot. Adam had seen that look before. Maybe she had changed, as she said, but as far as he could see, the past was repeating itself, as the past often did on Abaddon.

He should have married someone modest and demure—not this wild, warrior woman who had only minimal ties to the faith of her ancestors. But Adam had been drawn to Magen, violently attracted by her recklessness, lured by their differences.

It seemed so strange to be sharing a meal with his wife again, after all this time. The meal itself seemed endless and unreal, even more unreal than the time storm outside. Magen remained fixed and rigid, trapped in amber, hissing and clicking, separated from Adam in ways she did not realize.

Adam looked away from Magen. He realized that her being here was not a coincidence at all, but rather the product of some enormous effort on her part.

Magen seemed to resent Adam's insistence on observing the ancient laws under these bizarre circumstances, but she didn't understand how terrible and hopeless their situation was. They had nothing but faith and observance to keep them from madness, and no hope for deliverance outside of a miracle. He felt a sudden, profound gratitude for his dinner of weeds.

Adam was glad that he had kept the kosher laws on Abaddon. Now he and his wife had their own food stores and would not have to join the battle for sustenance raging outside. He could eat his simple dinner in the shadows, sheltered from Hell. The weeds had almost no taste, except for a slight hint of bitterness. They had a rubbery texture that made them difficult to chew. Still, the weeds would sustain them.

God did not reveal himself through miracles, nor through human introspection. God did not reveal himself in coincidences, or in chaos. God did not even reveal himself in nature, as Adam once supposed. He revealed himself by hiding. And here, on Abaddon, where God was most hidden, Adam found God most revealed. In a vacuum, where there should have been no proper tools for Jewish worship, Adam found God growing in the weeds.

* * *

As Magen came back into sync with Adam, she asked, "How can I tell you I am sorry?"

She reached across the table and took both of his hands in hers. "Come closer," she said.

He stood and crossed over to her. He couldn't disobey, even if he wanted to.

The smells of her body, once so familiar to him, had been intensified by the long period she had gone without washing. Her pungent musk invaded his nostrils, provoking him. He pulled her close and their lips met. The gamy taste of her mouth sent jolts through his abdomen. His passions quickened.

The way he grabbed her was crude and insensitive, but he couldn't help himself. He was desperate for her. Yet he was terrified of contact. Lovemaking opened windows into the soul. He was afraid that even the smallest of intimate contact would allow her to see the ruins of his will.

"Wait . . ." she protested.

He pulled back, his arms dropping to his sides.

"You don't have to be so rushed."

"Just tell me what you want."

"Adam!"

"I mean I just want to make you happy."

"Let's get clean."

He escorted her to a small shower stall at the rear of the exploratory station. Slowly, she peeled off her sticky garments. Her body still retained its severe beauty. The tight panels of her abdomen rippled with her heavy breathing. The sculpted forms of her belly and hips led his eyes to her loins. Already he could see desire glistening on her brown tuft of hair.

"Adam, it is so strange the way you look at me."

He turned his eyes away.

"No, look at me, please, just stop staring. And stop staring there."

He stepped out of his clothes and stood naked in front of his wife. Now she was staring, as if seeing his body for the first time.

Together, they climbed under the running water. She lathered up her hands with a bar of soap that smelled of flammable disinfectant; then she smeared the soapy foam on his belly. As she worked the lather over his body hair, it turned grey as the dust of Abaddon. He took the soap from her and greased her breasts with it. He felt her nipples pointing into the palms of his hands, tracing designs on his slippery caresses. Their mouths met.

He lathered her thighs, then found her center. She felt rough and viscous as he washed her. She soaped him in reciprocity, her fingers lubricated with alcoholic foam.

She cupped her hands to catch water from the shower, then poured it warmly over him, washing away the lather. He swept the soap from her body with his wet hands.

He ached, mad with desire.

"What are you waiting for?" she asked.

"You said to wait . . ." The words involuntarily escaped from his lips.

She laughed. She thought he was joking. "Well, if you need to be told when to stop waiting, then you can just wait."

He broke from the embrace.

"Adam, I was joking."

She climbed him like a ladder into a chair made of his arms. The shower sprayed on them. "We've been waiting too long. We don't have to wait anymore." Her long legs wrapped around his, and she enveloped him.

* * *

Magen awoke to find her husband naked and asleep beside her, the two of them cramped on a simple cot. She touched him gently, to test the depth of his slumber. At the contact of their skin, a warm, fluid sensation fluttered in her abdomen. He continued to sleep. She crept out of bed without disturbing him.

Her stomach began to growl. She crossed over to a rear corridor, looking for something to eat. At that moment, she felt hungrier than she had ever felt in her life. The dented metal walls of the exploratory station had faded to a pale yellow, except for black streaks of baked-on tar, splatters from an ancient explosion. Magen peeled off a long strip of tar, and found a military shade of avocado lurking underneath. The place had once housed soldiers or mercs.

Magen crossed from room to room, checking for food bins. She found some bags that were supposed to contain dehydrated food. The powder inside tasted like chalk. For all she knew, she was eating dirt, but she ate it anyway, greedily stuffing handfuls into her mouth.

A battery of laser cannons, all equipped with telescopic sights, lined the rear barricade. She paused at the laser cannons. They appeared to be in good condition. Even the subspace aimers still worked, antique defenses against invading warships.

As she took a look through the high-powered telescopic aiming device, the broken towers rolled into view. The image of her ship crashing still played across the sky above the towers. Perversely, she adjusted the telescopics for a clearer view of herself. Regarding the shadow of her former folly between the crosshairs of the laser cannon, she saw her own lips stretched thin, her eyes wide behind green-tinted goggles during the approach to Hell. Magen laughed at herself and all of her old determination. Young girl, young fool, charging into Hell.

She looked past herself, up to the grey sky, where the access hole was closing again and again. She readjusted the telescopics, and the spiral-shaped hole came into sharp focus. For the first time in an eternity, she saw outer space: black and silver, infinite depth speckled with points of light. She lingered there, watching the heavens like a child with a kaleidoscope.

Then a searing flash of laser light blurred the scene. A ship drifted into view, flying in slow motion. Amelia's assault craft. She saw a terrified expression gradually playing over Amelia's features.

She tested the cannon. It could still fire. She adjusted the fine-tuning on the blue beam. In an effort to warn Amelia away, she shot bits and pieces of nonessential machinery off her ship. It didn't seem to dissuade her.

She waited and waited.

Amelia kept coming, diving toward the planet. Then, aiming directly at Amelia's face, Magen opened fire again. It took her an hour or more to burn her warning across her windshield.

TURN BACK.


Amelia showed up one day, unannounced, at the headquarters of the Slavers Bod on the Summer World. Her hair had been elaborately braided. Her gown was shockingly cut to show off her firm flesh. She wanted to look her best for this occasion. Dawson stood armed at her side.

She presented herself to the slave at the receptionist booth and demanded to see Chadwick Hubbel. She met the usual bureaucratic resistance.

Amelia pounded on the Plexiglas wire mesh window of the booth. With deliberately inappropriate volume, flushed in the face, she shouted to the slave, "Tell your supervisor and your supervisor's supervisor, and his supervisor too, that Amelia Strados brings news about Magen Hirsch. I must see Chadwick Hubbel within the next ten minutes!''

The tone caught the receptionist's attention. Within moments from the receptionist's call, Hubbel emerged from the elevator bank in the lobby, a vaguely irritated falseness shining through his smile. He looked magnificent, dressed in prime director's robes of royal blue velvet with copper brocades.

Hubbel personally escorted Amelia to his office in the left eyeball of Bacchus.

Amelia glanced around and ran a finger along marbled paneling. ''Nice, real nice,'' she said. ''Olagy made you chief of operations after all. That must have been a hard sell.''

''Very hard. I had to kill him. Three times, in fact. Then I finally found one of the clones willing to give me the appointment.''

'I am glad for you.''

''I thought you were dead,'' said Hubbel.

''I've just been through a long run of bad luck. Really awful rotten luck.''

Hubbel raised an eyebrow. ''That boy. What was his name? He lasted such a long time with you. A lot longer than I did.''

''He lasted too long. Much too long. He's gone now. You want to hear something silly? I thought I was in love. I thought I had stumbled onto some long-lost ancient secret. It was just some silly behavior pattern I picked up from Magen. It ended up killing her.''

''Hirsch is dead? Are you sure? Her raids haven't stopped.''

''She's dead. Someone's taken her place.''

''I'm glad to have the information. Perhaps I can exploit it in some way.'' Hubbel scribbled a note on a small tablet.

"She was shot down over Abaddon—supposedly chasing some lead on her husband that you gave her. Is it true?"

"I told her Adam Hirsch is on Abaddon. Yes. That is what my sources reported. He was supposed to be alive, too, if you consider being on Abaddon life."

"Now I understand why love is so poorly regarded."

"Actually, I'd like to try it sometime. I hear it is a potent aphrodisiac."

Settling back into her chair, eyes gleaming, she asked, "Did you forget our deal?"

"No. But I wasn't about to volunteer anything—especially if you forgot. But we did have a deal. You did what I asked, I remember."

"You'll have all the sanctions lifted against me? I can do business with the bods again?"

"Yes." He jotted down some more notes.

"You'll give me my ten thousand slaves?"

"That was our deal. We have plenty to spare."

Amelia smiled, an easy, confident smile. She never expected things to be this easy. Perhaps her luck had changed at last.

Hubbel glanced up from his note scribbling, catching Amelia midgaze, looking deep into her eyes to reinforce the appearance of sincerity. "I shall have the sanctions lifted against you at once; however, I am going to delay delivery of the slaves. Only for a short time, perhaps. I am not reneging on our deal. There are a lot of forms to fill out."

"I want my slaves by tomorrow, Hubbel, or I will distribute across the entire system specific instructions on how to successfully deprogram your slaves."

"Tomorrow, then." He turned his attention to his scribbling, and away from her. His face flushed with repressed rage.

She left the office, quickly returning to Dawson's protection. He escorted her from the building.

"You heard what I said in there?" she asked.

"I did. Auditory monitoring—for your protection, of course."

"I wasn't bluffing. I know how to free slaves. Do you want your freedom, old friend?"

"What would I do with it? What would I do different with the rest of my life—besides trying to keep you happy?"

"You're not just saying that because of your conditioning?"

"Is that a question or an order?"

She took his impertinence as a sign that he had more than enough will to make this decision on his own.


Inside her diamond mansion, Amelia took a long, leisurely swim, nude in a pool filled with pink-tinged carbonated water. Overhead, the lights shone gloriously, photon-filtered and wave-controlled.

The water, gently heated to her body temperature, soothed her joints. She had toned up, looking better and firmer, still one of the most beautiful women in the Draconian system. Her swim was part of a new routine of strenuous exercises. When she finished swimming, she tackled a set of weight-lifting devices that adjusted automatically to her fatigue levels. She spent anywhere from six to eight hours a day swimming, cycling, walking, and weight lifting. Amelia had been watching herself transform from wretchedness to strength. This transformation made her think of what Magen had said back on the Autumn World about using times of loss as opportunities to grow. Magen was wrong, Amelia decided. Deprivation did not promote growth. Pain was just pain, not a fire that transmuted base mettle into sterner stuff. Losses only made one poorer. Personal growth needed to be taken leisurely. It couldn't be rushed. It needed to be cultivated in the proper environment, in places like the mansion, accommodations that delighted the eye and stimulated the mind.

Amelia had needed to come home. It gave her the strength and cunning to force Hubbel into upholding his bargain. Under the right conditions, there were no limits to what the human will could accomplish.

That is what aristocracy is all about, she thought.

She stepped onto her balcony, where she could see the large bod ships unloading their cargo of fresh slaves. Magen and Veil would disapprove. Amelia reflected on her dealings with those two. They had been enlightening—but also tedious, costly, and trying.

The old notions about a hidden order lying beneath the chaos of perception still held a disquieting appeal. God made sense in a simplistic way. What if Amelia were truly special to God, as Veil claimed? What had been lost in the cosmic scheme of things? Amelia shuddered, remembering Veil's warnings about the Devil, and the creature she had seen in her dreams.

Perhaps someday Amelia would give this atonement thing another try. Someday. But for now, she planned to travel, pursue expensive entertainments, and indulge in the luxuries she had always loved.

Magen turned to find Adam standing beside her.

She said, "We have to find a way out of here." Her voice held a note of forced, strained control.

"I spent months thinking about escape. I couldn't find a way to get off this planet, except through the spiral hole and it was too well guarded. There was only one way out. Magen, you destroyed it. There is no way to repair the towers. There is no escape."

"Everyone said it was impossible to find you. I am not the kind of person who quits."

"This is different."

"Yes, the stakes are higher, now."

He began to beat his forehead with the heel of his palm, as if pain could undo the infirmity of his thought process. Nothing seemed to change. He tried hitting harder. And harder.

"Stop it," she said.

He immediately stopped.

"Adam, I don't understand these things at all. I don't understand why we can't just fly out or blast our way out."

"Take my word for it. It can't be done so easily."

"Then, since you understand it so well, you've got to think of a way to get us off this world. You have to," she said.

Obediently, he walked back into the office, sat down at the table, and folded his hands in front of him.

Magen tried talking to Adam, but she found that he had slipped into a different time frame. She could tell he was talking when his lips blurred to a pinkish smudge, but she could not tell if he was trying to talk to her, or if he was praying. His eyelids, rapidly blinking, had become faintly visible, peach-tone veils.

Then she heard a voice speaking in deep, time-dragged tones. The pace of syllables accelerated as Adam came back into sync with her. ". . . You see how time is distorted here. Perhaps we can find some area on the planet's surface where the past has been preserved, or perhaps we can find a stream of time that will carry us far back. This world wasn't always enclosed. There might be a spot of preserved past where the sky is open."

"I don't know anything about such things, Adam. It sounds so strange to me."

Something flickered in Adam's eyes, a trace of hope, a faint recollection. "There are many places where Abaddon's past is preserved—but I have never seen any sky but the hard grey shell. I don't know if we will be able to find an opening, but we have no other chance."

Magen began to gather her belongings, her weapons and food. Determined to endure Adam's weeds for as long as possible, she stuffed them into her backpack. Preparing for temptation, she also packed the portions of unkosher meat.

Magen crossed the space that separated her from Adam—only a few feet, but it took her a long time to cross.

They stepped outside together.

Vicious battles over food raged all around, but a quirk of time flow had changed a field of slaughter into a field of miracles. Time flowed in reverse. Like a preview of Judgment Day, the dead flew up from the ground, landing on their feet like cats. Their reversed falls looked like gravity-defying leaps. Those who had died by laser blast emerged from coalescing crimson clouds. Sprays of blood snaked back into opened veins and arteries. Cyanotic cheeks pinked.

Clouds of flies dropped like rain, becoming maggots on impact with the ground. Then the maggots would spread skin back onto faces, like workers rolling down carpets, or vomit lungs back into the dustbowls of empty rib cages.

Carrion birds were spitting toes back onto cold, dead feet.

The victim of an acid sword lay on the ground, his skin unburning, regenerating, the acid rolling upward and off him in a sizzling tide, spreading an abdomen of beautifully toned sweat-glazed muscles over the girdle of a gore-blackened skeleton.

On the field of battle mortal enemies embraced, extracted knives from one another's kidneys, cauterizing wounds with backhand motions of their blades.

Magen trod carefully, cautious of light blasts that whistled backward around her, unsure whether or not they could still inflict injury.

The spectacle of battle became a spectacle of peace, a vision of a perfect world of brotherly love, a foreshadow of the messianic era—men forsaking war, the dead waking. Guns repented of their anger, pulling back spears of light and returning forever to their holsters. The smells of putrescence reformed and sweetened in the air. Soldiers were revived by inhaling their own death screams. Men were healing each other's wounds, reconciling their differences, and exchanging food. Resurrections churned the mud around them. It was moving, in a way, beautiful.

As they left the battle behind them, Magen walked with surer steps. The brittle ground crackled like frying grease as her pace quickened. A thousand shifting smells cascaded through the air, a bouquet of history. Some distant time long ago, there had been flowers in the desert. And trees. She could smell echoes of ancient garbage, snow, sulfur—and long, long ago there had been an ocean.

# 11

## THE ARK

Out in the desert, Magen could feel time distortions vibrating across her face. In a valley far from the exploratory station, they found a wrecked cruiser lying twisted between boulders. The ship's fins, slender as razors, bent at odd angles along the fuselage. Scrape marks scored the hull. Paint had been scratched from the nose and wings in long swaths.

The remains of two pilots rested inside. Scum-coated bones tangled beneath the canopy blister. They had obviously been testing themselves against the grey scud. Though the pilots had failed to breach the barrier, they managed an astounding escape of another kind. The skeletons lay still, truly dead. The eyes, runny as oysters, fixated on one another. The mouths gaped open, rejoicing the miracle of nonresurrection, singing silence. The dead pilots seemed to have died embracing one another, their stiff white fingers now interlocked. It was the first sign of true death that Magen had seen since coming to Abaddon. No tremors stirred these corpses. No false life. Not even a twitch. Perhaps these stubborn bones had achieved their measure of peace because they had died so close to the time wall, pounding themselves against the shell.

Magen pried the skeletons from their sticky, leather thrones. She took the larger of the two flak jackets and handed it to Adam. The jacket fit him fine. The helmet also fit him. The coincidence troubled her.

"What is wrong?" asked Adam.

"I am terrified of what I feel for you, Adam. In so many ways, we are almost strangers. I haven't seen you for five years."

"When I think of all you have done for me, for the sake of our love and marriage, I am overwhelmed. It makes the old passions seem vapid and unworthy. I cannot tell you how very much I love you at this moment."

She cut in, "Is that why you say yes to everything I ask?" She laughed, for a moment, then sobered.

Magen asked Adam to help fix the ship. He nodded stiffly. Using dry white stones that powdered and chipped on impact, he hammered the bent fins back into place. Magen peeled back the hood cover. She spliced wires and rerouted gas pipes. Cannibalizing components from some of the luxury systems, like the auto-aimers and the climate controls, she fed the ship's essentials. She disassembled her guns and culled parts from them as well. Magen had been trained by her bod to make spot repairs. She could patch the insides of a ship with her eyes closed. Her fingers moved on automatic, even though she understood almost nothing of the mechanics involved. The work went quickly.

She began to get frustrated when she tried to make the final linkup between the engine and the control console.

The genders of the outlets and plugs, the colors of the wire coverings, would not match up. She suspected the ship had already gone through a fair amount of customizing before it had fallen into her hands. Every time she loosened a screw, foreign parts revealed themselves, many from older models she couldn't even recognize. As she fiddled with the circuitry, Magen got lost in a maze of purple and green wires and silver circuit chips. She banged at a ceramic socket that was so old, it could have come from Earth. She tried to bluff her way through the problem, or solve it by blind luck.

Adam was still straightening the fins, clanging as he bent out the metal. Magen's hands tugged at the wire jungle.

Suddenly overwhelmed by the difficulty of the task, she pulled loose a handful of connections and tossed them in the dust. Cursing, she kicked the ship.

"Maybe we should try to find a different ship," suggested Adam.

Magen waved away the notion, scattering dust motes that hovered in front of her face. "I am not giving up, Adam. I don't care how long it takes. We are going to work this through. What is time on Abaddon that we should worry about wasting it?" She laughed at herself, a forced, ugly laugh. "You almost made me lose hope, you know. Don't try it again! Make me keep working on this ship until I can get it to fly. Even if I change my mind, don't listen to me. I don't care how long it takes."

He nodded stiffly, then turned his attention to the exposed engine circuitry, prodding wires with his dusty fingers.

Adam and Magen sat on the crusted ground together, trying to decipher form and function.

* * *

Beyond the valley where they worked, the lines of vision divided into two half-planes, one grey, the other dull yellow. The bisecting horizon blurred at the edge where the desert met the sky. Cracks of varying size veined the ground, distorting perspectives. A fine, grey powder spewed from the cracks.

After an undetermined time, working on the ship's engine, dust invaded Magen's eyes, gathering in muddy balls along her lashes. It caked in her hair and stuffed her ears. Her feet began to ache; then the pain spread to her knees and thighs. Her tendons felt like piano wires slicing through muscle and nerve. Adam's knuckles were making popping sounds whenever he moved his hands. His fingernails were scratching staccato whispers over the surface of the engine's firewall. An impassive mask of dust covered his face. He caught saw-edged breaths between fits of coughing. If he felt pain, he didn't show it.

Magen collapsed. Adam stopped working when she did, dropping to the ground behind her, like a shadow.

When Magen awoke, she continued her efforts to repair the electrical system. She struggled to find meaning in the mechanical hieroglyphs. Slowly the male, the female, and the bisexual outlets linked up in ways that seemed to be correct.

Suddenly she saw dark lines drawing around the horizon, marching threads etching new divisions on the monotonous landscape. As the lines drew closer, they knitted into human forms. At least a hundred men were tramping toward them.

Magen reached for her guns, but found her holsters empty. Her pistols and rifles lay in heaps of junk on the ground, their jeweled hearts beating inside the ship engine, which was nearly repaired. Magen shook Adam awake. She said, "We've got to get out of here."

Hurriedly, they made a few last-minute adjustments to the engine, then climbed into the cockpit together. Magen pulled back on the starter. Metal parts scraped under the hood; then the engine gasped. She pumped in more gas and a fist of kerosene fumes hit her face. Sputtering sounds followed. She had been too impatient and flooded the engine. The ignition would not turn over.

Magen threw open the canopy blister. She said to Adam, "Get out slowly and walk away. There's plenty of distance between us and them. Don't run. They'll think we have something valuable. If they have lasers, they'll be able to cut us down from where they stand."

"Who knows?" said Adam. "Those men could be from a hundred years ago. When they reach us, they could be bones. Or we could be bones. Or they could never reach us."

"We can't take any chances."

"But I can't leave this place."

"We have to."

"I can't, Magen. You ordered me to stay until the ship was repaired."

"What do you mean?" Her eyes widened. Suddenly it became obvious to her.

"I can't leave. I'm under orders. You said even if you changed your mind, I am not to leave until the ship is repaired."

"They made you a slave."

"Yes. I lied to you. I am sorry."

"God damn you, Adam! I don't have the strength to carry you. How can I undo this order?"

"I don't think you can."

"God damn you! Why didn't you be honest with me? It wouldn't have made any difference to me! God damn it! I was expecting you should be a slave!" She threw up her hands, exasperated.

As the forms drew closer, the sound of jangling chains

drifted through the time currents. Then the images thrust forward faster than Magen had expected, moving through accelerated time.

Suddenly, they were surrounded.

Defensively, Magen affected the listless amble and indifferent stare of a slave. She copied the look convincingly.

A group of six gunmen led a procession of shackled slaves and walking corpses. The marching footsteps fluffed up sheets of low-lying dust over the brittle plane. At the head of the procession, the leader shouted commands that whistled through small, sharp teeth.

"Olagy," said Magen, trying hard not to let her surprise ruin her impersonation of a slave.

Olagy approached her, took her face into his webbed hand. He looked her up and down. "You know me?" he hissed.

"Everyone in the system knows about Olagy," she replied.

"They know my clones. No one knows me, the real Olagy. Olagy the first. They exiled me to Abaddon; a long time ago, I guess."

One of the gunmen started pulling weapons off Magen. Quill implants striped his spine and arms. His eyes were purple. "I am the duke of Abaddon," he said.

"We have been gathering slaves," said Olagy. "Establishing a way of doing things, here. A new way like the old way, based on slavery." His slit eyes took on a nostalgic cast. "This reminds me of the old days, when I first wanted to be the chairman of the Slavers Bod. Now, there was an Olagy to be feared." He pointed over his shoulder with his thumb to three identical boys with hair close-cropped to a fine fuzz, triplets or clones. "These are the barons." Then, gesturing toward a fat male, Olagy said, "And that's the queen. These men are my chiefs, with slaves of their own. Obey them. They serve me."

Olagy slapped a wrist shackle on Magen, adding her to the procession like a new charm on a bracelet.

Magen froze with her head cocked in Olagy's direction as he finished frisking her. Adam was chained as well.

The aristocrats of Abaddon herded their slaves off to one side and left them standing. They tested the half-repaired ship, listening to the gunning engine.

While the aristocrats played with the ship, Adam maneuvered past the other slaves and brought himself close to Magen's side. "I'm sorry," he whispered. "I wish I could have been of more help. I should have tried to escape with you, or I should have fought them, but I could not."

"I don't expect you should fight for me, Adam. If I had wanted a fight, there would have been a fight. I should have known that they made you into a slave. I should have known it."

"I don't understand why he has put us in chains. He doesn't need them. We're slaves. Perhaps the symbolism appeals to him. Or perhaps he suspects you."

"I don't mind the chains," she said, jangling a six-inch length while she toyed with the small locks that linked them together. "They give me a weapon."

The aristocrats found that the ship wouldn't work. They had no interest in attempting repairs. With prodding lasers, they drove the slaves back into motion. The chained slaves ambled wearily. At least half of them were mush-skinned Abaddon corpses, walking dead.

"Stop," said Adam. "We cannot leave this place."

"What do you mean?" asked Olagy, surprised by the slave's impertinence.

"We have to stay here."

Magen cursed under her breath.

"I say no."

"We have to leave Abaddon!" shouted Adam.

"I don't want to leave," said Olagy matter-of-factly. He was unholstering his gun, an irritated look on his face.

"I can't leave this place," said Adam. "I was ordered to stay."

"Yeah? Who ordered you?" Olagy had enough of this. He leveled his pistol at Adam.

Magen snapped her chain loose. The aristocrats were unprepared for the sudden, skilled attack. With a flick of her wrist, she blinded the duke, splattering jelly and bony orbital fragments as the chain whipped across his face. Magen spun the chain over to one of the barons, snaking it around his neck. She jerked him forward, cracking his cervical spine. She pulled the cooling body into collision with Olagy, who lost balance.

Magen lunged for the dead baron's handgun. She grabbed it with her right hand, using a scooping gesture as she hit the ground rolling. Then she bounced to her feet, aiming the gun.

And she stood there.

And stood there.

And stood.

Poised, she pointed her gun at Olagy's head. A battle cry was sounding on her lips in slow hisses and clicks. Magen was frozen in a block of slow-moving time, trapped like a fly in amber.

Her left hand dangled in real time, spastically shaking as if it had been severed. The chain linked to her wrist shackle jangled softly.

Olagy peeled off a shot at her. The other aristocrats opened fire as well. Three red beams flashed toward Magen. All three beams slowed to a creep as they crossed the perimeters of the time block. The aristocrats shrieked with delight.

"Leave her alone!" shouted Adam.

"Keep out of this," Olagy replied, and his words fell with the full force of a command.

The sluggish deadly beams seemed to ooze their way toward Magen through the medium of aberrant time.

The aristocrats were laughing at the image, which had been fixed at an unexpected moment, like an embarrassing photograph.

Now one of the beams wormed past Magen's temple, bathing her forehead with a crimson glow. A straight line of blistered weals slowly bubbled over her eyebrows.

The next beam plodded on a track toward Magen's heart.

Adam began to sweat. He could almost feel the heat searing across his wife's skin.

A moment before the beam could lacerate Magen's breast, Olagy grabbed the end of her chain and pulled hard. She jerked sideways, back into real time, stunned. Her eyes rolled, unfocused. Before she could recover, one of the remaining barons threw a snap kick to her midriff, propelling her back into the time block. Magen froze in midair, bent at the waist, just above the original laser beams, which were about to finish their crawl. As the beams touched the invisible outer shell of the block, they squirted out across the plains, bright flashes escaping to the horizon.

Olagy fired at Magen's frozen form once again. A new red beam inched toward her face.

Adam was shaking now. His head burned. He couldn't think. He couldn't act. Disassociated anger sat in abstract chunks in his wounded mind. Caught in crossfires of mixed messages, his nerves just shook.

The aristocrats waited until the bar of light painted a soft pink glow on Magen's lips; then they jerked her out again.

Olagy let her stay in real time for just a second, then he threw her back in. Olagy fired a new laser shot. It seemed he reserved this pleasure for himself, a privilege of rank.

They pulled Magen out again, then they tossed her back in. The aristocrats laughed like children.

Adam felt he was dying. His larynx constricted. Pressure built in his heart. He gripped his chains as if they were a lifeline.

Adam squeezed the rough, rusty metal into the palms of his sweaty hands.

By this time, Magen hung in the block, curled in a fetal position. A line of laser light was creeping toward her spine.

Adam heard the sound of the aristocrats laughing and shooting their jeweled guns. He heard the crackling of laser beams as they zapped through real space and smacked with dull thuds against the walls of the time block. He heard the hissing and clicking of Magen's battle yell. Or was she sobbing now?

This was Adam's fault. He had taken this woman out of her natural element and plunged her into the rigors of his ancient customs. He had let himself be captured. He had let himself become a slave. He hated himself, an utterly useless, shaking thing.

He spoke to God. "Punish me, don't punish her. She doesn't deserve this. She came to this world, this hell, to rescue me. She was trying to do a mitzvah. I am the one who committed the blasphemies. Not her. Punish me."

A line of laser light was plodding toward Magen.

"Can you hear me, God?" whispered Adam.

No answer.

"Are you there?"

No answer.

Adam would make God listen to his pleas. He tried to shout, he tried to make a sound that would penetrate Abaddon's shell. His throat was too tight. Blood frothed on his lips and made small popping sounds, that was all. He gripped his chains and shook them. The links rattled and clanked. It still wasn't enough sound to attract God's attention.

Adam pulled on his chains until one link snapped. He whipped the chains, sent them whistling through the air. Centrifugal force tugged at his shoulders. He smacked the chains into Olagy's ribs, which yielded a great, cracking sound. Then he swung out wildly in all directions, harvesting screams. The screams, the loud, agonized screams, the whistling links, the jangling of metal, it still wasn't enough sound. He kept beating the air, and anything that occupied the air. His own voice failed him.

And then it was quiet again, so quiet he could hear Magen hissing from her separate time. He pulled her out of the block.

The aristocrats of Abaddon lay on the floor of the desert, soaked in blood. Only the blind duke remained alive, sobbing in the dust. The surrounding slaves began to murmur.

Confusion swept through Adam, a deep disorientation that confounded even dream chaos. His brain hurt. Even though he knew the human brain contained no nerve endings and was not supposed to feel pain directly, he believed that his brain was the source of his agony, and not the tissues surrounding the interior of his skull. His brain, not his eyes, though they throbbed, too. His brain. He had resisted a command and the effort of breaking his conditioning seemed to have ripped vital tissue in his thought centers.

Raw animal rage had broken his programming. Not prayer. Not divine intervention. A fury that put him back to his origins. It was as if he had been suddenly set free and his first human response was to kill.

Magen slowly came back into sync with him. "What happened?" she asked.

"We should get out of here."

They tried the ship again. This time it took flight with ferocious ignition. They ripped into the sky.

Magen could see a hunched figure on horseback herding up the stray slaves. Reptilian scales twinkled under Abaddon's grey glow, as Olagy shouted commands and gestured angrily. Maybe it was a time replay, or another clone.

Even before the ship hit Abaddon's barrier, the cruiser was vibrating like a banner in a storm. It would fly, but for how long?

Magen cruised around as high as she could get under the envelope, looking for an opening, a patch of blue or black.

From the air, traveling at high speeds, they could read the history of Abaddon. The past flickered beneath them. A city began to rise on the ground, its structures spreading like fast-forming crystals on the continent. In an instant, the structures collapsed. A ravenous jungle erupted, swallowing the ruins. Then the green, rolling vistas shimmered into oceans, and the oceans vanished like mirages. Magen poured on the speed, even though they were running short of fuel. The grey scud, the shell of Hell, went on forever.

"It's impossible," said Magen. "This world wasn't always closed off. It could not be that it was always shut. Why can't we find an opening?"

"I think we have gone past a million years or more."

She accelerated again, bringing the slender fins of the ship so close to the boundaries of the sky that they etched a trail of sparks. Recklessly, she let the ship's nose bounce off the barrier.

Adam shouted, "It does no good."

She ignored him. She bounced against the shell even harder this time, trying to crash through or die trying.

She lost control. The ship slammed upward. On impact with the walled-off sky, the fins bent at awkward angles and the windows exploded.

They smacked into the shell three times, then plummeted downward. The ground flew up to embrace them.

Adam climbed from the wreckage. He fell to his knees as he touched the ground. Magen struggled at the console, slamming the accelerator, tugging on the steering column. She pulled until her knuckles blanched, as if she were trying to lift the ship back into the sky with her bare hands.

"It is hopeless," said Adam.

Magen clawed her way up through the twisted brambles of the shattered canopy blister. "We'll get another ship," she announced.

"It is hopeless."

"No. It was a good idea."

"Now it is time for us to give up. I am finally free enough to disobey your command. I give up, Magen! I have been watching the shell, Magen. I believe it is part of the ecology of this place. The times may change on the ground, but the shell holds everything in. Like the banks of a river. There is no escape from Abaddon."

Magen started to laugh hysterically. "There is a way."

"No; Magen. Never. We are trapped here forever."

"There is a way." Her eyes were wide and full of awe, as if she were looking straight into the eyes of the Almighty. She was going into shock.

Adam hit her. She kept on laughing and repeating, "There is a way." He hit her again, and again. He knew she was the better fighter—she could kill him if she wanted to, but he kept on hitting her. She never hit back, never made any threats. She just kept on laughing. He stopped hitting her. He could not tell if he had been trying to slap her to her senses, or if he had just been venting all his frustration on the nearest target.

Then she stopped laughing. She was making an intense effort to bring herself under control.

"There is a way," she said, straight-faced. But the laughter snorted out through her nose, and broke out again all over, an instant after the words were out of her mouth.

Adam sadly shook his head.

Magen couldn't talk anymore, she was laughing too hard. She grabbed Adam by the collar of his flak jacket and she pointed.

Adam saw a ship poised against the horizon. Enormous gantries flanked the ship on either side like the frame of an incomplete cathedral.

Even though it was far away, Adam could see much of its design because the ship was so huge—at least forty stories tall. The decorative architecture along the enormous vistaview windows suggested ancient artistry. Its golden skin shined under the grey skies. The lines were sleek, but the forms seemed to rotate around a longitudinal axis. It looked more like a stationary monument than something that could fly. The retros and thrusters were tiny in scale, almost out of place—like vestigial remains of a primitive technology, clearly incapable of bearing the ship any significant distance.

"There is a way is a way is way is way . . . there is . . ."

Adam stared.

They had stumbled upon a warship.

Magen and Adam ran toward the warship. They held hands, screaming for joy, as their feet slammed furiously against the crusted ground, raising clouds of dust.

The ship began to move in time.

Pockmarks of corrosion were dulling the metal. Magen dropped Adam's hand and ran faster, hoping to outrace the deterioration. The faster she ran, the faster the corrosion spread. Adam's pace slowed to a leisurely amble. His eyes stayed fixed on the warship. The pockmarks on the metal blistered, then popped open into lacy clusters of small rust holes. The holes widened, feeding into one another.

She kicked the fuselage of the warpship and rust flakes sprayed on impact. Then she beat her fists on the old hulk, as if trying to resuscitate it. Her blows rang and bellowed with hollow metal echoes.

Magen cried, "Why does nothing good ever happen on this world? It seems wicked by design, made to torment you with false hope."

Adam had reached her side. He commented, in a detached tone, "You are right. Nothing good ever seems to happen here." Then he thought about her observation. His mind felt strong and unburdened, hopeful, curious. He had been engaged intellectually by the chain of adverse coincidences that had befallen them, and it distracted him from the grimness of their situation. He felt hope when he had every reason to despair, and he felt determined to uncover a means to escape their plight. Was this the product of Magen's former, unretracted commands? Or was it the product of free will? He couldn't tell.

He continued, "It seems that there should occasionally be some pleasant by-products of these disturbed time currents—like a return to youth, or a chance to right a past mistake. But such things never happen here. I suppose if there were positive effects from warp travel, mankind would have never given it up. You see, God does let his will be known."

"We are trapped here forever. That is what God is telling us."

"No, we'll find a way."

Magen shook her head sadly. "It will never hold air. Nothing good ever happens here. Nothing. The ship is just one more torment. It is good for one thing only. It is a way to kill ourselves. We can escape from Hell, Adam. But not to life."

Adam approached the ship. He reached for a handful of ancient metal and let it crumble in his fingertips.

Magen continued, "At least we will die together." She began to cry. "Death is not so terrible. It is better than staying here."

"We can try to make a new outer shell."

"Adam, if there is even a tiny hole, the ship will burst in space. Where will we get the machinery to make a flawless hull? Now you are getting . . . you are getting crazy about keeping hope alive."

"I won't give up."

"This isn't giving up. This is a kind of victory. This is the end we have been heading for, Adam. Not a good end, but not so terrible an end either. This is our destiny."

"Yes."

"Are you ready?"

"Give me a minute."

"I am ready. We should not delay, Adam. It makes it harder."

"Not yet . . ."

"Now."

He studied the ruined outer sheath, waiting for a miracle. On one part of the ship, the erosion seemed to be reversing, a trick of the time currents. Perhaps if he waited long enough, the sheath would be regenerated by backward-moving time.

Now Magen's tears were crawling back up her cheeks. He could hear her cheering along with himself as they ran toward the ship, uncountable moments ago, their shouts drifting forward and back.

". . . this is a kind of victory," Magen repeated.

The sheath was rebuilding itself. One minute, and it was glistening and whole.

The next minute, it crumbled away again.

Nothing good ever came from the contrary time currents of Abaddon. Only torture through hope.

". . . this is a kind of victory . . ."

Was Magen repeating herself? Or was it a loop of time?

"You told me never to give up," said Adam. He didn't know if it was a new thought, or a replay of an old one.

"Adam, the ship will never hold air."

He thought about trying to follow a time current back to the moment when the ship was whole. Another impossibility. Nothing good ever came from Abaddon. He thought about taking Magen's hand and shooting them into the vacuum. It would be painless. The moment they came out of subspace, they would burst in the vacuum of space.

The concept of death in space replayed in Adam's mind. He thought about bursting open in the vacuum like a popcorn kernel filled with gore.

Then he said, "It doesn't have to hold air. It is a warpship. We don't have to travel through space."

"I don't know about this." She thought about it for a minute. "Even if it doesn't have to hold air in subspace, so what. We are still trapped here. What do you know about traveling between worlds?"

"Enough."

"This would be easy if all we had to do was get past Abaddon's shell. That I could handle. We could get out to space, and then I could get our bearings. Without a shell, in order to live, we must come out of subspace on a world with air. There are things you need to have in advance when you plot a course, Adam. You need to know where you are. You need to know how fast you will be going. And you need to know your starting time. How are you going to find out these things, Adam?"

"These old ships had computers."

They climbed up the side of the ship, using sections of the exposed frame as a ladder. Then, one at a time, they swung through one of the larger rust holes. They found the main computer terminal in the center of the cockpit, draped in the remains of a rotted g-web, beside the tilted console.

Magen and Adam stared at the glowing multicolored readout screen of the computer. Like many of the old Earth models of its time, the computer was almost absurdly simple in its operations. As Adam suspected, it could calculate all the necessary information for subspace travel.

"We should aim for the Autumn World," said Magen. "There's no radar to track us. No bod installations. And I have friends there."

Magen pulled up a screen of star charts. She punched in a series of coordinates. The computer automatically accommodated spatial distortions. The sensors had some difficulty fixing the position of the gantries—but fortunately that information was retrievable from the memory banks. The gantries had not moved in three hundred years.

The computer figured the warp parallaxes, the travel time to the Autumn World, the logarithmic scales, the speed curves.

But the computer couldn't tell time.

The chrono calculator stayed frozen on a date over two centuries old.

Magen said, "Without the exact time, Adam, we can't go anywhere. The computer cannot fix our position if it doesn't know the time. With a broken chronometer, it is just the same as aiming at random."

"Maybe it isn't broken."

"It doesn't even measure seconds, Adam."

"Maybe time isn't passing. Look at the mechanism, Magen. It looks as if it is new. Maybe time isn't passing at all. Abaddon is a singularity. I think we have been trapped inside a moment, a slice of time. That is why Abaddon doesn't orbit. That is why nothing dies."

"Adam—even if you are right . . . what day is it outside

the shell of Abaddon? The Autumn World—every world in the system is changing position all the time. Maybe the computer can aim at the place the Autumn World was two hundred years ago—but does that help us? We will still end up in deep space. We will end up dead.''

Adam sat back and studied the frozen chronometer. He drummed his fingers. "There has to be some kind of mechanism built into the computer to allow the chronometer to readjust before it leaves subspace. There has to be; otherwise, our ancestors would not have been able to navigate these old ships. Remember, they were coming from Earth, where the light from this system did not even register as stars. They were aiming themselves through a void, crossing vast gulfs of incalculable light-years. Earth time had no meaning by the end of the voyage. I believe the chronometer will readjust before we hit real space. Just tell the computer where we want to go.''

"You talk like you are so sure, but you are really guessing about a lot of this.''

"We have nothing to lose.''

She punched in the coordinates for the Autumn World.

Adam and Magen sat down together, sharing the frame of a single strapless, cushionless chair.

Magen squeezed her eyes shut, as if expecting an explosion; then she hit the starter. The engine rumbled, sending shivers through the antique frame.

Magen feared the ship would shake apart before the engine kicked over. She cocked her head, listening intently for the sound of ignition. It was hard to hear over the clattering of disjointed metal seams. She relaxed the starter, then hesitantly tested it again.

Another rush of chattering rippled through the cockpit; then, beneath the ship, a soft rasping sound whispered.

Magen and Adam gulped air. She reached for him and found fingers groping for her. They reeled in one another's arms, pulling close.

Suddenly the world flashed away. A sweep of lights and sound, a rush of void, and they found themselves engulfed in emptiness. This was worse than Abaddon. Nothingness, absolute nothingness, and it seemed that Adam and Magen had become nothingness as well, losing substance.

The journey took no time at all. They might not have even been aware of their passage, but their time perceptions had been skewed to adjust to the caprices of Abaddon. Part of them remained intact, at least enough to apprehend their surroundings.

Unreal colors pulsated on Adam's retinas, a neurologic reaction to the absolute nothingness, like the formless music pounding on his eardrums. A terrible cold numbed his sense of touch, but not completely. Certain tactile sensations lingered like an afterthought, frozen at the moment they reached his brain, textures signaling through his nerves: the roughness of the corroded floor beneath his legs, the teeth of rust holes biting into skin, the pressure of his wife's embrace.

The air Adam held in his chest seemed to warm his insides without any hint of pressure.

He tried to speak, but could not. Perhaps Magen was trying to speak as well. The medium of nothingness conducted neither particle nor wave to their deprived sensory organs. They pulled closer, seeking shelter from the ambient void.

They sped through the underbelly of creation, the primal stuff of raw chaos that existed for an eternity before the coming of light. This was the forbidden realm. They were committing the greatest sin of their culture—traveling faster than light.

What was waiting for Adam and Magen at the end of their trespass? They had as much chance of landing in deep space as they had of reaching the Autumn World. Adam had made many assumptions. There would be no way of knowing if he was right until they reached the end of the void. Perhaps there would be no way of knowing at all.

There was nothing for a while, cracked time and empty space. Nothing but the ancient collapsing ship, the sea of chaos, the waves of abstraction. Nothing but each other. Nothing but a need to hold and be held that went beyond the necessities of love or lust. Nothing but male and female, the flicker of life under the shadow of death.

Suddenly gravity grabbed them.

Time was moving again. They found themselves sheltered in a knot of limbs, a frost from nowhere spreading over the parts of their bodies that weren't touching, hair crinkling as it froze, their back muscles constricting and shivering. The rust holes lit up, filled with bright azure. Air blew into their lungs.

Magen twisted loose from Adam's embrace as the ship dropped. Her fingers scrambled over the console, then hit the retro switches. Their descent slowed.

The rotted old ship floated like a leaf, weeping parts of itself onto the Autumn forests below.

Magen still shivered from the chill of subspace, even though the sun had begun to beat upon the hull and warm the ship.

The old engines began to quake under the demands of flight. Magen dumped altitude. Time was taking its toll, and a ripple of ruin shook the deteriorating frame like a death rattle. Slowly and carefully, she brought the great antique to a landing.

Magen pulled herself free of her chair. She stood in the center of a giant rust hole, brightness all around, gulping air like a newborn.

"God has been kind to us," she said.

"Very kind, it would seem. But this is mostly your

doing, Magen. Because you did not forget me, as so many other women would have. God has blessed me with good fortune, but mostly, he has blessed me with you."

"I am just stubborn. I don't like people should take what is mine." Then emotion began to overwhelm her. Adam took her into his embrace before she began to weep.

He said, "Perhaps God has new joys for us, and new sorrows. At least we have some part to play in his future. I don't wonder about his motives anymore." The rhythm of his wife's breathing, the beat of his own heart, gave form and moment to their return to reality. Then he added, "The passage of time is welcome, even with all of its consequences."

A child appeared, stepping from the shade of a great oak. One of the children from the slave settlement.

The sound of crunching leaves warned that more people were coming.

A crowd of former slaves began to gather around the great warship. They stood barefoot in evenly spaced geometric rows. All wore simple, colorless, hand-stitched uniforms made from flax they grew themselves.

Most of the former slaves had lost the listless stares of slavery—but they seemed to lack individuated responses, adopting group expressions, as if they shared a single mind. Now they were transfixed by the presence of the warship.

Word of the ship's arrival seemed to be spreading silently, telepathically. More and more of the former slaves began to appear, some in their nightclothes, some dirty with topsoil. Their lot seemed to have improved in Magen's absence. The parasites had been plucked from their hair. They demonstrated some new connection to life with their frank reverence for the ancient ruin.

The fields and dormitories must have been empty. The forest had filled with free slaves.